The Amateur Gentleman

by

Jeffery Farnol et al

The Echo Library 2007

Published by

The Echo Library

Echo Library
131 High St.
Teddington
Middlesex TW11 8HH

www.echo-library.com

Please report serious faults in the text to complaints@echo-library.com

ISBN 978-1-40686-369-7

CONTENTS

CHAPTER

CHAPTER I

IN WHICH BABNABAS KNOCKS DOWN HIS FATHER, THOUGH AS DUTIFULLY AS MAY BE

John Barty, ex-champion of England and landlord of the "Coursing Hound," sat screwed round in his chair with his eyes yet turned to the door that had closed after the departing lawyer fully five minutes ago, and his eyes were wide and blank, and his mouth (grim and close-lipped as a rule) gaped, becoming aware of which, he closed it with a snap, and passed a great knotted fist across his brow.

"Barnabas," said he slowly, "I beant asleep an' dreaming be I, Barnabas?"

"No, father!"

"But—seven—'undred—thousand—pound. It were seven—'undred thousand pound, weren't it, Barnabas?"

"Yes, father!"

"Seven—'undred—thou—! No! I can't believe it, Barnabas my bye."

"Neither can I, father," said Barnabas, still staring down at the papers which littered the table before him.

"Nor I aren't a-going to try to believe it, Barnabas."

"And yet—here it is, all written down in black and white, and you heard what Mr. Crabtree said?"

"Ah,—I heered, but arter all Crabtree's only a lawyer—though a good un as lawyers go, always been honest an' square wi' me—leastways I 've never caught him trying to bamboozle John Barty yet—an' what the eye don't ob-serve the heart don't grieve, Barnabas my bye, an' there y'are. But seven 'undred thousand pound is coming it a bit too strong—if he'd ha' knocked off a few 'undred thousand I could ha' took it easier Barnabas, but, as it is—no, Barnabas!"

"It's a great fortune!" said Barnabas in the same repressed tone and with his eyes still intent.

"Fortun'," repeated the father, "fortun'—it's fetched me one in the ribs—low, Barnabas, low!—it's took my wind an' I'm a-hanging on to the ropes, lad. Why, Lord love me! I never thought as your uncle Tom 'ad it in him to keep hisself from starving, let alone make a fortun'! My scapegrace brother Tom—poor Tom as sailed away in a emigrant ship (which is a un-common bad kind of a ship to sail in—so I've heered, Barnabas) an' now, to think as he went an' made all that fortun'—away off in Jamaiky—out o' vegetables."

"And lucky speculation, father—!"

"Now, Barnabas," exclaimed his father, beginning to rasp his fingers to and fro across his great, square, shaven chin, "why argufy? Your uncle Tom was a planter—very well! Why is a man a planter—because he plants things, an' what should a man plant but vegetables? So Barnabas, vegetables I says, an' vegetables I abide by, now an' hereafter. Seven 'undred thousand pound all made in Jamaiky—out o' vegetables—an' there y' are!"

Here John Barty paused and sat with his chin 'twixt finger and thumb in expectation of his son's rejoinder, but finding him silent, he presently continued:

"Now what astonishes an' fetches me a leveller as fair doubles me up is—why should my brother Tom leave all this money to a young hop o' me thumb like you, Barnabas? you, as he never see but once and you then a infant (and large for your age) in your blessed mother's arms, Barnabas, a-kicking an' a-squaring away wi' your little pink fists as proper as ever I seen inside the Ring or out. Ah, Barnabas!" sighed his father shaking his head at him, "you was a promising infant, likewise a promising bye; me an' Natty Bell had great hopes of ye, Barnabas; if you'd been governed by me and Natty Bell you might ha' done us all proud in the Prize Ring. You was cut out for the 'Fancy.' Why, Lord! you might even ha' come to be Champion o' England in time—you 're the very spit o' what I was when I beat the Fighting Quaker at Dartford thirty years ago."

"But you see, father—"

"That was why me an' Natty Bell took you in hand—learned you all we knowed o' the game—an' there aren't a fighting man in all England as knows so much about the Noble Art as me an' Natty Bell."

"But father—"

"If you 'd only followed your nat'ral gifts, Barnabas, I say you might ha' been Champion of England to-day, wi' Markisses an' Lords an' Earls proud to shake your hand—if you'd only been ruled by Natty Bell an' me, I'm disappointed in ye, Barnabas—an' so's Natty Bell."

"I'm sorry, father—but as I told you—"

"Still Barnabas, what ain't to be, ain't—an' what is, is. Some is born wi' a nat'ral love o' the 'Fancy' an' gift for the game, like me an' Natty Bell—an' some wi' a love for reading out o' books an' a-cyphering into books—like you: though a reader an' a writer generally has a hard time on it an' dies poor—which, arter all, is only nat'ral—an' there y' are!"

Here John Barty paused to take up the tankard of ale at his elbow, and pursed up his lips to blow off the foam, but in that moment, observing his son about to speak, he immediately set down the ale untasted and continued:

"Not as I quarrels wi' your reading and writing, Barnabas, no, and because why? Because reading and writing is apt to be useful now an' then, and because it were a promise—as I made—to—your mother. When—your mother were alive, Barnabas, she used to keep all my accounts for me. She likewise larned me to spell my own name wi' a capital G for John, an' a capital B for Barty, an' when she died, Barnabas (being a infant, you don't remember), but when she died, lad! I was that lost—that broke an' helpless, that all the fight were took out o' me, and it's a wonder I didn't throw up the sponge altogether. Ah! an' it's likely I should ha' done but for Natty Bell."

"Yes, father—"

"No man ever 'ad a better friend than Natty Bell—Ah! yes, though I did beat him out o' the Championship which come very nigh breaking his heart at the time, Barnabas; but—as I says to him that day as they carried him out of the ring—it was arter the ninety-seventh round, d' ye see, Barnabas—'what is to be, is, Natty Bell,' I says, 'an' what ain't, ain't. It were ordained,' I says, 'as I should be Champion o' England,' I says—'an' as you an' me should be friends—now an' hereafter,' I says—an' right good friends we have been, as you know, Barnabas."

"Indeed, yes, father," said Barnabas, with another vain attempt to stem his father's volubility.

"But your mother, Barnabas, your mother, God rest her sweet soul!—your mother weren't like me—no nor Natty Bell—she were away up over me an' the likes o' me—a wonderful scholard she were, an'—when she died, Barnabas—" here the ex-champion's voice grew uncertain and his steady gaze wavered—sought the sanded floor—the raftered ceiling—wandered down the wall and eventually fixed upon the bell-mouthed blunderbuss that hung above the mantel, "when she died," he continued, "she made me promise as you should be taught to read an' cypher—an' taught I've had you according—for a promise is a promise, Barnabas—an' there y' are."

"For which I can never be sufficiently grateful, both to her—and to you!" said Barnabas, who sat with his chin propped upon his hand, gazing through the open lattice to where the broad white road wound away betwixt blooming hedges, growing ever narrower till it vanished over the brow of a distant hill. "Not as I holds wi' eddication myself, Barnabas, as you know," pursued his father, "but that's why you was sent to school, that's why me an' Natty Bell sat by quiet an' watched ye at your books. Sometimes when I've seen you a-stooping your back over your reading, or cramping your fist round a pen, Barnabas, why—I've took it hard, Barnabas, hard, I'll not deny—But Natty Bell has minded me as it was her wish and so—why—there y' are."

It was seldom his father mentioned to Barnabas the mother whose face he had never seen, upon which rare occasions John Barty's deep voice was wont to take on a hoarser note, and his blue eyes, that were usually so steady, would go wandering off until they fixed themselves on some remote object. Thus he sat now, leaning back in his elbow chair, gazing in rapt attention at the bell-mouthed blunderbuss above the mantel, while his son, chin on fist, stared always and ever to where the road dipped, and vanished over the hill—leading on and on to London, and the great world beyond.

"She died, Barnabas—just twenty-one years ago—buried at Maidstone where you were born. Twenty-one years is a longish time, lad, but memory's longer, an' deeper,—an' stronger than time, arter all, an' I know that her memory will go wi' me—all along the way—d' ye see lad: and so Barnabas," said John Barty lowering his gaze to his son's face, "so Barnabas, there y' are."

"Yes, father!" nodded Barnabas, still intent upon the road.

"And now I come to your uncle Tom—an' speaking of him—Barnabas my lad,—what are ye going to do wi' all this money?"

Barnabas turned from the window and met his father's eye.

"Do with it," he began, "why first of all—"

"Because," pursued his father, "we might buy the 'White Hart'—t' other side o' Sevenoaks,—to be sure you're over young to have any say in the matter—still arter all the money's yours, Barnabas—what d' ye say to the 'White Hart'?"

"A very good house!" nodded Barnabas, stealing a glance at the road again—"but—"

"To be sure there's the 'Running Horse,'" said his father, "just beyond Purley on the Brighton Road—a coaching-house, wi' plenty o' custom, what d' ye think o' the 'Running Horse'?"

"Any one you choose, father, but—"

"Then there's the 'Sun in the Sands' on Shooter's Hill—a fine inn an' not to be sneezed at, Barnabas—we might take that."

"Just as you wish, father, only—"

"Though I've often thought the 'Greyhound' at Croydon would be a comfortable house to own."

"Buy whichever you choose, father, it will be all one to me!"

"Good lad!" nodded John, "you can leave it all to Natty Bell an' me."

"Yes," said Barnabas, rising and fronting his father across the table, "you see I intend to go away, sir."

"Eh?" exclaimed his father, staring—"go away—where to?"

"To London!"

"London? and what should you want in London—a slip of a lad like you?"

"I'm turned twenty-two, father!"

"And what should a slip of a lad of twenty-two want in London? You leave London alone, Barnabas. London indeed! what should you want wi' London?"

"Learn to be a gentleman."

"A—what?" As he spoke, John Barty rose up out of his chair, his eyes wide, his mouth agape with utter astonishment. As he encountered his son's look, however, his expression slowly changed from amazement to contempt, from contempt to growing ridicule, and from ridicule to black anger. John Barty was a very tall man, broad and massive, but, even so, he had to look up to Barnabas as they faced each other across the table. And as they stood thus eye to eye, the resemblance between them was marked. Each possessed the same indomitable jaw, the same square brow and compelling eyes, the same grim prominence of chin; but there all likeness ended. In Barnabas the high carriage of the head, the soft brilliancy of the full, well-opened gray eye, the curve of the sensitive nostrils, the sweet set of the firm, shapely mouth—all were the heritage of that mother who was to him but a vague memory. But now while John Barty frowned upon his son, Barnabas frowned back at his father, and the added grimness of his chin offset the sweetness of the mouth above.

"Barnabas," said his father at last, "did you say a—gentleman, Barnabas?"

"Yes."

"What—you?" Here John Barty's frown vanished suddenly and, expanding his great chest, he threw back his head and roared with laughter. Barnabas clenched his fists, and his mouth lost something of its sweetness, and his eyes glinted through their curving lashes, while his father laughed and laughed till the place rang again, which of itself stung Barnabas sharper than any blow could have done.

But now having had his laugh out, John Barty frowned again blacker than ever, and resting his two hands upon the table, leaned towards Barnabas with his great, square chin jutted forward, and his deep-set eyes narrowed to shining slits—the "fighting face" that had daunted many a man ere now.

"So you want to be a gentleman—hey?"

"Yes."

"You aren't crazed in your 'ead, are ye, Barnabas?"

"Not that I know of, father."

"This here fortun' then—it's been an' turned your brain, that's what it is."

Barnabas smiled and shook his head.

"Listen, father," said he, "it has always been the dream and ambition of my life to better my condition, to strive for a higher place in the world—to be a gentleman. This was why I refused to become a pugilist, as you and Natty Bell desired, this was why I worked and studied—ah! a great deal harder than you ever guessed—though up till to-day I hardly dared hope my dream would ever be realized—but now—"

"Now you want to go to London and be a gentleman—hey?"

"Yes."

"Which all comes along o' your reading o' fool book! Why, Lord! you can no more become a gentleman than I can or the—blunderbuss yonder. And because why? Because a gentleman must be a gentleman born, and his father afore him, and *his* father afore him. You, Barnabas, you was born the son of a Champion of England, an' that should be enough for most lads; but your head's chock full o' fool's notions an' crazy fancies, an' as your lawful father it's my bounden duty to get 'em out again, Barnabas my lad." So saying, John Barty proceeded to take off his coat and belcher neckerchief, and rolled his shirt sleeves over his mighty forearms, motioning Barnabas to do the like.

"A father's duty be a very solemn thing, Barnabas," he continued slowly, "an' your 'ead being (as I say) full o' wild idees, I'm going to try to punch 'em out again as a well-meaning father should, so help me back wi' the table out o' the road, an' off wi' your coat and neckercher."

Well knowing the utter futility of argument with his father at such a time, Barnabas obediently helped to set back the table, thus leaving the floor clear, which done, he, in turn, stripped off coat and neckcloth, and rolled up his sleeves, while his father watched him with sharply appraising eye.

"You peel well, Barnabas," he nodded. "You peel like a fighting man, you've a tidy arm an' a goodish spread o' shoulder, likewise your legs is clean an' straight, but your skin's womanish, Barnabas, womanish, an' your muscles soft wi' books. So, lad!—are ye ready? Then come on."

Thus, without more ado they faced each other foot to foot, bare-armed and alert of eye. For a moment they sparred watchfully, then John Barty feinted Barnabas into an opening, in that same moment his fist shot out and Barnabas measured his length on the floor.

"Ah—I knowed as much!" John sighed mournfully as he aided Barnabas to his feet, "and 't were only a love-tap, so to speak,—this is what comes o' your book reading."

"Try me again," said Barnabas.

"It'll be harder next time!" said his father.

"As hard as you like!" nodded Barnabas.

Once more came the light tread of quick-moving feet, once more John Barty feinted cunningly—once more his fist shot out, but this time it missed its mark, for, ducking the blow, Barnabas smacked home two lightning blows on his father's ribs and danced away again light and buoyant as a cork.

"Stand up an' fight, lad!" growled his father, "plant your feet square—never go hopping about on your toe-points like a French dancing-master."

"Why as to that, father, Natty Bell, as you know, holds that it is the quicker method," here Barnabas smote his father twice upon the ribs, "and indeed I think it is," said he, deftly eluding the ex-champion's return.

"Quicker, hey?" sneered his father, and with the words came his fist—to whizz harmlessly past Barnabas's ear—"we'll prove that."

"Haven't we had almost enough?" inquired Barnabas, dropping his fists.

"Enough? why we aren't begun yet, lad."

"Then how long are we to go on?"

"How long?" repeated John, frowning; "why—that depends on you, Barnabas."

"How on me, father?"

"Are ye still minded to go to London?"

"Of course."

"Then we'll go on till you think better of it—or till you knock me down, Barnabas my lad."

"Why then, father, the sooner I knock you down the better!"

"What?" exclaimed John Barty, staring, "d' ye mean to say—you think you can?—me?—you?"

"Yes," nodded Barnabas.

"My poor lad!" sighed his father, "your head's fair crazed, sure as sure, but if you think you can knock John Barty off his pins, do it, and there y' are."

"I will," said Barnabas, "though as gently as possible."

And now they fell to it in silence, a grim silence broken only by the quick tread and shuffle of feet and the muffled thud of blows. John Barty, resolute of jaw, indomitable and calm of eye, as in the days when champions had gone down before the might of his fist; Barnabas, taller, slighter, but full of the supreme confidence of youth. Moreover, he had not been the daily pupil of two such past masters in the art for nothing; and now he brought to bear all his father's craft and cunning, backed up by the lightning precision of Natty Bell. In all his many hard-fought battles John Barty had ever been accounted most dangerous when he smiled, and he was smiling now. Twice Barnabas staggered back to the wall, and there was an ugly smear upon his cheek, yet as they struck and parried, and feinted, Barnabas, this quick-eyed, swift-footed Barnabas, was smiling also. Thus, while they smiled upon and smote each other, the likeness between them was more apparent than ever, only the smile of Barnabas was the smile of youth, joyous, exuberant, unconquerable. Noting which Experienced Age laughed short and fierce, and strode in to strike Youth down—then came a rush of feet, the panting hiss of breath, the shock of vicious blows, and John Barty, the unbeaten ex-champion of all England, threw up his arms, staggered back the length of the room, and went down with a crash.

For a moment Barnabas stood wide-eyed, panting, then ran towards him with hands outstretched, but in that moment the door was flung open, and Natty Bell stood between them, one hand upon the laboring breast of Barnabas, the other stretched down to the fallen ex-champion.

"Man Jack," he exclaimed, in his strangely melodious voice. "Oh, John!—John Barty, you as ever was the king o' the milling coves, here's my hand, shake it. Lord, John, what a master o' the Game we've made of our lad. He's stronger than you and quicker than ever I was. Man Jack, 'twas as sweet, as neat, as pretty a knockdown as ever we gave in our best days, John. Man Jack, 'tis proud you should be to lie there and know as you have a son as can stop even *your* rush wi' his left an' down you wi' his right as neat and proper, John, as clean an' delicate as ever man saw. Man Jack, God bless him, and here's my hand, John."

So, sitting there upon the floor, John Barty solemnly shook the hand Natty Bell held out to him, which done, he turned and looked at his son as though he had never seen him before.

"Why, Barnabas!" said he; then, for all his weight, sprang nimbly to his feet and coming to the mantel took thence his pipe and began to fill it, staring at Barnabas the while.

"Father," said Barnabas, advancing with hand outstretched, though rather diffidently—"Father!"

John Barty pursed up his lips into a soundless whistle and went on filling his pipe.

"Father," said Barnabas again, "I did it—as gently—as I could." The pipe shivered to fragments on the hearth, and Barnabas felt his fingers caught in his father's mighty grip.

"Why, Barnabas, lad, I be all mazed like; there aren't many men as have knocked me off my pins, an' I aren't used to it, Barnabas, lad, but 't was a clean blow, as Natty Bell says, and why—I be proud of thee, Barnabas, an'—there y' are."

"Spoke like true fighting men!" said Natty Bell, standing with a hand on the shoulder of each, "and, John, we shall see this lad, this Barnabas of ours, Champion of England yet." John frowned and shook his head.

"No," said he, "Barnabas'll never be Champion, Natty Bell—there aren't a fighting man in the Ring to-day as could stand up to him, but he'll never be Champion, an' you can lay to that, Natty Bell. And if you ask me why," said he, turning to select another pipe from the sheaf in the mantel-shelf, "I should tell you because he prefers to go to London an' try to turn himself into a gentleman."

"London," exclaimed Natty Bell, "a gentleman—our Barnabas—what?"

"Bide an' listen, Natty Bell," said the ex-champion, beginning to fill his new pipe.

"I'm listening, John."

"Well then, you must know, then, his uncle, my scapegrace brother Tom—you'll mind Tom as sailed away in a emigrant ship—well, Natty Bell, Tom has took an' died an' left a fortun' to our lad here."

"A fortun', John!—how much?"

"Seven—'undred—thousand—pound," said John, with a ponderous nod after each word, "seven—'undred—thousand—pound, Natty Bell, and there y' are."

Natty Bell opened his mouth, shut it, thrust his hands down into his pockets and brought out a short clay pipe.

"Man Jack," said he, beginning to fill the pipe, yet with gaze abstracted, "did I hear you say aught about a—gentleman?"

"Natty Bell, you did; our lad's took the idee into his nob to be a gentleman, an' I were trying to knock it out again, but as it is. Natty Bell, I fear me," and John Barty shook his handsome head and sighed ponderously.

"Why then, John, let's sit down, all three of us, and talk this matter over."

CHAPTER II

IN WHICH IS MUCH UNPLEASING MATTER REGARDING SILK PURSES, SOWS' EARS, MEN, AND GENTLEMEN

A slender man was Natty Bell, yet bigger than he looked, and prodigiously long in the reach, with a pair of very quick, bright eyes, and a wide, good-humored mouth ever ready to curve into a smile. But he was solemn enough now, and there was trouble in his eyes as he looked from John to Barnabas, who sat between them, his chair drawn up to the hearth, gazing down into the empty fireplace.

"An' you tell me, John," said he, as soon as his pipe was well alight,—"you tell me that our Barnabas has took it into his head to set up as a gentleman, do you?"

"Ah!" nodded John. Whereupon Natty Bell crossed his legs and leaning back in his chair fell a-singing to himself in his sweet voice, as was his custom when at all inclined to deep thought:

"A true Briton from Bristol, a rum one to fib, He's Champion of England, his name is Tom Cribb;"

"Ah! and you likewise tell me as our Barnabas has come into a fortun'."

"Seven—'undred—thousand—pound."

"Hum!" said Natty Bell,—"quite a tidy sum, John."

"Come list, all ye fighting gills
 And coves of boxing note, sirs,
While I relate some bloody mills
 In our time have been fought, sirs."

"Yes, a good deal can be done wi' such a sum as that, John."

"But it can't make a silk purse out of a sow's ear, Natty Bell,—nor yet a gentlemen out o' you or me—or Barnabas here."

"For instance," continued Natty Bell, "for instance, John:

"Since boxing is a manly game,
 And Britain's recreation,
By boxing we will raise our fame
 'Bove every other nation."

"As I say, John, a young and promising life can be wrecked, and utterly blasted by a much less sum than seven hundred thousand pound."

"Ah!" nodded John, "but a sow's ear aren't a silk purse, Natty Bell, no, nor never can be."

"True, John; but, arter all, a silk purse ain't much good if 't is empty—it's the gold inside of it as counts."

"But a silk purse is ever and always a silk purse—empty or no, Natty Bell."

"An' a man is always a man, John, which a gentleman often ain't."

"But surely," said Barnabas, speaking for the first time, "a gentleman is both."

"No—not nohow, my lad!" exclaimed John, beginning to rasp at his chin again. "A man is ever and allus a man—like me and you, an' Natty Bell, an' a gentleman's a gentleman like—Sir George Annersley—up at the great house yonder."

"But—" began Barnabas.

"Now, Barnabas"—remonstrated his father, rasping his chin harder than ever—"wherefore argufy—if you do go for to argufy—"

"We come back to the silk purses and the sows' ears," added Natty Bell.

"And I believe," said Barnabas, frowning down at the empty hearth, "I'm sure, that gentility rests not so much on birth as upon hereditary instinct."

"Hey?" said his father, glancing at him from the corners of his eyes—"go easy, Barnabas, my lad—give it time—on what did 'ee say?"

"On instinct, father."

"Instinct!" repeated John Barty, puffing out a vast cloud of smoke—"instinct does all right for 'osses, Barnabas, dogs likewise; but what's nat'ral to 'osses an' dogs aren't nowise nat'ral to us! No, you can't come instinct over human beings,—not nohowsoever, Barnabas, my lad. And, as I told you afore, a gentleman is nat'rally born a gentleman an' his feyther afore him an' his grand-feyther afore him, back an' back—"

"To Adam?" inquired Barnabas; "now, if so, the question is—was Adam a gentleman?"

"Lord, Barnabas!" exclaimed John Barty, with a reproachful look— "why drag in Adam? You leave poor old Adam alone, my lad. Adam indeed! What's Adam got to do wi' it?"

"Everything, we being all his descendants,—at least the Bible says so.—Lords and Commons, Peers and Peasants—all are children of Adam; so come now, father, was Adam a gentleman, Yes or No?"

John Barty frowned up at the ceiling, frowned down at the floor, and finally spoke:

"What do you say to that, Natty Bell?"

"Why, I should say, John—hum!"

"Pray haven't you heard of a jolly young coal-heaver,
Who down at Hungerford used for to ply,
His daddles he used with such skill and dexterity
Winning each mill, sir, and blacking each eye."

"Ha!—I should say, John, that Adam being in the habit o' going about—well, as you might put it—in a free and easy, airy manner, fig leaves an' suchlike, John,—I should say as he didn't have no call to be a gentleman, seeing as there weren't any tailors."

"Tailors!" exclaimed John, staring. "Lord! and what have tailors got to do wi' it, Natty Bell?"

"A great deal more than you 'd think, John; everything, John, seeing 't was tailors as invented gentlemen as a matter o' trade, John. So, if Barnabas wants to have a try at being one—he must first of all go dressed in the fashion."

"That is very true," said Barnabas, nodding.

"Though," pursued Natty Bell, "if you were the best dressed, the handsomest, the strongest, the bravest, the cleverest, the most honorable man in the world—that wouldn't make you a gentleman. I tell you, Barnabas, if you went among 'em and tried to be one of 'em,—they'd find you out some day an' turn their gentlemanly backs on you."

"Ah," nodded John, "and serve you right, lad,—because if you should try to turn yourself into a gentleman, why, Lord, Barnabas!—you'd only be a sort of a amitoor arter all, lad."

"Then," said Barnabas, rising up from his chair and crossing with resolute foot to the door, "then, just so soon as this law business is settled and the money mine, an Amateur Gentleman I'll be."

CHAPTER III

HOW BARNABAS SET OUT FOR LONDON TOWN

It was upon a certain glorious morning, some three weeks later, that Barnabas fared forth into the world; a morning full of the thousand scents of herb and flower and ripening fruits; a morning glad with the song of birds. And because it was still very early, the dew yet lay heavy, it twinkled in the grass, it sparkled in the hedges, and gemmed every leaf and twig with a flaming pendant. And amidst it all, fresh like the morning and young like the sun, came Barnabas, who, closing the door of the "Coursing Hound" behind him, leapt lightly down the stone steps and, turning his back upon the ancient inn, set off towards that hill, beyond which lay London and the Future. Yet—being gone but a very little way—he halted suddenly and came striding back again. And standing thus before the inn he let his eyes wander over its massive crossbeams, its leaning gables, its rows of gleaming lattices, and so up to the great sign swinging above the door—an ancient sign whereon a weather-beaten hound, dim-legged and faded of tail, pursued a misty blur that, by common report, was held to be a hare. But it was to a certain casement that his gaze oftenest reverted, behind whose open lattice he knew his father lay asleep, and his eyes, all at once, grew suffused with a glittering brightness that was not of the morning, and he took a step forward, half minded to clasp his father's hand once more ere he set out to meet those marvels and wonders that lay waiting for him over the hills—London-wards. Now, as he stood hesitating, he heard a voice that called his name softly, and, glancing round and up, espied Natty Bell, bare of neck and touzled of head, who leaned far out from the casement of his bedchamber above.

"Ah, Barnabas, lad!" said he with a nod—"So you're going to leave us, then?"

"Yes!" said Barnabas.

"And all dressed in your new clothes as fine as ever was!—stand back a bit and let me have a look at you."

"How are they, Natty Bell?" inquired Barnabas with a note of anxiety in his voice—"the Tenderden tailor assured me they were of the very latest cut and fashion—what do you think, Natty Bell?"

"Hum!" said the ex-pugilist, staring down at Barnabas, chin in hand. "Ha! they're very good clothes, Barnabas, yes indeed; just the very thing—for the country."

"The country!—I had these made for London, Natty Bell."

"For London, Barnabas—hum!"

"What do you mean by 'hum,' Natty Bell?"

"Why—look ye now—'t is a good sensible coat, I'll not deny, Barnabas; likewise the breeches is serviceable—but being only a coat and breeches, why—they ain't per-lite enough. For in the world of London, the per-lite world, Barnabas, clothes ain't garments to keep a man warm—they're works of art; in the country a man puts 'em on, and forgets all about 'em—in the per-lite world he has 'em put on for him, and remembers 'em. In the country a man wears his clothes, in the per-lite world his clothes wears him, ah! and they're often the perlitest thing about him, too!"

"I suppose," sighed Barnabas, "a man's clothes are very important—in the fashionable world?"

"Important! They are the most importantest part o' the fashionable world, lad. Now there's Mr. Brummell—him as they call the 'Beau'—well, he ain't exactly a Lord Nelson nor yet a Champion of England, he ain't never done nothing, good, bad, or indifferent—but he does know how to wear his clothes—consequently he's a very famous gentleman indeed—in the per-lite world, Barnabas." Here there fell a silence while Barnabas stared up at the inn and Natty Bell stared down at him. "To be sure, the old 'Hound' ain't much of a place, lad—not the kind of inn as a gentleman of quality would go out of his way to seek and search for, p'r'aps—but there be worse places in London, Barnabas, I was born there and I know. There, there! dear lad, never hang your head—youth must have its dreams I've heard; so go your ways, Barnabas. You're a master wi' your fists, thanks to John an' me—and you might have been Champion of England if you hadn't set your heart on being only a gentleman. Well, well, lad! don't forget as there are two old cocks o' the Game down here in Kent as will think o' you and talk o' you, Barnabas, and what you might have been if you hadn't happened to—Ah well, let be. But wherever you go and whatever you come to be—you're our lad still, and so, Barnabas, take this, wear it in memory of old Natty Bell—steady—catch!" And, with the word, he tossed down his great silver watch.

"Why, Natty Bell!" exclaimed Barnabas, very hoarse of voice. "Dear old Natty—I can't take this!"

"Ah, but you can—it was presented to me twenty and one years ago, Barnabas, the time I beat the Ruffian on Bexley Heath."

"But I can't—I couldn't take it," said Barnabas again, looking down at the broad-faced, ponderous timepiece in his hand, which he knew had long been Natty Bell's most cherished possession.

"Ay, but you can, lad—you must—'t is all I have to offer, and it may serve to mind you of me, now and then, so take it! take it! And, Barnabas, when you're tired o' being a fine gentleman up there in London, why—come back to us here at the old 'Hound' and be content to be just—a man. Good-by, lad; good-by!" saying which, Natty Bell nodded, drew in his head and vanished, leaving Barnabas to stare up at the closed lattice, with the ponderous timepiece ticking in his hand.

So, in a while, Barnabas slipped it into his pocket and, turning his back upon the "Coursing Hound," began to climb that hill beyond which lay the London of his dreams. Therefore as he went he kept his eyes lifted up to the summit of the hill, and his step grew light, his eye brightened, for Adventure lay in wait for him; Life beckoned to him from the distance; there was magic in the air. Thus

Barnabas strode on up the hill full of expectancy and the blind confidence in destiny which is the glory of youth.

Oh, Spirit of Youth, to whose fearless eyes all things are matters to wonder at; oh, brave, strong Spirit of Youth, to whom dangers are but trifles to smile at, and death itself but an adventure; to thee, since failure is unknown, all things are possible, and thou mayest, peradventure, make the world thy football, juggle with the stars, and even become a Fine Gentleman despite thy country homespun—and yet—

But as for young Barnabas, striding blithely upon his way, he might verily have been the Spirit of Youth itself—head high, eyes a-dance, his heart light as his step, his gaze ever upon the distance ahead, for he was upon the road at last, and every step carried him nearer the fulfilment of his dream.

"At Tonbridge he would take the coach," he thought, or perhaps hire a chaise and ride to London like a gentleman. A gentleman! and here he was whistling away like any ploughboy. Happily the road was deserted at this early hour, but Barnabas shook his head at himself reproachfully, and whistled no more—for a time.

But now, having reached the summit of the hill, he paused and turned to look back. Below him lay the old inn, blinking in its many casements in the level rays of the newly risen sun; and now, all at once, as he gazed down at it from this eminence, it seemed, somehow, to have shrunk, to have grown more weather-beaten and worn—truly never had it looked so small and mean as it did at this moment. Indeed, he had been wont to regard the "Coursing Hound" as the very embodiment of what an English inn should be—but now! Barnabas sighed—which was a new thing for him. "Was the change really in the old inn, or in himself?" he wondered. Hereupon he sighed again, and turning, went on down the hill. But now, as he went, his step lagged and his head drooped. "Was the change in the inn, or could it be that money can so quickly alter one?" he wondered. And straightway the coins in his pocket chinked and jingled "yes, yes!" wherefore Barnabas sighed for the third time, and his head drooped lower yet.

Well then, since he was rich, he would buy his father a better inn—the best in all England. A better inn! and the "Coursing Hound" had been his home as long as he could remember. A better inn! Here Barnabas sighed for the fourth time, and his step was heavier than ever as he went on down the hill.

CHAPTER IV

HOW BARNABAS FELL IN WITH A PEDLER OF BOOKS, AND PURCHASED A "PRICELESS WOLLUM"

"Heads up, young master, never say die! and wi' the larks and the throstles a-singing away so inspiring too—Lord love me!"

Barnabas started guiltily, and turning with upflung head, perceived a very small man perched on an adjacent milestone, with a very large pack at his feet, a very large hunk of bread and cheese in his hand, and with a book open upon his knee.

"Listen to that theer lark," said the man, pointing upwards with the knife he held.

"Well?" said Barnabas, a trifle haughtily perhaps.

"There's music for ye; there's j'y. I never hear a lark but it takes me back to London—to Lime'us, to Giles's Rents, down by the River."

"Pray, why?" inquired Barnabas, still a trifle haughtily.

"Because it's so different; there ain't much j'y, no, nor yet music in Giles's Rents, down by the River."

"Rather an unpleasant place!" said Barnabas.

"Unpleasant, young sir. I should say so—the worst place in the world—but listen to that theer blessed lark; there's a woice for ye; there's music with a capital M.; an' I've read as they cooks and eats 'em."

"Who do?"

"Nobs do—swells—gentlemen—ah, an' ladies, too!"

"More shame to them, then."

"Why, so says I, young master, but, ye see, beef an' mutton, ducks an' chicken, an' sich, ain't good enough for your Nobs nowadays, oh no! They must dewour larks wi' gusto, and French hortolons wi' avidity, and wi' a occasional leg of a frog throw'd in for a relish—though, to be sure, a frog's leg ain't over meaty at the best o' times. Oh, it's all true, young sir; it's all wrote down here in this priceless wollum." Here he tapped the book upon his knee. "Ye see, with the Quality it is quality as counts—not quantity. It's flavor as is their constant want, or, as you might say, desire; flavor in their meat, in their drink, and above all, in their books; an' see you, I sell books, an' I know."

"What kind of flavor?" demanded Barnabas, coming a step nearer, though in a somewhat stately fashion.

"Why, a gamey flavor, to be sure, young sir; a 'igh flavor—ah! the 'igher the better. Specially in books. Now here," continued the Chapman, holding up the volume he had been reading. "'Ere's a book as ain't to be ekalled nowheers nor nohow—not in Latin nor Greek, nor Persian, no, nor yet 'Indoo. A book as is fuller o' information than a egg is o' meat. A book as was wrote by a person o' quality, therefore a elewating book; wi' nice bold type into it—ah! an' wood-cuts—picters an' engravin's, works o' art as is not to be beat nowheers nor nohow; not in China, Asia, nor Africa, a book therefore as is above an' beyond all price."

"What book is it?" inquired Barnabas, forgetting his haughtiness, and coming up beside the Chapman.

"It's a book," said the Chapman; "no, it's THE book as any young gentleman a-going out into the world ought to have wi' him, asleep or awake."

"But what is it all about?" inquired Barnabas a trifle impatiently.

"Why, everything," answered the Chapman; "an' I know because I 've read it—a thing I rarely do."

"What's the title?"

"The title, young sir; well theer! read for yourself."

And with the words the Chapman held up the book open at the title-page, and Barnabas read:

HINTS ON ETIQUETTE,

OR

THE COMPLEAT ART OF A GENTLEMANLY DEPORTMENT
BY A PERSON OF QUALITY.

"You'll note that theer Person o' Quality, will ye?" said the Chapman.

"Strange!" said Barnabas.

"Not a bit of it!" retorted the Chapman. "Lord, love me! any one could be a gentleman by just reading and inwardly di-gesting o' this here priceless wollum; it's all down here in print, an' nice bold type, too—pat as you please. If it didn't 'appen as my horryscope demands as I should be a chapman, an' sell books an' sich along the roads, I might ha' been as fine a gentleman as any on 'em, just by follering the directions printed into this here blessed tome, an' in nice large type, too, an' woodcuts."

"This is certainly very remarkable!" said Barnabas.

"Ah!" nodded the Chapman, "it's the most remarkablest book as ever was!—Lookee—heer's picters for ye—lookee!" and he began turning over the pages, calling out the subject of the pictures as he did so.

"Gentleman going a walk in a jerry 'at. Gentleman eating soup! Gentleman kissing lady's 'and. Gentleman dancing with lady—note them theer legs, will ye—theer's elegance for ye! Gentleman riding a 'oss in one o' these 'ere noo buckled 'ats. Gentleman shaking 'ands with ditto—observe the cock o' that little finger, will ye! Gentleman eating ruffles—no, truffles, which is a vegetable, as all pigs is uncommon partial to. Gentleman proposing lady's 'ealth in a frilled shirt an' a pair o' skin-tights. Gentleman making a bow."

"And remarkably stiff in the legs about it, too!" nodded Barnabas.

"Stiff in the legs!" cried the Chapman reproachfully. "Lord love you, young sir! I've seen many a leg stiffer than that."

"And how much is the book?"

The Chapman cast a shrewd glance up at the tall youthful figure, at the earnest young face, at the deep and solemn eyes, and coughed behind his hand.

"Well, young sir," said he, gazing thoughtfully up at the blue sky—"since you are you, an' nobody else—an' ax me on so fair a morning, wi' the song o' birds filling the air—we'll charge you only—well—say ten shillings: say eight, say seven-an'-six—say five—theer, make it five shillings, an' dirt-cheap at the price, too."

Barnabas hesitated, and the Chapman was about to come down a shilling or two more when Barnabas spoke.

"Then you're not thinking of learning to become a gentleman yourself?"

"O Lord love you—no!"

"Then I'll buy it," said Barnabas, and forthwith handed over the five shillings. Slipping the book into his pocket, he turned to go, yet paused again and addressed the Chapman over his shoulder.

"Shouldn't you like to become a gentleman?" he inquired.

Again the Chapman regarded him from the corners of his eyes, and again he coughed behind his hand.

"Well," he admitted, "I should an' I shouldn't. O' course it must be a fine thing to bow to a duchess, or 'and a earl's daughter into a chariot wi' four 'orses an' a couple o' footmen, or even to sit wi' a markus an' eat a French hortolon (which never 'aving seen, I don't know the taste on, but it sounds promising); oh yes, that part would suit me to a T; but then theer's t'other part to it, y' see."

"What do you mean?"

"Why, a gentleman has a great deal to live up to—theer's his dignity, y' see."

"Yes, I suppose so," Barnabas admitted.

"For instance, a gentleman couldn't very well be expected to sit in a ditch and enj'y a crust o' bread an' cheese; 'is dignity wouldn't allow of it, now would it?"

"Certainly not," said Barnabas.

"Nor yet drink 'ome-brewed out of a tin pot in a inn kitchen."

"Well, he might, if he were very thirsty," Barnabas ventured to think. But the Chapman scouted the idea.

"For," said he, "a gentleman's dignity lifts him above inn kitchens and raises him superior to tin pots. Now tin pots is a perticler weakness o' mine, leastways when theer's good ale inside of 'em. And then again an' lastly," said the Chapman, balancing a piece of cheese on the flat of his knife-blade, "lastly theer's his clothes, an', as I've read somewhere, 'clothes make the man'—werry good—chuck in dignity an' theer's your gentleman!"

"Hum," said Barnabas, profoundly thoughtful.

"An' a gentleman's clothes is a world o' trouble and anxiety to him, and takes up most o' his time, what wi' his walking breeches an' riding breeches an' breeches for dancing; what wi' his coats cut 'igh an' his coats cut low; what wi' his flowered satin weskits; what wi' his boots an' his gloves, an' his cravats an' his 'ats, why, Lord love ye, he passes his days getting out o' one suit of clothes an' into another. And it's just this clothes part as I can't nowise put up wi', for I'm one as loves a easy life, I am."

"And is your life so easy?" inquired Barnabas, eyeing the very small Chapman's very large pack.

"Why, to be sure theer's easier," the Chapman admitted, scratching his ear and frowning; "but then," and here his brow cleared again, "I've only got this one single suit of clothes to bother my 'ead over, which, being wore out as you can see, don't bother me at all."

"Then are you satisfied to be as you are?"

"Well," answered the Chapman, clinking the five shillings in his pocket, "I aren't one to grumble at fate, nor yet growl at fortun'."

"Why, then," said Barnabas, "I wish you good morning."

"Good morning, young sir, and remember now, if you should ever feel like being a gentleman—it's quite easy—all as you've got to do is to read the instructions in that theer priceless wollum—mark 'em—learn 'em, and inwardly di-gest 'em, and you'll be a gentleman afore you know it."

Now hereupon Barnabas smiled, a very pleasant smile and radiant with youth, whereat the Chapman's pinched features softened for pure good fellowship, and for the moment he almost wished that he had charged less for the "priceless wollum," as, so smiling, Barnabas turned and strode away, London-wards.

CHAPTER V

IN WHICH THE HISTORIAN SEES FIT TO INTRODUCE A LADY OF QUALITY; AND FURTHER NARRATES HOW BARNABAS TORE A WONDERFUL BOTTLE-GREEN COAT

Now in a while Barnabas came to where was a stile with a path beyond—a narrow path that led up over a hill until it lost itself in a wood that crowned the ascent; a wood where were shady dells full of a quivering green twilight; where broad glades led away beneath leafy arches, and where a stream ran gurgling in the shade of osiers and willows; a wood that Barnabas had known from boyhood. Therefore, setting his hand upon the stile, he vaulted lightly over, minded to go through the wood and join the high road further on. This he did by purest chance, and all unthinking followed the winding path.

Now had Barnabas gone on by the road how different this history might have been, and how vastly different his career! But, as it happened, moved by Chance, or Fate, or Destiny, or what you will, Barnabas vaulted over the stile and strode on up the winding path, whistling as he went, and, whistling, plunged into the green twilight of the wood, and, whistling still, swung suddenly into a broad and grassy glade splashed green and gold with sunlight, and then stopped all at once and stood there silent, dumb, the very breath in check between his lips.

She lay upon her side—full length upon the sward, and her tumbled hair made a glory in the grass, a golden mane. Beneath this silken curtain he saw dark brows that frowned a little—a vivid mouth, and lashes thick and dark like her eyebrows, that curled upon the pallor of her cheek.

Motionless stood Barnabas, with eyes that wandered from the small polished riding-boot, with its delicately spurred heel, to follow the gracious line that swelled voluptuously from knee to rounded hip, that sank in sweetly to a slender waist, yet rose again to the rounded beauty of her bosom.

So Barnabas stood and looked and looked, and looking sighed, and stole a step near and stopped again, for behold the leafy screen was parted suddenly, and Barnabas beheld two boots—large boots they were but of exquisite shape—boots that strode strongly and planted themselves masterfully; Hessian boots, elegant, glossy and betasselled. Glancing higher, he observed a coat of a bottle-green, high-collared, close-fitting and silver-buttoned; a coat that served but to make more apparent the broad chest, powerful shoulders, and lithe waist of its wearer. Indeed a truly marvellous coat (at least, so thought Barnabas), and in that moment, he, for the first time, became aware how clumsy and ill-contrived were his own garments; he understood now what Natty Bell had meant when he had said they were not polite enough; and as for his boots—blunt of toe, thick-soled and ponderous—he positively blushed for them. Here, it occurred to him that the wearer of the coat possessed a face, and he looked at it accordingly. It was a handsome face he saw, dark of eye, square-chinned and full-lipped. Just now the eyes were lowered, for their possessor stood apparently lost in leisurely contemplation of her who lay outstretched between them; and as his gaze wandered to and fro over her defenceless beauty, a glow dawned in the eyes, and the full lips parted in a slow smile, whereat Barnabas frowned darkly, and his cheeks grew hot because of her too betraying habit.

"Sir!" said he between snapping teeth.

Then, very slowly and unwillingly, the gentleman raised his eyes and stared across at him.

"And pray," said he carelessly, "pray who might you be?"

At his tone Barnabas grew more angry and therefore more polite.

"Sir, that—permit me to say—does not concern you."

"Not in the least," the other retorted, "and I bid you good day; you can go, my man, I am acquainted with this lady; she is quite safe in my care."

"That, sir, I humbly beg leave to doubt," said Barnabas, his politeness growing.

"Why—you impudent scoundrel!"

Barnabas smiled.

"Come, take yourself off!" said the gentleman, frowning, "I'll take care of this lady."

"Pardon me! but I think not."

The gentleman stared at Barnabas through suddenly narrow lids, and laughed softly, and Barnabas thought his laugh worse than his frown.

"Ha! d' you mean to say you—won't go?"

"With all the humility in the world, I do, sir."

"Why, you cursed, interfering yokel! must I thrash you?"

Now "yokel" stung, for Barnabas remembered his blunt-toed boots, therefore he smiled with lips suddenly grim, and his politeness grew almost aggressive.

"Thrash me, sir!" he repeated, "indeed I almost venture to fear that you must." But the gentleman's gaze had wandered to the fallen girl once more, and the glow was back in his roving eyes.

"Pah!" said he, still intent, "if it is her purse you are after—here, take mine and leave us in peace." As he spoke, he flung his purse towards Barnabas, and took a long step nearer the girl. But in that same instant Barnabas strode forward also and, being nearer, reached her first, and, stepping over her, it thus befell that they came face to face within a foot of one another. For a moment they stood thus, staring into each other's eyes, then without a word swift and sudden they closed and grappled.

The gentleman was very quick, and more than ordinarily strong, so also was Barnabas, but the gentleman's handsome face was contorted with black rage, whereas Barnabas was smiling, and therein seemed the only difference between them as they strove together breast to breast, now in sunlight, now in shadow, but always grimly silent.

So, within the glory of the morning, they reeled and staggered to and fro, back and forth, trampling down the young grass, straining, panting, swaying—the one frowning and determined, the other smiling and grim.

Suddenly the bottle-green coat ripped and tore as its wearer broke free; there was the thud of a blow, and Barnabas staggered back with blood upon his face—staggered, I say, and in that moment, as his antagonist rushed, laughed fierce and short, and stepped lightly aside and smote him clean and true under the chin, a little to one side.

The gentleman's fists flew wide, he twisted upon his heels, pitched over upon his face, and lay still.

Smiling still, Barnabas looked down upon him, then grew grave.

"Indeed," said he, "indeed it was a great pity to spoil such a wonderful coat."

So he turned away, and coming to where she, who was the unwitting cause of all this, yet lay, stopped all at once, for it seemed to him that her posture was altered; her habit had become more decorous, and yet the lashes, so dark in contrast to her hair, those shadowy lashes yet curled upon her cheek. Therefore, very presently, Barnabas stooped, and raising her in his arms bore her away through the wood towards the dim recesses where, hidden in the green shadows, his friend the brook went singing upon its way.

And in a while the gentleman stirred and sat up, and, beholding his torn coat, swore viciously, and, chancing upon his purse, pocketed it, and so went upon his way, and by contrast with the glory of the morning his frown seemed the blacker.

CHAPTER VI

OF THE BEWITCHMENT OF BLACK EYELASHES; AND OF A FATEFUL LACE HANDKERCHIEF

Let it be understood that Barnabas was not looking at her as she lay all warm and yielding in his embrace, on the contrary, he walked with his gaze fixed pertinaciously upon the leafy path he followed, nevertheless he was possessed, more than once, of a sudden feeling that her eyes had opened and were watching him, therefore, after a while be it noted, needs must he steal a downward glance at her beauty, only to behold the shadowy lashes curling upon her cheeks, as was but natural, of course. And now he began to discover that these were, indeed, no ordinary lashes (though to be sure his experience in such had been passing small), yet the longer he gazed upon them the more certain he became that these were, altogether and in all respects, the most demurely tantalizing lashes in the world. Then, again, there was her mouth—warmly red, full-lipped and sensitive like the delicate nostrils above; a mouth all sweet curves; a mouth, he thought, that might grow firm and proud, or wonderfully tender as the case might be, a mouth of scarlet bewitchment; a mouth that for some happy mortal might be—here our Barnabas came near blundering into a tree, and thenceforth he kept his gaze upon the path again. So, strong armed and sure of foot, he bore her through the magic twilight of the wood until he reached the brook. And coming to where the bending willows made a leafy bower he laid her there, then, turning, went down to the brook and drawing off his neckerchief began to moisten it in the clear, cool water.

And lo! in the same minute, the curling lashes were lifted suddenly, and beneath their shadow two eyes looked out—deep and soft and darkly blue, the eyes of a maid—now frank and ingenuous, now shyly troubled, but brimful of witchery ever and always. And pray what could there be in all the fair world more proper for a maid's eyes to rest upon than young Alcides, bare of throat, and with the sun in his curls, as he knelt to moisten the neckerchief in the brook?

Therefore, as she lay, she gazed upon him in her turn, even as he had first looked upon her, pleased to find his face so young and handsome, to note the breadth of his shoulders, the graceful carriage of his limbs, his air of virile strength and latent power, yet doubting too, because of her sex, because of the loneliness, and because he was a man; thus she lay blushing a little, sighing a little, fearing a little, waiting for him to turn. True, he had been almost reverent so far, but then the place was so very lonely. And yet—

Barnabas turned and came striding up the bank. And how was he to know anything of all this, as he stood above her with his dripping neckerchief in his hand, looking down at her lying so very still, and pitying her mightily because her lashes showed so dark against the pallor of her cheek? How was he to know how her heart leapt in her white bosom as he sank upon his knees beside her? Therefore he leaned above her closer and raised the dripping neckerchief. But in that moment she (not minded to be wet) sighed, her white lids fluttered, and, sitting up, she stared at him for all the world as though she had never beheld him until that very moment.

"What are you going to do?" she demanded, drawing away from the streaming neckerchief. "Who are you? Why am I here?—what has happened?"

Barnabas hesitated, first because he was overwhelmed by this sudden torrent of questions, and secondly because he rarely spoke without thinking; therefore, finding him silent, she questioned him again—

"Where am I?"

"In Annersley Wood, madam."

"Ah, yes, I remember, my horse ran away."

"So I brought you here to the brook."

"Why?"

"You were hurt; I found you bleeding and senseless."

"Bleeding!" And out came a dainty lace handkerchief on the instant.

"There," said Barnabas, "above your eyebrow," and he indicated a very small trickle of blood upon the snow of her temple.

"And you—found me, sir?"

"Beneath the riven oak in the Broad Glade—over yonder."

"That is a great way from here, sir!"

"You are not—heavy!" Barnabas explained, a little clumsily perhaps, for she fell silent at this, and stooped her head the better to dab tenderly at the cut above her eyebrow; also the color deepened in her cheeks.

"Madam," said Barnabas, "that is the wrong eyebrow."

"Then why don't you tell me where I'm hurt?" she sighed. For answer, after a moment's hesitation, Barnabas reached out and taking her hand, handkerchief and all, laid it very gently upon the cut, though to be sure it was a very poor thing, as cuts go, after all.

"There," said he again, "though indeed it is very trifling."

"Indeed, sir, it pains atrociously!" she retorted, and to bear out her words showed him her handkerchief, upon whose snow was a tiny vivid stain.

"Then perhaps," ventured Barnabas, "perhaps I'd better bathe it with this!" and he held up his dripping handkerchief.

"Nay, sir, I thank you," she answered, "keep it for your own wounds—there is a cut upon your cheek."

"A cut!" repeated Barnabas—bethinking him of the gentleman's signet ring.

"Yes, a cut, sir," she repeated, and stole a glance at him under her long lashes; "pray did *your* horse run away also?"

Barnabas was silent again, this time because he knew not how to answer—therefore he began rubbing at his injured cheek while she watched him—and after a while spoke.

"Sir," said she, "that is the wrong cheek."

"Then, indeed, this must be very trifling also," said Barnabas, smiling.

"Does it pain you, sir?"

"Thank you—no."

"Yet it bleeds! You say it was not your horse, sir?" she inquired, wonderfully innocent of eye.

"No, it was not my horse."

"Why, then—pray, how did it happen?"

"Happen, madam?—why, I fancy I must have—scratched myself," returned Barnabas, beginning to wring out his neckerchief.

"Scratched yourself. Ah! of course!" said she, and was silent while Barnabas continued to wring the water from his neckerchief.

"Pray," she inquired suddenly, "do you often scratch yourself—until you bleed?—'t is surely a most distressing habit." Now glancing up suddenly, Barnabas saw her eyes were wonderfully bright for all her solemn mouth, and suspicion grew upon him.—"Did she know? Had she seen?" he wondered.

"Nevertheless, sir—my thanks are due to you—"

"For what?" he inquired quickly.

"Why—for—for—"

"For bringing you here?" he suggested, beginning to wring out his neckerchief again.

"Yes; believe me I am more than grateful for—for—"

"For what, madam?" he inquired again, looking at her now.

"For—your—kindness, sir."

"Pray, how have I been kind?—you refused my neckerchief."

Surely he was rather an unpleasant person after all, she thought, with his persistently direct eyes, and his absurdly blunt mode of questioning—and she detested answering questions.

"Sir," said she, with her dimpled chin a little higher than usual, "it is a great pity you troubled yourself about me, or spoilt your neckerchief with water."

"I thought you were hurt, you see—"

"Oh, sir, I grieve to disappoint you," said she, and rose, and indeed she gained her feet with admirable grace and dignity notwithstanding her recent fall, and the hampering folds of her habit; and now Barnabas saw that she was taller than he had thought.

"Disappoint me!" repeated Barnabas, rising also; "the words are unjust."

For a moment she stood, her head thrown back, her eyes averted disdainfully, and it was now that Barnabas first noticed the dimple in her chin, and he was yet observing it very exactly when he became aware that her haughtiness was gone again and that her eyes were looking up at him, half laughing, half shy, and of course wholly bewitching.

"Yes, I know it was," she admitted, "but oh! won't you please believe that a woman can't fall off her horse without being hurt, though it won't bleed much." Now as she spoke a distant clock began to strike and she to count the strokes, soft and mellow with distance.

"Nine!" she exclaimed with an air of tragedy—"then I shall be late for breakfast, and I'm ravenous—and gracious heavens!"

"What now, madam?"

"My hair! It's all come down—look at it!"

"I've been doing so ever since I—met you," Barnabas confessed.

"Oh, have you! Then why didn't you tell me of it—and I've lost nearly all my hairpins—and—oh dear! what will they think?"

"That it is the most beautiful hair in all the world, of course," said Barnabas. She was already busy twisting it into a shining rope, but here she paused to look up at him from under this bright nimbus, and with two hair-pins in her mouth.

"Oh!" said she again very thoughtfully, and then "Do you think so?" she inquired, speaking over and round the hairpins as it were.

"Yes," said Barnabas, steady-eyed; and immediately down came the curling lashes again, while with dexterous white fingers she began to transform the rope into a coronet.

"I'm afraid it won't hold up," she said, giving her head a tentative shake, "though, fortunately, I haven't far to go."

"How far?" asked Barnabas.

"To Annersley House, sir."

"Yes," said Barnabas, "that is very near—the glade yonder leads into the park."

"Do you know Annersley, then, sir?"

Barnabas hesitated and, having gone over the question in his mind, shook his head.

"I know of it," he answered.

"Do you know Sir George Annersley?"

Again Barnabas hesitated. As a matter of fact he knew as much of Sir George as he knew of the "great house," as it was called thereabouts, that is to say he had seen him once or twice—in the distance. But it would never do to admit as much to her, who now looked up at him with eyes of witchery as she waited for him to speak. Therefore Barnabas shook his head, and answered airily enough:

"We are not exactly acquainted, madam."

Yesterday he would have scorned the subterfuge; but to-day there was money in his purse; London awaited him with expectant arms, the very air was fraught with a magic whereby the impossible might become concrete fact, wherein dreams might become realities; was not she herself, as she stood before him lithe and vigorous in all the perfection of her warm young womanhood—was she not the very embodiment of those dreams that had haunted him sleeping and waking? Verily. Therefore with this magic in the air might he not meet Sir George Annersley at the next cross-roads or by-lane, and strike up an enduring friendship on the spot—truly, for anything was possible to-day. Meanwhile my lady had gathered up the folds of her riding-habit, and yet in the act of turning into the leafy path, spoke:

"Are you going far, sir?"

"To London."

"Have you many friends there?"

"None,—as yet, madam."

After this they walked on in silence, she with her eyes on the lookout for obstacles, he lost to all but the beauty of the young body before him—the proud carriage of the head, the sway of the hips, the firm poise of the small and slender foot—all this he saw and admired, yet (be it remarked) his face bore nothing of the look that had distorted the features of the gentleman in the bottle-green coat—though to be sure our Barnabas was but an amateur at best—even as Natty Bell had said. So at last she reached the fateful glade beyond which, though small with distance, was a noble house set upon a gentle hill that rose above the swaying green of trees. Here my lady paused; she looked up the glade and down the glade, and finally at him. And her eyes were the eyes of a maid, shy, mischievous, demure, challenging.

"Sir," said she, shyly, demurely—but with eyes still challenging— "sir, I have to thank you. I do thank you—more than these poor lips can tell. If there is anything I could—do—to—to prove my gratitude, you—have but to—name it."

"Do," stammered Barnabas. "Do—indeed—I—no."

The challenging eyes were hidden now, but the lips curved wonderfully tempting and full of allurement. Barnabas clenched his fists hard.

"I see, sir, your cheek has stopped bleeding, 't is almost well. I think—there are others—whose hurts will not heal—quite so soon—and, between you and me, sir, I'm glad—glad! Good-by! and may you find as many friends in London as you deserve." So saying, she turned and went on down the glade.

And in a little Barnabas sighed, and turning also, strode on London-wards.

Now when she had gone but a very short way, my lady must needs glance back over her shoulder, then, screened to be sure by a convenient bramble-bush, she stood to watch him as he swung along, strong, graceful, but with never a look behind.

"Who was he?" she wondered. "What was he? From his clothes he might be anything between a gamekeeper and a farmer."

Alas! poor Barnabas! To be sure his voice was low and modulated, and his words well chosen—who was he, what was he? And he was going to London where he had no friends. And he had never told his name, nor, what was a great deal worse, asked for hers! Here my lady frowned, for such indifference was wholly new in her experience. But on went long-legged Barnabas, all unconscious, striding through sunlight and shadow, with step blithe and free—and still (Oh! Barnabas) with never a look behind. Therefore, my lady's frown grew more portentous, and she stamped her foot at his unconscious back; then all at once the frown vanished in a sudden smile, and she instinctively shrank closer into cover, for Barnabas had stopped.

"Oh, indeed, sir!" she mocked, secure behind her leafy screen, nodding her head at his unconscious back; "so you've actually thought better of it, have you?"

Here Barnabas turned.

"Really, sir, you will even trouble to come all the way back, will you, just to learn her name—or, perhaps to—indeed, what condescension. But, dear sir, you're too late; oh, yes, indeed you are! 'for he who will not when he may, when he will he shall have nay.' I grieve to say you are too late—quite too late! Good morning, Master Shill-I-shall-I." And with the word she turned, then hastily drew a certain lace handkerchief from her bosom, and set it very cleverly among the thorns of a bramble, and so sped away among the leaves.

CHAPTER VII

IN WHICH MAY BE FOUND DIVERS RULES AND MAXIMS FOR THE ART OF BOWING

"Now, by the Lord!" said Barnabas, stopping all at once, "forgetful fool that I am! I never bowed to her!" Therefore, being minded to repair so grave an omission, he turned sharp about, and came striding back again, and thus it befell that he presently espied the lace handkerchief fluttering from the bramble, and having extricated the delicate lace from the naturally reluctant thorns with a vast degree of care and trouble, he began to look about for the late owner. But search how he might, his efforts proved unavailing—Annersley Wood was empty save for himself. Having satisfied himself of the fact, Barnabas sighed again, thrust the handkerchief into his pocket, and once more set off upon his way.

But now, as he went, he must needs remember his awkward stiffness when she had thanked him; he grew hot all over at the mere recollection, and, moreover, he had forgotten even to bow! But there again, was he quite sure that he could bow as a gentleman should? There were doubtless certain rules and maxims for the bow as there were for mathematics—various motions to be observed in the making of it, of which Barnabas confessed to himself his utter ignorance. What then was a bow? Hereupon, bethinking him of the book in his pocket, he drew it out, and turning to a certain page, began to study the "stiff-legged-gentleman" with a new and enthralled interest. Now over against this gentleman, that is to say, on the opposite page, he read these words:—

"THE ART OF BOWING."

"To know how, and when, and to whom to bow, is in itself an art. The bow is, indeed, an all-important accomplishment,—it is the 'Open Sesame' of the 'Polite World.' To bow gracefully, therefore, may be regarded as the most important part of a gentlemanly deportment."

"Hum!" said Barnabas, beginning to frown at this; and yet, according to the title-page, these were the words of a "Person of Quality."

"To bow gracefully,"—the Person of Quality chattered on,—"the feet should be primarily disposed as in the first position of dancing."

Barnabas sighed, frowning still.

"The left hand should be lifted airily and laid upon the bosom, the fingers kept elegantly spread.

The head is now stooped forward, the body following easily from the hips, the right hand, at the same moment, being waved gracefully in the air. It is, moreover, very necessary that the expression of the features should assume as engaging an air as possible. The depth of the bow is to be regulated to the rank of the person saluted."

And so forth and so on for two pages more.

Barnabas sighed and shook his head hopelessly.

"Ah!" said he, "under these circumstances it is perhaps just as well that I forgot to try. It would seem I should have bungled it quite shamefully. Who would have thought a thing so simple could become a thing so very complicated!" Saying which, he shut the book, and thrust it back into his pocket, and thus became aware of a certain very small handful of dainty lace and cambric, and took it out, and, looking at it, beheld again the diminutive stain, while there stole to his nostrils a perfume, faint and very sweet.

"I wonder," said he to himself. "I wonder who she was—I might have asked her name but, fool that I am, I even forgot that!"

Here Barnabas sighed, and, sighing, hid the handkerchief in his pocket.

"And yet," he pursued, "had she told me her name, I should have been compelled to announce mine, and—Barnabas Barty—hum! somehow there is no suggestion about it of broad acres, or knightly ancestors; no, Barty will never do." Here Barnabas became very thoughtful. "Mortimer sounds better," said he, after a while, "or Mandeville. Then there's Neville, and Desborough, and Ravenswood—all very good names, and yet none of them seems quite suitable. Still I must have a name that is beyond all question!" And Barnabas walked on more thoughtful than ever. All at once he stopped, and clapped hand to thigh.

"My mother's name, of course—Beverley; yes, it is an excellent name, and, since it was hers, I have more right to it than to any other. So Beverley it shall be—Barnabas Beverley—good!" Here Barnabas stopped and very gravely lifted his hat to his shadow.

"Mr. Beverley," said he, "I salute you, your very humble obedient servant, Mr. Beverley, sir, God keep you!" Hereupon he put on his hat again, and fell into his swinging stride.

"So," said he, "that point being settled it remains to master the intricacies of the bow." Saying which, he once more had recourse to the "priceless wollum," and walked on through the glory of the morning, with his eyes upon the valuable instructions of the "Person of Quality."

Now, as he went, chancing to look up suddenly, he beheld a gate-post. A very ancient gate-post it was—a decrepit gate-post, worn and heavy with years, for it leaned far out from the perpendicular. And with his gaze upon this, Barnabas halted suddenly, clapped the book to his bosom, and raising his hat with an elegant flourish, bowed to that gnarled and withered piece of timber as though it had been an Archduke at the very least, or the loveliest lady in the land.

"Ha! by Thor and Odin, what's all this?" cried a voice behind him. "I say what the devil's all this?"

Turning sharp about, Barnabas beheld a shortish, broad-shouldered individual in a befrogged surtout and cords, something the worse for wear, who stood with his booted legs wide apart and stared at him from a handsome bronzed face, with a pair of round blue eyes; he held a broad-brimmed hat in his hand—the other, Barnabas noticed, was gone from the elbow.

"Egad!" said he, staring at Barnabas with his blue eyes. "What's in the wind? I say, what the devil, sir—eh, sir?"

Forthwith Barnabas beamed upon him, and swept him another bow almost as low as that he had bestowed upon the gate-post.

"Sir," said he, hat gracefully flourished in the air, "your very humble obedient servant to command."

"A humble obedient fiddlestick, sir!" retorted the new comer. "Pooh, sir!—I say dammit!—are ye mad, sir, to go bowing and scraping to a gate-post, as though it were an Admiral of the Fleet or Nelson himself—are ye mad or only drunk, sir? I say, what d' ye mean?"

Here Barnabas put on his hat and opened the book.

"Plainly, sir," he answered, "being overcome with a sudden desire to bow to something or other, I bowed to that gate-post in want of a worthier object; but now, seeing you arrive so very opportunely, I' 11 take the liberty of trying another. Oblige me by observing if my expression is sufficiently engaging," and with the words Barnabas bowed as elaborately as before.

"Sink me!" exclaimed the one-armed individual, rounder of eye than ever, "the fellow's mad—stark, staring mad."

"No, indeed, sir," smiled Barnabas, reassuringly, "but the book here—which I am given to understand is wholly infallible—says that to bow is the most important item of a gentlemanly equipment, and in the World of Fashion—"

"In the World of Fashion, sir, there are no gentlemen left," his hearer broke in.

"How, sir—?"

"I say no, sir, no one. I say, damme, sir—"

"But, sir—"

"I say there are no gentlemen in the fashionable world—they are all blackguardly Bucks, cursed Corinthians, and mincing Macaronies nowadays, sir. Fashionable world—bah, sir!"

"But, sir, is not the Prince himself—"

"The Prince, sir!" Here the one-armed gentleman clapped on his hat and snorted, "The Prince is a—prince, sir; he's also an authority on sauce and shoe-buckles. Let us talk of something more interesting—yourself, for instance."

Barnabas bowed.

"Sir," said he, "my name is Barnabas—Barnabas Beverley."

"Hum!" said the other, thoughtfully, "I remember a Beverley—a lieutenant under Hardy in the 'Agamemnon'—though, to be sure, he spelt his name with an 'l-e-y.'"

"So do I, sir," said Barnabas.

"Hum!"

"Secondly, I am on my way to London."

"London! Egad! here's another of 'em! London, of course—well?"

"Where I hope to cut some figure in the—er—World of Fashion."

"Fashion—Gog and Magog!—why not try drowning. 'T would be simpler and better for you in the long run. London! Fashion! in that hat, that coat, those—"

"Sir," said Barnabas, flushing, "I have already—"

"Fashion, eh? Why, then, you must cramp that chest into an abortion, all collar, tail, and buttons, and much too tight to breathe in; you must struggle into breeches tight enough to burst, and cram your feet into bepolished torments—"

"But, sir," Barnabas ventured again, "surely the Prince himself is accountable for the prevailing fashion, and as you must know, he is said to be the First Gentleman in Europe and—"

"Fiddle-de-dee and the devil, sir!—who says he is? A set of crawling sycophants, sir—a gang of young reprobates and bullies. First Gentleman in—I say pish, sir! I say bah! Don't I tell you that gentlemen went out o' fashion when Bucks came in? I say there isn't a gentleman left in England except perhaps one or two. This is the age of your swaggering, prize-fighting Corinthians. London swarms with 'em, Brighton's rank with 'em, yet they pervade even these solitudes, damme! I saw one of 'em only half an hour ago, limping out of a wood yonder. Ah! a polished, smiling rascal—a dangerous rogue! One of your sleepy libertines—one of your lucky gamblers—one of your conscienceless young reprobates equally ready to win your money, ruin your sister, or shoot you dead as the case may be, and all in the approved way of gallantry, sir; and, being all this, and consequently high in royal favor, he is become a very lion in the World of Fashion. Would you succeed, young sir, you must model yourself upon him as nearly as may be."

"And he was limping, you say?" inquired Barnabas, thoughtfully.

"And serve him right, sir—egad! I say damme! he should limp in irons to Botany Bay and stay there if I had my way."

"Did you happen to notice the color of his coat?" inquired Barnabas again.

"Ay, 't was green, sir; but what of it—have you seen him?"

"I think I have, sir," said Barnabas, "if 't was a green coat he wore. Pray, sir, what might his name be?"

"His name, sir, is Carnaby—Sir Mortimer Carnaby."

"Sir Mortimer Carnaby!" said Barnabas, nodding his head.

"And, sir," pursued his informant, regarding Barnabas from beneath his frowning brows, "since it is your ambition to cut a figure in the World of Fashion, your best course is to cultivate him, frequent his society as much as possible, act upon his counsel, and in six months, or less, I don't doubt you'll be as polished a young blackguard as any of 'em. Good morning, sir."

Here the one-armed gentleman nodded and turned to enter the field.

"Sir," said Barnabas, "one moment! Since you have been so obliging as to describe a Buck, will you tell me who and what in your estimation is a gentleman?"

"A gentleman? Egad, sir! must I tell you that? No, I say I won't—the Bo'sun shall." Hereupon the speaker faced suddenly about and raised his voice: "Aft there!" he bellowed. "Pass the word for the Bo'sun—I say where's Bo'sun Jerry?"

Immediately upon these words there came another roar surprisingly hoarse, deep, and near at hand.

"Ay, ay, sir! here I be, Cap'n," the voice bellowed back. "Here I be, sir, my helm hard a-starboard, studden sails set, and all a-drawing alow and aloft, but making bad weather on it on account o' these here furrers and this here jury-mast o' mine, but I'll fetch up alongside in a couple o' tacks."

Now glancing in the direction of the voice, Barnabas perceived a head and face that bobbed up and down on the opposite side of the hedge. A red face it was, a jovial, good-humored face, lit up with quick, bright eyes that twinkled from under a prodigious pair of eyebrows; a square honest face whose broad good nature beamed out from a mighty bush of curling whisker and pigtail, and was surmounted by a shining, glazed hat.

Being come opposite to them, he paused to mop at his red face with a neckerchief of vivid hue, which done, he touched the brim of the glazed hat, and though separated from them by no more than the hedge and ditch, immediately let out another roar—for all the world as though he had been hailing the maintop of a Seventy-four in a gale of wind.

"Here I be, Cap'n!" he bellowed, "studden sails set an' drawing, tho' obleeged to haul my wind, d'ye see, on account o' this here spar o' mine a-running foul o' the furrers." Having said the which, he advanced again with a heave to port and a lurch to starboard very like a ship in a heavy sea; this peculiarity of gait was explained as he hove into full view, for then Barnabas saw that his left leg was gone from the knee and had been replaced by a wooden one.

"Bo'sun," said the Captain, indicating Barnabas, with a flap of his empty sleeve, "Bo'sun—favor me, I say oblige me by explaining to this young gentleman your opinion of a gentleman—I say tell him who you think is the First Gentleman in Europe!"

The Bo'sun stared from Barnabas to the Captain and back again.

"Begging your Honor's parding," said he, touching the brim of the glazed hat, "but surely nobody don't need to be told that 'ere?"

"It would seem so, Jerry."

"Why then, Cap'n—since you ax me, I should tell you—bold an' free like, as the First Gentleman in Europe—ah! or anywhere else—was Lord Nelson an' your Honor."

As he spoke the Bo'sun stood up very straight despite his wooden leg, and when he touched his hat again, his very pigtail seemed straighter and stiffer than ever.

"Young sir," said the Captain, regarding Barnabas from the corners of his eyes, "what d' ye say to that?"

"Why," returned Barnabas, "now I come to think of it, I believe the Bo'sun is right."

"Sir," nodded the Captain, "the Bo'sun generally is; my Bo'sun, sir, is as remarkable as that leg of his which he has contrived so that it will screw on or off—in sections sir—I mean the wooden one."

"But," said Barnabas, beginning to stroke his chin in the argumentative way that was all his father's, "but, sir, I was meaning gentlemen yet living, and Lord Nelson, unfortunately, is dead."

"Bo'sun," said the Captain, "what d' ye say to that?"

"Why, Cap'n, axing the young gentleman's pardon, I beg leave to remark, or as you might say, ob-serve, as men like 'im don't die, they jest gets promoted, so to speak."

"Very true, Jerry," nodded the Captain again, "they do, but go to a higher service, very true. And now, Bo'sun, the bread!"

"Ay, ay, sir!" said the Bo'sun, and, taking the neat parcel the Captain held out, dropped it forthwith into the crown of the glazed hat.

"Bo'sun, the meat! the young fool will be hungry by now, poor lad!"

"Ay, ay, Cap'n!" And, the meat having disappeared into the same receptacle, the Bo'sun resumed his hat. Now turning to Barnabas, the Captain held out his hand.

"Sir," said he, "I wish you good-by and a prosperous voyage, and may you find yourself too much a man ever to fall so low as 'fashion,'—I say dammit! The bread and meat, sir, are for a young fool who thinks, like yourself, that the World of Fashion is *the* world. By heaven, sir, I say by Gog and Magog! if I had a son with fashionable aspirations, I'd have him triced up to the triangles and flogged with the 'cat'—I say with the cat-o'-ninetails, sir, that is—no I wouldn't, besides I—never had a son—she—died, sir—and good-by!"

"Stay," said Barnabas, "pray tell me to whom I am indebted for so much good instruction."

"My name, sir, is Chumly—plain Chumly—spelt with a U and an M, sir; none of your *olmondeleys* for me, sir, and I beg you to know that I have no crest or monogram or coat of arms; there's neither or, azure, nor argent about me; I'm neither rampant, nor passant, nor even regardant. And I want none of your sables, ermines, bars, escallops, embattled fiddle-de-dees, or dencette tarradiddles, sir. I'm Chumly, Captain John Chumly, plain and without any fashionable varnish. Consequently, though I have commanded many good ships, sloops, frigates, and even one Seventy-four—"

"The 'Bully-Sawyer,' Trafalgar!" added the Bo'sun.

"Seeing I am only John Chumly, with a U and an M, I retire still a captain. Now, had I clapped in an *olmondeley* and the rest of the fashionable gewgaws, I should now be doubtless a Rear Admiral at the very least, for the polite world—the World of Fashion is rampant, sir, not to mention passant and regardant. So, if you would achieve a reputation among Persons of Quality nowadays—bow, sir, bow everywhere day in and day out—keep a supple back, young sir, and spell your name with as many unnecessary letters as you can. And as regards my idea of a gentleman, he is, I take it, a man—who is gentle—I say good morning, young sir." As he ended, the Captain took off his hat, with his remaining arm put it on again, and then reached out, suddenly, and clapped Barnabas upon the shoulder. "Here's wishing you a straight course, lad," said he with a smile, every whit as young and winning as that which curved the lips of Barnabas, "a fair course and a good, clean wind to blow all these fashionable fooleries out of your head. Good-by!" So he nodded, turned sharp about and went upon his way.

Hereupon the Bo'sun shook his head, took off the glazed hat, stared into it, and putting it on again, turned and stumped along beside Barnabas.

CHAPTER VIII

CONCERNING THE CAPTAIN'S ARM, THE BOSUN'S LEG, AND THE "BELISARIUS," SEVENTY-FOUR

"The 'Bully-Sawyer,' Trafalgar!" murmured the Bo'sun, as they went on side by side; "you've 'eerd o' the 'Bully-Sawyer,' Seventy-four, o' course, young sir?"

"I'm afraid not," said Barnabas, rather apologetically.

"Not 'eerd o' the 'Bully-Sawyer,' Seventy-four, Lord, young sir! axing your pardon, but—not 'eerd o' the—why, she were in the van that day one o' the first to engage the enemy—but a cable's length to wind'ard o' the 'Victory'—one o' the first to come up wi' the Mounseers, she were. An' now you tell me as you ain't 'eerd o' the—Lord, sir!" and the Bo'sun sighed, and shook his head till it was a marvel how the glazed hat kept its position.

"Won't you tell me of her, Bo'sun?"

"Tell you about the old 'Bully-Sawyer,' Seventy-four, ay surely, sir, surely. Ah! 't were a grand day for us, a grand day for our Nelson, and a grand day for England—that twenty-first o' October—though 't were that day as they French and Spanishers done for the poor old 'Bully-Sawyer,' Seventy-four, and his honor's arm and my leg, d' ye see. The wind were light that day as we bore down on their line—in two columns, d' ye see, sir—we was in Nelson's column, the weather line 'bout a cable's length astarn o' the 'Victory.' On we went, creeping nearer and nearer—the 'Victory,' the old 'Bully-Sawyer,' and the 'Temeraire'—and every now and then the Mounseers trying a shot at us to find the range, d' ye see. Right ahead o' us lay the 'Santissima Trinidado'—a great four-decker, young sir—astarn o' her was the 'Beaucenture,' and astarn o' her again, the 'Redoutable,' wi' eight or nine others. On we went wi' the Admiral's favorite signal flying, 'Engage the enemy more closely.' Ah, young sir, there weren't no stand-offishness about our Nelson, God bless him! As we bore closer their shot began to come aboard o' us, but the old 'Bully-Sawyer' never took no notice, no, not so much as a gun. Lord! I can see her now as she bore down on their line; every sail drawing aloft, the white decks below—the gleam o' her guns wi' their crews stripped to the waist, every eye on the enemy, every man at his post—very different she looked an hour arterwards. Well, sir, all at once the great 'Santissima Trinidado' lets fly at us wi' her whole four tiers o' broadside, raking us fore and aft, and that begun it; down comes our foretopmast wi' a litter o' falling spars and top-hamper, and the decks was all at once splashed, here and there, wi' ugly blotches. But, Lord! the old 'Bully-Sawyer' never paid no heed, and still the men stood to the guns, and his Honor, the Captain, strolled up and down, chatting to his flag officer. Then the enemy's ships opened on us one arter another, the 'Beaucenture,' the 'San Nicholas,' and the 'Redoutable' swept and battered us wi' their murderous broadsides; the air seemed full o' smoke and flame, and the old 'Bully-Sawyer' in the thick o' it. But still we could see the 'Victory' through the drifting smoke ahead o' us wi' the signal flying, 'Engage the enemy more closely,' and still we waited and waited very patient, and crept down on the enemy nearer and nearer."

"And every minute their fire grew hotter, and their aim truer—down came our mizzen-topgallant-mast, and hung down over our quarter; away went our bowsprit—but we held on till we struck their line 'twixt the 'Santissima Trinidado' and the 'Beaucenture,' and, as we crossed the Spanisher's wake, so close that our yard-arms grazed her gilded starn, up flashed his Honor's sword, 'Now, lads!' cried he, hailing the guns—and then—why then, afore I'd took my whistle from my lips, the old 'Bully-Sawyer,' as had been so patient, so very patient, let fly wi' every starboard gun as it bore, slap into the great Spanisher's towering starn, and, a moment arter, her larboard guns roared and flamed as her broadside smashed into the 'Beaucenture,' and 'bout five minutes arterwards we fell aboard o' the 'Fougeux,' and there we lay, young sir, and fought it out yard-arm to yard-arm, and muzzle to muzzle, so close that the flame o' their guns blackened and scorched us, and we was obliged to heave buckets o' water, arter every discharge, to put out the fire. Lord! but the poor old 'Bully-Sawyer' were in a tight corner then, what wi' the 'Fougeux' to port, the 'Beaucenture' to starboard, and the great Spanisher hammering us astarn, d' ye see. But there was our lads—what was left o' 'em—reeking wi' sweat, black wi' powder, splashed wi' blood, fighting the guns; and there was his Honor the Cap'n, leaning against the quarter-rail wi' his sword in one hand, and his snuff-box in t' other—he had two hands then, d'ye see, young sir; and there was me, hauling on the tackle o' one o' the quarter-guns—it happened to be short-handed, d'ye see—when, all at once, I felt a kind o' shock, and there I was flat o' my back, and wi' the wreckage o' that there quarter-gun on this here left leg o' mine, pinning me to the deck. As I lay there I heerd our lads a cheering above the roar and din, and presently, the smoke lifting a bit, I see the Spanisher had struck, but I likewise see as the poor old 'Bully-Sawyer' were done for; she lay a wreck—black wi' smoke, blistered wi' fire, her decks foul wi' blood, her fore and mainmasts beat overboard, and only the mizzen standing. All this I see in a glance—ah! and something more—for the mizzen-topgallant had been shot clean through at the cap, and hung dangling. But now, what wi' the quiver o' the guns and the roll o' the vessel, down she come sliding, and sliding, nearer and nearer, till the splintered end brought up ag'in the wreck o' my gun. But presently I see it begin to slide ag'in nearer to me—very slow, d'ye see—inch by inch, and there's me pinned on the flat o' my back, watching it come. 'Another foot,' I sez, 'and there's an end o' Jerry Tucker—another ten inches, another eight, another six.' Lord, young sir, I heaved and I strained at that crushed leg o' mine; but there I was, fast as ever, while down came the t'gallant—inch by inch. Then, all at once, I kinder let go o' myself. I give a shout, sir, and then—why then—there's his Honor the Cap'n leaning over me. 'Is that you, Jerry?' sez he—for I were black wi' powder, d' ye see, sir. 'Is that you, Jerry?' sez he. 'Ay, ay, sir,' sez I, 'it be me surely, till this here spar slips down and does for me.' 'It shan't do that,' sez he, very square in the jaw. 'It must,' sez I. 'No,' sez he. 'Nothing to stop it, sir,' sez I. 'Yes, there is,' sez he. 'What's that,' sez I. 'This,' sez he, 'twixt his shut teeth, young sir. And then, under that there hellish, murdering piece of timber, the Cap'n sets his hand and arm—his naked hand and arm, sir!' In the name o' God!' I sez, 'let it come, sir!' 'And lose my Bo'sun?—not me!' sez he. Then, sir, I see his face go white—and whiter. I heerd the bones o' his hand and arm crack—like so many sticks—and down he falls atop o' me in a dead faint, sir."

"But the t'gallant were stopped, and the life were kept in this here carcase o' mine. So—that's how the poor old 'Bully-Sawyer,' Seventy-four, were done for—that's how his Honor lost his arm, and me my leg, sir. And theer be the stocks, and theer be our young gentleman inside o' 'em, as cool and smiling and comfortable as you please."

CHAPTER IX

WHICH CONCERNS ITSELF, AMONG OTHER MATTERS, WITH THE VIRTUES OF A PAIR OF STOCKS AND THE PERVERSITY OF FATHERS

Before them was a church, a small church, gray with age, and, like age, lonely. It stood well back from the road which wound away down the hill to the scattered cottages in the valley below.

About this church was a burial ground, upon whose green mounds and leaning headstones the great square tower cast a protecting shadow that was like a silent benediction. A rural graveyard this, very far removed from the strife and bustle of cities, and, therefore, a good place to sleep in.

A low stone wall was set about it, and in the wall was a gate with a weather-beaten porch, and beside the gate were the stocks, and in the stocks, with his hands in his pockets, and his back against the wall, sat a young gentleman.

A lonely figure, indeed, whose boots, bright and polished, were thrust helplessly enough through the leg-holes of the stocks, as though offering themselves to the notice of every passer-by. Tall he was, and *point-de-vice* from those same helpless boots to the gleaming silver buckle in his hat band.

Now observing the elegance of his clothes, and the modish languor of his lounging figure, Barnabas at once recognized him as a gentleman par excellence, and immediately the memory of his own country-made habiliments and clumsy boots arose and smote him. The solitary prisoner seemed in no whit cast down by his awkward and most undignified situation, indeed, as they drew nearer, Barnabas could hear him whistling softly to himself. At the sound of their approach, however, he glanced up, and observed them from under the brim of the buckled hat with a pair of the merriest blue eyes in the world.

"Aha, Jerry!" he cried, "whom do you bring to triumph over me in my abasement? For shame, Jerry! Is this the act of a loving and affectionate Bo'sun, the Bo'sun of my innocent childhood? Oh, bruise and blister me!"

"Why, sir," answered the Bo'sun, beaming through his whiskers, "this be only a young genelman, like yourself, as be bound for Lonnon, Master Horatio."

The face, beneath the devil-may-care rake of the buckled hat, was pale and handsome, and, despite its studied air of gentlemanly weariness, the eyes were singularly quick and young, and wholly ingenuous.

Now, as they gazed at each other, eye to eye—the merry blue and the steadfast gray—suddenly, unaffectedly, as though drawn by instinct, their hands reached out and met in a warm and firm clasp, and, in that instant, the one forgot his modish languor, and the other his country clothes and blunt-toed boots, for the Spirit of Youth stood between them, and smile answered smile.

"And so you are bound for London, sir; pray, are you in a hurry to get there?"

"Not particularly," Barnabas rejoined.

"Then there you have the advantage of me, for I am, sir. But here I sit, a martyr for conscience sake. Now, sir, if you are in no great hurry, and have a mind to travel in company with a martyr, just as soon as I am free of these bilboes, we'll take the road together. What d' ye say?"

"With pleasure!" answered Barnabas.

"Why then, sir, pray sit down. I blush to offer you the stocks, but the grass is devilish dewy and damp, and there's deuce a chair to be had—which is only natural, of course; but pray sit somewhere until the Bo'sun, like the jolly old dog he is, produces the key, and lets me out."

"Bo'sun, you'll perceive the gentleman is waiting, and, for that matter, so am I. The key, Jerry, the key."

"Axing your pardons, gentlemen both," began the Bo'sun, taking himself by the starboard whisker, "but orders is orders, and I was to tell you, Master Horatio, sir, as there was firstly a round o' beef cold, for breakfus!"

"Beef!" exclaimed the prisoner, striking himself on the crown of the hat.

"Next a smoked tongue—" continued the Bo'sun.

"Tongue!" sighed the prisoner, turning to Barnabas. "You hear that, sir, my unnatural father and uncle batten upon rounds of beef, and smoked tongues, while I sit here, my legs at a most uncomfortable angle, and my inner man as empty as a drum; oh, confound and curse it!"

"A brace o' cold fowl," went on the Bo'sun inexorably; "a biled 'am—"

"Enough, Jerry, enough, lest I forget filial piety and affection and rail upon 'em for heartless gluttons."

"And," pursued the Bo'sun, still busy with his whisker and abstracted of eye—"and I were to say as you was now free to come out of they stocks—"

"Aha, Jerry! even the most Roman of fathers can relent, then. Out with the key, Jerry! Egad! I can positively taste that beef from here; unlock me, Jerry, that I may haste to pay my respects to Roman parent, uncle, and beef—last, but not least, Jerry—"

"Always supposing," added the Bo'sun, giving a final twist to his whisker, "that you've 'ad time to think better on it, d' ye see, and change your mind, Master Horatio, my Lord."

Barnabas pricked up his ears; a lord, and in the stocks! preposterous! and yet surely these were the boots, and clothes, and hat of a lord.

"Change my mind, Jerry!" exclaimed his Lordship, "impossible; you know I never change my mind. What! yield up my freedom for a mess of beef and tongue, or even a brace of cold fowl—"

"Not to mention a cold biled 'am, Master Horatio, sir."

"No, Jerry, not for all the Roman parents, rounds of beef, tyrannical uncles and cold hams in England. Tempt me no more, Jerry; Bo'sun, avaunt, and leave me to melancholy and emptiness."

"Why then," said the Bo'sun, removing the glazed hat and extracting therefrom the Captain's meat packages, "I were to give you this meat, Master Horatio, beef and bread, my Lord."

"From the Captain, I'll be sworn, eh, Jerry?"

"Ay, ay, my Lord, from his Honor the Cap'n."

"Now God bless him for a tender-hearted old martinet, eh, Bo'sun?"

"Which I begs to say, amen, Master Horatio, sir."

"To be sure there is nothing Roman about my uncle." Saying which, his Lordship, tearing open the packages, and using his fingers as forks, began to devour the edibles with huge appetite.

"There was a tongue, I think you mentioned, Jerry," he inquired suddenly.

"Ay, sir, likewise a cold biled 'am."

His Lordship sighed plaintively.

"And yet," said he, sandwiching a slice of beef between two pieces of bread with great care and nicety, "who would be so mean-spirited as to sell that freedom which is the glorious prerogative of man (and which I beg you to notice is a not unpleasing phrase, sir) who, I demand, would surrender this for a base smoked tongue?"

"Not forgetting a fine, cold biled 'am, Master Horatio, my Lord. And now, wi' your permission, I'll stand away for the village, leaving you to talk wi' this here young gentleman and take them vittles aboard, till I bring up alongside again, Cap'n's orders, Master Horatio." Saying which, the Bo'sun touched the glazed hat, went about, and, squaring his yards, bore away for the village.

"Sir," said his Lordship, glancing whimsically at Barnabas over his fast-disappearing hunch of bread and meat, "you have never been—called upon to—sit in the stocks, perhaps?"

"Never—as yet," answered Barnabas, smiling.

"Why, then, sir, let me inform you the stocks have their virtues. I'll not deny a chair is more comfortable, and certainly more dignified, but give me the stocks for thought, there's nothing like 'em for profound meditation. The Bible says, I believe, that one should seek the seclusion of one's closet, but, believe me, for deep reverie there's nothing like the stocks. You see, a poor devil has nothing else to do, therefore he meditates."

"And pray," inquired Barnabas, "may I ask what brings you sitting in this place of thought?"

"Three things, sir, namely, matrimony, a horse race, and a father. Three very serious matters, sir, and the last the gravest of all. For you must know I am, shall I say—blessed? yes, certainly, blessed in a father who is essentially Roman, being a man of his word, sir. Now a man of his word, more especially a father, may prove a very mixed blessing. Speaking of fathers, generally, sir, you may have noticed that they are the most unreasonable class of beings, and delight to arrogate to themselves an authority which is, to say the least, trying; my father especially so—for, as I believe I hinted before, he is so infernally Roman."

"Indeed," smiled Barnabas, "the best of fathers are, after all, only human."

"Aha!" cried his Lordship, "there speaks experience. And yet, sir, these human fathers, one and all, believe in what I may term the divine right of fathers to thwart, and bother, and annoy sons old enough to be—ha—"

"To know their own minds," said Barnabas.

"Precisely," nodded his Lordship. "Consequently, my Roman father and I fell out—my honored Roman and I frequently do fall out—but this morning, sir, unfortunately 't was before breakfast." Here his Lordship snatched a hasty bite of bread and meat with great appetite and gusto, while Barnabas sat, dreamy of eye, staring away across the valley.

"Pray," said he suddenly, yet with his gaze still far away, "do you chance to be acquainted with a Sir Mortimer Carnaby?"

"Acquainted," cried his Lordship, speaking with his mouth full. "Oh, Gad, sir, every one who *is* any one is acquainted with Sir Mortimer Carnaby."

"Ah!" said Barnabas musingly, "then you probably know him."

"He honors me with his friendship."

"Hum!" said Barnabas.

Here his Lordship glanced up quickly and with a slight contraction of the brow.

"Sir," he retorted, with a very creditable attempt at dignity, despite the stocks and his hunch of bread and meat, "Sir, permit me to add that I am proud of his friendship."

"And pray," inquired Barnabas, turning his eyes suddenly to his companion's face, "do you like him?"

"Like him, sir!"

"Or trust him!" persisted Barnabas, steadfast-eyed.

"Trust him, sir," his Lordship repeated, his gaze beginning to wander, "trust him!" Here, chancing to espy what yet remained of the bread and meat, he immediately took another bite, and when he spoke it was in a somewhat muffled tone in consequence. "Trust him? Egad, sir, the boot's on t'other leg, for 'twixt you and me, I owe him a cool thousand, as it is!"

"He is a great figure in the fashionable world, I understand," said Barnabas.

"He is the most admired Buck in London, sir," nodded his Lordship, "the most dashing, the most sought after, a boon companion of Royalty itself, sir, the Corinthian of Corinthians."

"Do you mean," said Barnabas, with his eyes on the distance again, "that he is a personal friend of the Prince?"

"One of the favored few," nodded his Lordship, "and, talking of him, brings us back to my honored Roman."

"How so?" inquired Barnabas, his gaze on the distance once more.

"Because, sir, with that unreasonableness peculiar to fathers, he has taken a violent antipathy to my friend Carnaby, though, as far as I know, he has never met my friend Carnaby. This morning, sir, my father summoned me to the library. 'Horatio,' says he, in his most Roman manner,—he never calls me Horatio unless about to treat me to the divine right of fathers,—'Horatio,' says he, 'you're old enough to marry.' 'Indeed, I greatly fear so, sir,' says I. 'Then,' says he, solemn as an owl, 'why not settle down here and marry?' Here he named a certain lovely person whom, 'twixt you and me, sir, I have long ago determined to marry, but, in my own time, be it understood. 'Sir,' said I, 'believe me I would ride over and settle the matter with her this very morning, only that I am to race

'Moonraker' (a horse of mine, you'll understand, sir) against Sir Mortimer Carnaby's 'Clasher' and if I should happen to break my neck, it might disappoint the lady in question, or even break her heart.' 'Horatio,' says my Roman—more Roman than ever—'I strongly disapprove of your sporting propensities, and, more especially, the circle of acquaintances you have formed in London.' 'Blackguardedly Bucks and cursed Corinthians!' snarls my uncle, the Captain, flapping his empty sleeve at me. 'That, sirs, I deeply regret,' says I, preserving a polite serenity, 'but the match is made, and a man must needs form some circle of acquaintance when he lives in London.' 'Then,' says my honored Roman, with that lack of reasonableness peculiar to fathers, 'don't live in London, and as for the horse match give it up.' 'Quite impossible, sir,' says I, calmly determined, 'the match has been made and recorded duly at White's, and if you were as familiar with the fashionable sporting set as I, you would understand.' 'Pish, boy,' says my Roman—'t is a trick fathers have at such times of casting one's youth in one's teeth, you may probably have noticed this for yourself, sir—'Pish, boy,' says he, 'I know, I know, I've lived in London!' 'True, sir,' says I, 'but things have changed since your day, your customs went out with your tie-wigs, and are as antiquated as your wide-skirted coats and buckled shoes'—this was a sly dig at my worthy uncle, the Captain, sir. 'Ha!' cries he, flapping his empty sleeve at me again, 'and nice figure-heads you made of yourselves with your ridiculous stocks and skin-tight breeches,' and indeed," said his Lordship, stooping to catch a side-view of his imprisoned legs, "they are a most excellent fit, I think you'll agree."

"Marvellous!" sighed Barnabas, observing them with the eyes of envy.

"Well, sir," pursued his Lordship, "the long and short of it was—my honored Roman, having worked himself into a state of 'divine right' necessary to the occasion, vows that unless I give up the race and spend less time and money in London, he will clap me into the stocks. 'Then, sir,' says I, smiling and unruffled, 'pray clap me in as soon as you will'; and he being, as I told you, a man of his word,—well—here I am."

"Where I find you enduring your situation with a remarkable fortitude," said Barnabas.

"Egad, sir! how else should I endure it? I flatter myself I am something of a philosopher, and thus, enduring in the cause of freedom and free will, I scorn my bonds, and am consequently free. Though, I'll admit, 'twixt you and me, sir, the position cramps one's legs most damnably."

"Now in regard to Sir Mortimer Carnaby," persisted Barnabas, "your father, it would seem, neither likes nor trusts him."

"My father, sir, is—a father, consequently perverse. Sir Mortimer Carnaby is my friend, therefore, though my father has never met Sir Mortimer Carnaby, he takes a mortal antipathy to Sir Mortimer Carnaby, Q.E.D., and all the rest of it."

"On the other hand," pursued Barnabas the steadfast-eyed, "you—admire, respect, and honor your friend Sir Mortimer Carnaby!"

"Admire him, sir, who wouldn't? There isn't such another all-round sportsman in London—no, nor England. Only last week he drove cross-country in his tilbury over hedges and ditches, fences and all, and never turned a hair.

Beat the 'Fighting Tanner' at Islington in four rounds, and won over ten thousand pounds in a single night's play from Egalité d'Orléans himself. Oh, egad, sir! Carnaby's the most wonderful fellow in the world!"

"Though a very indifferent boxer!" added Barnabas.

"Indiff—!" His Lordship let fall the last fragments of his bread and meat, and stared at Barnabas in wide-eyed amazement. "Did you say—indifferent?"

"I did," nodded Barnabas, "he is much too passionate ever to make a good boxer."

"Why, deuce take me! I tell you there isn't a pugilist in England cares to stand up to him with the muffles, or bare knuckles!"

"Probably because there are no pugilists left in England, worth the name," said Barnabas.

"Gad, sir! we are all pugilists nowadays—the Manly Art is all the fashion—and, I think, a very excellent fashion. And permit me to tell you I know what I'm talking of, I have myself boxed with nearly all the best 'milling coves' in London, and am esteemed no novice at the sport. Indeed love of the 'Fancy' was born in me, for my father, sir—though occasionally Roman—was a great patron of the game, and witnessed the great battle between 'Glorious John Barty' and Nathaniel Bell—"

"At Dartford!" added Barnabas.

"And when Bell was knocked down, at the end of the fight—"

"After the ninety-seventh round!" nodded Barnabas.

"My father, sir, was the first to jump into the ring and clasp the Champion's fist—and proud he is to tell of it!"

"Proud!" said Barnabas, staring.

"Proud, sir—yes, why not? so should I have been—so would any man have been. Why let me tell you, sir, at home, in the hall, between the ensign my uncle's ship bore through Trafalgar, and the small sword my grandfather carried at Blenheim, we have the belt John Barty wore that day."

"His belt!" exclaimed Barnabas, "my—John Barty's belt?"

"So you see I should know what I am talking about. Therefore, when you condemn such a justly celebrated man of his hands as my friend Carnaby, I naturally demand to know who you are to pronounce judgment?"

"I am one," answered Barnabas, "who has been taught the science by that very Nathaniel Bell and 'Glorious John' you mention."

"Hey—what?—what?" cried his Lordship.

"I have boxed with them regularly every day," Barnabas continued, "and I have learned that strength of arm, quickness of foot, and a true eye are all unavailing unless they be governed by a calm, unruffled temper, for passion clouds the judgment, and in fighting as in all else, it is judgment that tells in the long run."

"Now, by heaven!" exclaimed his Lordship, jerking his imprisoned legs pettishly, "if I didn't happen to be sitting trussed up here, and we had a couple of pair of muffles, why we might have had a friendly 'go' just to take each other's measures; as it is—"

But at this moment they heard a hoarse bellow, and, looking round, beheld the Bo'sun who, redder of face than ever and pitching and rolling in his course, bore rapidly down on them, and hauling his wind, took off the glazed hat.

"Ha, Jerry!" exclaimed his Lordship, "what now? If you happen to have anything else eatable in that hat of yours, out with it, for I am devilish sharp-set still."

"Why, I have got summat, Master Horatio, but it aren't bread nor yet beef, nor yet again biled 'am, my Lord—it can't be eat nor it can't be drank—and here it be!" and with the words the Bo'sun produced a ponderous iron key.

"Why, my dear old Jerry—my lovely Bo'sun—"

"Captured by his Honor, Master Horatio—carried off by the Cap'n under your own father's very own nose, sir—or as you might say, cut out under the enemy's guns, my Lord!" With which explanation the old sailor unfastened the padlock, raised the upper leg-board, and set the prisoner free.

"Ah!—but it's good to have the use of one's legs again!" exclaimed his Lordship, stretching the members in question, "and that," said he, turning to Barnabas with his whimsical smile, "that is another value of the stocks—one never knows how pleasant and useful a pair of legs can be until one has sat with 'em stretched out helplessly at right angles for an hour or two." Here, the Bo'sun having stowed back the key and resumed his hat, his Lordship reached out and gripped his hand. "So it was Uncle John, was it, Jerry—how very like Uncle John—eh, Jerry?"

"Never was nobody born into this here vale o' sorrer like the Cap'n—no, nor never will be—nohow!" said the Bo'sun with a solemn nod.

"God bless him, eh, Jerry?"

"Amen to that, my Lord."

"You'll let him know I said 'God bless him,' Jerry?"

"I will, my Lord, ay, ay, God bless him it is, Master Horatio!"

"Now as to my Roman—my father, Jerry, tell him—er—"

"Be you still set on squaring away for London, then, sir?"

"As a rock, Jerry, as a rock!"

"Then 't is 'good-by,' you're wishing me?"

"Yes, 'good-by,' Jerry, remember 'God bless Uncle John,' and—er—tell my father that—ah, what the deuce shall you tell him now?—it should be something a little affecting—wholly dutiful, and above all gently dignified—hum! Ah, yes—tell him that whether I win or lose the race, whether I break my unworthy neck or no, I shall never forget that I am the Earl of Bamborough's son. And as for you, Jerry, why, I shall always think of you as the jolly old sea dog who used to stoop down to let me get at his whiskers, they were a trifle blacker in those days. Gad! how I did pull 'em, Jerry, even then I admired your whiskers, didn't I? I swear there isn't such another pair in England. Good-by, Jerry!" Saying which his Lordship turned swiftly upon his heel and walked on a pace or two, while Barnabas paused to wring the old seaman's brown hand; then they went on down the hill together.

And the Bo'sun, sitting upon the empty stocks with his wooden pin sticking straight out before him, sighed as he watched them striding London-wards, the Lord's son, tall, slender, elegant, a gentleman to his finger tips, and the commoner's son, shaped like a young god, despite his homespun, and between them, as it were linking them together, fresh and bright and young as the morning, went the joyous Spirit of Youth.

Now whether the Bo'sun saw aught of this, who shall say, but old eyes see many things. And thus, perhaps, the sigh that escaped the battered old man-o'-war's man's lips was only because of his own vanished youth—his gray head and wooden leg, after all.

CHAPTER X

WHICH DESCRIBES A PERIPATETIC CONVERSATION

"Sir," said his Lordship, after they had gone some way in silence, "you are thoughtful, not to say, devilish grave!"

"And you," retorted Barnabas, "have sighed—three times."

"No, did I though?—why then, to be candid,—I detest saying 'Good-by!'—and I have been devoutly wishing for two pair of muffles, for, sir, I have taken a prodigious liking to you—but—"

"But?" inquired Barnabas.

"Some time since you mentioned the names of two men—champions both—ornaments of the 'Fancy'—great fighters of unblemished reputation."

"You mean my—er—that is, Natty Bell and John Barty."

"Precisely!—you claim to have—boxed with them, sir?"

"Every day!" nodded Barnabas.

"With both of them,—I understand?"

"With both of them."

"Hum!"

"Sir," said Barnabas, growing suddenly polite, "do you doubt my word?"

"Well," answered his Lordship, with his whimsical look, "I'll admit I could have taken it easier had you named only one, for surely, sir, you must be aware that these were Masters of the Fist—the greatest since the days of Jack Broughton and Mendoza."

"I know each had been champion—but it would almost seem that I have entertained angels unawares!—and I boxed with both because they happened to live together."

"Then, sir," said the Viscount, extending his hand in his frank, impetuous manner, "you are blest of the gods. I congratulate you and, incidentally, my desire for muffles grows apace,—you must positively put 'em on with me at the first opportunity."

"Right willingly, sir," said Barnabas.

"But deuce take me!" exclaimed the Viscount, "if we are to become friends, which I sincerely hope, we ought at least to know each other's name. Mine, sir, is Bellasis, Horatio Bellasis; I was named Horatio after Lord Nelson, consequently my friends generally call me Tom, Dick, or Harry, for with all due respect to his Lordship, Horatio is a very devil of a name, now isn't it? Pray what's yours?"

"Barnabas—Beverley. At your service."

"Barnabas—hum! Yours isn't much better. Egad! I think 't is about as bad. Barnabas!—No, I'll call you Bev, on condition that you make mine Dick; what d' ye say, my dear Bev?"

"Agreed, Dick," answered Barnabas, smiling, whereupon they stopped, and having very solemnly shaken hands, went on again, merrier than ever.

"Now what," inquired the Viscount, suddenly, "what do you think of marriage, my dear Bev?"

"Marriage?" repeated Barnabas, staring.

"Marriage!" nodded his Lordship, airily, "matrimony, Bev,—wedlock, my dear fellow?"

"I—indeed I have never had occasion to think of it."

"Fortunate fellow!" sighed his companion.

"Until—this morning!" added Barnabas, as his fingers encountered a small, soft, lacy bundle in his pocket.

"Un-fortunate fellow!" sighed the Viscount, shaking his head. "So you are haunted by the grim spectre, are you? Well, that should be an added bond between us. Not that I quarrel with matrimony, mark you, Bev; in the abstract it is a very excellent institution, though—mark me again!—when a man begins to think of marriage it is generally the beginning of the end. Ah, my dear fellow! many a bright and promising career has been blighted—sapped—snapped off—and—er—ruthlessly devoured by the ravenous maw of marriage. There was young Egerton with a natural gift for boxing, and one of the best whips I ever knew—we raced our coaches to Brighton and back for a thousand a side and he beat me by six yards—a splendid all round sportsman—ruined by matrimony! He's buried somewhere in the country and passing his days in the humdrum pursuit of being husband and father. Oh, bruise and blister me! it's all very pitiful, and yet"—here the Viscount sighed again—"I do not quarrel with the state, for marriage has often proved a—er—very present help in the time of trouble, Bev."

"Trouble?" repeated Barnabas.

"Money-troubles, my dear Bev, pecuniary unpleasantnesses, debts, and duns, and devilish things of that kind."

"But surely," said Barnabas, "no man—no honorable man would marry and burden a woman with debts of his own contracting?"

At this, the Viscount looked at Barnabas, somewhat askance, and fell to scratching his chin. "Of course," he continued, somewhat hurriedly, "I shall have all the money I need—more than I shall need some day."

"You mean," inquired Barnabas, "when your father dies?"

Here the Viscount's smooth brow clouded suddenly.

"Sir," said he, "we will not mention that contingency. My father is a great Roman, I'll admit, but, 'twixt you and me,—I—I'm devilish fond of him, and, strangely enough, I prefer to have him Romanly alive and my purse empty—than to possess his money and have him dea—Oh damn it! let's talk of something else,—Carnaby for instance."

"Yes," nodded Barnabas, "your friend, Carnaby."

"Well, then, in the first place, I think I hinted to you that I owe him five thousand pounds?"

"Five thousand! indeed, no, it was only one, when you mentioned it to me last."

"Was it so? but then, d'ye see, Bev, we were a good two miles nearer my honored Roman when I mentioned the matter before, and trees sometimes have ears, consequently I—er—kept it down a bit, my dear Bev, I kept it down a bit;

but the fact remains that it's five, and I won't be sure but that there's an odd hundred or two hanging on to it somewhere, beside."

"You led your father to believe it was only one thousand, then?"

"I did, Bev; you see money seems to make him so infernally Roman, and I've been going the pace a bit these last six months. There's another thousand to Jerningham, but he can wait, then there's six hundred to my tailor, deuce take him!"

"Six hundred!" exclaimed Barnabas, aghast.

"Though I won't swear it isn't seven."

"To be sure he is a very excellent tailor," Barnabas added.

"Gad, yes! and the fellow knows it! Then, let's see, there's another three hundred and fifty to the coach builders, how much does that make, Bev?"

"Six thousand, nine hundred and fifty pounds!"

"So much—deuce take it! And that's not all, you know."

"Not?"

"No, Bev, I dare say I could make you up another three or four hundred or so if I were to rake about a bit, but six thousand is enough to go on with, thank you!"

"Six thousand pounds is a deal of money to owe!" said Barnabas.

"Yes," answered the Viscount, scratching his chin again, "though, mark me, Bev, it might be worse! Slingsby, a friend of mine, got plucked for fifteen thousand in a single night last year. Oh! it might be worse. As it is, Bev, the case lies thus: unless I win the race some three weeks from now—I've backed myself heavily, you'll understand—unless I win, I am between the deep sea of matrimony and the devil of old Jasper Gaunt."

"And who is Jasper Gaunt?"

"Oh, delicious innocence! Ah, Bev! it's evident you are new to London. Gaunt is an outcome of the City, as harsh and dingy as its bricks, as flinty and hard as its pavements. Gad! most of our set know Jasper Gaunt—to their cost! Who is Jasper Gaunt, you ask; well, my dear fellow, question Slingsby of the Guards, he's getting deeper every day, poor old Sling! Ask it, but in a whisper, at Almack's, or White's, or Brooke's, and my Lord this, that, or t'other shall tell you pat and to the point in no measured terms. Ask it of wretched debtors in the prisons, of haggard toilers in the streets, of pale-faced women and lonely widows, and they'll tell you, one and all, that Jasper Gaunt is the harshest, most merciless bloodsucker that ever battened and grew rich on the poverty and suffering of his fellow men, and—oh here we are!"

Saying which, his Lordship abruptly turned down an unexpected and very narrow side lane, where, screened behind three great trees, was a small inn, or hedge tavern with a horse-trough before the door and a sign whereon was the legend, "The Spotted Cow," with a representation of that quadruped below, surely the very spottiest of spotted cows that ever adorned an inn sign.

"Not much to look at, my dear Bev," said the Viscount, with a wave of his hand towards the inn, "but it's kept by an old sailor, a shipmate of the Bo'sun's. I can at least promise you a good breakfast, and the ale you will find excellent. But first I want to show you a very small demon of mine, a particularly diminutive fiend; follow me, my dear fellow."

So, by devious ways, the Viscount led Barnabas round to the back of the inn, and across a yard to where, beyond a gate, was a rick-yard, and beyond that again, a small field or paddock. Now, within this paddock, the admired of a group of gaping rustics, was the very smallest groom Barnabas had ever beheld, for, from the crown of his leather postilion's hat to the soles of his small top boots, he could not have measured more than four feet at the very most.

"There he is, Bev, behold him!" said the Viscount, with his whimsical smile, "the very smallest fiend, the most diminutive demon that ever wore top boots!"

The small groom was engaged in walking a fine blood horse up and down the paddock, or rather the horse was walking the groom, for the animal being very tall and powerful and much given to divers startings, snortings, and tossings of the head, it thus befell that to every step the diminutive groom marched on terra firma, he took one in mid-air, at which times, swinging pendulum-like, he poured forth a stream of invective that the most experienced ostler, guard, or coachman might well have envied, and all in a voice so gruff, so hoarse and guttural, despite his tender years, as filled the listening rustics with much apparent awe and wonder.

"And he can't be a day older than fourteen, my dear Bev," said the Viscount, with a complacent nod, as they halted in the perfumed shade of an adjacent rick; "that's his stable voice assumed for the occasion, and, between you and me, I can't think how he does it. Egad! he's the most remarkable boy that ever wore livery, the sharpest, the gamest. I picked him up in London, a ragged urchin—caught him picking my pocket, Been with me ever since, and I wouldn't part with him for his weight in gold."

"Picking your pocket!" said Barnabas, "hum!"

The Viscount looked a trifle uncomfortable. "Why you see, my dear fellow," he explained, "he was so—so deuced—small, Bev, a wretched little pale-faced, shivering atomy, peeping up at me over a ragged elbow waiting to be thrashed, and I liked him because he didn't snivel, and he was too insignificant for prison, so, when he told me how hungry he was, I forgot to cuff his shrinking, dirty little head, and suggested a plate of beef at one of the à la mode shops. 'Beef?' says he. 'Yes, beef,' says I, 'could you eat any?' 'Beef?' says he again, 'couldn't I? why, I could eat a ox whole, I could!' So I naturally dubbed him Milo of Crotona on the spot."

"And has he ever tried to pick your pocket since?"

"No, Bev; you see, he's never hungry nowadays. Gad!" said the Viscount, taking Barnabas by the arm, "I've set the fashion in tigers, Bev. Half the fellows at White's and Brooke's are wild to get that very small demon of mine; but he isn't to be bought or bribed or stolen—for what there is of him is faithful, Bev,—and now come in to breakfast."

So saying, the Viscount led Barnabas across the yard to a certain wing or off-shoot of the inn, where beneath a deep, shadowy gable was a door. Yet here he must needs pause a moment to glance down at himself to settle a ruffle and adjust his hat ere, lifting the latch, he ushered Barnabas into a kitchen.

A kitchen indeed? Ay, but such a kitchen! Surely wood was never whiter, nor pewter more gleaming than in this kitchen; surely no flagstones ever glowed a warmer red; surely oak panelling never shone with a mellower lustre; surely no viands could look more delicious than the great joint upon the polished sideboard, flanked by the crisp loaf and the yellow cheese; surely no flowers could ever bloom fairer or smell sweeter than those that overflowed the huge punch bowl at the window and filled the Uncle Toby jugs upon the mantel; surely nowhere could there be at one and the same time such dainty orderliness and comfortable comfort as in this kitchen.

Indeed the historian is bold to say that within no kitchen in this world were all things in such a constant state of winking, twinkling, gleaming and glowing purity, from the very legs of the oaken table and chairs, to the hacked and battered old cutlass above the chimney, as in this self-same kitchen of "The Spotted Cow."

And yet—and yet! Sweeter, whiter, warmer, purer, and far more delicious than anything in this kitchen (or out of it) was she who had started up to her feet so suddenly, and now stood with blushing cheeks and hurried bosom, gazing shy-eyed upon the young Viscount; all dainty grace from the ribbons in her mob-cap to the slender, buckled shoe peeping out beneath her print gown; and Barnabas, standing between them, saw her flush reflected as it were for a moment in the Viscount's usually pale cheek.

"My Lord!" said she, and stopped.

"Why, Clemency, you—you are—handsomer than ever!" stammered the Viscount.

"Oh, my Lord!" she exclaimed; and as she turned away Barnabas thought there were tears in her eyes.

"Did we startle you, Clemency? Forgive me—but I—that is, we are—hungry, ravenous. Er—this is a friend of mine—Mr. Beverley—Mistress Clemency Dare; and oh, Clemency, I've had no breakfast!"

But seeing she yet stood with head averted, the Viscount with a freedom born of long acquaintance, yet with a courtly deference also, took the hand that hung so listless, and looked down into the flushed beauty of her face, and, as he looked, beheld a great tear that crept upon her cheek.

"Why, Clemency!" he exclaimed, his raillery gone, his voice suddenly tender, "Clemency—you're crying, my dear maid; what is it?"

Now, beholding her confusion, and because of it, Barnabas turned away and walked to the other end of the kitchen, and there it chanced that he spied two objects that lay beneath the table, and stooping, forthwith, he picked them up. They were small and insignificant enough in themselves—being a scrap of crumpled paper, and a handsome embossed coat button; yet as Barnabas gazed upon this last, he smiled grimly, and so smiling slipped the objects into his pocket.

"Come now, Clemency," persisted the Viscount, gently, "what is wrong?"

"Nothing; indeed, nothing, my Lord."

"Ay, but there is. See how red your eyes are; they quite spoil your beauty—"

"Beauty!" she cried. "Oh, my Lord; even you!"

"What? What have I said? You are beautiful you know, Clem, and—"

"Beauty!" she cried again, and turned upon him with clenched hands and dark eyes aflame. "I hate it—oh, I hate it!" and with the words she stamped her foot passionately, and turning, sped away, banging the door behind her.

"Now, upon my soul!" said the Viscount, taking off his hat and ruffling up his auburn locks, "of all the amazing, contradictory creatures in the world, Bev! I've known Clemency—hum—a goodish time, my dear fellow; but never saw her like this before, I wonder what the deuce—"

But at this juncture a door at the further end of the kitchen opened, and a man entered. He, like the Bo'sun, was merry of eye, breezy of manner, and hairy of visage; but there all similarity ended, for, whereas the Bo'sun was a square man, this man was round—round of head, round of face, and round of eye. At the sight of the Viscount, his round face expanded in a genial smile that widened until it was lost in whisker, and he set two fingers to his round forehead and made a leg.

"Lord love me, my Lord, and is it you?" he exclaimed, clasping the hand the Viscount had extended. "Now, from what that imp of a bye—axing his parding—your tiger, Mr. Milo, told me, I were to expect you at nine sharp—and here it be nigh on to ten—"

"True, Jack; but then both he and I reckoned without my father. My father had the bad taste to—er—disagree with me, hence I am late, Jack, and breakfastless, and my friend Mr. Beverley is as hungry as I am. Bev, my dear fellow, this is a very old friend of mine—Jack Truelove, who fought under my uncle at Trafalgar."

"Servant, sir!" says Jack, saluting Barnabas.

"The 'Belisarius,' Seventy-four!" smiled Barnabas.

"Ay, ay," says Jack, with a shake of his round head, "the poor old 'Bully-Sawyer'—But, Lord love me! if you be hungry—"

"Devilish!" said the Viscount, "but first, Jack—what's amiss with Clemency?"

"Clemency? Why, where be that niece o' mine?"

"She's run away, Jack. I found her in tears, and I had scarce said a dozen words to her when—hey presto! She's off and away."

"Tears is it, my Lord?—and 'er sighed, too, I reckon. Come now—'er sighed likewise. Eh, my Lord?"

"Why, yes, she may have sighed, but—"

"There," says Jack, rolling his round head knowingly, "it be nought but a touch o' love, my Lord."

"Love!" exclaimed the Viscount sharply.

"Ah, love! Nieces is difficult craft, and very apt to be took all aback by the wind o' love, as you might say—but Lord! it's only natural arter all. Ah! the rearing o' motherless nieces is a ticklish matter, gentlemen—as to nevvys, I can't say, never 'aving 'ad none *to* rear—but nieces—Lord! I could write a book on 'em, that is, s'posing I could write, which I can't; for, as I've told you many a time, my Lord, and you then but a bye over here on a visit, wi' the Bo'sun, or his Honor the Cap'n, and you no older then than—er—Mr. Milo, though longer in the leg, as I 've told you many a time and oft—a very ob-servant man I be in most things, consequent' I aren't observed this here niece—this Clem o' mine fair weather and foul wi'out larning the kind o' craft nieces be. Consequent', when you tell me she weeps, and likewise sighs, then I make bold to tell you she's got a touch o' love, and you can lay to that, my Lord."

"Love," exclaimed the Viscount again, and frowning this time; "now, who the devil should she be in love with!"

"That, my Lord, I can't say, not having yet observed. But now, by your leave, I'll pass the word for breakfast."

Hereupon the landlord of "The Spotted Cow" opened the lattice, and sent a deep-lunged hail across the yard.

"Ahoy!" he roared, "Oliver, Penelope, Bess—breakfast ho!—breakfast for the Viscount—and friend. They be all watching of that theer imp—axing his pardon—that theer groom o' yours, what theer be of him, which though small ain't by no means to be despised, him being equally ready wi' his tongue as his fist."

Here entered two maids, both somewhat flushed with haste but both equally bright of eye, neat of person, and light of foot, who very soon had laid a snowy cloth and duly set out thereon the beef, the bread and cheese, and a mighty ham, before which the Viscount seated himself forthwith, while their sailor host, more jovial than ever, pointed out its many beauties with an eloquent thumb. And so, having seen his guests seated opposite each other, he pulled his forelock at them, made a leg to them, and left them to their breakfast.

CHAPTER XI

IN WHICH FISTS ARE CLENCHED; AND OF A SELFISH MAN, WHO WAS AN APOSTLE OF PEACE

Conversation, though in itself a blessed and delightful thing, yet may be sometimes out of place, and wholly impertinent. If wine is a loosener of tongues, surely food is the greatest, pleasantest, and most complete silencer; for what man when hunger gnaws and food is before him—what man, at such a time, will stay to discuss the wonders of the world, of science—or even himself?

Thus our two young travellers, with a very proper respect for the noble fare before them, paid their homage to it in silence—but a silence that was eloquent none the less. At length, however, each spoke, and each with a sigh.

The Viscount. "The ham, my dear fellow—!"

Barnabas. "The beef, my dear Dick—!"

The Viscount and Barnabus. "Is beyond words."

Having said which, they relapsed again into a silence, broken only by the occasional rattle of knife and fork.

The Viscount (hacking at the loaf). "It's a grand thing to be hungry, my dear fellow."

Barnabas (glancing over the rim of his tankard). "When you have the means of satisfying it—yes."

The Viscount (becoming suddenly abstracted, and turning his piece of bread over and over in his fingers). "Now regarding—Mistress Clemency, my dear Bev; what do you think of her?"

Barnabas (helping himself to more beef). "That she is a remarkably handsome girl!"

The Viscount (frowning at his piece of bread). "Hum! d'you think so?"

Barnabas. "Any man would. I'll trouble you for the mustard, Dick."

The Viscount. "Yes; I suppose they would."

Barnabas. "Some probably do—especially men with an eye for fine women."

The Viscount (frowning blacker than ever). "Pray, what mean you by that?"

Barnabas. "Your friend Carnaby undoubtedly does."

The Viscount (starting). "Carnaby! Why what the devil put him into your head? Carnaby's never seen her."

Barnabas. "Indeed, I think it rather more than likely."

The Viscount (crushing the bit of bread suddenly in his fist). "Carnaby! But I tell you he hasn't—he's never been near this place."

Barnabas. "There you are quite wrong."

The Viscount (flinging himself back in his chair). "Beverley, what the devil are you driving at?"

Barnabas. "I mean that he was here this morning."

The Viscount. "Carnaby? Here? Impossible! What under heaven should make you think so?"

"This," said Barnabas, and held out a small, crumpled piece of paper. The Viscount took it, glanced at it, and his knife clattered to the floor.

"Sixty thousand pounds!" he exclaimed, and sat staring down at the crumpled paper, wide-eyed. "Sixty thousand!" he repeated. "Is it sixty or six, Bev? Read it out," and he thrust the torn paper across to Barnabas, who, taking it up, read as follows:—

—felicitate you upon your marriage with the lovely
heiress, Lady M., failing which I beg most humbly to remind
you, my dear Sir Mortimer Carnaby, that the sixty thousand
pounds must be paid back on the day agreed upon, namely
July 16,

Your humble, obedient Servant,
JASPER GAUNT.

"Jasper Gaunt!" exclaimed the Viscount. "Sixty thousand pounds! Poor Carnaby! Sixty thousand pounds payable on July sixteenth! Now the fifteenth, my dear Bev, is the day of the race, and if he should lose, it looks very much as though Carnaby would be ruined, Bev."

"Unless he marries 'the lovely heiress'!" added Barnabas.

"Hum!" said the Viscount, frowning. "I wish I'd never seen this cursed paper, Bev!" and as he spoke he crumpled it up and threw it into the great fireplace. "Where in the name of mischief did you get it?"

"It was in the corner yonder," answered Barnabas. "I also found this." And he laid a handsomely embossed coat button on the table. "It has been wrenched off you will notice."

"Yes," nodded the Viscount, "torn off! Do you think—"

"I think," said Barnabas, putting the button back into his pocket, "that Mistress Clemency's tears are accounted for—"

"By God, Beverley," said the Viscount, an ugly light in his eyes, "if I thought that—!" and the hand upon the table became a fist.

"I think that Mistress Clemency is a match for any man—or brute," said Barnabas, and drew his hand from his pocket.

Now the Viscount's fist was opening and shutting convulsively, the breath whistled between his teeth, he glanced towards the door, and made as though he would spring to his feet; but in that moment came a diversion, for Barnabas drew his hand from his pocket, and as he did so, something white fluttered to the floor, close beside the Viscount's chair. Both men saw it and both stooped to recover it, but the Viscount, being nearer, picked it up, glanced at it, looked at Barnabas with a knowing smile, glanced at it again, was arrested by certain initials embroidered in one corner, stooped his head suddenly, inhaling its subtle perfume, and so handed it back to Barnabas, who took it with a word of thanks and thrust it into an inner pocket, while the Viscount stared at him under his drawn brows. But Barnabas, all unconscious, proceeded to cut himself another slice of beef, offering to do the same for the Viscount.

"Thank you—no," said he.

"What—have you done, so soon?"

"Yes," said he, and thereafter sat watching Barnabas ply knife and fork, who, presently catching his eye, smiled.

"Pray," said the Viscount after a while, "pray are you acquainted with the Lady Cleone Meredith?"

"No," answered Barnabas. "I'll trouble you for the mustard, Dick."

"Have you ever met the Lady Cleone Meredith?"

"Never", answered Barnabas, innocent of eye.

Hereupon the Viscount rose up out of the chair and leaned across the table.

"Sir," said he, "you are a most consummate liar!"

Hereupon Barnabas helped himself to the mustard with grave deliberation, then, leaning back in his chair, he smiled up into the Viscount's glowing eyes as politely and with as engaging an air as might be.

"My Lord," said he gently, "give me leave to remark that he who says so, lies himself most foully." Having said which Barnabas set down the mustard, and bowed.

"Mr. Beverley," said the Viscount, regarding him calm-eyed across the table, "there is a place I know of near by, a very excellent place, being hidden by trees, a smooth, grassy place—shall we go?"

"Whenever you will, my Lord," said Barnabas, rising.

Forthwith having bowed to each other and put on their hats, they stepped out into the yard, and so walked on side by side, a trifle stiffer and more upright than usual maybe, until they came to a stile. Here they must needs pause to bow once more, each wishful to give way to the other, and, having duly crossed the stile, they presently came to a place, even as the Viscount had said, being shady with trees, and where a brook ran between steep banks. Here, too, was a small foot-bridge, with hand-rails supported at either end by posts. Now upon the right-hand post the Viscount set his hat and coat, and upon the left, Barnabas hung his. Then, having rolled up their shirt-sleeves, they bowed once more, and coming to where the grass was very smooth and level they faced each other with clenched fists.

"Mr. Beverley," said the Viscount, "you will remember I sighed for muffles, but, sir, I count this more fortunate, for to my mind there is nothing like bare fists, after all, to try a man's capabilities."

"My Lord," said Barnabas, "you will also remember that when I told you I had boxed daily both with 'Glorious John' and Nathaniel Bell, you doubted my word? I therefore intend to try and convince you as speedily as may be."

"Egad!" exclaimed the Viscount, his blue eyes a-dance, "this is positively more than I had ventured to hope, my dear fell—Ah! Mr. Beverley, at your service, sir?"

And, after a season, Barnabas spoke, albeit pantingly, and dabbing at his bloody mouth the while.

"Sir," said he, "I trust—you are not—incommoded at all?" whereupon the Viscount, coming slowly to his elbow and gazing round about him with an expression of some wonder, made answer, albeit also pantingly and short of breath:

"On the contrary, sir, am vastly—enjoying myself—shall give myself the pleasure—of continuing—just as soon as the ground subsides a little."

Therefore Barnabas, still dabbing at his mouth, stepped forward being minded to aid him to his feet, but ere he could do so, a voice arrested him.

"Stop!" said the voice.

Now glancing round, Barnabas beheld a man, a small man and slender, whose clothes, old and worn, seemed only to accentuate the dignity and high nobility of his face.

Bareheaded he advanced towards them and his hair glistened silver white in the sunshine, though his brows were dark, like the glowing eyes below. Upon his cheek was the dark stain of blood, and on his lips was a smile ineffably sweet and gentle as he came forward, looking from one to the other.

"And pray, sir," inquired the Viscount, sitting cross-legged upon the green, "pray, who might you be?"

"I am an apostle of peace, young sir," answered the stranger, "a teacher of forgiveness, though, doubtless, an unworthy one."

"Peace, sir!" cried the Viscount, "deuce take me!—but you are the most warlike Apostle of Peace that eyes ever beheld; by your looks you might have been fighting the Seven Champions of Christendom, one down, t' other come on—"

"You mean that I am bleeding, sir; indeed, I frequently do, and therein is my joy, for this is the blood of atonement."

"The blood of atonement?" said Barnabas.

"Last night," pursued the stranger in his gentle voice, "I sought to teach the Gospel of Mercy and Universal Forgiveness at a country fair not so very far from here, and they drove me away with sticks and stones; indeed, I fear our rustics are sometimes woefully ignorant, and Ignorance is always cruel. So, to-day, as soon as the stiffness is gone from me, I shall go back to them, sirs, for even Ignorance has ears."

Now whereupon, the Viscount got upon his legs, rather unsteadily, and bowed.

"Sir," said he, "I humbly ask your pardon; surely so brave an apostle should do great works."

"Then," said the stranger, drawing nearer, "if such is your thought, let me see you two clasp hands."

"But, sir," said the Viscount, somewhat taken aback, "indeed we have—scarcely begun—"

"So much the better," returned the teacher of forgiveness with his gentle smile, and laying a hand upon the arm of each.

"But, sir, I went so far as to give this gentleman the lie!" resumed the Viscount.

"Which I went so far as to—return," said Barnabas.

"But surely the matter can be explained?" inquired the stranger.

"Possibly!" nodded the Viscount, "though I generally leave explanations until afterwards."

"Then," said the stranger, glancing from one proud young face to the other, "in this instance, shake hands first. Hate and anger are human attributes, but to forgive is Godlike. Therefore now, forget yourselves and in this thing be gods. For, young sirs, as it seems to me, it was ordained that you two should be friends. And you are young and full of great possibilities and friendship is a mighty factor in this hard world, since by friendship comes self-forgetfulness, and no man can do great works unless he forgets Self. So, young sirs, shake hands!"

Now, as they looked upon each other, of a sudden, despite his split lip, Barnabas smiled and, in that same moment, the Viscount held out his hand.

"Beverley," said he, as their fingers gripped, "after your most convincing—shall we say, argument?—if you tell me you have boxed with all and every champion back to Mendoza, Jack Slack, and Broughton, egad! I'll believe you, for you have a devilish striking and forcible way with you at times!" Here the Viscount cherished his bruised ribs with touches of tender inquiry. "Yes," he nodded, "there is a highly commendable thoroughness in your methods, my dear Bev, and I'm free to confess I like you better and better—but—!"

"But?" inquired Barnabas.

"As regards the handkerchief now—?"

"I found it—on a bramble-bush—in a wood," said Barnabas.

"In a wood!"

"In Annersley Wood; I found a lady there also."

"A lady—oh, egad!"

"A very beautiful woman," said Barnabas thoughtfully, "with wonderful yellow hair!"

"The Lady Cleone Meredith!" exclaimed the Viscount, "but in a—wood!"

"She had fallen from her horse."

"How? When? Was she hurt?"

"How, I cannot tell you, but it happened about two hours ago, and her hurt was trifling."

"And you—found her?"

"I also saw her safely out of the wood."

"And you did not know her name?"

"I quite—forgot to ask it," Barnabas admitted, "and I never saw her until this morning."

"Why, then, my dear Bev," said the Viscount, his brow clearing, "let us go back to breakfast, all three of us."

But, now turning about, they perceived that the stranger was gone, yet, coming to the bridge, they presently espied him sitting beside the stream laving his hurts in the cool water.

"Sir," said Barnabas, "our thanks are due to you—"

"And you must come back to the inn with us," added the Viscount; "the ham surpasses description."

"And I would know what you meant by the 'blood of atonement,'" said Barnabas, the persistent.

"As to breakfast, young sirs," said the stranger, shaking his head, "I thank you, but I have already assuaged my hunger; as to my story, well, 'tis not over long, and indeed it is a story to think upon—a warning to heed, for it is a story of Self, and Self is the most insidious enemy that man possesses. So, if you would listen to the tale of a selfish man, sit down here beside me, and I'll tell you."

CHAPTER XII

OF THE STRANGER'S TALE, WHICH, BEING SHORT, MAY PERHAPS MEET WITH THE READER'S KIND APPROBATION.

"In ancient times, sirs," began the stranger, with his gaze upon the hurrying waters of the brook, "when a man had committed some great sin he hid himself from the world, and lashed himself with cruel stripes, he walked barefoot upon sharp flints and afflicted himself with grievous pains and penalties, glorying in the blood of his atonement, and wasting himself and his remaining years in woeful solitude, seeking, thereby, to reclaim his soul from the wrath to come. But, as for me, I walk the highways preaching always forgiveness and forgetfulness of self, and if men grow angry at my teaching and misuse me, the pain of wounds, the hardships, the fatigue, I endure them all with a glad and cheerful mind, seeking thereby to work out my redemption and atonement, for I was a very selfish man." Here the stranger paused, and his face seemed more lined and worn, and his white hair whiter, as he stared down into the running waters of the brook.

"Sirs," he continued, speaking with bent head, "I once had a daughter, and I loved her dearly, but my name was dearer yet. I was proud of her beauty, but prouder of my ancient name, for I was a selfish man."

"We lived in the country, a place remote and quiet, and consequently led a very solitary, humdrum life, because I was ever fond of books and flowers and the solitude of trees—a selfish man always. And so, at last, because she was young and high-spirited, she ran away from my lonely cottage with one who was a villain. And I grieved for her, young sirs, I grieved much and long, because I was lonely, but I grieved more for my name, my honorable name that she had besmirched, because, as I told you, I was a selfish man." Again the stranger was silent, sitting ever with bent head staring down at the crystal waters of the brook, only he clasped his thin hands and wrung them as he continued:

"One evening, as I sat among my roses with a book in my hand, she came back to me through the twilight, and flung herself upon her knees before me, and besought my forgiveness with sobs and bitter, bitter tears. Ah, young sirs! I can hear her weeping yet. The sound of it is always in my ears. So she knelt to me in her abasement with imploring hands stretched out to me. Ah, the pity of those white appealing hands, the pity of them! But I, sirs, being as I say a selfish man and remembering only my proud and honorable name, I, her father, spurned her from me with reproaches and vile words, such burning, searing words as no daughter should hear or father utter."

"And so, weeping still, she turned away wearily, hopelessly, and I stood to watch her bowed figure till she had crept away into the evening and was gone."

"Thus, sirs, I drove her from me, this wounded lamb, this poor broken-hearted maid—bone of my bone, flesh of my flesh—I drove her from me, I who should have comforted and cherished her, I drove her out into the night with hateful words and bitter curses. Oh, was ever sin like mine? Oh, Self, Self!

In ancient times, sirs, when a man had committed some great sin he lashed himself with cruel stripes, but I tell you no rod, no whip of many thongs ever stung or bit so sharp and deep as remorse—it is an abiding pain. Therefore I walk these highways preaching always forgiveness and forgetfulness of self, and so needs must I walk until my days be done, or until—I find her again." The stranger rose suddenly and so stood with bent head and very still, only his hands griped and wrung each other. Yet when he looked up his brow was serene and a smile was on his lips."

"But you, sirs, you are friends again, and that is good, for friendship is a blessed thing. And you have youth and strength, and all things are possible to you, therefore. But oh, beware of self, take warning of a selfish man, forget self, so may you achieve great things."

"But, as for me, I never stand upon a country road when evening falls but I see her, a broken, desolate figure, creeping away from me, always away from me, into the shadows, and the sound of her weeping comes to me in the night silences." So saying, the stranger turned from them and went upon his way, limping a little because of his hurts, and his hair gleamed silver in the sunshine as he went.

CHAPTER XIII

IN WHICH BARNABAS MAKES A CONFESSION

"A very remarkable man!" said the Viscount, taking up his hat.

"And a very pitiful story!" said Barnabas, thoughtfully.

"Though I could wish," pursued the Viscount, dreamy of eye, and settling his hat with a light tap on the crown, "yes, I do certainly wish that he hadn't interfered quite so soon, I was just beginning to—ah—enjoy myself."

"It must be a terrible thing to be haunted by remorse so bitter as his, 'to fancy her voice weeping in the night,' and to see her creeping on into the shadows always—away from him," said Barnabas.

But now, having helped each other into their coats, they set off back to the inn.

"My ribs," said the Viscount, feeling that region of his person with tender solicitude as he spoke, "my ribs are infernally sore, Bev, though it was kind of you not to mark my face; I'm sorry for your lip, my dear fellow, but really it was the only opening you gave me; I hope it isn't painful?"

"Indeed I had forgotten it," returned Barnabas.

"Then needs must I try to forget my bruised ribs," said the Viscount, making a wry face as he clambered over the stile.

But here Barnabas paused to turn and look back at the scene of their encounter, quite deserted now, for the stranger had long since disappeared in the green.

"Yes, a very remarkable man!" sighed Barnabas, thoughtfully. "I wish he had come back with us to the inn and—Clemency. Yes, a very strange man. I wonder now—"

"And I beg you to remember," added the Viscount, taking him by the arm, "he said that you and I were ordained to be friends, and by Gad! I think he spoke the truth, Bev."

"I feel sure of it, Viscount," Barnabas nodded.

"Furthermore, Bev, if you are 'Bev' to me, I must be 'Dick' to you henceforth—amen and so forth!"

"Agreed, Dick."

"Then, my dear Bev?" said the Viscount impulsively.

"Yes, my dear Dick?"

"Suppose we shake hands on it?"

"Willingly, Dick, yet, first, I think it but honorable to tell you that I—love the Lady Cleone Meredith."

"Eh—what?" exclaimed the Viscount, falling back a step, "you love her? the devil you do! since when?"

"Since this morning."

"Love her!" repeated the Viscount, "but you've seen her but once in your life."

"True," said Barnabas, "but then I mean to see her many times, henceforth."

"Ah! the deuce you do!"

"Yes," answered Barnabas. "I shall possibly marry her—some day."

The Viscount laughed, and frowned, and laughed again, then noting the set mouth and chin of the speaker, grew thoughtful, and thereafter stood looking at Barnabas with a new and suddenly awakened interest. Who was he? What was he? From his clothes he might have been anything between a gentleman farmer and a gamekeeper.

As for Barnabas himself, as he leaned there against the stile with his gaze on the distance, his eyes a-dream, he had clean forgotten his awkward clothes and blunt-toed boots.

And after all, what can boots or clothes matter to man or woman? indeed, they sink into insignificance when the face of their wearer is stamped with the serene yet determined confidence that marked Barnabas as he spoke.

"Marry—Cleone Meredith?" said the Viscount at last.

"Marry her—yes," said Barnabas slowly.

"Why then, in the first place let me tell you she's devilish high and proud."

"'T is so I would have her!" nodded Barnabas.

"And cursedly hard to please."

"So I should judge her," nodded Barnabas.

"And heiress to great wealth."

"No matter for that," said Barnabas.

"And full of whims and fancies."

"And therefore womanly," said Barnabas.

"My dear Beverley," said the Viscount, smiling again, "I tell you the man who wins Cleone Meredith must be stronger, handsomer, richer, and more accomplished than any 'Buck,' 'Corinthian,' or 'Macaroni' of 'em all—"

"Or more determined!" added Barnabas.

"Or more determined, yes," nodded the Viscount.

"Then I shall certainly marry her—some day," said Barnabas.

Again the Viscount eyed Barnabas a while in silence, but this time, be it noted, he smiled no more.

"Hum!" said he at last, "so it seems in finding a friend I have also found myself another rival?"

"I greatly fear so," said Barnabas, and they walked on together.

But when they had gone some distance in moody silence, the Viscount spoke:

"Beverley," said he, "forewarned is forearmed!"

"Yes," answered Barnabas, "that is why I told you."

"Then," said the Viscount, "I think we'll—shake hands—after all."

The which they did forthwith.

Now it was at this moment that Milo of Crotona took it upon himself to become visible.

CHAPTER XIV

CONCERNING THE BUTTONS OF ONE MILO OF CROTONA

Never did a pair of top boots, big or little, shine with a lustre more resplendent; never was postilion's jacket more excellent of fit, nattier, or more carefully brushed; and nowhere could there be found two rows of crested silver buttons with such an air of waggish roguery, so sly, so knowing, and so pertinaciously on the everlasting wink, as these same eight buttons that adorned the very small person of his groomship, Milo of Crotona. He had slipped out suddenly from the hedge, and now stood cap in hand, staring from the Viscount to Barnabas, and back again, with his innocent blue eyes, and with every blinking, twinkling button on his jacket. And his eyes were wide and guileless—the eyes of a cherub; but his buttons!

Yea, forsooth, it was all in his buttons as they winked slyly one to another as much as to say:

"Aha! we don't know why his Lordship's nankeens are greened at the knees, not we! nor why the gent's lower lip is unduly swelled. Lord love your eyes and limbs, oh no!"

"What, my imp of innocence!" exclaimed the Viscount. "Where have you sprung from?"

"'Edge, m'lud."

"Ah! and what might you have been doing in the hedge now?"

"Think'n', m'lud."

"And what were you thinking?"

"I were think'n', m'lud, as the tall genelman here is a top-sawyer wi' 'is daddies, m'lud. I was."

"Aha! so you've been watching, eh?"

"Not watchin'—oh no, m'lud; I just 'appened ter notice—that's all, m'lud."

"Ha!" exclaimed the Viscount; "then I suppose you happened to notice me being—knocked down?"

"No, m'lud; ye see, I shut my eyes—every time."

"Every time, eh!" said his Lordship, with his whimsical smile. "Oh Loyalty, thy name is Milo! But hallo!" he broke off, "I believe you've been fighting again—come here!"

"Fightin', m'lud! What, me?"

"What's the matter with your face—it's all swollen; there, your cheek?"

"Swellin', m'lud; I don't feel no swellin'."

"No, no; the other cheek."

"Oh, this, m'lud. Oh, 'e done it, 'e did; but I weren't fightin'."

"Who did it?"

"S' Mortimer's friend, 'e done it, 'e did."

"Sir Mortimer's friend?"

"Ah, 'im, m'lud."

"But, how in the world—"

"Wi' his fist, m'lud."

"What for?"

"'Cos I kicked 'im, I did."

"You—kicked Sir Mortimer Carnaby's friend!" exclaimed the Viscount. "What in heaven's name did you do that for?"

"'Cos you told me to, m'lud, you did."

"I told you to kick—"

"Yes, m'lud, you did. You sez to me, last week—arter I done up that butcher's boy—you sez to me, 'don't fight 'cept you can't 'elp it,' you sez; 'but allus pertect the ladies,' you sez, 'an if so be as 'e's too big to reach wi' your fists—why, use your boots,' you sez, an' so I did, m'lud."

"So you were protecting a lady, were you, Imp?"

"Miss Clemency, mam; yes, m'lud. She's been good ter me, Miss Clemency, mam 'as—an' so when I seen 'im strugglin' an' a-tryin' to kiss 'er—when I 'eered 'er cry out—I came in froo de winder, an' I kicked 'im, I did, an' then—"

"Imp," said the Viscount gravely, "you are forgetting your aitches! And so Sir Mortimer's friend kissed her, did he? Mind your aitches now!"

"Yes, m' lud; an' when Hi seen the tears hin her eyes—"

"Now you are mixing them, Imp!—tears in her eyes. Well?"

"Why then I kicked him, m' lud, an' he turned round an' give me this 'ere."

"And what was Sir Mortimer's friend like?"

"A tall—werry sleepy gentleman, wot smiled, m' lud."

"Ha!" exclaimed the Viscount, starting; "and with a scar upon one cheek?"

"Yes, m'lud."

His Lordship frowned. "That would be Chichester," said he thoughtfully. "Now I wonder what the devil should bring that fellow so far from London?"

"Well, m' lud," suggested Milo, shaking his golden curls, "I kind of 'specks there's a woman at the bottom of it. There mostly generally is."

"Hum!" said the Viscount.

"'Sides, m' lud, I 'eard 'im talkin' 'bout a lady to S' Mortimer!"

"Did they mention her name?"

"The sleepy one 'e did, m' lud. Jist as S' Mortimer climbed into the chaise—'Here's wishing you luck wi' the lovely Meredyth,' 'e sez."

"Meredith!" exclaimed the Viscount.

"Meredith, m' lud; 'the lovely Meredith,' 'e sez, an' then, as he stood watchin' the chaise drive away, 'may the best man win,' sez 'e to himself, 'an' that's me,' sez'e."

"Boy," said the Viscount, "have the horses put to—at once."

"Werry good, m' lud," and, touching his small hat, Milo of Crotona turned and set off as fast as his small legs would carry him.

"Gad!" exclaimed his Lordship, "this is more than I bargained for. I must be off."

"Indeed!" said Barnabas, who for the last minute or so had been watching a man who was strolling idly up the lane, a tall, languid gentleman in a jaunty hat. "You seem all at once in a mighty hurry to get to London."

"London!" repeated the Viscount, staring blankly. "London? Oh, why yes, to be sure, I was going to London; but—hum—fact of the matter is, I've changed my mind about it, my dear Bev; I'm going—back. I'm following Carnaby."

"Ah!" said Barnabas, still intent upon the man in the lane, "Carnaby again."

"Oh, damn the fellow!" exclaimed the Viscount.

"But—he is your friend."

"Hum!" said the Viscount; "but Carnaby is always—Carnaby, and she—"

"Meaning the Lady Cleone," said Barnabas.

"Is a woman—"

"'The lovely Meredith'!" nodded Barnabas.

"Exactly!" said the Viscount, frowning; "and Carnaby is the devil with women."

"But not this woman," answered Barnabas, frowning a little also.

"My dear fellow, men like Carnaby attract all women—"

"That," said Barnabas, shaking his head, "that I cannot believe."

"Have you known many women, Bev?"

"No," answered Barnabas; "but I have met the Lady Cleone—"

"Once!" added the Viscount significantly.

"Once!" nodded Barnabas.

"Hum," said the Viscount. "And, therefore," added Barnabas, "I don't think that we need fear Sir Mortimer as a rival."

"That," retorted the Viscount, shaking his head, "is because you don't know him—either."

Hereupon, having come to the inn and having settled their score, the Viscount stepped out to the stables accompanied by the round-faced landlord, while Barnabas, leaning out from the open casement, stared idly into the lane. And thus he once more beheld the gentleman in the jaunty hat, who stood lounging in the shade of one of the great trees that grew before the inn, glancing up and down the lane in the attitude of one who waits. He was tall and slender, and clad in a tight-fitting blue coat cut in the extreme of the prevailing fashion, and beneath his curly-brimmed hat, Barnabas saw a sallow face with lips a little too heavy, nostrils a little too thin, and eyes a little too close together, at least, so Barnabas thought, but what he noticed more particularly was the fact that one of the buttons of the blue coat had been wrenched away.

Now, as the gentleman lounged there against the tree, he switched languidly at a bluebell that happened to grow within his reach, cut it down, and with gentle, lazy taps beat it slowly into nothingness, which done, he drew out his watch, glanced at it, frowned, and was in the act of thrusting it back into his fob when the hedge opposite was parted suddenly and a man came through. A wretched being he looked, dusty, unkempt, unshorn, whose quick, bright eyes gleamed in the thin oval of his pallid face. At sight of this man the gentleman's lassitude vanished, and he stepped quickly forward.

"Well," he demanded, "did you find her?"

"Yes, sir."

"And a cursed time you've been about it."

"Annersley is further than I thought, sir, and—"

"Pah! no matter, give me her answer," and the gentleman held out a slim white hand.

"She had no time to write, sir," said the man, "but she bid me tell you—"

"Damnation!" exclaimed the gentleman, glancing towards the inn, "not here, come further down the lane," and with the word he turned and strode away, with the man at his heels.

"Annersley," said Barnabas, as he watched them go; "Annersley."

But now, with a prodigious clatter of hoofs and grinding of wheels, the Viscount drove round in his curricle, and drew up before the door in masterly fashion; whereupon the two high-mettled bloods immediately began to rear and plunge (as is the way of their kind), to snort, to toss their sleek heads, and to dance, drumming their hoofs with a sound like a brigade of cavalry at the charge, whereupon the Viscount immediately fell to swearing at them, and his diminutive groom to roaring at them in his "stable voice," and the two ostlers to cursing them, and one another; in the midst of which hubbub out came Barnabas to stare at them with the quick, appraising eye of one who knows and loves horses.

To whom, thusly, the Viscount, speaking both to him and the horses:

"Oh, there you are, Bev—stand still, damn you! There's blood for you, eh, my dear fellow—devil burn your hide! Jump up, my dear fellow—Gad, they're pulling my arms off."

"Then you want me to come with you, Dick?"

"My dear Bev, of course I do—stand still, damn you—though we are rivals, we're friends first—curse your livers and bones—so jump up, Bev, and—oh dammem, there's no holding 'em—quick, up with you."

Now, as Barnabas stepped forward, afar off up the lane he chanced to espy a certain jaunty hat, and immediately, acting for once upon impulse, he shook his head.

"No, thanks," said he.

"Eh—no?" repeated the Viscount, "but you shall see her, I'll introduce you myself."

"Thanks, Dick, but I've decided not to go back."

"What, you won't come then?"

"No."

"Ah, well, we shall meet in London. Inquire for me at White's or Brooke's, any one will tell you where to find me. Good-by!"

Then, settling his feet more firmly, he took a fresh grip upon the reins, and glanced over his shoulder to where Milo of Crotona sat with folded arms in the rumble.

"All right behind?"

"Right, m'lud."

"Then give 'em their heads, let 'em go!"

The grooms sprang away, the powerful bays reared, once, twice, and then, with a thunder of hoofs, started away at a gallop that set the light vehicle rocking and swaying, yet which in no whit seemed to trouble Milo of Crotona, who sat upon his perch behind with folded arms as stiff and steady as a small graven image, until he and the Viscount and the curricle had been whirled into the distance and vanished in a cloud of dust.

CHAPTER XV

IN WHICH THE PATIENT READER MAY LEARN SOMETHING OF THE GENTLEMAN IN THE JAUNTY HAT

"Lord, but this is a great day for the old 'Cow,' sir," said the landlord, as Barnabas yet stood staring down the road, "we aren't had so many o' the quality here for years. Last night the young Vi-count, this morning, bright and early, Sir Mortimer Carnaby and friend, then the Vi-count again, along o' you, sir, an' now you an' Sir Mortimer's friend; you don't be no ways acquainted wi' Sir Mortimer's friend, be you, sir?"

"No," answered Barnabas, "what is his name?"

"Well, Sir Mortimer hailed him as 'Chichester,' I fancy, sir, though I aren't prepared to swear it, no more yet to oath it, not 'aving properly ob-served, but 'Chichester,' I think it were; and, 'twixt you an' me, sir, he be one o' your fine gentlemen as I aren't no wise partial to, an' he's ordered dinner and supper."

"Has he," said Barnabas, "then I think I'll do the same."

"Ay, ay, sir, very good."

"In the meantime could you let me have pen, ink and paper?"

"Ay, sir, surely, in the sanded parlor, this way, sir."

Forthwith he led Barnabas into a long, low panelled room, with a wide fireplace at the further end, beside which stood a great high-backed settle with a table before it. Then Barnabas sat down and wrote a letter to his father, as here follows:—

My Dear Father and Natty Bell,—I have read somewhere in my books that 'adventures are to the adventurous,' and, indeed, I have already found this to be true. Now, since I am adventuring the great world, I adventure lesser things also.

Thus I have met and talked with an entertaining pedler, from whom I have learned that the worst place in the world is Giles's Rents down by the River; from him, likewise, I purchased a book as to the merits of which I begin to entertain doubts.

Then I have already thrashed a friend of the Prince Regent, and somewhat spoiled a very fine gentleman, and, I fear, am like to be necessitated to spoil another before the day is much older; from each of whom I learn that a Prince's friend may be an arrant knave.

Furthermore, I have become acquainted with the son of an Earl, and finding him a man also, have formed a friendship with him, which I trust may endure.

Thus far, you see, much has happened to me; adventures have befallen me in rapid succession. 'Wonderful!' say you. 'Not at all,' say I, since I have found but what I sought after, for, as has been said—'adventures are to the adventurous.' Therefore, within the next few hours, I confidently expect other, and perchance weightier, happenings to overtake me because—I intend them to. So much for myself.

Now, as for you and Natty Bell, it is with deep affection that I think of you—an affection that shall abide with me always. Also, you are both in my thoughts continually. I remember our bouts with the 'muffles,' and my wild gallops on unbroken horses with Natty Bell; surely he knows a horse better than any, and is a better rider than boxer, if that could well be. Indeed, I am fortunate in having studied under two such masters.

Furthermore, I pray you to consider that this absence of mine will only draw us closer together, in a sense. Indeed, now, when I think of you both, I am half-minded to give up this project and come back to you. But my destiny commands me, and destiny must be obeyed. Therefore I shall persist unto the end; but whether I succeed or no, remember, I pray of you, that I am always,

Your lover and friend,
Barnabas.

P.S.—Regarding the friend of the Prince Regent, I could wish now that I had struck a little harder, and shall do so next time, should the opportunity be given.

B.

Having finished this letter, in which it will be seen he made no mention of the Lady Cleone, though his mind was yet full of her, having finished his letter I say, Barnabas sanded it, folded it, affixed wafers, and had taken up his pen to write the superscription, when he was arrested by a man's voice speaking in a lazy drawl, just outside the open lattice behind him.

"Now 'pon my soul and honor, Beatrix—so much off ended virtue for a stolen kiss—begad! you were prodigal of 'em once—"

"How-dare you! Oh, coward that you are!" exclaimed another voice, low and repressed, yet vibrant with bitter scorn; "you know that I found you out—in time, thank God!"

"Beatrix?" said Barnabas to himself.

"In time; ah! and pray who'd believe it? You ran away from me—but you ran away with me—first! In time? Did your father believe it, that virtuous old miser?

would any one, who saw us together, believe it? No, Beatrix, I tell you all the world knows you for my—"

"Stop!" A moment's silence and then came a soft, gently amused laugh.

"Lord, Beatrix, how handsome you are!—handsomer than ever, begad! I'm doubly fortunate to have found you again. Six years is a long time, but they've only matured you—ripened you. Yes, you're handsomer than ever; upon my life and soul you are!"

But here came the sudden rush of flying draperies, the sound of swift, light footsteps, and Barnabas was aware of the door behind him being opened, closed and bolted, and thereafter, the repressed sound of a woman's passionate weeping. Therefore he rose up from the settle, and glancing over its high back, beheld Clemency.

Almost in the same moment she saw him, and started back to the wall, glanced from Barnabas to the open lattice, and covered her face with her hands. And now not knowing what to do, Barnabas crossed to the window and, being there, looked out, and thus espied again the languid gentleman, strolling up the lane, with his beaver hat cocked at the same jaunty angle, and swinging his betasselled stick as he went.

"You—you heard, then!" said Clemency, almost in a whisper.

"Yes," answered Barnabas, without turning; "but, being a great rascal he probably lied."

"No, it is—quite true—I did run away with him; but oh! indeed, indeed I left him again before—before—"

"Yes, yes," said Barnabas, a little hurriedly, aware that her face was still hidden in her hands, though he kept his eyes studiously averted. Then all at once she was beside him, her hands were upon his arm, pleading, compelling; and thus she forced him to look at her, and, though her cheeks yet burned, her eyes met his, frank and unashamed.

"Sir," said she, "you do believe that I—that I found him out in time—that I—escaped his vileness—you must believe—you shall!" and her slender fingers tightened on his arm. "Oh, tell me—tell me, you believe!"

"Yes," said Barnabas, looking down into the troubled depths of her eyes; "yes, I do believe."

The compelling hands dropped from his arm, and she stood before him, staring out blindly into the glory of the morning; and Barnabas could not but see how the tears glistened under her lashes; also he noticed how her brown, shapely hands griped and wrung each other.

"Sir," said she suddenly; "you are a friend of—Viscount Devenham."

"I count myself so fortunate."

"And—therefore—a gentleman."

"Indeed, it is my earnest wish."

"Then you will promise me that, should you ever hear anything spoken to the dishonor of Beatrice Darville, you will deny it."

"Yes," said Barnabas, smiling a little grimly, "though I think I should do—more than that."

Now when he said this, Clemency looked up at him suddenly, and in her eyes there was a glow no tears could quench; her lips quivered but no words came, and then, all at once, she caught his hand, kissed it, and so was gone, swift and light, and shy as any bird.

And, in a while, happening to spy his letter on the table, Barnabas sat down and wrote out the superscription with many careful flourishes, which done, observing his hat near by, he took it up, brushed it absently, put it on, and went out into the sunshine.

Yet when he had gone but a very little way, he paused, and seeing he still carried the letter in his hand, thrust it into his breast, and so remained staring thoughtfully towards that spot, green and shady with trees, where he and the Viscount had talked with the Apostle of Peace. And with his gaze bent thitherwards he uttered a name, and the name was—

"Beatrix."

CHAPTER XVI

IN WHICH BARNABAS ENGAGES ONE WITHOUT A CHARACTER

Barnabas walked on along the lane, head on breast, plunged in a profound reverie, and following a haphazard course, so much so that, chancing presently to look about him, he found that the lane had narrowed into a rough cart track that wound away between high banks gay with wild flowers, and crowned with hedges, a pleasant, shady spot, indeed, as any thoughtful man could wish for.

Now as he walked, he noticed a dry ditch—a grassy, and most inviting ditch; therefore Barnabas sat him down therein, leaning his back against the bank.

"Beatrix!" said he, again, and thrusting his hands into his pockets he became aware of the "priceless wollum." Taking it out, he began turning its pages, idly enough, and eventually paused at one headed thus:

THE CULT OF DRESS.

But he had not read a dozen words when he was aware of a rustling of leaves, near by, that was not of the wind, and then the panting of breath drawn in painful gasps; and, therefore, having duly marked his place with a finger, he raised his head and glanced about him. As he did so, the hedge, almost opposite, was burst asunder and a man came slipping down the bank, and, regaining his feet, stood staring at Barnabas and panting. A dusty, bedraggled wretch he looked, unshaven and unkempt, with quick, bright eyes that gleamed in the pale oval of his face.

"What do you want?" Barnabas demanded.

"Everything!" the man panted, with the ghost of a smile on his pallid lips; "but—the ditch would do."

"And why the ditch?"

"Because they're—after me."

"Who are?"

"Gamekeepers!"

"Then, you're a poacher?"

"And a very clumsy one—they had me once—close on me now."

"How many?"

"Two."

"Then—hum!—get into the ditch," said Barnabas.

Now the ditch, as has been said, was deep and dry, and next moment, the miserable fugitive was hidden from view by reason of this, and of the grasses and wild flowers that grew luxuriantly there; seeing which, Barnabas went back to his reading.

"It is permitted," solemnly writes the Person of Quality, "that white waistcoats be worn,—though sparingly, for caution is always advisable, and a buff waistcoat therefore is recommended as safer. Coats, on the contrary, may occasionally vary both as to the height of the collar, which must, of course, roll, and the number of buttons—"

Thus far the Person of Quality when:
"Hallo, theer" roared a stentorian voice.

"Breeches, on the other hand," continues the Person of Quality gravely, "are governed as inexorably as the Medes and Persians; thus, for mornings they must be either pantaloons and Hessians—"

"Hallo theer! oho!—hi!—waken oop will 'ee!"

"Or buckskins and top boots—"

"Hi!" roared the voice, louder than ever, "you theer under th' 'edge,—oho!"

Once more Barnabas marked the place with his finger, and glancing up, straightway espied Stentor, somewhat red-faced, as was but natural, clad in a velveteen jacket and with a long barrelled gun on his shoulder.

"Might you be shouting at me?" inquired Barnabas.

"Well," replied Stentor, looking up and down the lane, "I don't see nobody else to shout at, so let's s'pose as I be shouting at ye, bean't deaf, be ye?"

"No, thank God."

"'Cause if so be as y' are deaf, a can shout a tidy bit louder nor that a reckon."

"I can hear you very well as it is."

"Don't go for to be too sartin, now; ye see I've got a tidy voice, I have, which I aren't noways afeared o' usin'!"

"So it would appear!" nodded Barnabas.

"You're quite sure as ye can 'ear me, then?"

"Quite."

"Werry good then, if you are sure as you can 'ear me I'd like to ax 'ee a question, though, mark me, I'll shout it, ah! an' willin'; if so be you're minded, say the word!"

But, before Barnabas could reply, another man appeared, being also clad in velveteens and carrying a long barrelled gun.

"Wot be doin', Jarge?" he inquired of Stentor, in a surly tone, "wot be wastin' time for"

"W'y, lookee, I be about to ax this 'ere deaf chap a question, though ready, ah! an' willin' to shout it, if so be 'e gives the word."

"Stow yer gab, Jarge," retorted Surly, more surly than ever, "you be a sight too fond o' usin' that theer voice o' your'n!" saying which he turned to Barnabas:

"Did ye see ever a desprit, poachin' wagabone run down this 'ere lane, sir?" he inquired.

"No," answered Barnabas.

"Well, did ye see ever a thievin' wastrel run oop this 'ere lane?" demanded Stentor.

"No," answered Barnabas.

"But we seen 'im run this way," demurred Surly.

"Ah!—he must ha' run oop or down this 'ere lane," said Stentor.

"He did neither," said Barnabas.

"Why, then p'r'aps you be stone blind as well as stone deaf?" suggested Stentor.

"Neither one nor the other," answered Barnabas, "and now, since I have answered all your questions, suppose you go and look somewhere else?"

"Look, is it?—look wheer—d'ye mean—?"

"I mean—go."

"Go!" repeated Stentor, round of eye, "then s'pose you tell us—wheer!"

"Anywhere you like, only—be off!"

"Now you can claw me!" exclaimed Stentor with an injured air, nodding to his gun, seeing his companion had already hurried off, "you can grab and duck me if this don't beat all!—you can burn an' blister me if ever I met a deaf cove as was so ongrateful as this 'ere deaf cove,—me 'avin' used this yer v'ice o' mine for 'is be'oof an' likewise benefit; v'ices like mine is a gift as was bestowed for deaf 'uns like 'im;—I've met deaf 'uns afore, yes,—but such a ongrateful deaf 'un as 'im,—no. All I 'opes is as 'e gets deafer an' deafer, as deaf as a stock, as a stone, as a—dead sow,—that's all I 'opes!"

Having said which, Stentor nodded to his gun again, glanced at Barnabas again, and strode off, muttering, after his companion.

Hereupon Barnabas once more opened his book; yet he was quite aware that the fugitive had thrust his head out of the ditch, and having glanced swiftly about, was now regarding him out of the corners of his eyes.

"Why do you stare at me?" he demanded suddenly.

"I was wondering why you took the trouble and risk of shielding such a thing as I am," answered the fugitive.

"Hum!" said Barnabas, "upon my soul,—I don't know."

"No," said the man, with the ghostly smile upon his lips again, "I thought not."

Now, as he looked at the man, Barnabas saw that his cheeks, beneath their stubble, were hollow and pinched, as though by the cruel hands of want and suffering. And yet in despite of all this and of the grizzled hair at his temples, the face was not old, moreover there was a merry twinkle in the eye, and a humorous curve to the wide-lipped mouth that appealed to Barnabas.

"And you are a poacher, you say?"

"Yes, sir, and that is bad, I confess, but, what is worse, I was, until I took to poaching, an honest man without a shred of character."

"How so?"

"I was discharged—under a cloud that was never dispelled."

"To be sure, you don't look like an ordinary poacher."

"That is because I am an extraordinary one."

"You mean?"

"That I poach that I may live to—poach again, sir. I am, at once, a necessitous poacher, and a poacher by necessity."

"And what by choice?"

"A gentleman, sir, with plenty of money and no ambitions."

"Why deny ambition?"

"Because I would live a quiet life, and who ever heard of an ambitious man ever being quiet, much less happy and contented?"

"Hum!" said Barnabas, "and what were you by profession?"

"My calling, sir, was to work for, think for, and shoulder the blame for others—generally fools, sir. I was a confidential servant, a valet, sir. And I have worked, thought, and taken the blame for others so very successfully, that I must needs take to poaching that I may live."

"But—other men may require valets!"

"True, sir, and there are plenty of valets to be had—of a sort; but the most accomplished one in the world, if without a character, had better go and hang himself out of the way, and have done with it. And indeed, I have seriously contemplated so doing."

"You rate yourself very highly."

"And I go in rags! Though a professed thief may do well in the world, though the blackest rascal, the slyest rogue, may thrive and prosper, the greatest of valets being without a character, may go in rags and starve—and very probably will."

"Hum!" said Barnabas.

"Now, to starve, sir, is unpleasant; thus I, having a foolish, though very natural, dread of it, poach rabbits that I may exist. I possess also an inborn horror of rags and dirt, therefore I—exchanged this coat and breeches from a farmhouse, the folk being all away in the fields, and though they are awkward, badly-made garments, still beggars—and—"

"Thieves!" added Barnabas.

"And thieves, sir, cannot always be choosers, can they?"

"Then you admit you are a thief?"

Here the fugitive glanced at Barnabas with a wry smile.

"Sir, I fear I must. Exchange is no robbery they say; but my rags were so very ragged, and these garments are at least wearable."

"You have also been a—great valet, I understand?"

"And have served many gentlemen in my time."

"Then you probably know London and the fashionable world?"

"Yes, sir," said the man, with a sigh.

"Now," pursued Barnabas, "I am given to understand, on the authority of a Person of Quality, that to dress properly is an art."

The fugitive nodded. "Indeed, sir, though your Person of Quality should rather have called it the greatest of all the arts."

"Why so?"

"Because by dress it is possible to make—something out of nothing!"

"Explain yourself."

"Why, there was the case of young Lord Ambleside, a nobleman remarkable for a vague stare, and seldom saying anything but 'What!' or 'Dey-vil take me!' though I'll admit he could curse almost coherently—at times. I found him nothing but a lord, and very crude material at that, yet in less than six months he was made."

"Made?"

"Made, sir," nodded the fugitive. "I began him with a cravat, an entirely original creation, which drew the approval of Brummell himself, and, consequently, took London by storm, and I continued him with a waistcoat."

"Not a—white one?" Barnabas inquired.

"No, sir, it was a delicate pink, embroidered with gold, and of quite a new cut and design, which was the means of introducing him to the notice of Royalty itself. The Prince had one copied from it, and wore it at a state reception. And I finished him with a pair of pantaloons which swept the world of fashion clean off its legs, and brought him into lasting favor with the Regent. So my Lord was made, and eventually I married him to an heiress."

"You married him?"

"That is to say, I dictated all his letters, and composed all his verses, which speedily brought the affair to a happy culmination."

"You seem to be a man of many and varied gifts?"

"And one—without a character, sir."

"Nevertheless," said Barnabas, "I think you are the very man I require."

"Sir," exclaimed the fugitive, staring, "sir?"

"And therefore," continued Barnabas, "you may consider yourself engaged."

"Engaged, sir—engaged!" stammered the man—"me?"

"As my valet," nodded Barnabas.

"But, sir, I told you—I was—a thief!"

"Yes," said Barnabas, "and therefore I have great hopes of your future honesty."

Now hereupon the man, still staring, rose up to his knees, and with a swift, appealing gesture, stretched out his hands towards Barnabas, and his hands were trembling all at once.

"Sir!" said he, "oh, sir—d'ye mean it? You don't know, you can't know what such an offer means to me. Sir, you're not jesting with me?"

"No," answered Barnabas, calmly serious of eye, "no, I'm not jesting; and to prove it, here is an advance of wages." And he dropped two guineas into the man's open palm.

The man stared down at the coins in his hand, then rose abruptly to his feet and turned away, and when he spoke again his voice was hoarse.

"Sir," said he, jerkily, "for such trust I would thank you, only words are too poor. But if, as I think, it is your desire to enter the World of Fashion, it becomes my duty, as an honest man, to tell you that all your efforts, all your money, would be unavailing, even though you had been introduced by Barrymore, or Hanger, or Vibart, or Brummell himself."

"Ah," said Barnabas, "and why?"

"Because you have made a fatal beginning."

"How?"

"By knocking down the Prince's friend and favorite—Sir Mortimer Carnaby."

CHAPTER XVII

IN WHICH BARNABAS PARTS COMPANY WITH THE PERSON OF QUALITY

For a long moment the two remained silent, each staring at the other, Barnabas still seated in the ditch and the man standing before him, with the coins clutched in his hand.

"Ah!" said Barnabas, at last, "then you were in the wood?"

"I lay hidden behind a bush, and watched you do it, sir."

"And what were you doing in Annersley Wood?"

"I bore a message, sir, for the lady."

"Ah!" said Barnabas, "the lady—yes."

"Who lay watching you, also."

"No," said Barnabas, "the lady was unconscious."

"Yet recovered sufficiently to adjust her habit, and to watch you knock him down."

"Hum!" said Barnabas, and was silent a while. "Have you heard such a name as Chichester?" he inquired suddenly.

"No, sir."

"And did you deliver the letter?"

"I did, sir."

"And she—sent back an answer?"

"Yes, sir."

"The gentleman who sent the letter was tall and slender, I think, with dark hair, and a scar on his cheek?"

"Yes, sir."

"And when you came back with her answer, he met you down the lane yonder, and I heard you say that the lady had no time to write."

"Yes, sir; but she promised to meet him at a place called Oakshott's Barn."

"Ah!" said Barnabas, "I think I know it."

"At sunset, sir!"

"That would be somewhere about half past seven," mused Barnabas, staring blankly, down at the book on his knee.

"Yes, sir."

"How came you to be carrying his letter?"

"He offered me five shillings to go and bring her answer."

"Did you know the lady?"

"No, sir, but he described her."

"To be sure." said Barnabas; "he mentioned her hair, perhaps?"

"Yes, sir."

"Her—eyelashes, perhaps?"

"And her eyes also, sir."

"Yes, her eyes, of course. He seemed to know her well, perhaps?"

"Yes, sir."

"And she—promised to meet him—in a very lonely place?"

"At Oakshott's Barn, sir."

Once again Barnabas stared down at his book, and was silent so long that his new servant wondered, grew fidgety, coughed, and at last spoke.

"Sir," said he, "what are your orders?"

Barnabas started and looked up.

"Orders?" he repeated; "why, first of all, get something to eat, then find yourself a barber, and wait for me at 'The Spotted Cow.'"

"Yes, sir." The man bowed, turned away, took three or four steps, and came back again.

"Sir," said he, "I have two guineas of yours, and you have never even asked my name."

"True," said Barnabas.

"Supposing I go, and never come back?"

"Then I shall be two guineas the poorer, and you will have proved yourself a thief; but until you do, you are an honest man, so far as I am concerned."

"Sir, said the fugitive, hoarsely, but with a new light in his face," for that, if I were not your servant—I—should like to—clasp your hand; and, sir, my name is John Peterby."

"Why, then," said Barnabas, smiling all at once, "why then, John Peterby, here it is!"

So, for a moment their hands met, and then John Peterby turned sharp about and strode away down the lane, his step grown light and his head held high.

But as for Barnabas, he sat there in the ditch, staring at nothing; and as he stared his brow grew black and ever blacker, until chancing at last to espy the "priceless wollum," where it lay beside him, he took it up, balanced it in his hand, then hurled it over the opposite hedge: which done, he laughed sudden and harsh, and clenched his fists.

"God!" he exclaimed, "a goddess and a satyr!" and so sat staring on at nothingness again.

CHAPTER XVIII

HOW BARNABAS CAME TO OAKSHOTT'S BARN

The sun was getting low, as Barnabas parted the brambles, and looking about him, frowned. He stood in a grassy glade or clearing, a green oasis hemmed in on every side with bushes. Before him was Oakshott's Barn, an ancient structure, its rotting thatch dishevelled, its doors gone long since, its aged walls cracked and scarred by years, a very monument of desolation; upon its threshold weeds had sprung up, and within its hoary shadow breathed an air damp, heavy, and acrid with decay.

It was indeed a place of solitude full of the "hush" of leaves, shut out from the world, close hidden from observation, a place apt for the meetings of lovers. And, therefore, leaning in the shadow of the yawning doorway, Barnabas frowned.

Evening was falling, and from shadowy wood, from dewy grass and flower, stole wafts of perfume, while from some thicket near by a blackbird filled the air with the rich note of his languorous song; but Barnabas frowned only the blacker, and his hand clenched itself on the stick he carried, a heavy stick, that he had cut from the hedge as he came.

All at once the blackbird's song was hushed, and gave place to a rustle of leaves that drew nearer and nearer; yet Barnabas never moved, not even when the bushes were pushed aside and a man stepped into the clearing—a tall, elegant figure, who having paused to glance sharply about him, strolled on again towards the barn, swinging his tasselled walking-cane, and humming softly to himself as he came. He was within a yard of Barnabas when he saw him, and stopped dead.

"Ah!" he exclaimed, softly; and thereafter the two eyed each other in an ominous silence.

"And who the devil are you?" he inquired at length, his eyes still intent.

"Sir," said Barnabas, yet leaning in the doorway—"your name I think, is Chichester?"

"Well?"

"Permit me to return your coat button!" and Barnabas held out the article in question, but Mr. Chichester never so much as glanced at it.

"What do you want here?" he demanded, soft of voice.

"To tell you that this dismal place is called Oakshott's Barn, sir."

"Well?"

"To warn you that Oakshott's Barn is an unhealthy place—for your sort, sir."

"Ha!" said Mr. Chichester, his heavy-lidded eyes unwinking, "do you threaten?"

"Let us rather say—I warn!"

"So you do threaten!"

"I warn!" repeated Barnabas.

"To the devil with you and your warning!" All this time neither of them had moved or raised his voice, only Mr. Chichcster's thin, curving nostrils began to twitch all at once, while his eyes gleamed beneath their narrowed lids. But now Barnabas stepped clear of the doorway, the heavy stick swinging in his hand.

"Then, sir," said he, "let me advise. Let me advise you to hurry from this solitude."

Mr. Chichester laughed—a low, rippling laugh.

"Ah!" said he, "ah, so that's it!"

"Yes," nodded Barnabas, shifting his gaze to Mr. Chichester's right hand, a white beringed hand, whose long, slender fingers toyed with the seals that dangled at his fob, "so pray take up your button and go!"

Mr. Chichester glanced at the heavy stick; at the powerful hand, the broad shoulders and resolute face of him who held it, and laughed again, and, laughing, bowed.

"Your solicitude for my health—touches me, sir,—touches me, my thanks are due to you, for my health is paramount. I owe you a debt which I shall hope to repay. This place, as you say, is dismal. I wish you good evening!" saying which, Mr. Chichester turned away. But in that same instant, swift and lithe as a panther, Barnabas leapt, and dropping his stick, caught that slender, jewelled hand, bent it, twisted it, and wrenched the weapon from its grasp. Mr. Chichester stood motionless, white-lipped and silent, but a devil looked out of his eyes.

"Ah!" said Barnabas, glancing down at the pistol he held, "I judged you would not venture into these wilds without something of the sort. The path, you will notice, lies to your left; it is a winding path, I will go with you therefore, to see that you do not lose your way, and wander—back here again."

Without a word Mr. Chichester turned, and coming to the path followed it, walking neither fast nor slow, never once looking to where Barnabas strode behind, and heedless of briar or bramble that dragged at him as he passed. On they went, until the path lost itself in a grassy lane, until the lane ended in a five-barred gate. Now, having opened the gate, Mr. Chichester passed through into the high road, and then, for one moment he looked at Barnabas, a long, burning look that took in face, form and feature, and so, still without uttering a word, he went upon his way, walking neither fast nor slow, and swinging his tasselled cane as he went, while Barnabas, leaning upon the gate, watched him until his tall, slender figure had merged into the dusk, and was gone.

Then Barnabas sighed, and becoming aware of the pistol in his hand, smiled contemptuously, and was greatly minded to throw it away, but slipped it into his pocket instead, for he remembered the devil in the eyes of Mr. Chichester.

CHAPTER XIX

WHICH TELLS HOW BARNABAS TALKS WITH MY LADY CLEONE FOR THE SECOND TIME

It was dark among the trees, but, away to his left, though as yet low down, the moon was rising, filling the woods with mystery, a radiant glow wherein objects seemed to start forth with a new significance; here the ragged hole of a tree, gnarled, misshapen; there a wide-flung branch, weirdly contorted, and there again a tangle of twigs and strange, leafy shapes that moved not. And over all was a deep and brooding quietude.

Yes, it was dark among the trees, yet not so black as the frown that clouded the face of Barnabas as he strode on through the wood, and so betimes reached again the ancient barn of Oakshott. And lo! even as he came there, it was night, and because the trees grew tall and close together, the shadows lay thicker than ever save only in one place where the moon, finding some rift among the leaves, sent down a shaft of silvery light that made a pool of radiance amid the gloom. Now, as Barnabas gazed at this, he stopped all at once, for, just within this patch of light, he saw a foot. It was a small foot, proudly arched, a shapely foot and slender, like the ankle above; indeed, a haughty and most impatient foot, that beat the ground with angry little taps, and yet, in all and every sense, surely, and beyond a doubt, the most alluring foot in the world. Therefore Barnabas sighed and came a step nearer, and in that moment it vanished; therefore Barnabas stood still again. There followed a moment's silence, and then:

"Dear," said a low, thrilling voice, "have you come—at last? Ah! but you are late, I began to fear—" The soft voice faltered and broke off with a little gasp, and, as Barnabas stepped out of the shadows, she shrank away, back and back, to the mossy wall of the barn, and leaned there staring up at him with eyes wide and fearful. Her hood, close drawn, served but to enhance the proud beauty of her face, pale under the moon, and her cloak, caught close in one white hand, fell about her ripe loveliness in subtly revealing folds. Now in her other hand she carried a silver-mounted riding-whip. And because of the wonder of her beauty, Barnabas sighed again, and because of the place wherein they stood, he frowned; yet, when he spoke, his voice was gentle:

"Don't be afraid, madam, he is gone."

"Gone!" she echoed, faintly.

"Yes, we are quite alone; consequently you have no more reason to be afraid."

"Afraid, sir? I thought—why, 'twas you who startled me."

"Ay," nodded Barnabas, "you expected—him!"

"Where is he? When did he go?"

"Some half-hour since."

"Yet he expected me; he knew I should come; why did he go?"

Now hereupon Barnabas lifted a hand to his throat, and loosened his neckcloth.

"Why then," said he slowly, "you have—perhaps—met him hereabouts—before to-night?"

"Sir," she retorted, "you haven't answered me; why did he go so soon?"

"He was—forced to, madam."

"Forced to go,—without seeing me,—without one word! Oh, impossible!"

"I walked with him to the cross-roads, and saw him out of sight."

"But I—I came as soon as I could! Ah! surely he gave you some message—some word for me?"

"None, madam!" said Barnabas evenly, but his hand had clenched itself suddenly on the stick he held.

"But I—don't understand!" she sighed, with a helpless gesture of her white hands, "to hurry away like this, without a word! Oh, why—why did he go?"

"Madam," said Barnabas, "it was because I asked him to."

"You—asked him to?"

"I did."

"But why—why?"

"Because, from what little I know of him, I judged it best."

"Sir," she said, softly, "sir—what do you mean?"

"I mean, that this is such a very lonely place for any woman and—such as he."

Now even as Barnabas uttered the words she advanced upon him with upflung head and eyes aflame with sudden passionate scorn.

"Insolent," she exclaimed. "So it was you—you actually dared to interfere?"

"Madam," said Barnabas, "I did."

Very straight and proud she stood, and motionless save for the pant and tumult of her bosom, fierce-eyed and contemptuous of lip.

"And remained to insult me—with impunity."

"To take you home again," said Barnabas, "therefore pray let us begone."

"Us? Sir, you grow presumptuous."

"As you will," said Barnabas, "only let us go."

"With you?" she exclaimed.

"With me."

"No—not a step, sir; When I choose to go, I go alone."

"But to-night," said Barnabas, gentle of voice but resolute of eye, "to-night—I go with you."

"You!" she cried, "a man I have seen but once, a man who may be anything, a—a thief, a ploughman, a runaway groom for aught I know." Now, watching him beneath disdainful drooping lashes, she saw Barnabas flinch at this, and the curve of her scornful lips grew more bitter.

"And now I'm going—alone. Stand aside, and let me pass."

"No, madam."

"Let me pass, I warn you!"

For a minute they fronted each other, eye to eye, very silent and still, like two antagonists that measure each other's strength; then Barnabas smiled and shook his head. And in that very instant, quick and passionate, she raised her whip and struck him across the cheek. Then, as she stood panting, half fearful of what she had done, Barnabas reached out and took the whip, and snapped it between his hands.

"And now," said he, tossing aside the broken pieces, "pray let us go."

"No."

"Why, then," sighed Barnabas, "I must carry you again."

Once more she shrank away from him, back and back to the crumbling wall, and leaned there. But now because of his passionless strength, she fell a-trembling and, because of his calmly resolute eyes and grimly smiling mouth, fear came upon her, and therefore, because she could not by him, because she knew herself helpless against him, she suddenly covered her face from his eyes, and a great sob burst from her.

Barnabas stopped, and looking at her bowed head and shrinking figure, knew not what to do. And as he stood there within a yard of her, debating within himself, upon the quiet broke a sudden sound—a small, sharp sound, yet full of infinite significance—the snapping of a dry twig among the shadows; a sound that made the ensuing silence but the more profound, a breathless quietude which, as moment after moment dragged by, grew full of deadly omen. And now, even as Barnabas turned to front these menacing shadows, the moon went out.

CHAPTER XX

OF THE PROPHECY OF ONE BILLY BUTTON, A MADMAN

Upon the quiet stole a rustle of leaves, a whisper that came and went, intermittently, that grew louder and louder, and so was gone again; but in place of this was another sound, a musical jingle like the chime of fairy bells, very far, and faint, and sweet. All at once Barnabas knew that his companion's fear of him was gone, swallowed up—forgotten in terror of the unknown. He heard a slow-drawn, quivering sigh, and then, pale in the dimness, her hand came out to him, crept down his arm, and finding his hand, hid itself in his warm clasp; and her hand was marvellous cold, and her fingers stirred and trembled in his.

Came again a rustling in the leaves, but louder now, and drawing nearer and nearer, and ever the fairy chime swelled upon the air. And even as it came Barnabas felt her closer, until her shoulder touched his, until the fragrance of her breath fanned his cheek, until the warmth of her soft body thrilled through him, until, loud and sudden in the silence, a voice rose—a rich, deep voice:

"'Now is the witching hour when graveyards yawn'—the witching hour—aha!—Oh! poor pale ghost, I know thee—by thy night-black hair and sad, sweet eyes—I know thee. Alas, so young and dead—while I, alas, so old and much alive! Yet I, too, must die some day—soon, soon, beloved shadow. Then shall my shade encompass thine and float up with thee into the infinite. But now, aha! now is the witching hour! Oh! shades and phantoms, I summon thee, fairies, pixies, ghosts and goblins, come forth, and I will sing you and dance you."

"Tis a rare song, mine—and well liked by the quality,—you've heard it before, perchance—ay, ay for you, being dead, hear and see all things, oh, Wise Ones! Come, press round me, so. Now, hearkee, 'Oysters! oysters! and away we go."

"'Many a knight and lady fair
  My oysters fine would try,
They are the finest oysters, sir,
  That ever you did buy.
Oysters! who'll buy my oysters, oh!'"

The bushes rustled again, and into the dimness leapt a tall, dark figure that sang in a rich, sweet voice, and capered among the shadows with a fantastic dancing step, then grew suddenly silent and still. And in that moment the moon shone out again, shone down upon a strange, wild creature, bareheaded and bare of foot. A very tall man he was, with curling gray hair that hung low upon his shoulders, and upon his coat were countless buttons of all makes and kinds that winked and glittered in the moonlight, and jingled faintly as he moved. For a moment he stood motionless and staring, then, laying one hand to the gleaming buttons on his bosom, bowed with an easy, courtly grace.

"Who are you?" demanded Barnabas.

"Billy, sir, poor Billy—Sir William, perhaps—but, mum for that; the moon knows, but cannot tell, then why should I?"

"And what do you want—here?"

"To sing, sir, for you and the lady, if you will. I sing for high folk and low folk. I have many songs, old and new, grave and gay, but folk generally ask for my Oyster Song. I sing for rich and poor, for the sad and for the merry. I sing at country fairs sometimes, and sometimes to trees in lonely places—trees are excellent listeners always. But to-night I sing for—Them."

"And who are they?"

"The Wise Ones, who, being dead, know all things, and live on for ever. Ah, but they're kind to poor Billy, and though they have no buttons to give him, yet they tell him things sometimes. Aha! such things!—things to marvel at! So I sing for them always when the moon is full, but, most of all, I sing for Her."

"Who is she?"

"One who died, many years ago. Folk told her I was dead, killed at sea, and her heart broke—hearts will break—sometimes. So when she died, I put off the shoes from my feet, and shall go barefoot to my grave. Folk tell me that poor Billy's mad—well, perhaps he is—but he sees and hears more than folk think; the Wise Ones tell me things. You now; what do they tell me of you? Hush! You are on your way to London, they tell me—yes—yes, to London town; you are rich, and shall feast with princes, but youth is over-confident, and thus shall you sup with beggars. They tell me you came here to-night—oh, Youth!—oh, Impulse!—hasting—hasting to save a wanton from herself."

"Fool!" exclaimed Barnabas, turning upon the speaker in swift anger; for my lady's hand had freed itself from his clasp, and she had drawn away from him.

"Fool?" repeated the man, shaking his head, "nay, sir, I am only mad, folk tell me. Yet the Wise Ones make me their confidant, they tell me that she—this proud lady—is here to aid an unworthy brother, who sent a rogue instead."

"Brother!" exclaimed Barnabas, with a sudden light in his eyes.

"Who else, sir?" demands my lady, very cold and proud again all at once.

"But," stammered Barnabas, "but—I thought—"

"Evil of me!" says she.

"No—that is—I—I—Forgive me!"

"Sir, there are some things no woman can forgive; you dared to think—"

"Of the rogue who came instead," said Barnabas.

"Ah!—the rogue?"

"His name is Chichester," said Barnabas.

"Chichester!" she repeated, incredulously. "Chichester!"

"A tall, slender, dark man, with a scar on his cheek," added Barnabas.

"Do you mean he was here—here to meet me—alone?"

Now, at this she seemed to shrink into herself; and, all at once, sank down, crouching upon her knees, and hid her face from the moon.

"My lady!"

"Oh!" she sighed, "oh, that he should have come to this!"

"My Lady Cleone!" said Barnabas, and touched her very gently.

"And you—you!" she cried, shuddering away from him, "you thought me what—he would have made me! You thought I—Oh, shame! Ah, don't touch me!"

But Barnabas stooped and caught her hands, and sank upon his knees, and thus, as they knelt together in the moonlight, he drew her so that she must needs let him see her face.

"My lady," said he, very reverently, "my thought of you is this, that, if such great honor may be mine, I will marry you—to-night."

But hereupon, with her two hands still prisoned in his, and with the tears yet thick upon her lashes, she threw back her head, and laughed with her eyes staring into his. Thereat Barnabas frowned blackly, and dropped her hands, then caught her suddenly in his long arms, and held her close.

"By God!" he exclaimed, "I'd kiss you, Cleone, on that scornful, laughing mouth, only—I love you—and this is a solitude. Come away!"

"A solitude," she repeated; "yes, and he sent me here, to meet a beast—a satyr! And now—you! You drove away the other brute, oh! I can't struggle—you are too strong—and nothing matters now!" And so she sighed, and closed her eyes. Then gazing down upon her rich, warm beauty, Barnabas trembled, and loosed her, and sprang to his feet.

"I think," said he, turning away to pick up his cudgel, "I think—we had—better—go."

But my lady remained crouched upon her knees, gazing up at him under her wet lashes.

"You didn't—kiss me!" she said, wonderingly.

"You were so—helpless!" said Barnabas. "And I honor you because it was—your brother."

"Ah! but you doubted me first, you thought I came here to meet that—beast!"

"Forgive me," said Barnabas, humbly.

"Why should I?"

"Because I love you."

"So many men have told me that," she sighed.

"But I," said Barnabas, "I am the last, and it is written 'the last shall be first,' and I love you because you are passionate, and pure, and very brave."

"Love!" she exclaimed, "so soon; you have seen me only once!"

"Yes," he nodded, "it is, therefore, to be expected that I shall worship you also—in due season."

Now Barnabas stood leaning upon his stick, a tall, impassive figure; his voice was low, yet it thrilled in her ears, and there was that in his steadfast eyes before which her own wavered and fell; yet, even so, from the shadow of her hood, she must needs question him further.

"Worship me? When?"

"When you are—my—wife."

Again she was silent, while one slender hand plucked nervously at the grass.

"Are you so sure of me?" she inquired at last.

"No; only of myself."

"Ah! you mean to—force a promise from me—here?"

"No."

"Why not?"

"Because it is night, and you are solitary; I would not have you fear me again. But I shall come to you, one day, a day when the sun is in the sky, and friends are within call. I shall come and ask you then."

"And if I refuse?"

"Then I shall wait."

"Until I wed another?"

"Until you change your mind."

"I think I shall—refuse you."

"Indeed, I fear it is very likely."

"Why?"

"Because of my unworthiness; and, therefore, I would not have you kneel while I stand."

"And the grass is very damp," she sighed.

So Barnabas stepped forward with hand outstretched to aid her, but, as he did so, the wandering singer was between them, looking from one to the other with his keen, bright eyes.

"Stay!" said he. "The Wise Ones have told me that she who kneels before you now, coveted for her beauty, besought for her money, shall kneel thus in the time to come; and one—even I, poor Billy—shall stand betwixt you and join your hands thus, and bid you go forth trusting in each other's love and strength, even as poor Billy does now. And, mayhap, in that hour you shall heed the voice, for time rings many changes; the proud are brought low, the humble exalted. Hush! the Wise Ones grow impatient for my song; I hear them calling from the trees, and must begone. But hearkee! they have told me your name, Barnabas? yes, yes; Barn—, Barnabas; for the other, no matter—mum for that! Barnabas, aha! that minds me—at Barnaby Bright we shall meet again, all three of us, under an orbed moon, at Barnaby Bright:—"

"Oh, Barnaby Bright, Barnaby Bright,
The sun's awake, and shines all night!"

"Ay, ay, 't is the night o' the fairies—when spirits pervade the air. Then will I tell you other truths; but now—They call me. She is fair, and passing fair, and by her beauty, suffering shall come upon thee; but 'tis by suffering that men are made, and because of pride, shame shall come on her; but by shame cometh humility. Farewell; I must begone—farewell till Barnaby Bright. We are to meet again in London town, I think—yes, yes—in London. Oho! oysters! oysters, sir?"

"Many a knight and lady gay
My oysters fine would try,
They are the finest oysters
That ever you could buy!
Oysters! Oysters."

And so he bowed, turned, and danced away into the shadows, and above the hush of the leaves rose the silvery jingle of his many buttons, that sank to a chime, to a murmur, and was gone. And now my lady sighed and rose to her feet, and looking at Barnabas, sighed again—though indeed a very soft, little sigh this time. As for Barnabas, he yet stood wondering, and looking after the strange creature, and pondering his wild words. Thus my lady, unobserved, viewed him at her leisure; noted the dark, close-curled hair, the full, well-opened, brilliant eye, the dominating jaw, the sensitive nostrils, the tender curve of the firm, strong mouth. And she had called him "a ploughman—a runaway footman," and had even—she could see the mark upon his cheek—how red it glowed! Did it hurt much, she wondered?

"Mad of course—yes a madman, poor fellow!" said Barnabas, thoughtfully.

"And he said your name is Barnabas."

"Why, to be sure, so he did," said Barnabas, rubbing his chin as one at a loss, "which is very strange, for I never saw or heard of him before."

"So then, your name is—Barnabas?"

"Yes. Barnabas Bar—Beverley."

"Beverley?"

"Yes—Beverley. But we must go."

"First, tell me how you learned my name?"

"From the Viscount—Viscount Devenham?"

"Then, you know the Viscount?"

"I do; we also know each other as rivals."

"Rivals? For what?"

"Yourself."

"For me? Sir—sir—what did you tell him?"

"My name is Barnabas. And I told him that I should probably marry you, some day."

"You told him—that?"

"I did. I thought it but honorable, seeing he is my friend."

"Your friend!—since when, sir?"

"Since about ten o'clock this morning."

"Sir—sir—are you not a very precipitate person?"

"I begin to think I am. And my name is Barnabas."

"Since ten o'clock this morning! Then you knew—me first?"

"By about an hour."

Swiftly she turned away, yet not before he had seen the betraying dimple in her cheek. And so, side by side, they came to the edge of the clearing.

Now as he stooped to open a way for her among the brambles, she must needs behold again the glowing mark upon his cheek, and seeing it, her glance fell, and her lips grew very tender and pitiful, and, in that moment, she spoke.

"Sir," she said, very softly, "sir?"

"My name is Barnabas."

"I fear—I—does your cheek pain you very much, Mr. Beverley?"

"Thank you, no. And my name is Barnabas."

"I did not mean to—to—"

"No, no, the fault was mine—I—I frightened you, and indeed the pain is quite gone," he stammered, holding aside the brambles for her passage. Yet she stood where she was, and her face was hidden in her hood. At last she spoke and her voice was very low.

"Quite gone, sir?"

"Quite gone, and my name is—"

"I'm very—glad—Barnabas."

Four words only, be it noted; yet on the face of Barnabas was a light that was not of the moon, as they entered the dim woodland together.

CHAPTER XXI

IN WHICH BARNABAS UNDERTAKES A MISSION

Their progress through the wood was slow, by reason of the undergrowth, yet Barnabas noticed that where the way permitted, she hurried on at speed, and moreover, that she was very silent and kept her face turned from him; therefore he questioned her.

"Are you afraid of these woods?"

"No."

"Of me?"

"No."

"Then, I fear you are angry again."

"I think Barnab—your name is—hateful!"

"Strange!" said Barnabas, "I was just thinking how musical it was—as you say it."

"I—oh! I thought your cheek was paining you," said she, petulantly.

"My cheek?—what has that to do with it?"

"Everything, sir!"

"That," said Barnabas, "that I don't understand."

"Of course you don't!" she retorted.

"Hum!" said Barnabas.

"And now!" she demanded, "pray how did you know I was to be at Oakshott's Barn to-night?"

"From my valet."

"Your valet?"

"Yes; though to be sure, he was a poacher, then."

"Sir, pray be serious!"

"I generally am."

"But why have a poacher for your valet?"

"That he might poach no more; and because I understand that he is the best valet in the world."

Here she glanced up at Barnabas and shook her head: "I fear I shall never understand you, Mr. Beverley."

"That time will show; and my name is Barnabas."

"But how did—this poacher—know?"

"He was the man who brought you the letter from Mr. Chichester."

"It was written by my—brother, sir."

"He was the man who gave you your brother's letter in Annersley Wood."

"Yes—I remember—in the wood."

"Where I found you lying quite unconscious."

"Where you found me—yes."

"Lying—quite unconscious!"

"Yes," she answered, beginning to hasten her steps again. "And where you left me without telling me your name—or—even asking mine."

"For which I blamed myself—afterwards," said Barnabas.

"Indeed, it was very remiss of you."

"Yes," sighed Barnabas, "I came back to try and find you."

"Really, sir?" said she, with black brows arched—"did you indeed, sir?"

"But I was too late, and I feared I had lost you—"

"Why, that reminds me, I lost my handkerchief."

"Oh!" said Barnabas, staring up at the moon.

"I think I must have dropped it—in the wood."

"Then, of course, it is gone—you may depend upon that," said Barnabas, shaking his head at the moon.

"It had my monogram embroidered in one corner."

"Indeed!" said Barnabas.

"Yes; I was—hoping—that you had seen it, perhaps?"

"On a bramble-bush," said Barnabas, nodding at the moon.

"Then—you did find it, sir?"

"Yes; and I beg to remind you that my name—"

"Where is it?"

"In my pocket."

"Then why couldn't you say so before?"

"Because I wished to keep it there."

"Please give it to me!"

"Why?"

"Because no man shall have my favors to wear until he has my promise, also."

"Then, since I have the one—give me the other."

"Mr. Beverley, you will please return my handkerchief," and stopping all at once, she held out her hand imperiously.

"Of course," sighed Barnabas, "on a condition—"

"On no condition, sir!"

"That you remember my name is Barnabas."

"But I detest your name."

"I am hoping that by use it may become a little less objectionable," said he, rather ponderously.

"It never can—never; and I want my handkerchief,—Barnabas."

So Barnabas sighed again, and perforce gave the handkerchief into her keeping. And now it was she who smiled up at the moon; but as for Barnabas, his gaze was bent earthwards. After they had gone some way in silence, he spoke.

"Have you met—Sir Mortimer Carnaby—often?" he inquired.

"Yes," she answered, then seeing his scowling look, added, "very often, oh, very often indeed, sir!"

"Ha!" said frowning Barnabas, "and is he one of the many who have—told you their love?"

"Yes."

"Hum," said Barnabas, and strode on in gloomy silence. Seeing which she smiled in the shadow of her hood, and thereafter grew angry all at once.

"And pray, why not, sir?" she demanded, haughtily, "though, indeed, it does not at all concern you; and he is at least a gentleman, and a friend of the Prince—"

"And has an excellent eye for horseflesh—and women," added Barnabas.

Now when he said this, she merely looked at him once, and thereafter forgot all about him, whereby Barnabas gradually perceived that his offence was great, and would have made humble atonement, yet found her blind and deaf, which was but natural, seeing that, for her, he had ceased to exist.

But they reached a stile. It was an uncommonly high stile, an awkward stile at any time, more especially at night. Nevertheless, she faced it resolutely, even though Barnabas had ceased to exist. When, therefore, having vaulted over, he would have helped her, she looked over him, and past him, and through him, and mounted unaided, confident of herself, proud and supremely disdainful both of the stile and Barnabas; and then—because of her pride, or her disdain, or her long cloak, or all three—she slipped, and to save herself must needs catch at Barnabas, and yield herself to his arm; so, for a moment, she lay in his embrace, felt his tight clasp about her, felt his quick breath upon her cheek. Then he had set her down, and was eyeing her anxiously.

"Your foot, is it hurt?" he inquired.

"Thank you, no," she answered, and turning with head carried high, hurried on faster than ever.

"You should have taken my hand," said he; but he spoke to deaf ears.

"You will find the next stile easier, I think," he ventured; but still she hurried on, unheeding.

"You walk very fast!" said he again, but still she deigned him no reply; therefore he stooped till he might see beneath her hood.

"Dear lady," said he very gently, "if I offended you a while ago—forgive me—Cleone."

"Indeed," said she, looking away from him; "it would seem I must be always forgiving you, Mr. Beverley."

"Why, surely it is a woman's privilege to forgive, Cleone—and my name—"

"And a man's prerogative to be forgiven, I suppose, Mr. Beverley."

"When he repents as I do, Cleone; and my—"

"Oh! I forgive you," she sighed.

"Yet you still walk very fast."

"It must be nearly ten o'clock."

"I suppose so," said Barnabas, "and you will, naturally, be anxious to reach home again."

"Home," she said bitterly; "I have no home."

"But—"

"I live in a gaol—a prison. Yes, a hateful, hateful prison, watched by a one-legged gaoler, and guarded by a one-armed tyrant—yes, a tyrant!" Here, having stopped to stamp her foot, she walked on faster than ever.

"Can you possibly mean old Jerry and the Captain?"

Here my lady paused in her quick walk, and even condescended to look at Barnabas.

"Do you happen to know them too, sir?"

"Yes; and my name is—"

"Perhaps you met them also this morning, sir?"

"Yes; and my—"

"Indeed," said she, with curling lip; "this has been quite an eventful day for you."

"On the whole, I think it has; and may I remind you that my—"

"Perhaps you don't believe me when I say he is a tyrant?"

"Hum," said Barnabas.

"You don't, do you?"

"Why, I'm afraid not," he admitted.

"I'm nineteen!" said she, standing very erect.

"I should have judged you a little older," said Barnabas.

"So I am—in mind, and—and experience. Yet here I live, prisoned in a dreary old house, and with nothing to see but trees, and toads, and cows and cabbages; and I'm watched over, and tended from morning till night, and am the subject of more councils of war than Buonaparte's army ever was."

"What do you mean by councils of war?"

"Oh! whenever I do anything my tyrant disapproves of, he retires to what he calls the 'round house,' summons the Bo'sun, and they argue and talk over me as though I were a hostile fleet, and march up and down forming plans of attack and defence, till I burst in on them, and then—and then—Oh! there are many kinds of tyrants, and he is one. And so to-night I left him; I ran away to meet—" She stopped suddenly, and her head drooped, and Barnabas saw her white hands clench themselves.

"Your brother," said he.

"Yes, my—brother," but her voice faltered at the word, and she went on through the wood, but slowly now, and with head still drooping. And so, at last, they came out of the shadows into the soft radiance of the moon, and thus Barnabas saw that she was weeping; and she, because she could no longer hide her grief, turned and laid a pleading hand upon his arm.

"Pray, think of him as kindly as you can," she sighed, "you see—he is only a boy—my brother."

"So young?" said Barnabas.

"Just twenty, but younger than his age—much younger. You see," she went on hastily, "he went to London a boy—and—and he thought Mr. Chichester was his friend, and he lost much money at play, and, somehow, put himself in Mr. Chichester's power. He is my half-brother, really; but I—love him so, and I've tried to take care of him—I was always so much stronger than he—and—and so I would have you think of him as generously as you can."

"Yes," said Barnabas, "yes." But now she stopped again so that he must needs stop too, and when she spoke her soft voice thrilled with a new intensity.

"Will you do more? You are going to London—will you seek him out, will you try to—save him from himself? Will you promise me to do this—will you?"

Now seeing the passionate entreaty in her eyes, feeling it in the twitching fingers upon his arm, Barnabas suddenly laid his own above that slender hand, and took it into his warm clasp.

"My lady," said he, solemnly, "I will." As he spoke he stooped his head low and lower, until she felt his lips warm upon her palm, a long, silent pressure, and yet her hand was not withdrawn.

Now although Barnabas had clean forgotten the rules and precepts set down in the "priceless wollum," he did it all with a graceful ease which could not have been bettered—no, not even by the Person of Quality itself.

"But it will be difficult," she sighed, as they went on together. "Ronald is very headstrong and proud—it will be very difficult!"

"No matter," said Barnabas.

"And—dangerous, perhaps."

"No matter for that either," said Barnabas.

"Does it seem strange that I should ask so much of you?"

"The most natural thing in the world," said Barnabas.

"But you are a stranger—almost!"

"But I—love you, Cleone."

After this there fell a silence between them; and so having crossed the moonlit meadow, they came to a tall hedge beyond whose shadow the road led away, white under the moon; close by the ways divided, and here stood a weather-beaten finger-post. Now beneath this hedge they stopped, and it is to be noted that neither looked at the other.

"Sir," said she, softly, "we part here, my home lies yonder," and she pointed to where above the motionless tree-tops rose the gables and chimneys of a goodly house.

"It would seem to be fairly comfortable as prisons go," said Barnabas; but my lady only sighed.

"Do you start for London—soon?"

"To-night," nodded Barnabas.

"Sir," said she, after a pause, "I would thank you, if I could, for—for all that you have done for me."

"No, no," said Barnabas, hastily.

"Words are poor things, I know, but how else may I show my gratitude?"

And now it was Barnabas who was silent; but at last—

"There is a way," said he, staring at the finger-post.

"How—what way?"

"You might—kiss me—once, Cleone."

Now here she must needs steal a swift look at him, and thus she saw that he still stared at the ancient finger-post, but that his hands were tight clenched.

"I only ask," he continued heavily, "for what I might have taken."

"But didn't!" she added, with lips and eyes grown suddenly tender.

"No," sighed Barnabas, "nor shall I ever,—until you will it so,—because, you see, I love you."

Now as he gazed at the finger-post, even so she gazed at him; and thus she saw again the mark upon his cheek, and looking, sighed; indeed, it was the veriest ghost of a sigh, yet Barnabas heard it, and straightway forgot the finger-post, forgot the world and all things in it, save her warm beauty, the red allurement of her mouth, and the witchery of her drooping lashes; therefore he reached out his hands to her, and she saw that they were trembling.

"Cleone," he murmured, "oh, Cleone—look up!"

But even as he spoke she recoiled from his touch, for, plain and clear, came the sound of footsteps on the road near by. Sighing, Barnabas turned thitherwards and beheld advancing towards them one who paused, now and then, to look about him as though at a loss, and then hurried on again. A very desolate figure he was, and quaintly pathetic because of his gray hair, and the empty sleeve that flapped helplessly to and fro with the hurry of his going—a figure, indeed, that there was no mistaking. Being come to the finger-post, he paused to look wistfully on all sides, and Barnabas could see that his face was drawn and haggard. For a moment he gazed about him wild-eyed and eager, then with a sudden, hopeless gesture, he leaned his one arm against the battered sign-post and hid his face there.

"Oh, my lass—my dear!" he cried in a strangled voice, "why did you leave me? Oh, my lass!"

Then all at once came a rustle of parting leaves, the flutter of flying draperies, and Cleone had fled to that drooping, disconsolate figure, had wreathed her protecting arms about it, and so all moans, and sobs, and little tender cries, had drawn her tyrant's head down upon her gentle bosom and clasped it there.

CHAPTER XXII

IN WHICH THE READER IS INTRODUCED TO AN ANCIENT FINGER-POST

"Why, Cleone!" exclaimed the Captain, and folded his solitary arm about her; but not content with this, my lady must needs take his empty sleeve also, and, drawing it close about her neck, she held it there.

"Oh, Cleone!" sighed the Captain, "my dear, dear lass!"

"No," she cried, "I'm a heartless savage, an ungrateful wretch! I am, I am—and I hate myself!" and here, forthwith, she stamped her foot at herself.

"No, no, you're not—I say no! You didn't mean to break my heart. You've come back to me, thank God, and—and—Oh, egad, Cleone, I swear—I say I swear—by Gog and Magog, I'm snuffling like a birched schoolboy; but then I—couldn't bear to—lose my dear maid."

"Dear," she sighed, brushing away his tears with the cuff of his empty sleeve, "dear, if you'd only try to hate me a little—just a little, now and then, I don't think I should be quite such a wretch to you." Here she stood on tip-toe and kissed him on the chin, that being nearest. "I'm a cat—yes, a spiteful cat, and I must scratch sometimes; but ah! if you knew how I hated myself after! And I know you'll go and forgive me again, and that's what makes it so hard to bear."

"Forgive you, Clo'—ay, to be sure! You've come back to me, you see, and you didn't mean to leave me solitary and—"

"Ah, but I did—I did! And that's why I am a wretch, and a cat, and a savage! I meant to run away and leave you for ever and ever!"

"The house would be very dark without you, Cleone."

"Dear, hold me tighter—now listen! There are times when I hate the house, and the country, and—yes, even you. And at such times I grow afraid of myself—hold me tighter!—at such times I long for London—and—and—Ah, but you do love me, don't you?"

"Love you—my own lass!" The Captain's voice was very low, yet eloquent with yearning tenderness; but even so, his quick ear had caught a rustle in the hedge, and his sharp eye had seen Barnabas standing in the shadow. "Who's that?" he demanded sharply.

"Why, indeed," says my lady, "I had forgotten him. 'Tis a friend of yours, I think. Pray come out, Mr. Beverley."

"Beverley!" exclaimed the Captain. "Now sink me! what's all this? Come out, sir,—I say come out and show yourself!"

So Barnabas stepped out from the hedge, and uncovering his head, bowed low.

"Your very humble, obedient servant, sir," said he.

"Ha! by Thor and Odin, so it's you again, is it, sir? Pray, what brings you still so far from the fashionable world? What d'ye want, sir, eh, sir?"

"Briefly, sir," answered Barnabas, "your ward."

"Eh—what? what?" cried the Captain.

"Sir," returned Barnabas, "since you are the Lady Cleone's lawful guardian, it is but right to tell you that I hope to marry her—some day."

"Marry!" exclaimed the Captain. "Marry my—damme, sir, but you're cool—I say cool and devilish impudent, and—and—oh, Gad, Cleone!"

"My dear," said she, smiling and stroking her tyrant's shaven cheek, "why distress ourselves, we can always refuse him, can't we?"

"Ay, to be sure, so we can," nodded the Captain, "but oh! sink me,—I say sink and scuttle me, the audacity of it! I say he's a cool, impudent, audacious fellow!"

"Yes, dear, indeed I think he's all that," said my lady, nodding her head at Barnabas very decidedly, "and I forgot to tell you that beside all this, he is the—gentleman who—saved me from my folly to-night, and brought me back to you."

"Eh? eh?" cried the Captain, staring.

"Yes, dear, and this is he who—" But here she drew down her tyrant's gray head, and whispered three words in his ear. Whatever she said it affected the Captain mightily, for his frown changed suddenly into his youthful smile, and reaching out impulsively, he grasped Barnabas by the hand.

"Aha, sir!" said he, "you have a good, big fist here!"

"Indeed," said Barnabas, glancing down at it somewhat ruefully, "it is—very large, I fear."

"Over large, sir!" says my lady, also regarding it, and with her head at a critical angle, "it could never be called—an elegant hand, could it?"

"Elegant!" snorted the Captain, "I say pooh! I say pish! Sir, you must come in and sup with us, my house is near by. Good English beef and ale, sir."

Barnabas hesitated, and glanced toward Cleone, but her face was hidden in the shadow of her hood, wherefore his look presently wandered to the finger-post, near by, upon whose battered sign he read the words:—

TO HAWKHURST. TO LONDON.

"Sir," said he, "I would, most gratefully, but that I start for London at once." Yet while he spoke, he frowned blackly at the finger-post, as though it had been his worst enemy.

"London!" exclaimed the Captain, "so you are still bound for the fashionable world, are ye?"

"Yes," sighed Barnabas, "but I—"

"Pish, sir, I say fiddle-de-dee!"

"I have lately undertaken a mission."

"Ha! So you won't come in?"

"Thank you, no; this mission is important, and I must be gone;" and here again Barnabas sighed.

Then my lady turned and looked at Barnabas, and, though she uttered no word, her eyes were eloquent; so that the heart of him was uplifted, and he placed his hand upon the finger-post as though it had been his best friend.

"Why then, so be it, young sir," said the Captain, "it remains only to thank you, which I do, I say which I do most heartily, and to bid you good-by."

"Until we meet again, Captain."

"Eh—what, sir? meet when?"

"At 'Barnaby Bright,'" says my lady, staring up at the moon.

"In a month's time," added Barnabas.

"Eh?" exclaimed the Captain, "what's all this?"

"In a month's time, sir, I shall return to ask Cleone to be my wife," Barnabas explained.

"And," said my lady, smiling at the Captain's perplexity, "we shall be glad to see him, shan't we, dear? and shall, of course, refuse him, shan't we, dear?"

"Refuse him? yes—no—egad! I don't know," said the Captain, running his fingers through his hair, "I say, deuce take me—I'm adrift; I say where's the Bo'sun?"

"Good-by, sir!" says my lady, very seriously, and gave him her hand; "good-by."

"Till 'Barnaby Bright,'" said Barnabas.

At this she smiled, a little tremulously perhaps.

"May heaven prosper you in your mission," said she, and turned away.

"Young sir," said the Captain, "always remember my name is Chumly, John Chumly, plain and unvarnished, and, whether we refuse you or not, John Chumly will ever be ready to take you by the hand. Farewell, sir!"

So tyrant and captive turned away and went down the by-road together, and his solitary arm was close about her. But Barnabas stood there under the finger-post until a bend in the road hid them; then he, too, sighed and turned away. Yet he had gone only a little distance when he heard a voice calling him, and, swinging round, he saw Cleone standing under the finger-post.

"I wanted to give you—this," said she, as he came striding back, and held out a folded paper. "It is his—my brother's—letter. Take it with you, it will serve to show you what a boy he is, and will tell you where to find him."

So Barnabas took the letter and thrust it into his pocket. But she yet stood before him, and now, once again, their glances avoided each other.

"I also wanted to—ask you—about your cheek," said she at last.

"Yes?" said Barnabas.

"You are quite sure it doesn't—pain you, Mr. Bev—"

"Must I remind you that my name—"

"Are you quite sure—Barnabas?"

"Quite sure—yes, oh yes!" he stammered.

"Because it—glows very red!" she sighed, though indeed she still kept her gaze averted, "so will you please—stoop your head a little?"

Wonderingly Barnabas obeyed, and then—even as he did so, she leaned swiftly towards him, and for an instant her soft, warm mouth rested upon his cheek. Then, before he could stay her, she was off and away; and her flying feet had borne her out of sight.

Then Barnabas sighed, and would have followed, but the ancient finger-post barred his way with its two arms pointing:—

TO HAWKHURST. TO LONDON.

So he stopped, glanced about him to fix the hallowed place in his memory, and, obeying the directing finger, set off London-wards.

CHAPTER XXIII

HOW BARNABAS SAVED HIS LIFE—BECAUSE HE WAS AFRAID

On went Barnabas swift of foot and light of heart, walking through a World of Romance, and with his eyes turned up to the luminous heaven. Yet it was neither of the moon, nor the stars, nor the wonder thereof that he was thinking, but only of the witchery of a woman's eyes, and the thrill of a woman's lips upon his cheek; and, indeed, what more natural, more right, and altogether proper? Little recked he of the future, of the perils and dangers to be encountered, of the sorrows and tribulations that lay in wait for him, or of the enemies that he had made that day, for youth is little given to brooding, and is loftily indifferent to consequences.

So it was of Lady Cleone Meredith he thought as he strode along the moonlit highway, and it was of her that he was thinking as he turned into that narrow by-lane where stood "The Spotted Cow." As he advanced, he espied some one standing in the shadow of one of the great trees, who, as he came nearer, stepped out into the moonlight; and then Barnabas saw that it was none other than his newly engaged valet. The same, yet not the same, for the shabby clothes had given place to a sober, well-fitting habit, and as he took off his hat in salutation, Barnabas noticed that his hollow cheeks were clean and freshly shaved; he was, indeed, a new man.

But now, as they faced each other, Barnabas observed something else; John Peterby's lips were compressed, and in his eye was anxiety, the which had, somehow, got into his voice when he spoke, though his tone was low and modulated: "Sir, if you are for London to-night, we had better start at once, the coach leaves Tenterden within the hour."

"But," says Barnabas, setting his head aslant, and rubbing his chin with the argumentative air that was so very like his father, "I have ordered supper here, Peterby."

"Which—under the circumstances—I have ventured to countermand, sir."

"Oh?" said Barnabas, "pray, what circumstances?"

"Sir, as I told you, the mail—"

"John Peterby, speak out—what is troubling you?"

But now, even while Peterby stood hesitating, from the open casement of the inn, near at hand, came the sound of a laugh: a soft, gentle, sibilant laugh which Barnabas immediately recognized.

"Ah!" said he, clenching his fist. "I think I understand." As he turned towards the inn, Peterby interposed.

"Sir," he whispered, "sir, if ever a man meant mischief—he does. He came back an hour ago, and they have been waiting for you ever since."

"They?"

"He and the other."

"What other?"

"Sir, I don't know."

"Is he a very—young man, this other?"

"Yes, sir, he seems so. And they have been drinking together and—I've heard enough to know that they mean you harm." But here Master Barnabas smiled with all the arrogance of youth and shook his head.

"John Peterby," said he, "learn that the first thing I desire in my valet is obedience. Pray stand out of my way!" So, perforce Peterby stood aside, yet Barnabas had scarce taken a dozen strides ere Clemency stood before him.

"Go back," she whispered, "go back!"

"Impossible," said Barnabas, "I have a mission to fulfil."

"Go back!" she repeated in the same tense whisper, "you must—oh, you must! I've heard he has killed a man before now—"

"And yet I must see and speak with his companion."

"No, no—ah! I pray you—"

"Nay," said Barnabas, "if you will, and if need be, pray for me." So saying he put her gently aside, and entering the inn, came to the door of that room wherein he had written the letter to his father.

"I tell you I'll kill him, Dalton," said a soft, deliberate voice.

"Undoubtedly; the light's excellent; but, my dear fellow, why—?"

"I object to him strongly, for one thing, and—"

The voice was hushed suddenly, as Barnabas set wide the door and stepped into the room, with Peterby at his heels.

Mr. Chichester was seated at the table with a glass beside him, but Barnabas looked past him to his companion who sprawled on the other side of the hearth—a sleepy, sighing gentleman, very high as to collar, very tight as to waist, and most ornate as to waistcoat; young he was certainly, yet with his first glance, Barnabas knew instinctively that this could not be the youth he sought. Nevertheless he took off his hat and saluted him with a bow that for stateliness left the "stiff-legged gentleman" nowhere.

"Sir," said he, "pray what might your name be?"

Instead of replying, the sleepy gentleman opened his eyes rather wider than was usual and stared at Barnabas with a growing surprise, stared at him from head to foot and up again, then, without changing his lounging attitude, spoke:

"Oh, Gad, Chichester!—is this the—man?"

"Yes."

"But—my dear Chit! Surely you don't propose to—this fellow! Who is he? What is he? Look at his boots—oh, Gad!"

Hereupon Barnabas resumed his hat, and advancing leaned his clenched fists on the table, and from that eminence smiled down at the speaker, that is to say his lips curled and his teeth gleamed in the candle-light.

"Sir," said he gently, "you will perhaps have the extreme condescension to note that my boots are strong boots, and very serviceable either for walking, or for kicking an insolent puppy."

"If I had a whip, now," sighed the gentleman, "if I only had a whip, I'd whip you out of the room. Chichester,—pray look at that coat, oh, Gad!"

But Mr. Chichester had risen, and now crossing to the door, he locked it, and dropped the key into his pocket.

"As you say, the light is excellent, my dear Dalton," said he, fixing Barnabas with his unwavering stare.

"But my dear Chit, you never mean to fight the fellow—a—a being who wears such a coat! such boots! My dear fellow, be reasonable! Observe that hat! Good Gad! Take your cane and whip him out—positively you cannot fight this bumpkin."

"None the less I mean to shoot him—like a cur, Dalton." And Mr. Chichester drew a pistol from his pocket, and fell to examining flint and priming with a practised eye. "I should have preferred my regular tools; but I dare say this will do the business well enough; pray, snuff the candles."

Now, as Barnabas listened to the soft, deliberate words, as he noted Mr. Chichester's assured air, his firm hand, his glowing eye and quivering nostrils, a sudden deadly nausea came over him, and he leaned heavily upon the table.

"Sirs," said he, uncertainly, and speaking with an effort, "I have never used a pistol in my life."

"One could tell as much from his boots," murmured Mr. Dalton, snuffing the candles.

"You have another pistol, I think, Dalton; pray lend it to him. We will take opposite corners of the room, and fire when you give the word."

"All quite useless, Chit; this fellow won't fight."

"No," said Barnabas, thrusting his trembling hands into his pockets, "not—in a corner."

Mr. Chichester shrugged his shoulders, sat down, and leaning back in his chair stared up at pale-faced Barnabas, tapping the table-edge softly with the barrel of his weapon.

"Not in a corner—I told you so, Chit. Oh, take your cane and whip him out!"

"I mean," said Barnabas, very conscious of the betraying quaver in his voice, "I mean that, as I'm—unused to—shooting, the corner would be—too far."

"Too far? Oh, Gad!" exclaimed Mr. Dalton. "What's this?"

"As for pistols, I have one here," continued Barnabas, "and if we must shoot, we'll do it here—across the table."

"Eh—what? Across the table! but, oh, Gad, Chichester! this is madness!" said Mr. Dalton.

"Most duels are," said Barnabas, and as he spoke he drew from his pocket the pistol he had taken from Mr. Chichester earlier in the evening and, weapon in hand, sank into a chair, thus facing Mr. Chichester across the table.

"But this is murder—positive murder!" cried Mr. Dalton.

"Sir," said Barnabas, "I am no duellist, as I told you; and it seems to me that this equalizes our chances, for I can no more fail of hitting my man at this distance than he of shooting me dead across the width of the room. And, sir—if I am to—die to-night, I shall most earnestly endeavor to take Mr. Chichester with me."

There was a tremor in his voice again as he spoke, but his eye was calm, his brow serene, and his hand steady as he cocked the pistol, and leaning his elbow upon the table, levelled it within six inches of Mr. Chichester's shirt frill. But hereupon Mr. Dalton sprang to his feet with a stifled oath:

"I tell you it's murder—murder!" he exclaimed, and took a quick step towards them.

"Peterby!" said Barnabas.

"Sir?" said Peterby, who had been standing rigid beside the door.

"Take my stick," said Barnabas, holding it out towards him, but keeping his gaze upon Mr. Chichester's narrowed eyes; "it's heavy you'll find, and should this person presume to interfere, knock him down with it."

"Yes, sir," said Peterby, and took the stick accordingly.

"But—oh, Gad!" exclaimed Dalton, "I tell you this can't go on!"

"Indeed, I hope not," said Barnabas; "but it is for Mr. Chichester to decide. I am ready for the count when he is."

But Mr. Chichester sat utterly still, his chin on his breast, staring at Barnabas under his brows, one hand tight clenched about the stock of his weapon on the table before him, the other hanging limply at his side. So for an interval they remained thus, staring into each other's eyes, in a stillness so profound that it seemed all four men had ceased breathing. Then Mr. Chichester sighed faintly, dropped his eyes to the muzzle of the weapon so perilously near, glanced back at the pale, set face and unwinking eyes of him who held it, and sighed again.

"Dalton," said he, "pray open the door, and order the chaise," and he laid the key upon the table.

"First," said Barnabas, "I will relieve you of that—encumbrance," and he pointed to the pistol yet gripped in Mr. Chichester's right hand. Without a word Mr. Chichester rose, and leaving the weapon upon the table, turned and walked to the window, while Mr. Dalton, having unlocked the door, hurried away to the stable-yard, and was now heard calling for the ostlers.

"Peterby," said Barnabas, "take this thing and throw it into the horse-pond; yet, no, give it to the gentleman who just went out."

"Yes, sir," said Peterby, and, taking up the pistol, he went out, closing the door behind him.

Mr. Chichester still lounged in the window, and hummed softly to himself; but as for Barnabas, he sat rigid in his chair, staring blankly at the opposite wall, his eyes wide, his lips tense, and with a gleam of moisture amid the curls at his temples. So the one lounged and hummed, and the other glared stonily before him until came the grind of wheels and the stamping of hoofs. Then Mr. Chichester took up his hat and cane, and, humming still, crossed to the door, and lounged out into the yard.

Came a jingle of harness, a sound of voices, the slam of a door, and the chaise rolled away down the lane, farther and farther, until the rumble of its wheels died away in the distance. Then Barnabas laughed—a sudden shrill laugh—and clenched his fists, and strove against the laughter, and choked, and so sank forward with his face upon his arms as one that is very weary. Now, presently, as he sat thus, it seemed to him that one spoke a long way off, whereupon, in a little, he raised his head, and beheld Clemency.

"You—are not hurt?" she inquired anxiously.

"Hurt?" said Barnabas, "no, not hurt, Mistress Clemency, not hurt, I thank you; but I think I have grown a—great deal—older."

"I saw it all, through the window, and yet I—don't know why you are alive."

"I think because I was so very much—afraid," said Barnabas.

"Sir," said she, with her brown hands clasped together, "was it for—if it was for—my sake that you—quarrelled, and—"

"No," said Barnabas, "it was because of—another."

Now, when he said this, Clemency stared at him wide-eyed, and, all in a moment, flushed painfully and turned away, so that Barnabas wondered.

"Good-by!" said she, suddenly, and crossed to the door, but upon the threshold paused; "I did pray for you," she said, over her shoulder.

"Ah!" said Barnabas, rising, "you prayed for me, and behold, I am alive."

"Good-by!" she repeated, her face still averted.

"Good-by!" said Barnabas, "and will you remember me in your prayers—sometimes?"

"My prayers! Why?"

"Because the prayers of a sweet, pure woman may come between man and evil—like a shield."

"I will," said she, very softly. "Oh, I will," and so, with a swift glance, was gone.

Being come out of the inn, Barnabas met with his valet, John Peterby.

"Sir," he inquired, "what now?"

"Now," said Barnabas, "the Tenterden coach, and London."

CHAPTER XXIV

WHICH RELATES SOMETHING OF THE "WHITE LION" AT TENTERDEN

Of all the lions that ever existed, painted or otherwise, white lions, blue lions, black, green, or red lions, surely never was there one like the "White Lion" at Tenterden. For he was such a remarkably placid lion, although precariously balanced upon the extreme point of one claw, and he stared down at all and sundry with such round, inquiring eyes, as much as to say:

"Who are you? What's your father? Where are you going?" Indeed, so very inquisitive was he that his very tail had writhed itself into a note of interrogation, and, like a certain historical personage, was forever asking a question. To-night he had singled out Barnabas from the throng, and was positively bombarding him with questions, as:

"Dark or fair? Tall or short? Does she love you? Will she remember you? Will she kiss you—next time? Aha! will she, will she?"

But here, feeling a touch upon his arm, Barnabas turned to find Peterby at his elbow, and thus once more became aware of the hubbub about him.

"Box seat, sir; next to the coachman!" says Peterby above the din, for voices are shouting, horses snorting and stamping, ostlers are hurrying here, running there, and swearing everywhere; waiters and serving-maids are dodging to and fro, and all is hurry and bustle, for the night mail is on the eve of departure for London.

Throned above all this clamor, calmly aloof, yet withal watchful of eye, sits the coachman, beshawled to the ears of him, hatted to the eyes of him, and in a wondrous coat of many capes; a ponderous man, hoarse of voice and mottled of face, who, having swallowed his hot rum and water in three leisurely gulps, tosses down the glass to the waiting pot-boy (and very nearly hits a fussy little gentleman in a green spencer, who carries a hat-box in one hand and a bulging valise in the other, and who ducks indignantly, but just in time), sighs, shakes his head, and proceeds to rewind the shawl about his neck and chin, and to belt himself into his seat, throwing an occasional encouraging curse to the perspiring ostlers below.

"Coachman!" cries the fussy gentleman, "hi, coachman!"

"The 'Markis' seems a bit fresh to-night, Sam," says Mottle-face affably to one of the ostlers.

"Fresh!" exclaims that worthy as the 'Marquis' rears again, "fresh, I believe you—burn 'is bones!"

"Driver!" shouts the fussy gentleman, "driver!"

"Why then, bear 'im up werry short, Sam."

"Driver!" roars the fussy little gentleman, "driver! coachman! oh, driver!"

"Vell, sir, that's me?" says Mottle-face, condescending to become aware of him at last.

"Give me a hand up with my valise—d'ye hear?"

"Walise, sir? No, sir, can't be done, sir. In the boot, sir; guard, sir."

"Boot!" cries the fussy gentleman indignantly. "I'll never trust my property in the boot!"

"Then v'y not leave it be'ind, sir, and stay vith it, or—"

"Nonsense!" exclaimed the little man, growing angry. "I tell you this is valuable property. D'ye know who I am?"

"Or ye might climb into the boot along vith it, sir—"

"Do you know who I am?"

"All aboard—all aboard for London!" roared the guard, coming up at the instant.

"Valter!" cried Mottle-face.

"Ay, ay, Joe?"

"Gentleman's walise for the boot, Valter; and sharp's the vord!"

"Ay, ay, Joe!" and, as he spoke, the guard caught the valise from the protesting small gentleman with one hand, and the hat-box with the other, and, forthwith, vanished. Hereupon the fussy gentleman, redder of face, and more angry than ever, clambered to the roof, still loudly protesting; all of which seemed entirely lost upon Mottle-face, who, taking up the reins and settling his feet against the dash-board, winked a solemn, owl-like eye at Barnabas sitting beside him, and carolled a song in a husky voice, frequently interrupting himself to admonish the ostlers, in this wise:—

"She vore no 'at upon 'er 'ead,
Nor a cap, nor a—"

"Bear the 'Markis' up werry short, Sam, vill 'ee?

"—dandy bonnet,
But 'er 'air it 'ung all down 'er back,
Like a—"

"Easy—easy now! Hold on to them leaders, Dick!

"—bunch of carrots upon it.
Ven she cried 'sprats' in Vestminister,
Oh! sich a sveet loud woice, sir,
You could 'ear 'er all up Parlyment Street,
And as far as Charing Cross, sir."

"All aboard, all aboard for London!" roars the guard, and roaring, swings himself up into the boot.

"All right be'ind?" cries Mottle-face.

"All right, Joe!" sings the guard.

"Then—leggo, there!" cries Mottle-face.

Back spring the ostlers, forward leap the four quivering horses, their straining hoofs beating out showers of sparks from the cobbles; the coach lurches forward and is off, amid a waving of hats and pocket-handkerchiefs, and Barnabas, casting a farewell glance around, is immediately fixed by the gaze of the "White Lion," as inquiring of eye and interrogatory of tail as ever.

"Tall or short? Dark or fair? Will she kiss you—next time—will she, will she? Will she even be glad to see you again—will she, now will she?"

Whereupon Barnabas must needs become profoundly thoughtful all at once.

"Now—I wonder?" said he to himself.

CHAPTER XXV

OF THE COACHMAN'S STORY

Long before the lights of the "White Lion" had vanished behind them, the guard blows a sudden fanfare on the horn, such a blast as goes echoing merrily far and wide, and brings folk running to open doors and lighted windows to catch a glimpse of the London Mail ere it vanishes into the night; and so, almost while the cheery notes ring upon the air, Tenterden is behind them, and they are bowling along the highway into the open country beyond. A wonderful country this, familiar and yet wholly new; a nightmare world where ghosts and goblins flit under a dying moon; where hedge and tree become monsters crouched to spring, or lift knotted arms to smite; while in the gloom of woods beyond, unimagined horrors lurk.

But, bless you, Mottle-face, having viewed it all under the slant of his hat-brim, merely settles his mottled chin deeper in his shawls, flicks the off ear of the near leader with a delicate turn of the wrists, and turning his owl-like eye upon Barnabas, remarks that "It's a werry fine night!" But hereupon the fussy gentleman, leaning over, taps Mottle-face upon the shoulder.

"Coachman," says he, "pray, when do you expect to reach The Borough, London?"

"Vich I begs to re-mark, sir," retorts Mottle-face, settling his curly-brimmed hat a little further over his left eye, "vich I 'umbly begs to re-mark as I don't expect nohow!"

"Eh—what! what! you don't expect to—"

"Vich I am vun, sir, as don't novise expect nothin', consequent am never novise disapp'inted," says Mottle-face with a solemn nod; "but, vind an' veather permittin', ve shall be at the 'George' o' South'ark at five, or thereabouts!"

"Ha!" says the fussy gentleman, "and what about my valise? is it safe?"

"Safe, ah! safe as the Bank o' England, unless ve should 'appen to be stopped—"

"Stopped? stopped, coachman? d' you mean—?"

"Ah! stopped by Blue-chinned Jack o' Brockley, or Gallopin' Toby o' Tottenham, or—"

"Eh—what! what! d' you mean there are highwaymen on this road?"

"'Ighvaymen!" snorted Mottle-face, winking ponderously at Barnabas, "by Goles, I should say so, it fair bristles vith 'em."

"God bless my soul!" exclaimed the fussy gentleman in an altered tone, "but you are armed, of course?"

"Armed?" repeated Mottle-face, more owl-like of eye than ever, "armed, sir, Lord love me yes! my guard carries a brace o' barkers in the boot."

"I'm glad of that," said the fussy gentleman, "very!"

"Though," pursued Mottle-face, rolling his head heavily, "Joe ain't 'zactly what you might call a dead shot, nor yet a ex-pert, bein' blind in 'is off blinker, d'ye see."

"Eh—blind, d'ye say—blind?" exclaimed the fussy gentleman.

"Only in 'is off eye," nodded Mottle-face, reassuringly, "t'other 'un's as good as yours or mine, ven 'e ain't got a cold in it."

"But this—this is an outrage!" spluttered the fussy gentleman, "a guard blind in one eye! Scandalous! I shall write to the papers of this. But you—surely you carry a weapon too?"

"A vepping? Ay, to be sure, sir, I've got a blunder-bush, under this 'ere werry seat, loaded up to the muzzle wi' slugs too,—though it von't go off."

"Won't—eh, what? Won't go off?"

"Not on no account, sir, vich ain't to be 'spected of it, seeing as it ain't got no trigger."

"But—heaven preserve us! why carry such a useless thing?"

"Force of 'abit, sir; ye see, I've carried that theer old blunderbush for a matter of five-an'-twenty year, an' my feyther 'e carried it afore me."

"But suppose we are attacked?"

"Vich I begs to re-mark, sir, as I don't never suppose no such thing, like my feyther afore me. Brave as a lion were my feyther, sir, an' bred up to the road; v'y, Lord! 'e were born vith a coachman's v'ip in 'is mouth—no, I mean 'is fist, as ye might say; an' 'e were the boldest—"

"But what's your father got to do with it?" cried the fussy gentleman. "What about my valise?"

"Your walise, sir? we'm a-coming to that;" and here, once more, Mottle-face slowly winked his owl-like eye at Barnabas. "My feyther, sir," he continued, "my feyther, 'e druv' the Dartford Mail, an' 'e were the finest v'ip as ever druv' a coach, Dartford or otherwise; 'Andsome 'Arry' 'e vere called, though v'y 'andsome I don't know, seeing as 'is nose veren't all it might ha' been, on account o' a quart pot; an' v'y 'Arry I don't know, seeing as 'is name vos Villiam; but, "Andsome 'Arry' 'e vere called, an' werry much respected 'e vere too. Lord! there vos never less than a dozen or so young bloods to see 'im start. Ah! a great favorite 'e vere vith them, an' no error, an' werry much admired; admired? I should say so. They copied 'is 'at they copied 'is boots, they copied 'is coat, they'd a copied 'im inside as well as out if they could."

"Hum!" said the fussy gentleman. "Ha!"

"Oh, 'e vos a great fav'rite vith the Quality," nodded Mottle-face. "Ah! it vos a dream to see 'im 'andle the ribbons,—an' spit? Lord! it vos a eddication to see my feyther spit, I should say so! Vun young blood—a dock's son he vere too—vent an' 'ad a front tooth drawed a purpose, but I never 'eard as it done much good; bless you, to spit like my feyther you must be born to it!" (here Mottle-face paused to suit the action to the word). "And, mark you! over an' above all this, my feyther vere the boldest cove that ever—"

"Yes, yes!" exclaimed the fussy gentleman impatiently, "but where does my valise come in?"

"Your walise, sir," said Mottle-face, deftly flicking the off wheeler, "your walise comes in—at the end, sir, and I'm a-comin' to it as qvick as you'll let me."

"Hum!" said the gentleman again.

"Now, in my feyther's time," resumed Mottle-face serenely, "the roads vos vorse than they are to-day, ah! a sight vorse, an' as for 'ighvaymen—Lord! they vos as thick as blackberries—blackberries? I should say so! Theer vos footpads be'ind every 'edge—gangs of 'em—an' 'ighvaymen on every 'eath—"

"God bless my soul!" exclaimed the fussy gentleman, "so many?"

"Many?" snorted Mottle-face, "there vos armies of 'em. But my feyther, as I think I mentioned afore, vere the bravest, boldest, best-plucked coachman as ever sat on a box."

"I hope it runs in the family."

"Sir, I ain't one give to boastin', nor yet to blowin' my own 'orn, but truth is truth, and—it do!"

"Good!" said the fussy gentleman, "very good!"

"Now the vorst of all these rogues vos a cove called Black Dan, a thieving, murdering, desprit wagabone as vere ewentually 'ung sky-'igh on Pembury 'Ill—"

"Good!" said the fussy gentleman louder than before, "good! Glad of it!"

"An' yet," sighed Mottle-face, "'e 'ad a werry good 'eart—as 'ighvaymen's 'earts go; never shot nobody unless 'e couldn't help it, an' ven 'e did, 'e allus made a werry neat job of it, an' polished 'em off nice an' qvick."

"Hum!" said the fussy gentleman, "still, I'm glad he's hanged."

"Black Dan used to vork the roads south o' London,

"Kent an' Surrey mostly, conseqvent it vere a long time afore 'im an' my feyther met; but at last vun night, as my feyther vos driving along—a good fifteen mile an hour, for it vere a uncommon fine night, vith a moon, like as it might be now—"

"Ah?" said the fussy gentleman.

"An' presently 'e came to vere the road narrered a bit, same as it might be yonder—"

"Ah!" murmured the fussy gentleman again.

"An' vith a clump o' trees beyond, nice, dark, shady trees—like it might be them werry trees ahead of us—"

"Oh!" exclaimed the fussy gentleman.

"An' as 'e come up nearer an' nearer, all at vunce 'e made out a shadder in the shade o' them trees—"

"Dear me!" exclaimed the fussy gentleman uneasily, staring very hard at the trees in front.

"A shadder as moved, although the leaves vos all dead still. So my feyther—being a bold cove—reached down for 'is blunderbush—this werry same old blunderbush as I 've got under the box at this i-dentical minute, (though its trigger veren't broke then) but, afore 'e can get it out, into the road leaps a man on a great black 'oss—like it might be dead ahead of us, a masked man, an' vith a pistol in each fist as long as yer arm."

"Good Lord!" exclaimed the fussy gentleman.

"'Stand an' deliver!' roars the masked man, so my feyther, cocking 'is heye at the pistols, pulls up, an' there 'e is, starin' down at the 'ighvayman, an' the 'ighvayman staring up at 'im. 'You 're 'Andsome 'Arry, ain't you?' sez the 'ighvayman. 'Ay,' sez my feyther, 'an' I guess you 're Black Dan.' 'Sure as you 're born!' sez Black Dan, 'I've 'eered o' you before to-day, 'Andsome 'Arry,' sez 'e, 'an' meant to make your acquaintance afore this, but I 've been kep' too busy till to-night,' sez 'e, 'but 'ere ve are at last,' 'e sez, 'an' now—vot d' ye think o' that?' sez 'e, an' pi'nts a pistol under my feyther's werry nose. Now, as I think I 've 'inted afore, my feyther vere a nat'rally bold, courage-ful cove, so 'e took a look at the murderous vepping, an' nodded. 'It's a pistol, ain't it?' sez 'e. 'Sure as you're settin' on that there box, it is,' sez Black Dan, 'an' 'ere's another.' 'An' werry good veppings too,' sez my feyther, 'but vot might you be vanting vith me, Black Dan?' 'First of all, I vants you to come down off that box,' sez Black Dan. 'Oh?' sez my feyther, cool as a coocumber. 'Ah!' sez Black Dan. 'Verefore an' v'y?' enkvires my feyther, but Black Dan only vagged 'is veppings in my feyther's face, an' grinned under 'is mask. 'I vants you, so, 'Andsome 'Arry—come down!' sez 'e. Now I've told you as my feyther vos the boldest—"

"Yes, yes," cried the fussy gentleman. "Well?"

"Vell, sir, my feyther stared at them murderous pistols, stared at Black Dan, an' being the werry gamest an' bravest cove you ever see, didn't 'esitate a second."

"Well," cried the fussy gentleman, "what did he do then?"

"Do, sir—v'y I'll tell you—my feyther—come down."

"Yes, yes," said the fussy gentleman, as Mottle-face paused. "Go on, go on!"

"Go on v'ere, sir?"

"Go on with your story. What was the end of it?"

"V'y, that's the end on it."

"But it isn't; you haven't told us what happened after he got down. What became of him after?"

"Took the 'Ring o' Bells,' out Islington vay, an' drank hisself to death all quite nat'ral and reg'lar."

"But that's not the end of your story."

"It vere the end o' my feyther though—an' a werry good end it vere, too."

Now here there ensued a silence, during which the fussy gentleman stared fixedly at Mottle-face, who chirruped to the horses solicitously, and turned a serene but owl-like eye up to the waning moon.

"And pray," said the fussy gentleman at length, very red in the face, and more indignant than ever, "pray what's all this to do with my valise, I should like to know?"

"So should I," nodded Mottle-face—"ah, that I should."

"You—you told me," spluttered the fussy gentleman, in sudden wrath, "that you were coming to my valise."

"An' so ve have," nodded Mottle-face, triumphantly. "Ve're at it now; ve've been a-coming to that theer blessed walise ever since you come aboard."

"Well, and what's to be done about it?" snapped the fussy gentleman.

"Vell," said Mottle-face, with another ponderous wink at Barnabas, "if it troubles you much more, sir, if I vos you I should get a werry strong rope, and a werry large stone, and tie 'em together werry tight, an' drop that theer blessed walise into the river, and get rid of it that way."

Hereupon the fussy gentleman uttered an inarticulate exclamation, and, throwing himself back in his seat, tugged his hat over his eyes, and was heard no more.

But Mottle-face, touching up the near leader with deft and delicate play of wrist, or flicking the off wheeler, ever and anon gave vent to sounds which, though somewhat muffled, on account of coat-collar and shawl, were uncommonly like a chuckle. Yet if this were so or no, Barnabas did not trouble to ascertain, for he was already in that dreamy state 'twixt sleeping and waking, drowsily conscious of being borne on through the summer night, past lonely cottage and farmhouse, past fragrant ricks and barns, past wayside pools on whose still waters stars seemed to float—on and ever on, rumbling over bridges, clattering through sleeping hamlets and villages, up hill and down hill, on and ever on toward London and the wonders thereof. But, little by little, the chink and jingle of the harness, the rumble of the wheels, the rhythmic beat of the sixteen hoofs, all became merged into a drone that gradually softened to a drowsy murmur, and Barnabas fell into a doze; yet only to be awakened, as it seemed to him, a moment later by lights and voices, and to find that they were changing horses once more. Whereupon Mottle-face, leaning over, winked his owl-like eye, and spoke in a hoarse, penetrating whisper:

"Ten mile, sir, an' not a vord out o' old Walise so far!" saying which he jerked his head towards the huddled form of the fussy gentleman, winked again, and turned away to curse the hurrying ostlers, albeit in a tone good-natured and jovial.

And so, betimes, off they went again, down hill and up, by rolling meadow and winding stream, 'neath the leafy arches of motionless trees, through a night profoundly still save for the noise of their own going, the crow of a cock, or the bark of a dog from some farmyard. The moon sank and was gone, but on went the London Mail swirling through eddying mist that lay in every hollow like ghostly pools. Gradually the stars paled to the dawn, for low down in the east was a gray streak that grew ever broader, that changed to a faint pink, deepening to rose, to crimson, to gold—an ever brightening glory, till at last up rose the sun, at whose advent the mists rolled away and vanished, and lo! day was born.

Yawning, Barnabas opened drowsy eyes, and saw that here and there were houses in fair gardens, yet as they went the houses grew thicker and the gardens more scant. And now Barnabas became aware of a sound, soft with distance, that rose and fell—a never-ceasing murmur; therefore, blinking drowsily at Mottle-face, he inquired what this might be.

"That, sir, that's London, sir—cobble-stones, sir, cart-vheels, sir, and—Lord love you!"—here Mottle-face leaned over and once more winked his owl-like eye—"but 'e ain't mentioned the vord 'walise' all night, sir—so 'elp me!" Having said which, Mottle-face vented a throaty chuckle, and proceeded to touch up his horses.

And now as one in a dream, Barnabas is aware that they are threading streets, broad streets and narrow, and all alive with great wagons and country wains; on they go, past gloomy taverns, past churches whose gilded weather-cocks glitter in the early sunbeams, past crooked side-streets and dark alley-ways, and so, swinging suddenly to the right, have pulled up at last in the yard of the "George."

It is a great inn with two galleries one above another and many windows, and here, despite the early hour, a motley crowd is gathered. Forthwith Barnabas climbs down, and edging his way through the throng, presently finds Peterby at his elbow.

"Breakfast, sir?"

"Bed, Peterby."

"Very good—this way, sir."

Thereafter, though he scarcely knows how, he finds himself following a trim-footed damsel, who, having shown him up a winding stair, worn by the tread of countless travellers, brings him to a smallish, dullish chamber, opening upon the lower gallery. Hereupon Barnabas bids her "good night," but, blinking in the sunlight, gravely changes it to "good morning." The trim-footed maid smiles, curtsies, and vanishes, closing the door behind her.

Now upon the wall of the chamber, facing the bed, hangs the picture of a gentleman in a military habit with an uncomfortably high stock. He is an eagle-nosed gentleman with black whiskers, and a pair of remarkably round wide-awake eyes, which stare at Barnabas as much as to say—

"And who the devil are you, sir?"

Below him his name and titles are set forth fully and with many flourishes, thus—

LIEUTENANT-GENERAL THE RIGHT HONORABLE THE EARL OF POMFROY, K.G., K.T.S., etc., etc., etc.

So remarkably wide-awake is he, indeed, that it seems to drowsy Barnabas as if these round eyes wait to catch him unawares and follow him pertinaciously about the smallish, dullish chamber. Nevertheless Barnabas yawns, and proceeds to undress, which done, remembering he is in London, he takes purse and valuables and very carefully sets them under his pillow, places Mr. Chichester's pistol on the small table conveniently near, and gets into bed.

Yet now, sleepy though he is, he must needs turn to take another look at the Honorable the Earl of Pomfroy, wonders idly what the three "etc.'s" may mean, admires the glossy curl of his whiskers, counts the medals and orders on his bulging breast, glances last of all at his eyes, and immediately becomes aware that they are curiously like those of the "White Lion" at Tenterden, in that they are plying him with questions.

"Tall or short? dark or fair? Will she kiss you—next time, sir? Will she even be glad to see you again, you presumptuous young dog—will she—will she, confound you?"

"Ah!" sighed Barnabas. "Next time—I wonder!"

So saying, he sighed again, once, twice, and with the third fell fast asleep, and dreamed that a certain White Lion, clad in a Lieutenant-General's uniform, and with a pair of handsome black whiskers, stood balancing himself upon a single claw on the rail of the bed.

CHAPTER XXVI

CONCERNING THE DUTIES OF A VALET—AND A MAN

"And now, Peterby," said Barnabas, pushing his chair from the breakfast table, "the first thing I shall require is—a tailor."

"Very true, sir."

"These clothes were good enough for the country, Peterby, but—"

"Exactly, sir!" answered Peterby, bowing.

"Hum!" said Barnabas, with a quick glance. "Though mark you," he continued argumentatively,—"they might be worse, Peterby; the fit is good, and the cloth is excellent. Yes, they might be a great deal worse."

"It is—possible, sir," answered Peterby, with another bow. Hereupon, having glanced at his solemn face, Barnabas rose, and surveyed himself, as well as he might, in the tarnished mirror on the wall.

"Are they so bad as all that?" he inquired.

Peterby's mouth relaxed, and a twinkle dawned in his eye.

"As garments they are—serviceable, sir," said he, gravely, "but as clothes they—don't exist."

"Why then," said Barnabas, "the sooner we get some that do,—the better. Do you know of a good tailor?"

"I know them all, sir."

"Who is the best—the most expensive?"

"Stultz, sir, in Clifford Street; but I shouldn't advise you to have him."

"And why not?"

"Because he *is* a tailor."

"Oh?" said Barnabas.

"I mean that the clothes he makes are all stamped with his individuality, as it were,—their very excellence damns them. They are the clothes of a tailor instead of being simply a gentleman's garments."

"Hum!" said Barnabas, beginning to frown at this, "it would seem that dress can be a very profound subject, Peterby."

"Sir," answered Peterby, shaking his head, "it is a life study, and, so far as I know, there are only two people in the world who understand it aright; Beau Brummell was one, and, because he was the Beau, had London and the World of Fashion at his feet."

"And who was the other?"

Peterby took himself by the chin, and, though his mouth was solemn, the twinkle was back in his eye as he glanced at Barnabas.

"The other, sir," he answered, "was one who, until yesterday, was reduced to the necessity of living upon poached rabbits."

Here Barnabas stared thoughtfully up at the ceiling.

"I remember you told me you were the best valet in the world," said he.

"It is my earnest desire to prove it, sir."

"And yet," said Barnabas, with his gaze still turned ceiling-wards, "I would have you—even more than this, Peterby."

"More, sir?"

"I would have you, sometimes, forget that you are only 'the best valet in the world,' and remember that you are—a man: one in whom I can confide; one who has lived in this great world, and felt, and suffered, and who can therefore advise me; one I may trust to in an emergency; for London is a very big place, they tell me, and my friends are few—or none—and—do you understand me, Peterby?"

"Sir," said Peterby in an altered tone, "I think I do."

"Then—sit down, John, and let us talk."

With a murmur of thanks Peterby drew up a chair and sat watching Barnabas with his shrewd eyes.

"You will remember," began Barnabas, staring up at the ceiling again, "that when I engaged you I told you that I intended to—hum! to—cut a figure in the fashionable world?"

"Yes, sir; and I told you that,—after what happened in a certain wood,—it was practically impossible."

"You mean because I thrashed a scoundrel?"

"I mean because you knocked down a friend of the Prince Regent."

"And is Carnaby so very powerful, Peterby?"

"Sir, he is—the Prince's friend! He is also as great a Buck as George Hanger, as Jehu, or Jockey of Norfolk, and as famous, almost, as the late Sir Maurice Vibart."

"Ah!" said Barnabas.

"And since the retirement of Mr. Brummell, he and the Marquis of Jerningham have to some extent taken his place and become the Arbiters of Fashion."

"Oh!" said Barnabas.

"And furthermore, sir, I would warn you that he is a dangerous enemy, said to be one of the best pistol-shots in England."

"Hum," said Barnabas, "nevertheless, I mean to begin—"

"To begin, sir?"

"At once, Peterby."

"But—how, sir?"

"That is for you to decide, Peterby."

"Me, sir?"

"You, Peterby."

Here Peterby took himself by the chin again, and looked at Barnabas with thoughtful eyes and gloomy brow.

"Sir," said he, "the World of Fashion is a trivial world where all must appear trivial; it is a place where all must act a part, and where those are most regarded who are most affected; it is a world of shams and insincerity, and very jealously guarded."

"So I have heard," nodded Barnabas.

"To gain admission you must, first of all, have money."

"Yes," said Barnabas.

"Birth—if possible."

"Hum," said Barnabas.

"Wit and looks may be helpful, but all these are utterly useless unless you have what I may call the magic key."

"And what is that?"

"Notoriety, sir."

"For what?"

"For anything that will serve to lift you out of the ruck—to set you above the throng,—you must be one apart—an original."

"Originality is divine!" said Barnabas.

"More or less, sir," added Peterby, "for it is very easily achieved. Lord Alvanly managed it with apricot tarts; Lord Petersham with snuff-boxes; Mr. Mackinnon by his agility in climbing round drawing-rooms on the furniture; Jockey of Norfolk by consuming a vast number of beef-steaks, one after the other; Sir George Cassilis, who was neither rich nor handsome nor witty, by being insolent; Sir John Lade by dressing like a stagecoach-man, and driving like the devil; Sir George Skeffington by inventing a new color and writing bad plays; and I could name you many others beside—"

"Why then, Peterby—what of Sir Mortimer Carnaby?"

"He managed it by going into the ring with Jack Fearby, the 'Young Ruffian,' and beating him in twenty-odd rounds for one thing, and winning a cross-country race—"

"Ha!" exclaimed Barnabas, "a race!" and so he fell to staring up at the ceiling again.

"But I fear, sir," continued Peterby, "that in making him your enemy, you have damned your chances at the very outset, as I told you."

"A race!" said Barnabas again, vastly thoughtful.

"And therefore," added Peterby, leaning nearer in his earnestness, "since you honor me by asking my advice, I would strive with all my power to dissuade you."

"John Peterby—why?"

"Because, in the first place, I know it to be impossible."

"I begin to think not, John."

"Why, then, because—it's dangerous!"

"Danger is everywhere, more or less, John."

"And because, sir, because you—you—" Peterby rose, and stood with bent head and hands outstretched, "because you gave a miserable wretch another chance to live; and therefore I—I would not see you crushed and humiliated. Ah, sir! I know this London, I know those who make up the fashionable world. Sir, it is a heartless world, cruel and shallow, where inexperience is made a mock of—generosity laughed to scorn; where he is most respected who can shoot the straightest; where men seldom stoop to quarrel, but where death is frequent, none the less—and, sir, I could not bear—I—I wouldn't have you cut off thus—!"

Peterby stopped suddenly, and his head sank lower; but as he stood Barnabas rose, and coming to him, took his hand into his own firm clasp.

"Thank you, John Peterby," said he. "You may be the best valet in the world—I hope you are—but I know that you are a man, and, as a man, I tell you that I have decided upon going on with the adventure."

"Then I cannot hope to dissuade you, sir?"

"No, John!"

"Indeed, I feared not."

"It was for this I came to London, and I begin—at once."

"Very good, sir."

"Consequently, you have a busy day before you; you see I shall require, first of all, clothes, John; then—well, I suppose a house to live in—"

"A—house, sir?"

"In a fashionable quarter, and furnished, if possible."

"A lodging, St. James's Street way, is less expensive, sir, and more usual."

"Good!" said Barnabas; "to buy a house will be more original, at least. Then there must be servants, horses—vehicles—but you will understand—"

"Certainly, sir."

"Well then, John—go and get 'em."

"Sir?" exclaimed Peterby.

"Go now, John," said Barnabas, pulling out his purse, "this very moment."

"But," stammered Peterby, "but, sir—you will—"

"I shall stay here—I don't intend to stir out until you have me dressed as I should be—in 'clothes that exist,' John!"

"But you—don't mean to—to entrust—everything—to—me?"

"Of course, John."

"But sir—"

"I have every confidence in your judgment, you see. Here is money, you will want more, of course, but this will do to go on with."

But Peterby only stared from Barnabas to the money on the table, and back again.

"Sir," said he at last, "this is—a great deal of money."

"Well, John?"

"And I would remind you that we are in London, sir, and that yesterday I—was a poacher—a man of no character—a—"

"But to-day you are my valet, John. So take the money and buy me whatever I require, but a tailor first of all."

Then, as one in a dream, Peterby took up the money, counted it, buttoned it into his pocket, and crossed to the door; but there he paused and turned.

"Sir," said he slowly, "I'll bring you a man who, though he is little known as yet, will be famous some day, for he is what I may term an artist in cloth. And sir,"—here Peterby's voice grew uncertain—"you shall find me worthy of your trust, so help me God!" Then he opened the door, went out, and closed it softly behind him. But as for Barnabas, he sat with his gaze fixed on the ceiling again, lost in reverie and very silent. After a while he spoke his thoughts aloud.

"A race!" said he.

CHAPTER XXVII

HOW BARNABAS BOUGHT AN UNRIDABLE HORSE—AND RODE IT

The coffee-room at the "George" is a longish, narrowish, dullish chamber, with a row of windows that look out upon the yard,—but upon this afternoon they looked at nothing in particular; and here Barnabas found a waiter, a lonely wight who struck him as being very like the room itself, in that he, also, was long, and narrow, and dull, and looked out upon the yard at nothing in particular; and, as he gazed, he sighed, and tapped thoughtfully at his chin with a salt-spoon. As Barnabas entered, however, he laid down the spoon, flicked an imaginary crumb from the table-cloth with his napkin, and bowed.

"Dinner, sir?" he inquired in a dullish voice, and with his head set engagingly to one side, while his sharp eyes surveyed Barnabas from boots to waistcoat, from waistcoat to neckcloth, and stayed there while he drew out his own shirt-frill with caressing fingers, and coughed disapprobation into his napkin. "Did you say dinner, sir?" he inquired again.

"Thank you, no," answered Barnabas.

"Perhaps cheese an' a biscuit might be nearer your mark, and say—a half of porter?"

"I've only just had breakfast," said Barnabas, aware of the waiter's scrutiny.

"Ah!" sighed the waiter, still caressing his shirt-frill, "you're Number Four, I think—night coach?"

"Yes."

"From the country of course, sir?"

"Yes—from the country," said Barnabas, beginning to frown a little, "but how in the world did you guess that?"

"From your 'toot example,' sir, as they say in France—from your appearance, sir."

"You are evidently a very observant man!" said Barnabas.

"Well," answered the waiter, with his gaze still riveted upon the neckcloth—indeed it seemed to fascinate him, "well, I can see as far through a brick wall as most,—there ain't much as I miss, sir."

"Why, then," said Barnabas, "you may perhaps have noticed a door behind you?"

The waiter stared from the neckcloth to the door and back again, and scratched his chin dubiously.

"Door, sir—yessir!"

"Then suppose you go out of that door, and bring me pens, and ink, and paper."

"Yessir!"

"Also the latest newspapers."

"Yessir—certainly, sir;" and with another slight, though eloquent cough into his napkin, he started off upon his errand. Hereupon, as soon as he was alone,

Barnabas must needs glance down at that offending neckcloth, and his frown grew the blacker.

"Now, I wonder how long Peterby will be?" he said to himself. But here came the creak of the waiter's boots, and that observant person reappeared, bearing the various articles which he named in turn as he set them on the table.

"A bottle of ink, sir; pens and writing-paper, sir; and the Gazette."

"Thank you," said Barnabas, very conscious of his neckcloth still.

"And now, sir," here the waiter coughed into his napkin again, "now—what will you drink, sir; shall we say port, or shall we make it sherry?"

"Neither," said Barnabas.

"Why, then, we 'ave some rare old burgundy, sir—'ighly esteemed by connysoors and (cough again) other—gentlemen."

"No, thank you."

"On the other 'and—to suit 'umbler tastes, we 'ave,"—here the waiter closed his eyes, sighed, and shook his head—"ale, sir, likewise beer, small and otherwise."

"Nothing, thank you," said Barnabas; "and you will observe the door is still where it was."

"Door, sir, yessir—oh, certainly, sir!" said he, and stalked out of the room.

Then Barnabas set a sheet of paper before him, selected a pen, and began to write as follows:—

George Inn,
Borough.
June 2, 18—.

To VISCOUNT DEVENHAM,

MY DEAR DICK,—I did not think to be asking favors of you so soon, but—(here a blot).

"Confound it!" exclaimed Barnabas, and taking out his penknife he began to mend the spluttering quill. But, in the midst of this operation, chancing to glance out of the window, he espied a long-legged gentleman with a remarkably fierce pair of whiskers; he wore a coat of ultra-fashionable cut, and stood with his booted legs wide apart, staring up at the inn from under a curly-brimmed hat. But the hat had evidently seen better days, the coat was frayed at seam and elbow, and the boots lacked polish; yet these small blemishes were more than offset by his general dashing, knowing air, and the untamable ferocity of his whiskers. As Barnabas watched him, he drew a letter from the interior of his shabby coat, unfolded it with a prodigious flourish, and began to con it over. Now, all at once, Barnabas dropped knife and pen, thrust a hand into his own breast and took thence a letter also, at sight of which he straightway forgot the bewhiskered gentleman; for what he read was this:—

Dearest and Best of Sisters,—Never, in all this world was there such an unfortunate, luckless dog as I—were it not for your unfailing love I should have made an end of it all, before now.

I write this letter to beg and implore you to grant me another interview, anywhere and at any time you may name. Of course you will think it is more money I want—so I do; I'm always in need of it, and begin to fear I always shall be. But my reasons for wishing this meeting are much more than this—indeed, *most urgent*! (this underlined). I am threatened by a GRAVE DANGER (this doubly underlined). I am at my wit's end, and only you can save me, Cleone—you and you only. Chichester has been more than kind, *indeed, a true friend to me*! (this also underlined). I would that you could feel kinder towards him.

This letter must reach you where none of your guardian's spies can intercept it; your precious Captain has always hated me, damn him! (this scratched out). Oh, shame that he, a stranger, should ever have been allowed to come between brother and sister. I shall journey down to Hawkhurst to see you and shall stay about until you can contrive to meet me. Chichester may accompany me, and if he should, try to be kinder to your brother's only remaining friend. How different are our situations! you surrounded by every luxury, while I—yet heaven forbid I should forget my manhood and fill this letter with my woes. But if you ever loved your unfortunate brother, do not fail him in this, Cleone.

Your loving, but desperate,
RONALD BARRYMAINE.

Having read this effusion twice over, and very carefully, Barnabas was yet staring at the last line with its scrawling signature, all unnecessary curls and flourishes, when he heard a slight sound in the adjacent box, and turning sharply, was just in time to see the top of a hat ere it vanished behind the curtain above the partition.

Therefore he sat very still, waiting. And lo! after the lapse of half a minute, or thereabouts, it reappeared, slowly and by degrees—a beaver hat, something the worse for wear. Slowly it rose up over the curtain—the dusty crown, the frayed band, the curly brim, and eventually a pair of bold, black eyes that grew suddenly very wide as they met the unwinking gaze of Barnabas. Hereupon the lips, as yet unseen, vented a deep sigh, and, thereafter, uttered these words:

"The same, and yet, curse me, the nose!—y-e-s, the nose seems, on closer inspection, a trifle too aquiline, perhaps; and the chin—y-e-s, decidedly a thought too long! And yet—!" Here another sigh, and the face rising into full view, Barnabas recognized the bewhiskered gentleman he had noticed in the yard.

"Sir," continued the stranger, removing the curly-brimmed hat with a flourish, and bowing over the partition as well as he could, "you don't happen to be a sailor—Royal Navy, do you?"

"No, sir," answered Barnabas.

"And your name don't happen to be Smivvle, does it?"

"No, sir," said Barnabas again.

"And yet," sighed the bewhiskered gentleman, regarding him with half-closed eyes, and with his head very much on one side, "in spite of your nose, and in spite of your chin, you are the counterpart, sir, the facsimile—I might say the breathing image of a—ha!—of a nephew of mine; noble youth, handsome as Adonis—Royal Navy—regular Apollo; went to sea, sir, years ago; never heard of more; tragic, sir—devilish tragic, on my soul and honor."

"Very!" said Barnabas; "but—"

"Saw you from the yard, sir, immediately struck by close resemblance; flew here, borne on the wings of hope, sir; you 're quite sure your name ain't Smivvle, are you?"

"Quite sure."

"Ah, well—mine is; Digby Smivvle, familiarly known as 'Dig,' at your service, sir. Stranger to London, sir?"

"Yes," said Barnabas.

"Ha! Bad place, London, sink of iniquity! Full of rogues, rascals, damn scoundrels,—by heaven, sharks, sir! confounded cannibals, by George!—eat you alive. Stranger myself, sir; just up from my little place in Worcestershire—King's Heath,—know it, perhaps? No? Charming village! rural, quiet; mossy trees, sir; winding brooks, larks and cuckoos carolling all day long. Sir, there has been a Smivvle at the Hall since before the Conquest! Fine old place, the Hall; ancient, sir, hoary and historic—though devilish draughty, upon my soul and honor!"

Here, finding that he still held the open letter in his hand, Barnabas refolded it and thrust it into his pocket, while Mr. Smivvle smilingly caressed his whiskers, and his bold, black eyes darted glances here and there, from Barnabas mending his pen to the table, from the table to the walls, to the ceiling, and from that altitude they dropped to the table again, and hovered there.

"Sir," said Barnabas without looking up, "pray excuse the blot, the pen was a bad one; I am making another, as you see."

Mr. Smivvle started, and raised his eyes swiftly. Stared at unconscious Barnabas, rubbed his nose, felt for his whisker, and, having found it, tugged it viciously.

"Blot, sir!" he exclaimed loudly; "now, upon my soul and honor—what blot, sir?"

"This," said Barnabas, taking up his unfinished letter to the Viscount—"if you've finished, we may as well destroy it," and forthwith he crumpled it into a ball, and tossed it into the empty fireplace.

"Sir!" exclaimed Mr. Smivvle, louder than before, "'pon my soul, now, if you mean to insinuate—" Here he paused, staring at Barnabas, and with his whiskers fiercer than ever.

"Well, sir?" inquired Barnabas, still busily trimming his quill.

Mr. Smivvle frowned; but finding Barnabas was quite unconscious of it, shook his head, felt for his whisker again, found it, tugged it, and laughed jovially.

"Sir," said he, "you are a devilish sharp fellow, and a fine fellow. I swear you are. I like your spirit, on my soul and honor I do, and, as for blots, I vow to you I never write a letter myself that I don't smear most damnably—curse me if I don't. That blot, sir, shall be another bond between us, for I have conceived a great regard for you. The astounding likeness between you and one who—was snatched away in the flower of his youth—draws me, sir, draws me most damnably; for I have a heart, sir, a heart—why should I disguise it?" Here Mr. Smivvle tapped the third left-hand button of his coat. "And so long as that organ continues its functions, you may count Digby Smivvle your friend, and at his little place in Worcestershire he will be proud to show you the hospitality *of* a Smivvle. Meanwhile, sir, seeing we are both strangers in a strange place, supposing we—join forces and, if you are up for the race, I propose—"

"The race!" exclaimed Barnabas, looking up suddenly.

"Yes, sir, devilish swell affair, with gentlemen to ride, and Royalty to look on—a race of races! London's agog with it, all the clubs discuss it, coffee houses ring with it, inns and taverns clamor with it—soul and honor, betting—everywhere. The odds slightly favor Sir Mortimer Carnaby's 'Clasher'; but Viscount Devenham's 'Moonraker' is well up. Then there's Captain Slingsby's 'Rascal,' Mr. Tressider's 'Pilot,' Lord Jerningham's 'Clinker,' and five or six others. But, as I tell you, 'Clasher' and 'Moonraker' carry the money, though many knowing ones are sweet on the 'Rascal.' But, surely, you must have heard of the great steeplechase? Devilish ugly course, they tell me."

"The Viscount spoke of it, I remember," said Barnabas, absently.

"Viscount, sir—not—Viscount Devenham?"

"Yes."

Here Mr. Smivvle whistled softly, took off the curly-brimmed hat, looked at it, and put it on again at a more rakish angle than ever.

"Didn't happen to mention my name, did he—Smivvle, sir?"

"No."

"Nor Dig, perhaps?"

"No, sir."

"Remarkable—hum!" exclaimed Mr. Smivvle, shaking his head; "but I'm ready to lay you odds that he *did* speak of my friend Barry. I may say my bosom companion—a Mr. Ronald Barrymaine, sir."

"Ronald Barrymaine," repeated Barnabas, trying the new point of his pen upon his thumb-nail, yet conscious of the speaker's keen glance, none the less. "No, he did not."

"Astounding!" exclaimed Mr. Smivvle.

"Why so?"

"Because my friend Barrymaine was particularly intimate with his Lordship, before he fell among the Jews, dammem! My friend Barry, sir, was a dasher, by George! a regular red-hot tearer, by heaven! a Go, sir, a Tippy, a bang up Blood, and would be still if it were not for the Jews—curse 'em!"

"And is Mr. Barrymaine still a friend of yours?"

At this Mr. Smivvle took off his hat again, clapped it to his bosom, and bowed.

"Sir," said he, "for weal or woe, in shadow or shine, the hand of a Smivvle, once given, is given for good."

As he spoke, Mr. Smivvle stretched out the member in question, which Barnabas observed was none too clean.

"The hand of a Smivvle, sir," pursued that gentleman, "the hand of a Smivvle is never withdrawn either on account of adversity, plague, poverty, pestilence, or Jews—dammem! As for my friend Barrymaine; but, perhaps, you are acquainted with him, sir."

"No," answered Barnabas.

"Ah! a noble fellow, sir! Heroic youth, blood, birth, and breeding to his finger-tips, sir. But he is, above all else, a brother to a—a sister, sir. Ah! what a creature! Fair, sir? fair as the immortal Helena! Proud, sir? proud as an arch-duchess! Handsome, sir? handsome, sir, as—as—oh, dammit, words fail me; but go, sir, go and ransack Olympus, and you couldn't match her, 'pon my soul! Diana, sir? Diana was a frump! Venus? Venus was a dowdy hoyden, by George! and as for the ox-eyed Juno, she was a positive cow to this young beauty! And then—her heart, sir!"

"Well, what of it?" inquired Barnabas, rather sharply.

"Utterly devoted—beats only for my friend—"

"You mean her brother?"

"I mean her brother, yes, sir; though I have heard a rumor that Sir Mortimer Carnaby—"

"Pooh!" said Barnabas.

"With pleasure, sir; but the fact remains that it was partly on his account, and partly because of another, that she was dragged away from London—"

"What other?"

"Well, let us say—H.R.H."

"Sir," inquired Barnabas, frowning, "do you mean the Prince?"

"Sir," said Mr. Smivvle, with a smiling shake of the head, "I prefer the letters H.R.H. Anyhow, there were many rumors afloat at the time, and her guardian—

a regular, tarry old sea dog, by George—drags her away from her brother's side, and buries her in the country, like the one-armed old pirate he is, eye to her money they tell me; regular old skinflint; bad as a Jew—damn him! But speaking of the race, sir, do you happen to—know anything?"

"I know that it is to be run on the fifteenth of July," said Barnabas abstractedly.

"Oh, very good!" exclaimed Mr. Smivvle—"ha! ha!—excellent! knows it is to be run on the fifteenth; very facetious, curse me! But, joking apart, sir, have you any private knowledge? The Viscount, now, did he happen to tell you anything that—"

But, at this juncture, they were interrupted by a sudden tumult in the yard outside, a hubbub of shouts, the ring and stamp of hoofs, and, thereafter, a solitary voice upraised in oaths and curses. Barnabas sprang to his feet, and hurrying out into the yard, beheld a powerful black horse that reared and plunged in the grip of two struggling grooms; in an adjacent corner was the late rider, who sat upon a pile of stable-sweepings and swore, while, near by, perched precariously upon an upturned bucket, his slim legs stretched out before him, was a young exquisite—a Corinthian from top to toe—who rocked with laughter, yet was careful to keep his head rigid, so as to avoid crushing his cravat, a thing of wonder which immediately arrested the attention of Barnabas, because of its prodigious height, and the artful arrangement of its voluminous folds.

"Oh, dooce take me," he exclaimed in a faint voice, clapping a hand to his side, "I'll be shot if I saw anything neater, no, not even at Sadler's Wells! Captain Slingsby of the Guards in his famous double somersault! Oh, damme, Sling! I'd give a hundred guineas to see you do it again—I would, dooce take me!"

But Captain Slingsby continued to shake his fist at the great, black horse, and to swear with unabated fervor.

"You black devil!" he exclaimed, "you four-legged imp of Satan! So, you're up to your tricks again, are you? Well, this is the last chance you shall have to break my neck, b'gad! I'm done with you for a—"

Here the Captain became extremely fluent, and redder of face than ever, as he poured forth a minute description of the animal; he cursed him from muzzle to crupper and back again; he damned his eyes, he damned his legs, individually and collectively, and reviled him, through sire and dam, back to the Flood.

Meanwhile Barnabas turned from raging Two-legs to superbly wrathful Four-legs; viewed him from sweeping tail to lofty crest; observed his rolling eye and quivering nostril; took careful heed of his broad chest, slender legs, and powerful, sloping haunches with keen, appraising eyes, that were the eyes of knowledge and immediate desire. And so, from disdainful Four-legs he turned back to ruffled Two-legs, who, having pretty well sworn himself out by this time, rose gingerly to his feet, felt an elbow with gentle inquiry, tenderly rubbed a muddied knee, and limped out from the corner.

Now, standing somewhat apart, was a broad-shouldered man, a rough-looking customer in threadbare clothes, whose dusty boots spoke of travel. He was an elderly man, for the hair, beneath the battered hat, was gray, and he leaned wearily upon a short stick. Very still he stood, and Barnabas noticed that he kept his gaze bent ever upon the horse; nor did he look away even when the Captain began to speak again.

"B'gad!" exclaimed the Captain, "I'll sell the brute to the highest bidder. You, Jerningham, you seem devilish amused, b'gad! If you think you can back him he's yours for what you like. Come, what's the word?"

"Emphatically no, my dear, good Sling," laughed the young Corinthian, shaking his curly head. "I don't mean to risk this most precious neck of mine until the fifteenth, dear fellow, dooce take me if I do!"

"Why then, b'gad! I'll sell him to any one fool enough to bid. Come now," cried the Captain, glancing round the yard, "who'll buy him? B'gad! who'll give ten pounds for an accursed brute that nobody can possibly ride?"

"I will!" said Barnabas.

"Fifteen, sir!" cried the shabby man on the instant, with his gaze still on the horse.

"Twenty!" said Barnabas, like an echo.

"Twenty-five, sir!" retorted the shabby man.

"Hey?" cried the Captain, staring from one to the other. "What's all this? B'gad! I say stop a bit—wait a minute! Bob, lend me your bucket."

Hereupon the Corinthian obligingly vacating that article. Captain Slingsby incontinent stood upon it, and from that altitude began to harangue the yard, flourishing his whip after the manner of an auctioneer's hammer.

"Now here you are, gentlemen!" he cried. "I offer you a devilishly ugly, damnably vicious brute, b'gad! I offer you a four-legged demon, an accursed beast that nobody can ever hope to ride—a regular terror, curse me! Killed one groom already, will probably kill another. Now, what is your price for this lady's pet? Look him over and bid accordingly."

"Twenty-five pound, sir," said the shabby man.

"Thirty!" said Barnabas.

"Thirty-one, sir."

"Fifty!" said Barnabas.

"Fifty!" cried the Captain, flourishing his whip. "Fifty pounds from the gentleman in the neckcloth—fifty's the figure. Any more? Any advance on fifty? What, all done! Won't any one go another pound for a beast fit only for the knacker's yard? Oh, Gad, gentlemen, why this reticence? Are you all done?"

"I can't go no higher, sir," said the shabby man, shaking his gray head sadly.

"Then going at fifty—at fifty! Going! Going! Gone, b'gad! Sold to the knowing young cove in the neckcloth."

Now, at the repetition of this word, Barnabas began to frown.

"And b'gad!" exclaimed the Captain, stepping down from the bucket, "a devilish bad bargain he's got, too."

"That, sir, remains to be seen," said Barnabas, shortly.

"Why, what do you mean to do with the brute?"

"Ride him."

"Do you, b'gad?"

"I do."

"Lay you ten guineas you don't sit him ten minutes."

"Done!" said Barnabas, buttoning up his coat.

But now, glancing round, he saw that the shabby man had turned away, and was trudging heavily out of the yard, therefore Barnabas hastened after him, and touched him upon the arm.

"I'm sorry you were disappointed," said he.

"Is it about the 'oss you mean, sir?" inquired the shabby man, touching his hat.

"Yes."

"Why, it do come a bit 'ard-like to ha' lost 'im, sir, arter waiting my chance so long. But fifty guineas be a sight o' money to a chap as be out of a job, though 'e's dirt-cheap at the price. There ain't many 'osses like 'im, sir."

"That was why I should have bought him at ten times the price," said Barnabas.

The man took off his hat, ran his stubby fingers through his grizzled hair, and stared hard at Barnabas.

"Sir," said he, "even at that you couldn't ha' done wrong. He ain't a kind 'oss—never 'aving been understood, d' ye see; but take my word for it, 'e's a wonder, that 'oss!"

"You know him, perhaps?"

"Since 'e were foaled, sir. I was stud-groom; but folks think I'm too old for the job, d' ye see, sir?"

"Do you think he 'd remember you?"

"Ay, that 'e would!"

"Do you suppose—look at him!—do you suppose you could hold him quieter than those ostlers?"

"'Old 'im, sir!" exclaimed the man, throwing back his shoulders. "'Old 'im—ah, that I could! Try me!"

"I will," said Barnabas. "How would forty shillings a week suit you?"

"Sir?" exclaimed the old groom, staring.

"Since you need a job, and I need a groom, I'll have you—if you're willing."

The man's square jaw relaxed, his eyes glistened; then all at once he shook his head and sighed.

"Ah! sir," said he, "ah! young sir, my 'air's gray, an' I'm not so spry as I was—nobody wants a man as old as I be, and, seeing as you've got the 'oss, you ain't got no call to make game o' me, young sir. You 've got—the 'oss!"

Now at this particular moment Captain Slingsby took it into his head to interrupt them, which he did in characteristic fashion.

"Hallo!—hi there!" he shouted, flourishing his whip.

"But I'm not making game of you," said Barnabas, utterly unconscious of the Captain, at least his glance never wavered from the eager face of the old groom.

"Hallo, there!" roared the Captain, louder than ever.

"And to prove it," Barnabas continued, "here is a guinea in advance," and he slipped the coin into the old groom's lax hand.

"Oh, b'gad," cried the Captain, hoarsely, "don't you hear me, you over there? Hi! you in the neckcloth!"

"Sir," said Barnabas, turning sharply and frowning again at the repetition of the word, "if you are pleased to allude to me, I would humbly inform you that my name is Beverley."

"Oh!" exclaimed the Captain, "I see—young Beverley, son of old Beverley—and a devilish good name too!"

"Sir, I'm vastly relieved to hear you say so," retorted Barnabas, with a profound obeisance. Then taking out his purse, he beckoned his new groom to approach.

"What is your name?" he inquired, as he counted out a certain sum.

"Gabriel Martin, sir."

"Then, Martin, pray give the fellow his money."

"Sir?"

"I mean the red-faced man in the dirty jacket, Martin," added Barnabas.

The old groom hesitated, glanced from the Captain's scowling brow to the smiling lips of Barnabas.

"Very good, sir," said he, touching his shabby hat, and taking the money Barnabas held out, he tendered it to the Captain, who, redder of face than ever, took it, stared from it to Barnabas, and whistled.

"Now, damme!" he exclaimed, "damme, if I don't believe the fellow means to be offensive!"

"If so, sir, the desire would seem to be mutual!" returned Barnabas.

"Yes, b'gad! I really believe he means to be offensive!" repeated the Captain, nodding as he pocketed the money.

"Of that you are the best judge, sir," Barnabas retorted. Captain Slingsby whistled again, frowned, and tossing aside his whip, proceeded to button up his coat.

"Why then," said he, "we must trouble this offensive person to apologize or—or put 'em up, begad!"

But hereupon the young Corinthian (who had been watching them languidly through the glass he carried at the end of a broad ribbon) stepped forward, though languidly, and laid a white and languid hand upon the Captain's arm.

"No, no, Sling," said he in a die-away voice, "he's a doocid fine 'bit of stuff'—look at those shoulders! and quick on his pins—remark those legs! No, no, my dear fellow, remember your knee, you hurt it, you know—fell on it when you were thrown,—must be doocid painful! Must let me take your place. Shall insist! Pleasure's all mine, 'sure you."

"Never, Jerningham!" fumed the Captain, "not to be thought of, my dear Bob—no begad, he's mine; why you heard him, he—he positively called me a—a fellow!"

"So you are, Sling," murmured the Corinthian, surveying Barnabas with an approving eye, "dev'lish dashing fellow, an 'out-and-outer' with the 'ribbons'—

fiddle it with any one, by George, but no good with your mauleys, damme if you are! Besides, there's your knee, you know—don't forget your knee—"

"Curse my knee!"

"Certainly, dear fellow, but—"

"My knee's sound enough to teach this countryman manners, b'gad; you heard him say my coat was filthy?"

"So it is, Sling, my boy, devilish dirty! So are your knees—look at 'em! But if you will dismount head over heels into a muck-heap, my dear fellow, what the dooce can you expect?" The Captain merely swore.

"Doocid annoying, of course," his friend continued, "I mean your knee, you know, you can hardly walk, and this country fellow looks a regular, bang up milling cove. Let me have a try at him, do now. Have a little thought for others, and don't be so infernally selfish, Sling, my boy."

As he spoke, the Corinthian took off his hat, which he forced into the Captain's unwilling grasp, drew off his very tight-fitting coat, which he tossed over the Captain's unwilling arm, and, rolling back his snowy shirt-sleeves, turned to Barnabas with shining eyes and smiling lips.

"Sir," said he, "seeing my friend's knee is not quite all it should be, perhaps you will permit me to take his place, pleasure's entirely mine, 'sure you. Shall we have it here, or would you prefer the stables—more comfortable, perhaps—stables?"

Now while Barnabas hesitated, somewhat taken aback by this unlooked-for turn of events, as luck would have it, there came a diversion. A high, yellow-wheeled curricle swung suddenly into the yard, and its two foam-spattered bays were pulled up in masterly fashion, but within a yard of the great, black horse, which immediately began to rear and plunge again; whereupon the bays began to snort, and dance, and tremble (like the thoroughbreds they were), and all was uproar and confusion; in the midst of which, down from the rumble of the dusty curricle dropped a dusty and remarkably diminutive groom, who, running to the leader's head, sprang up and, grasping the bridle, hung there manfully, rebuking the animal, meanwhile, in a voice astonishingly hoarse and gruff for one of his tender years.

"Dooce take me," exclaimed the Corinthian, feeling for his eye-glass, "it's Devenham!"

"Why, Dicky!" cried the Captain, "where have you sprung from?" and, forgetful of Barnabas, they hurried forward to greet the Viscount, who, having beaten some of the dust from his driving coat, sprang down from his high seat and shook hands cordially.

Then, finding himself unnoticed, Barnabas carefully loosed his neckerchief, and drew out the ends so that they dangled in full view.

"I've been rusticating with my 'Roman,'" the Viscount was proceeding to explain, keeping his eye upon his horses, "but found him more Roman than usual—Gad, I did that! Have 'em well rubbed down, Milo," he broke off suddenly, as the bays were led off to the stables, "half a bucket of water apiece, no more, mind, and—say, a dash of brandy!"

"Werry good, m'lud!" This from Milo of Crotona, portentous of brow and stern of eye, as he overlooked the ostlers who were busily unbuckling straps and traces.

"My 'Roman,' as I say," continued the Viscount, "was rather more so than usual, actually wanted me to give up the Race! After that of course I had to be firm with him, and we had a slight—ah, misunderstanding in consequence—fathers, as a rule, are so infernally parental and inconsiderate! Met Carnaby on the road, raced him for a hundred; ding-dong all the way, wheel and wheel to Bromley, though he nearly ditched me twice, confound him! Coming down Mason's Hill I gave him my dust, up the rise he drew level again. 'Ease up for the town, Carnaby,' says I, 'Be damned if I do!' says he, so at it we went, full tilt. Gad! to see the folk jump! Carnaby drove like a devil, had the lead to Southend, but, mark you, his whip was going! At Catford we were level again. At Lewisham I took the lead and kept it, and the last I saw of him he was cursing and lashing away at his cattle, like a brute. Carnaby's a devilish bad loser, I've noticed, and here I am. And oh! by the way—he's got a devil of an eye, and a split lip. Says he fell out of his curricle, but looks as though some one had—thrashed him."

"But my very dear fellow!" exclaimed the Corinthian, "thrash Carnaby? pooh!"

"Never in the world!" added the Captain.

"Hum!" said the Viscount, feeling a tender part of his own ribs thoughtfully, "ha! But, hallo, Jerningham! have you been at it too? Why are you buffed?" And he nodded to the Corinthian's bare arms.

"Oh, dooce take me, I forgot!" exclaimed the Marquis, looking about; "queer cove, doocid touchy, looks as if he might fib though. Ah, there he is! talking to the rough-looking customer over yonder;" and he pointed to Barnabas, who stood with his coat thrown open, and the objectionable neckcloth in full evidence. The Viscount looked, started, uttered a "view hallo," and, striding forward, caught Barnabas by the hand.

"Why, Bev, my dear fellow, this is lucky!" he exclaimed. Now Barnabas was quick to catch the glad ring in the Viscount's voice, and to notice that the neckcloth was entirely lost upon him, therefore he smiled as he returned the Viscount's hearty grip.

"When did you get here? what are you doing? and what the deuce is the trouble between you and Jerningham?" inquired the Viscount all in a breath. But before Barnabas could answer, the great, black horse, tired of comparative inaction, began again to snort and rear, and jerk his proud head viciously, whereupon the two ostlers fell to swearing, and the Viscount's bays at the other end of the yard to capering, and the Viscount's small groom to anathematizing, all in a moment.

"Slingsby!" cried his Lordship, "look to that black demon of yours!"

"He is no concern of mine, Devenham," replied the Captain airily, "sold him, b'gad!"

"And I bought him," added Barnabas.

"You did?" the Viscount exclaimed, "in heaven's name, what for?"

"To ride—"

"Eh? my dear fellow!"

"I should like to try him for the race on the fifteenth, if it could be managed, Dick."

"The race!" exclaimed the Viscount, staring.

"I 've been wondering if you could—get me entered for it," Barnabas went on, rather diffidently, "I'd give anything for the chance."

"What—with that brute! my dear fellow, are you mad?"

"No, Dick."

"But he's unmanageable, Bev; he's full of vice—a killer—look at him now!"

And indeed at this moment, as if to bear out this character, up went the great, black head again, eyes rolling, teeth gleaming, and ears laid back.

"I tell you, Bev, no one could ride that devil!" the Viscount repeated.

"But," said Barnabas, "I've bet your friend Captain Slingsby that I could."

"It would be madness!" exclaimed the Viscount. "Ha! look out! There—I told you so!" For in that moment the powerful animal reared suddenly—broke from the grip of one ostler, and swinging the other aside, stood free, and all was confusion. With a warning shout, the old groom sprang to his head, but Barnabas was beside him, had caught the hanging reins, and swung himself into the saddle.

"I've got him, sir," cried Martin, "find yer stirrups!"

"Your stick," said Barnabas, "quick, man! Now—let go!"

For a moment the horse stood rigid, then reared again, up and up—his teeth bared, his forefeet lashing; but down came the heavy stick between the flattened ears, once—twice, and brought him to earth again.

And now began a struggle between the man and the brute—each young, each indomitable, for neither had as yet been mastered, and therefore each was alike disdainful of the other. The head of the horse was high and proud, his round hoofs spurned the earth beneath, fire was in his eye, rage in his heart—rage and scorn of this presumptuous Two-legs who sought to pit his puny strength against his own quivering, four-legged might. Therefore he mocked Two-legs, scorned and contemned him, laughed ha! ha! (like his long-dead ancestor among the Psalmist's trumpets) and gathered himself together—eager for the battle.

But the eyes of Barnabas were wide and bright, his lips were curved, his jaw salient—his knees gripped tight, and his grasp was strong and sure upon the reins.

And now Four-legs, having voiced his defiance, tossed his crest on high, then plunged giddily forward, was checked amid a whirlwind of lashing hoofs, rose on his hind legs higher and higher, swinging giddily round and round, felt a stunning blow, staggered, and dropping on all fours, stove in the stable door with a fling of his hind hoofs. But the eyes of Barnabas were glowing, his lips still curved, and his grip upon the reins was more masterful. And, feeling all this, Four-legs, foaming with rage, his nostrils flaring, turned upon his foe with snapping teeth, found him out of reach, and so sought to play off an old trick that had served him more than once; he would smash his rider's leg against a post or wall, or brush him off altogether and get rid of him that way. But lo! even as he leapt in fulfilment of this manoeuvre, his head was wrenched round, further and further, until he must perforce, stop—until he was glaring up into the face above, the face of his bitter foe, with its smiling mouth, its glowing eye, its serene brow.

"Time's up!" cried the Captain, suddenly; "b'gad, sir, you win the bet!" But Barnabas scarcely heard.

"You've done it—you win; eleven and a half minutes, b'gad!" roared the Captain again—"don't you hear, sir?—come off, before he breaks your neck!"

But Barnabas only shook his head, and, dropping the stick, leaned over and laid his hand upon that proud, defiant crest, a hand grown suddenly gentle, and drew it down caressingly from ear to quivering nostril, once, twice, and spoke words in a soft tone, and so, loosed the cruel grip upon the rein, and sat back—waiting. But Four-legs had become thoughtful; true, he still tossed his head and pawed an impatient hoof, but that was merely for the sake of appearances—Four-legs was thoughtful. No one had ever touched him so, before—indeed blows had latterly been his portion—but this Two-legs was different from his kind, besides, he had a pleasing voice—a voice to soothe ragged nerves—there it was again! And then surely, the touch of this hand awoke dim memories, reminded him of far-off times when two-legged creatures had feared him less; and there was the hand again! After all, things might be worse—the hand that could be so gentle could be strong also; his mouth was sore yet, and a strong man, strong-handed and gentle of voice, was better than—oh, well!

Whether of all this, or any part of it, the great, black horse was really thinking, who shall say? Howbeit Barnabas presently turned in his saddle and beckoned the old groom to his stirrup.

"He'll be quiet now, I think," said he.

"Ah! that he will, sir. You've larned the trick o' voice an' hand—it ain't many as has it—must be born in a man, I reckon, an' 'tis that as does more nor all your whips and spurs, an' curb-bits, sir. 'E'll be a babe wi' you arter this, sir, an' I'm thinkin' as you won't be wantin' me now, maybe? I ain't young enough nor smart enough, d' ye see."

Here Barnabas dismounted, and gave the reins into the old groom's eager hand.

"I shan't be wanting him for—probably three or four days, Gabriel, until then—look after him, exercise him regularly, for I'm hoping to do great things with him, soon, Gabriel, perhaps." And so Barnabas smiled, and as Martin led the horse to the stables, turned to find the young Corinthian at his elbow; he had resumed hat and coat, and now regarded Barnabas as smiling and imperturbable as ever.

"Sir," said he, "I congratulate you heartily. Sir, any friend of Viscount Devenham is also mine, I trust; and I know your name, and—hem!—I swear Slingsby does! Beverley, I think—hem!—son of old Beverley, and a devilish good name too! Eh, Sling my boy?"

Hereupon the Captain limped forward, if possible redder of face than ever, very much like a large schoolboy in fault.

"Sir," he began, "b'gad—!" here he paused to clear his throat loudly once or twice—"a devil incarnate! Fourteen minutes and a half, by my watch, and devil a spur! I'd have lent you my boots had there been time, I would, b'gad! As it is, if you've any desire to shake hands with a—ha!—with a fellow—hum!—in a dirty coat—why—here's mine, b'gad!"

"Captain the Honorable Marmaduke Slingsby—Mr. Beverley—The Marquis of Jerningham—Mr. Beverley. And now," said the Viscount, as Barnabas shook hands, "now tell 'em why you bought the horse, Bev."

"I was hoping, sirs," said Barnabas, rather diffidently, "that I might perhaps have the honor of riding in the Steeplechase on the fifteenth."

Hereupon the Captain struck his riding boot a resounding blow with his whip, and whistled; while the Marquis dangled his eyeglass by its riband, viewing it with eyes of mild surprise, and the Viscount glanced from one to the other with an enigmatical smile upon his lips.

"That would rest with Carnaby to decide, of course," said the Captain at last.

"Why so?" inquired Barnabas.

"Because—well, because he—is Carnaby, I suppose," the Captain answered.

"Though Jerningham has the casting-vote," added the Viscount.

"True," said the Marquis, rearranging a fold of his cravat with a self-conscious air, "but, as Sling says—Carnaby is—Carnaby."

"Sirs," began Barnabas, very earnestly, "believe me I would spare no expense—"

"Expense, sir?" repeated the Marquis, lifting a languid eyebrow; "of course it is no question of 'expense'!" Here the Viscount looked uncomfortable all at once, and Barnabas grew suddenly hot.

"I mean," he stammered, "I mean that my being entered so late in the day—the fees might be made proportionately heavier—double them if need be—I should none the less be—be inestimably indebted to you; indeed I—I cannot tell you—" Now as Barnabas broke off, the Marquis smiled and reached out his hand—a languid-seeming hand, slim and delicate, yet by no means languid of grip.

"My dear Beverley," said he, "I like your earnestness. A race—especially this one—is a doocid serious thing; for some of us, perhaps, even more serious than we bargain for. It's going to be a punishing race from start to finish, a test of endurance for horse and man, over the worst imaginable country. It originated in a match between Devenham on his 'Moonraker' and myself on 'Clinker,' but Sling here was hot to match his 'Rascal,' and Carnaby fancied his 'Clasher,' and begad! applications came so fast that we had a field in no time."

"Good fellows and sportsmen all!" nodded the Captain. "Gentlemen riders—no tag-rag, gamest of the game, sir."

"Now, as to yourself, my dear Beverley," continued the Marquis authoritatively, "you 're doocid late, y' know; but then—"

"He can ride," said the Viscount.

"And he's game," nodded the Captain.

"And, therefore," added the Marquis, "we'll see what can be done about it."

"And b'gad, here's wishing you luck!" said the Captain.

At this moment Peterby entered the yard, deep in converse with a slim, gentleman-like person, whose noble cravat immediately attracted the attention of the Marquis.

"By the way," pursued the Captain, "we three are dining together at my club; may I have a cover laid for you, Mr. Beverley?"

"Sir," answered Barnabas, "I thank you, but, owing to—circumstances" —here he cast a downward glance at his neckerchief—"I am unable to accept. But, perhaps, you will, all three of you, favor me to dinner at my house—say, in three days' time?"

The invitation was no sooner given than accepted.

"But," said the Viscount, "I didn't know that you had a place here in town, Bev. Where is it?"

"Why, indeed, now you come to mention it, I haven't the least idea; but, perhaps, my man can tell me."

"Eh—what?" exclaimed the Captain. "Oh, b'gad, he's smoking us!"

"Peterby!"

"Sir?" and having saluted the company, Peterby stood at respectful attention.

"I shall be giving a small dinner in three days' time."

"Certainly, sir."

"At my house, Peterby,—consequently I desire to know its location. Where do I live now, Peterby?"

"Number five, St. James's Square, sir."

"Thank you, Peterby."

"An invaluable fellow, that of yours," laughed the Marquis, as Peterby bowed and turned away.

"Indeed, I begin to think he is, my Lord," answered Barnabas, "and I shall expect you all, at six o'clock, on Friday next." So, having shaken hands again, Captain Slingsby took the arm of the Marquis, and limped off.

Now, when they were alone, the Viscount gazed at Barnabas, chin in hand, and with twinkling eyes.

"My dear Bev," said he, "you can hang me if I know what to make of you. Egad, you're the most incomprehensible fellow alive; you are, upon my soul! If I may ask, what the deuce did it all mean—about this house of yours?"

"Simply that until this moment I wasn't sure if I had one yet."

"But—your fellow—"

"Yes. I sent him out this morning to buy me one."

"To buy you—a house?"

"Yes; also horses and carriages, and many other things, chief among them—a tailor."

The Viscount gasped.

"But—my dear fellow—to leave all that to your—servant! Oh, Gad!"

"But, as the Marquis remarked, Peterby is an inestimable fellow."

The Viscount eyed Barnabas with brows wrinkled in perplexity; then all at once his expression changed.

"By the way," said he, "talking of Carnaby, he's got the most beautiful eye you ever saw!"

"Oh?" said Barnabas, beginning to tuck in the ends of his neckerchief.

"And a devil of a split lip!"

"Oh?" said Barnabas again.

"And his coat had been nearly ripped off him; I saw it under his cape!"

"Ah?" said Barnabas, still busy with his neckcloth.

"And naturally enough," pursued the Viscount, "I've been trying to imagine—yes, Bev, I've been racking my brain most damnably, wondering why you—did it?

"It was in the wood," said Barnabas.

"So it *was* you, then?"

"Yes, Dick."

"But—he didn't even mark you?"

"He lost his temper, Dick."

"You thrashed—Carnaby! Gad, Bev, there isn't a milling cove in England could have done it."

"Yes—there are two—Natty Bell, and Glorious John."

"And I'll warrant he deserved it, Bev."

"I think so," said Barnabas; "it was in the wood, Dick."

"The wood? Ah! do you mean where you—"

"Where I found her lying unconscious."

"Unconscious! And with him beside her! My God, man!" cried the Viscount, with a vicious snap of his teeth. "Why didn't you kill him?"

"Because I was beside her—first, Dick."

"Damn him!" exclaimed the Viscount bitterly.

"But he is your friend, Dick."

"Was, Bev, was! We'll make it in the past tense hereafter."

"Then you agree with your father after all?"

"I do, Bev; my father is a cursed, long-sighted, devilish observant man! I'll back him against anybody, though he is such a Roman. But oh, the devil!" exclaimed the Viscount suddenly, "you can never ride in the race after this."

"Why not?"

"Because you'll meet Carnaby; and that mustn't happen."

"Why not?"

"Because he'll shoot you."

"You mean he'd challenge me? Hum," said Barnabas, "that is awkward! But I can't give up the race."

"Then what shall you do?"

"Risk it, Dick."

But now, Mr. Smivvle, who from an adjoining corner had been an interested spectator thus far, emerged, and flourishing off the curly-brimmed hat, bowed profoundly, and addressed himself to the Viscount.

"I believe," said he, smiling affably, "that I have the pleasure to behold Viscount Devenham?"

"The same, sir," rejoined the Viscount, bowing stiffly.

"You don't remember me, perhaps, my Lord?"

The Viscount regarded the speaker stonily, and shook his head.

"No, I don't, sir."

Mr. Smivvle drew himself up, and made the most of his whiskers.

"My Lord, my name is Smivvle, Digby Smivvle, at your service, though perhaps you don't remember my name, either?"

The Viscount took out his driving gloves and began to put them on.

"No, I don't, sir!" he answered dryly.

Mr. Smivvle felt for his whisker, found it, and smiled.

"Quite so, my Lord, I am but one of the concourse—the multitude—the ah—the herd, though, mark me, my Lord, a Smivvle, sir, —a Smivvle, every inch of me,—while you are the owner of 'Moonraker,' and Moonraker's the word just now, I hear. But, sir, I have a friend—"

"Indeed, sir," said the Viscount, in a tone of faint surprise, and beckoning a passing ostler, ordered out his curricle.

"As I say," repeated Mr. Smivvle, beginning to search for his whisker again, "I have a friend, my Lord—"

"Congratulate you," murmured the Viscount, pulling at his glove.

"A friend who has frequently spoken of your Lordship—"

"Very kind of him!" murmured the Viscount.

"And though, my Lord, though my name is not familiar, I think you will remember his; the name of my friend is "—here Mr. Smivvle, having at length discovered his whisker, gave it a fierce twirl,— "Ronald Barrymaine."

The Viscount's smooth brow remained unclouded, only the glove tore in his fingers; so he smiled, shook his head, and drawing it off, tossed it away.

"Hum?" said he, "I seem to have heard some such name—somewhere or other—ah! there's my Imp at last, as tight and smart as they make 'em, eh, Bev? Well, good-by, my dear fellow, I shan't forget Friday next." So saying, the Viscount shook hands, climbed into his curricle, and, with a flourish of his whip, was off and away in a moment.

"A fine young fellow, that!" exclaimed Mr. Smivvle; "yes, sir, regular out-and-outer, a Bang up! by heaven, a Blood, sir! a Tippy! a Go! a regular Dash! High, sir, high, damned high, like my friend Barrymaine,—indeed, you may have remarked a similarity between 'em, sir?"

"You forget, I have never met your friend," said Barnabas.

"Ah, to be sure, a great pity! You'd like him, for Barrymaine is a cursed fine fellow in spite of the Jews, dammem! yes,—you ought to know my friend, sir."

"I should be glad to," said Barnabas.

"Would you though, would you indeed, sir? Nothing simpler; call a chaise! Stay though, poor Barry's not himself to-day, under a cloud, sir. Youthful prodigalities are apt to bring worries in their train—chiefly in the shape of Jews, sir, and devilish bad shapes too! Better wait a day—say to-morrow, or Thursday—or even Friday would do."

"Let it be Saturday," said Barnabas.

"Saturday by all means, sir, I'll give myself the pleasure of calling upon you."

"St. James's Square," said Barnabas, "number five."

But now Peterby, who had been eyeing Mr. Smivvle very much askance, ventured to step forward.

"Sir," said he, "may I remind you of your appointment?"

"I hadn't forgotten, Peterby; and good day, Mr. Smivvle."

"Au revoir, sir, delighted to have had the happiness. If you *should* chance ever to be in Worcestershire, the Hall is open to you. Good afternoon, sir!" And so, with a prodigious flourish of the hat, Mr. Smivvle bowed, smiled, and swaggered off. Then, as he turned to follow Peterby into the inn, Barnabas must needs pause to glance towards the spot where lay the Viscount's torn glove.

CHAPTER XXVIII

CONCERNING, AMONG OTHER THINGS, THE LEGS OF A GENTLEMAN-IN-POWDER

In that delightful book, "The Arabian Nights' Entertainments," one may read of Spirits good, and bad, and indifferent; of slaves of lamps, of rings and amulets, and talismanic charms; and of the marvels and wonders they performed. But never did Afrit, Djinn, or Genie perform greater miracles than steady-eyed, soft-voiced Peterby. For if the far away Orient has its potent charms and spells, so, in this less romantic Occident, have we also a spell whereby all things are possible, a charm to move mountains—a spell whereby kings become slaves, and slaves, kings; and we call it Money.

Aladdin had his wonderful Lamp, and lo! at the Genie's word, up sprang a palace, and the wilderness blossomed; Barnabas had his overflowing purse, and behold! Peterby went forth, and the dull room at the "George" became a mansion in the midst of Vanity Fair.

Thus, at precisely four o'clock on the afternoon of the third day, Barnabas stood before a cheval mirror in the dressing-room of his new house, surveying his reflection with a certain complacent satisfaction.

His silver-buttoned blue coat, high-waisted and cunningly rolled of collar, was a sartorial triumph; his black stockinette pantaloons, close-fitting from hip to ankle and there looped and buttoned, accentuated muscled calf and virile thigh in a manner somewhat disconcerting; his snowy waistcoat was of an original fashion and cut, and his cravat, folded and caressed into being by Peterby's fingers, was an elaborate masterpiece, a matchless creation never before seen upon the town. Barnabas had become a dandy, from the crown of his curly head to his silk stockings and polished shoes, and, upon the whole, was not ill-pleased with himself.

"But they're—dangerously tight, aren't they, Peterby?" he inquired suddenly, speaking his thought aloud.

"Tight, sir!" repeated Mr. Barry, the tailor, reproachfully, and shaking his gentleman-like head, "impossible, sir,—with such a leg inside 'em."

"Tight, sir?" exclaimed Peterby, from where he knelt upon the floor, having just finished looping and buttoning the garments in question, "indeed, sir, since you mention it, I almost fear they are a trifle too—roomy. Can you raise your bent knee, sir?"

"Only with an effort, John."

"That settles it, Barry," said Peterby with a grim nod, "you must take them in at least a quarter of an inch."

"Take 'em in?" exclaimed Barnabas, aghast, "no, I'll be shot if you do,—not a fraction! I can scarcely manage 'em as it is." Peterby shook his head in grave doubt, but at this juncture they were interrupted by a discreet knock, and the door opening, a Gentleman-in-Powder appeared. He was a languid gentleman, an extremely superior gentleman, but his character lay chiefly in his nose, which was remarkably short and remarkably supercilious of tip, and his legs which were large and nobly shaped; they were, in a sense, eloquent legs, being given to divers tremors and quiverings when their possessor labored under any strong feeling or excitement; but, above all, they were haughty legs, contemptuous of this paltry world and all that therein is, yea, even of themselves, for their very calves seemed striving to turn their backs upon each other.

"Are you in, sir?" he inquired in an utterly impersonal tone.

"In?" repeated Barnabas, with a quick downward glance at his tight nether garments, "in?—in what?—in where?"

"Are you at 'ome, sir?"

"At home? Of course,—can't you see that?"

"Yes, sir," returned the Gentleman-in-Powder, his legs growing a little agitated.

"Then why do you ask?"

"There is a—person below, sir."

"A person?"

"Yes, sir,—very much so! Got 'is foot in the door—wouldn't take it out—had to let 'em in—waiting in the 'all, sir."

"What's he like, who is he?"

"Whiskers, sir,—name of Snivels,—no card!" Here might have been observed the same agitation of the plump legs.

"Ask him to wait."

"Beg pardon, sir—did you say—to wait?" (Agitation growing.)

"Yes. Say I'll be down at once." (Agitation extreme.)

"Meaning as you will—see 'im, sir?" (Agitation indescribable.)

"Yes," said Barnabas, "yes, of course."

The Gentleman-in-Powder bowed; his eye was calm, his brow unruffled, but his legs!!! And his nose was more supercilious than ever as he closed the door upon it.

Mr. Smivvle, meanwhile, was standing downstairs before a mirror, apparently lost in contemplation of his whiskers, and indeed they seemed to afford him a vast degree of pleasure, for he stroked them with caressing fingers, and smiled upon them quite benevolently.

"Six pair of silver candlesticks!" he murmured. "Persian rugs! Bric-a-brac, rare—costly pictures! He's a Nabob, by heaven,—yes he is,—a mysterious young Nabob, wallowing in wealth! Five shillings? —preposterous! we'll make it—ten,—and—yes, shall we say another five for the pampered menial? By all means let us make it another five shillings for the cursed flunkey,—here he comes!"

And indeed, at that moment the legs of the Gentleman-in-Powder might have been descried descending the stair rather more pompously than usual. As soon as they had become stationary, Mr. Smivvle directed a glance at the nearest, and addressed it.

"James!" said he.

The Gentleman-in-Powder became lost in dreamy abstraction, with the exception of his legs which worked slightly. Hereupon Mr. Smivvle reached out and poked him gently with the head of his tasselled cane.

"Awake, James?" said he.

"Name of Harthur—*if* you please, sir!" retorted the Gentleman-in-Powder, brushing away the touch of the cane, and eyeing the place with much concern.

"If, James," continued Mr. Smivvle, belligerent of whisker, "if you would continue to ornament this lordly mansion, James, be more respectful, hereafter, to your master's old and tried friends," saying which Mr. Smivvle gave a twirl to each whisker, and turned to inspect a cabinet of old china.

"Sevres, by George!" he murmured, "we'll make it a pound!" He was still lost in contemplation of the luxurious appointments that everywhere met his view, and was seriously considering the advisability of "making it thirty shillings," when the appearance of Barnabas cut him short, and he at once became all smiles, flourishes and whiskers.

"Ah, Beverley, my boy!" he cried heartily, "pray forgive this horribly unseasonable visit, but—under the circumstances—I felt it my duty to—ah—to drop in on you, my dear fellow."

"What circumstances?" demanded Barnabas, a little stiffly, perhaps.

"Circumstances affecting our friend Barrymaine, sir."

"Ah?" said Barnabas, his tone changing, "what of him? though you forget, Mr. Barrymaine and I are still strangers."

"By heaven, you are right, sir, though, egad! I'm only a little previous,—eh, my dear fellow?" and, smiling engagingly, Mr. Smivvle followed Barnabas into a side room, and shutting the door with elaborate care, immediately shook his whiskers and heaved a profound sigh. "My friend Barrymaine is low, sir,—devilish low," he proceeded to explain, "indeed I'm quite distressed for the poor fellow, 'pon my soul and honor I am,—for he is—in a manner of speaking—in eclipse as it were, sir!"

"I fear I don't understand," said Barnabas.

"Why, then—in plain words, my dear Beverley,—he's suffering from an acute attack of the Jews, dammem!—a positive seizure, sir!"

"Do you mean he has been taken—for debt?"

"Precisely, my dear fellow. An old affair—ages ago—a stab in the dark! Nothing very much, in fact a mere bagatelle, only, as luck will have it, I am damnably short myself just now."

"How much is it?"

"Altogether exactly twenty-five pound ten. An absurd sum, but all my odd cash is on the race. So I ventured here on my young friend's behalf to ask for a trifling loan,—a pound—or say thirty shillings would be something."

Barnabas crossed to a cabinet, unlocked a drawer, and taking thence a smallish bag that jingled, began to count out a certain sum upon the table.

"You said twenty-five pounds ten, I think?" said Barnabas, and pushed that amount across the table. Mr. Smivvle stared from the money to Barnabas and back again, and felt for his whisker with fumbling fingers.

"Sir," he said, "you can't—you don't mean to—to—"

"Yes," said Barnabas, turning to re-lock the drawer. Mr. Smivvle's hand dropped from his whiskers, indeed, for the moment he almost seemed to have forgotten their existence.

"Sir," he stammered, "I cannot allow—no indeed, sir! Mr. Beverley, you overwhelm me—"

"Debts are necessary evils," said Barnabas, "and must be paid." Mr. Smivvle stared at Barnabas, his brow furrowed by perplexity, —stared like one who is suddenly at a loss; and indeed his usual knowing air was quite gone. Then, dropping his gaze to the money on the table, he swept it into his pocket, almost furtively, and took up his hat and cane, and, it is worthy of note, that he did it all without a flourish.

"Mr. Beverley," said he, "in the name of my friend Barrymaine, I thank you, and—I—I thank you!" So he turned and went out of the room, and, as he went, he even forgot to swagger.

Then Barnabas crossed to a mirror, and, once more, fell to studying his reflection with critical eyes, in the midst of which examination he looked up to find Peterby beside him.

"Are you quite satisfied, sir?"

"They are wonderful, John."

"The coat," said Peterby, "y-e-s, the coat will pass well enough, but I have grave doubts as regard the pantaloons."

"I refuse to have 'em touched, John. And Natty Bell was quite right."

"Sir?" said Peterby.

"You don't know Natty Bell as yet, John, but you may; he is a very remarkable man! He told me, I remember, that in Town, a man had his clothes put on for him, and—remembered them,—and so he does,—the difficulty will be ever to forget 'em, they"—here Barnabas stole a glance at his legs—"they positively obtrude themselves, John! Yes, clothes are wonderful things, but I fear they will take a great deal of living up to!"

Here Barnabas drew a long sigh, in the midst of which he was interrupted by the calves of the Gentleman-in-Powder, which presented themselves at the doorway with the announcement:

"Viscount Deafenem, sir!"

Barnabas started and hurried forward, very conscious, very nervous, and for once uncertain of himself by reason of his new and unaccustomed splendor. But the look in the Viscount's boyish eyes, his smiling nod of frank approval, and the warm clasp of his hand, were vastly reassuring.

"Why, Bev, that coat's a marvel!" he exclaimed impulsively, "it is, I swear it is; turn round—so! Gad, what a fit!"

"I hoped you 'd approve of it, Dick," said Barnabas, a little flushed, "you see, I know very little about such things, and—"

"Approve of it! My dear fellow! And the cut!"

"Now—as for these—er—pantaloons, Dick—?"

"Dashing, my dear fellow,—devilish dashing!"

"But rather too—too tight, don't you think?"

"Can't be, Bev, tighter the better,—have 'em made too tight to get into, and you're right; look at mine, if I bend, I split,—deuced uncomfortable but all the mode, and a man must wear something! My fellow has the deuce of a time getting me into 'em, confound 'em. Oh, for ease, give me boots and buckskins!" Hereupon the Viscount having walked round Barnabas three times, and viewed him critically from every angle, nodded with an air of finality. "Yes, they do you infinite credit, my dear fellow,—like everything else;" and he cast a comprehensive glance round the luxurious apartment.

"The credit of it all rests entirely with Peterby," said Barnabas. "John—where are you?" But Peterby had disappeared.

"You're the most incomprehensible fellow, Bev," said the Viscount, seating himself on the edge of the table and swinging his leg. "You have been a constant surprise to me ever since you found me—er—let us say—ruminating in the bilboes, and now"—here he shook his head gravely—"and now it seems you are to become a source of infernal worry and anxiety as well."

"I hope not, Dick."

"You are, though," repeated the Viscount, looking graver than ever.

"Why?"

"Because—well, because you are evidently bent upon dying young."

"How so, Dick?"

"Well, if you ride in the race and don't break your neck, Carnaby will want a word with you; and if he doesn't shoot you, why then Chichester certainly will—next time, damn him!"

"Next time?"

"Oh, I know all about your little affair with him—across the table. Gad, Beverley, what a perfectly reckless fellow you are!"

"But—how do you know of this?"

"From Clemency."

"So you've seen her again, Dick?"

"Yes, of course; that is, I took 'Moonraker' for a gallop yesterday, and—happened to be that way."

"Ah!" said Barnabas.

"And she told me—everything," said the Viscount, beginning to stride up and down the room, with his usual placidity quite gone, "I mean about—about the button you found, it was that devil Chichester's it seems, and—and—Beverley, give me your hand! She told me how you confronted the fellow. Ha! I'll swear you had him shaking in his villain's shoes, duellist as he is."

"But," said Barnabas, as the Viscount caught his hand, "it was not altogether on Clemency's account, Dick."

"No matter, you frightened the fellow off. Oh, I know—she told me; I made her! She had to fight with the beast, that's how he lost his button. I tell you, if ever I get the chance at him, he or I shall get his quietus. By God, Bev, I'm half-minded to send the brute a challenge, as it is."

"Because of Clemency, Dick?"

"Well—and why not?"

"The Earl of Bamborough's son fight a duel over the chambermaid of a hedge tavern!"

The Viscount's handsome face grew suddenly red, and as suddenly pale again, and his eyes glowed as he fronted Barnabas across the hearth.

"Mr. Beverley," said he very quietly, "how am I to take that?"

"In friendship, Dick, for the truth of it is that—though she is as brave, as pure, as beautiful as any lady in the land, she is a chambermaid none the less."

The Viscount turned, and striding to the window stood there, looking out with bent head.

"Have I offended you?" inquired Barnabas.

"You go—too far, Beverley."

"I would go farther yet for my friend, Viscount, or for our Lady Cleone."

Now when Barnabas said this, the Viscount's head drooped lower yet, and he stood silent. Then, all at once, he turned, and coming to the hearth, the two stood looking at each other.

"Yes, I believe you would, Beverley. But you have a way of jumping to conclusions that is—devilish disconcerting. As for Chichester, the world would be well rid of him. And, talking of him, I met another rascal as I came—I mean that fellow Smivvle; had he been here?"

"Yes."

"Begging, I suppose?"

"He borrowed some money for his friend Barrymaine."

The Viscount flushed hotly, and looked at Barnabas with a sudden frown.

"Perhaps you are unaware, that is a name I never allow spoken in my presence, Mr. Beverley."

"Indeed, Viscount, and pray, why not?"

"For one thing, because he is—what he is—"

"Lady Cleone's brother."

"Half-brother, sir, and none the less a—knave."

"How—?"

"I mean that he is a card-sharper, a common cheat."

"Her brother—?"

"Half-brother!"

"A cheat! Are you sure?"

"Certain! I had the misfortune to make the discovery. And it killed him in London, all the clubs shut their doors upon him of course, he was cut in the streets,—it is damning to be seen in his company or even to mention his name—now."

"And you—you exposed him?"

"I said I made the discovery; but I kept it to myself. The stakes were unusually high that night, and we played late. I went home with him, but Chichester was there, waiting for him. So I took him aside, and, in as friendly a spirit as I could, told him of my discovery. He broke down, and, never attempting a denial, offered restitution and promised amendment. I gave my word to keep silent and, on one pretext or another, the loser's money was returned. But next week, the whole town hummed with the news. One night—it was at White's—he confronted me, and—he gave me—the lie!" The Viscount's fists were tight clenched, and he stared down blindly at the floor. "And, sir, though you'll scarcely credit it of course, I—there, before them all—I took it."

"Of course," said Barnabas, "for Her sake."

"Beverley!" exclaimed the Viscount, looking up with a sudden light in his eyes. "Oh, Bev!" and their hands met and gripped.

"You couldn't do anything else, Dick."

"No, Bev, no, but I'm glad you understand. Later it got about that I—that I was—afraid of the fellow—he's a dead shot, they say, young as he is—and—well, it—it wasn't pleasant, Bev. Indeed it got worse until I called out one of Chichester's friends, and winged him—a fellow named Dalton."

"I think I've seen him," said Barnabas, nodding.

"Anyhow, Barrymaine was utterly discredited and done for—he's an outcast, and to be seen with him, or his friends, is to be damned also."

"And yet," said Barnabas, sighing and shaking his head, "I must call upon him to-morrow."

"Call upon him! Man—are you mad?"

"No; but he is her brother, and—"

"And, as I tell you, he is banned by society as a cheat!"

"And is that so great a sin, Dick?"

"Are there any—worse?"

"Oh, yes; one might kill a man in a duel, or dishonor a trusting woman, or blast a man's character; indeed it seems to me that there are many greater sins!"

The Viscount dropped back in his chair, and stared at Barnabas with horrified eyes.

"My—dear—Beverley," said he at last, "are you—serious?"

"My dear Viscount—of course I am."

"Then let me warn you, such views will never do here: any one holding such views will never succeed in London."

"Yet I mean to try," said Barnabas, squaring his jaw.

"But why," said the Viscount, impatiently, "why trouble yourself about such a fellow?"

"Because She loves him, and because She asked me to help him."

"She asked—you to?"

"Yes."

"And—do you think you can?"

"I shall try."

"How?"

"First, by freeing him from debt."

"Do you know him—have you ever met him?"

"No, Dick, but I love his sister."

"And because of this, you'd shoulder his debts? Ah, but you can't, and if you ask me why, I tell you, because Jasper Gaunt has got him, and means to keep him. To my knowledge Barrymaine has twice had the money to liquidate his debt—but Gaunt has put him off, on one pretext or another, until the money has all slipped away. I tell you, Bev, Jasper Gaunt has got him in his clutches—as he's got Sling, and poor George Danby, and—God knows how many more—as he'd get me if he could, damn him! Yes, Gaunt has got his claws into him, and he'll never let him go again—never."

"Then," said Barnabas, "I must see Jasper Gaunt as soon as may be."

"Oh, by all means," nodded the Viscount, "if you have a taste for snakes, and spiders, and vermin of that sort, Slingsby will show you where to find him—Slingsby knows his den well enough, poor old Sling! But look to yourself, for spiders sting and snakes bite, and Jasper Gaunt does both."

The knuckles of the Gentleman-in-Powder here made themselves heard, and thereafter the door opened to admit his calves, which were immediately eclipsed by the Marquis, who appeared to be in a state of unwonted hurry.

"What, have I beat Slingsby, then?" he inquired, glancing round the room, "he was close behind me in Piccadilly—must have had a spill—that's the worst of those high curricles. As a matter of fact," he proceeded to explain, "I rushed round here—that is we both did, but I've got here first, to tell you that—Oh, dooce take me!" and out came the Marquis's eyeglass. "Positively you must excuse me, my dear Beverley. Thought I knew 'em all, but no—damme if I ever saw the fellow to yours! Permit me!" Saying which the Marquis gently led Barnabas to the window, and began to study his cravat with the most profound interest.

"By George, Devenham," he exclaimed suddenly,—"it's new!"

"Gad!" said the Viscount, "now you come to mention it,—so it is!"

"Positively—new!" repeated the Marquis in an awestruck voice, staring at the Viscount wide-eyed. "D'you grasp the importance of this, Devenham?—d'you see the possibilities, Dick? It will create a sensation,—it will set all the clubs by the ears, by George! We shall have the Prince galloping up from Brighton. By heaven, it's stupendous! Permit me, my dear Beverley. See—here we have three folds and a tuck, then—oh, Jupiter, it's a positive work of art, —how the deuce d'you tie it? Never saw anything approaching this, and I've tried 'em all,—the Mail-coach, the Trone d'Amour, the Osbaldistone, the Napoleon, the Irish tie, the Mathematical tie, and the Oriental,—no, 'pon my honor it's unique, it's—it's—" the Marquis sighed, shook his head, and words failing him, took out his enamelled snuff-box. "Sir," said he, "I have the very highest regard for a man of refined taste, and if there is one thing in which that manifests itself more than another, it is the cravat. Sir, I make you free of my box, pray honor me." And the Marquis flicked open his snuff-box and extended it towards Barnabas with a bow.

"My Lord," said Barnabas, shaking his head, "I appreciate the honor you do me, but pray excuse me,—I never take it."

"No?" said the Marquis with raised brows, "you astonish me; but then—between ourselves—neither do I. Can't bear the infernal stuff. Makes me sneeze most damnably. And then, it has such a cursed way of blowing about! Still, one must conform to fashion, and—"

"Captain Slingsby!"

The Gentleman-in-Powder had scarcely articulated the words, when the Captain had gripped Barnabas by the hand.

"Congratulate you, Beverley, heartily."

"Thank you, but why?" inquired Barnabas.

"Eh—what? Hasn't Jerningham told you? B'gad, is it possible you don't know—"

"Why, dooce take me, Sling, if I didn't forget!" said the Marquis, clapping hand to thigh, "but his cravat put everything else out of my nob, and small wonder either! You tell him."

"No," answered the Captain. "I upset a cursed apple-stall on my way here—you got in first—tell him yourself."

"Why, then, Beverley," said the Marquis, extending his hand, in his turn, as he spoke, "we have pleasure, Sling and I, to tell you that you are entered for the race on the fifteenth."

"The race!" exclaimed Barnabas, flushing. "You mean I'm to ride then?"

"Yes," nodded the Captain, "but b'gad! we mean more than that, we mean that you are one of us, that Devenham's friend must be ours because he's game—"

"And can ride," said the Viscount.

"And is a man of taste," added the Marquis.

Thus it was as one in a dream that Barnabas beheld the legs of the Gentleman-in-Powder, and heard the words:

"Dinner is served, gentlemen!"

But scarcely had they taken their places at the table when the Marquis rose, his brimming glass in his hand.

"Mr. Beverley," said he, bowing, "when Devenham, Slingsby, and I meet at table, it is our invariable custom to drink to one whom we all—hum—"

"Admire!" said the Viscount, rising.

"Adore!" said the Captain, rising also.

"Therefore, gentlemen," pursued the Marquis, "with our host's permission, we will—"

"Stay a moment, Jerningham," said the Viscount,—"it is only right to tell you that my friend Beverley is one with us in this,—he also is a suitor for the hand of Lady Cleone."

"Is he, b'gad!" exclaimed the Captain. "Dooce take me!" said the Marquis, "might have known it though. Ah, well! one more or less makes small difference among so many."

So Barnabas rose, and lifting his glass with the others, drank to—

"Our Lady Cleone—God bless her!"

CHAPTER XXIX

WHICH DESCRIBES SOMETHING OF THE MISFORTUNES OF RONALD BARRYMAINE

Holborn was in full song,—a rumbling, roaring melody, a clattering, rushing, blaring symphony made up of the grind of wheels upon resounding cobble-stones, the thudding beat of horse-hoofs, the tread of countless feet, the shrill note of voices; it was all there, the bass and the treble blending together, harsh, discordant, yet the real symphony of life.

And, amidst it all, of it all, came Barnabas, eager-eyed, forgetful of his companion, lost to all but the stir and bustle, the rush and roar of the wonderful city about him. The which Mr. Smivvle duly remarked from under the curly-brimmed hat, but was uncommonly silent. Indeed, though his hat was at its usual rakish angle, though he swung his cane and strode with all his ordinary devil-may-care swagger, though his whiskers were as self-assertive as ever, yet Mr. Smivvle himself was unusually pensive, and in his bold black eyes was a look very like anxiety. But in a while, as they turned out of the rush of Holborn Hill, he sighed, threw back his shoulders, and spoke.

"Nearly there now, my dear fellow, this is the Garden."

"Garden?" said Barnabas, glancing about. "Where?"

"Here, sir; we're in it,—Hatton Garden. Charmingly rustic spot, you'll observe, delightfully rural retreat! Famous for strawberries once, I believe,—flowers too, of course. Talking of flowers, sir, a few of 'em still left to—ah—blush unseen? I'm one, Barrymaine's another—a violet? No. A lily? No. A blush-rose? Well, let us say a blush-rose, but damnably run to seed, like the rest of us. And—ah—talking of Barrymaine, I ought, perhaps, to warn you that we may find him a trifle—queer—a leetle touched perhaps." And Mr. Smivvle raised an invisible glass, and tossed down its imaginary contents with an expression of much beatitude.

"Is he given to—that sort of thing?"

"Sir," said Mr. Smivvle, "can you blame one who seeks forgetfulness in the flowing bowl—and my friend Barry has very much to forget—can you blame him?"

"No, poor fellow!"

"Sir, allow me to tell you my friend Barry needs no man's pity, though I confess I could wish Chichester was not quite so generous—in one respect."

"How?"

"In—ah—in keeping the flowing bowl continually brimming, my dear fellow."

"Is Mr. Chichester a friend of his?"

"The only one, with the exception of yours obediently, who has not deserted him in his adversity."

"Why?"

"Because, well,—between you and me, my dear fellow, I believe his regard for Barry's half-sister, the Lady Cleone, is largely accountable in Chichester's case; as for myself, because, as I think I mentioned, the hand of a Smivvle once given, sir, is never withdrawn, either on account of plague, poverty, pestilence, or Jews, —dammem! This way, my dear fellow!" and turning into Cross Street, up towards Leather Lane, Mr. Smivvle halted at a certain dingy door, opened it, and showed Barnabas into a dingier hall, and so, leading the way up the dingiest stairs in the world, eventually ushered him into a fair-sized, though dingy, room; and being entered, immediately stood upon tip-toe and laid a finger on his lips.

"Hush! the poor fellow's asleep, but you'll excuse him, I know."

Barnabas nodded, and, softly approaching the couch, looked down upon the sleeper, and, with the look, felt his heart leap.

A young face he saw, delicately featured, a handsome face with disdainful lips that yet drooped in pitiful weariness, a face which, for all its youth, was marred by the indelible traces of fierce, ungoverned passions. And gazing down upon these features, so dissimilar in expression, yet so strangely like in their beauty and lofty pride, Barnabas felt his heart leap,—because of the long lashes that curled so black against the waxen pallor of the cheek; for in that moment he almost seemed to be back in the green, morning freshness of Annersley Wood, and upon his lips there breathed a name—"Cleone."

But all at once the sleeper stirred, frowned, and started up with a bitter imprecation upon his lips that ended in a vacant stare.

"Why, Barry," cried Mr. Smivvle leaning over him, "my dear boy, did we disturb you?"

"Ah, Dig—is that you? Fell asleep—brandy, perhaps, and—ha,—your pardon, sir!" and Ronald Barrymaine rose, somewhat unsteadily, and, folding his threadbare dressing-gown about him, bowed, and so stood facing Barnabas, a little drunk and very stately.

"This is my friend Beverley, of whom I told you," Mr. Smivvle hastened to explain. "Mr. Barnabas Beverley,—Mr. Ronald Barrymaine."

"You are—welcome, sir," said Mr. Barrymaine, speaking with elaborate care, as if to make quite sure of his utterance. "Pray be seated, Mr. Bev'ley. We—we are a little crowded I f-fear. Move those boots off the chair, Dig. Indeed my apartment might be a little more commodious, but it's all I have at p-present, and by God!" he cried, suddenly fierce, "I shouldn't have even this but for Dig here! Dig's the only f-friend I have in the world—except Chichester. Push the brandy over, Dig. Of course there's—Cleone, but she's only a sister, after all. Don't know what I should do if it wasn't for Dig—d-do I, Dig? And Chichester of course. Give Mr. Bev'ley a chair. Dig. I'll get him—glass!" Hereupon Mr. Smivvle hurried forward with a chair which, like all the rest of the furniture, had long ago seen its best days, during which manoeuvre he contrived to whisper hurriedly:

"Poor Barry's decidedly 'touched' to-day, a little more so than usual, but you'll excuse him I know, my dear fellow. Hush!" for Barrymaine, who had crossed to the other end of the room, now turned and came towards them, swaying a little, and with a glass in his hand.

"It's rickety, sir, you'll notice," said he, nodding. "I—I mean that chair—dev'lish rickety, like everything else 'bout here—especially myself, eh, Dig? B-but don't be alarmed, it—will bear you, sir. D-devil of a place to ask—gentleman to sit down in, —but the Spanswick hasn't been round to clean the place this week—damn her! S-scarcely blame her, though—never gets paid—except when Dig remembers it. Don't know what I should do without D-Dig,—raised twenty pounds yesterday, damme if I know where! said it was watch—but watch went weeks ago. Couldn't ever pay the Spanswick. That's the accursed part of it—pay, pay! debt on debt, and—n-nothing to pay with. All swallowed up by that merciless bloodsucker—that—"

"Now, Barry!" Mr. Smivvle expostulated, "my dear boy—"

"He's a cursed v-vampire, I tell you!" retorted Barrymaine, his pale cheeks suddenly flushed, and his dark eyes flashing in swift passion, —"he's a snake."

"Now, my dear fellow, calm yourself."

"Calm myself. How can I, when everything I have is his, when everything I g-get belongs to him before—curse him—even before I get it! I tell you, Dig, he's—he's draining my life away, drop by drop! He's g-got me down with his foot on my neck—crushing me into the mud. I say he's stamping me down into hell—damn him!"

"Restrain yourself, Barry, my dear boy, remember Mr. Beverley is our guest—"

"Restrain myself—yes, Dig, yes. B-beg Mr. Beverley's pardon for me, Dig. Not myself to-day,—but must restrain myself—certainly. Give me some more brandy—ha! and pass bottle to Mr. Bev'ley, Dig. No, sir? Ah well, help yourself, Dig. Must forgive exhibition of feeling, sir, but I always do get carried away when I remember that inhuman monster—God's curse on him!"

"Sir," said Barnabas, "whom do you mean?"

"Mean? ha! ha! oh damme, hark to that, Dig! Dev'lish witty I call that—oh c-cursed rich! Whom do I mean? Why," cried Barrymaine, starting up from the couch, "whom should I mean but Gaunt! Gaunt! Gaunt!" and he shook his clenched fists passionately in the air. Then, as suddenly he turned upon Barnabas with a wild, despairing gesture, and stretching out his arms, pointed to each wrist in turn. "D'ye see 'em?" he cried, "d'ye hear 'em; jangle? No? Ah, but they *are* there! riveted on, never to come off, eating deeper into my flesh every day! I'm shackled, I tell you,—fettered hand and foot. Oh! egad, I'm an object lesson!—point a moral and adorn a tale, —beware of p-prodigality and m-money lenders. Shackled—shackled hand and foot, and must drag my chain until I f-fall into a debtor's grave."

"No!" cried Barnabas, so suddenly that Ronald Barrymaine started, and thereafter grew very high and haughty.

"Sir," said he with upflung head, "I don't permit my word to be—to be—contra—dicted,—never did and never will. Though you see before you a m-miserable wretch, yet that wretch is still a gentleman at heart, and that wretch tells you again he's shackled, sir, hand and foot—yes, damme, and so I am!"

"Well then," said Barnabas, "why not free yourself?"

Ronald Barrymaine sank down upon the couch, looked at Barnabas, looked at Smivvle, drained his glass and shook his head.

"My dear Dig," said he, "your friend's either mad or drunk—mos' probably drunk. Yes, that's it,—or else he's smoking me, and I won't be smoked, no man shall laugh at me now that I'm down. Show him the door, Dig. I—I won't have my private affairs discussed by s-strangers, no, by heaven!"

"Now, Barry," exclaimed Mr. Smivvle, "do be calm, Mr. Beverley only wants to help you—er—that is, in a friendly way, of course, and I 'm sure—"

"Damn his help! I'd rather die in the g-gutter than ask help or charity of any one."

"Yes, yes—of course, my dear fellow! But you're so touchy, Barry, so infernally proud, my dear boy. Mr. Beverley merely wishes to—"

"Be honored with your friendship," said Barnabas with his ingenuous smile.

"Why then, Dig," says his youthful Mightiness, beginning to relent, "pray beg Mr. Bev'ley's pardon for me again, and 'sure him the honor is mine."

"And I would have you trust me also," Barnabas pursued.

"Trust you?" repeated Barrymaine with a sudden laugh. "Gad, yes, willingly! Only it happens I've n-noth-ing left to trust you with, —no, not enough to pay the Spanswick."

"And yet, if you will, you may be free," said Barnabas the persistent.

"Free! He's at it again, Dig."

"Believe me it is my earnest desire to help you,—to—"

"Help me, sir! a stranger! by heaven,—no! A stranger, damme!"

"Let us say your friend."

"I tell you, sir," said Barrymaine, starting up unsteadily, "I seek no man's aid—s-scorn it! I'm not one to weep out my misfortunes to strangers. Damme, I'm man enough to manage my own affairs, what's left of 'em. I want nobody's accursed pity either—pah!" and he made a gesture of repudiation so fierce that he staggered and recovered himself only by clutching at Mr. Smivvle's ready arm. "The Past, sir," said he, supporting himself by that trusty arm, "the Past is done with, and the F-Future I'll face alone, as I have done all along, eh, Dig?"

"But surely—"

"Ay, surely, sir, I'm no object of charity whining for alms, no, by Gad! I—I'm—Dig, push the brandy!"

"If you would but listen—" Barnabas began again.

"Not—not a word. Why should I? Past's dead, and damn the Future. Dig, pass the brandy."

"And I tell you," said Barnabas, "that in the future are hope and the chance of a new life, once you are free of Gaunt."

"Free of Gaunt! Hark to that, Dig. Must be dev'lish drunk to talk such cursed f-folly! Why, I tell you again," he cried in rising passion, "that I couldn't get free of Gaunt's talons even if I had the money, and mine's all gone long ago, and half Cleone's beside, —her Guardian's tied up the rest. She can't touch another penny without his consent, damn him!—so I'm done. The future? In the future is a debtor's prison that opens for me whenever Jasper Gaunt says the word. Hope? There can be no hope for me till Jasper Gaunt's dead and shrieking in hell-fire."

"But your debts shall be paid,—if you will."

"Paid? Who—who's to pay 'em?"

"I will."

"You!—you?"

"Yes," nodded Barnabas, "on a condition."

Ronald Barrymaine sank back upon the couch, staring at Barnabas with eyes wide and with parted lips; then, leaned suddenly forward, sobered by surprise.

"Ah-h!" said he slowly. "I think I begin to understand. You have seen my—my sister."

"Yes."

"Do you know—how much I owe?"

"No, but I'll pay it,—on a condition."

"A condition?" For a long moment the passionate dark eyes met and questioned the steady gray; then Barrymaine's long lashes fluttered and fell.

"Of course it would be a loan. I—I'd pay you back," he muttered.

"At your own convenience."

"And you would advance the money at once?"

"On a condition!"

Once again their eyes met, and once again Barrymaine's dropped; his fingers clenched and unclenched themselves, he stirred restlessly, and, finally, spoke.

"And your condition. Is it—Cleone?"

"No!" said Barnabas vehemently.

"Then, what is it?"

"That from this hour you give up brandy and Mr. Chichester—both evil things."

"Well, and what more,—what—for yourself? How can this benefit you? Come, speak out,—what is your real motive?"

"The hope that you may, some day, be worthy of your sister's love."

"Worthy, sir!" exclaimed Barrymaine, flushing angrily. "Poverty is no crime!"

"No; but there remain brandy and Mr. Chichester."

"Ha! would you insult m-my friend?"

"Impossible. You have no friend, unless it be Mr. Smivvle here."

"Now by heaven," began Barrymaine passionately, "I tell you—"

"And I tell you that these are my only conditions," said Barnabas. "Accept them and you may begin a new life. It is in your power to become the man you might be, to regain the place in men's esteem that you have lost, for if you are but sufficiently determined, nothing is impossible."

Now as he spoke, Barnabas beheld Barrymaine's drooping head uplifted, his curving back grew straight, and a new light sprang into his eyes.

"A new life," he muttered, "to come back to it all, to outface them all after their cursed sneers and slights! Are you sure you don't promise too much,—are you sure it's not too late?"

"Sure and certain!" said Barnabas. "But remember the chance of salvation rests only with and by yourself, after all," and he pointed to the half-emptied bottle. "Do you agree to my conditions?"

"Yes, yes, by God I do!"

"Then, friend, give me your hand. To-day I go to see Jasper Gaunt."

So Ronald Barrymaine, standing square upon his feet, gave Barnabas his hand. But even in that moment Barnabas was conscious that the door had opened softly behind him, saw the light fade out of Barrymaine's eyes, felt the hand grow soft and lax, and turning about, beheld Mr. Chichester smiling at them from the threshold.

CHAPTER XXX

IN WHICH RONALD BARRYMAINE MAKES HIS CHOICE

There was a moment of strained silence, then, as Barnabas sank back on the rickety chair, Mr. Chichester laughed softly, and stepped into the room.

"Salvation, was it, and a new life?" he inquired, "are you the one to be saved, Ronald, or Smivvle here, or both?"

Ronald Barrymaine was dumb, his eyes sought the floor, and his pale cheek became, all at once, suffused with a burning, vivid scarlet.

"I couldn't help but overhear as I came upstairs," pursued Mr. Chichester pleasantly, "and devilish dark stairs they are—"

"Though excellent for eavesdropping, it appears!" added Barnabas.

"What?" cried Barrymaine, starting up, "listening, were you—s-spying on me—is that your game, Chichester?" But hereupon Mr. Smivvle started forward.

"Now, my dear Barry," he remonstrated, "be calm—"

"Calm? I tell you nobody's going to spy on me,—no, by heaven! neither you, nor Chichester, nor the d-devil himself—"

"Certainly not, my dear fellow," answered Mr. Smivvle, drawing Barrymaine's clenched fist through his arm and holding it there, "nobody wants to. And, as for you, Chichester—couldn't come at a better time—let me introduce our friend Mr. Beverley—"

"Thank you, Smivvle, but we've met before," said Mr. Chichester dryly, "last time he posed as Rustic Virtue in homespun, to-day it seems he is the Good Samaritan in a flowered waistcoat, very anxiously bent on saving some one or other—conditionally, of course!"

"And what the devil has it to do with you?" cried Barrymaine passionately.

"Nothing, my dear boy, nothing in the world,—except that until to-day you have been my friend, and have honored me with your confidence."

"Yes, by heavens! So I have—utterly—utterly,—and what I haven't told you—y-you've found out for yourself—though God knows how. N-not that I've anything to f-fear,—not I!"

"Of course not," smiled Mr. Chichester, "I am—your friend, Ronald, —and I think you will always remember that." Mr. Chichester's tone was soothing, and the pat he bestowed upon Barrymaine's drooping shoulder was gentle as a caress, yet Barrymaine flinched and drew away, and the hand he stretched out towards the bottle was trembling all at once.

"Yes," Mr. Chichester repeated more softly than before, "yes, I am your friend, Ronald, you must always remember that, and indeed I—fancy—you always will." So saying, Mr. Chichester patted the drooping shoulder again, and turned to lay aside his hat and cane. Barrymaine was silent, but into his eyes had crept a look—such a look as Barnabas had never seen—such a look as Barnabas could never afterwards forget; then Barrymaine stooped to reach for the bottle.

"Well," said he, without looking up again, "s-suppose you are my friend,—what then?"

"Why, then, my dear fellow, hearing you are to be saved—on a condition—I am, naturally enough, anxious to know what that condition may be?"

"Sir," said Barnabas, "let me hasten to set your anxiety at rest. My condition is merely that Mr. Barrymaine gives up two evil things—namely, brandy and yourself."

And now there fell a silence so utter that Barnabas could distinctly hear the tick of Natty Bell's great watch in his fob; a silence in which Mr. Smivvle stared with wide-eyed dismay, while Barrymaine sat motionless with his glass half-way to his lips. Then Mr. Chichester laughed again, but the scar glowed upon his pallid cheek, and the lurking demon peeped out of his narrowed eyes.

"And for this," said he, shaking his head in gentle disbelief, "for this our young Good Samaritan is positively eager to pay twenty thousand odd pounds--"

"As a loan," muttered Barrymaine, "it would be only a loan, and I—I should be free of Jasper Gaunt f-for good and all, damn him!"

"Let us rather say you would try a change of masters—"

"Now—by God—Chichester—!"

"Ah!—ah, to be sure, Ronald, our young Good Samaritan having purchased the brother, would naturally expect the sister—"

"Have a c-care, Chichester, I say!"

"The sister to be grateful, my dear boy. Pah! don't you see it, Ronald? a sprat to catch a whale! The brother saved, the sister's gratitude gained—Oh, most disinterested, young Good Samaritan!"

"Ha! by heaven, I never thought of that!" cried Barrymaine, turning upon Barnabas, "is it Cleone—is it? is it?"

"No," said Barnabas, folding his arms—a little ostentatiously, "I seek only to be your friend in this."

"Friend!" exclaimed Mr. Chichester, laughing again, "friend, Ronald? Nay, let us rather say your guardian angel in cords and Hessians."

"Since you condescend to mention my boots, sir," said Barnabas growing polite, "may I humbly beg you to notice that, in spite of their polish and tassels, they are as strong, as serviceable for kicking purposes as those I wore when we last—sat at table together."

Mr. Chichester's iron self-control wavered for a moment, his brows twitched together, and he turned upon Barnabas with threatening gesture but, reading the purpose in the calm eye and smiling lip of Barnabas, he restrained himself; yet seeming aware of the glowing mark upon his cheek, he turned suddenly and, coming to the dingy casement, stood with his back to the room, staring down into the dingy street. Then Barnabas leaned forward and laid his hand upon Barrymaine's, and it so happened it was the hand that yet held the slopping wineglass.

"Think—think!" said Barnabas earnestly, "once you are free of Gaunt, life will begin afresh for you, you can hold up your head again—"

"Though never in London, Ronald, I fear," added Mr. Chichester over his shoulder.

"Once free of Gaunt, you may attain to higher things than you ever did," said Barnabas.

"Unless the dead past should happen to come to life again, and find a voice some day," added Mr. Chichester over his shoulder.

"No, no!" said Barnabas, feeling the quiver of the fingers within his own, "I tell you it would mean a new beginning—a new life—a new ending for you—"

"And for Cleone!" added Mr. Chichester over his shoulder, "our young, disinterested Good Samaritan knows she is too proud to permit a stranger to shoulder her brother's responsibilities—"

"Proud, eh?" cried Barrymaine, leaping up in sudden boyish passion, "well, am I not proud? Did you ever know me anything else—did you?"

"Never, my dear Ronald," cried Mr. Chichester, turning at last. "You are unfortunate, but you have always met disaster—so far, with the fortitude of a gentleman, scorning your detractors and—abominating charity."

"C-charity! damn you, Chichester, d' ye think I-I'd accept any man's c-charity? D' you think I'd ever drag Cleone to that depth—do you?"

"Never, Barrymaine, never, I swear."

"Why then—leave me alone, I can m-manage my own affairs—" "Perfectly, my dear fellow, I am sure of it."

"Then sir," said Barnabas, rising, "seeing it really is no concern of yours, after all, suppose you cease to trouble yourself any further in the matter, and allow Mr. Barrymaine to choose for himself—"

"I—I have decided!" cried Barrymaine, "and I tell you—"

"Wait!" said Barnabas.

"Speak!" said Mr. Chichester.

"Wait!" repeated Barnabas, "Mr. Chichester is—going, I think. Let us wait until we are alone." Then, bowing to Mr. Chichester, Barnabas opened the door wide. "Sir," said he, "may I venture to suggest that your presence is—not at all necessary?"

"Ah!" said Mr. Chichester, "you will certainly compel me to kill you, some day."

"'Sufficient unto the day,' sir!" Barnabas retorted; "in the meantime I shall most certainly give myself the pleasure of kicking you downstairs unless you choose to walk—at once."

As he spoke, Barnabas took a stride towards Mr. Chichester's rigid figure, but, in that moment, Barrymaine snatched up the bottle and sprang between them.

"Ah!—would you?" he cried, "who are you to order my f-friends about—and in m-my own place too! Ha! did you think you could buy me, d-did you? Did you think I—I'd sacrifice my sister—did you? Ha! drunk, am I? Well, I'm sober enough to—to 'venge my honor and hers; by God I'll kill you! Ah—let go, Dig! Let go, I say! Didn't you hear? Tempt me with his cursed money, will he! Oh, let go my arm! Damn him, I say—I'll kill him!"

But, as he struck, Mr. Smivvle caught his wrist, the bottle crashed splintering to the floor, and they were locked in a fierce grapple.

"Beverley—my dear fellow—go!" panted Mr. Smivvle, "must forgive—poor Barry—not himself. Go—go,—I can—manage him. Now Barry, do be calm! Go, my dear fellow—leave him to me—go!" So, perforce, Barnabas turned away and went down the dingy stairs, and in his ears was the echo of the boy's drunken ravings and Mr. Chichester's soft laughter.

And presently, being come into the dingy street, Barnabas paused to look up at the dingy house, and looking, sighed.

"She said it would be 'difficult, and dangerous, perhaps,'" said he to himself, "and indeed I think she was right."

Then he turned and went upon his way, heavy-footed and chin on breast. On he went, plunged in gloomy abstraction, turning corners at random, lost to all but the problem he had set himself, which was this:

How he might save Ronald Barrymaine in spite of Ronald Barrymaine.

CHAPTER XXXI

WHICH DESCRIBES SOME OF THE EVILS OF VINDICTIVENESS

Barnabas stumbled suddenly, dropped his cane, saw his hat spin through the air and roll on before him; staggered sideways, was brought up by a wall, and turning, found three men about him, —evil-faced men whose every move and look held a menace. A darting hand snatched at his fob-seals, but Barnabas smote, swift and hard, and the three were reduced, for the moment, to two. Thus with his back to the wall stood Barnabas, fists clenched, grim of mouth, and with eyes quick and bright; wherefore, beholding him in this posture, his assailants hesitated. But the diamonds sparkled at them from his cravat, the bunch of seals gleamed at them from his fob, and the fallen man having risen, albeit unsteadily, they began to close in upon him. Then, all at once, even as he poised himself to meet their rush, a distant voice uttered a sharp, warning cry, whereat the three, spattering curses, incontinent took to their heels, and were gone with a thud of flying feet.

For a moment Barnabas stood dazed by the suddenness of it all, then, stooping to recover hat and cane, glanced about, and saw that he was in a dirty, narrow street, or rather alley. Now up this alley a man was approaching, very deliberately, for as he came, he appeared to be perusing a small book. He was a short, broad-shouldered man, a mild-faced man of a sober habit of dress, with a broad-brimmed hat upon his head—a hat higher in the crown than was the custom, and a remarkably nobbly stick beneath his arm; otherwise, and in all respects, he was a very ordinary-looking man indeed, and as he walked, book in hand, might have been some small tradesman busily casting up his profit and loss, albeit he had a bright and roving eye.

Being come up with Barnabas, he stopped, closed his book upon his finger, touched the broad rim of his hat, and looked at Barnabas, or to be exact, at the third left-hand button of his coat.

"Anything stole, sir?" he inquired hopefully.

"No," answered Barnabas, "no, I think not."

"Ah, then you won't be vantin' to mek a charge ag'in 'em, sir?"

"No,—besides, they've escaped."

"Escaped, Lord no, sir, they've only run avay, I can allus put my 'ooks on 'em,—I spotted 'em, d'ye see. And I know 'em, Lord love you! —like a feyther! They vas Bunty Fagan, Dancin' James, and Vistlin' Dick, two buzmen an' a prig."

"What do you mean?" inquired Barnabas, beginning to eye the man askance for all his obtrusive mildness.

"I means two pickpockets and a thief, sir. It vas Vistlin' Dick as you give such a 'leveller' to,—a rare pretty knock-down I vill say, sir,—never saw a cleaner—Oh! they're a bad lot, they are, 'specially Vistlin' Dick, an' it's lucky for you as I 'appened to come this vay."

"Why, do you mean to say," said Barnabas, staring at the mild-faced man, "do you want me to believe that it was the sight of you that sent them running?"

"Vell, there veren't nobody else to, as I could see, sir," said the man, with a gentle smile and shake of the head. "Volks ain't partial to me in these yere parts, and as to them three, they're a bad lot, they are, but Vistlin' Dick's the vorst—mark my vords, 'e'll come to be topped yet."

"What do you mean by 'topped'?"

"V'y, I means scragged, sir," answered the man, his roving eye glancing continually up and down the alley,

"I means 'anged, sir,—Lord love you, it's in 'is face—never see a more promising mug, consequent, I 've got Vistlin' Dick down in my little book 'ere, along vith a lot of other promising vuns."

"But why in your book?"

"Veil, d' ye see, I keeps a record of all the likely coves, Capital Coves as you might call 'em—" Here the mild man jerked his head convulsively to one side, rolled up his eyes, and protruded his tongue, all in hideous pantomime, and was immediately his placid self again.

"Ah! you mean—hanged?" said Barnabas.

"As ever vas, sir, capital punishment. And I goes round reg'lar jest to keep an eye on my capital coves. Lord! I vatches over 'em all—like a feyther. Theer's some volks as collects books, an' some volks as collects picters an' old coins, but I collects capital coves,—names and faces. The faces I keeps 'ere," and he tapped his placid forehead, "the names I keeps 'ere," and he tapped the little book. "It's my trade d' ye see, and though there's better trades, still there's trades as is vorse, an' that's summat, ain't it?"

"And what might your trade be?" inquired Barnabas, as they walked on together along the narrow alley.

"Veil, sir, I'm vot they calls a bashaw of the pigs—but I'm more than that."

"Pray," said Barnabas, "what do you mean?" For answer the man smiled, and half drew from his pocket a short staff surmounted by a crown.

"Ah!" said Barnabas, "a Bow Street Runner?"

"And my name is Shrig, sir, Jasper Shrig. You'll have heard it afore, o'course."

"No!" said Barnabas. Mr. Shrig seemed placidly surprised, and vented a gentle sigh.

"It's pretty vell known, in London, sir, though it ain't a pretty name, I'll allow. Ye-es, I've 'eard prettier, but then it's better than a good many, and that's sum-mat, ain't it? And then, as I said afore, it's pretty vell known."

"How so?"

"Vell, sir, there be some as 'as a leanin' to one branch o' the profession, and some to another,—now mine's murders."

"Murders?" said Barnabas, staring.

"Vith a werry big M., sir. V'y, Lord love you, there's been more murderers took and topped through me than any o' the other traps in London, it's a nat'ral gift vith me. Ye see, I collects 'em—afore the fact, as ye might say. I can smell 'em out, feel 'em out, taste 'em out, it's jest a nat'ral gift."

"But—how? What do you mean?"

"I means as I'll be valking along a street, say, looking at every face as I pass. Vell, all at once I'll spot a cove or covess vith vot I calls a capital mug, I'll follow that cove or covess, and by 'ook or by crook I'll find out that there cove or covess's name, and—down it goes in my little book, d' ye see?" and he tapped the little book.

"But surely," said Barnabas, "surely they don't all prove to be murderers?"

"Vell no, sir—that's hardly to be expected,—ye see, some on 'em wanishes away, an' some goes an' dies, but they mostly turns out true capitals—if I only vaits for 'em long enough, and—up they goes."

"And are you always on the lookout for such faces?"

"Yes, sir,—v'en I ain't busy on some case. A man must 'ave some little relaxation, and that's mine. Lord love you, sir, scarcely a day goes by that I don't spot one or two. I calls 'em my children, an' a werry large, an' a werry mixed lot they are too! Rich an' poor, men an' women,—rolling in their coaches an' crawling along the kennel. Aha! if you could look into my little reader an' see the names o' some o' my most promisin' children they'd as-tonish you. I've been to 'ave a look at a couple of 'em this mornin'. Aha! it would a-maze you if you could look into my little reader."

"I should like to," said Barnabas, eyeing the small, shabby book with a new interest. But Mr. Shrig only blinked his wide, innocent eyes, and slipping the book into his pocket, led the way round a sudden corner into another alley narrower than the last, and, if possible, dirtier.

"Where are we going?" Barnabas demanded, for Mr. Shrig, though always placid, had suddenly taken on an air that was almost alert, his bright, roving eye wandered more than ever, and he appeared to be hearkening to distant sounds. "Where are we going?" repeated Barnabas.

"Gray's Inn is 'andiest, sir, and I must ask you to step out a bit, they're a rough crowd as lives 'ereabouts,—scamps an' hunters, didlers an' cly-fakers, so I must ask you to step out a bit, this is a bad country for me."

"Bad for you? Why?"

"On account o' windictiveness, sir!"

"Of what?"

"Windictiveness, sir—windictiveness in every shape an' form, but brick-ends mostly—vith a occasional chimbley-pot."

"I'm afraid I don't understand," Barnabas began.

"Veil then," explained Mr. Shrig as they strode along, "I vere the means o' four coves bein' topped d' ye see, 'ighvay robbery vith wiolence,—'bout a month ago, used to live round 'ere, they did, an' their famblies an' friends is windictive against me accordingly, an' werry nat'ral too, for 'uman natur' is only 'uman natur', ain't it? Werry good then. Now their windictiveness,—or as you might say, 'uman natur',—generally takes the shape of chimbley-pots and brick-ends, though I 'ave met windictiveness in the form o' b'iling vater and flat-irons, not to mention saucepans an' sich, afore now, and vunce a arm-cheer, all of vich is apt to vorry you a bit until you gets used to it. Then there's knives—knives is allus awk'ard, and bludgeons ain't to be sneezed at, neither. But, Lord! every perfession and trade 'as its drawbacks, an' there's a sight o' comfort in that, ain't there?"

All this time the eyes of Mr. Shrig were roving here, wandering there, now apparently glancing up at the strip of sky between the dingy house tops, now down at the cobbles beneath their feet; also Barnabas noticed that his step, all at once, grew slower and more deliberate, as one who hesitates, uncertain as to whether he shall go on, or turn back. It was after one of those swift, upward glances, that Mr. Shrig stopped all at once, seized Barnabas by the middle and dragged him into an adjacent doorway, as something crashed down and splintered within a yard of them.

"What now—what is it?" cried Barnabas.

"Win-dictiveness!" sighed Mr. Shrig, shaking his head at the missile, "a piece o' coping-stone, thirty pound if a ounce—Lord! Keep flat agin the door sir, same as me, they may try another—I don't think so—still they may, so keep close ag'in the door. A partic'lar narrer shave I calls it!" nodded Mr. Shrig; "shook ye a bit sir?"

"Yes," said Barnabas, wiping his brow.

"Ah well, it shook me—and I'm used to windictiveness. A brick now," he mused, his eyes wandering again, "a brick I could ha' took kinder, bricks an' sich I'm prepared for, but coping-stones—Lord love me!"

"But a brick would have killed you just the same—"

"Killed me? A brick? Oh no, sir!"

"But, if it had hit you on the head—"

"On the 'at sir, the 'at—or as you might say—the castor—this, sir," said Mr. Shrig; and glancing furtively up and down the gloomy alley he took off the broad-brimmed hat; "just run your ogles over this 'ere castor o' mine, an' you'll understand, perhaps."

"It's very heavy," said Barnabas, as he took the hat.

"Ah, it is a bit 'eavyish, sir. Peep inside of it."

"Why," exclaimed Barnabas, "it's lined with—"

"Iron, sir. My own inwention ag'in windictiveness in the shape o' bricks an' bludgeons, an' werry useful an comfortin' I've found it. But if they're going to begin on me vith coping-stones,—v'y Lord!" And Mr. Shrig sighed his gentle sigh, and rubbed his placid brow, and once more covered it with the "inwention."

"And now sir, you've got a pair o' good, long legs—can ye use 'em?"

"Use them,—yes. Why?"

"Because it's about time as we cut our stick an' run for it."

"What are we to run for?"

"Because they're arter me,—nine on 'em,—consequent they're arter you too, d' ye see. There's four on 'em be'ind us, an' five on 'em in front. You can't see 'em because they're layin' low. And they're bad uns all, an' they means business."

"What—a fight?"

"As ever vas, sir. I've 'ad my eye on 'em some time. That 'ere coping-stone vas the signal."

"Ha!" said Barnabas, buttoning up his coat.

"Now, are ye ready, sir?"

"Quite!"

"Then keep close be'ind me—go!" With the word Mr. Shrig began to run, always keeping close beside the wall; indeed he ran so fast and was so very nimble that Barnabas had some ado to keep up with him. They had gone but a little distance when five rough looking fellows started into view further up the alley, completely blocking their advance, and by the clatter of feet behind, Barnabas knew that their retreat was cut off, and instinctively he set his teeth, and gripped his cane more firmly. But on ran Mr. Shrig, keeping close beside the wall, head low, shoulders back, elbows well in, for all the world as if he intended to hurl himself upon his assailants in some desperate hope of breaking through them; but all at once, like a rabbit into his burrow, he turned short off in mid career, and vanished down a dark and very narrow entry or passage, and, as Barnabas followed, he heard, above the vicious thud of footsteps, hoarse cries of anger and disappointment. Half-way down the passage Mr. Shrig halted abruptly and turned, as the first of their pursuers appeared.

"This'll do!" he panted, swinging the nobbly stick in his hand, "can't come on more nor two at vunce. Be ready vith your stick—at their eyes—poke at 'em—no 'itting—" the rest was drowned in the echoing rush of heavy feet and the boom of hoarse voices. But now, seeing their quarry stand on the defensive, the pursuers checked their advance, their cries sank to growling murmurs, till, with a fierce shout, one of their number rushed forward brandishing a heavy stick, whereupon the others followed, and there, in the echoing dimness, the battle was joined, and waxed furious and grim.

Almost at the first onset the slender cane Barnabas wielded broke short off, and he was borne staggering back, the centre of a panting, close-locked, desperate fray. But in that narrow space his assailants were hampered by their very numbers, and here was small room for bludgeon-play,—and Barnabas had his fists.

There came a moment of thudding blows, trampling feet, oaths, cries, —and Barnabas was free, staring dazedly at his broken knuckles. He heard a sudden shout, a vicious roar, and the Bow Street Runner, dropping the nobbly stick, tottered weakly and fell,—strove to rise, was smitten down again, and, in that moment, Barnabas was astride him; felt the shock of stinging blows, and laughing fierce and short, leapt in under the blows, every nerve and muscle braced and quivering; saw a scowling face,—smote it away; caught a bony wrist, wrenched the bludgeon from the griping fingers, struck and parried and struck again with untiring arm, felt the press thin out before him as his assailants gave back, and so, stood panting.

"Run! Run!" whispered Mr. Shrig's voice behind him. "Ve can do it now, —run!"

"No!" panted Barnabas, wiping the blood from his cheek. "Run!" cried Mr. Shrig again, "there's a place I knows on close by—ve can reach it in a jiff—this vay,—run!"

"No!"

"Not run? then v'ot vill ye do?"

"Make them!"

"Are ye mad? Ha!—look out!" Once more the echoing passage roared with the din of conflict, as their assailants rushed again, were checked, smote and were smitten, and fell back howling before the thrust of the nobbly stick and the swing of the heavy bludgeon.

"Now vill ye run?" panted Mr. Shrig, straightening the broad-brimmed hat.

"No!"

"V'y then, I vill!" which Mr. Shrig immediately proceeded to do.

But the scowl of Barnabas grew only the blacker, his lips but curled the fiercer, and his fingers tightened their grip upon the bludgeon as, alone now, he fronted those who remained of the nine.

Now chancing to glance towards a certain spot, he espied something that lay in the angle of the wall, and, instinctively stooping, he picked up Mr. Shrig's little book, slipped it into his pocket, felt a stunning blow, and reeled back, suddenly faint and sick. And now a mist seemed to envelop him, but in the mist were faces above, below, around him, faces to be struck at. But his blows grew weak and ever weaker, the cudgel was torn from his lax grip, he staggered back on stumbling feet knowing he could fight no more, and felt himself caught by a mighty arm, saw a face near by, comely and dimpled of chin, blue-eyed, and with whiskers trimmed into precise little tufts on either cheek. Thereafter he was aware of faint cries and shouts, of a rushing patter like rain among leaves, and of a voice speaking in his ear.

"Right about face,—march! Easy does it! mind me 'ook, sir, the p'int's oncommon sharp like. By your left—wheel! Now two steps up, sir—that's it! Now three steps down, easy does it! and 'ere we are. A cheer, sir, now water and a sponge!"

Here Barnabas, sinking back in the chair, leaned his head against the wall behind him, and the mist grew more dense, obliterating all things.

CHAPTER XXXII

OF CORPORAL RICHARD ROE, LATE OF THE GRENADIERS; AND FURTHER CONCERNING MR. SHRIG'S LITTLE READER

A small, dim chamber, with many glasses and bottles arrayed very precisely on numerous shelves; a very tall, broad-shouldered man who smiled down from the rafters while he pulled at a very precise whisker with his right hand, for his left had been replaced by a shining steel hook; and Mr. Shrig who shook his placid head as he leaned upon a long musket whose bayonet twinkled wickedly in the dim light; all this Barnabas saw as, sighing, he opened his eyes.

"'E's all right now!" nodded the smiling giant.

"Ha!" exclaimed Mr. Shrig, "but vith a lump on 'is 'ead like a negg. 'Run!' I sez. 'No!' sez 'e,—and 'ere's me vith vun eye a-going into mourning, and 'im vith a lump on 'is nob like a noo-laid egg!"

"'E's game though, Jarsper," said the benevolent giant.

"Game! I believe you, Corp!" nodded Mr. Shrig. "Run!' I sez. 'No!' sez 'e. 'Then v'ot vill you do?' sez I. 'Make them!' sez 'e. Game? Lord love me, I should say so!" Here, seeing Barnabas sit upright, Mr. Shrig laid by the musket and came towards him with his hand out.

"Sir," said he, "when them raskels got me down they meant to do for me; ah! they'd ha' given me my quietus for good an' all if you 'adn't stood 'em off. Sir, if it ain't too much, I should like to shake your daddle for that!"

"But you saved my life twice," said Barnabas, clasping the proffered hand.

"V'y the coping-stone I'll not go for to deny, sir," said Mr. Shrig, stroking his smooth brow, "but t'other time it were my friend and pal the Corp 'ere,—Corporal Richard Roe, late Grenadiers. 'E's only got an 'ook for an 'and, but vith that 'ook 'e's oncommonly 'andy, and as a veapon it ain't by no means to be sneezed at. No, 'e ain't none the worse for that 'ook, though they thought so in the army, and it vere 'im as brought you off v'ile I vos a-chasing of the enemy vith 'is gun, yonder."

"Why, then I should like to thank Corporal Richard Roe," said Barnabas,—(here the Corporal tugged at his precise and carefully trimmed whisker again), "and to shake his hand as well." Here the giant blushed and extended a huge fist.

"Honored, sir," said he, clicking his heels together.

"And now," said Mr. Shrig, "ve're all a-going to drink—at my expense."

"No, at mine," said Barnabas.

"Sir," said Mr. Shrig, round and placid of eye, "ven I says a thing I means it. Consequent you are now a-going to sluice your ivory vith a glass of the Vun an' Only, at my expense,—you must and you shall."

"Yes," said Barnabas, feeling in his pockets. "I must, my purse is gone."

"Purse!" exclaimed Mr. Shrig, his innocent eyes rounder than ever, "gone, sir?"

"Stolen," nodded Barnabas.

"Think o' that now!" sighed Mr. Shrig, "but I ain't surprised, no, I ain't surprised, and—by Goles!"

"What now?"

"Your cravat-sparkler!—that's wanished too!" Barnabas felt his rumpled cravat, and nodded. "And your vatch, now—don't tell me as they 've took—"

"Yes, my watch also," sighed Barnabas.

"A great pity!" said Mr. Shrig, "though it ain't to be vondered at,—not a bit."

"I valued the watch greatly, because it was given me by a very good friend," said Barnabas, sighing again.

"Walleyed it, hey?" exclaimed Mr. Shrig, "walleyed it, sir?—v'y then, 'ere it be!" and from a capacious side-pocket he produced Natty Bell's great watch, seals and all.

"Why—!" exclaimed Barnabas, staring.

"Also your purse, sir,—not forgetting the sparkler." Mr. Shrig continued, producing each article in turn.

"But—how in the world—?" began Barnabas.

"I took 'em from you v'ile you vos a-lookin' at my castor. Lord love me, a babe could ha' done it,—let alone a old 'and, like me!"

"Do you mean—?" began Barnabas, and hesitated.

"In my young days, sir," explained Mr. Shrig with his placid smile, "I vere a champion buzman, ah! and a prime rook at queering the gulls, too, but I ewentually turned honest all along of a flash, morning-sneak covess as got 'erself conwerted."

"What do you mean by a morning-sneak covess?"

"I means a area-sneak, sir, as vorks werry early in the morning. A fine 'andsome gal she vere, and vith nothing of the flash mollisher about 'er, either, though born on the streets, as ye might say, same as me. Vell, she gets con-werted, and she's alvays napping 'er bib over me,—as you'd say, piping 'er eye, d'ye see? vanting me to turn honest and be con-werted too. 'Turn honest,' says she, 'and ve'll be married ter-morrow,' says she."

"So you turned honest and married her?" said Barnabas, as Mr. Shrig paused.

"No, sir, I turned honest and she married a coal-v'ipper, v'ich, though it did come a bit 'ard on me at first, vos all for the best in the end, for she deweloped a chaffer,—as you might say, a tongue, d' ye see, sir, and I'm vun as is fond of a quiet life, v'en I can get it. Howsomever, I turned honest, and come werry near starving for the first year, but I kept honest, and I ain't never repented it—so fur. So, as for the prigs, and scamps, and buzmen, and flash leary coves, I'm up to all their dodges, 'aving been one of them, d'ye see. And now," said Mr. Shrig, as the big Corporal having selected divers bottles from his precise array, took himself off to concoct a jorum of the One and Only—"now sir, what do you think o' my pal Corporal Dick?"

"A splendid fellow!" said Barnabas.

"'E is that, sir,—so 'e is,—a giant, eh sir?"

"A giant, yes, and handsome too!" said Barnabas.

"V'y you're a sizable cove yourself, sir," nodded Mr. Shrig, "but you ain't much alongside my pal the Corp, are you? I'm nat'rally proud of 'im, d'ye see, for 't were me as saved 'im."

"Saved him from what? How?"

"Me being only a smallish chap myself, I've allus 'ad a 'ankering arter sizable coves. But I never seen a finer figger of a man than Corporal Dick—height, six foot six and a quarter, chest, fifty-eight and a narf, and sir—'e were a-going to drownd it all in the River, all along o' losing his 'and and being drove out o' the army, v'ich vould ha' been a great vaste of good material, as ye might say, seeing as there's so much of 'im. It vas a dark night, the night I found 'im, vith vind and rain, and there vos me and 'im a-grappling on the edge of a vharf—leastvays I vere a-holding onto 'is leg, d'ye see—ah, and a mortal 'ard struggle it vere too, and in the end I didn't save 'im arter all."

"What do you mean?"

"I mean as it vere 'im as saved me, for v'ot vith the vind, and the rain, and the dark, ve lost our footing and over ve vent into the River together—down and down till I thought as ve should never come up again, but ve did, o' course, and then, jest as 'ard as 'e'd struggled to throw 'imself in, 'e fought to get me out, so it vere 'im as really saved me, d'ye see?"

"No," said Barnabas, "it was you who really saved him."

"V'y, I'm as glad as you think so, sir, only d'ye see, I can't svim, and it vos 'im as pulled me out. And it all come along of 'im losing 'is 'and—come nigh to breaking 'is 'eart to be discharged, it did."

"Poor fellow!" said Barnabas, "and how did he lose his hand?"

"V'y, I could tell you, or you could read of it in the Gazette—jest three or four lines o' printing—and they've spelt 'is name wrong at that, curse 'em! But Corporal Dick can tell you best. Let 'im. 'Ere 'e comes, vith a steaming brew o' the Vun and Only."

And indeed, at this moment the Corporal re-entered, bearing a jug that gave forth a most enticing and delicious aroma, and upon which Mr. Shrig cast amorous glances, what time he reached three glasses from the marshalled array on the shelves.

And now, sitting at the small table that stood in a snug corner beside the chimney, Mr. Shrig, having filled the three glasses with all due care, tendered one to Barnabas with the words:

"Jest give that a snuff with your sneezer, sir,—there's perfume, there's fray-grance for ye! There ain't a man in London as can brew a glass o' rum-punch like the Corp,—though 'e 'as only got vun 'and. And now, Corporal Dick, afore ve begin, three steamers."

"Ay, for sure, Jarsper!" said the Corporal; and opening a small corner cupboard he took thence three new pipes and a paper of tobacco.

"Will you smoke, sir?" he inquired diffidently of Barnabas.

"Thank you, yes, Corporal," said Barnabas, and taking the proffered pipe he filled and lighted it.

Now when the pipes were in full blast, when the One and Only had been tasted, and pronounced by Mr. Shrig to be "up to the mark," he nodded to Corporal Dick with the words:

"Tell our young gent 'ow you lost your 'and, Corp."

But hereupon the Corporal frowned, shuffled his feet, stroked his trim whiskers with his hook, and finally addressed Barnabas.

"I aren't much of a talker, sir,—and it aren't much of a story, but if you so wish—"

"I do so wish," said Barnabas heartily.

"Why, very good, sir!" Saying which the Corporal sat up, squared his mighty shoulders, coughed, and began:

"It was when they Cuirassiers broke our square at Quatre-bras, sir,—fine fellows those Cuirassiers! They rode into us, through us, over us,—the square was tottering, and it was 'the colors—rally!' Ah, sir! the colors means the life or death of a square at such times. And just then, when horses was a-trampling us and the air full o' the flash o' French steel, just then I see our colors dip and sway, and down they went. But still it's 'the colors—rally!' and there's no colors to rally to; and all the time the square is being cut to pieces. But I, being nearest, caught up the colors in this here left hand," here the Corporal raised his gleaming hook, "but a Cuirassier, 'e caught them too, and there's him at one end o' the staff and me at t'other, pulling and hauling, and then—all at once he'd got 'em. And because why? Because I hadn't got no left 'and to 'old with. But I'd got my right, and in my right was 'Brown Bess' there," and the Corporal pointed to the long musket in the corner. "My bayonet was gone, and there weren't no time to reload, so—I used the butt. Then I picked up the colors again and 'eld 'em high over my head, for the smoke were pretty thick, and, 'To the colors,' I shouted,' Rally, lads, rally!' And oh, by the Lord, sir,—to hear our lads cheer! And so the square formed up again—what was left of it—formed up close and true round me and the colors, and the last thing I mind was the cheering. Ah! they was fine fellows, they Cuirassiers!"

"So that vere the end o' the Corp's soldiering!" nodded Mr. Shrig.

"Yes," sighed the Corporal, "a one-handed soldier ain't much good, ye see, sir."

"So they—throwed 'im out!" snarled Mr. Shrig.

"Now Jarsper," smiled the giant, shaking his head. "Why so 'ard on the sarvice? They give me m' stripe."

"And your dis-charge!" added Mr. Shrig.

"And a—pension," said the soldier.

"Pension," sniffed Mr. Shrig, "a fine, large vord, Dick, as means werry little to you!"

"And they mentioned me in the Gazette, Jarsper," said the Corporal looking very sheepish, and stroking his whisker again with his hook.

"And a lot o' good that done you, didn't it? Your 'eart vos broke the night I found you—down by the River."

"Why, I did feel as I weren't much good, Jarsper, I'll admit. You see, I 'adn't my hook then, sir. But I think I'd ha' give my other 'and—ah! that I would—to ha' been allowed to march on wi' the rest o' the lads to Waterloo."

"So you vos a-going to throw yerself into the River!"

"I were, Jarsper, should ha' done it but for you, comrade."

"But you didn't do it, so later on ve took this 'ere place."

"You did, Jarsper—"

"Ve took it together, Dick. And werry vell you're a-doing vith it, for both of us."

"I do my best, Jarsper."

"V'ich couldn't be bettered, Dick. Then look how you 'elp me vith my cases."

"Do I, Jarsper?" said the Corporal, his blue eyes shining.

"That you do, Dick. And now I've got another case as I'm a-vaiting for,—a extra-special Capital case it is too!"

"Another murder, Jarsper?"

"Ah, a murder, Dick,—a murder as ain't been committed yet, a murder as I'm expecting to come off in—say a month, from information received this 'ere werry arternoon. A murder, Dick, as is going to be done by a capital cove as I spotted over a month ago. Now v'ot I 'm going to tell you is betwixt us—private and confidential and—" But here Barnabas pushed back his chair.

"Then perhaps I had better be going?" said he.

"Going, sir? and for v'y?"

"That you may be more private, and talk more freely."

"Sir," said Mr. Shrig. "I knows v'en to speak and v'en not. My eyes tells me who I can trust and who not. And, sir, I've took to you, and so's the Corp,—ain't you, Dick?"

"Yes, sir," said the giant diffidently.

"Sir," pursued Mr. Shrig, "you're a Nob, I know, a Corinthian by your looks, a Buck, sir, a Dash, a 'eavy Toddler, but also, I takes the liberty o' telling you as you're only a man, arter all, like the rest on us, and it's that man as I'm a-talking to. Now v'en a man 'as stood up for me, shed 'is good blood for me, I makes that man my pal, and my pal I allus trusts."

"And you shall find me worthy of your confidence," said Barnabas, "and there's my hand on it, though, indeed, you hardly know me—really."

"More than you think, sir. Besides, it ain't v'ot a cove tells me about 'imself as matters, nor v'ot other coves tell me about a cove, as matters, it's v'ot a cove carries in 'is face as I goes by,—the cock of 'is eye, an' all the rest of it. And then, I knows as your name's Barnabas Barty—"

"Barty!—you know that?" exclaimed Barnabas, starting,—"how—how in the world did you find out?"

"Took the liberty to look at your vatch, sir."

"Watch!" said Barnabas, drawing it from his fob, "what do you mean?"

"Give it 'ere, and I'll show ye, sir." So saying, Mr. Shrig took the great timepiece and, opening the back, handed it to Barnabas. And there, in the cavity between the two cases was a very small folded paper, and upon this paper, in Natty Bell's handwriting, these words:

"To my dear lad Barnabas Barty, hoping that he may prove as fine a gentleman as he is—a man."

Having read this, Barnabas folded the paper very gently, and putting it back, closed the watch, and slipped it into his fob.

"And now," said Mr. Shrig, exhaling a vast cloud of smoke, "afore I go on to tell you about this 'ere murder as I'm a-vaiting for, I must show ye my little reader." Here Mr. Shrig thrust a hand into his pocket,—then his pipe shivered to fragments on the stone floor and he started up, mouth agape and eyes staring.

"Lord, Jarsper!" cried the Corporal, "what is it, comrade?"

"It's gone, Dick!" he gasped, "my little reader's been stole."

But now, even as he turned towards the door, Barnabas laid a detaining hand upon his arm.

"Not stolen—lost!" said he, "and indeed, I'm not at all surprised!" Here Barnabas smiled his quick, bright smile.

"Sir—sir?" stammered Mr. Shrig, "oh, Pal, d'ye mean—?"

"That I found it, yes," said Barnabas, "and here it is."

Mr. Shrig took his little book, opened it, closed it, thrust it into his pocket, and took it out again.

"Sir," said he, catching Barnabas by the hand, "this here little book is more to me nor gold or rubies. Sir, you are my pal,—and consequent the Corp's also, and this 'ere chaffing-crib is allus open to you. And if ever you want a man at your back—I'm your man, and v'en not me—there's my pal Dick, ain't there, Di—"

Mr. Shrig stopped suddenly and stood with his head to one side as one that listens. And thus, upon the stillness came the sound of one who strode along the narrow passage-way outside, whistling as he went.

"'Sally in our Alley,' I think?" said Mr. Shrig.

"Yes," said Barnabas, wondering.

"V'ich means as I'm vanted, ah!—and vanted precious qvick too," saying which, Mr. Shrig caught up his "castor," seized the nobbly stick, crossed to the door, and came back again.

"Dick," said he, "I'll get you to look after my little reader for me, —I ain't a-going to risk losing it again."

"Right you are, Jarsper," nodded the Corporal.

"And sir," continued Mr. Shrig, turning towards Barnabas with the book in his hand, "you said, I think, as you'd like to see what I'd got inside o' this 'ere.—If so be you're in the same mind about it, why—'ere it is." And Mr. Shrig laid the little book on the table before Barnabas. "And v'ot's more, any time as you're passing, drop in to the 'Gun,' and drink a glass o' the Vun and Only vith Dick and me." So Mr. Shrig nodded, unlocked the door, shut it very gently behind him, and his footsteps died away along the echoing passage.

Then, while the Corporal puffed at his long pipe, Barnabas opened the little book, and turning the pages haphazard presently came to one where, painfully written in a neat, round hand, he read this:

CAPITAL COVES

EXTRA-SPECIALS

Name.	When spotted.	Date of Murder.	Sentence.	Date of Execution.
James Aston (Porter)	Feb. 2	March 30	Hanged	April 5
Digbeth Andover (Gent)	March 3	April 28	Transported	May 5
John Barnes (Sailor)	March 10	Waiting	Waiting	Waiting
Sir Richard Brock(Bart)	April 5	May 3	Hanged	May 30
Thomas Beal (Tinker)	March 23	April 15	Hanged	May 30

There were many such names all carefully set down in alphabetical order, and Barnabas read them through with perfunctory interest. But—half-way down the list of B's his glance was suddenly arrested, his hands clenched themselves, and he grew rigid in his chair—staring wide-eyed at a certain name. In a while he closed the little book, yet sat there very still, gazing at nothing in particular, until the voice of the Corporal roused him somewhat.

"A wonderful man, my comrade Jarsper, sir?"

"Yes," said Barnabas absently.

"Though he wouldn't ha' passed as a Grenadier,—not being tall enough, you see."

"No," said Barnabas, his gaze still fixed.

"But as a trap, sir,—as a limb o' the law, he ain't to be ekalled—nowheres nor nohow."

"No," said Barnabas, rising.

"What? are you off, sir—must you march?"

"Yes," said Barnabas, taking up his hat, "yes, I must go."

"'Olborn way, sir?"

"Yes."

"Why then—foller me, sir,—front door takes you into Gray's Inn Lane—by your left turn and 'Olborn lays straight afore you,—this way, sir." But, being come to the front door of the "Gun," Barnabas paused upon the threshold, lost in abstraction again, and staring at nothing in particular while the big Corporal watched him with a growing uneasiness.

"Is it your 'ead, sir?" he inquired suddenly.

"Head?" repeated Barnabas.

"Not troubling you, is it, sir?"

"No,—oh no, thank you," answered Barnabas, and stretched out his hand. "Good-by, Corporal, I'm glad to have met you, and the One and Only was excellent."

"Thankee, sir. I hope as you'll do me and my comrade the honor to try it again—frequent. Good-by, sir." But standing to watch Barnabas as he went, the Corporal shook his head and muttered to himself, for Barnabas walked with a dragging step, and his chin upon his breast.

Holborn was still full of the stir and bustle, the rush and roar of thronging humanity, but now Barnabas was blind and deaf to it all, for wherever he looked he seemed to see the page of Mr. Shrig's little book with its list of carefully written names,—those names beginning with B.—thus:

Name.	When spotted.	Date of Murder.	Sentence.	Date of Execution.
Sir Richard Brock (Bart.)	April 5	May 3	Hanged	May 30
Thomas Beal (Tinker)	March 23	April 15	Hanged	May 30
Ronald Barrymaine	May 12	Waiting	Waiting	Waiting

CHAPTER XXXIII

CONCERNING THE DUTY OF FATHERS; MORE ESPECIALLY THE VISCOUNT'S "ROMAN"

It was about two o'clock in the afternoon that Barnabas knocked at the door of the Viscount's chambers in Half-moon Street and was duly admitted by a dignified, albeit somewhat mournful gentleman in blue and silver, who, after a moment of sighing hesitancy, ushered him into a small reception room where sat a bullet-headed man with one eye and a remarkably bristly chin, a sinister looking person who stared very hard with his one eye, and sucked very hard, with much apparent relish and gusto, at the knob of the stick he carried. At sight of this man the mournful gentleman averted his head, and vented a sound which, despite his impressive dignity, greatly resembled a sniff, and, bowing to Barnabas, betook himself upstairs to announce the visitor. Hereupon the one-eyed man having surveyed Barnabas from head to foot with his solitary orb, drew the knob of his stick from his mouth, dried it upon his sleeve, looked at it, gave it a final rub, and spoke.

"Sir," said he in a jovial voice that belied his sinister aspect, "did you 'ear that rainbow sniff?"

"Rainbow?" said Barnabas.

"Well,—wallet, then,—footman—the ornamental cove as jest popped you in 'ere. Makes one 'undred and eleven of 'em!"

"One hundred and eleven what?"

"Sniffs, sir,—s-n-i-double-f-s! I've took the trouble to count 'em, —nothing else to do. I ain't got a word out of 'im yet, an' I've been sittin' 'ere ever since eight o'clock s'mornin'. I'm a conwivial cock, I am,—a sociable cove, yes, sir, a s-o-s-h-able cove as ever wore a pair o' boots. Wot I sez is,—though a bum, why not a sociable bum, and try to make things nice and pleasant, and I does my best, give you my word! But Lord! all my efforts is wasted on that 'ere rainbow—nothing but sniffs!"

"Why then—who—what are you?"

"I'm Perks and Condy, wines and sperrits,—eighty-five pound, eighteen, three—that's me, sir."

"Do you mean that you are—in possession—here?"

"Just that, sir,—ever since eight o'clock s'morning—and nothing but sniffs—so fur." Here the bullet-headed man nodded and eyed the knob of his stick hungrily. But at this moment the door opened, and the dignified (though mournful) gentleman appeared, and informed Barnabas (with a sigh) that "his Lordship begged Mr. Beverley would walk upstairs."

Upstairs accordingly Barnabas stepped, and guided by a merry whistling, pushed open a certain door, and so found the Viscount busily engaged in the manufacture of a paper dart, composed of a sheet of the Gazette, in the midst of which occupation he paused to grip Barnabas by the hand.

"Delighted to see you, Bev," said he heartily, "pray sit down, my dear fellow—sit anywhere—no, not there—that's the toast, deuce take it! Oh, never mind a chair, bed'll do, eh? Yes, I'm rather late this morning, Bev,—but then I was so late last night that I was devilish early, and I'm making up for it,—must have steady nerves for the fifteenth, you know. Ah, and that reminds me!" Here the Viscount took up his unfinished dart and sighed over it. "I'm suffering from a rather sharp attack of Romanism, my dear fellow, my Honored Parent has been at it again, Bev, and then, I dropped two hundred pounds in Jermyn Street last night."

"Dropped it! Do you mean you lost it, or were you robbed?" inquired Barnabas the Simple. Now when he said this, the Viscount stared at him incredulously, but, meeting the clear gaze of the candid gray eyes, he smiled all at once and shook his head.

"Gad!" he exclaimed, "what a strange fellow you are, Bev. And yet I wouldn't have you altered, no, damme! you're too refreshing. You ask me 'did I lose it, or was I robbed?' I answer you,—both, my dear fellow. It was a case of sharps and flats, and—I was the flat."

"Ah,—you mean gambling, Dick?"

"Gambling, Bev,—at a hell in Jermyn Street."

"Two hundred pounds is a great deal of money to lose at cards," said Barnabas, shaking his head gravely.

"Humph!" murmured the Viscount, busied upon his paper dart again, "you should congratulate me, I think, that it was no more,—might just as easily have been two thousand, you see, indeed I wonder it wasn't. Egad! the more I think of it, the more fortunate I consider myself. Yes, I certainly think you should congratulate me. Now—watch me hit Sling!" and the Viscount poised his completed dart.

"Captain Slingsby—here?" exclaimed Barnabas, glancing about.

"Under the settee, yonder," nodded the Viscount, "wrapped up in the table-cloth."

"Table-cloth!" repeated Barnabas.

"By way of military cloak," explained the Viscount. "You see—Sling was rather—mellow, last night, and—at such times he always imagines he's campaigning again—insists upon sleeping on the floor."

Now, looking where the Viscount pointed, Barnabas espied the touzled head of Captain Slingsby of the Guards protruding from beneath the settee, and reposing upon a cushion. The Captain's features were serene, and his breathing soft and regular, albeit deepening, ever and anon, into a gentle snore.

"Poor old Sling!" said the Viscount, leaning forward the better to aim his missile, "in two hours' time he must go and face the Ogre, —poor old Sling! Now watch me hit him!" So saying Viscount Devenham launched his paper dart which, gliding gracefully through the air, buried its point in the Captain's whisker, whereupon that warrior, murmuring plaintively, turned over and fell once more gently a-snoring.

"Talking about the Ogre—" began the Viscount.

"You mean—Jasper Gaunt?" Barnabas inquired.

"Precisely, dear fellow, and, talking of him, did you happen to notice a—fellow, hanging about downstairs,—a bristly being with one eye, Bev?"

"Yes, Dick."

"Ha!" said the Viscount nodding, "and talking of him, brings me back to my Honored Roman—thus, Bev. Chancing to find myself in—ha—hum—a little difficulty, a—let us say—financial tightness, Bev. I immediately thought of my father, which,—under the circumstances was, I think, very natural—and filial, my dear fellow. I said to myself, here is a man, the author of my being, who, though confoundedly Roman, is still my father, and, as such, owes certain duties to his son, sacred duties, Bev, not to be lightly esteemed, blinked, or set aside,—eh, Bev?"

"Undoubtedly!" said Barnabas.

"I, therefore, ventured to send him a letter, post-haste, gently reminding him of those same duties, and acquainting him with my—ah—needy situation,—which was also very natural, I think."

"Certainly!" said Barnabas, smiling.

"But—would you believe it, my dear fellow, he wrote, or rather, indited me an epistle, or, I should say, indictment, in his most Roman manner which—but egad! I'll read it to you, I have it here somewhere." And the Viscount began to rummage among the bedclothes, to feel and fumble under pillow and bolster, and eventually dragged forth a woefully crumpled document which he smoothed out upon his knees, and from which he began to read as follows:

MY DEAR HORATIO.

"As soon as I saw that' t—i—o,' Bev, I knew it was no go. Had it been merely a—c—e I should have nourished hopes, but the 't—i—o' slew 'em—killed 'em stone dead and prepared me for a screed in my Honored Roman's best style, bristling with the Divine Right of Fathers, and, Bev—I got it. Listen:"

Upon reading your long and very eloquent letter, I was surprised to learn, firstly, that you required money, and secondly to observe that you committed only four solecisms in spelling,

("Gives me one at the very beginning, you'll notice, Bev.")

As regards the money, you will, I am sure, be amazed, nay astounded, to learn that you have already exceeded your allowance by some five hundred pounds—

("So I was, Bev, begad—I thought it was eight.")

As regards your spelling—

("Ah! here he leads again with his left, and gets one in,—low, Bev, low!")

As regards your spelling, as you know, I admire originality in
all things; but it has, hitherto, been universally conceded that the
word "eliminate" shall not and cannot begin with the letters i-l-l!
"Vanquish" does not need a k. "Apathy" is spelled with but one p—
while never before have I beheld "anguish" with a w.

("Now, Bev, that's what I call coming it a bit too strong!" sighed the Viscount, shaking his head; "'anguish' is anguish however you spell it! And, as for the others, let me tell you when a fellow has a one-eyed being with bristles hanging about his place, he isn't likely to be over particular as to his p's and q's, no, damme! Let's see, where were we? ah! here it is,—'anguish' with a 'w'!")

I quite agree with your remarks, viz. that a father's duties to his son are sacred and holy—

("This is where I counter, Bev, very neatly,—listen! He quite agrees that,—")

—a father's duties to his son are sacred and holy, and not to be lightly esteemed, blinked, or set aside—

("Aha! had him there, Bev,—inside his guard, eh?")

I also appreciate, and heartily endorse your statement that it is to his father that a son should naturally turn for help—

("Had him again—a leveller that time, egad!")

naturally turn for help, but, when the son is constantly turning,
then, surely, the father may occasionally turn too, like the worm.
The simile, though unpleasant, is yet strikingly apt.

("Hum! there he counters me and gets one back, I suppose, Bev? Oh, I'll admit the old boy is as neat and quick with his pen as he used to be with his hands. He ends like this:")

I rejoice to hear that you are well in health, and pray that,
despite the forthcoming steeplechase, dangerous as I hear it is, you
may so continue. Upon this head I am naturally somewhat anxious,
since I possess only one son. And I further pray that, wilfully
reckless though he is, he may yet be spared to be worthy of the name
that will be his when I shall have risen beyond it.

BAMBOROUGH AND REVELSDEN.

The Viscount sighed, and folded up his father's letter rather carefully.

"He's a deuced old Roman, of course," said he, "and yet—!" Here the Viscount turned, and slipped the letter back under his pillow with a hand grown suddenly gentle. "But there you are, Bev! Not a word about money,—so downstairs Bristles must continue to sit until—"

"If," said Barnabas diffidently, "if you would allow me to lend—"

"No, no, Bev—though I swear it's uncommon good of you. But really I couldn't allow it. Besides, Jerningham owes me something, I believe, at least, if he doesn't he did, and it's all one anyway. I sent the Imp over to him an hour ago; he'll let me have it, I know. Though I thank you none the less, my dear fellow, on my soul I do! But—oh deuce take me—you've nothing to drink! what will you take—?"

"Nothing, thanks, Dick. As a matter of fact, I came to ask you a favor—"

"Granted, my dear fellow!"

"I want you to ask Captain Slingsby to introduce me to Jasper Gaunt."

"Ah?" said the Viscount, coming to his elbow, "you mean on behalf of that—"

"Of Barrymaine, yes."

"It's—it's utterly preposterous!" fumed the Viscount.

"So you said before, Dick."

"You mean to—go on with it?"

"Of course!"

"You are still determined to befriend a—"

"More than ever, Dick."

"For—Her sake?"

"For Her sake. Yes, Dick," said Barnabas, beginning to frown a little. "I mean to free him from Gaunt, and rescue him from Chichester—if I can."

"But Chichester is about the only friend he has left, Bev."

"On the contrary, I think Chichester is his worst enemy."

"But—my dear fellow! Chichester is the only one who has stood by him in his disgrace, though why, I can't imagine."

"I think I can tell you the reason, and in one word," said Barnabas, his face growing blacker.

"Well, Bev,—what is it?"

"Cleone!" The Viscount started.

"What,—you think—? Oh, impossible! The fellow would never have a chance, she despises him, I know."

"And fears him too, Dick."

"Fears him? Gad! what do you mean, Bev?"

"I mean that, unworthy though he may be, she idolizes her brother."

"Half-brother, Bev."

"And for his sake, would sacrifice her fortune,—ah! and herself!"

"Well?"

"Well, Dick, Chichester knows this, and is laying his plans accordingly."

"How?"

"He's teaching Barrymaine to drink, for one thing—"

"He didn't need much teaching, Bev."

"Then, he has got him in his power,—somehow or other, anyhow, Barrymaine fears him, I know. When the time comes, Chichester means to reach the sister through her love for her brother, and—before he shall do that, Dick—" Barnabas threw up his head and clenched his fists.

"Well, Bev?"

"I'll—kill him, Dick."

"You mean—fight him, of course?"

"It would be all one," said Barnabas grimly.

"And how do you propose to—go about the matter—to save Barrymaine?"

"I shall pay off his debts, first of all."

"And then?"

"Take him away with me."

"When?"

"To-morrow, if possible—the sooner the better."

"And give up the race, Bev?"

"Yes," said Barnabas, sighing, "even that if need be."

Here the Viscount lay back among his pillows and stared up at the tester of the bed, and his gaze was still directed thitherwards when he spoke:

"And you would do all this—"

"For—Her sake," said Barnabas softly, "besides, I promised, Dick."

"And you have seen her—only once, Bev!"

"Twice, Dick."

Again there was silence while the Viscount stared up at the tester and Barnabas frowned down at the clenched fist on his knee.

"Gad!" said the Viscount suddenly, "Gad, Beverley, what a deuced determined fellow you are!"

"You see—I love her, Dick."

"And by the Lord, Bev, shall I tell you what I begin to think?"

"Yes, Dick."

"Well, I begin to think that in spite of—er—me, and hum—all the rest of 'em, in spite of everything—herself included, if need be, —you'll win her yet."

"And shall I tell you what I begin to think, Dick?"

"Yes."

"I begin to think that you have never—loved her at all."

"Eh?" cried the Viscount, starting up very suddenly, "what?—never lov—oh, Gad, Beverley! what the deuce should make you think that?"

"Clemency!" said Barnabas.

The Viscount stared, opened his mouth, shut it, ran his fingers through his hair, and fell flat upon his pillows again.

"So now," said Barnabas the persistent, "now you know why I am so anxious to meet Jasper Gaunt."

"Gaunt!" said the Viscount dreamily, "Gaunt!"

"Captain Slingsby has to see him this afternoon,—at least so you said, and I was wondering—"

"Slingsby! Oh, egad I forgot! so he has,—curricle's ordered for half-past three. Will you oblige me by prodding him with your cane, Bev? Don't be afraid,—poke away, my dear fellow, Sling takes a devil of a lot of waking."

Thus admonished, Barnabas presently succeeded in arousing the somnolent Slingsby, who, lifting a drowsy head, blinked sleepily, and demanded in an injured tone:

"Wha' the dooce it was all about, b'gad?" Then having yawned prodigiously and come somewhat to himself, he proceeded to crawl from under the settee, when, catching sight of Barnabas, he sprang lightly to his feet and greeted him cordially.

"Ah, Beverley!" he cried,—"how goes it? Glad you woke me—was having a devil of a dream. Thought the 'Rascal' had strained his 'off' fore-leg, and was out of the race! What damnable things dreams are, b'gad!"

"My dear Sling," said the Viscount, "it is exactly a quarter past three."

"Oh, is it, b'gad! Well?"

"And at four o'clock I believe you have an appointment with Gaunt."

"Gaunt!" repeated the Captain, starting, and Barnabas saw all the light and animation die out of his face, "Gaunt,—yes, I—b'gad!—I 'd forgotten, Devenham."

"You ordered your curricle for half-past three, didn't you?"

"Yes, and I've no time to bathe—ought to shave, though, and oh, damme,—look at my cravat!"

"You'll find everything you need in my dressing-room, Sling."

The Captain nodded his thanks, and forthwith vanished into the adjacent chamber, whence he was to be heard at his ablutions, puffing and blowing, grampus-like. To whom thus the Viscount, raising his voice: "Oh, by the way, Sling, Beverley wants to go with you." Here the Captain stopped, as it seemed in the very middle of a puff, and when he spoke it was in a tone of hoarse incredulity:

"Eh,—b'gad, what's that?"

"He wants you to introduce him to Jasper Gaunt."

Here a sudden explosive exclamation, and, thereafter, the Captain appeared as in the act of drying himself, his red face glowing from between the folds of the towel while he stared from the Viscount to Barnabas with round eyes.

"What!" he exclaimed at last, "you, too, Beverley! Poor devil, have you come to it—and so soon?"

"No," said Barnabas, shaking his head, "I wish to see him on behalf of another—"

"Eh? Another? Oh—!"

"On behalf of Mr. Ronald Barrymaine."

"Of Barrym—" Here the Captain suddenly fell to towelling himself violently, stopped to stare at Barnabas again, gave himself another futile rub or two, and, finally, dropped the towel altogether. "On behalf of—oh b'gad!" he exclaimed, and incontinent vanished into the dressing-room. But, almost immediately he was back again, this time wielding a shaving brush. "Wish to see—Gaunt, do you?" he inquired.

"Yes," said Barnabas.

"And," said the Captain, staring very hard at the shaving brush, "not—on your own account?"

"No," answered Barnabas.

"But on behalf—I think you said—of—"

"Of Ronald Barrymaine," said Barnabas.

"Oh!" murmured the Captain, and vanished again. But now Barnabas followed him.

"Have you any objection to my going with you?" he inquired.

"Not in the least," answered the Captain, making hideous faces at himself in the mirror as he shaved, "oh, no—delighted, 'pon my soul, b'gad—only—"

"Well?"

"Only, if it's time you're going to ask for—it's no go, my boy—hard-fisted old rasper, you know the saying,—(Bible, I think), figs, b'gad, and thistles, bread from stones, but no mercy from Jasper Gaunt."

"I don't seek his mercy," said Barnabas.

"Why, then, my dear Beverley—ha! there's Jenk come up to say the curricle's at the door."

Sure enough, at the moment, the Viscount's gentleman presented himself to announce the fact, albeit mournfully and with a sigh. He was about to bow himself out again when the Viscount stayed him with an upraised finger.

"Jenkins," said he, "my very good Jenk!"

"Yes, m'lud?" said Jenkins.

"Is the person with the—ah—bristles—still downstairs?"

"He is, m'lud," said Jenkins, with another sigh.

"Then tell him to possess his soul in patience, Jenk,—for I fear he will remain there a long, long time."

CHAPTER XXXIV

OF THE LUCK OF CAPTAIN SLINGSBY, OF THE GUARDS

"You don't mind if we—drive about a bit, do you, Beverley?"

"Not in the least."

"I—er—I generally go the longest way round when I have to call on—"

"On Gaunt?"

"Yes."

Now as they went, Barnabas noticed that a change had come over his companion, his voice had lost much of its jovial ring, his eye its sparkle, while his ruddy cheeks were paler than their wont; moreover he was very silent, and sat with bent head and with his square shoulders slouched dejectedly. Therefore Barnabas must needs cast about for some means of rousing him from this depression.

"You drive a very handsome turnout," said he at last.

"It is neat, isn't it?" nodded Slingsby, his eye brightening.

"Very!" said Barnabas, "and the horses—"

"Horses!" cried the Captain, almost himself again, "ha, b'gad—there's action for you—and blood too! I was a year matching 'em. Cost me eight hundred guineas—and cheap at the money—but—"

"Well?"

"After all, Beverley, they—aren't mine, you see."

"Not yours?"

"No. They're—his!"

"You mean—Gaunt's?"

The Captain nodded gloomily.

"Yes," said he, "my horses are his, my curricle's his, my clothes are his—everything's his. So am I, b'gad! Oh, you needn't look so infernal incredulous—fact, I assure you. And, when you come to think of it—it's all cursed humorous, isn't it?" and here the Captain contrived to laugh, though it rang very hollow, to be sure.

"You owe—a great deal then?" said Barnabas.

"Owe?" said the Captain, turning to look at him, "I'm in up to my neck, and getting deeper. Owe! B'gad, Beverley—I believe you!" But now, at sight of gravefaced Barnabas, he laughed again, and this time it sounded less ghoul-like. "Debt is a habit," he continued sententiously, "that grows on one most damnably, and creditors are the most annoying people in the world—so confoundedly unreasonable! Of course I pay 'em—now and then—deserving cases, y' know. Fellow called on me t' other day,—seemed to know his face. 'Who are you?' says I. 'I'm the man who makes your whips, sir,' says he. 'And devilish good whips too!' says I, 'how much do I owe you?' 'Fifteen pounds, sir,' says he, 'I wouldn't bother you only'—well, it seemed his wife was sick—fellow actually blubbered! So of course I rang for my rascal Danby, Danby's my valet, y' know. 'Have you any money, Danby?' says I. 'No sir,' says he; queer thing, but

Danby never has, although I pay him regularly—devilish improvident fellow, Danby! So I went out and unearthed Jerningham—and paid the fellow on the spot—only right, y' know."

"But why not pay your debts with your own money?" Barnabas inquired.

"For the very good reason that it all went,—ages ago!"

"Why, then," said Barnabas, "earn more."

"Eh?" said the Captain, staring, "earn it? My dear Beverley, I never earned anything in my life, except my beggarly pay, and that isn't enough even for my cravats."

"Well, why not begin?"

"Begin? To earn money? How?"

"You might work," suggested Barnabas.

"Work?" repeated the Captain, starting, "eh, what? Oh, I see, you're joking, of course,—deuced quaint, b'gad!"

"No, I'm very serious," said Barnabas thoughtfully.

"Are you though! But what the deuce kind of work d'you suppose I'm fit for?"

"All men can work!" said Barnabas, more thoughtfully than before.

"Well,—I can ride, and shoot, and drive a coach with any one."

"Anything more?"

"No,—not that I can think of."

"Have you never tried to work, then,—hard work, I mean?"

"Oh Lord, no! Besides, I've always been too busy, y'know. I've never had to work. Y' see, as luck would have it, I was born a gentleman, Beverley."

"Yes," nodded Barnabas, more thoughtful than ever, "but—what is a gentleman?"

"A gentleman? Why—let me think!" said the Captain, manoeuvring his horses skilfully as they swung into the Strand.

And when he had thought as far as the Savoy he spoke:

"A gentleman," said he, "is a fellow who goes to a university, but doesn't have to learn anything; who goes out into the world, but doesn't have to—work at anything; and who has never been blackballed at any of the clubs. I've done a good many things in my time, but I've never had to work."

"That is a great pity!" sighed Barnabas.

"Oh! is it, b'gad! And why?"

"Because hard work ennobles a man," said Barnabas.

"Always heard it was a deuce of a bore!" murmured the Captain.

"Exertion," Barnabas continued, growing a little didactic perhaps, "exertion is—life. By idleness come degeneration and death."

"Sounds cursed unpleasant, b'gad!" said the Captain.

"The work a man does lives on after him," Barnabas continued, "it is his monument when he is no more, far better than your high-sounding epitaphs and stately tombs, yes, even though it be only the furrow he has ploughed, or the earth his spade has turned."

"But,—my dear fellow, you surely wouldn't suggest that I should take up—digging?"

"You might do worse," said Barnabas, "but—"

"Ha!" said the Captain, "well now, supposing I was a—deuced good digger,—a regular rasper, b'gad! I don't know what a digger earns, but let's be moderate and say five or six pounds a week. Well, what the deuce good d'you suppose that would be to me? Why, I still owe Gaunt, as far as I can figure it up, about eighty thousand pounds, which is a deuced lot more than it sounds. I should have been rotting in the Fleet, or the Marshalsea, years ago if it hadn't been for my uncle's gout, b'gad!"

"His gout?"

"Precisely! Every twinge he has—up goes my credit. I'm his only heir, y'know, and he's seventy-one. At present he's as sound as a bell, —actually rode to hounds last week, b'gad! Consequently my credit's—nowhere. Jolly old boy, though—deuced fond of him—ha! there's Haynes! Over yonder! Fellow driving the phaeton with the black-a-moor in the rumble."

"You mean the man in the bright green coat?"

"Yes. Call him 'Pea-green Haynes'—one of your second-rate, ultra dandies. Twig his vasty whiskers, will you! Takes his fellow hours to curl 'em. And then his cravat, b'gad!"

"How does he turn his head?" inquired Barnabas.

"Never does,—can't! I lost a devilish lot to him at hazard a few years ago—crippled me, y' know. But talking of my uncle—devilish fond of him—always was."

"But mark you, Beverley, a man has no right—no business to go on living after he's seventy, at least, it shows deuced bad taste, I think—so thoughtless, y'know. Hallo! why there's Ball Hughes—driving the chocolate-colored coach, and got up like a regular jarvey. Devilish rich, y'know—call him 'The Golden Ball'—deuce of a fellow! Pitch and toss, or whist at five pound points, damme! Won small fortune from Petersham at battledore and shuttlecock,—played all night too."

"And have you lost to him also?"

"Of course?"

"Do you ever win?"

"Oh, well—now and then, y'know, though I'm generally unlucky. Must have been under—Aldeboran, is it?—anyhow, some cursed star or other. Been dogged by ill-luck from my cradle, b'gad! On the turf, in the clubs and bells, even in the Peninsular!"

"So you fought in the Peninsular?"

"Oh, yes."

"And did you gamble there too?"

"Naturally—whenever I could."

"And did you lose?"

"Generally. Everything's been against me, y'know—even my size."

"How so?"

"Well, there was a fellow in the Eighty-eighth, name of Crichton. I'd lost to him pretty heavily while we were before Ciudad Rodrigo. The night before the storming—we both happened to have volunteered, y'know—'Crichton,' says I, 'I'll go you double or quits I'm into the town to-morrow before you are.' 'Done!' says he. Well, we advanced to the attack about dawn, about four hundred of us. The breach was wide enough to drive a battery through, but the enemy had thrown up a breast-work and fortified it during the night. But up we went at the 'double,' Crichton and I in front, you may be sure. As soon as the Frenchies opened fire, I began to run,—so did Crichton, but being longer in the leg, I was at the breach first, and began to scramble over the débris. Crichton was a little fellow, y' know, but game all through, and active as a cat, and b'gad, presently above the roar and din, I could hear him panting close behind me. Up we went, nearer and nearer, with our fellows about a hundred yards in our rear, clambering after us and cheering as they came. I was close upon the confounded breastwork when I took a musket-ball through my leg, and over I went like a shot rabbit, b'gad! Just then Crichton panted up. 'Hurt?' says he. 'Only my leg,' says I, 'go on, and good luck to you.' 'Devilish rough on you, Sling!' says he, and on he went. But he'd only gone about a couple of yards when he threw up his arms and pitched over on his face. 'Poor Crichton's done for!' says I to myself, and made shift to crawl over to him. But b'gad! he saw me coming, and began to crawl too. So there we were, on our hands and knees, crawling up towards the Frenchies as hard as we could go. My leg was deuced—uncomfortable, y' know, but I put on a spurt, and managed to draw level with him. 'Hallo, Sling!' says he, 'here's where you win, for I'm done!' and over he goes again. 'So am I, for that matter,' says I—which was only the truth, Beverley. So b'gad, there we lay, side by side, till up came our fellows, yelling like fiends, past us and over us, and charged the breastwork with the bayonet,—and carried it too! Presently, up came two stragglers,—a corporal of the Eighty-eighth and a sergeant of 'Ours.' 'Hi, Corporal,' yells Crichton, 'ten pounds if you can get me over the breastwork—quick's the word!' 'Sergeant,' says I, 'twenty pounds if you get me over first.' Well, down went the Corporal's musket and the Sergeant's pike, and on to their backs we scrambled—a deuced painful business for both of us, I give you my word, Beverley. So we began our race again—mounted this time. But it was devilish bad going, and though the Sergeant did his best, I came in a very bad second. You see, I'm no light weight, and Crichton was."

"You lost, then?"

"Oh, of course, even my size is against me, you see." Hereupon, once more, and very suddenly, the Captain relapsed into his gloomy mood, nor could Barnabas dispel it; his efforts were rewarded only by monosyllables until, swinging round into a short and rather narrow street, he brought his horses to a walk.

"Here we are, Beverley!"

"Where?" Barnabas inquired.

"Kirby Street,—his street. And there's the house,—his house," and Captain Slingsby pointed his whip at a high, flat-fronted house. It was a repellent-looking place with an iron railing before it, and beyond this railing a deep and narrow area, where a flight of damp steps led down to a gloomy door. The street was seemingly a quiet one, and, at this hour, deserted save for themselves and a solitary man who stood with his back to them upon the opposite side of the way, apparently lost in profound thought. A very tall man he was, and very upright, despite the long white hair that showed beneath his hat, which, like his clothes, was old and shabby, and Barnabas noticed that his feet were bare. This man Captain Slingsby incontinent hailed in his characteristic fashion.

"Hi,—you over there!" he called. "Hallo!" The man never stirred. "Oho! b'gad, are you deaf? Just come over here and hold my horses for me, will you?" The man raised his head suddenly and turned. So quickly did he turn that the countless gleaming buttons that he wore upon his coat rang a jingling chime. Now, looking upon this strange figure, Barnabas started up, and springing from the curricle, crossed the street and looked upon the man with a smile.

"Have you forgotten me?" said Barnabas. The man smiled in turn, and sweeping off the weather-beaten hat, saluted him with an old-time bow of elaborate grace.

"Sir." he answered in his deep, rich voice, "Billy Button never forgets—faces. You are Barnaby Bright—Barnabas, 't is all the same. Sir, Billy Button salutes you."

"Why, then," said Barnabas, rather diffidently, seeing the other's grave dignity, "will you oblige me by—by holding my friend's horses? They are rather high-spirited and nervous."

"Nervous, sir? Ah, then they need me. Billy Button shall sing to them, horses love music, and, like trees, are excellent listeners." Forthwith Billy Button crossed the street with his long, stately stride, and taking the leader's bridle, fell to soothing the horses with soft words, and to patting them with gentle, knowing hands.

"B'gad!" exclaimed the Captain, staring, "that fellow has been used to horses—once upon a time. Poor devil!" As he spoke he glanced from Billy Button's naked feet and threadbare clothes to his own glossy Hessians and immaculate garments, and Barnabas saw him wince as he turned towards the door of Jasper Gaunt's house. Now when Barnabas would have followed, Billy Button caught him suddenly by the sleeve.

"You are not going—there?" he whispered, frowning and nodding towards the house.

"Yes."

"Don't!" he whispered, "don't! An evil place, a place of, sin and shadows, of sorrow, and tears, and black despair. Ah, an evil place! No place for Barnaby Bright."

"I must," said Barnabas.

"So say they all. Youth goes in, and leaves his youth behind; men go in, and leave all strength and hope behind; age goes in, and creeps out—to a grave. Hear me, Barnaby Bright. There is one within there already marked for destruction. Death follows at his heel, for evil begetteth evil, and the sword, the sword. He is already doomed. Listen,—blood! I've seen it upon the door yonder,—a bloody hand! I know, for They have told me—They—the Wise Ones. And so I come here, sometimes by day, sometimes by night, and I watch—I watch. But this is no place for you,—'t is the grave of youth, don't go—don't go!"

"I must," repeated Barnabas, "for another's sake."

"Then must the blighting shadow fall upon you, too,—ah, yes, I know. Oh, Barnaby,—Barnaby Bright!"

Here, roused by the Captain's voice, rather hoarser than usual, Barnabas turned and saw that the door of the house was open, and that Captain Slingsby stood waiting for him with a slender, youthful-seeming person who smiled; a pale-faced, youngish man, with colorless hair, and eyes so very pale as to be almost imperceptible in the pallor of his face. Now, even as the door closed, Barnabas could hear Billy Button singing softly to the horses.

CHAPTER XXXV

HOW BARNABAS MET JASPER GAUNT, AND WHAT CAME OF IT

Barnabas followed the Captain along a somewhat gloomy hall, up a narrow and winding staircase, and here, halfway up, was a small landing with an alcove where stood a tall, wizen-faced clock with skeleton hands and a loud, insistent, very deliberate tick; so, up more stairs to another hall, also somewhat gloomy, and a door which the pale-eyed, smiling person obligingly opened, and, having ushered them into a handsomely furnished chamber, disappeared. The Captain crossed to the hearth, and standing before the empty grate, put up his hand and loosened his high stock with suddenly petulant fingers, rather as though he found some difficulty in breathing; and, looking at him, Barnabas saw that the debonair Slingsby had vanished quite; in his place was another—a much older man, haggard of eye, with a face peaked, and gray, and careworn beneath the brim of the jaunty hat.

"My dear Beverley," said he, staring down into the empty grate, "if you 're ever in need—if you're ever reduced to—destitution, then, in heaven's name, go quietly away and—starve! Deuced unpleasant, of course, but it's—sooner over, b'gad!"

At this moment the smiling person reappeared at a different door, and uttered the words:

"Captain Slingsby,—if *you* please." Hereupon the Captain visibly braced himself, squared his shoulders, took off his hat, crossed the room in a couple of strides, and Barnabas was alone.

Now as he sat there waiting, he gradually became aware of a sound that stole upon the quiet, a soft, low sound, exactly what he could not define, nevertheless it greatly perturbed him. Therefore he rose, and approaching that part of the room whence it proceeded, he saw another door. And then, all at once, as he stood before this door, he knew what the sound was, and why it had so distressed him; and, even as the knowledge came, he opened the door and stepped into the room beyond.

And this is what he saw:

A bare little room, or office; the pale, smiling gentleman, who lounged in a cushioned chair, a comb in one hand, and in the other a small pocket mirror, by the aid of which he was attending to a diminutive tuft of flaxen whisker; and a woman, in threadbare garments, who crouched upon a bench beside the opposite wall, her face bowed upon her hands, her whole frame shaken by great, heart-broken, gasping sobs,—a sound full of misery, and of desolation unutterable.

At the opening of the door, the pale gentleman started and turned, and the woman looked up with eyes swollen and inflamed by weeping.

"Sir," said the pale gentleman, speaking softly, yet in the tone of one used to command, "may I ask what this intrusion means?" Now as he looked into the speaker's pallid eyes, Barnabas saw that he was much older than he had thought.

He had laid aside the comb and mirror, and now rose in a leisurely manner, and his smile was more unpleasant than ever as he faced Barnabas.

"This place is private, sir—you understand, private, sir. May I suggest that you—go, that you—leave us?" As he uttered the last two words, he thrust out his head and jaw in a very ugly manner, therefore Barnabas turned and addressed himself to the woman.

"Pray, madam," said he, "tell me your trouble; what is the matter?" But the woman only wrung her hands together, and stared with great, frightened eyes at the colorless man, who now advanced, smiling still, and tapped Barnabas smartly on the shoulder.

"The trouble is her own, sir, the matter is—entirely a private one," said he, fixing Barnabas with his pale stare, "I repeat, sir,—a private one. May I, therefore, suggest that you withdraw—at once?"

"As often as you please, sir," retorted Barnabas, bowing.

"Ah!" sighed the man, thrusting out his head again, "and what do you want—here?"

"First, is your name Jasper Gaunt?"

"No; but it is as well known as his—better to a great many."

"And your name is—?"

"Quigly."

"Then, Mr. Quigly, pray be seated while I learn this poor creature's sorrow."

"I think—yes, I think you'd better go," said Mr. Quigly,—"ah, yes—and at once, or—"

"Or?" said Barnabas, smiling and clenching his fists.

"Or it will be the worse—for you—"

"Yes?"

"And for your friend the Captain."

"Yes?"

"And you will give this woman more reason for her tears!"

Then, looking from the pale, threatening eyes, and smiling lips of the man, to the trembling fear of the weeping woman, and remembering Slingsby's deathly cheek and shaking hand, a sudden, great anger came upon Barnabas; his long arm shot out and, pinning Mr. Quigly by the cravat, he shook him to and fro in a paroxysm of fury. Twice he raised his cane to strike, twice he lowered it, and finally loosing his grip, Mr. Quigly staggered back to the opposite wall, and leaned there, panting.

Hereupon Barnabas, somewhat shocked at his own loss of self-restraint, re-settled his cuff, straightened his cravat, and, when he spoke, was more polite than ever.

"Mr. Quigly, pray sit down," said he; "I have no wish to thrash you,—it would be a pity to spoil my cane, so—oblige me by sitting down."

Mr. Quigly opened his mouth as if to speak, but, glancing at Barnabas, thought better of it; yet his eyes grew so pale that they seemed all whites as he sank into the chair.

"And now," said Barnabas, turning to the crouching woman, "I don't think Mr. Quigly will interrupt us again, you may freely tell your trouble—if you will."

"Oh, sir,—it's my husband! He's been in prison a whole year, and now—now he's dying—they've killed him. It was fifty pounds a year ago. I saved, and scraped, and worked day and night, and a month ago—I brought the fifty pounds. But then—Oh, my God!—then they told me I must find twenty more—interest, they called it. Twenty pounds! why, it would take me months and months to earn so much, —and my husband was dying!—dying! But, sir, I went away despairing. Then I grew wild,—desperate—yes, desperate—oh, believe it, sir, and I,—I—Ah, sir—what won't a desperate woman do for one she loves? And so I—trod shameful ways! To-day I brought the twenty pounds, and now—dear God! now they say it must be twenty-three. Three pounds more, and I have no more—and I can't—Oh, I—can't go back to it again—the shame and horror—I—can't, sir!" So she covered her face again, and shook with the bitter passion of her woe.

And, after a while, Barnabas found voice, though his voice was very hoarse and uneven.

"I think," said he slowly, "yes, I think my cane could not have a worthier end than splintering on your villain's back, Mr. Quigly."

But, even as Barnabas advanced with very evident purpose, a tall figure stood framed in the open doorway.

"Ah, Quigly,—pray what is all this?" a chill, incisive voice demanded. Barnabas turned, and lowering the cane, stood looking curiously at the speaker. A tall, slender man he was, with a face that might have been any age,—a mask-like face, smooth and long, and devoid of hair as it was of wrinkles; an arresting face, with its curving nostrils, thin-lipped, close-shut mouth, high, prominent brow, and small, piercingly-bright eyes; quick eyes, that glinted between their red-rimmed, hairless lids, old in their experience of men and the ways of men. For the rest, he was clad in a rich yet sober habit, unrelieved by any color save for the gleaming seals at his fob, and the snowy lace at throat and wrist; his hair—evidently a wig—curled low on either cheek, and his hands were well cared for, with long, prehensile fingers.

"You are Jasper Gaunt, I think?" said Barnabas at last.

"At your service, sir, and you, I know, are Mr. Barnabas Beverley."

So they stood, fronting each other, the Youth, unconquered as yet, and therefore indomitable, and the Man, with glittering eyes old in their experience of men and the ways of men.

"You wished to see me on a matter of business, Mr. Beverley?"

"Yes."

"Then pray step this way."

"No," said Barnabas, "first I require your signature to this lady's papers."

Jasper Gaunt smiled, and shrugged his shoulders slightly.

"Such clients as this, sir,—I leave entirely to Mr. Quigly."

"Then, in this instance, sir, you will perhaps favor me by giving the matter your personal attention!"

Jasper Gaunt hesitated, observed the glowing eye, flushed cheek, and firm-set lips of the speaker, and being wise in men and their ways,—bowed.

"To oblige you, Mr. Beverley, with pleasure. Though I understand from Mr. Quigly that she is unable to meet—"

"Seventy-eight pounds, sir! She can pay it all—every blood-stained, tear-soaked farthing. She should meet it were it double—treble the sum!" said Barnabas, opening his purse.

"Ah, indeed, I see! I see!" nodded Jasper Gaunt. "Take the money, Quigly, I will make out the receipt. If you desire, you shall see me sign it, Mr. Beverley." So saying, he crossed to the desk, wrote the document, and handed it to Barnabas, with a bow that was almost ironical.

Then Barnabas gave the precious paper into the woman's eager fingers, and looked down into the woman's shining eyes.

"Sir," said she between trembling lips, "I cannot thank you,—I—I cannot. But God sees, and He will surely repay."

"Indeed," stammered Barnabas, "I—it was only three pounds, after all, and—there,—go,—hurry away to your husband, and—ah! that reminds me,—he will want help, perhaps!" Here Barnabas took out his card, and thrust it into her hand. "Take that to my house, ask to see my Steward, Mr. Peterby,—stay, I'll write the name for you, he will look after you, and—good-by!"

"It is a truly pleasant thing to meet with heartfelt gratitude, sir," said Jasper Gaunt, as the door closed behind the woman. "And now I am entirely at your service,—this way, sir."

Forthwith Barnabas followed him into another room, where sat the Captain, his long legs stretched out before him, his chin on his breast, staring away at vacancy.

"Sir," said Jasper Gaunt, glancing from Barnabas to the Captain and back again, "he will not trouble us, I think, but if you wish him to withdraw—?"

"Thank you—no," answered Barnabas, "Captain Slingsby is my friend!" Jasper Gaunt bowed, and seated himself at his desk opposite Barnabas. His face was in shadow, for the blind had been half-drawn to exclude the glare of the afternoon sun, and he sat, or rather lolled, in a low, deeply cushioned chair, studying Barnabas with his eyes that were so bright and so very knowing in the ways of mankind; very still he sat, and very quiet, waiting for Barnabas to begin. Now on the wall, immediately behind him, was a long, keen-bladed dagger, that glittered evilly where the light caught it; and as he sat there so very quiet and still, with his face in the shadow, it seemed to Barnabas as though he lolled there dead, with the dagger smitten sideways through his throat, and in that moment Barnabas fancied he could hear the deliberate tick-tock of the wizen-faced clock upon the stairs.

"I have come," began Barnabas at last, withdrawing his eyes from the glittering steel with an effort, "I am here on behalf of one—in whom I take an interest—a great interest."

"Yes, Mr. Beverley?"

"I have undertaken to—liquidate his debts."

"Yes, Mr. Beverley."

"To pay—whatever he may owe, both principal and interest."

"Indeed, Mr. Beverley! And—his name?"

"His name is Ronald Barrymaine."

"Ronald—Barrymaine!" There was a pause between the words, and the smooth, soft voice had suddenly grown so harsh, so deep and vibrant, that it seemed incredible the words could have proceeded from the lips of the motionless figure lolling in the chair with his face in the shadow and the knife glittering behind him.

"I have made out to you a draft for more than enough, as I judge, to cover Mr. Barrymaine's liabilities."

"For how much, sir?"

"Twenty-two thousand pounds."

Then Jasper Gaunt stirred, sighed, and leaned forward in his chair.

"A handsome sum, sir,—a very handsome sum, but—" and he smiled and shook his head.

"Pray what do you mean by 'but'?" demanded Barnabas.

"That the sum is—inadequate, sir."

"Twenty-two thousand pounds is not enough then?"

"It is—not enough, Mr. Beverley."

"Then, if you will tell me the precise amount, I will make up the deficiency." But, here again, Jasper Gaunt smiled his slow smile and shook his head.

"That, I grieve to say, is quite impossible, Mr. Beverley."

"Why?"

"Because I make it a rule never to divulge my clients' affairs to a third party; and, sir,—I never break my rules."

"Then—you refuse to tell me?"

"It is—quite impossible."

So there fell a silence while the wide, fearless eyes of Youth looked into the narrow, watchful eyes of Experience. Then Barnabas rose, and began to pace to and fro across the luxurious carpet; he walked with his head bent, and the hands behind his back were tightly clenched. Suddenly he stopped, and throwing up his head faced Jasper Gaunt, who sat lolling back in his chair again.

"I have heard," said he, "that this sum was twenty thousand pounds, but, as you say, it may be more,—a few pounds more, or a few hundreds more."

"Precisely, Mr. Beverley."

"I am, therefore, going to make you an offer—"

"Which I must—refuse."

"And my offer is this: instead of twenty thousand pounds I will double the sum."

Jasper Gaunt's lolling figure grew slowly rigid, and leaning across the desk, he stared up at Barnabas under his hairless brows. Even Captain Slingsby stirred and lifted his heavy head.

"Forty thousand pounds!" said Jasper Gaunt, speaking almost in a whisper.

"Yes," said Barnabas, and sitting down, he folded his arms a little ostentatiously. Jasper Gaunt's head drooped, and he stared down at the papers on the desk before him, nor did he move, only his long, white fingers began to tap softly upon his chair-arms, one after the other.

"I will pay you forty thousand pounds," said Barnabas. Then, all in one movement as it seemed, Gaunt had risen and turned to the window, and stood there awhile with his back to the room.

"Well?" inquired Barnabas at last.

"I—cannot, sir."

"You mean—will not!" said Barnabas, clenching his fists.

"Cannot, sir." As Gaunt turned, Barnabas rose and approached him until barely a yard separated them, until he could look into the eyes that glittered between their hairless lids, very like the cruel-looking dagger on the wall.

"Very well," said Barnabas, "then I'll treble it. I'll pay you sixty thousand pounds! What do you say? Come—speak!" But now, the eyes so keen and sharp to read men and the ways of men wavered and fell before the indomitable steadfastness of unconquered Youth; the long, white hands beneath their ruffles seemed to writhe with griping, contorted fingers, while upon his temple was something that glittered a moment, rolled down his cheek, and so was gone.

"Speak!" said Barnabas.

Yet still no answer came, only Jasper Gaunt sank down in his chair with his elbows on the desk, his long, white face clasped between his long, white hands, staring into vacancy; but now his smooth brow was furrowed, his narrow eyes were narrower yet, and his thin lips moved as though he had whispered to himself "sixty thousand pounds!"

"Sir,—for the last time—do you accept?" demanded Barnabas.

Without glancing up, or even altering the direction of his vacant stare, and with his face still framed between his hands, Jasper Gaunt shook his head from side to side, once, twice, and thrice; a gesture there was no mistaking.

Then Barnabas fell back a step, with clenched fist upraised, but in that moment the Captain was before him and had caught his arm.

"By Gad, Beverley!" he exclaimed in a shaken voice, "are you mad?"

"No," said Barnabas, "but I came here to buy those bills, and buy them I will! If trebling it isn't enough, then—"

"Ah!" cried Slingsby, pointing to the usurer's distorted face, "can't you see? Don't you guess? He can't sell! No money-lender of 'em all could resist such an offer. I tell you he daren't sell, the bills aren't his! Come away—"

"Not his!" cried Barnabas, "then whose?"

"God knows! But it's true,—look at him!"

"Tell me," cried Barnabas, striving to see Gaunt's averted eyes, "tell me who holds these bills,—if you have one spark of generosity—tell me!"

But Jasper Gaunt gave no sign, only the writhing fingers crept across his face, over staring eyes and twitching lips.

So, presently, Barnabas suffered Captain Slingsby to lead him from the room, and down the somewhat dark and winding stair, past the wizen-faced clock, out into the street already full of the glow of evening.

"It's a wonder to me," said the Captain, "yes, it's a great wonder to me, that nobody has happened to kill Gaunt before now."

So the Captain frowned, sighed, and climbed up to his seat. But, when Barnabas would have followed, Billy Button touched him on the arm.

"Oh, Barnaby!" said he, "oh, Barnaby Bright, look—the day is dying, the shadows are coming,—in a little while it will be night. But, oh Youth, alas! alas! I can see the shadows have touched you already!" And so, with a quick upflung glance at the dismal house, he turned, waved his hand, and sped away on noiseless feet, and so was gone.

CHAPTER XXXVI

OF AN ETHICAL DISCUSSION, WHICH THE READER IS ADVISED TO SKIP

Oho! for the rush of wind in the hair, for the rolling thunder of galloping hoofs, now echoing on the hard, white road, now muffled in dewy grass.

Oho! for the horse and his rider and the glory of them; for the long, swinging stride that makes nothing of distance, for the tireless spring of the powerful loins, for the masterful hand on the bridle, strong, yet gentle as a caress, for the firm seat—the balance and sway that is an aid to speed, and proves the born rider. And what horse should this be but Four-legs, his black coat glossy and shining in the sun, his great, round hoofs spurning the flying earth, all a-quiver with high courage, with life and the joy of it? And who should be the rider but young Barnabas?

He rides with his hat in his whip-hand, that he may feel the wind, and with never a look behind, for birds are carolling from the cool freshness of dewy wood and copse, in every hedge and tree the young sun has set a myriad gems flashing and sparkling; while, out of the green distance ahead, Love is calling; brooks babble of it, birds sing of it, the very leaves find each a small, soft voice to whisper of it.

So away—away rides Barnabas by village green and lonely cot, past hedge and gate and barn, up hill and down hill,—away from the dirt and noise of London, away from its joys and sorrows, its splendors and its miseries, and from the oncoming, engulfing shadow. Spur and gallop, Barnabas,—ride, youth, ride! for the shadow has already touched you, even as the madman said.

Therefore while youth yet abides, while the sun yet shines,—ride, Barnabas, ride!

Now as he went, Barnabas presently espied a leafy by-lane, and across this lane a fence had been erected,—a high fence, but with a fair "take-off" and consequently, a most inviting fence. At this, forthwith, Barnabas rode, steadied Four-legs in his stride, touched him with the spur, and cleared it with a foot to spare. Then, all at once, he drew rein and paced over the dewy grass to where, beneath the hedge, was a solitary man who knelt before a fire of twigs fanning it to a blaze with his wide-eaved hat.

He was a slender man, and something stooping of shoulder, and his hair shone silver-white in the sunshine. Hearing Barnabas approach, he looked up, rose to his feet, and so stood staring as one in doubt. Therefore Barnabas uncovered his head and saluted him with grave politeness.

"Sir," said he, reining in his great horse, "you have not forgotten me, I hope?"

"No indeed, young sir," answered the Apostle of Peace, with a dawning smile of welcome. "But you are dressed very differently from what I remember. The quiet, country youth has become lost, and transfigured into the dashing Corinthian. What a vast difference clothes can make in one! And yet your face is the same, your expression unchanged. London has not altered you yet, and I hope it never may. No, sir, your face is not one to be forgotten,—indeed it reminds me of other days."

"But we have only met once before," said Barnabas.

"True! And yet I seem to have known you years ago,—that is what puzzles me! But come, young sir,—if you have time and inclination to share a vagrant's breakfast, I can offer you eggs and new milk, and bread and butter,—simple fare, but more wholesome than your French ragouts and highly-seasoned dishes."

"You are very kind," said Barnabas, "the ride has made me hungry, — besides, I should like to talk with you."

"Why, then—light down from that great horse of yours, and join me. The grass must be both chair and table, but here is a tree for your back, and the bank for mine."

So, having dismounted and secured his horse's bridle to a convenient branch, Barnabas sat himself down with his back to the tree, and accepted the wandering Preacher's bounty as freely as it was offered. And when the Preacher had spoken a short grace, they began to eat, and while they ate, to talk, as follows:

Barnabas. "It is three weeks, I think, since we met?"

The Preacher. "A month, young sir."

Barnabas. "So long a time?"

The Preacher. "So short a time. You have been busy, I take it?"

Barnabas. "Yes, sir. Since last we met I have bought a house and set up an establishment in London, and I have also had the good fortune to be entered for the Gentleman's Steeplechase on the fifteenth."

The Preacher. "You are rich, young sir?"

Barnabas. "And I hope to be famous also."

The Preacher. "Then indeed do I begin to tremble for you."

Barnabas (staring). "Why so?"

The Preacher. "Because wealth is apt to paralyze effort, and Fame is generally harder to bear, and far more dangerous, than failure."

Barnabas. "How dangerous, sir?"

The Preacher. "Because he who listens too often to the applause of the multitude grows deaf to the voice of Inspiration, for it is a very small, soft voice, and must be hearkened for, and some call it Genius, and some the Voice of God—"

Barnabas. "But Fame means Power, and I would succeed for the sake of others beside myself. Yes,—I must succeed, and, as I think you once said, all things are possible to us! Pray, what did you mean?"

The Preacher. "Young sir, into each of us who are born into this world God puts something of Himself, and by reason of this Divine part, all things are possible."

Barnabas. "Yet the world is full of failures."

The Preacher. "Alas! yes; but only because men do not realize power within them. For man is a selfish creature, and Self is always grossly blind. But let a man look within himself, let him but become convinced of this Divine power, and the sure and certain knowledge of ultimate success will be his. So, striving diligently, this power shall grow within him, and by and by he shall achieve great things, and the world proclaim him a Genius."

Barnabas. "Then—all men might succeed."

The Preacher. "Assuredly! for success is the common heritage of Man. It is only Self, blind, ignorant Self, who is the coward, crying 'I cannot! I dare not! It is impossible!'"

Barnabas. "What do you mean by 'Self'?"

The Preacher. "I mean the grosser part, the slave that panders to the body, a slave that, left unchecked, may grow into a tyrant, a Circe, changing Man to brute."

Here Barnabas, having finished his bread and butter, very thoughtfully cut himself another slice.

Barnabas (still thoughtful). "And do you still go about preaching Forgetfulness of Self, sir?"

The Preacher. "And Forgiveness, yes. A good theme, young sir, but—very unpopular. Men prefer to dwell upon the wrongs done them, rather than cherish the memory of benefits conferred. But, nevertheless, I go up and down the ways, preaching always."

Barnabas. "Why, then, I take it, your search is still unsuccessful."

The Preacher. "Quite! Sometimes a fear comes upon me that she may be beyond my reach—"

Barnabas. "You mean—?"

The Preacher. "Dead, sir. At such times, things grow very black until I remember that God is a just God, and therein lies my sure and certain hope. But I would not trouble you with my griefs, young sir, more especially on such a glorious morning,—hark to the throstle yonder, he surely sings of Life and Hope. So, if you will, pray tell me of yourself, young sir, of your hopes and ambitions."

Barnabas. "My ambitions, sir, are many, but first,—I would be a gentleman."

The Preacher (nodding). "Good! So far as it goes, the ambition is a laudable one."

Barnabas (staring thoughtfully at his bread and butter). "The first difficulty is to know precisely what a gentleman should be. Pray, sir, what is your definition?"

The Preacher. "A gentleman, young sir, is (I take it) one born with the Godlike capacity to think and feel for others, irrespective of their rank or condition."

Barnabas. "Hum! One who is unselfish?"

The Preacher. "One who possesses an ideal so lofty, a mind so delicate, that it lifts him above all things ignoble and base, yet strengthens his hands to raise those who are fallen—no matter how low. This, I think, is to be truly a gentleman, and of all gentle men Jesus of Nazareth was the first."

Barnabas (shaking his head). "And yet, sir, I remember a whip of small cords."

The Preacher. "Truly, for Evil sometimes so deadens the soul that it can feel only through the flesh."

Barnabas. "Then—a man may fight and yet be a gentleman?"

The Preacher. "He who can forgive, can fight."

Barnabas. "Sir, I am relieved to know that. But must Forgiveness always come after?"

The Preacher. "If the evil is truly repented of."

Barnabas. "Even though the evil remain?"

The Preacher. "Ay, young sir, for then Forgiveness becomes truly divine."

Barnabas. "Hum!"

The Preacher. "But you eat nothing, young sir."

Barnabas. "I was thinking."

The Preacher. "Of what?"

Barnabas. "Sir, my thought embraced you."

The Preacher. "How, young sir?"

Barnabas. "I was wondering if you had ever heard of a man named Chichester?"

The Preacher (speaking brokenly, and in a whisper). "Sir!—young sir,—you said—?"

Barnabas (rising). "Chichester!"

The Preacher (coming to his knees). "Sir,—oh, sir,—this man—Chichester is he who stole away—my daughter,—who blasted her honor and my life,—who—"

Barnabas. "No!"

The Preacher (covering his face). "Yes,—yes! God help me, it's true! But in her shame I love her still, oh, my pride is dead long ago. I remember only that I am her father, with all a father's loving pity, and that she—"

Barnabas. "And that she is the stainless maid she always was—"

"Sir," cried the Preacher, "oh, sir,—what do you mean?" and Barnabas saw the thin hands clasp and wring themselves, even as he remembered Clemency's had done.

"I mean," answered Barnabas, "that she fled from pollution, and found refuge among honest folk. I mean that she is alive and well, that she lives but to bless your arms and feel a father's kiss of forgiveness. If you would find her, go to the 'Spotted Cow,' near Frittenden, and ask for 'Clemency'!"

"Clemency!" repeated the Preacher, "Clemency means mercy. And she called herself—Clemency!" Then, with a sudden, rapturous gesture, he lifted his thin hands, and with his eyes upturned to the blue heaven, spoke.

"Oh, God!" he cried, "Oh, Father of Mercy, I thank Thee!" And so he arose from his knees, and turning about, set off through the golden morning towards Frittenden, and Clemency.

CHAPTER XXXVII

IN WHICH THE BO'SUN DISCOURSES ON LOVE AND ITS SYMPTOMS

Oho! for the warmth and splendor of the mid-day sun; for the dance and flurry of leafy shadows on the sward; for stilly wayside pools whose waters, deep and dark in the shade of overhanging boughs, are yet dappled here and there with glory; for merry brooks leaping and laughing along their stony beds; for darkling copse and sunny upland,—oho! for youth and life and the joy of it.

To the eyes of Barnabas, the beauty of the world about him served only to remind him of the beauty of her who was compounded of all things beautiful,—the One and Only Woman, whose hair was yellow like the ripening corn, whose eyes were deep and blue as the infinite heaven, whose lips were red as the poppies that bloomed beside the way, and whose body was warm with youth, and soft and white as the billowy clouds above.

Thus on galloped Barnabas with the dust behind and the white road before, and with never a thought of London, or its wonders, or the gathering shadow.

It was well past noon when he beheld a certain lonely church where many a green mound and mossy headstone marked the resting-place of those that sleep awhile. And here, beside the weather-worn porch, were the stocks, that "place of thought" where Viscount Devenham had sat in solitary, though dignified meditation. A glance, a smile, and Barnabas was past, and galloping down the hill towards where the village nestled in the valley. Before the inn he dismounted, and, having seen Four-legs well bestowed, and given various directions to a certain sleepy-voiced ostler, he entered the inn, and calling for dinner, ate it with huge relish. Now, when he had done, came the landlord to smoke a pipe with him,—a red-faced man, vast of paunch and garrulous of tongue.

"Fine doin's there be up at t' great 'ouse, sir," he began.

"You mean Annersley House?"

"Ay, sir. All the quality is there,—my son's a groom there an' 'e told me, so 'e did. Theer ain't nobody as ain't either a Markus or a Earl or a Vi'count, and as for Barry-nets, they're as thick as flies, they are,—an' all to meet a little, old 'ooman as don't come up to my shoulder! But then—she's a Duchess, an' that makes all the difference!"

"Yes, of course," said Barnabas.

"A little old 'ooman wi' curls, as don't come no-wise near so 'igh as my shoulder! Druv up to that theer very door as you see theer, in 'er great coach an' four, she did,—orders the steps to be lowered, —comes tapping into this 'ere very room with 'er little cane, she do, —sits down in that theer very chair as you're a-sittin' in, she do, fannin' 'erself with a little fan—an' calls for—now, what d' ye suppose, sir?"

"I haven't the least idea."

"She calls, sir,—though you won't believe me, it aren't to be expected,—no, not on my affer-daver,—she being a Duchess, ye see—"

"Well, what did she call for?" inquired Barnabas, rising.

"Sir, she called for—on my solemn oath it's true—though I don't ax ye to believe me, mind,—she sat in that theer identical chair,—an' mark me, 'er a Duchess,—she sat in that cheer, a-fannin' 'erself with 'er little fan, an' calls for a 'arf of Kentish ale—'Westerham brew,' says she; an' 'er a Duchess! In a tankard! But I know as you won't believe me,—nor I don't ax any man to,—no, not if I went down on my bended marrer-bones—"

"But I do believe you," said Barnabas.

"What—you do?" cried the landlord, almost reproachfully.

"Certainly! A Duchess is, sometimes, almost human."

"But you—actooally—believe me?"

"Yes."

"Well—you surprise me, sir! Ale! A Duchess! In a tankard! No, it aren't nat'ral. Never would I ha' believed as any one would ha' believed such a—"

But here Barnabas laughed, and taking up his hat, sallied out into the sunshine.

He went by field paths that led him past woods in whose green twilight thrushes and blackbirds piped, by sunny meadows where larks mounted heavenward in an ecstasy of song, and so, eventually he found himself in a road where stood a weather-beaten finger-post, with its two arms wide-spread and pointing:

TO LONDON. TO HAWKHURST

Here Barnabas paused a while, and bared his head as one who stands on hallowed ground. And looking upon the weather-worn finger-post, he smiled very tenderly, as one might who meets an old friend. Then he went on again until he came to a pair of tall iron gates, hospitable gates that stood open as though inviting him to enter. Therefore he went on, and thus presently espied a low, rambling house of many gables, about which were trim lawns and stately trees. Now as he stood looking at this house, he heard a voice near by, a deep, rolling bass upraised in song, and the words of it were these:

"What shall we do with the drunken sailor,
Heave, my lads, yo-ho!
Why, put him in the boat and roll him over,
Put him in the boat till he gets sober,
Put him in the boat and roll him over,
With a heave, my lads, yo-ho!"

Following the direction of this voice, Barnabas came to a lawn screened from the house by hedges of clipped yew. At the further end of this lawn was a small building which had been made to look as much as possible like the after-cabin of a ship. It had a door midway, with a row of small, square windows on either side, and was flanked at each end by a flight of wooden steps, with elaborately carved hand-rails, that led up to the quarterdeck above, which was protected by more carved posts and rails. Here a stout pole had been erected and rigged with block and fall, and from this, a flag stirred lazily in the gentle wind.

Now before this building, his blue coat laid by, his shirt sleeves rolled up, his glazed hat on the back of his head, was the Bo'sun, polishing away at a small, brass cannon that was mounted on a platform, and singing lustily as he worked. So loudly did he sing, and so engrossed was he, that he did not look up until he felt Barnabas touch him. Then he started, turned, stared, hesitated, and, finally, broke into a smile.

"Ah, it's you, sir,—the young gemman as bore away for Lon'on alongside Master Horatio, his Lordship!"

"Yes," said Barnabas, extending his hand, "how are you, Bo'sun?"

"Hearty, sir, hearty, I thank ye!" Saying which he touched his forehead, rubbed his hand upon his trousers, looked at it, rubbed it again, and finally gave it to Barnabas, though with an air of apology. "Been making things a bit ship-shape, sir, 'count o' this here day being a occasion,—but I'm hearty, sir, hearty, I thank ye."

"And the Captain," said Barnabas with some hesitation. "How is the Captain?"

"The Cap'n, sir," answered the Bo'sun, "the Cap'n is likewise hearty."

"And—Lady Cleone—is she well, is she happy?"

"Why, sir, she's as 'appy as can be expected—under the circumstances."

"What circumstances?"

"Love, sir."

"Love!" exclaimed Barnabas, "why, Bo'sun—what do you mean?"

"I mean, sir, as she's fell in love at last—

"How do you know—who with—where is she—?"

"Well, sir, I know on account o' 'er lowness o' sperrits,—noticed it for a week or more. Likewise I've heered 'er sigh very frequent, and I've seen 'er sit a-staring up at the moon—ah, that I have! Now lovers is generally low in their sperrits, I've heered tell, and they allus stare very 'ard at the moon,—why, I don't know, but they do,—leastways, so I've—"

"But—in love—with whom? Can I see her? Where is she? Are you sure?"

"And sartain, sir. Only t' other night, as I sat a-smoking my pipe on the lawn, yonder,—she comes out to me, and nestles down under my lee—like she used to years ago. 'Jerry, dear,' says she, 'er voice all low and soft-like, 'look at the moon,—how beautiful it is!' says she, and—she give a sigh. 'Yes, my lady,' says I. 'Oh, Jerry,' says she, 'call me Clo, as you used to do.' 'Yes, my Lady Clo,' says I. But she grapples me by the collar, and stamps 'er foot at me, all in a moment. 'Leave out the 'lady," says she. 'Yes, Clo,' says I. So she nestles an' sighs and stares at the moon again. 'Jerry, dear,' says she after a bit, 'when will the moon be at the full?' 'To-morrer, Clo,' says I. And after she's stared and sighed a bit longer—'Jerry, dear,' says she again, 'it's sweet to think that while we are looking up at the moon—others perhaps are looking at it too, I mean others who are far away. It—almost seems to bring them nearer, doesn't it? Then I knowed as 't were love, with a big L, sartin and sure, and—"

"Bo'sun," said Barnabas, catching him by the arm, "who is it she loves?"

"Well, sir,—I aren't quite sure, seeing as there are so many on 'em in 'er wake, but I think,—and I 'ope, as it's 'is Lordship, Master Horatio."

"Ah!" said Barnabas, his frowning brow relaxing.

"If it ain't 'im,—why then it's mutiny,—that's what it is, sir!"

"Mutiny?"

"Ye see, sir," the Bo'sun went on to explain, "orders is orders, and if she don't love Master Horatio—well, she ought to."

"Why?"

"Because they was made for each other. Because they was promised to each other years ago. It were all arranged an' settled 'twixt Master Horatio's father, the Earl, and Lady Cleone's guardian, the Cap'n."

"Ah!" said Barnabas, "and where is she—and the Captain?"

"Out, sir; an' she made him put on 'is best uniform, as he only wears on Trafalgar Day, and such great occasions. She orders out the fam'ly coach, and away they go, 'im the very picter o' what a post-captain o' Lord Nelson should be (though to be sure, there's a darn in his white silk stocking—the one to starboard, just abaft the shoe-buckle, and, therefore, not to be noticed, and I were allus 'andy wi' my needle), and her—looking the picter o' the handsomest lady, the loveliest, properest maid in all this 'ere world. Away they go, wi' a fair wind to sarve 'em, an' should ha' dropped anchor at Annersley House a full hour ago."

"At Annersley?" said Barnabas. "There is a reception there, I hear?"

"Yes, sir, all great folk from Lon'on, besides country folk o' quality,—to meet the Duchess o' Camberhurst, and she's the greatest of 'em all. Lord! There's enough blue blood among 'em to float a Seventy-four. Nat'rally, the Cap'n wanted to keep a good offing to windward of 'em. 'For look ye, Jerry,' says he, 'I'm no confounded courtier to go bowing and scraping to a painted old woman, with a lot of other fools, just because she happens to be a duchess,—no, damme!' and down 'e sits on the breech o' the gun here. But, just then, my lady heaves into sight, brings up alongside, and comes to an anchor on his knee. 'Dear,' says she, with her round, white arm about his neck, and her soft, smooth cheek agin his, 'dear, it's almost time we began to dress.' 'Dress?' says he, 'what for, Clo,—I say, what d'ye mean?' 'Why, for the reception,' says she. 'To-day is my birthday' (which it is, sir, wherefore the flag at our peak, yonder), 'and I know you mean to take me,' says she, 'so I told Robert we should want the coach at three. So come along and dress,—like a dear.' The Cap'n stared at 'er, dazed-like, give me a look, and,—well—" the Bo'sun smiled and shook his head. "Ye see, sir, in some ways the Cap'n 's very like a ordinary man, arter all!"

CHAPTER XXXVIII

HOW BARNABAS CLIMBED A WALL

Now presently, as he went, he became aware of a sound that was not the stir of leaves, nor the twitter of birds, nor the music of running waters, though all these were in his ears,—for this was altogether different; a distant sound that came and went, that swelled to a murmur, sank to a whisper, yet never wholly died away. Little by little the sound grew plainer, more insistent, until, mingled with the leafy stirrings, he could hear a plaintive melody, rising and falling, faint with distance.

Hereupon Barnabas halted suddenly, his chin in hand, his brow furrowed in thought, while over his senses stole the wailing melody of the distant violins. A while he stood thus, then plunged into the cool shadow of a wood, and hurried on by winding tracks, through broad glades, until the wood was left behind, until the path became a grassy lane; and ever the throbbing melody swelled and grew. It was a shady lane, tortuous and narrow, but on strode Barnabas until, rounding a bend, he beheld a wall, an ancient, mossy wall of red brick; and with his gaze upon this, he stopped again. But the melody called to him, louder now and more insistent, and mingled with the throb of the violins was the sound of voices and laughter.

Then, standing on tip-toe, Barnabas set his hands to the coping of the wall, and drawing himself up, caught a momentary vision of smiling gardens, of green lawns where bright figures moved, of winding walks and neat trimmed hedges, ere, swinging himself over, he dropped down among a bed of Sir George Annersley's stocks.

Before him was a shady walk winding between clipped yews, and, following this, Barnabas presently espied a small arbor some distance away. Now between him and this arbor was a place where four paths met, and where stood an ancient sun-dial with quaintly carved seats. And here, the sun making a glory of her wondrous hair, was my Lady Cleone, with the Marquis of Jerningham beside her. She sat with her elbow on her knee and her dimpled chin upon her palm, and, even from where he stood, Barnabas could see again the witchery of her lashes that drooped dark upon the oval of her cheek.

The Marquis was talking earnestly, gesturing now and then with his slender hand that had quite lost its habitual languor, and stooping that he might look into the drooping beauty of her face, utterly regardless of the havoc he thus wrought upon the artful folds of his marvellous cravat. All at once she looked up, laughed and shook her head, and, closing her fan, pointed with it towards the distant house, laughing still, but imperious. Hereupon the Marquis rose, albeit unwillingly, and bowing, hurried off to obey her behest. Then Cleone rose also, and turning, went on slowly toward the arbor, with head drooping as one in thought.

And now, with his gaze upon that shapely back, all youthful loveliness from slender foot to the crowning glory of her hair, Barnabas sighed, and felt his heart leap as he strode after her. But, even as he followed, oblivious of all else under heaven, he beheld another back that obtruded itself suddenly upon the scene, a broad, graceful back in a coat of fine blue cloth,—a back that bore itself with a masterful swing of the shoulders. And, in that instant, Barnabas recognized Sir Mortimer Carnaby.

Cleone had reached the arbor, but on the threshold turned to meet Sir Mortimer's sweeping bow. And now she seemed to hesitate, then extended her hand, and Sir Mortimer followed her into the arbor. My lady's cheeks were warm with rich color, her eyes were suddenly and strangely bright as she sank into a chair, and Sir Mortimer, misinterpreting this, had caught and imprisoned her hands.

"Cleone," said he, "at last!" The slender hands fluttered in his grasp, but his grasp was strong, and, ere she could stay him, he was down before her on his knee, and speaking quick and passionately.

"Cleone!—hear me! nay, I will speak! All the afternoon I have tried to get a word with you, and now you must hear me—you shall. And yet you know what I would say. You know I love you, and have done from the first hour I saw you. And from that hour I've hungered for your, Cleone, do you hear? Ah, tell me you love me!"

But my lady sat wide-eyed, staring at the face amid the leaves beyond the open window,—a face so handsome, yet so distorted; saw the gleam of clenched teeth, the frowning brows, the menacing gray eyes.

Sir Mortimer, all unconscious, had caught her listless hands to his lips, and was speaking again between his kisses.

"Speak, Cleone! You know how long I have loved you,—speak and bid me hope! What, silent still? Why, then—give me that rose from your bosom,—let it be hope's messenger, and speak for you."

But still my lady sat dumb, staring up at the face amid the leaves, the face of Man Primeval, aglow with all the primitive passions; beheld the drawn lips and quivering nostrils, the tense jaw savage and masterful, and the glowing eyes that threatened her. And, in that moment, she threw tip her head rebellious, and sighed, and smiled,—a woman's smile, proud, defiant; and, uttering no word, gave Sir Mortimer the rose. Then, even as she did so, sprang to her feet, and laughed, a little tremulously, and bade Sir Mortimer Go! Go! Go! Wherefore, Sir Mortimer, seeing her thus, and being wise in the ways of women, pressed the flower to his lips, and so turned and strode off down the path. And when his step had died away Cleone sank down in the chair, and spoke.

"Come out—spy!" she called. And Barnabas stepped out from the leaves. Then, because she knew what look was in his eyes, she kept her own averted; and because she was a woman young, and very proud, she lashed him with her tongue.

"So much for your watching and listening!" said she.

"But—he has your rose!" said Barnabas.

"And what of that?"

"And he has your promise!"

"I never spoke—"

"But the rose did!"

"The rose will fade and wither—"

"But it bears your promise—"

"I gave no promise, and—and—oh, why did you—look at me!"

"Look at you?"

"Why did you frown at me?"

"Why did you give him the rose?"

"Because it was so my pleasure. Why did you frown at me with eyes like—like a devil's?"

"I wanted to kill him—then!"

"And now?"

"Now, I wish him well of his bargain, and my thanks are due to him."

"Why?"

"Because, without knowing it, he has taught me what women are."

"What do you mean?"

"I—loved you, Cleone. To me you were one apart—holy, immaculate—"

"Yes?" said Cleone very softly.

"And I find you—"

"Only a—woman, sir,—who will not be watched, and frowned at, and spied upon."

"—a heartless coquette—" said Barnabas.

"—who despises eavesdroppers, and will not be spied upon, or frowned at!"

"I did not spy upon you," cried Barnabas, stung at last, "or if I did, God knows it was well intended."

"How, sir?"

"I remembered the last time we three were together,—in Annersley Wood." Here my lady shivered and hid her face. "And now, you gave him the rose! Do you want the love of this man, Cleone?"

"There is only one man in all the world I despise more, and his name is—Barnabas," said she, without looking up.

"So you—despise me, Cleone?"

"Yes—Barnabas."

"And I came here to tell you that I—loved you—to ask you to be my wife--"

"And looked at me with Devil's eyes—"

"Because you were mine, and because he—"

"Yours, Barnabas? I never said so."

"Because I loved you—worshipped you, and because—"

"Because you were—jealous, Barnabas!"

"Because I would have my wife immaculate—"

"But I am not your—wife."

"No," said Barnabas, frowning, "she must be immaculate."

Now when he said this he heard her draw a long, quivering sigh, and with the sigh she rose to her feet and faced him, and her eyes were wide and very bright, and the fan she held snapped suddenly across in her white fingers.

"Sir," she said, very softly, "I whipped you once, if I had a whip now, your cheek should burn again."

"But I should not ask you to kiss it,—this time!" said Barnabas.

"Yes," she said, in the same soft voice, "I despise you—for a creeping spy, a fool, a coward—a maligner of women. Oh, go away,—pray go. Leave me, lest I stifle."

But now, seeing the flaming scorn of him in her eyes, in the passionate quiver of her hands, he grew afraid, cowed by her very womanhood.

"Indeed," he stammered, "you are unjust. I—I did not mean—"

"Go!" said she, cold as ice, "get back over the wall. Oh! I saw you climb over like a—thief! Go away, before I call for help—before I call the grooms and stable-boys to whip you out into the road where you belong—go, I say!" And frowning now, she stamped her foot, and pointed to the wall. Then Barnabas laughed softty, savagely, and, reaching out, caught her up in his long arms and crushed her to him.

"Call if you will, Cleone," said he, "but listen first! I said to you that my wife should come to me immaculate—fortune's spoiled darling though she be,—petted, wooed, pampered though she is,—and, by God, so you shall! For I love you, Cleone, and if I live, I will some day call you 'wife,'—in spite of all your lovers, and all the roses that ever bloomed. Now, Cleone,—call them if you will." So saying he set her down and freed her from his embrace. But my lady, leaning breathless in the doorway, only looked at him once,—frowning a little, panting a little,—a long wondering look beneath her lashes, and, turning, was gone among the leaves. Then Barnabas picked up the broken fan, very tenderly, and put it into his bosom, and so sank down into the chair, his chin propped upon his fist, frowning blackly at the glory of the afternoon.

CHAPTER XXXIX

IN WHICH THE PATIENT READER IS INTRODUCED TO AN ALMOST HUMAN DUCHESS

"Very dramatic, sir! Though, indeed, you missed an opportunity, and—gracious heaven, how he frowns!" A woman's voice, sharp, high-pitched, imperious.

Barnabas started, and glancing up, beheld an ancient lady, very small and very upright; her cheeks were suspiciously pink, her curls suspiciously dark and luxuriant, but her eyes were wonderfully young and handsome; one slender mittened hand rested upon the ivory head of a stick, and in the other she carried a small fan.

"Now, he stares!" she exclaimed, as she met his look. "Lud, how he stares! As if I were a ghost, or a goblin, instead of only an old woman with raddled cheeks and a wig. Oh, yes! I wear a wig, sir, and very hideous I look without it! But even I was young once upon a time—many, many years ago, and quite as beautiful as She, indeed, rather more so, I think,—and I should have treated you exactly as She did—only more so,—I mean Cleone. Your blonde women are either too cold or overpassionate,—I know, for my hair was as yellow as Cleone's, hundreds of years ago, and I think, more abundant. To-day, being only a dyed brunette, I am neither too cold nor over-passionate, and I tell you, sir, you deserved it, every word."

Here Barnabas rose, and, finding nothing to say, bowed.

"But," continued the ancient lady, sweeping him with a quick, approving gaze, "I like your face, and y-e-s, you have a very good leg. You also possess a tongue, perhaps, and can speak?"

"Given the occasion, madam," said Barnabas, smiling.

"Ha, sir! do I talk so much then? Well, perhaps I do, for when a woman ceases to talk she's dead, and I'm very much alive indeed. So you may give me your arm, sir, and listen to me, and drop an occasional remark while I take breath,—your arm, sir!" And here the small, ancient lady held out a small, imperious hand, while her handsome young eyes smiled up into his.

"Madam, you honor me!"

"But I am only an old woman,—with a wig!"

"Age is always honorable, madam."

"Now that is very prettily said, indeed you improve, sir. Do you know who I am?"

"No, madam; but I can guess."

"Ah, well,—you shall talk to me. Now, sir,—begin. Talk to me of Cleone."

"Madam—I had rather not."

"Eh, sir,—you won't?"

"No, madam."

"Why, then, I will!" Here the ancient lady glanced up at Barnabas with a malicious little smile. "Let me see, now—what were her words? 'Spy,' I think.

Ah, yes—'a creeping spy,' 'a fool' and 'a coward.' Really, I don't think I could have bettered that—even in my best days,—especially the 'creeping spy.'"

"Madam," said Barnabas in frowning surprise, "you were listening?"

"At the back of the arbor," she nodded, "with my ear to the panelling, —I am sometimes a little deaf, you see."

"You mean that you were—actually prying—?"

"And I enjoyed it all very much, especially your 'immaculate' speech, which was very heroic, but perfectly ridiculous, of course. Indeed, you are a dreadfully young, young sir, I fear. In future, I warn you not to tell a woman, too often, how much you respect her, or she'll begin to think you don't love her at all. To be over-respectful doesn't sit well on a lover, and 'tis most unfair and very trying to the lady, poor soul!"

"To hearken to a private conversation doesn't sit well on a lady, madam, or an honorable woman."

"No, indeed, young sir. But then, you see, I'm neither. I'm only a Duchess, and a very old one at that, and I think I told you I wore a wig? But 'all the world loves a lover,' and so do I. As soon as ever I saw you I knew you for a lover of the 'everything-or-nothing' type. Oh, yes, all lovers are of different types, sir, and I think I know 'em all. You see, when I was young and beautiful—ages ago—lovers were a hobby of mine,—I studied them, sir. And, of 'em all, I preferred the 'everything-or-nothing, fire-and-ice, kiss-me-or-kill-me' type. That was why I followed you, that was why I watched and listened, and, I grieve to say, I didn't find you as deliciously brutal as I had hoped."

"Brutal, madam? Indeed, I—"

"Of course! When you snatched her up in your arms,—and I'll admit you did it very well,—when you had her there, you should have covered her with burning kisses, and with an oath after each. Girls like Cleone need a little brutality and—Ah! there's the Countess! And smiling at me quite lovingly, I declare! Now I wonder what rod she has in pickle for me? Dear me, sir, how dusty your coat is! And spurred boots and buckskins are scarcely the mode for a garden fête. Still, they're distinctive, and show off your leg to advantage, better than those abominable Cossack things,—and I doat upon a good leg—" But here she broke off and turned to greet the Countess,—a large, imposing, bony lady in a turban, with the eye and the beak of a hawk.

"My dearest Letitia!"

"My dear Duchess,—my darling Fanny, you 're younger than ever, positively you are,—I'd never have believed it!" cried the Countess, more hawk-like than ever. "I heard you were failing fast, but now I look at you, dearest Fanny, I vow you don't look a day older than seventy."

"And I'm seventy-one, alas!" sighed the Duchess, her eyes young with mischief. "And you, my sweetest creature,—how well you look! Who would ever imagine that we were at school together, Letitia!"

"But indeed I was—quite an infant, Fanny."

"Quite, my love, and used to do my sums for me. But let me present to you a young friend of mine, Mr.—Mr.—dear, dear! I quite forget—my memory is going, you see, Letitia! Mr.—"

"Beverley, madam," said Barnabas.

"Thank you,—Beverley, of course! Mr. Beverley—the Countess of Orme."

Hereupon Barnabas bowed low before the haughty stare of the keen, hawk-like eyes.

"And now, my sweet Letty," continued the Duchess, "you are always so delightfully gossipy—have you any news,—any stories to laugh over?"

"No, dear Fanny, neither the one nor the other—only—"

"'Only,' my love?"

"Only—but you've heard it already, of course,—you would be the very first to know of it!"

"Letitia, my dear—I always hated conundrums, you'll remember."

"I mean, every one is talking of it, already."

"Heigho! How warm the sun is!"

"Of course it may be only gossip, but they do say Cleone Meredith has refused the hand of your grandnephew."

"Jerningham, oh yes," added the Duchess, "on the whole, it's just as well."

"But I thought—" the hawk-eyes were very piercing indeed. "I feared it would be quite a blow to you—"

The Duchess shook her head, with a little ripple of laughter.

"I had formed other plans for him weeks ago,—they were quite unsuited to each other, my love."

"I'm delighted you take it so well, my own Fanny," said the Countess, looking the reverse. "We leave almost immediately,—but when you pass through Sevenoaks, you must positively stay with me for a day or two. Goodby, my sweet Fanny!" So the two ancient ladies gravely curtsied to each other, pecked each other on either cheek, and, with a bow to Barnabas, the Countess swept away with an imposing rustle of her voluminous skirts.

"Cat!" exclaimed the Duchess, shaking her fan at the receding figure; "the creature hates me fervently, and consequently, kisses me—on both cheeks. Oh, yes, indeed, sir, she detests me—and quite naturally. You see, we were girls together,—she's six months my junior, and has never let me forget it,—and the Duke—God rest him—admired us both, and, well,—I married him. And so Cleone has actually refused poor Jerningham,—the yellow-maned minx!"

"Why, then—you didn't know of it?" inquired Barnabas.

"Oh, Innocent! of course I didn't. I'm not omniscient, and I only ordered him to propose an hour ago. The golden hussy! the proud jade! Refuse my grand-nephew indeed! Well, there's one of your rivals disposed of, it seems,—count that to your advantage, sir!"

"But," said Barnabas, frowning and shaking his head, "Sir Mortimer Carnaby has her promise!"

"Fiddlesticks!"

"She gave him the rose!" said Barnabas, between set teeth. The Duchess tittered.

"Dear heart! how tragic you are!" she sighed. "Suppose she did,—what then? And besides—hum! This time it is young D'Arcy, it seems,—callow, pink, and quite harmless."

"Madam?" said Barnabas, wondering.

"Over there—behind the marble faun,—quite harmless, and very pink, you'll notice. I mean young D'Arcy—not the faun. Clever minx! Now I mean Cleone, of course—there she is!" Following the direction of the Duchess's pointing fan, Barnabas saw Cleone, sure enough. Her eyes were drooped demurely before the ardent gaze of the handsome, pink-cheeked young soldier who stood before her, and in her white fingers she held—a single red rose. Now, all at once, (and as though utterly unconscious of the burning, watchful eyes of Barnabas) she lifted the rose to her lips, and, smiling, gave it into the young soldier's eager hand. Then they strolled away, his epaulette very near the gleaming curls at her temple.

"Lud, young sir!" exclaimed the Duchess, catching Barnabas by the coat, "how dreadfully sudden you are in your movements—"

"Madam, pray loose me!"

"Why?"

"I'm going—I cannot bear—any more!"

"You mean—?"

"I mean that—she has—"

"A very remarkable head, she is as resourceful as I was—almost."

"Resourceful!" exclaimed Barnabas, "she is—"

"An extremely clever girl—"

"Madam, pray let me go."

"No, sir! my finger is twisted in your buttonhole,—if you pull yourself away I expect you'll break it, so pray don't pull; naturally, I detest pain. And I have much to talk about."

"As you will, madam," said Barnabas, frowning.

"First, tell me—you're quite handsome when you frown,—first, sir, why weren't you formally presented to me with the other guests?"

"Because I'm not a guest, madam."

"Sir—explain yourself."

"I mean that I came—over the wall, madam."

"The wall! Climbed over?"

"Yes, madam!"

"Dear heaven! The monstrous audacity of the man! You came to see Cleone, of course?"

"Yes, madam."

"Ah, very right,—very proper! I remember I had a lover—in the remote ages, of course,—who used to climb—ah, well,—no matter! Though his wall was much higher than yours yonder." Here the Duchess sighed tenderly. "Well, you came to see Cleone, you found her,—and nicely you behaved to each other when you met! Youth is always so dreadfully tragic! But then what would love be without a little tragedy? And oh—dear heaven!—how you must adore each other! Oh, Youth! Youth!—and there's Sir George Annersley—!"

"Then, madam, you must excuse me!" said Barnabas, glancing furtively from the approaching figures to the adjacent wall.

"Oh dear, no. Sir George is with Jerningharn and Major Piper, a heavy dragoon—the heaviest in all the world, I'm sure. You must meet them."

"No, indeed—I—"

"Sir," said the Duchess, buttonholing him again, "I insist! Oh, Sir George—gentlemen!" she called. Hereupon three lounging figures turned simultaneously, and came hurrying towards them.

"Why, Duchess!" exclaimed Sir George, a large, mottled gentleman in an uncomfortable cravat, "we have all been wondering what had become of your Grace, and—" Here Sir George's sharp eye became fixed upon Barnabas, upon his spurred boots, his buckskins, his dusty coat; and Sir George's mouth opened, and he gave a tug at his cravat.

"Deuce take me—it's Beverley!" exclaimed the Marquis, and held out his hand.

"What—you know each other?" the Duchess inquired.

"Mr. Beverley is riding in the steeplechase on the fifteenth," the Marquis answered. Hereupon Sir George stared harder than ever, and gave another tug at his high cravat, while Major Piper, who had been looking very hard at nothing in particular, glanced at Barnabas with a gleam of interest and said "Haw!"

As for the Duchess, she clapped her hands.

"And he never told me a word of it!" she exclaimed. "Of course all my money is on Jerningham,—though 'Moonraker' carries the odds, but I must have a hundred or two on Mr. Beverley for—friendship's sake."

"Friendship!" exclaimed the Marquis, "oh, begad!" Here he took out his snuff-box, tapped it, and put it in his pocket again.

"Yes, gentlemen," smiled the Duchess, "this is a friend of mine who—dropped in upon me, as it were, quite unexpectedly—over the wall, in fact."

"Wall!" exclaimed Sir George.

"The deuce you did, Beverley!" said the Marquis.

As for Major Piper, he hitched his dolman round, and merely said:

"Haw!"

"Yes," said Barnabas, glancing from one to the other, "I am a trespasser here, and, Sir George, I fear I damaged some of your flowers!"

"Flowers!" repeated Sir George, staring from Barnabas to the Duchess and back again, "Oh!"

"And now—pray let me introduce you," said the Duchess. "My friend Mr. Beverley—Sir George Annersley. Mr. Beverley—Major Piper."

"A friend of her Grace is always welcome here, sir," said Sir George, extending a mottled hand.

"Delighted!" smiled the Major, saluting him in turn. "Haw!"

"But what in the world brings you here, Beverley?" inquired the Marquis.

"I do," returned his great-aunt. "Many a man has climbed a wall on my account before to-day, Marquis, and remember I'm only just—seventy-one, and growing younger every hour,—now am I not, Major?"

"Haw!—Precisely! Not a doubt, y' Grace. Soul and honor! Haw!"

"Marquis—your arm, Mr. Beverley—yours! Now, Sir George, show us the way to the marquee; I'm dying for a dish of tea, I vow I am!"

Thus, beneath the protecting wing of a Duchess was Barnabas given his first taste of Quality and Blood. Which last, though blue beyond all shadow of doubt, yet manifested itself in divers quite ordinary ways as,—in complexions of cream and roses; in skins sallow and wrinkled; in noses haughtily Roman or patricianly Greek, in noses mottled and unclassically uplifted; in black hair, white hair, yellow, brown, and red hair;—such combinations as he had seen many and many a time on village greens, and at country wakes and fairs. Yes, all was the same, and yet—how vastly different! For here voices were softly modulated, arms and hands gracefully borne, heads carried high, movement itself an artful science. Here eyes were raised or lowered with studied effect; beautiful shoulders, gracefully shrugged, became dimpled and irresistible; faces with perfect profiles were always—in profile. Here, indeed, Age and Homeliness went clothed in magnificence, and Youth and Beauty walked hand in hand with Elegance; while everywhere was a graceful ease that had been learned and studied with the Catechism. Barnabas was in a world of silks and satins and glittering gems, of broadcloth and fine linen, where such things are paramount and must be lived up to; a world where the friendship of a Duchess may transform a nobody into a SOMEBODY, to be bowed to by the most elaborate shirtfronts, curtsied to by the haughtiest of turbans, and found worthy of the homage of bewitching eyes, seductive dimples, and entrancing profiles.

In a word, Barnabas had attained—even unto the World of Fashion.

CHAPTER XL

WHICH RELATES SUNDRY HAPPENINGS AT THE GARDEN FÊTE

"Gad, Beverley! how the deuce did y' do it?"

"Do what, Marquis?"

"Charm the Serpent! Tame the Dragon!"

"Dragon?"

"Make such a conquest of her Graceless Grace of Camberhurst, my great-aunt? I didn't know you were even acquainted,—how long have you known her?"

"About an hour," said Barnabas.

"Eh—an hour? But, my dear fellow, you came to see her—over the wall, you know,—she said so, and—"

"She said so, yes, Marquis, but—"

"But? Oh, I see! Ah, to be sure! She is my great-aunt, of course, and my great-aunt, Beverley, generally thinks, and does, and says—exactly what she pleases. Begad! you never can tell what she' 11 be up to next,—consequently every one is afraid of her, even those high goddesses of the beau monde, those exclusive grandes dames, my Ladies Castlereagh, Jersey, Cowper and the rest of 'em—they're all afraid of my small great-aunt, and no wonder! You see, she's old—older than she looks, and—with a perfectly diabolical memory! She knows not only all their own peccadillos, but the sins of their great-grandmothers as well. She fears nothing on the earth, or under the earth, and respects no one—not even me. Only about half an hour ago she informed me that I was a—well, she told me precisely what I was,—and she can be painfully blunt, Beverley,—just because Cleone happens to have refused me again."

"Again?" said Barnabas inquiringly.

"Oh, yes! She does it regularly. Begad! she's refused me so often that it's grown into a kind of formula with us now. I say, 'Cleone, do!' and she answers, 'Bob, don't!' But even that's something,—lots of 'em haven't got so far as that with her."

"Sir Mortimer Carnaby, for instance!" said Barnabas, biting his lip.

"Hum!" said the Marquis dubiously, deftly re-settling his cravat, "and what of—yourself, Beverley?"

"I have asked her—only twice, I think."

"Ah, and she—refused you?"

"No," sighed Barnabas, "she told me she—despised me."

"Did she so? Give me your hand—I didn't think you were so strong in the running. With Cleone's sort there's always hope so long as she isn't sweet and graciously indifferent."

"Pray," said Barnabas suddenly, "pray where did you get that rose, Marquis?"

"This? Oh, she gave it to me."

"Cleone?"

"Of course."

"But—I thought she'd refused you?"

"Oh, yes—so she did; but that's just like Cleone, frowning one moment, smiling the next—April, you know."

"And did she—kiss it first?"

"Kiss it? Why—deuce take me, now I come to think of it,—so she did,—at least—What now, Beverley?"

"I'm—going!" said Barnabas.

"Going? Where?"

"Back—over the wall!"

"Eh!—run away, is it?"

"As far," said Barnabas, scowling, "as far as possible. Good-by, Marquis!" And so he turned and strode away, while the Marquis stared after him, open-mouthed. But as he went, Barnabas heard a voice calling his name, and looking round, beheld Captain Chumly coming towards him. A gallant figure he made (despite grizzled hair and empty sleeve), in all the bravery of his white silk stockings, and famous Trafalgar coat, which, though a little tarnished as to epaulettes and facings, nevertheless bore witness to the Bo'sun's diligent care; he was, indeed, from the crown of his cocked hat down to his broad, silver shoe-buckles, the very pattern of what a post-captain of Lord Nelson should be.

"Eh, sir!" he exclaimed, with his hand outstretched in greeting, "are ye blind, I say are ye blind and deaf? Didn't you hear her Grace hailing you? Didn't ye see me signal you to 'bring to'?"

"No, sir," answered Barnabas, grasping the proffered hand.

"Oho!" said the Captain, surveying Barnabas from head to foot, "so you've got 'em on, I see, and vastly different you look in your fine feathers. But you can sink me,—I say you can scuttle and sink me if I don't prefer you in your homespun! You'll be spelling your name with as many unnecessary letters, and twirls, and flourishes as you can clap in, nowadays, I'll warrant."

"Jack Chumly, don't bully the boy!" said a voice near by; and looking thitherward, Barnabas beheld the Duchess seated at a small table beneath a shady tree, and further screened by a tall hedge; a secluded corner, far removed from the throng, albeit a most excellent place for purposes of observation, commanding as it did a wide view of lawns and terraces. "As for you, Mr. Beverley," continued the Duchess, with her most imperious air, "you may bring a seat—here, beside me,—and help the Captain to amuse me."

"Madam," said Barnabas, his bow very solemn and very deep, "I am about to leave, and—with your permission—I—"

"You have my permission to—sit here beside me, sir. So! A dish of tea? No? Ah, well—we were just talking of you; the Captain was describing how he first met you—"

"Bowing to a gate-post, mam,—on my word as a sailor and a Christian, it was a gate-post,—I say, an accurs—a confoundedly rotten old stick of a gate-post."

"I remember," sighed Barnabas.

"And to-day, sir," continued the Captain, "to-day you must come clambering over a gentleman's garden wall to bow and scrape to a—"

"Don't dare to say—another stick, Jack Chumly!" cried the Duchess.

"I repeat, sir, you must come trespassing here, to bow—I say bah! and scrape—"

"I say tush!" interpolated the Duchess demurely.

"To an old—"

"Painted!" suggested the Duchess.

"Hum!" said the Captain, a little hipped, "I say—ha!—lady, sir—"

"With a wig!" added the Duchess.

"And with a young and handsome,—I say a handsome and roguish pair of eyes, sir, that need no artificial aids, mam, nor ever will!"

"Three!" cried the Duchess, clapping her hands. "Oh, Jack! Jack Chumly! you, like myself, improve with age! As a midshipman you were too callow, as a lieutenant much too old and serious, but now that you are a battered and wrinkled young captain, you can pay as pretty a compliment as any other gallant youth. Actually three in one hour, Mr. Beverley."

"Compliments, mam!" snorted the Captain, with an angry flap of his empty sleeve, "Compliments, I scorn 'em! I say pish, mam,—I say bah! I speak only the truth, mam, as well you know."

"Four!" cried the Duchess, with a gurgle of youthful laughter. "Oh, Jack! Jack! I protest, as you sit there you are growing more youthful every minute."

"Gad so, mam! then I'll go before I become a mewling infant—I say a puling brat, mam."

"Stay a moment, Jack. I want you to explain your wishes to Mr. Beverley in regard to Cleone's future."

"Certainly, your Grace—I say by all means, mam."

"Very well, then I'll begin. Listen—both of you. Captain Chumly, being a bachelor and consequently an authority on marriage, has, very properly, chosen whom his ward must marry; he has quite settled and arranged it all, haven't you, Jack?"

"Quite, mam, quite."

"Thus, Cleone is saved all the bother and worry of choosing for herself, you see, Mr. Beverley, for the Captain's choice is fixed,— isn't it, Jack?"

"As a rock, mam—I say as an accurs—ha! an adamantine crag, mam. My ward shall marry my nephew, Viscount Devenham, I am determined on it—"

"Consequently, Mr. Beverley, Cleone will, of course, marry—whomsoever she pleases!"

"Eh, mam? I say, what?—I say—"

"Like the feminine creature she is, Mr. Beverley!"

"Now by Og,—I say by Og and Gog, mam! She is my ward, and so long as I am her guardian she shall obey—"

"I say boh! Jack Chumly,—I say bah!" mocked the Duchess, nodding her head at him. "Cleone is much too clever for you—or any other man, and there is only one woman in this big world who is a match for her, and that woman is—

me. I've watched her growing up—day by day—year after year into—just what I was—ages ago,—and to-day she is—almost as beautiful,—and—very nearly as clever!"

"Clever, mam? So she is, but I'm her guardian and—she loves me—I think, and—"

"Of course she loves you, Jack, and winds you round her finger whenever she chooses—"

"Finger, mam! finger indeed! No, mam, I can be firm with her."

"As a candle before the fire, Jack. She can bend you to all the points of your compass. Come now, she brought you here this afternoon against your will,—now didn't she?"

"Ah!—hum!" said the Captain, scratching his chin.

"And coaxed you into your famous Trafalgar uniform, now didn't she?"

"Why as to that, mam, I say—"

"And petted you into staying here much longer than you intended, now didn't she?"

"Which reminds me that it grows late, mam," said the Captain, taking out his watch and frowning at it. "I must find my ward. I say I will bring Cleone to make you her adieux." So saying, he bowed and strode away across the lawn.

"Poor Jack," smiled the Duchess, "he is such a dear, good, obedient child, and he doesn't know it. And so your name is Beverley, hum! Of the Beverleys of Ashleydown? Yet, no,—that branch is extinct, I know. Pray what branch are you? Why, here comes Sir Mortimer Carnaby,—heavens, how handsome he is! And you thrashed him, I think? Oh, I know all about it, sir, and I know—why!"

"Then," said Barnabas, somewhat taken aback, "you'll know he deserved it, madam."

"Mm! Have you met him since?"

"No, indeed, nor have I any desire to!"

"Oh, but you must," said the Duchess, and catching Sir Mortimer's gaze, she smiled and beckoned him, and next moment he was bowing before her. "My dear Sir Mortimer," said she, "I don't think you are acquainted with my friend, Mr. Beverley?"

"No," answered Sir Mortimer with a perfunctory glance at Barnabas.

"Ah! I thought not. Mr. Beverley—Sir Mortimer Carnaby."

"Honored, sir," said Sir Mortimer, as they bowed.

"Mr. Beverley is, I believe, an opponent of yours, Sir Mortimer?" pursued the Duchess, with her placid smile.

"An opponent! indeed, your Grace?" said he, favoring Barnabas with another careless glance.

"I mean—in the race, of course," smiled the Duchess. "But oh, happy man! So you have been blessed also?"

"How, Duchess?"

"I see you wear Cleone's favor,—you've been admitted to the Order of the Rose, like all the others." And the Duchess tittered.

"Others, your Grace! What others?"

"Oh, sir, their name is Legion. There's Jerningham, and young Denton, and Snelgrove, and Ensign D'Arcy, and hosts beside. Lud, Sir Mortimer, where are your eyes? Look there! and there! and there again!" And, with little darting movements of her fan, she indicated certain young gentlemen, who strolled to and fro upon the lawn; now, in the lapel of each of their coats was a single, red rose. "There's safety in numbers, and Cleone was always cautious!" said the Duchess, and tittered again.

Sir Mortimer glanced from those blooms to the flower in his own coat, and his cheek grew darkly red, and his mouth took on a cruel look.

"Ah, Duchess," he smiled, "it seems our fair Cleone has an original idea of humor,—very quaint, upon my soul!" And so he laughed, and bowing, turned away.

"Now—watch!" said the Duchess, "there!" As she spoke, Sir Mortimer paused, and with a sudden fierce gesture tore the rose from his coat and tossed it away. "Now really," said the Duchess, leaning back and fanning herself placidly, "I think that was vastly clever of me; you should be grateful, sir, and so should Cleone—hush!—here she comes, at last."

"Where?" inquired Barnabas, glancing up hastily.

"Ssh! behind us—on the other side of the hedge—clever minx!"

"Why then—"

"Sit still, sir—hush, I say!"

"So that is the reason," said Cleone's clear voice, speaking within a yard of them, "that is why you dislike Mr. Beverley?"

"Yes, and because of his presumption!" said a second voice, at the sound of which Barnabas flushed and started angrily, whereupon the Duchess instantly hooked him by the buttonhole again.

"His presumption in what, Mr. Chichester?"

"In his determined pursuit of you."

"Is he in pursuit of me?"

"Cleone—you know he is!"

"But how do you happen to know?"

"From his persecution of poor Ronald, for one thing."

"Persecution, sir?"

"It amounted to that. He found his way to Ronald's wretched lodging, and tempted the poor fellow with his gold,—indeed almost commanded Ronald to allow him to pay off his debts—"

"But Ronald refused, of course?" said Cleone quickly.

"Of course! I was there, you see, and this Beverley is a stranger!"

"A stranger—yes."

"And yet, Cleone, when your unfortunate brother refused his money,—this utter stranger, this Good Samaritan,—actually went behind Ronald's back and offered to buy up his debts! Such a thing might be done by father for son, or brother for brother, but why should any man do so much for an utter stranger—?"

"Either because he is very base, or very—noble!" said Cleone.

"Noble! I tell you such a thing is quite impossible—unheard of! No man would part with a fortune to benefit a stranger—unless he had a powerful motive!"

"Well?" said Cleone softly.

"Well, Cleone, I happen to know that motive is—yourself!" Here the Duchess, alert as usual, caught Barnabas by the cravat, and only just in time.

"Sit still—hush!" she whispered, glancing up into his distorted face, for Mr. Chichester was going on in his soft, deliberate voice:

"Oh, it is all very simple, Cleone, and very clumsy,—thus, see you. In the guise of Good Samaritan this stranger buys the debts of the brother, trusting to the gratitude of the sister. He knows your pride, Cleone, so he would buy your brother and put you under lasting obligation to himself. The scheme is a little coarse, and very clumsy,—but then, he is young."

"And you say—he tried to pay these debts—without Ronald's knowledge? Are you sure—quite sure?"

"Quite! And I know, also, that when Ronald's creditor refused, he actually offered to double—to treble the sum! But, indeed, you would be cheap at sixty thousand pounds, Cleone!"

"Oh—hateful!" she cried.

"Crude, yes, and very coarse, but, as I said before, he is young—what, are you going?"

"Yes—no. Pray find my guardian and bring him to me."

"First, tell me I may see you again, Cleone, before I leave for London?"

"Yes," said Cleone, after a momentary hesitation.

Thereafter came the tread of Mr. Chichester's feet upon the gravel, soft and deliberate, like his voice.

Then Barnabas sighed, a long, bitter sigh, and looking up—saw Cleone standing before him.

"Ah, dear Godmother!" said she lightly, "I hope your Grace was able to hear well?"

"Perfectly, my dear, thank you—every word," nodded the Duchess, "though twice Mr. Beverley nearly spoilt it all. I had to hold him dreadfully tight,—see how I've crumpled his beautiful cravat. Dear me, how impetuous you are, sir! As for you, Cleone, sit down, my dear,—that's it!—positively I'm proud of you,—kiss me,—I mean about the roses. It was vastly clever! You are myself over again."

"Your Grace honors me!" said Cleone, her eyes demure, but with a dimple at the corner of her red mouth.

"And I congratulate you. I was a great success—in my day. Ah me! I remember seeing you—an hour after you were born. You were very pink, Cleone, and as bald as—as I am, without my wig. No—pray sit still,—Mr. Beverley isn't looking at you, and he was just as bald, once, I expect—and will be again, I hope. Even at that early age you pouted at me, Cleone, and I liked you for it. You are pouting now, Miss! To-day Mr. Beverley frowns at me, and I like him for it,—besides, he's very handsome when he frowns, don't you think, Cleone?"

"Madam—" began Barnabas, with an angry look.

"Ah! now you're going to quarrel with me,—well there's the Major,—I shall go. If you must quarrel with some one,—try Cleone, she's young, and, I think, a match for you. Oh, Major! Major Piper, pray lend your arm and protection to a poor, old, defenceless woman." So saying, the Duchess rose, and the Major, bowing gallantly gave her the limb she demanded, and went off with her, 'haw'-ing in his best and most ponderous manner.

Barnabas sat, chin in hand, staring at the ground, half expecting that Cleone would rise and leave him. But no! My lady sat leaning back in her chair, her head carelessly averted, but watching him from the corners of her eyes. A sly look it was, a searching, critical look, that took close heed to all things, as—the fit and excellence of his clothes; the unconscious grace of his attitude; the hair that curled so crisp and dark at his temples; the woeful droop of his lips;—a long, inquisitive look, a look wholly feminine. Yes, he was certainly handsome, handsomer even than she had thought. And finding him so, she frowned, and, frowning, spoke:

"So you meant to buy me, sir—as you would a horse or dog?"

"No," said Barnabas, without looking up, and speaking almost humbly.

"It would have been the same thing, sir," she continued, a little more haughtily in consequence. "You would have put upon me an obligation I could never, never have hoped to repay?"

"Yes, I see my error now," said Barnabas, his head sinking lower. "I acted for the best, but I am a fool, and a clumsy one it seems. I meant only to serve you, to fulfil the mission you gave me, and I blundered—because I am—very ignorant. If you can forgive me, do so."

Now this humility was new in him, and because of this, and because she was a woman, she became straightway more exacting, and questioned him again.

"But why—why did you do it?"

"You asked me to save your brother, and I could see no other way—"

"How so? Please explain."

"I meant to free him from the debt which is crushing him down and unmanning him."

"But—oh, don't you see—he would still be in debt—to you?"

"I had forgotten that!" sighed Barnabas.

"Forgotten it?" she repeated.

"Quite!"

Surely no man could lie, whose eyes were so truthful and steadfast.

"And so you went and offered to—buy up his debts?"

"Yes."

"For three times the proper sum?"

"I would have paid whatever was asked."

"Why?"

"Because I promised you to help him," answered Barnabas, staring at the ground again.

"You must be—very rich?" said Cleone, stealing another look at him.

"I am."

"And—supposing you had taken over the debt, who did you think would ever repay you?"

"It never occurred to me."

"And you would have done—all this for a—stranger?"

"No, but because of the promise I gave."

"To me?"

"Yes,—but, as God sees me, I would have looked for no recompense at your hands."

"Never?"

"Never—unless—"

"Unless, sir?"

"Unless I—I had dreamed it possible that you—could ever have—loved me." Barnabas was actually stammering, and he was looking at her—pleadingly, she knew, but this time my lady kept her face averted, of course. Wherefore Barnabas sighed, and his head drooping, stared at the ground again. And after he had stared thus, for perhaps a full minute, my lady spoke, but with her face still averted.

"The moon is at the full to-night, I think?"

Barnabas (lifting his head suddenly). "Yes."

Cleone (quite aware of his quick glance). "And—how do you like—the Duchess?"

Barnabas (staring at the ground again). "I don't know."

Cleone (with unnecessary emphasis). "Why, she is the dearest, best, cleverest old godmother in all the world, sir!"

Barnabas (humbly). "Yes."

Cleone (with a side glance). "Are you riding back to London to-night?"

Barnabas (nodding drearily). "Yes."

Cleone (watching him more keenly). "It should be glorious to gallop under a—full-orbed moon."

Barnabas (shaking his head mournfully). "London is a great way from—here."

Cleone (beginning to twist a ring on her finger nervously). "Do you remember the madman we met—at Oakshott's Barn?"

Barnabas (sighing). "Yes. I met him in London, lately."

Cleone (clasping her hands together tightly). "Did he talk about—the moon again?"

Barnabas (still sighing, and dense), "No, it was about some shadow, I think."

Cleone (frowning at him a little). "Well—do you remember what he prophesied—about—an 'orbed moon'—and 'Barnaby Bright'?"

Barnabas (glancing up with sudden interest). "Yes,—yes, he said we should meet again at Barnaby Bright—under an orbed moon!"

Cleone (head quite averted now, and speaking over her shoulder). "Do you remember the old finger-post—on the Hawkhurst road?"

Barnabas (leaning towards her eagerly). "Yes—do you mean—Oh, Cleone-?"

Cleone (rising, and very demure). "Here comes the Duchess with my Guardian—hush! At nine o'clock, sir."

CHAPTER XLI

IN WHICH BARNABAS MAKES A SURPRISING DISCOVERY, THAT MAY NOT SURPRISE THE READER IN THE LEAST

Evening, with the promise of a glorious night later on; evening, full of dewy scents, of lengthening shadows, of soft, unaccountable noises, of mystery and magic; and, over all, a rising moon, big and yellow. Thus, as he went, Barnabas kept his eyes bent thitherward, and his step was light and his heart sang within him for gladness, it was in the very air, and in the whole fair world was no space for care or sorrow, for his dreams were to be realized at a certain finger-post on the Hawkhurst road, on the stroke of nine. Therefore, as he strode along, being only human after all, Barnabas fell a whistling to himself under his breath. And his thoughts were all of Cleone, of the subtle charm of her voice, of the dimple in her chin, of her small, proud feet, and her thousand sly bewitchments; but, at the memory of her glowing beauty, his flesh thrilled and his breath caught. Then, upon the quietude rose a voice near by, that spoke from where the shadows lay blackest,—a voice low and muffled, speaking as from the ground:

"How long, oh Lord, how long?"

And, looking within the shadow, Barnabas beheld one who lay face down upon the grass, and coming nearer, soft-footed, he saw the gleam of silver hair, and stooping, touched the prostrate figure. Wherefore the heavy head was raised, and the mournful voice spoke again:

"Is it you, young sir? You will grieve, I think, to learn that my atonement is not complete, my pilgrimage unfinished. I must wander the roads again, preaching Forgiveness, for, sir,—Clemency is gone, my Beatrix is vanished. I am—a day too late! Only one day, sir, and there lies the bitterness."

"Gone!" cried Barnabas, "gone?"

"She left the place yesterday, very early in the morning,—fled away none knows whither,—I am too late! Sir, it is very bitter, but God's will be done!"

Then Barnabas sat down in the shadow, and took the Preacher's hand, seeking to comfort him:

"Sir," said he gently, "tell me of it."

"Verily, for it is soon told, sir. I found the place you mentioned, I found there also, one—old like myself, a sailor by his look, who sat bowed down with some grievous sorrow. And, because of my own joy, I strove to comfort him, and trembling with eagerness, hearkening for the step of her I had sought so long, I told him why I was there. So I learned I was too late after all,—she had gone, and his grief was mine also. He was very kind, he showed me her room, a tiny chamber under the eaves, but wondrous fair and sweet with flowers, and all things orderly, as her dear hands had left them. And so we stayed there a while,—two old men, very silent and full of sorrow. And in a while, though he would have me rest there the night, I left, and walked I cared not whither, and, being weary, lay down here wishful to die. But I may not die until my atonement be complete, and mayhap—some day I shall find her yet. For God is a just God, and His will be done. Amen!"

"But why—why did she go?" cried Barnabas.

"Young sir, the answer is simple, the man Chichester had discovered her refuge. She was afraid!" Here the Apostle of Peace fell silent, and sat with bent head and lips moving as one who prayed. When at last he looked up, a smile was on his lips. "Sir," said he, "it is only the weak who repine, for God is just, and I know I shall find her before I die!" So saying he rose, though like one who is very weary, and stood upon his feet.

"Where are you going?" Barnabas inquired.

"Sir, my trust is in God, I take to the road again."

"To search for her?"

"To preach for her. And when I have preached sufficiently, God will bring me to her. So come, young sir, if you will, let us walk together as far as we may." Thus, together, they left the shadow and went on, side by side, in the soft radiance of the rising moon.

"Sir," said Barnabas after a while, seeing his companion was very silent, and that his thin hands often griped and wrung each other, —that gesture which was more eloquent than words,—"Sir, is there anything I can do to lighten your sorrow?"

"Yes, young sir, heed it well, let it preach to you this great truth, that all the woes arid ills we suffer are but the necessary outcome of our own acts. Oh sir,—young sir, in you and me, as in all other men, there lies a power that may help to make or mar the lives of our fellows, a mighty power, yet little dreamed of, and we call it Influence. For there is no man but he must, of necessity, influence, to a more or less degree, the conduct of those he meets, whether he will or no,—and there lies the terror of it! Thus, to some extent, we become responsible for the actions of our neighbors, even after we are dead, for Influence is immortal. Man is a pebble thrown into the pool of Life,—a splash, a bubble, and he is gone! But—the ripples of Influence he leaves behind go on widening and ever widening until they reach the farthest bank. Oh, had I but dreamed of this in my youth, I might have been—a happy man to-night, and—others also. In helping others we ourselves are blessed, for a noble thought, a kindly word, a generous deed, are never lost; such things cannot go to waste, they are our monuments after we are dead, and live on forever."

So, talking thus, they reached a gate, and, beyond the gate, a road, white beneath the moon, winding away between shadowy hedges.

"You are for London, I fancy, young sir?"

"Yes."

"Then we part here. But before I bid you God speed, I would know your name; mine is Darville—Ralph Darville."

"And mine, sir, is Barnabas—Beverley."

"Beverley!" said the Preacher, glancing up quickly, "of Ashleydown?"

"Sir," said Barnabas, "surely they are all dead?"

"True, true!" nodded the Preacher, "the name is extinct. That is how the man—Chichester came into the inheritance. I knew the family well, years ago. The brothers died abroad, Robert, the elder, with his regiment in the Peninsula, Francis, in battle at sea, and Joan—like my own poor Beatrix, was unhappy, and ran away, but she was never heard of again."

"And her name was Joan?" said Barnabas slowly, "Joan—Beverley?"

"Yes."

"Sir, Joan Beverley was my mother! I took her name—Beverley—for a reason."

"Your mother! Ah, I understand it now; you are greatly like her, at times, it was the resemblance that puzzled me before. But, sir—if Joan Beverley was your mother, why then—"

"Then, Chichester has no right to the property?"

"No!"

"And—I have?"

"If you can prove your descent."

"Yes," said Barnabas, "but—to whom?"

"You must seek out a Mr. Gregory Dyke, of Lincoln's Inn; he is the lawyer who administered the estate—"

"Stay," said Barnabas, "let me write it down."

"And now, young sir," said the Preacher, when he had answered all the eager questions of Barnabas as fully as he might, "now, young sir, you know I have small cause to love the man—Chichester, but, remember, you are rich already, and if you take this heritage also,—he will be destitute."

"Sir," said Barnabas, frowning, "better one destitute and starving, than that many should be wretched, surely."

The Preacher sighed and shook his head.

"Young sir, good-by," said he, "I have a feeling we may meet again, but life is very uncertain, therefore I would beg of you to remember this: as you are strong, be gentle; as you are rich, generous; and as you are young, wise. But, above all, be merciful, and strive to forgive wrongs." So they clasped hands, then, sighing, the Preacher turned and plodded on his lonely way. But, long after he had vanished down the moonlit road, Barnabas stood, his fists clenched, his mouth set, until he was roused by a sound near by, a very small sound like the jingle of distant spurs. Therefore, Barnabas lifted his head, and glanced about him, but seeing no one, presently went his way, slow of foot and very thoughtful.

CHAPTER XLII

IN WHICH SHALL BE FOUND FURTHER MENTION OF A FINGER-POST

The hands of Natty Bell's great watch were pointing to the hour of nine, what time Barnabas dismounted at the cross-roads, and tethering Four-legs securely, leaned his back against the ancient finger-post to wait the coming of Cleone.

Now being old, and having looked upon many and divers men (and women) in its day, it is to be supposed that the ancient finger-post took more or less interest in such things as chanced in its immediate vicinity. Thus, it is probable that it rightly defined why this particular long-legged human sighed so often, now with his gaze upon the broad disc of the moon, now upon a certain point of the road ahead, and was not in the least surprised to see Barnabas start forward, bareheaded, to meet her who came swift and light of foot; to see her pause before him, quick-breathing, blushing, sighing, trembling; to see how glance met glance; to see him stoop to kiss the hand she gave him, and all—without a word. Surprised? not a bit of it, for to a really observant finger-post all humans (both he and she) are much alike at such times.

"I began to fear you wouldn't come," said Barnabas, finding voice at last.

"But to-night is—Barnaby Bright, and the prophecy must be fulfilled, sir. And—oh, how wonderful the moon is!" Now, lifting her head to look at it, her hood must needs take occasion to slip back upon her shoulders, as if eager to reveal her loveliness,—the high beauty of her face, the smooth round column of her throat, and the shining wonder of her hair.

"Cleone—how beautiful you are!"

And here ensued another silence while Cleone gazed up at the moon, and Barnabas at Cleone.

But the ancient finger-post (being indeed wonderfully knowing—for a finger-post) well understood the meaning of such silences, and was quite aware of the tremble of the strong fingers that still held hers, and why, in the shadow of her cloak, her bosom hurried so. Oh! be sure the finger-post knew the meaning of it all, since humans, of every degree, are only men and women after all.

"Cleone, when will you—marry me?"

Now here my lady stole a quick glance at him, and immediately looked up at the moon again, because the eyes that could burn so fiercely could hold such ineffable tenderness also.

"You are very—impetuous, I think," she sighed.

"But I—love you," said Barnabas, "not only for your beauty, but because you are Cleone, and there is no one else in the world like you. But, because I love you so much, it—it is very hard to tell you of it. If I could only put it into fine-sounding phrases—"

"Don't!" said my lady quickly, and laid a slender (though very imperious) finger upon his lips.

"Why?" Barnabas inquired, very properly kissing the finger and holding it there.

"Because I grow tired of fine phrases and empty compliments, and because, sir—"

"Have you forgotten that my name is Barnabas?" he demanded, kissing the captive finger again, whereupon it struggled—though very feebly, to be sure.

"And because, Barnabas, you would be breaking your word."

"How?"

"You must only tell me—that, when 'the sun is shining, and friends are within call,'—have you forgotten your own words so soon?"

Now, as she spoke Barnabas beheld the dimple—that most elusive dimple, that came and went and came again, beside the scarlet lure of her mouth; therefore he drew her nearer until he could look, for a moment, into the depths of her eyes. But here, seeing the glowing intensity of his gaze, becoming aware of the strong, compelling arm about her, feeling the quiver of the hand that held her own, lo! in that instant my lady, with her sly bewitchments, her coquettish airs and graces, was gone, and in her place was the maid—quick-breathing, blushing, trembling, all in a moment.

"Ah, no!" she pleaded, "Barnabas, no!" Then Barnabas sighed, and loosed his clasp—but behold! the dimple was peeping at him again. And in that moment he caught her close, and thus, for the first time, their lips met.

Oh, privileged finger-post to have witnessed that first kiss! To have seen her start away and turn; to have felt her glowing cheek pressed to thy hoary timbers; to have felt the sweet, quick tumult of her bosom! Oh, thrice happy finger-post! To have seen young Barnabas, radiant-faced, and with all heaven in his eyes! Oh, most fortunate of finger-posts to have seen and felt all this, and to have heard the rapture thrilling in his voice:

"Cleone!"

"Oh!" she whispered, "why—why did you?"

"Because I love you!"

"No other man ever dared to—"

"Heaven be praised!"

"Upon—the mouth!" she added, her face still hidden.

"Then I have set my seal upon it."

"And now,—am I—immaculate?"

"Oh—forgive me!"

"No!"

"Look at me."

"No!"

"Are you angry?"

"Yes, I—think I am, Barnabas,—oh, very!"

"Forgive me!" said Barnabas again.

"First," said my lady, throwing up her head, "am I—heartless and a—coquette?"

"No, indeed, no! Oh, Cleone, is it possible you could learn to—love me, in time?"

"I—I don't know."

"Some day, Cleone?"

"I—I didn't come to answer—idle questions, sir," says my lady, suddenly demure. "It must be nearly half-past nine—I must go. I forgot to tell you—Mr. Chichester is coming to meet me to-night—"

"To meet you? Where?" demanded Barnabas, fierce-eyed all at once.

"Here, Barnabas. But don't look so—so murderous!"

"Chichester—here!"

"At a quarter to ten, Barnabas. That is why I must go at—half-past nine—Barnabas, stop! Oh, Barnabas, you're crushing me! Not again, sir,—I forbid you—please, Barnabas!"

So Barnabas loosed her, albeit regretfully, and stood watching while she dexterously twisted, and smoothed, and patted her shining hair into some semblance of order; and while so doing, she berated him, on this wise:

"Indeed, sir, but you're horribly strong. And very hasty. And your hands are very large. And I fear you have a dreadful temper. And I know my hair is all anyhow,—isn't it?"

"It is beautiful!" sighed Barnabas.

"Mm! You told me that in Annersley Wood, sir."

"You haven't forgotten, then?"

"Oh, no," answered Cleone, shaking her head, "but I would have you more original, you see,—so many men have told me that. Ah! now you're frowning again, and it's nearly time for me to go, and I haven't had a chance to mention what I came for, which, of course, is all your fault, Barnabas. To-day, I received a letter from Ronald. He writes that he has been ill, but is better. And yet, I fear, he must be very weak still, for oh! it's such poor, shaky writing. Was he very ill when you saw him?"

"No," answered Barnabas.

"Here is the letter,—will you read it? You see, I have no one who will talk to me about poor Ronald, no one seems to have any pity for him,—not even my dear Tyrant."

"But you will always have me, Cleone!"

"Always, Barnabas?"

"Always."

So Barnabas took Ronald Barrymaine's letter, and opening it, saw that it was indeed scrawled in characters so shaky as to be sometimes almost illegible; but, holding it in the full light of the moon, he read as follows:

DEAREST OF SISTERS,—I was unable to keep the appointment I begged for in my last, owing to a sudden indisposition, and, though better now, I am still ailing. I fear my many misfortunes are rapidly undermining my health, and sometimes I sigh for Death and Oblivion. But, dearest Cleone, I forbid you to grieve for me, I am man enough, I hope, to endure my miseries uncomplainingly, as a man and a gentleman should. Chichester, with his unfailing kindness, has offered me an asylum at his country place near Headcorn, where I hope to regain something of my wonted health. But for Chichester I tremble to think what would have been my fate long before this. At Headcorn I shall at least be nearer you, my best of sisters, and it is my hope that you may be persuaded to steal away now and then, to spend an hour with two lonely bachelors, and cheer a brother's solitude. Ah, Cleone! Chichester's devotion to you is touching, such patient adoration must in time meet with its reward. By your own confession you have nothing against him but the fact that he worships you too ardently, and this, most women would think a virtue. And remember, he is your luckless brother's only friend. This is the only man who has stood by me in adversity, the only man who can help me to retrieve the past, the only man a truly loving sister should honor with her regard. All women are more or less selfish. Oh, Cleone, be the exception and give my friend the answer he seeks, the answer he has sought of you already, the answer which to your despairing brother means more than you can ever guess, the answer whereby you can fulfil the promise you gave our dying mother to help

Your unfortunate brother,
RONALD BARRYMAINE.

Now, as he finished reading, Barnabas frowned, tore the letter across in sudden fury, and looked up to find Cleone frowning also:

"You have torn my letter!"

"Abominable!" said Barnabas fiercely.

"How dared you?"

"It is the letter of a coward and weakling!"

"My brother, sir!"

"Half-brother."

"And you insult him!"

"He would sell you to a—" Barnabas choked.

"Mr. Chichester is my brother's friend."

"His enemy!"

"And poor Ronald is sick—"

"With brandy!"

"Oh—not that!" she cried sharply, "not that!"

"Didn't you know?"

"I only—dreaded it. His father—died of it. Oh, sir—oh, Barnabas! there is no one else who will help him—save him from—that! You will try, won't you?"

"Yes," said Barnabas, setting his jaw, "no one can help a man against his will, but I'll try. And I ask you to remember that if I succeed or not, I shall never expect any recompense from you, never!"

"Unless, Barnabas—" said Cleone, softly.

"Unless—oh, Cleone, unless you should—some day learn to—love me—just a little, Cleone?"

"Would—just a little, satisfy you?"

"No," said Barnabas, "no, I want you all—all—all. Oh, Cleone, will you marry me?"

"You are very persistent, sir, and I must go."

"Not yet,—pray not yet."

"Please, Barnabas. I would not care to see Mr. Chichester—to-night."

"No," sighed Barnabas, "you must go. But first,—will you—?"

"Not again, Barnabas!" And she gave him her two hands. So he stopped and kissed them instead. Then she turned and left him standing bareheaded under the finger-post. But when she had gone but a little way she paused and spoke to him over her shoulder:

"Will you—write to me—sometimes?"

"Oh—may I?"

"Please, Barnabas,—to tell me of—my brother."

"And when can I see you again?"

"Ah! who can tell?" she answered. And so, smiling a little, blushing a little, she hastened away.

Now, when she was gone, Barnabas stooped, very reverently, and pressed his lips to the ancient finger-post, on that spot where her head had rested, and sighed, and turned towards his great, black horse.

But, even as he did so, he heard again that soft sound that was like the faint jingle of spurs, the leaves of the hedge rustled, and out into the moonlight stepped a tall figure, wild of aspect, bareheaded and bare of foot; one who wore his coat wrong side out, and who, laying his hand upon his bosom, bowed in stately fashion, once to the moon and once to him.

"Oh, Barnaby Bright, Barnaby Bright,
The moon's awake, and shines all night!"

"Do you remember, Barnaby Bright, how I foretold we should meet again—under an orbed moon? Was I not right? She's fair, Barnaby, and passing fair, and very proud,—but all good, beautiful women are proud, and hard in the winning,—oh, I know! Billy Button knows! My buttons jingled, so I turned my coat, though I'm no turn-coat; once a friend, always a friend. So I followed you, Barnaby Bright, I came to warn you of the shadow,—it grows blacker every day,—back there in the great city, waiting for you, Barnaby Bright, to smother you—to quench hope, and light, and life itself. But I shall be there, —and She. Aha! She shall forget all things then—even her pride. Shadows have their uses, Barnaby, even the blackest. I came a long way—oh, I followed you. But poor Billy is never weary, the Wise Ones bear him up in their arms sometimes. So I followed you—and another, also, though he didn't know it. Oho! would you see me conjure you a spirit from the leaves yonder,—ah! but an evil spirit, this! Shall I? Watch now! See, thus I set my feet! Thus I lift my arms to the moon!"

So saying, the speaker flung up his long arms, and with his gaze fixed upon a certain part of the hedge, lifted his voice and spoke:

"Oho, lurking spirit among the shadows! Ho! come forth, I summon ye. The dew is thick amid the leaves, and dew is an evil thing for purple and fine linen. Oho, stand forth, I bid ye."

There followed a moment's utter silence, then—another rustle amid the leaves, and Mr. Chichester stepped out from the shadows.

"Ah, sir," said Barnabas, consulting his watch, "you are just twenty-three minutes before your time. Nevertheless you are, I think, too late."

Mr. Chichester glanced at Barnabas from head to foot, and, observing his smile, Barnabas clenched his fists.

"Too late, sir?" repeated Mr. Chichester softly, shaking his head, "no,—indeed I think not. Howbeit there are times and occasions when solitude appeals to me; this is one. Pray, therefore, be good enough to—go, and—ah—take your barefooted friend with you."

"First, sir," said Barnabas, bowing with aggressive politeness, "first, I humbly beg leave to speak with you, to—"

"Sir," said Mr. Chichester, gently tapping a nettle out of existence with his cane, "sir, I have no desire for your speeches, they, like yourself, I find a little trying, and vastly uninteresting. I prefer to stay here and meditate a while. I bid you good night, sir, a pleasant ride."

"None the less, sir," said Barnabas, beginning to smile, "I fear I must inflict myself upon you a moment longer, to warn you that I—"

"To warn me? Again? Oh, sir, I grow weary of your warnings, I do indeed! Pray go away and warn somebody else. Pray go, and let me stare upon the moon and twiddle my thumbs until—"

"If it is the Lady Cleone you wait for, she is gone!" said Youth, quick and impetuous.

"Ah!" sighed Mr. Chichester, viewing Barnabas through narrowed eyes, "gone, you say? But then, young sir," here he gently poked a dock-leaf into ruin, "but then, Cleone is one of your tempting, warm, delicious creatures! Cleone is a skilled coquette to whom all men are—men. To-night it is—you, to-morrow—" Mr. Chichester's right hand vanished into his bosom as Barnabas strode forward, but, on the instant, Billy Button was between them.

"Stay, my Lord!" he cried, "look upon this face,—'t is the face of my friend Barnaby Bright, but, my Lord, it is also the face of Joan's son. You've heard tell of Joan, poor Joan who was unhappy, and ran away, and got lost,—you'll mind Joan Beverley?" Now, in the pause that followed, as Mr. Chichester gazed at Barnabas, his narrowed eyes opened, little by little, his compressed lips grew slowly loose, and the tasselled cane slipped from his fingers, and lay all neglected.

"Sir," said Barnabas at last, "this is what I would have told you. I am the lawful son of Joan Beverley, whose maiden name I took for—a purpose. I have but to prove my claim and I can dispossess you of the inheritance you hold, which is mine by right. But, sir, I have enough for my needs, and I am, therefore, prepared to forego my just claim—on a condition."

Mr. Chichester neither moved nor spoke.

"My condition," Barnabas continued, "is this. That, from this hour, you loose whatever hold you have upon Ronald Barrymaine,—that you have no further communication with him, either by word or letter. Failing this, I institute proceedings at once, and will dispossess you as soon as may be. Sir, you have heard my condition, it is for you to answer."

But, as he ended, Billy Button pointed a shaking finger downwards at the grass midway between them, and spoke:

"Look!" he whispered, "look! Do you not see it—bubbling so dark, —down there among the grass? Ah! it reaches your feet, Barnaby Bright. But—look yonder! it rises to his heart,—look!" and with a sudden, wild gesture, he pointed to Chichester's rigid figure. "Blood!" he cried, "blood!—cover it up! Oh, hide it—hide it!" Then, turning about, he sped away, his muffled buttons jingling faintly as he went, and so was presently gone.

Then Barnabas loosed his horse and mounted, and, with never a glance nor word to the silent figure beneath the finger-post, galloped away London-wards.

Now, had it been possible for a worn and decrepit finger-post to be endued with the faculty of motion (which, in itself, is a ridiculous thought, of course), it is probable that this particular one would have torn itself up bodily, and hastened desperately after Barnabas to point him away—away, east or west, or north or south,—anywhere, so long as it was far enough from him who stood so very still, and who stared with such eyes so long upon the moon, with his right hand still hidden in his breast, while the vivid mark glowed, and glowed upon the pallor of his cheek.

CHAPTER XLIII

IN WHICH BARNABAS MAKES A BET, AND RECEIVES A WARNING

The fifteenth of July was approaching, and the Polite World, the World of Fashion, was stirred to its politest depths. In the clubs speculation was rife, the hourly condition of horses and riders was discussed gravely and at length, while betting-books fluttered everywhere. In crowded drawing-rooms and dainty boudoirs, love and horse-flesh went together, and everywhere was a pleasurable uncertainty, since there were known to be at least four competitors whose chances were practically equal. Therefore the Polite World, gravely busied with its cards or embroidery, and at the same time striving mentally to compute the exact percentage of these chances, was occasionally known to revoke, or prick its dainty finger.

Even that other and greater world, which is neither fashionable nor polite,—being too busy gaining the wherewithal to exist,—even in fetid lanes and teeming streets, in dingy offices and dingier places still, the same excitement prevailed; busy men forgot their business awhile; crouching clerks straightened their stooping backs, became for the nonce fabulously rich, and airily bet each other vast sums that Carnaby's "Clasher" would do it in a canter, that Viscount Devenham's "Moonraker" would have it in a walk-over, that the Marquis of Jerningham's "Clinker" would leave the field nowhere, and that Captain Slingsby's "Rascal" would run away with it.

Yes, indeed, all the world was agog, rich and poor, high and low. Any barefooted young rascal scampering along the kennel could have named you the four likely winners in a breath, and would willingly have bet his ragged shirt upon his choice, had there been any takers.

Thus, then, the perspicacious waiter at the "George" who, it will be remembered, on his own avowal usually kept his eyes and ears open, and could, therefore, see as far through a brick wall as most, knew at once that the tall young gentleman in the violet coat with silver buttons, the buckled hat and glossy Hessians, whose sprigged waistcoat and tortuous cravat were wonders among their kind, was none other than a certain Mr. Beverley, who had succeeded in entering his horse at the last possible moment, and who, though an outsider with not the remotest chance of winning, was, nevertheless, something of a buck and dandy, the friend of a Marquis and Viscount, and hence worthy of all respect. Therefore the perspicacious waiter at the "George" viewed Barnabas with the eye of reverence, his back was subservient, and his napkin eloquent of eager service, also he bowed as frequently and humbly as such expensive and elegant attire merited; for the waiter at the "George" had as just and reverent a regard for fine clothes as any fine gentleman in the Fashionable World.

"A chair, sir!" Here a flick of the officious napkin. "Now shall we say a chop, sir?" Here a smiling obeisance. "Or shall we make it a steak, sir—cut thick, sir—medium done, and with—"

"No, thank you," said Barnabas, laying aside hat and cane.

"No, sir? Very good, sir! Certainly not, sir! A cut o' b'iled beef might suit, p'raps,—with carrots? or shall we say—"

"Neither, thank you, but you can bring me a bottle of Burgundy and the Gazette."

"Burgundy, sir—Gazette? Certainly, sir—"

"And—I'm expecting a gentleman here of the name of Smivvle—"

"Certainly, sir! Burgundy, Gazette, Gent name of Sniffle, yessir! Hanythink else, sir?"

"Yes, I should like pens and ink and paper."

"Yessir—himmediately, sir." Hereupon, and with many and divers bows and flicks of the napkin, the waiter proceeded to set out the articles in question, which done, he flicked himself out of the room. But he was back again almost immediately, and had uncorked the bottle and filled the glass with a flourish, a dexterity, a promptness, accorded only to garments of the very best and most ultra-fashionable cut. Then, with a bow that took in bestarched cravat, betasselled Hessians, and all garments between, the waiter fluttered away. So, in a while, Barnabas took pen and paper, and began the following letter:

MY DEAR FATHER AND NATTY BELL,—Since writing my last letter to you, I have bought a house near St. James's, and set up an establishment second to none. I will confess that I find myself like to be overawed by my retinue of servants, and their grave and decorous politeness; I also admit that dinner is an ordeal of courses,— each of which, I find, requires a different method of attack; for indeed, in the Polite World, it seems that eating is cherished as one of its most important functions, hence, dining is an art whereof the proper manipulation of the necessary tools is an exact science. However, by treating my servants with a dignified disregard, and by dint of using my eyes while at table, I have committed no great solecism so far, I trust, and am rapidly gaining in knowledge and confidence.

I am happy to tell you that I have the good fortune to be entered for the Gentlemen's Steeplechase, a most exclusive affair, which is to be brought off at Eltham on the fifteenth of next month. From all accounts it will be a punishing Race, with plenty of rough going,— plough, fallow, hedge and ditch, walls, stake-fences and water. The walls and water-jump are, I hear, the worst.

Now, although I shall be riding against some of the best horsemen in England, still I venture to think I can win, and this for three reasons. First, because I intend to try to the uttermost—with hand and heel and head. Secondly, because I have bought a horse—such a horse as I have only dreamed of ever possessing,—all fire and courage, with a long powerful action—Oh, Natty Bell, if you could but see him! Rising six, he is, with tushes well through,—even your keen eye could find no flaw in him, though he is, perhaps, a shade long in the cannon. And, thirdly, I am hopeful to win because I was taught horse-craft by that best, wisest of riders, Natty Bell. Very often, I remember, you have told me, Natty Bell, that races are won more by judgment of the rider than by the speed of the horse, nor shall I forget this. Thus then, sure of my horse, sure of myself, and that kind Destiny which has brought me successfully thus far, I shall ride light-hearted and confident.

Yet, my dears, should I win or lose, I would have you remember me always as

Your dutiful, loving
BARNABAS.

Now, as Barnabas laid down his pen, he became aware of voices and loud laughter from the adjacent coffee-room, and was proceeding to fold and seal his letter when he started and raised his head, roused by the mention of his own name spoken in soft, deliberate tones that he instantly recognized:

"Ah, so you have met this Mr. Beverley?"

"Yes," drawled another, deeper voice, "the Duchess introduced him to me. Who the deuce is he, Chichester?"

"My dear Carnaby, pray ask Devenham, or Jerningham, he's their protege—not mine."

"Sir," broke in the Viscount's voice, speaking at its very iciest,— "Mr. Beverley is—my friend!"

"And mine also, I trust!" thus the Marquis.

"Exactly!" rejoined Mr. Chichester's smooth tones, "and, consequently, despite his mysterious origin, he is permitted to ride in the Steeplechase among the very élite of the sporting world—"

"And why not, b'gad?" Captain Slingsby's voice sounded louder and gruffer than usual, "I'll warrant him a true-blue,—sportsman every inch, and damme! one of the right sort too,—sit a horse with any man,—bird at a fence, and ready to give or take odds on his chances, I'll swear—"

"Now really," Mr. Chichester's tone was softer than ever, "he would seem to be a general favorite here. Still, it would, at least, be—interesting to know exactly who and what he is."

"Yes," Sir Mortimer's voice chimed in, "and only right in justice to ourselves. Seems to me, now I come to think of it, I've seen him somewhere or other, before we were introduced,—be shot if I know where, though."

"In the—country, perhaps?" the Viscount suggested.

"Like as not," returned Sir Mortimer carelessly. "But, as Chichester says, it *is* devilish irregular to allow any Tom, Dick, or Harry to enter for such a race as this. If, as Sling suggests, the fellow is willing to back himself, it would, at least, be well to know that he could cover his bets."

"Sir Mortimer!" the Viscount's tone was colder and sharper than before, "you will permit me, in the first place, to tell you that his name is neither Tom, nor Dick, nor Harry. And in the second place, I would remind you that the gentleman honors me with his friendship. And in the third place, that I suffer no one to cast discredit upon my friends. D'you take me, Sir Mortimer?"

There followed a moment of utter stillness, then the sudden scrape and shuffle of feet, and thereafter Carnaby's voice, a little raised and wholly incredulous:

"What, Viscount,—d'you mean to take this fellow's part—against me?"

"Most certainly, if need be."

But here, before Sir Mortimer could reply, all five started and turned as the door opened and Barnabas appeared on the threshold.

"Viscount," said he, "for that I thank you most sincerely, most deeply. But, indeed, it will not be necessary, seeing I am here to do it for myself, and to answer such questions as I think—proper."

"Ah, Mr.—Beverley!" drawled Sir Mortimer, seating himself on the tale and crossing his legs, "you come pat, and since you are here, I desire a word with you."

"As many as you wish, sir," answered Barnabas, and he looked very youthful as he bowed his curly head.

"It would seem, Mr. Beverley, that you are something of a mystery, and I, for one, don't like mysteries. Then it has been suggested that you and I have met before our introduction, and, egad! now I come to look at you more attentively, your face does seem familiar, and I am curious to know who you may happen to be?"

"Sir," said Barnabas, looking more youthful than ever, "such rare condescension, such lively interest in my concerns, touches me—touches me deeply," and he bowed, lower than before.

"Suppose, sir," retorted Sir Mortimer, his cheek flushing a little, "suppose you answer my question, and tell me plainly who and what you are?" and he stared at Barnabas, swinging his leg to and fro as he awaited his reply.

"Sir," said Barnabas, "I humbly beg leave to remark, that as to who I am can concern only my—friends. As to what I am concerns only my Maker and myself—"

"Oh, vastly fine," nodded Sir Mortimer, "but that's no answer."

"And yet I greatly fear it must suffice—for you, sir," sighed Barnabas. Sir Mortimer's swinging foot grew still, and he frowned suddenly.

"Now look you, sir," said he slowly, and with a menace in his eyes, "when I trouble to ask a question, I expect an answer—"

"Alas, sir,—even your expectations may occasionally be disappointed," said Barnabas, beginning to smile aggressively. "But, as to my resources, I do not lack for money, and am ready, here and now, to lay you, or any one else, a thousand guineas that I shall be one of the first three to pass the winning-post on the fifteenth."

Sir Mortimer's frown grew more ominous, the flush deepened in his cheeks, and his powerful right hand clenched itself, then he laughed.

"Egad! you have plenty of assurance, sir. It is just possible that you may have ridden—now and then?"

"Sufficiently to know one end of a horse from the other, sir," retorted Barnabas, his smile rather grim.

"And you are willing to bet a thousand guineas that you ride third among all the best riders in the three kingdoms, are you?"

"No, sir," said Barnabas, shaking his head, "the bet was a rash one, —I humbly beg leave to withdraw it. Instead, I will bet five thousand guineas that I pass the winning-post before you do, Sir Mortimer."

Carnaby's smile vanished, and he stared up at calm-eyed Barnabas in open-mouthed astonishment.

"You're not mad, are you?" he demanded at last, his red under-lip curling.

"Sir," said Barnabas, taking out his memorandum, "it is now your turn to answer. Do you take my bet?"

"Take it!" cried Sir Mortimer fiercely, "yes! I'll double it—make it ten thousand guineas, sir!"

"Fifteen if you wish," said Barnabas, his pencil poised.

"No, by God! but I'll add another five and make it an even twenty thousand!"

"May I suggest you double instead, and make it thirty?" inquired Barnabas.

"Ha!—may I venture to ask how much higher you are prepared to go?"

"Why, sir," said Barnabas thoughtfully, "I have some odd six hundred thousand pounds, and I am prepared to risk—a half."

"Vastly fine, sir!" laughed Sir Mortimer, "why not put it at a round million and have done with it. No, egad! I want something more than your word—"

"You might inquire of my bankers," Barnabas suggested.

"Twenty thousand will suit me very well, sir!" nodded Sir Mortimer.

"Then you take me at that figure, Sir Mortimer?"

"Yes, I bet you twenty thousand guineas that you do not pass the winning-post ahead of me! And what's more,—non-starters to forfeit their money! Oh, egad,—I'll take you!"

"And I also," said Mr. Chichester, opening his betting-book. "Gentlemen, you are all witnesses of the bet. Come, Viscount,—Slingsby,—here's good money going a-begging—why not gather it in—eh, Marquis?" But the trio sat very silent, so that the scratch of Sir Mortimer's pencil could be plainly heard as he duly registered his bet, which done, he turned his attention to Barnabas again, looking him up and down with his bold, black eyes.

"Hum!" said he musingly, "it sticks in my mind that I have seen you—somewhere or other, before we met at Sir George Annersley's. Perhaps you will tell me where?"

"With pleasure, sir," answered Barnabas, putting away his memorandum book, "it was in Annersley Wood, rather early in the morning. And you wore—"

"Annersley—Wood!" Sir Mortimer's careless, lounging air vanished, and he stared at Barnabas with dilating eyes.

"And you wore, I remember, a bottle-green coat, which I had the misfortune to tear, sir."

And here there fell a silence, once more, but ominous now, and full of menace; a pregnant stillness, wherein the Viscount sat leaned forward, his hands clutching his chair-arms, his gaze fixed upon Barnabas; as for the Marquis, he had taken out his snuff-box and, in his preoccupation, came very near inhaling a pinch; while Captain Slingsby sat open-mouthed. Then, all at once, Sir Mortimer was on his feet and had caught up a heavy riding-whip, and thus he and Barnabas fronted each other, eye to eye,—each utterly still, yet very much on the alert.

But now upon this tense silence came the soft, smooth tones of Mr. Chichester:

"Pray, Mr. Beverley, may I speak a word with you—in private?"

"If the company will excuse us," Barnabas replied; whereupon Mr. Chichester rose and led the way into the adjoining room, and, closing the door, took a folded letter from his pocket.

"Sir," said he, "I would remind you that the last time we met, you warned me,—indeed you have a weakness for warning people, it seems,—you also threatened me that unless I agreed to—certain conditions, you would dispossess me of my inheritance—"

"And I repeat it," said Barnabas.

"Oh, sir, save your breath and listen," smiled Mr. Chichester, "for let me tell you, threats beget threats, and warnings, warnings! Here is one, which I think—yes, which I venture to think you will heed!" So saying, he unfolded the letter and laid it upon the table. Barnabas glanced at it, hesitated, then stooping, read as follows:

DEAR LADY CLEONE,—I write this to warn you that the person calling himself Mr. Beverley, and posing as a gentleman of wealth and breeding, is, in reality, nothing better than a rich vulgarian, one Barnabas Barty, son of a country inn-keeper. The truth of which shall be proved to your complete satisfaction whenever you will, by:

Yours always humbly to command,
WILFRED CHICHESTER.

Now when he had finished reading, Barnabas sank down into a chair, and, leaning his elbows upon the table, hid his face between his hands; seeing which, Mr. Chichester laughed softly, and taking up the letter, turned to the door. "Sir," said he, "as I mentioned before, threats beget threats. Now,—you move, and I move. I tell you, if you presume to interfere with me again in any way,—or with my future plans in any way, then, in that same hour, Cleone shall know you for the impudent impostor you are!" So Mr. Chichester laughed again, and laid his hand upon the latch of the door. But Barnabas sat rigid, and did not move or lift his heavy head even when the door opened and closed, and he knew he was alone.

Very still lie sat there, crouched above the table, his face hidden in his hands, until he was roused by a cough, the most perfectly discreet and gentleman-like cough in the world, such a cough, indeed, as only a born waiter could emit.

"Sir," inquired the waiter, his napkin in a greater flutter than ever, as Barnabas looked up, "sir,—is there hanythink you're wanting, sir?"

"Yes," said Barnabas, heavily, "you can—give me—my hat!"

CHAPTER XLIV

OF THE TRIBULATIONS OF THE LEGS OF THE GENTLEMAN-IN-POWDER

The Gentleman-in-Powder, aware of a knocking, yawned, laid aside the "Gazette," and getting upon his legs (which, like all things truly dignified, were never given to hurry), they, in due season, brought him to the door, albeit they shook with indignant quiverings at the increasing thunder of each repeated summons. Therefore the Gentleman-in-Powder, with his hand upon the latch, having paused long enough to vindicate and compose his legs, proceeded to open the portal of Number Five, St. James's Square; but, observing the person of the importunate knocker, with that classifying and discriminating eye peculiar to footmen, immediately frowned and shook his head:

"The hother door, me man,—marked 'tradesmen,'" said he, the angle of his nose a little more supercilious than usual, "and ring only, *if* you please." Having said which, he shut the door again; that is to say,—very nearly, for strive as he might, his efforts were unavailing, by reason of a round and somewhat battered object which, from its general conformation, he took to be the end of a formidable bludgeon or staff. But, applying his eye to the aperture, he saw that this very obtrusive object was nothing more or less than a leg (that is to say, a wooden one), which was attached to the person of a burly, broad-shouldered, fiercely bewhiskered man in clothes of navy-blue, a man whose hairy, good-natured visage was appropriately shaded by a very shiny glazed hat.

"Avast there!" said this personage in deep, albeit jovial tones, "ease away there, my lad,—stand by and let old Timbertoes come aboard!"

But the Gentleman-in-Powder was not to be cajoled. He sniffed.

"The hother door, me good feller!" he repeated, relentless but dignified, "and ring only, *if* you pl—"

The word was frozen upon his horrified lip, for Timbertoes had actually set his blue-clad shoulder to the door, and now, bending his brawny back, positively began to heave at it with might and main, cheering and encouraging himself meanwhile with sundry nautical "yo ho's." And all this in broad daylight! In St. James's Square!

Whereupon ensued the following colloquy:

The Gentleman-in-Powder (pushing from within. Shocked and amazed). "Wot's this? Stop it! Get out now, d'ye hear!"

Timbertoes (pushing from without. In high good humor). "With a ho, my hearties, and a merrily heave O!"

The Gentleman-in-Powder (struggling almost manfully, though legs highly agitated). "I—I'll give you in c-charge! I'll—"

Timbertoes (encouraging an imaginary crew). "Cheerily! Cheerily! heave yo ho!"

The Gentleman-in-Powder (losing ground rapidly. Condition of legs indescribable). "I never—see nothing—like this here! I'll—"

Timbertoes (all shoulders, whiskers and pig-tail). "With a heave and a ho, and up she rises O!"

The Gentleman-in-Powder (extricating his ruffled dignity from between wall and door). "Oh, very good,—I'll give you in charge for this, you—you feller! Look at me coat! I'll send for a constable. I'll—"

Timbertoes. "Belay, my lad! This here's Number Five, ain't it?"

The Gentleman-in-Powder (glancing down apprehensively at his quivering legs). "Yes,—and I'll—"

Timbertoes. "Cap'n Beverley's craft, ain't it?"

The Gentleman-in-Powder (re-adjusting his ruffled finery). "*Mister* Beverley occipies this here res-eye-dence!"

Timbertoes (*nodding*). "Mister Beverley,—oh, ah, for sure. Well, is 'e aboard?"

The Gentleman-in-Powder (with lofty sarcasm). "No, 'e ain't! Nor a stick, nor a stock, nor yet a chair, nor a table. And, wot's more, 'e ain't one to trouble about the likes o' you, neether."

Timbertoes. "Belay, my lad, and listen. I'm Jerry Tucker, late Bo'sun in 'is Britannic Majesty's navy,—'Bully-Sawyer,' Seventy-four. D'ye get that? Well, now listen again. According to orders I hove anchor and bore up for London very early this morning, but being strange to these 'ere waters, was obleeged to haul my wind and stand off and on till I fell in with a pilot, d'ye see. But, though late, here I am all ship-shape and a-taunto, and with despatches safe and sound. Watch, now!" Hereupon the Bo'sun removed the glazed hat, held it to his hairy ear, shook it, nodded, and from somewhere in its interior took out and held up three letters.

"D'ye see those, my lad?" he inquired.

The Gentleman-in-Powder (haughtily). "I ain't blind!"

Timbertoes. "Why then—you'll know what they are, p'raps?"

The Gentleman-in-Powder (witheringly). "Nor I ain't a fool, neether."

Timbertoes (dubiously). "Ain't you, though?"

The Gentleman-in-Powder (legs again noticeably agitated). "No, I ain't. I've got all *my* faculties about *me*."

Timbertoes (shaking head incredulously). "Ah! but where do you stow 'em away?"

The Gentleman-in-Powder (legs convulsed). "And—wot's more, I've got my proper amount o' limbs too!"

Timbertoes. "Limbs? If it's legs you're meaning, I should say as you'd got more nor your fair share,—you're all legs, you are! Why, Lord! you're grow'd to legs so surprising, as I wonder they don't walk off with you, one o'these here dark nights, and—lose you!"

But at this juncture came Peterby, sedate, grave, soft of voice as became a major-domo and the pink of a gentleman's gentleman, before whose quick bright eye the legs of the Gentleman-in-Powder grew, as it were, suddenly abashed, and to whom the Bo'sun, having made a leg, forthwith addressed himself.

"Sarvent, sir—name o' Jerry Tucker, late Bo'sun, 'Bully-Sawyer,' Seventy-four; come aboard with despatches from his Honor Cap'n Chumly and my Lady Cleone Meredith. To see Mr. Barnabas Beverley, Esquire. To give these here despatches into Mr. Beverley Esquire's own 'and. Them's my orders, sir."

"Certainly, Bo'sun," said Peterby; and, to the Gentleman-in-Powder, his bow was impressive; "pray step this way."

So the Bo'sun, treading as softly as his wooden leg would allow, stumped after him upstairs and along a thickly carpeted corridor, to a certain curtained door upon which Peterby gently knocked, and thereafter opening, motioned the Bo'sun to enter.

It was a small and exquisitely furnished, yet comfortable room, whose luxurious appointments,—the rich hangings, the rugs upon the floor, the pictures adorning the walls,—one and all bore evidence to the rare taste, the fine judgment of this one-time poacher of rabbits, this quiet-voiced man with the quick, bright eyes, and the subtly humorous mouth. But, just now, John Peterby was utterly serious as he glanced across to where, bowed down across the writing-table, his head pillowed upon his arms, his whole attitude one of weary, hopeless dejection, sat Barnabas Beverley, Esquire. A pen was in his lax fingers, while upon the table and littering the floor were many sheets of paper, some half covered with close writing, some crumpled and torn, some again bearing little more than a name; but in each and every case the name was always the same. Thus, John Peterby, seeing this drooping, youthful figure, sighed and shook his head, and went out, closing the door behind him.

"Is that you, John?" inquired Barnabas, with bowed head.

"No, sir, axing your pardon, it be only me, Jerry Tucker, Bo'sun, —'Bully-Sawyer,' Seventy—"

"Bo'sun!" With the word Barnabas was upon his feet. "Why, Bo'sun," he cried, wringing the sailor's hand, "how glad I am to see you!"

"Mr. Beverley, sir," began the Bo'sun, red-faced and diffident by reason of the warmth of his reception, "I've come aboard with despatches, sir. I bring you a letter from his Honor the Cap'n, from 'er Grace the Duchess, and from Lady Cleone, God bless her!"

"A letter from—her!" Then taking the letters in hands that were strangely unsteady, Barnabas crossed to the window, and breaking the seal of a certain one, read this:

DEAR MR. BARNABAS (the 'Beverley' crossed out),—Her Grace, my dear god-mother, having bullied my poor Tyrant out of the house, and quarrelled with me until she is tired, has now fixed her mind upon you. She therefore orders her dutiful god-daughter to write you these, hoping that thereby you may be induced to yield yourself a willing slave to her caprices and come down here for a few days. Though the very dearest and best of women, my god-mother, as you may remember, possesses a tongue, therefore—be warned, sir! My Tyrant at this precise moment sits in the 'round house,' whither he has retreated to solace his ruffled feelings with tobacco. So, I repeat, sir, be warned! And yet, though indeed, 't is strange, and passing strange, she speaks of you often, and seems to hold you in her kind regard. But, for all that, do not be misled, sir; for the Duchess is always the Duchess,—even to poor me. A while ago, she insisted on playing a game of chess; as I write the pieces lie scattered on the floor. *I* shan't pick them up,—why should I? So you see her Grace is quite herself to-day. Nevertheless, should you determine to run the risk, you will, I think, find a welcome awaiting you from,

Yours, dear sir,
CLEONE MEREDITH.

P.S.—The Bo'sun assures me the moon will last another week.

This Postscript Master Barnabas must needs read three times over, and then, quick and furtive, press the letter to his lips ere he thrust it into his bosom, and opened and read the Captain's:

The Gables,
Hawkhurst.
Written in the Round-house,
June 29, 18—.

MY DEAR BEVERLEIGH,—How is Fashion and the Modish World? as trivial as usual, I'll warrant me. The latest sensation, I believe, is Cossack Trousers,—have you tried 'em yet? But to come to my mutton, as the Mounseers say.

The Duchess of Camberhurst, having honored my house with her presence—and consequently set it in an uproar, I am constantly running foul of her, though more often she is falling aboard of me. To put it plainly, what with cross-currents, head-seas, and shifting winds that come down suddenly and blow great guns from every point of the compass, I am continually finding myself taken all a-back, as it were, and since it is quite impossible to bring to and ride it out, am consequently forced to go about and run for it, and continually pooped, even then,—for a woman's tongue is, I'm sure, worse than any following sea.

Hence, my sweet Clo, with her unfailing solicitude for me, having observed me flying signals of distress, has contrived to put it into my head that your presence might have a calming effect. Therefore, my dear boy, if you can manage to cast off the grapples of the Polite World for a few days, to run down here and shelter a battered old hulk under your lee, I shall be proud to have you as my guest.

Yours faithfully to serve,
JOHN CHUMLY.

P.S.—Pray bring your valet; you will need him, her Grace insists on dressing for dinner. Likewise my Trafalgar coat begins to need skilled patching, here and there; it is getting beyond the Bo'sun.

Here again Barnabas must needs pause to read over certain of the Captain's scrawling characters, and a new light was in his eyes as he broke the seal of her Grace's epistle.

MY DEAR MR. BEVERLEY,—The country down here, though delightfully Arcadian and quite idyllic (hayricks are so romantic, and I always adored cows—in pictures), is dreadfully quiet, and I freely confess that I generally prefer a man to a hop-pole (though I do wear a wig), and the voice of a man to the babble of brooks, or the trill of a skylark,—though I protest, I wouldn't be without them (I mean the larks) for the world,—they make me long for London so.

Then again, the Captain (though a truly dear soul, and the most gallant of hosts) treats me very much as though I were a ship, and, beside, he is so dreadfully gentle.

As for Cleone, dear bird, she yawns until my own eyes water (though, indeed, she has very pretty teeth), and, on the whole, is very dutiful and quarrels with me whenever I wish. 'T is quite true she cannot play chess; she also, constantly, revokes at Whist, and is quite as bad-tempered over it as I am. Cards, I fear, are altogether beyond her at present,—she is young. Of course time may change this, but I have grave doubts. In this deplorable situation I turn to you, dear Mr. Beverley (Cleone knew your address, it seems), and write these hasty lines to ntreat,—nay, to command you to come and cheer our solitude.

Cleone has a new gown she is dying to wear, and I have much that you must patiently listen to, so that I may truly subscribe myself'

Your grateful friend,
FANNY CAMBERURST.

P.S.—I have seen the finger-post on the London Road.

And now, having made an end of reading, Barnabas sighed and smiled, and squared his stooping shoulders, and threw up his curly head, and turning, found the Bo'sun still standing, hat in fist, lost in contemplation of the gilded ceiling. Hereupon Barnabas caught his hand, and shook it again, and laughed for very happiness.

"Bo'sun, how can I thank you!" said he, "these letters have given me new hope—new life! and—and here I leave you to stand, dolt that I am! And with nothing to drink, careless fool that I am. Sit down, man, sit down—what will you take, wine? brandy?"

"Mr. Beverley, sir," replied the Bo'sun diffidently, accepting the chair that Barnabas dragged forward, "you're very kind, sir, but if I might make so bold,—a glass of ale, sir—?"

"Ale!" cried Barnabas. "A barrel if you wish!" and he tugged at the bell, at whose imperious summons the Gentleman-in-Powder appearing with leg-quivering promptitude, Barnabas forthwith demanded "Ale,—the best, and plenty of it! And pray ask Mr. Peterby to come here at once!" he added.

"Sir," said the Bo'sun as the door closed, "you'll be for steering a course for Hawkhurst, p'r'aps?"

"We shall start almost immediately," said Barnabas, busily collecting those scattered sheets of paper that littered floor and table; thus he was wholly unaware of the look that clouded the sailor's honest visage.

"Sir," said the Bo'sun, pegging thoughtfully at a rose in the carpet with his wooden leg, "by your good leave, I'd like to ax 'ee a question."

"Certainly, Bo'sun, what is it?" inquired Barnabas, looking up from the destruction of the many attempts of his first letter to Cleone.

"Mr. Beverley, sir," said the Bo'sun, pegging away at the carpet as he spoke, "is it—meaning no offence, and àxing your pardon,—but are you hauling your wind and standing away for Hawkhurst so prompt on 'account o' my Lady Cleone?"

"Yes, Bo'sun, on account of our Lady Cleone."

"Why, then, sir," said the Bo'sun, fixing his eyes on the ceiling again, "by your leave—but,—why, sir?"

"Because, Bo'sun, you and I have this in common, that we both—love her."

Here the Bo'sun dropped his glazed hat, and picking it up, sat turning it this way and that, in his big, brown fingers.

"Why, then, sir," said he, looking up at Barnabas suddenly, "what of Master Horatio, his Lordship?"

"Why, Bo'sun, I told him about it weeks ago. I had to. You see, he honors me with his friendship."

The Bo'sun nodded, and broke into his slow smile:

"Ah, that alters things, sir," said he. "As for loving my lady—why? who could help it?"

"Who, indeed, Bo'sun!"

"Though I'd beg to remind you, sir, as orders *is* orders, and consequently she's bound to marry 'is Lordship—some day—"

"Or—become a mutineer!" said Barnabas, as the door opened to admit Peterby, who (to the horror of the Gentleman-in-Powder, and despite his mutely protesting legs), actually brought in the ale himself; yet, as he set it before the Bo'sun, his sharp eyes were quick to notice his young master's changed air, and brightened as if in sympathy.

"I want you, John, to know my good friend Bo'sun Jerry," said Barnabas, "a Trafalgar man—"

"'Bully-Sawyer,' Seventy-four!" added the Bo'sun, rising and extending his huge hand.

"We are all going to Hawkhurst, at once, John," continued Barnabas, "so pack up whatever you think necessary—a couple of valises will do, and tell Martin I'll have the phaeton,—it's roomier; and I'll drive the bays. And hurry things, will you, John?"

So John Peterby bowed, solemn and sedate as ever, and went upon his errand. But it is to be remarked that as he hastened downstairs, his lips had taken on their humorous curve, and the twinkle was back in his eyes; also he nodded his head, as who would say:

"I thought so! The Lady Cleone Meredith, eh? Well,—the sooner the better!"

Thus the Bo'sun had barely finished his ale, when the Gentleman-in-Powder appeared to say the phaeton was at the door.

And a fine, dashing turn-out it was, too, with its yellow wheels, its gleaming harness, and the handsome thorough-breds pawing impatient hoofs.

Then, the Bo'sun having duly ensconced himself, with Peterby in the rumble as calm and expressionless as the three leather valises under the seat, Barnabas sprang in, caught up the reins, nodded to Martin the gray-haired head groom, and giving the bays their heads, they were off and away for Hawkhurst and the Lady Cleone Meredith, whirling round corners and threading their way through traffic at a speed that caused the Bo'sun to clutch the seat with one hand, and the glazed hat with the other, and to remark in his diffident way that:

"These here wheeled craft might suit some, but for comfort and safety give me an eight-oared galley!"

CHAPTER XLV

HOW BARNABAS SOUGHT COUNSEL OF THE DUCHESS "BO'SUN?"

"Sir?"

"Do you know the Duchess of Camberhurst well?"

"Know her, sir?" repeated the Bo'sun, giving a dubious pull at his starboard whisker; "why, Mr. Beverley, sir, there's two things as I knows on, as no man never did know on, nor never will know on,—and one on 'em's a ship and t' other's a woman."

"But do you know her well enough to like and—trust?"

"Why, Mr. Beverley, sir, since you ax me, I'll tell you—plain and to the p'int. We'll take 'er Grace the Duchess and say, clap her helm a-lee to tack up ag'in a beam wind, a wind, mind you, as ain't strong enough to lift her pennant,—and yet she'll fall off and miss her stays, d'ye see, or get took a-back and yaw to port or starboard, though, if you ax me why or wherefore, I'll tell you as how,—her being a woman and me only a man,—I don't know. Then, again, on the contrary, let it blow up foul—a roaring hurricane say, wi' the seas running high, ah! wi' the scud flying over her top-s'l yard, and she'll rise to it like a bird, answer to a spoke, and come up into the wind as sweet as ever you see. The Duchess ain't no fair-weather craft, I'll allow, but in 'owling, raging tempest she's staunch, sir, —ah, that she is,—from truck to keelson! And there y'are, Mr. Beverley, sir!"

"Do you mean," inquired Barnabas, puzzled of look, "that she is to be depended on—in an emergency?"

"Ay, sir—that she is!"

"Ah!" said Barnabas, nodding, "I'm glad to know that, Bo'sun,—very glad." And here he became thoughtful all at once. Yet after a while he spoke again, this time to Peterby.

"You are very silent, John."

"I am—your valet, sir!"

"Then, oh! man," exclaimed Barnabas, touching up the galloping bays quite unnecessarily, "oh, man—forget it a while! Here we sit—three men together, with London miles behind us, and the Fashionable World further still. Here we sit, three men, with no difference between us, except that the Bo'sun has fought and bled for this England of ours, you have travelled and seen much of the world, and I, being the youngest, have done neither the one nor the other, and very little else—as yet. So, John,—be yourself; talk, John, talk!"

Now hereupon John Peterby's grave dignity relaxed, a twinkle dawned in his eyes, and his lips took on their old-time, humorous curve. And lo! the valet became merged and lost in the cosmopolitan, the dweller in many cities, who had done and seen much, and could tell of such things so wittily and well that the miles passed unheeded, while the gallant bays whirled the light phaeton up hill and down dale, contemptuous of fatigue.

It needs not here to describe more fully this journey whose tedium was unnoticed by reason of good-fellowship. Nor of the meal they ate at the "Chequers" Inn at Tonbridge, and how they drank (at the Bo'sun's somewhat diffident suggestion) a health "to his Honor the Cap'n, and the poor old 'Bully-Sawyer,' Seventy-four."

And thus Barnabas, clad in purple and fine linen and driving his own blood horses, talked and laughed with a one-legged mariner, and sought the companionship of his own valet; which irregularity must be excused by his youth and inexperience, and the lamentable fact that, despite his purple and fine linen, he was, as yet, only a man, alas!

Thus, then, as evening fell, behold them spinning along that winding road where stood a certain ancient finger-post pointing the wayfarer:

TO LONDON. TO HAWKHURST

At sight of which weather-worn piece of timber. Barnabas must needs smile, though very tenderly, and thereafter fall a-sighing. But all at once he checked his sighs to stare in amazement, for there, demurely seated beneath the finger-post, and completely engrossed in her needlework, was a small, lonely figure, at sight of which Barnabas pulled up the bays in mid-career.

"Why—Duchess!" he exclaimed, and, giving Peterby the reins, stepped out of the phaeton.

"Ah! is that you, Mr. Beverley?" sighed the Duchess, looking up from her embroidery, which, like herself, was very elaborate, very dainty, and very small. "You find me here, sitting by the wayside,—and a very desolate figure I must look, I'm sure,—you find me here because I have been driven away by the tantrums of an undutiful god-daughter, and the barbarity of a bloodthirsty buccaneer. I mean the Captain, of course. And all because I had the forethought to tell Cleone her nose was red,—which it was,—sunburn you know, and because I remarked that the Captain was growing as rotund as a Frenchman, which he is,—I mean fat, of course. All Frenchmen are fat—at least some are. And then he will wear such a shabby old coat! So here I am, Mr. Beverley, very lonely and very sad, but industrious you see, quite as busy as Penelope, who used to spin webs all day long,—which sounds as though she were a spider instead of a classical lady who used to undo them again at night,—I mean the webs, not the spiders. But, indeed, you're very silent, Mr. Beverley, though I'm glad to see you are here so well to time."

"To time, madam?"

"Because, you see, I 've won my bet. Oh yes, indeed, I bet about everything nowadays,—oh, feverishly, sir, and shall do, until the race is over, I suppose."

"Indeed, Duchess?"

"Yes. I bet Cleone an Indian shawl against a pair of beaded mittens that you would be here, to-day, before ten o'clock. So you see, you are hours before your time, and the mittens are mine. Talking of Cleone, sir, she's in the orchard. She's also in a shocking temper—indeed quite cattish, so you'd better stay here and talk to me. But then—she's alone, and looking vastly handsome, I'll admit, so, of course, you're dying to be gone—now aren't you?"

"No," Barnabas replied, and turning, bade Peterby drive on to the house.

"Then you ought to be!" retorted the Duchess, shaking an admonitory finger at him, yet smiling also as the carriage rolled away. "Youth can never prefer to listen to a chattering old woman—in a wig!"

"But you see, madam, I need your help, your advice," said Barnabas gravely.

"Ah, now I love giving people advice! It's so pleasant and—easy!"

"I wish to confide in you,—if I may."

"Confidences are always interesting—especially in the country!"

"Duchess, I—I—have a confession to make."

"A confession, sir? Then I needn't pretend to work any longer—besides, I always prick myself. There!" And rolling the very small piece of embroidery into a ball, she gave it to Barnabas. "Pray sir, hide the odious thing in your pocket. Will you sit beside me? No? Very well—now, begin, sir!"

"Why, then, madam, in the first place, I—"

"Yes?"

"I—that is to say,—you—must understand that—in the first place—"

"You've said 'first place' twice!" nodded the Duchess as he paused.

"Yes—Oh!—Did I? Indeed I—I fear it is going to be even harder to speak of than I thought, and I have been nerving myself to tell you ever since I started from London."

"To tell me what?"

"That which may provoke your scorn of me, which may earn me Cleone's bitterest contempt."

"Why then, sir—don't say another word about it—"

"Ah, but I must—indeed I must! For I know now that to balk at it, to—to keep silent any longer would be dishonorable—and the act of a coward!"

"Oh dear me!" sighed the Duchess, "I fear you are going to be dreadfully heroic about something!"

"Let us say—truthful, madam!"

"But, sir,—surely Truthfulness, after all, is merely the last resource of the hopelessly incompetent! Anyhow it must be very uncomfortable, I'm sure," said the Duchess, nodding her head. Yet she was quick to notice the distress in his voice, and the gleam of moisture among the curls at his temple, hence her tone was more encouraging as she continued. "Still, sir, speak on if you wish, for even a Duchess may appreciate honor and truth—in another, of course,—though she does wear a wig!"

"Believe me," sighed Barnabas, beginning to stride restlessly to and fro, "the full significance of my conduct never occurred to me until it was forced on my notice by—by another, and then—" he paused and brushed the damp curls from his brow. "To-day I tried to write to Cleone—to tell her everything, but I—couldn't."

"So you decided to come and tell me first, which was very nice of you," nodded the Duchess, "oh, very right and proper! Well, sir, I'm listening."

"First, then," said Barnabas, coming to a halt, and looking down at her steadfast-eyed, "you must know that my real name is—Barty."

"Barty?" repeated the Duchess, raising her brows. "Mm! I like Beverley much better."

"Beverley was my mother's name. She was Joan Beverley."

"Joan? Joan Beverley? Why y-e-s, I think I remember her, and the talk there was. Joan? Ah yes, to be sure,—very handsome, and—disappeared. No one knew why, but now,—I begin to understand. You would suggest—"

"That she became the honorable wife of my father, John Barty, the celebrated pugilist and ex-champion of England, now keeper of a village inn," said Barnabas, speaking all in a breath, but maintaining his steadfast gaze.

"Eh?" cried the Duchess, and rose to her feet with astonishing ease for one of her years, "eh, sir, an innkeeper! And your mother—actually married him?" and the Duchess shivered.

"Yes, madam. I am their lawful son."

"Dreadful!" cried the Duchess, "handsome Joan Beverley—married to an—inn-keeper! Horrible! She'd much better have died—say, in a ditch—so much more respectable!"

"My father is an honorable man!" said Barnabas, with upflung head.

"Your father is—an inn-keeper!"

"And—my father, madam!"

"The wretch!" exclaimed the Duchess. "Oh, frightful!" and she shivered again.

"And his son—loves Cleone!"

"Dreadful! Frightful" cried the Duchess. "An inn-keeper's son! Beer and skittles and clay pipes! Oh, shocking!" And here, shuddering for the third time as only a great lady might, she turned her back on him.

"Ah," cried Barnabas, "so you scorn me—already?"

"Of course."

"For being—an inn-keeper's son?"

"For—telling of it!"

"And yet," said Barnabas, "I think Barnabas Barty is a better man than Barnabas Beverley, and a more worthy lover; indeed I know he is. And, as Barnabas Barty, I bid your Grace good-by!"

"Where are you going?"

"To the village inn, madam, my proper place, it seems. But—to-morrow morning, unless you have told Cleone, I shall. And now, if your Grace will have the kindness to send my servant to me—"

"But—why tell Cleone?" inquired the Duchess over her shoulder; "there is one alternative left to you."

"Then, madam, in heaven's name,—tell it me!" cried Barnabas eagerly.

"A ridiculously simple one, sir."

"Oh, madam—what can I do—pray tell me."

"You must—disown this inn-keeping wretch, of course. You must cast him off—now, at once, and forever!"

"Disown him—my father!"

"Certainly,"

Barnabas stared wide-eyed. Then he laughed, and uncovering his head, bowed deeply.

"Madam," said he, "I have the honor to bid your Grace good-by!"

"You—will tell Cleone then?"

"To-morrow morning."

"Why?"

"Because I love her. Because I, therefore, hate deceit, and because I—"

"Well?"

"And because Mr. Chichester knows already."

"Ah! You mean that he has forced your hand, sir, and now you would make the best of it—"

"I mean that he has opened my eyes, madam."

"And to-morrow you will tell Cleone?"

"Yes."

"And, of course, she will scorn you for an impudent impostor?"

Now at this Barnabas flinched, for these were Chichester's own words, and they bore a double sting.

"And yet—I must tell her!" he groaned.

"And afterwards, where shall you go?"

"Anywhere," he sighed, with a hopeless gesture.

"And—the race?"

"Will be run without me."

"And your friends—the Marquis, Viscount Devenham, and the rest?"

"Will, I expect, turn their gentlemanly backs upon me—as you yourself have done. So, madam, I thank you for your past kindness, and bid you—good-by"

"Stop, sir!"

"Of what avail, madam?" sighed Barnabas, turning away.

"Come back—I command you!"

"I am beneath your Grace's commands, henceforth," said Barnabas, and plodded on down the road.

"Then I—beg of you!"

"Why?" he inquired, pausing.

"Because—oh, because you are running off with my precious needlework, of course. In your pocket, sir,—the left one!" So, perforce, Barnabas came back, and standing again beneath the finger-post, gave the Duchess her very small piece of embroidery. But, behold! his hand was caught and held between two others, which, though very fragile, were very imperious.

"Barnabas," said the Duchess very softly, "oh, dear me, I'm glad you told me, oh very! I hoped you would!"

"Hoped? Why—why, madam, you—then you knew?"

"All about it, of course! Oh, you needn't stare—it wasn't witchcraft, it was this letter—read it." And taking a letter from her reticule, she gave it to Barnabas, and watched him while he read:

TO HER GRACE THE DUCHESS OF CAMBERHURST.

MADAM,—In justice to yourself I take occasion to warn your Grace against the person calling himself Barnabas Beverley. He is, in reality, an impudent impostor of humble birth and mean extraction. His real name and condition I will prove absolutely to your Grace at another time.

Your Grace's most humble obedt.
WILFRED CHICHESTER.

"So you see I'm not a witch, sir,—oh no, I'm only an old woman, with, among many other useful gifts, a very sharp eye for faces, a remarkable genius for asking questions, and the feminine capacity for adding two and two together and making them—eight. So, upon reading this letter, I made inquiries on my own account with the result that yesterday I drove over to a certain inn called the 'Coursing Hound,' and talked with your father. Very handsome he is too—as he always was, and I saw him in the hey-day of his fame, remember. Well, I sipped his ale,—very good ale I found it, and while I sipped, we talked. He is very proud of his son, it seems, and he even showed me a letter this son had written him from the 'George' inn at Southwark. Ha! Joan Beverley was to have married an ugly old wretch of a marquis, and John Barty is handsome still. But an inn-keeper, hum!"

"So—that was why my mother ran away, madam?"

"And Wilfred Chichester knows of this, and will tell Cleone, of course!"

"I think not—at least not yet," answered Barnabas thoughtfully,— "you see, he is using this knowledge as a weapon against me."

"Why?"

"I promised to help Ronald Barrymaine—"

"That wretched boy! Well?"

"And the only way to do so was to remove him from Chichester's influence altogether. So I warned Mr. Chichester that unless he forswore Barrymaine's society, I would, as Joan Beverley's son and heir to the Beverley heritage, prove my claim and dispossess him."

"You actually threatened Wilfred Chichester with this, and forgot that in finding you your mother's son, he would prove you to be your father's also?"

"Yes, I—I only remembered my promise."

"The one you gave Cleone, which she had no right to exact—as I told her—"

"But, madam—"

"Oh, she confessed to me all about it, and how you had tried to pay Ronald's debts for him out of your own pocket,—which was very magnificent but quite absurd."

"Yes," sighed Barnabas, "so now I am determined to free him from Chichester first—"

"By dispossessing Chichester?"

"Yes, madam."

"But—can't you see, if you force him to expose you it will mean your social ruin?"

"But then I gave—Her—my promise."

"Oh, Barnabas," said the Duchess, looking up at him with her young, beautiful eyes that were so like Cleone's, "what a superb fool you are! And your father *is* only a village inn-keeper!"

"No, madam,—he was champion of all England as well."

"Oh!" sighed the Duchess, shaking her head, "that poor Sir Mortimer Carnaby! But, as for you, sir, you 're a fool, either a very clumsy, or a very—unselfish one,—anyhow, you're a fool, you know!"

"Yes," sighed Barnabas, his head hanging, "I fear I am."

"Oh yes,—you're quite a fool—not a doubt of it!" said the Duchess with a nod of finality. "And yet, oh, dear me! I think it may be because I'm seventy-one and growing younger every day, or perhaps because I'm so old that I have to wear a wig, but my tastes are so peculiar that there are some fools I could almost—love. So you may give me your arm,—Barnabas."

He obeyed mechanically, and they went on down the road together in silence until they came to a pair of tall, hospitable gates, and here Barnabas paused, and spoke wonderingly:

"Madam, you—you surely forget I am the son of—"

"A champion of all England, Barnabas. But, though you can thrash Sir Mortimer Carnaby, Wilfred Chichester is the kind of creature that only a truly clever woman can hope to deal with, so you may leave him to me!"

"But, madam, I—"

"Barnabas, quite so. But Wilfred Chichester always makes me shudder, and I love to shudder—now and then, especially in the hot weather. And then everything bores me lately—Cleone, myself,—even Whist, so I'll try my hand at another game—with Wilfred Chichester as an opponent."

"But, Duchess, indeed I—"

"Very true, Barnabas! but the matter is quite settled. And now, you are still determined to—confess your father to Cleone, I suppose?"

"Yes, I dare not speak to her otherwise, how could I, knowing myself an—"

"Impudent impostor, sir? Quite so and fiddlesticks! Heigho! you are so abominably high-minded and heroic, Barnabas,—it's quite depressing. Cleone is only a human woman, who powders her nose when it's red, and quite right too—I mean the powder of course, not the redness. Oh! indeed she's very human, and after all, your mother was a Beverley, and I know you are rich and—ah! there she is—on the terrace with the Captain, and I'm sure she has seen you, Barnabas, because she's so vastly unconscious. Observe the pose of her head,—she has a perfect neck and shoulders, and she knows it. There! see her kissing the Captain,—that's all for my benefit, the yellow minx! just because I happened to call him a 'hunks,' and so he is—though I don't know what I meant,—because he refused to change that dreadful old service coat. There! now she's patting his cheek—the golden jade! Now—watch her surprise when she pretends to catch sight of us!"

Hereupon, as they advanced over the smooth turf, the Duchess raised her voice.

"My bird!" she called in dulcet tones, "Clo dear, Cleone my lamb, here is Barnabas, I found him—under the finger-post, my dove!"

My lady turned, gave the least little start in the world, was surprised, glad, demure, all in the self-same minute, and taking the arm of her Tyrant, who had already begun a truly nautical greeting, led him, forthwith, down the terrace steps, the shining curls at her temple brushing his shabby coat-sleeve as they came.

"Ha!" cried the Captain, "my dear fellow, we're glad—I say we're all of us glad to see you. Welcome to 'The Gables,'—eh, Clo?"

And Cleone? With what gracious ease she greeted him! With what clear eyes she looked at him! With what demure dignity she gave him her white hand to kiss! As though—for all the world as though she could ever hope to deceive anything so old and so very knowing as the ancient finger-post upon the London road!

"Clo dear," said the Duchess, "they're going to talk horses and racing, and bets and things,—I know they are,—your arm, my love. Now,—lead on, gentlemen. And now, my dear," she continued, speaking in Cleone's ear as Barnabas and the Captain moved on, "he simply—adores you!"

"Really, God-mother—how clever of you!" said Cleone, her eyes brim full of merriment, "how wonderful you are!"

"Yes, my lady Pert,—he worships you and, consequently, is deceiving you with every breath he draws!"

"Deceiving me—!"

"With every moment he lives!"

"But—oh, God-mother—!"

"Cleone,—he is not what he seems!"

"Deceiving me?"

"His very name is false!"

"What do you mean? Ah no, no—I'm sure he would not, and yet—oh, God-mother,—why?"

"Because—hush, Cleone—he's immensely rich, one of the wealthiest young men in London, and—hush! He would be—loved for himself alone. So, Cleone,—listen,—he may perhaps come to you with some wonderful story of poverty and humble birth. He may tell you his father was only a—a farmer, or a tinker, or a—an inn-keeper. Oh dear me,—so delightfully romantic! Therefore, loving him as you do—"

"I don't!"

"With every one of your yellow hairs—"

"I do—*not*!"

"From the sole of your foot—"

"God-mother!"

"To the crown of your wilful head,—oh, Youth, Youth!—you may let your heart answer as it would. Oh Fire! Passion! Romance! (yes, yes, Jack,—we're coming!) Your heart, I say, Cleone, may have its way, because with all his wealth he has a father who—hush!—at one time was the greatest man in all England,—a powerful man, Clo,—a famous man, indeed a man of the most—striking capabilities. So, when your heart—(dear me, how impatient Jack is!) Oh, supper? Excellent, for, child, now I come to think of it, I'm positively swooning with hunger!"

CHAPTER XLVI

WHICH CONCERNS ITSELF WITH SMALL THINGS IN GENERAL, AND A PEBBLE IN PARTICULAR

To those who, standing apart from the rush and flurry of life, look upon the world with a seeing eye, it is, surely, interesting to observe on what small and apparently insignificant things great matters depend. To the student History abounds with examples, and to the philosopher they are to be met with everywhere.

But how should Barnabas (being neither a student nor a philosopher) know, or even guess, that all his fine ideas and intentions were to be frustrated, and his whole future entirely changed by nothing more nor less than—a pebble, an ordinary, smooth, round pebble, as innocent-seeming as any of its kind, yet (like young David's) singled out by destiny to be one of these "smaller things"?

They were sitting on the terrace, the Duchess, Cleone, Barnabas, and the Captain, and they were very silent,—the Duchess, perhaps, because she had supped adequately, the Captain because of his long, clay pipe, Cleone because she happened to be lost in contemplation of the moon, and Barnabas, because he was utterly absorbed in contemplation of Cleone.

The night was very warm and very still, and upon the quietude stole a sound—softer, yet more insistent than the whisper of wind among leaves,—a soothing, murmurous sound that seemed to make the pervading quiet but the more complete.

"How cool the brook sounds!" sighed the Duchess at last, "and the perfume of the roses,—oh dear me, how delicious! Indeed I think the scent of roses always seems more intoxicating after one has supped well, for, after all, one must be well-fed to be really romantic,—eh, Jack?"

"Romantic, mam!" snorted the Captain, "romantic,—I say bosh, mam! I say—"

"And then—the moon, Jack!"

"Moon? And what of it, mam,—I say—"

"Roses always smell sweeter by moonlight, Jack, and are far more inclined to—go to the head—"

"Roses!" snorted the Captain, louder than before, "you must be thinking of rum, mam, rum—"

"Then, Jack, to the perfume of roses, add the trill of a nightingale—"

"And of all rums, mam, give me real old Jamaica—"

"And to the trill of a nightingale, add again the murmur of an unseen brook, Jack—"

"Eh, mam, eh? Nightingales, brooks? I say—oh, Gad, mam!" and the Captain relapsed into tobacco-puffing indignation.

"What more could youth and beauty ask? Ah, Jack, Jack!" sighed the Duchess, "had you paid more attention to brooks and nightingales, and stared at the moon in your youth, you might have been a green young grandfather to-night, instead of a hoary old bachelor in a shabby coat—sucking consolation from a clay pipe!"

"Consolation, mam! For what—I say, I demand to know for what?"

"Loneliness, Jack!"

"Eh, Duchess,—what, mam? Haven't I got my dear Clo, and the Bo'sun, eh, mam—eh?"

"The Bo'sun, yes,—he smokes a pipe, but Cleone can't, so she looks at the moon instead,—don't you dear?"

"The moon, God-mother?" exclaimed Cleone, bringing her gaze earthwards on the instant. "Why I,—I—the moon, indeed!"

"And she listens to the brook, Jack,—don't you, my dove?"

"Why, God-mother, I—the brook? Of course not!" said Cleone.

"And, consequently, Jack, you mustn't expect to keep her much longer—"

"Eh!" cried the bewildered Captain, "what's all this, Duchess,—I say, what d'ye mean, mam?"

"Some women," sighed the Duchess, "some women never know they're in love until they've married the wrong man, and then it's too late, poor things. But our sweet Clo, on the contrary—"

"Love!" snorted the Captain louder than ever, "now sink me, mam,—I say, sink and scuttle me; but what's love got to do with Clo, eh, mam?"

"More than you think, Jack—ask her!"

But lo! my lady had risen, and was already descending the terrace steps, a little hurriedly perhaps, yet in most stately fashion. Whereupon Barnabas, feeling her Grace's impelling hand upon his arm, obeyed the imperious command and rising, also descended the steps,—though in fashion not at all stately,—and strode after my lady, and being come beside her, walked on—yet found nothing to say, abashed by her very dignity. But, after they had gone thus some distance, venturing to glance at her averted face, Barnabas espied the dimple beside her mouth.

"Cleone," said he suddenly, "what *has* love to do with you?"

Now, for a moment, she looked up at him, then her lashes drooped, and she turned away.

"Oh, sir," she answered, "lift up your eyes and look upon the moon!"

"Cleone, has love—come to you—at last? Tell me!" But my lady walked on for a distance with head again averted, and—with never a word. "Speak!" said Barnabas, and caught her hand (unresisting now), and held it to his lips. "Oh, Cleone,—answer me!"

Then Cleone obeyed and spoke, though her voice was tremulous and low.

"Ah, sir," said she, "listen to the brook!"

Now it so chanced they had drawn very near this talkative stream, whose voice reached them—now in hoarse whisperings, now in throaty chucklings, and whose ripples were bright with the reflected glory of the moon. Just where they stood, a path led down to these shimmering waters,—a narrow and very steep path screened by bending willows; and, moved by Fate, or Chance, or Destiny, Barnabas descended this path, and turning, reached up his hands to Cleone.

"Come!" he said. And thus, for a moment, while he looked up into her eyes, she looked down into his, and sighed, and moved towards him, and—set her foot upon the pebble.

And thus, behold the pebble had achieved its purpose, for, next moment Cleone was lying in his arms, and for neither of them was life or the world to be ever the same thereafter.

Yes, indeed, the perfume of the roses was full of intoxication to-night; the murmurous brook whispered of things scarce dreamed of; and the waning moon was bright enough to show the look in her eyes and the quiver of her mouth as Barnabas stooped above her.

"Cleone!" he whispered, "Cleone—can you—do you—love me? Oh, my white lady,—my woman that I love,—do you love me?"

She did not speak, but her eyes answered him; and, in that moment Barnabas stooped and kissed her, and held her close, and closer, until she sighed and stirred in his embrace.

Then, all at once, he groaned and set her down, and stood before her with bent head.

"My dear," said he, "oh, my dear!"

"Barnabas?"

"Forgive me,—I should have spoken,—indeed, I meant to,—but I couldn't think,—it was so sudden,—forgive me! I didn't mean to even touch your hand until I had confessed my deceit. Oh, my dear, —I am not—not the fine gentleman you think me. I am only a very —humble fellow. The son of a village—inn-keeper. Your eyes were—kind to me just now, but, oh Cleone, if so humble a fellow is—unworthy, as I fear,—I—I will try to—forget."

Very still she stood, looking upon his bent head, saw the quiver of his lips, and the griping of his strong hands. Now, when she spoke, her voice was very tender.

"Can you—ever forget?"

"I will—try!"

"Then—oh, Barnabas, don't! Because I—think I could—love this—humble fellow, Barnabas."

The moon, of course, has looked on many a happy lover, yet where find one, before or since, more radiant than young Barnabas; and the brook, even in its softest, most tender murmurs, could never hope to catch the faintest echo of Cleone's voice or the indescribable thrill of it.

And as for the pebble that was so round, so smooth and innocent-seeming, whether its part had been that of beneficent sprite, or malevolent demon, he who troubles to read on may learn.

CHAPTER XLVII

HOW BARNABAS FOUND HIS MANHOOD

"Oh—hif you please, sir!"

Barnabas started, and looking about, presently espied a figure in the shadow of the osiers; a very small figure, upon whose diminutive jacket were numerous buttons that glittered under the moon.

"Why—it's Milo of Crotona!" said Cleone.

"Yes, my lady—hif you please, it are," answered Milo of Crotona, touching the peak of his leather cap.

"But—what are you doing here? How did you know where to find us?"

"'Cause as I came up the drive, m'lady, I jest 'appened to see you a-walking together,—so I followed you, I did, m'lady."

"Followed us?" repeated Cleone rather faintly. "Oh!"

"And then—when I seen you slip, m'lady, I thought as 'ow I'd better—wait a bit. So I waited, I did." And here, again, Milo of Crotona touched the peak of his cap, and looked from Barnabas to Cleone's flushing loveliness with eyes wide and profoundly innocent,—a very cherub in top-boots, only his buttons (Ah, his buttons!) seemed to leer and wink one to another, as much as to say: "Oh yes! Of course! to—be—sure?"

"And what brings you so far from London?" inquired Barnabas, rather hurriedly.

"Coach, sir,—box seat, sir!"

"And you brought your master with you, of course,—is the Viscount here?"

"No, m'lady. I 'ad to leave 'im be'ind 'count of 'im being unfit to travel—"

"Is he ill?"

"Oh, no, not hill, m'lady,—only shot, 'e is."

"Shot!" exclaimed Barnabas, "how—where?"

"In the harm, sir,—all on 'count of 'is 'oss,—'Moonraker' sir."

"His horse?"

"Yessir. 'S arternoon it were. Ye see, for a long time I ain't been easy in me mind about them stables where 'im and you keeps your 'osses, sir, 'count of it not being safe enough,—worritted I 'ave, sir. So 's arternoon, as we was passing the end o' the street, I sez to m'lud, I sez, 'Won't your Ludship jest pop your nob round the corner and squint your peepers at the 'osses?' I sez. So 'e laughs, easy like, and in we pops. And the first thing we see was your 'ead groom, Mr. Martin, wiv blood on 'is mug and one peeper in mourning a-wrastling wiv two coves, and our 'ead groom, Standish, wiv another of 'em. Jest as we run up, down goes Mr. Martin, but—afore they could maul 'im wiv their trotters, there's m'lud wiv 'is fists an' me wiv a pitchfork as 'appened to lie 'andy. And very lively it were, sir, for a minute or two. Then off goes a barker and off go the coves, and there's m'lud 'olding onto 'is harm and swearing 'eavens 'ard. And that's all, sir."

"And these men were—trying to get at the horses?"

"Ah! Meant to nobble 'Moonraker,' they did,—'im bein' one o' the favorites, d' ye see, sir, and it looked to me as if they meant to do for your 'oss, 'The Terror', as well."

"And is the Viscount much hurt?"

"Why no, sir. And it were only 'is whip-arm. 'Urts a bit o' course, but 'e managed to write you a letter, 'e did; an' 'ere it is."

So Barnabas took the letter, and holding it in the moonlight where Cleone could see it, they, together, made out these words:

MY DEAR BEV,—There is durty work afoot. Some Raskells have tried to lame 'Moonraker,' but thanks to my Imp and your man Martin, quite unsuccessfully. How-beit your man Martin—regular game for all his years—has a broken nob and one ogle closed up, and I a ball through my arm, but nothing to matter. But I am greatly pirtirbed for the safety of 'Moonraker' and mean to get him into safer quarters and advise you to do likewise. Also, though your horse 'The Terror,' as the stable-boys call him, is not even in the betting, it almost seems, from what I can gather, that they meant to nobble him also. Therefore I think you were wiser to return at once, and I am anxious to see you on another matter as well. Your bets with Carnaby and Chichester have somehow got about and are the talk of the town, and from what I hear, much to your disparagement, I fear.

A pity to shorten your stay in the country, but under the circumstances, most advisable.

Yours ever, etc.,

DICK.

P.S. My love and service to the Duchess, Cleone and the Capt.

Now here Barnabas looked at Cleone, and sighed, and Cleone sighing also, nodded her head:

"You must go," said she, very softly, and sighed again.

"Yes, I must go, and yet—it is so very soon, Cleone!"

"Yes, it is dreadfully soon, Barnabas. But what does he mean by saying that people are talking of you to your disparagement? How dare they? Why should they?"

"I think because I, a rank outsider, ventured to lay a wager against Sir Mortimer Carnaby."

"Do you mean you bet him that you would win the race, Barnabas?"

"No,—only that I would beat Sir Mortimer Carnaby."

"But, oh Barnabas,—he *is* the race! Surely you know he and the Viscount are favorites?"

"Oh, yes!"

"Then you do think you can win?"

"I mean to try—very hard!" said Barnabas, beginning to frown a little.

"And I begin to think," said Cleone, struck by his resolute eyes and indomitable mouth, "oh, Barnabas—I begin to think you—almost may."

"And if I did?"

"Then I should be very—proud of you."

"And if I lost?"

"Then you would be—"

"Yes?"

"Just—"

"Yes, Cleone?"

"My, Barnabas! Ah, no, no!" she whispered suddenly, "you are crushing me—dreadfully, and besides, that boy has terribly sharp eyes!" and Cleone nodded to where Master Milo stood, some distance away, with his innocent orbs lifted pensively towards the heavens, more like a cherub than ever.

"But he's not looking, and oh, Cleone,—how can I bear to leave you so soon? You are more to me than anything else in the world. You are my life, my soul,—my honor,—oh my dear!"

"Do you—love me so very much, Barnabas?" said she, with a sudden catch in her voice.

"And always must! Oh my dear, my dear,—don't you know? But indeed, words are so small and my love is so great that I fear you can never quite guess, or I tell it all."

"Then, Barnabas,—you will go?"

"Must I, Cleone? It will be so very hard to lose you—so soon."

"But a man always chooses the harder course, doesn't he, Barnabas? And, dear, you cannot lose me,—and so you will go, won't you?"

"Yes, I'll go—because I love you!"

Then Cleone drew him deeper into the shade of the willows, and with a sudden, swift gesture, reached up her hands and set them about his neck.

"Oh my dear," she murmured, "oh Barnabas dear, I think I can guess—now. And I'm sure—the boy—can't see us—here!"

No, surely, neither this particular brook nor any other water-brook, stream or freshet, that ever sang, or sighed, or murmured among the reeds, could ever hope to catch all the thrilling tenderness of the sweet soft tones of Cleone's voice.

A brook indeed? Ridiculous!

Therefore this brook must needs give up attempting the impossible, and betake itself to offensive chuckles and spiteful whisperings, and would have babbled tales to the Duchess had that remarkable, ancient lady been versed in the language of brooks. As it was, she came full upon Master Milo still intent upon the heavens, it is true, but in such a posture that his buttons stared point-blank and quite unblushingly towards a certain clump of willows.

"Oh Lud!" exclaimed the Duchess, starting back, "dear me, what a strange little boy! What do you want here, little man?"

Milo of Crotona turned and—looked at her. And though his face was as cherubic as ever, there was haughty reproof in every button.

"Who are you?" demanded the Duchess; "oh, gracious me, what a pretty child!"

Surely no cherub—especially one in such knowing top-boots—could be reasonably expected to put up with this! Master Milo's innocent brow clouded suddenly, and the expression of his glittering buttons grew positively murderous.

"I'm Viscount Devenham's con-fee-dential groom, mam, I am!" said he coldly, and with his most superb air.

"Groom?" said the Duchess, staring, "what a very small one, to be sure!"

"It ain't inches as counts wiv 'osses, mam,—or hany-think else, mam, —it's nerves as counts, it is."

"Why, yes, you seem to have plenty of nerve!"

"Well, mam, there ain't much as I trembles at, there ain't,—and when I do, I don't show it, I don't."

"And such a pretty child, too!" sighed the Duchess.

"Child, mam? I ain't no child, I'm a groom, I am. Child yourself, mam!"

"Lud! I do believe he's even paying me compliments! How old are you, boy?"

"A lot more 'n you think, and hoceans more 'n I look, mam."

"And what's your name?"

"Milo, mam,—Milo o' Crotona, but my pals generally calls me Tony, for short, they do."

"Milo of Crotona!" repeated the Duchess, with her eyes wider than ever, "but he was a giant who slew an ox with his fist, and ate it whole!"

"Why, mam, I'm oncommon fond of oxes,—roasted, I am."

"Well," said the Duchess, "you are the very smallest giant I ever saw."

"Why, you ain't werry large yourself, mam, you ain't."

"No, I fear I am rather petite," said the Duchess with a trill of girlish laughter. "And pray, Giant, what may you be doing here?"

"Come up on the coach, I did,—box seat, mam,—to take Mr. Beverley back wiv me 'cause 'is 'oss ain't safe, and—"

"Not safe,—what do you mean, boy?"

"Some coves got in and tried to nobble 'Moonraker' and 'im—"

"Nobble, boy?"

"Lame 'em, mam,—put 'em out o' the running."

"The wretches!"

"Yes'm. Ye see us sportsmen 'ave our worritting times, we do."

"But where is Mr. Beverley?"

"Why, I ain't looked, mam, I ain't,—but they're down by the brook—behind them bushes, they are."

"Oh, are they!" said the Duchess, "Hum!"

"No mam,—'e's a-coming, and so's she."

"Why, Barnabas," cried the Duchess, as Cleone and he stepped out of the shadow, "what's all this I hear about your horse,—what is the meaning of it?"

"That I must start for London to-night, Duchess."

"Leave to-night? Absurd!"

"And yet, madam, Cleone seems to think I must, and so does Viscount Devenham,—see what he writes." So the Duchess took the Viscount's letter and, having deciphered it with some difficulty, turned upon Barnabas with admonishing finger upraised:

"So you 've been betting, eh? And with Sir Mortimer Carnaby and Mr. Chichester of all people?"

"Yes, madam."

"Ah! You backed the Viscount, I suppose?"

"No,—I backed myself, Duchess."

"Gracious goodness—"

"But only to beat Sir Mortimer Carnaby—"

"The other favorite. Oh, ridiculous! What odds did they give you?"

"None."

"You mean—oh, dear me!—you actually backed yourself—at even money?"

"Yes, Duchess."

"But you haven't a chance, Barnabas,—not a chance! You didn't bet much, I hope?"

"Not so much as I intended, madam."

"Pray what was the sum?"

"Twenty thousand pounds."

"Not—each?"

"Yes, madam."

"Forty thousand pounds! Against a favorite! Cleone, my dear," said the Duchess, with one of her quick, incisive nods, "Cleone, this Barnabas of ours is either a madman or a fool! And yet—stoop down, sir,—here where I can see you,—hum! And yet, Cleone, there are times when I think he is perhaps a little wiser than he seems,—nothing is so baffling as simplicity, my dear! If you wished to be talked about, Barnabas, you have succeeded admirably,—no wonder all London is laughing over such a preposterous bet. Forty thousand pounds! Well, it will at least buy you notoriety, and that is next to fame."

"Indeed, I hadn't thought of that," said Barnabas.

"And supposing your horse had been lamed and you couldn't ride,—how then?"

"Why, then, I forfeit the money, madam."

Now here the Duchess frowned thoughtfully, and thereafter said "ha!" so suddenly, that Cleone started and hurried to her side.

"Dear God-mother, what is it?"

"A thought, my dear!"

"But—"

"Call it a woman's intuition if you will."

"What is your thought, dear?"

"That you are right, Cleone,—he must go—at once!"

"Go? Barnabas?"

"Yes; to London,—now—this very instant! Unless you prefer to forfeit your money, Barnabas?"

But Barnabas only smiled and shook his head.

"You would be wiser!"

"But I was never very wise, I fear," said Barnabas.

"And—much safer!"

"Oh, God-mother,—do you think there is—danger, then?"

"Yes, child, I do. Indeed, Barnabas, you were wiser and safer to forfeit your wagers and stay here with me and—Cleone!"

But Barnabas only sighed and shook his head.

"Cleone," said the Duchess, "speak to him."

So blushing a little, sighing a little, Cleone reached out her hand to Barnabas, while the Duchess watched them with her young, bright eyes.

"Oh, Barnabas, God-mother is very wise, and if—there is danger—you mustn't go—for my sake."

But Barnabas shook his head again, and taking in his strong clasp the pleading hand upon his arm, turned to the Duchess.

"Madam," said he, "dear Duchess, to-night I have found my manhood, for to-night I have learned that a man must ever choose the hardest course and follow it—to the end. To-night Cleone has taught me—many things."

"And you will—stay?" inquired the Duchess.

"I must go!" said Barnabas.

"Then good-by—Barnabas!" said her Grace, looking up at him with a sudden, radiant smile, "good-by!" said she very softly, "it is a fine thing to be a gentleman, perhaps,—but it is a godlike thing to be—a man!" So saying, she gave him her hand, and as Barnabas stooped to kiss those small, white fingers, she looked down at his curly head with such an expression as surely few had ever seen within the eyes of this ancient, childless woman, her Grace of Camberhurst.

"Now Giant!" she called, as Barnabas turned towards Cleone, "come here, Giant, and promise me to take care of Mr. Beverley."

"Yes, mam,—all right, mam,—you jest leave 'im to me," replied Master Milo with his superb air, "don't you worrit on 'is account, 'e'll be all right along o' me, mam, 'e will."

"For that," cried the Duchess, catching him by two of his gleaming buttons, "for that I mean to kiss you, Giant!" The which, despite his reproving blushes, she did forthwith.

And Cleone and Barnabas? Well, it so chanced, her Grace's back was towards them; while as for Master Milo—abashed, and for once forgetful of his bepolished topboots, he became in very truth a child, though one utterly unused to the motherly touch of a tender woman's lips; therefore he suffered the embrace with closed eyes,—even his buttons were eclipsed, and, in that moment, the Duchess whispered something in his ear. Then he turned and followed after Barnabas, who was already striding away across the wide lawn, his head carried high, a new light in his eyes and a wondrous great joy at his heart,

—a man henceforth—resolute to attempt all things, glorying in his strength and contemptuous of failure, because of the trill of a woman's voice and the quick hot touch of a woman's soft lips, whose caress had been in no sense—motherly. And presently, being come to the hospitable gates, he turned with bared head to look back at the two women, the one a childless mother, old and worn, yet wise with years, and the maid, strong and proud in all the glory of her warm, young womanhood. Side by side with arms entwined they stood, to watch young Barnabas, and in the eyes of each, an expression so much alike, yet so dissimilar. Then, with a flourish of his hat, Barnabas went on down the road, past the finger-post, with Milo of Crotona's small top-boots twinkling at his side.

"Sir," said he suddenly, speaking in an awed tone, "is she a real Doochess—the little old 'un?"

"Yes," nodded Barnabas, "very real. Why, Imp?"

"'Cos I called 'er a child, I did—Lord! An' then she—she kissed me, she did, sir—which ain't much in my line, it ain't. But she give me a guinea, sir, an' she likewise whispered in my ear, she did."

"Oh?" said Barnabas, thinking of Cleone—"whispered, did she?"

"Ah! she says to me—quick like, sir,—she says, 'tell 'im,' she says—meaning you, sir, 'tell 'im to beware o' Wilfred Chichester!' she says."

CHAPTER XLVIII

IN WHICH "THE TERROR," HITHERTO KNOWN AS "FOUR-LEGS," JUSTIFIES HIS NEW NAME

The chill of dawn was in the air as the chaise began to rumble over the London cobble-stones, whereupon Master Milo (who for the last hour had slumbered peacefully, coiled up in his corner like a kitten) roused himself, sat suddenly very upright, straightened his cap and pulled down his coat, broad awake all at once, and with his eyes as round and bright as his buttons.

"Are you tired, Imp?" inquired Barnabas, yawning.

"Tired, sir, ho no, sir—not a bit, I ain't."

"But you haven't slept much."

"Slep', sir? I ain't slep'. I only jest 'appened to close me eyes, sir. Ye see, I don't need much sleep, I don't,—four hours is enough for any man,—my pal Nick says so, and Nick knows a precious lot, 'e do."

"Who is Nick?"

"Nick's a cobbler, sir,—boots and shoes,—ladies' and gents', and a very good cobbler 'e is too, although a cripple wiv a game leg. Me and 'im's pals, sir, and though we 'as our little turn-ups 'count of 'im coming it so strong agin the Quality, I'm never very 'ard on 'im 'count of 'is crutch, d'ye see, sir."

"What do you mean by the 'Quality,' Imp?"

"Gentle-folks, sir,—rich folks like you an' m'lud. 'I'd gillertine the lot, if I'd my way,' he says, 'like the Frenchies did in Ninety-three,' 'e says. But 'e wouldn't reelly o'course, for Nick's very tender-hearted, though 'e don't like it known. So we 're pals, we are, and I often drop in to smoke a pipe wiv 'im—"

"What! Do you smoke, Imp?"

"Why, yes, o' course, sir,—all grooms smokes or chews, but I prefers a pipe—allus 'ave, ah! ever since I were a kid. But I mostly only 'as a pipe when I drop in on my pal Nick in Giles's Rents."

"Down by the River?" inquired Barnabas.

"Yessir. And now, shall I horder the post-boy to stop?"

"What for?"

"Well, the stables is near by, sir, and I thought as you might like to take a glimp at the 'osses,—just to make your mind easy, sir."

"Oh, very well!" said Barnabas, for there was something in the boy's small, eager face that he could not resist.

Therefore, having paid and dismissed the chaise, they turned into a certain narrow by-street. It was very dark as yet, although in the east was a faint, gray streak, and the air struck so chill, after the warmth of the chaise, that Barnabas shivered violently, and, happening to glance down, he saw that the boy was shivering also. On they went, side by side, between houses of gloom and silence, and thus, in a while, came to another narrow street, or rather, blind alley, at the foot of which were the stables.

"Hush, sir!" said the Imp, staring away to where the stable buildings loomed up before them, shadowy and indistinct in the dawn. "Hush, sir!" he repeated, and Barnabas saw that he was creeping forward on tip-toe, and, though scarce knowing why, he himself did the same.

They found the great swing doors fast, bolted from within, and, in this still dead hour, save for their own soft breathing, not a sound reached them. Then Barnabas laughed suddenly, and clapped Master Milo upon his small, rigid shoulder.

"There, Imp,—you see it's all right!" said he, and then paused, and held his breath.

"Did ye hear anythink?" whispered the boy.

"A chain—rattled, I think."

"And 't was in The Terror's' stall,—there? didn't ye hear somethink else, sir?"

"No!"

"I did,—it sounded like—" the boy's voice tailed off suddenly and, upon the silence, a low whistle sounded; then a thud, as of some one dropping from a height, quickly followed by another,—and thus two figures darted away, impalpable as ghosts in the dawn, but the alley was filled with the rush and patter of their flight. Instantly Barnabas turned in pursuit, then stopped and stood utterly still, his head turned, his eyes wide, glaring back towards the gloom of the stables. For, in that moment, above the sudden harsh jangling of chains from within, above the pattering footsteps of the fugitives without, was an appalling sound rising high and ever higher—shrill, unearthly, and full of horror and torment unspeakable. And now, sudden as it had come, it was gone, but in its place was another sound,—a sound dull and muffled, but continuous, and pierced, all at once, by the loud, hideous whinnying of a horse. Then Barnabas sprang back to the doors, beating upon them with his fists and calling wildly for some one to open.

And, in a while, a key grated, a bolt shrieked; the doors swung back, revealing Martin, half-dressed and with a lantern in his hand, while three or four undergrooms hovered, pale-faced, in the shadows behind.

"My horse!" said Barnabas, and snatched the lantern.

"'The Terror'!" cried Milo, "this way, sir!"

Coming to a certain shadowy corner, Barnabas unfastened and threw open the half-door; and there, rising from the gloom of the stall, was a fiendish, black head with ears laid back, eyes rolling, and teeth laid bare,—cruel teeth, whose gleaming white was hatefully splotched,—strong teeth, in whose vicious grip something yet dangled.

"Why—what's he got there!" cried Martin suddenly, and then— "Oh, my God! sir,—look yonder!" and, covering his eyes, he pointed towards a corner of the stall where the light of the lantern fell. And—twisted and contorted,—something lay there; something hideously battered, and torn, and trampled; something that now lay so very quiet and still, but which had left dark splashes and stains on walls and flooring; something that yet clutched the knife which was to have hamstrung and ended the career of Four-legs once and for all; something that had once been a man.

CHAPTER XLIX

WHICH, BEING SOMEWHAT IMPORTANT, IS CONSEQUENTLY SHORT

"My dear fellow," said the Viscount, stifling a yawn beneath the bedclothes, "you rise with the lark,—or should it be linnet? Anyhow, you do, you know. So deuced early!"

"I am here early because I haven't been to bed, Dick."

"Ah, night mail? Dev'lish uncomfortable! Didn't think you'd come back in such a deuce of a hurry, though!"

"But you wanted to see me, Dick, what is it?"

"Why,—egad, Bev, I'm afraid it's nothing much, after all. It's that fellow Smivvle's fault, really."

"Smivvle?"

"Fellow actually called here yesterday—twice, Bev. Dev'lish importunate fellow y'know. Wanted to see you,—deuced insistent about it, too!"

"Why?"

"Well, from what I could make out, he seemed to think—sounds ridiculous so early in the morning,—but he seemed to fancy you were in some kind of—danger, Bev."

"How, Dick?"

"Well, when I told him he couldn't see you because you had driven over to Hawkhurst, the fellow positively couldn't sit still—deuced nervous, y'know,—though probably owing to drink. 'Hawkhurst!' says he, staring at me as if I were a ghost, my dear fellow, 'yes,' says I, 'and the door's open, sir!' 'I see it is,' says he, sitting tight. 'But you must get him back!' 'Can't be done!' says I. 'Are you his friend?' says he. 'I hope so,' says I. 'Then,' says he, before I could remind him of the door again, 'then you must get him back— at once!' I asked him why, but he only stared and shook his head, and so took himself off. I'll own the fellow shook me rather, Bev, —he seemed so very much in earnest, but, knowing where you were, I wouldn't have disturbed you for the world if it hadn't been for the horses."

"Ah, yes—the horses!" said Barnabas thoughtfully. "How is your arm now, Dick?"

"A bit stiff, but otherwise right as a trivet, Bev. But now—about yourself, my dear fellow,—what on earth possessed you to lay Carnaby such a bet? What a perfectly reckless fellow you are! Of course the money is as good as in Carnaby's pocket already, not to mention Chichester's—damn him! As I told you in my letter, the affair has gone the round of the clubs,—every one is laughing at the 'Galloping Countryman,' as they call you. Jerningham came within an ace of fighting Tufton Green of the Guards about it, but the Marquis is deuced knowing with the barkers, and Tufton, very wisely, thought better of it. Still, I'm afraid the name will stick—!"

"And why not, Dick? I am a countryman, indeed quite a yokel in many ways, and I shall certainly gallop—when it comes to it."

"Which brings us back to the horses, Bev. I 've been thinking we ought to get 'em away—into the country—some quiet place like—say, the—the 'Spotted Cow,' Bev."

"Yes, the 'Spotted Cow' should do very well; especially as Clemency—"

"Talking about the horses, Bev," said the Viscount, sitting up in bed and speaking rather hurriedly, "I protest, since the rascally attempt on 'Moonraker' last night, I've been on pins and needles, positively,—nerve quite gone, y'know, Bev. If 'Moonraker' didn't happen to be a horse, he'd be a mare,—of course he would,—but I mean a nightmare. I've thought of him all day and dreamed of him all night, oh, most cursed, y'know! Just ring for my fellow, will you, Bev?—I'll get up, and we'll go round to the stables together."

"Quite unnecessary, Dick."

"Eh? Why?"

"Because I have just left there."

"Are the horses all right, Bev?"

"Yes, Dick."

"Ah!" sighed the Viscount, falling back among his pillows, "and everything is quite quiet, eh?"

"Very quiet,—now, Dick."

"Eh?" cried the Viscount, coming erect again, "Bev, what d' you mean?"

"I mean that three men broke in again to-night—"

"Oh, Lord!" exclaimed the Viscount, beginning to scramble out of bed.

"But we drove them off before they had done—what they came for."

"Did you, Bev,—did you? ah,—but didn't you catch any of 'em?"

"No; but my horse did."

"Your horse? Oh, Beverley,—d'you mean he—"

"Killed him, Dick!"

Once more the Viscount sank back among his pillows and stared up at the ceiling a while ere he spoke again—

"By the Lord, Bev," said he, at last, "the stable-boys might well call him 'The Terror'!"

"Yes," said Barnabas, "he has earned his name, Dick."

"And the man was—dead, you say?"

"Hideously dead, Dick,—and in his pocket we found this!" and Barnabas produced a dirty and crumpled piece of paper, and put it into the Viscount's reluctant hand. "Look at it, Dick, and tell me what it is."

"Why, Bev,—deuce take me, it's a plan of our stables! And they've got it right, too! Here's 'Moonraker's' stall marked out as pat as you please, and 'The Terror's,' but they've got his name wrong—"

"My horse had no name, Dick."

"But there's something written here."

"Yes, look at it carefully, Dick."

"Well, here's an H, and an E, and—looks like 'Hera,' Bev!"

"Yes, but it isn't. Look at that last letter again, Dick!"

"Why, I believe—by God, Bev,—it's an E!"

"Yes,—an E, Dick."

"'Here'!" said the Viscount, staring at the paper; "why, then—why, Bev,—it was—your horse they were after!"

"My horse,—yes, Dick."

"But he's a rank outsider—he isn't even in the betting! In heaven's name, why should any one—"

"Look on the other side of the paper, Dick."

Obediently, the Viscount turned the crumpled paper over, and thereafter sat staring wide-eyed at a name scrawled thereon, and from it to Barnabas and back again; for the name he saw was this:

RONALD BARRYMAINE ESQUIRE.

"And Dick," said Barnabas, "it is in Chichester's handwriting."

CHAPTER L

IN WHICH RONALD BARRYMAINE SPEAKS HIS MIND

The whiskers of Mr. Digby Smivvle were in a chastened mood, indeed their habitual ferocity was mitigated to such a degree that they might almost be said to wilt, or droop. Mr. Digby Smivvle drooped likewise; in a word, Mr. Smivvle was despondent.

He sat in one of the rickety chairs, his legs stretched out to the cheerless hearth, and stared moodily at the ashes of a long dead fire. At the opening of the door he started and half rose, but seeing Barnabas, sank back again.

"Beverley," he cried, "thank heaven you're safe back again—that is to say—" he went on, striving to speak in his ordinary manner, "that is to say,—I mean—ah—in short, my dear Beverley, I'm delighted to see you!"

"Pray what do you mean by safe?"

"What do I mean?" repeated Mr. Smivvle, beginning to fumble for his whisker with strangely clumsy fingers, "why, I mean—safe, sir,—a very natural wish, surely?"

"Yes," said Barnabas, "and you wished to see me, I think?"

"To see you?" echoed Mr. Smivvle, still feeling for his whisker,—"why, yes, of course—"

"At least, the Viscount told me so."

"Ah? Deuced obliging of the Viscount,—very!"

"Are you alone?" Barnabas inquired, struck by Mr. Smivvle's hesitating manner, and he glanced toward the door of what was evidently a bedroom.

"Alone, sir," said Mr. Smivvle, "is the precise and only word for it. You have hit the nail exactly—upon the nob, sir." Here, having found his whisker, Mr. Smivvle gave it a fierce wrench, loosed it, and clenching his fist, smote himself two blows in the region of the heart. "Sir," said he, "you behold in me a deserted and therefore doleful ruminant chewing reflection's solitary cud. And, sir,—it is a bitter cud, cursedly so,—wherein the milk of human kindness is curdled, sir, curdled most damnably, my dear Beverley! In a word, my friend Barry—wholly forgetful of those sacred bonds which the hammer of Adversity alone can weld,—scorning Friendship's holy obligations, has turned his back upon Smivvle,—upon Digby,—upon faithful Dig, and—in short has—ah—hopped the mutual perch, sir."

"Do you mean he has left you?"

"Yes, sir. We had words this morning—a good many and, the end of it was—he departed—for good, and all on your account!"

"My account?"

"And with a month's rent due, not to mention the Spanswick's wages, and she has a tongue! 'Oh, Death, where is thy sting?'"

"But how on my account?"

"Sir, in a word, he resented my friendship for you. Sir, Barrymaine is cursed proud, but so am I—as Lucifer! Sir, when the blood of a Smivvle is once curdled, it's curdled most damnably, and the heart of a Smivvle,—as all the world knows,—becomes a—an accursed flint, sir." Here Mr. Smivvle shook his head and sighed again. "Though I can't help wondering what the poor fellow will do without me at hand to—ah—pop round the corner for him. By the way, do you happen to remember if you fastened the front door securely?"

"No."

"I ask because the latch is faulty,—like most things about here,—and in this delightful Garden of Hatton and the—ah—hot-beds adjoining there are weeds, sir, of the rambling species which, given opportunity—will ramble anywhere. Several of 'em—choice exotics, too! have found their way up here lately,—one of 'em got in here this very morning after Barrymaine had gone,—characteristic specimen in a fur cap. But, as I was saying, you may have noticed that Chichester is not altogether—friendly towards you?"

"Chichester?" said Barnabas. "Yes!"

"And it would almost seem that he's determined that Barrymaine shall—be the same. Poor fellow's been very strange lately,—Gaunt's been pressing him again worse than ever,—even threatened him with the Marshalsea. Consequently, the flowing bowl has continually brimmed—Chichester's doing, of course,—and he seems to consider you his mortal enemy, and—in short, I think it only right to—put you on your guard."

"You mean against—Chichester?"

"I mean against—Barrymaine!"

"Ah!" said Barnabas, chin in hand, "but why?"

"Well, you'll remember that the only time you met him he was inclined to be—just a l-ee-tle—violent, perhaps?"

"When he attacked me with the bottle,—yes!" sighed Barnabas, "but surely that was only because he was drunk?"

"Y-e-s, perhaps so," said Mr. Smivvle, fumbling for his whisker again, "but this morning he—wasn't so drunk as usual."

"Well?"

"And yet he was more violent than ever—raved against you like a maniac."

"But—why?"

"It was just after he had received another of Jasper Gaunt's letters,—here it is!" and, stooping, Mr. Smivvle picked up a crumpled paper that had lain among the ashes, and smoothing it out, tendered it to Barnabas. "Read it, sir,—read it!" he said earnestly, "it will explain matters, I think,—and much better than I can. Yes indeed, read it, for it concerns you too!" So Barnabas took the letter, and this is what he read:

DEAR MR. BARRYMAINE,—In reply to your favor, *re* interest, requesting more time, I take occasion once more to remind you that I am no longer your creditor, being merely his agent, as Mr. Beverley himself could, and will, doubtless, inform you.

I am, therefore, compelled to demand payment within thirty days from date; otherwise the usual steps must be taken in lieu of same.

Yours obediently,
JASPER GAUNT.

Now when Barnabas had read the letter a sudden fit of rage possessed him, and, crumpling the paper in his fist, he dashed it down and set his foot upon it.

"A lie!" he cried, "a foul, cowardly lie!"

"Then you—you didn't buy up the debt, Beverley?"

"No! no!—I couldn't,—Gaunt had sold already, and by heaven I believe the real creditor is—"

"Ha!" cried Smivvle, pointing suddenly, "the door wasn't fastened, Beverley,—look there!"

Barnabas started, and glancing round, saw that the door was opening very slowly, and inch by inch; then, as they watched its stealthy movement, all at once a shaggy head slid into view, a round head, with a face remarkably hirsute as to eyebrow and whisker, and surmounted by a dingy fur cap.

"'Scuse me, gents!" said the head, speaking hoarsely, and rolling its eyes at them, "name o' Barrymaine,—vich on ye might that be, now?"

"Ha?" cried Mr. Smivvle angrily, "so you're here again, are you!"

"'Scuse me, gents!" said the head, blinking its round eyes at them, "name o' Barrymaine,—no offence,—vich?"

"Come," said Mr. Smivvle, beginning to tug at his whiskers,— "come, get out,—d'ye hear!"

"But, axing your pardons, gents,—vich on ye might be—name o' Barrymaine?"

"What do you want with him—eh?" demanded Mr. Smivvle, his whiskers growing momentarily more ferocious, "speak out, man!"

"Got a letter for 'im—leastways it's wrote to 'im," answered the head, "'ere's a B, and a Nay, and a Nar, and another on 'em, and a Vy,—that spells Barry, don't it? Then, arter that, comes a M., and a—"

"Oh, all right,—give it me!" said Mr. Smivvle, rising.

"Are you name o' Barrymaine?"

"No, but you can leave it with me, and I—"

"Leave it?" repeated the head, in a slightly injured tone, "leave it? axing your pardons, gents,—but burn my neck if I do! If you ain't name o' Barrymaine v'y then—p'r'aps this is 'im a-coming upstairs now,—and werry 'asty about it, too!" And, sure enough, hurried feet were heard ascending; whereupon Mr. Smivvle uttered a startled exclamation, and, motioning Barnabas to be seated in the dingiest corner, strode quickly to the door, and thus came face to face with Ronald Barrymaine upon the threshold.

"Why, Barry!" said he, standing so as to block Barrymaine's view of the dingy corner, "so you've come back, then?"

"Come back, yes!" returned the other petulantly, "I had to,—mislaid a letter, must have left it here, somewhere. Did you find it?"

"Axing your pardon, sir, but might you be name o' Barrymaine, no offence, but might you?"

The shaggy head had slid quite into the room now, bringing after it a short, thick-set person clad after the fashion of a bargeman.

"Yes; what do you want?"

"Might this 'ere be the letter as you come back for,—no offence, but might it?"

"Yes! yes," cried Barrymaine, and, snatching it, he tore it fiercely across and across, and made a gesture as if to fling the fragments into the hearth, then thrust them into his pocket instead. "Here's a shilling for you," said he, turning to the bargeman, "that is—Dig, l-lend me a shilling, I—" Ronald Barrymaine's voice ended abruptly, for he had caught sight of Barnabas sitting in the dingy corner, and now, pushing past Smivvle, he stood staring, his handsome features distorted with sudden fury, his teeth gleaming between his parted lips.

"So it's—you, is it?" he demanded.

"Yes," said Barnabas, and stood up.

"So—you're—back again, are you?"

"Thank you, yes," said Barnabas, "and quite safe!"

"S-safe?"

"As yet," answered Barnabas.

"You aren't d-drunk, are you?"

"No," said Barnabas, "nor are you, for once."

Barrymaine clenched his fists and took a step towards Barnabas, but spying the bargeman, who now lurched forward, turned upon him in a fury.

"What the d-devil d' you want? Get out of the way, d' ye hear?—get out, I say!"

"Axing your pardon, sir, an' meaning no offence, but summat was said about a bob, sir—vun shilling!"

"Damnation! Give the fellow his s-shilling, Dig, and then k-kick him out."

Hereupon Mr. Smivvle, having felt through his pockets, slowly produced the coin demanded, and handing it to the bargeman, pointed to the door.

"No,—see him downstairs—into the street, Dig. And you needn't hurry back, I'm going to speak my mind to this f-fellow—once and for all! So l-lock the street door, Dig."

Mr. Smivvle hesitated, glanced at Barnabas, shrugged his shoulders and followed the bargeman out of the room. As the door closed, Barrymaine sprang to it, and, turning the key, faced Barnabas with arms folded, head lowered, and a smile upon his lips:

"Now," said he, "you are going to listen to me—d'you hear? We are going to understand each other before you leave this room! D'you see?"

"Yes," said Barnabas.

"Oh!" he cried bitterly, "I know the sort of c-crawling thing you are, Gaunt has warned me—"

"Gaunt is a liar!" said Barnabas.

"I say,—he's told me,—are you listening? Y-you think, because you've bought my debts, you've bought me, too, body and soul, and—through me—Cleone! Ah, but you haven't,—before that happens y-you'll be dead and rotting—and I, and she as well. Are you listening?—she as well! You think you've g-got me—there beneath your foot—b-but you haven't, no, by God, you haven't—"

"I tell you Gaunt is a liar!" repeated Barnabas. "I couldn't buy your debts because he had sold them already. Come with me, and I'll prove it,—come and let me face him with the truth—"

"The truth? You? Oh, I might have guessed you'd come creeping round here to see S-Smivvle behind my back—as you do my sister—"

"Sir!" said Barnabas, flushing.

"What—do you dare deny it? Do you d-dare deny that you have met her—by stealth,—do you? do you? Oh, I know of your secret meetings with her. I know how you have imposed upon the credulity of a weak-minded old woman and a one-armed d-dotard sufficiently to get yourself invited to Hawkhurst. But I tell you this shall stop,—it shall! Yes, by God,—you shall give me your promise to c-cease your persecution of my sister before you leave this room, or—"

"Or?" said Barnabas.

"Or it will be the w-worse for you!"

"How?"

"I—I'll k-kill you!"

"Murder me?"

"It's no m-murder to kill your sort!"

"Then it *is* a pistol you have in your pocket, there?"

"Yes—l-look at it!" And, speaking, Barrymaine drew and levelled the weapon with practised hand. "Now listen!" said he. "You will s-sit down at that table there, and write Gaunt to g-give me all the time I need for your c-cursed interest—"

"But I tell you—"

"Liar!" cried Barrymaine, advancing a threatening step. "Liar,—I know! Then, after you've done that,—you will swear never to see or c-communicate with my sister again, or I'll shoot you dead where you stand,—s-so help me God!"

"You are mad," said Barnabas, "I am not your creditor, and—"

"Liar! I know!" repeated Barrymaine.

"And yet," said Barnabas, fronting him, white-faced, across the table, "I think—I'm sure, there are four things you don't know. The first is that Lady Cleone has promised to marry me—some day—"

"Go on to the next, liar!"

"The second is that my stables were broken into again, this morning,—the third is that my horse killed the man who was trying to hamstring him,—and the fourth is that in the dead man's pocket I found—this!" And Barnabas produced that crumpled piece of paper whereon was drawn the plan of the stables.

Now, at the sight of this paper, Barrymaine fell back a step, his pistol-hand wavered, fell to his side, and sinking into a chair, he seemed to shrink into himself as he stared dully at a worn patch in the carpet.

"Only one beside myself knows of this," said Barnabas.

"Well?" The word seemed wrung from Barrymaine's quivering lips. He lay back in the rickety chair, his arms dangling, his chin upon his breast, never lifting his haggard eyes, and, almost as he spoke, the pistol slipped from his lax fingers and lay all unheeded.

"Not another soul shall ever know," said Barnabas earnestly, "the world shall be none the wiser if you will promise to stop,—now, —to free yourself from Chichester's influence, now,—to let me help you to redeem the past. Promise me this, and I, as your friend, will tear up this damning evidence—here and now."

"And—if I—c-can't?"

Barnabas sighed, and folding up the crumpled paper, thrust it back into his pocket.

"You shall have—a week, to make up your mind. You know my address, I think,—at least, Mr. Smivvle does." So saying, Barnabas stepped towards the door, but, seeing the look on Barrymaine's face, he stooped very suddenly, and picked up the pistol. Then he unlocked the door and went out, closing it behind him. Upon the dark stairs he encountered Mr. Smivvle, who had been sitting there making nervous havoc of his whiskers.

"Gad, Beverley!" he exclaimed, "I ought not to have left you alone with him,—deuce of a state about it, 'pon my honor. But what could I do,—as I sat here listening to you both I was afraid."

"So was I," said Barnabas. "But he will be quiet now, I think. Here is one of his pistols, you'd better hide it. And—forget your differences with him, for if ever a man needed a friend, he does. As for your rent, don't worry about that, I'll send it round to you this evening. Good-by."

So Barnabas went on down the dark stairs, and being come to the door with the faulty latch, let himself out into the dingy street, and thus came face to face with the man in the fur cap.

"Lord, Mr. Barty, sir," said that worthy, glancing up and down the street with a pair of mild, round eyes, "you can burn my neck if I wasn't beginning to vorry about you, up theer all alone vith that 'ere child o' mine. For, sir, of all the Capital coves as ever I see, —'e's vun o' the werry capital-est."

CHAPTER LI

WHICH TELLS HOW AND WHY MR. SHRIG'S CASE WAS SPOILED

"Why," exclaimed Barnabas, starting, "is that you, Mr. Shrig?"

"As ever vas, sir. I ain't partial to disguises as a rule, but circumstances obleeges me to it now and then," sighed Mr. Shrig as they turned into Hatton Garden. "Ye see, I've been keeping a eye—or as you might say, a fatherly ogle on vun o' my fambly, vich is the v'y and the v'erefore o' these 'ere v'iskers. Yesterday, I vas a market gerdener, vith a basket o' fine wegetables as nobody 'ad ordered,—the day afore, a sailor-man out o' furrin parts, as vos a-seeking and a-searchin' for a gray-'eaded feyther as didn't exist,—to-day I'm a riverside cove as 'ad found a letter—a letter as I'd stole—"

"Stolen!" repeated Barnabas.

"Vell, let's say borreyed, sir,—borreyed for purposes o' obserwation, —out o' young Barrymaine's pocket, and werry neatly I done it too!" Here Mr. Shrig chuckled softly, checked himself suddenly, and shook his placid head. "But life ain't all lavender, sir,—not by no manner o' means, it ain't," said he dolefully. "Things is werry slack vith me,—nothing in the murder line this veek, and only vun sooicide, a couple o' 'ighvay robberies, and a 'sault and battery! You can scrag me if I know v'ot things is coming to. And then, to make it vorse, I 've jest 'ad a loss as vell."

"I'm sorry for that, Mr. Shrig, but—"

"A loss, sir, as I shan't get over in a 'urry. You'll remember V'istlin' Dick, p'r'aps,—the leary, flash cove as you give such a leveller to, the first time as ever I clapped my day-lights on ye?"

"Yes, I remember him."

"Veil sir,' e's been and took, and gone, and got 'isself kicked to death by an 'orse!"

"Eh,—a horse?" exclaimed Barnabas, starting.

"An 'orse, sir, yes. Vich I means to say is coming it a bit low down on *me*, sir,—sich conduct ain't 'ardly fair, for V'istlin' Dick vos a werry promising cove as Capitals go. And now to see 'im cut off afore 'is time, and in such a outrageous, onnat'ral manner, touches me up, Mr. Barty, sir,—touches me up werry sharp it do! For arter all, a nice, strong gibbet vith a good long drop is qvicker, neater, and much more pleasant than an 'orse's 'oof,—now ain't it? Still," said Mr. Shrig, sighing and shaking his head again, "things is allus blackest afore the dawn, sir, and—'twixt you and me,—I'm 'oping to bring off a nice little murder case afore long—"

"Hoping?"

"Veil—let's say—expecting, sir. Quite a bang up affair it'll be too,—nobs, all on 'em, and there's three on 'em concerned. I'll call the murderer Number Vun, Number Two is the accessory afore the fact, and Number Three is the unfort'nate wictim. Now sir, from private obserwation, the deed is doo to be brought off any time in the next three veeks, and as soon as it's done, v'y then I lays my right 'and on Number Vun, and my left 'and on Number Two, and—"

"But—what about Number Three?" inquired Barnabas.

Mr. Shrig paused, glanced at Barnabas, and scratched his ear, thoughtfully.

"V'y sir," said he at last, "Number Three vill be a corp."

"A what?" said Barnabas.

"A corp, sir—a stiff—"

"Do you mean—dead?"

"Ah,—I mean werry much so!" nodded Mr. Shrig.

"Number Three vill be stone cold,—somev'eres in the country it'll 'appen, I fancy,—say in a vood! And the leaves'll keep a-fluttering over 'im, and the birds'll keep a-singing to 'im,—oh, Number Three'll be comfortable enough,—'e von't 'ave to vorry about nothink no more, it'll be Number Vun and Number Two as'll do the vorrying, and me—till I gets my 'ooks on 'em, and then—"

"But," said Barnabas earnestly, "why not try to prevent it?"

"Prewent it, sir?" said Mr. Shrig, in a tone of pained surprise. "Prewent it? Lord, Mr. Barty, sir—then vere vould my murder case be? Besides, I ain't so onprofessional as to step in afore my time. Prewent it? No, sir. My dooty is to apprehend a man *arter* the crime, not afore it."

"But surely you don't mean to allow this unfortunate person to be done to death?"

"Sir," said Mr. Shrig, beginning to finger his ear again, "unfort'nate wictims is born to be—vell, let's say—unfort'nate. You can't 'elp 'em being born wictims. I can't 'elp it,—nobody can't, for natur' vill 'ave 'er own vay, sir, and I ain't vun to go agin natur' nor yet to spile a good case,—good cases is few enough. Oh, life ain't all lavender, as I said afore,—burn my neck if it is!" And here Mr. Shrig shook his head again, sighed again, and walked on in a somewhat gloomy silence.

Now, all at once, as they turned into the rush and roar of Holborn, Barnabas espied a face amid the hurrying throng; a face whose proud, dark beauty there was no mistaking despite its added look of sorrow; and a figure whose ripe loveliness the threadbare cloak could not disguise. For a moment her eyes looked up into his, dark and suddenly wide,—then, quick and light of foot, she was gone, lost in the bustling crowd.

But, even so, Barnabas turned and followed, striding on and on until at length he saw again the flutter of the threadbare cloak. And, because of its shabbiness, he frowned and hastened his steps, and because of the look he had read in her eyes, he paused again, yet followed doggedly nevertheless. She led him down Holborn Hill past the Fleet Market, over Blackfriars Bridge, and so, turning sharp to the right, along a somewhat narrow and very grimy street between rows of dirty, tumble-down houses, with, upon the right hand, numerous narrow courts and alley-ways that gave upon the turgid river. Down one of these alleys the fluttering cloak turned suddenly, yet when Barnabas reached the corner, behold the alley was quite deserted, save for a small and pallid urchin who sat upon a rotting stump, staring at the river, with a pallid infant in his arms.

"Which way did the lady go?" inquired Barnabas.

"Lady?" said the urchin, staring.

"Yes. She wore a cloak,—a gray cloak. Where did she go?" and Barnabas held up a shilling. Instantly the urchin rose and, swinging the pallid infant to his ragged hip, pattered over the cobbles with his bare feet, and with one small, dirty claw extended.

"A bob!" he cried in a shrill, cracked voice, "gimme it, sir! Yus, —yus,—I'll tell ye. She's wiv Nick—lives dere, she do. Now gimme th' bob,—she's in dere!" And he pointed to a narrow door at the further end of the alley. So Barnabas gave the shilling into the eager clutching fingers, and approaching the door, knocked upon the rotting timbers with the head of his cane.

"Come in!" roared a mighty voice. Hereupon Barnabas pushed open the crazy door, and descending three steps, found himself in a small, dark room, full of the smell of leather. And here, its solitary inmate, was a very small man crouched above a last, with a hammer in his hand and an open book before him. His head was bald save for a few white hairs that stood up, fiercely erect, and upon his short, pugnacious nose he wore a pair of huge, horn-rimmed spectacles.

"What's for you, sir?" he demanded in the same great, fierce voice, viewing Barnabas over his spectacles with sharp, bright eyes. "If it's a pair o' Hessians you'll be wanting—"

"It isn't," said Barnabas, "I—"

"Or a fine pair o' dancing shoes—?"

"No, thank you, I want to—"

"Or a smart pair o' bang up riding-jacks—?"

"No," said Barnabas again, "I came here to see—"

"You can't 'ave 'em! And because why?" demanded the little man, his fierce eyes growing fiercer as he stared at Barnabas from modish hat to flowered waistcoat, "because I don't make for the Quality. Quality—bah! If I 'ad my way, I'd gillertine 'em all,—ah, that I would! Like the Frenchies did when they revolutioned. I'd cut off their 'eads! By the dozen! With j'y!"

"You are Nick, the Cobbler, I think?"

"And what if I am? I'd chop off their 'eads, I tell ye,—with j'y and gusto!"

"And pray where is Clemency?"

"Eh?" exclaimed the little cobbler, pushing up his horn spectacles, "'oo did ye say?"

"Where is the lady who came in here a moment ago?"

"Lady?" said the cobbler, shaking his round, bald head, "Lord, sir, your heyes 'as been a-deceiving of you!"

"I am—her friend!"

"Friend!" exclaimed the cobbler, "to which I says—Hookey Walker, sir! 'Andsome gells don't want friends o' your kind. Besides, she ain't here—you can see that for yourself. Your heyes 'as been a-deceiving of you,—try next door."

"But I must see her," said Barnabas, "I wish to help her,—I have good news for her—"

"Noos?" said the cobbler, "Oh? Ah! Well go and tell your noos to someone else as ain't so 'andsome,—Mrs. Snummitt, say, as lives next door,—a widder,—respectable, but with only one heye,—try Mrs. Snummitt."

"Ah,—perhaps she's in the room yonder," said Barnabas, "anyhow, I mean to see—"

"No ye don't!" cried the little cobbler, seizing a crutch that leant near him, and springing up with astonishing agility, "no ye don't, my fine gentleman,—she ain't for you,—not while I'm 'ere to protect her!" and snatching up a long awl, he flourished it above his head. "I'm a cobbler, oh yes,—but then I'm a valiant cobbler, as valiant as Sir Bedevere, or Sir Lancelot, or any of 'em,—every bit,—come and try me!" and he made a pass in the air with the awl as though it had been a two-edged sword. But, at this moment, the door of the inner room was pushed open and Clemency appeared. She had laid aside her threadbare cloak, and Barnabas was struck afresh by her proud, dark loveliness.

"You good, brave Nick!" said she, laying her hand upon the little cripple's bent shoulder, "but we can trust this gentleman, I know."

"Trust him!" repeated the cobbler, peering at Barnahas, more particularly at his feet, "why, your boots *is* trustworthy—now I come to look at 'em, sir,"

"Boots?" said Barnabas.

"Ah," nodded the cobbler, "a man wears his character into 'is boots a sight quicker than 'e does into 'is face,—and I can read boots and shoes easier than I can print,—and that's saying summat, for I'm a great reader, I am. Why didn't ye show me your boots at first and have done with it?" saying which the cobbler snorted and sat down; then, having apparently swallowed a handful of nails, he began to hammer away lustily, while Barnabas followed Clemency into the inner room, and, being there, they stood for a long moment looking on each other in silence.

And now Barnabas saw that, with her apron and mobcap, the country serving-maid had vanished quite. In her stead was a noble woman, proud and stately, whose clear, sad eyes returned his gaze with a gentle dignity; Clemency indeed was gone, but Beatrix had come to life. Yet, when he spoke, Barnabas used the name he had known her by first.

"Clemency," said he, "your father is seeking for you."

"My—father!" she exclaimed, speaking in a whisper. "You have seen—my father? You know him?"

"Yes. I met him—not long ago. His name is Ralph Darville, he told me, and he goes up and down the countryside searching for you—has done so, ever since he lost you, and he preaches always Forgiveness and Forgetfulness of Self!"

"My father!" she whispered again with quivering lips. "Preaching?"

"He tramps the roads hoping to find you, Clemency, and he preaches at country wakes and fairs because, he told me, he was once a very selfish man, and unforgiving."

"And—oh, you have seen him, you say,—lately?" she cried.

"Yes. And I sent him to Frittenden—to the 'Spotted Cow.' But Clemency, he was just a day too late."

Now when Barnabas said this, Clemency uttered a broken cry, and covered her face.

"Oh, father!" she whispered, "if I had only known,—if I could but have guessed! Oh, father! father!"

"Clemency, why did you run away?"

"Because I—I was afraid!"

"Of Chichcster?"

"No!" she cried in sudden scorn, "him I only—hate!"

"Then—whom did you fear?"

Clemency was silent, but, all at once, Barnabas saw a burning flush that crept up, over rounded throat and drooping face, until it was lost in the dark shadow of her hair.

"Was it—the Viscount?" Barnabas demanded suddenly.

"No—no, I—I think it was—myself. Oh, I—I am very wretched and—lonely!" she sobbed, "I want—my father!"

"And he shall be found," said Barnabas, "I promise you! But, until then, will you trust me, Clemency, as—as a sister might trust her brother? Will you let me take you from this dreary place,—will you, Clemency? I—I'll buy you a house—I mean a—a cottage—in the country—or anywhere you wish."

"Oh, Mr. Beverley!" she sighed, looking up at him with tear-dimmed eyes, but with the ghost of a smile hovering round her scarlet lips, "I thank you,—indeed, indeed I do, but how can I? How may I?"

"Quite easily," said Barnabas stoutly, "oh quite—until I bring your father to you."

"Dear, dear father!" she sighed. "Is he much changed, I wonder? Is he well,—quite well?"

"Yes, he is very well," answered Barnabas, "but you—indeed you cannot stay here—"

"I must," she answered. "I can earn enough for my needs with my needle, and poor little Nick is very kind—so gentle and considerate in spite of his great, rough voice and fierce ways. I think he is the gentlest little man in all the world. He actually refused to take my money at first, until I threatened to go somewhere else."

"But how did you find your way to—such a place as this?"

"Milo brought me here."

"The Viscount's little imp of a groom?"

"Yes, though he promised never to tell—*him* where I was, and Milo always keeps his word. And you, Mr. Beverley, you will promise also, won't you?"

"You mean—never to tell the Viscount of your whereabouts?"

Clemency nodded.

"Yes," said Barnabas, "I will promise, but—on condition that you henceforth will regard me as a brother. That you will allow me the privilege of helping you whenever I may, and will always turn to me in your need. Will you promise me this, Clemency?" And Barnabas held out his hand.

"Yes," she answered, smiling up into his earnest eyes, "I think I shall be—proud to—have you for a brother." And she put her hand into his.

"Ah! so you're a-going, are ye?" demanded the cobbler, disgorging the last of the nails as Barnabas stepped into the dark little shop.

"Yes," said Barnabas, "and, if you think my boots sufficiently trustworthy, I should like to shake your hand."

"Eh?" exclaimed the cobbler, "shake 'ands with old Nick, sir? But you're one o' the Quality, and I 'ates the Quality—chop off their 'eads if I 'ad my way, I would! and my 'and's very dirty—jest let me wipe it a bit,—there sir, if you wish to! and 'ere's 'oping to see you again. Though, mark you, the Frenchies was quite right,—there's nothing like the gillertine, I say. Good arternoon, sir."

Then Barnabas went out into the narrow, grimy alley, and closed the crazy door behind him. But he had not gone a dozen yards when he heard Clemency calling his name, and hastened back.

"Mr. Beverley," said she, "I want to ask you—something else—about my father—"

"Yes," said Barnabas, as she hesitated.

"Does he think I am—does he know that—though I ran away with—a beast, I—ran away—from him, also,—does he know—?"

"He knows you for the sweet, pure woman you are," said Barnabas as she fell silent again, "he knows the truth, and lives but to find you again—my sister!" Now, when he said this, Barnabas saw within her tearful eyes the light of a joy unutterable; so he bared his head and, turning about, strode quickly away up the alley.

Being come into the narrow, dingy street, he suddenly espied Mr. Shrig who leaned against a convenient post and stared with round eyes at the tumble-down houses opposite, while upon his usually placid brow he wore a frown of deep perplexity.

"So you followed me?" exclaimed Barnabas.

"V'y, sir, since you mention it,—I did take that 'ere liberty. This is a werry on-savory neighborhood at most times, an' the air's werry bad for—fob-seals, say,—and cravat-sparklers at all times. Sich things 'as a 'abit o' wanishing theirselves avay." Having said which, Mr. Shrig walked on beside Barnabas as one who profoundly meditates, for his brow was yet furrowed deep with thought.

"Why so silent, Mr. Shrig?" inquired Barnabas as they crossed Blackfriars Bridge.

"Because I'm vorking out a problem, sir. For some time I've been trying to add two and two together, and now I'm droring my conclusions. So you know Old Nick the cobbler, do you, sir?"

"I didn't—an hour ago."

"Sir, when you vos in his shop, I took the liberty o' peeping in at the winder."

"Indeed?"

"And I seen that theer 'andsome gal."

"Oh, did you?"

"I likewise 'eered her call your name—Beverley, I think?"

"Yes,—well?"

"Beverley!" repeated Mr. Shrig.

"Yes."

"But your name's—Barty!"

"True, but in London I'm known as Beverley, Mr. Shrig."

"Not—not—*the* Beverley? Not the bang up Corinthian? Not the Beverley as is to ride in the steeplechase?"

"Yes," said Barnabas, "the very same,—why?"

"Now—dang me for a ass!" exclaimed Mr. Shrig, and, snatching off the fur cap, he dashed it to the ground, stooped, picked it up, and crammed it back upon his head,—all in a moment.

"Why—what's the matter?"

"Matter!" said Mr. Shrig, "matter, sir? Veil, vot vith your qviet, innocent looks and vays, and vot vith me a-adding two and two together and werry carefully making 'em—three, my case is spiled—won't come off,—can't come off,—mustn't come off!"

"What in the world do you mean?"

"Mean, sir? I mean as, if Number Vun is the murderer, and Number Two is the accessory afore the fact,—then Number Three—the unfort'nate wictim is—vait a bit!" Here, pausing in a quiet corner of Fleet Market, Mr. Shrig dived into his breast and fetched up his little book. "Sir," said he, turning over its pages with a questing finger, "v'en I borreyed that theer letter out o' young B.'s pocket, I made so free as to take a copy of it into my little reader,—'ere it is, —jest take a peep at it."

Then, looking where he pointed, Barnabas read these words, very neatly set down:

MY DEAR BARRYMAINE,—I rather suspect Beverley will not ride in the race on the Fifteenth. Just now he is at Hawkhurst visiting Cleone! He is with—your sister! If you are still in the same mind about a certain project, no place were better suited. If you are still set on trying for him, and I know how determined you are where your honor, or Cleone's, is concerned, the country is the place for it, and I will go with you, though I am convinced he is no fighter, and will refuse to meet you, on one pretext or another. However, you may as well bring your pistols,—mine are at the gun-smith's.—Yours always,

WILFRED CHICHESTER

"So you see, sir," sighed Mr. Shrig, as he put away the little book, "my case is spiled,—can't come off,—mustn't come off! For if young B. is Number Vun, the murderer, and C. is Number Two, the accessory afore the fact, v'y then Number Three, the unfort'nate wictim is—you, sir,—you! And you—" said Mr. Shrig, sighing deeper than ever, "you 'appen to be my pal!"

CHAPTER LII

OF A BREAKFAST, A ROMAN PARENT, AND A KISS

Bright rose the sun upon the "White Hart" tavern that stands within Eltham village, softening its rugged lines, gilding its lattices, lending its ancient timbers a mellower hue.

This inn of the "White Hart" is an ancient structure and very unpretentious (as great age often is), and being so very old, it has known full many a golden dawn. But surely never, in all its length of days, had it experienced quite such a morning as this. All night long there had been a strange hum upon the air, and now, early though the hour, Eltham village was awake and full of an unusual bustle and excitement. And the air still hummed, but louder now, a confused sound made up of the tramp of horse-hoofs, the rumble of wheels, the tread of feet and the murmur of voices. From north and south, from east and west, a great company was gathering, a motley throng of rich and poor, old and young: they came by high road and by-road, by lane and footpath, from sleepy village and noisy town,—but, one and all, with their faces set towards the ancient village of Eltham. For to-day is the fateful fifteenth of July; to-day the great Steeplechase is to be run—seven good miles across country from point to point; to-day the very vexed and all-important question as to which horse out of twenty-three can jump and gallop the fastest over divers awkward obstacles is to be settled once and for all.

Up rose the sun higher and higher, chasing the morning mists from dell and dingle, filling the earth with his glory and making glad the heart of man, and beast, and bird.

And presently, from a certain casement in the gable of the "White Hart," his curls still wet with his ablutions, Barnabas thrust his touzled head to cast an anxious glance first up at the cloudless blue of the sky, then down at the tender green of the world about, and to breathe in the sweet, cool freshness of the morning. But longest and very wistfully he gazed to where, marked out by small flags, was a track that led over field, and meadow, and winding stream, over brown earth newly turned by the plough, over hedge, and ditch, and fence, away to the hazy distance. And, as he looked, his eye brightened, his fingers clenched themselves and he frowned, yet smiled thereafter, and unfolding a letter he held, read as follows:

OUR DEAR LAD,—Yours received, and we are rejoyced to know you so successful so far. Yet be not over confident, says your father, and bids me remind you as a sow's ear ain't a silk purse, Barnabas, nor ever can be. Your description of horse reads well, though brief. But as to the Rayce, Barnabas, though you be a rider born, yet having ridden a many rayces in my day, I now offer you, my dear lad, a word of advice. In a rayce a man must think as quick as he sees, and act as quick as he thinks, and must have a nice judgment of payce. Now here comes my word of advice.

1. Remember that many riders beat themselves by over-eagerness. Well—let 'em, Barnabas.

2. Don't rush your fences, give your mount time, and steady him about twenty yards from the jump.

3. Remember that a balking horse generally swerves to the left, Barnabas.

4. Keep your eye open for the best take-offs and landings.

5. Gauge your payce, save your horse for raycing at finish.

6. Remember it's the last half-mile as counts, Barnabas.

7. So keep your spurs till they 're needed, my lad.

A rayce, Barnabas lad, is very like a fight, after all. Given a good horse it's the man with judgment and cool head as generally wins. So, Barnabas, keep your temper. This is all I have to say, or your father, only that no matter how near you come to turning yourself into a fine gentleman, we have faith as it won't spoil you, and that you may come a-walking into the old 'Hound' one of these days just the same dear Barnabas as we shall always love and remember.

Signed:
NATL. BELL.
GON BARTY.

Now, as he conned over these words of Natty Bell, a hand was laid upon his shoulder, and, glancing round, he beheld the Viscount in all the bravery of scarlet hunting frock, of snowy buckskins and spurred boots, a little paler than usual, perhaps, but as gallant a figure as need be.

"What, Bev!" he exclaimed, "not dressed yet?"

"Why I've only just woke up, Dick!"

"Woke up! D' you mean to say you've actually—been asleep?" demanded the Viscount reproachfully. "Gad! what a devilish cold-blooded fish you are, Bev! Haven't closed a peeper all night, myself. Couldn't, y' know, what with one deuced thing or another. So I got up, hours ago, went and looked at the horses. Found your man Martin on guard with a loaded pistol in each pocket, y' know,—deuced trustworthy fellow. The horses couldn't look better, Bev. Egad! I believe they know to-day is—the day! There's your 'Terror' pawing and fidgeting, and 'Moonraker' stamping and quivering—"

"But how is your arm, Dick?"

"Arm?" said the Viscount innocently. "Oh,—ah, to be sure,—thanks, couldn't be better, considering."

"Are you—quite sure?" persisted Barnabas, aware of the Viscount's haggard cheek and feverish eye.

"Quite, Bev, quite,—behold! feel!" and doubling his fist, he smote Barnabas a playful blow in the ribs. "Oh, my dear fellow, it's going to be a grand race though,—ding-dong to the finish! And it's dry, thank heaven, for 'Moonraker''s no mud-horse. But I shall be glad when we line up for the start, Bev."

"In about—four hours, Dick."

"Yes! Devilish long time till eleven o'clock!" sighed the Viscount, seating himself upon the bed and swinging his spurred heels petulantly to and fro. "And I hate to be kept waiting, Bev—egad, I do!"

"Viscount, do you love the Lady Cleone?"

"Eh? Who? Love? Now deuce take it, Beverley, how sudden you are!"

"Do you love her, Dick?"

"Love her—of course, yes—aren't we rivals? Love her, certainly, oh yes—ask my Roman parent!" And the Viscount frowned blackly, and ran his fingers through his hair.

"Why then," said Barnabas, "since you—honor me with your friendship, I feel constrained to tell you that she has given me to—to understand she will—marry me—some day."

"Eh? Oh! Marry you? The devil! Oh, has she though!" and hereupon the Viscount stared, whistled, and, in that moment, Barnabas saw that his frown had vanished.

"Will you—congratulate me, Dick?"

"My dear fellow," cried the Viscount, springing up, "with all my heart!"

"Dick," said Barnabas, as their hands met, "would you give me your hand as readily had it been—Clemency?"

Now here the Viscount's usually direct gaze wavered and fell, while his pallid cheek flushed a dull red. He did not answer at once, but his sudden frown was eloquent.

"Egad, Bev, I—since you ask me—I don't think I should."

"Why?"

"Oh well, I suppose—you see—oh, I'll be shot if I know!"

"You—don't love her, do you, Dick?"

"Clemency? Of course not—that is—suppose I do—what then?"

"Why then she'd make a very handsome Viscountess, Dick."

"Beverley," said the Viscount, staring wide-eyed, "are you mad?"

"No," Barnabas retorted, "but I take you to be an honorable man, my Lord."

The Viscount sprang to his feet, clenched his fists, then took two or three turns across the room.

"Sir," said he, in his iciest tones, "you presume too much on my friendship."

"My Lord," said Barnabas, "with your good leave I'll ring for my servant." Which he did, forthwith.

"Sir," said the Viscount, pale and stern, and with folded arms, "your remark was, I consider, a direct reflection upon my honor."

"My Lord," answered Barnabas, struggling with his breeches, "your honor is surely your friend's, also?"

"Sir," said the Viscount, with arms still folded, and sitting very upright on the bed, "were I to—call you out for that remark I should be only within my rights."

"My Lord," answered Barnabas, struggling with his shirt, "were you to call from now till doomsday—I shouldn't come."

"Then, sir," said the Viscount, cold and sneering, "a whip, perhaps,—or a cane might—"

But at this juncture, with a discreet knock, Peterby entered, and, having bowed to the scowling Viscount, proceeded to invest Barnabas with polished boots, waistcoat and scarlet coat, and to tie his voluminous cravat, all with that deftness, that swift and silent dexterity which helped to make him the marvel he was.

"Sir," said he, when Barnabas stood equipped from head to foot, "Captain Slingsby's groom called to say that his master and the Marquis of Jerningham are expecting you and Viscount Devenham to breakfast at 'The Chequers'—a little higher up the street, sir. Breakfast is ordered for eight o'clock."

"Thank you, Peterby," said Barnabas, and, bowing to the Viscount, followed him from the room and downstairs, out into the dewy freshness of the morning. To avoid the crowded street they went by a field-path behind the inn, a path which to-day was beset by, and wound between, booths and stalls and carts of all sorts. And here was gathered a motley crowd; bespangled tumblers and acrobats, dark-browed gipsy fortune-tellers and horse-coupers, thimble-riggers, showmen, itinerant musicians,—all those nomads who are to be found on every race-course, fair, and village green, when the world goes a-holiday making. Through all this bustling throng went our two young gentlemen, each remarkably stiff and upright as to back, and each excessively polite, yet walking, for the most part, in a dignified silence, until, having left the crowd behind, Barnabas paused suddenly in the shade of a deserted caravan, and turned to his companion.

"Dick!" said he smiling, and with hand outstretched.

"Sir?" said the Viscount, frowning and with eyes averted.

"My Lord," said Barnabas, bowing profoundly, "if I have offended your Lordship—I am sorry, but—"

"But, sir?"

"But your continued resentment for a fancied wrong is so much stronger than your avowed friendship for me, it would seem—that henceforth I—"

With a warning cry the Viscount sprang forward and, turning in a flash, Barnabas saw a heavy bludgeon in the air above him; saw the Viscount meet it with up-flung arm; heard the thud of the blow, a snarling curse; saw a figure dart away and vanish among the jungle of carts; saw the Viscount stagger against the caravan and lean there, his pale face convulsed with pain.

"Oh, Bev," he groaned, "my game arm, ye know. Hold me up, I—"

"Dick!" cried Barnabas, supporting the Viscount's writhing figure, "oh, Dick—it was meant for me! Are you much hurt?"

"No—nothing to—mention, my dear fellow. Comes a bit—sharp at first, y' know,—better in a minute or two."

"Dick—Dick, what can I do for you?"

"Nothing,—don't worry, Bev,—right as ninepence in a minute, y' know!" stammered the Viscount, trying to steady his twitching mouth.

"Come back," pleaded Barnabas, "come back and let me bathe it—have it attended to."

"Bathe it? Pooh!" said the Viscount, contriving to smile, "pain's quite gone, I assure you, my dear fellow. I shall be all right now, if—if you don't mind giving me your arm. Egad, Bev, some one seems devilish determined you shan't ride to-day!"

"But I shall—now, thanks to you, Dick!"

So they presently walked on together, but no longer unnaturally stiff as to back, for arm was locked in arm, and they forgot to be polite to each other.

Thus, in a while, they reached the "Chequers" inn, and were immediately shown into a comfortable sanded parlor where breakfast was preparing. And here behold Captain Slingsby lounging upon two chairs and very busily casting up his betting book, while the Marquis, by the aid of a small, cracked mirror, that chanced to hang against the wall, was frowning at his reflection and pulling at the folds of a most elaborate cravat with petulant fingers.

"Ah, Beverley—here's the dooce of a go!" he exclaimed, "that fool of a fellow of mine has actually sent me out to ride in a 'Trone d'Amour' cravat, and I've only just discovered it! The rascal knows I always take the field in an 'Osbaldistone' or 'Waterfall.' Now how the dooce can I be expected to ride in a thing like this! Most distressing, by Jove it is!"

"Eight thousand guineas!" said the Captain, yawning. "Steepish, b'gad, steepish! Eight thousand at ten to one—hum! Now, if Fortune should happen to smile on me to-day—by mistake, of course—still, if she does, I shall clear enough to win free of Gaunt's claws for good and all, b'gad!"

"Then I shall be devilish sorry to have to beat you, Sling, my boy!" drawled the Marquis, "yes, doocid sorry,—still—"

"Eh—what? Beat the 'Rascal,' Jerny? Not on your weedy 'Clinker,' b'gad—"

"Oh, but dooce take me, Sling, you'd never say the 'Rascal' was the better horse? Why, in the first place, there's too much daylight under him for your weight—besides—"

"But, my dear Jerny, you must admit that your 'Clinker' 's inclined to be just—a le-e-etle cow-hocked, come now, b'gad?"

"And then—as I've often remarked, my dear Sling, the 'Rascal' is too long in the pasterns, not to mention—"

"B'gad! give me a horse with good bellows,—round, d' ye see, well ribbed home—"

"My dear Sling, if you could manage to get your 'Rascal' four new legs, deeper shoulders, and, say, fuller haunches, he might possibly stand a chance. As it is, Sling, my boy, I commiserate you—but hallo! Devenham, what's wrong? You look a little off color."

"Well, for one thing, I want my breakfast," answered the Viscount.

"So do I!" cried the Captain, springing to his feet, "but, b'gad, Dick, you do look a bit palish round the gills, y' know."

"Effect of hunger and a bad night, perhaps."

"Had a bad night, hey, Dick? Why, so did I," said the Captain, frowning. "Dreamed that the 'Rascal' fell and broke his neck, poor devil, and that I was running like the wind—jumping hedges and ditches with Jasper Gaunt close at my heels—oh, cursed unpleasant, y'know! What—is breakfast ready? Then let's sit down, b'gad, I'm famished!"

So down they sat forthwith and, despite the Viscount's arm, and the Marquis of Jerningham's cravat, a very hearty and merry meal they made of it.

But lo! as they prepared to rise from the table, voices were heard beyond the door, whereupon the Viscount sat up suddenly to listen.

"Why—egad!" he exclaimed, "I do believe it's my Roman!"

"No, by heaven!" said the Marquis, also listening, "dooce take me if it isn't my great-aunt—her Graceless Grace, by Jove it is!"

Even as he spoke, the door opened and the Duchess swept in, all rustling silks and furbelows, very small, very dignified, and very imperious. Behind her, Barnabas saw a tall, graceful figure, strangely young-looking despite his white hair, which he wore tied behind in a queue, also his clothes, though elegant, were of a somewhat antiquated fashion; but indeed, this man with his kindly eyes and gentle, humorous mouth, was not at all like the Roman parent Barnabas had pictured.

"Ah, gentlemen!" cried the Duchess, acknowledging their four bows with a profound curtsy, "I am here to wish you success—all four of you—which is quite an impossible wish of course—still, I wish it. Lud, Captain Slingsby, how well you look in scarlet! Marquis—my fan! Mr. Beverley—my cane! A chair? thank you, Viscount. Yes indeed, gentlemen, I've backed you all—I shall gain quite a fortune if you all happen to win—which you can't possibly, of course,—still, one of you will, I hope,—and—oh, dear me, Viscount, how pale you are! Look at him, Bamborough—it's his arm, I know it is!"

"Arm, madam?" repeated the Viscount with an admirable look of surprise, "does your Grace suggest—"

But here the Earl of Bamborough stepped into the room and, closing the door, bowed to the company.

"Gentlemen," said he, "I have the honor to salute you! Viscount—your most dutiful, humble, obedient father to command."

"My Lord," answered the Viscount, gravely returning his father's bow, "your Lordship's most obliged and grateful son!"

"My dear Devenham," continued the Earl solemnly, "being, I fear, something of a fogy and fossil, I don't know if you Bucks allow the formality of shaking hands. Still, Viscount, as father and son—or rather son and father, it may perhaps be permitted us? How are you, Viscount?"

Now as they clasped hands, Barnabas saw the Viscount set his jaw grimly, and something glistened upon his temple, yet his smile was quite engaging as he answered:

"Thank you, my Lord,—never better!"

"Yes," said his Lordship, as he slowly relinquished the Viscount's hand, "your Grace was right, as usual,—it is his arm!"

"Then of course he cannot ride, Bamborough—you will forbid it?"

"On the contrary, madam, he must ride. Being a favorite, much money has changed hands already on his account, and, arm or no arm, he must ride now—he owes it to his backers. You intend to, of course, Horatio?"

"My Lord, I do."

"It's your right arm, luckily, and a horseman needs only his left. You ride fairly well, I understand, Viscount?"

"Oh, indifferent well, sir, I thank you. But allow me to present my friend to your Lordship,—Mr. Beverley—my father!"

So Barnabas shook hands with the Viscount's Roman parent, and, meeting his kindly eyes, saw that, for all their kindliness, they were eyes that looked deep into the heart of things.

"Come, gentlemen," cried the Duchess rising, "if you have quite finished breakfast, take me to the stables, for I'm dying to see the horses, I vow I am. Lead the way, Viscount. Mr. Beverley shall give me his arm."

So towards the stables they set forth accordingly, the Duchess and Barnabas well to the rear, for, be it remarked, she walked very slowly.

"Here it is, Barnabas," said she, as soon as the others were out of ear-shot.

"What, madam?"

"Oh, dear me, how frightfully dense you are, Barnabas!" she exclaimed, fumbling in her reticule. "What should it be but a letter, to be sure—Cleone's letter."

"A letter from Cleone! Oh, Duchess—"

"Here—take it. She wrote it last night—poor child didn't sleep a wink, I know, and—all on your account, sir. I promised I'd deliver it for her,—I mean the letter—that's why I made Bamborough bring me here. So you see I've kept my word as I always do—that is—sometimes. Oh, dear me, I'm so excited—about the race, I mean—and Cleone's so nervous—came and woke me long before dawn, and there were tears on her lashes—I know because I felt 'em when I kissed them—I mean her eyes. And Patten dressed me in such a hurry this morning—which was really my fault, and I know my wig's not straight—and there you stand staring at it as though you wanted to kiss it—I mean Cleone's letter, not my wig. That ridiculous Mr. Tressider told Cleone that it was the best course he ever hoped to ride over—meaning 'the worst' of course, so Cleone's quite wretched, dear lamb—but oh, Barnabas, it would be dreadful if— if you were—killed—oh!" And the Duchess shivered and turned away.

"Would you mind? So much, madam?"

"Barnabas—I never had a son—or a daughter—but I think I know just how—your mother would be feeling—now!"

"And I do not remember my mother!" said Barnabas.

"Poor, poor Joan!" sighed the Duchess, very gently. "Were she here I think she would—but then she was much taller than I, and—oh, boy, stoop—stoop down, you great, tall Barnabas—how am I ever to reach you if you don't?"

Then Barnabas stooped his head, and the Duchess kissed him—even as his own mother might have done, and so, smiling a little tremulously, turned away. "There! Barnabas," she sighed. "And now—oh, I know you are dying to read your letter—of course you are, so pray sir,—go back and fetch my fan,—here it is, it will serve as an excuse, while I go on to look at the horses." And with a quick, smiling nod, she hurried away across the paddock after the others. Then Barnabas broke the seal of Cleone's letter, and—though to be sure it might have been longer—he found it all sufficient. Here it is:

The Palace Grange,
Eltham,
Midnight.

Ever Dearest,—The race is to-morrow and, because I love you greatly, so am I greatly afraid for you. And dear, I love you because you are so strong, and gentle, and honorable. And therefore, here on my knees I have prayed God to keep you ever in his care, my Barnabas.

CLEONE.

CHAPTER LIII

IN WHICH SHALL BE FOUND SOME ACCOUNT OF THE GENTLEMAN'S STEEPLECHASE

Truly it is a great day for "The Terror," hitherto known as "Four-legs," and well he knows it.

Behold him as he stands, with his velvet muzzle upon old Martin's shoulder, the while the under-grooms, his two-legged slaves, hover solicitously about him! Behold the proud arch of his powerful neck, the knowing gleam of his rolling eye, the satiny sheen of his velvet coat! See how he flings up his shapely head to snuff the balmy air of morning, the while he paws the green earth with a round, bepolished hoof.

Yes, indeed, it is a great day for "The Terror," and well he knows it.

"He looks very well, Martin!" says Barnabas.

"And 'e's better than 'e looks, sir!" nods Martin. "And they're laying thirty to one ag'in you, sir!"

"So much, Martin?"

"Ah, but it'll be backed down a bit afore you get to the post, I reckon, so I got my fifty guineas down on you a good hour ago."

"Why, Martin, do you mean you actually backed me—to win—for fifty guineas?"

"Why, y'see sir," said Martin apologetically, "fifty guineas is all I've got, sir!"

Now at this moment, Barnabas became aware of a very shiny glazed hat, which bobbed along, among other hats of all sorts and shapes, now hidden, now rising again—very like a cock-boat in a heavy sea; and, presently, sure enough, the Bo'sun hove into view, and bringing himself to an anchor, made a leg, touched the brim of his hat, and gripped the hand Barnabas extended.

"Mr. Beverley, sir," said he, "I first of all begs leave to say as, arter Master Horatio his Lordship, it's you as I'd be j'yful to see come into port first, or—as you might say—win this 'ere race. Therefore and wherefore I have laid five guineas on you, sir, by reason o' you being you, and the odds so long. Secondly, sir, I were to give you this here, sir, naming no names, but she says as you'd understand."

Hereupon the Bo'sun took off the glazed hat, inserted a hairy paw, and brought forth a single, red rose.

So Barnabas took the rose, and bowed his head above it, and straightway forgot the throng and bustle about him, and all things else, yea even the great race itself until, feeling a touch upon his arm, he turned to find the Earl of Bamborough beside him.

"He is very pale, Mr. Beverley!" said his Lordship, and, glancing whither he looked, Barnabas saw the Viscount who was already mounted upon his bay horse "Moonraker."

"Can you tell me, sir," pursued the Earl, "how serious his hurt really is?"

"I know that he was shot, my Lord," Barnabas answered, "and that he received a violent blow upon his wounded arm this morning, but he is very reticent."

Here the Viscount chanced to catch sight of them, and, with his groom at "Moonraker's" head, paced up to them.

"Viscount," said his Lordship, looking up at his son with wise, dark eyes, "your arm is troubling you, I see."

"Indeed, sir, it might be—a great deal worse."

"Still, you will be under a disadvantage, for it will be a punishing race for horse and man."

"Yes, sir."

"And—you will do your best, of course, Horatio?"

"Of course, sir."

"But—Horace, may I ask you to remember—that your father has—only one son?"

"Yes, sir,—and, father, may I tell you that—that thoughtless though he may be, he never forgets that—he *is* your son!" Saying which the Viscount leaned down from his saddle, with his hand stretched out impulsively, and, this time, his father's clasp was very light and gentle. So the Earl bowed, and turning, walked away.

"He's—deuced Roman, of course, Bev," said the Viscount, staring hard after his father's upright figure, "but there are times when he's—rather more—than human!" And sighing, the Viscount nodded and rode off.

"Only ten minutes more, sir!" said Martin.

"Well, I'm ready, Martin," answered Barnabas, and, setting the rose in his breast very securely, he swung himself lightly into the saddle, and with the old groom at "The Terror's" head, paced slowly out of the paddock towards the starting post.

Here a great pavilion had been set up, an ornate contrivance of silk and gold cords, and gay with flags and bunting, above which floated the Royal Standard of England, and beneath which was seated no less ornate a personage than the First Gentleman in Europe—His Royal Highness the Prince Regent himself, surrounded by all that was fairest and bravest in the Fashionable and Sporting World. Before this pavilion the riders were being marshalled in line, a gallant sight in their scarlet coats, and, each and every, mounted upon a fiery animal every whit as high-bred as himself; which fact they manifested in many and divers ways, as—in rearing and plunging, in tossing of heads, in lashing of heels, in quivering, and snorting, and stamping—and all for no apparent reason, yet which is the prerogative of your thoroughbred all the world over.

Amidst this confusion of tossing heads and manes, Barnabas caught a momentary glimpse of the Viscount, some way down the line, his face frowning and pale; saw the Marquis alternately bowing gracefully towards the great, gaudy pavilion, soothing his plunging horse, and re-settling his cravat; caught a more distant view of Captain Slingsby, sitting his kicking sorrel like a centaur; and finally, was aware that Sir Mortimer Carnaby had ridden up beside him, who, handsome and debonair, bestrode his powerful gray with a certain air of easy assurance, and laughed softly as he talked with his other neighbor, a thinnish, youngish gentleman in sandy whiskers, who giggled frequently.

"....very mysterious person," Sir Mortimer was saying, "nobody knows him, devilish odd, eh, Tressider? Tufton Green dubbed him the 'Galloping Countryman,'—what do you think of the name?"

"Could have suggested a better, curse me if I couldn't, yes, Carnaby, oh damme! Why not 'the Prancing Ploughman,' or 'the Cantering Clodhopper'?" Here Sir Mortimer laughed loudly, and the thinnish, youngish gentleman giggled again.

Barnabas frowned, but looking down at the red rose upon his breast, he smiled instead, a little grimly, as he settled his feet in the stirrups, and shortening his reins, sat waiting, very patiently. Not so "The Terror." Patient, forsooth! He backed and sidled and tossed his head, he fidgeted with his bit, he glared viciously this way and that, and so became aware of other four-legged creatures like himself, notably of Sir Mortimer's powerful gray near by, and in his heart he scorned them, one and all, proud of his strength and might, and sure of himself because of the hand upon his bridle. Therefore he snuffed the air with quivering nostril, and pawed the earth with an impatient hoof,—eager for the fray.

Now all at once Sir Mortimer laughed again, louder than before, and in that same moment his gray swerved and cannoned lightly against "The Terror," and—reared back only just in time to avoid the vicious snap of two rows of gleaming teeth.

"Damnation!" cried Sir Mortimer, very nearly unseated, "can't you manage that brute of yours!" and he struck savagely at "The Terror" with his whip. But Barnabas parried the blow, and now—even as they stared and frowned upon each other, so did their horses, the black and the gray, glare at each other with bared teeth.

But, here, a sudden shout arose that spread and spread, and swelled into a roar; the swaying line of horsemen surges forward, bends, splits into plunging groups, and man and horse are off and away—the great Steeplechase has begun.

Half a length behind Carnaby's gray gallops "The Terror," fire in his eye, rage in his heart, for there are horses ahead of him, and that must not be. Therefore he strains upon the bit, and would fain lengthen his stride, but the hand upon his bridle is strong and compelling.

On sweeps the race, across the level and up the slope; twice Sir Mortimer glances over his shoulder, and twice he increases his pace, yet, as they top the rise, "The Terror" still gallops half a length behind.

Far in advance races Tressider, the thinnish, youngish gentleman in sandy whiskers, hotly pressed by the Marquis, and with eight or nine others hard in their rear; behind these again, rides the Viscount, while to the right of Barnabas races Slingsby on his long-legged sorrel, with the rest thundering on behind. And now before them is the first jump—a hedge with the gleam of water beyond; and the hedge is high, and the water broad. Nearer it looms, and nearer—half a mile away! a quarter! less! Tressider's horse rises to it, and is well over, with the

Marquis hard on his heels. But now shouts are heard, and vicious cries, as several horses, refusing, swerve violently; there is a crash! a muffled cry—some one is down. Then, as Barnabas watches, anxious-eyed, mindful of the Viscount's injured arm—"Moonraker" shoots forward and has cleared it gallantly.

And now it is that "The Terror" feels the restraining bit relax and thereupon, with his fierce eyes ever upon the gray flanks of his chosen foe, he tosses his great head, lengthens his stride, and with a snort of defiance sweeps past Carnaby's gray, on and on, with thundering hoofs and ears laid back, while Barnabas, eyeing the hedge with frowning brows, gauges his distance,—a hundred yards! fifty! twenty-five! steadies "The Terror" in his stride and sends him at it—feels the spring and sway of the powerful loins,—a rush of wind, and is over and away, with a foot to spare. But behind him is the sound of a floundering splash,—another! and another! The air is full of shouts and cries quickly lost in the rush of wind and the drumming of galloping hoofs, and, in a while, turning his head, he sees Slingsby's "Rascal" racing close behind.

"Bit of a rasper, that, b'gad!" bellows the Captain, radiant of face. "Thinned 'em out a bit, ye know, Beverley. Six of 'em—down and out of it b'gad! Carnaby's behind, too,—foot short at the water. Told you it would be—a good race, and b'gad—so it is!"

Inch by inch the great, black horse and the raking sorrel creep up nearer the leaders, and, closing in with the Viscount, Barnabas wonders to see the ghastly pallor of his cheek and the grim set of mouth and jaw, till, glancing at the sleeve of his whip-arm, he sees there a dark stain, and wonders no more. And the race is but begun!

"Dick!" he cried.

"That you, Bev?"

"Your arm, Dick,—keep your hand up!"

"Arm, Bev—right as a trivet!"

And to prove his words, the Viscount flourished his whip in the air.

"Deuce take me! but Jerningham's setting a devilish hot pace," he cried. "Means to weed out the unlikely ones right away. Gad! there's riding for you!—Tressider's 'Pilot"s blown already—Marquis hasn't turned a hair!"

And indeed the Marquis, it would seem, has at last ceased to worry over his cravat, and has taken the lead, and now, stooped low in the saddle, gallops a good twelve yards in front of Tressider.

"Come on Bev!" cries the Viscount and, uttering a loud "view hallo," flourishes his whip. "Moonraker" leaps forward, lengthens his stride, and away he goes fast and furious, filling the air with flying clods, on and on,—is level with Tressider,—is past, and galloping neck and neck with the Marquis.

Onward sweeps the race, over fallow and plough, over hedge and ditch and fence, until, afar off, Barnabas sees again the gleam of water—a jump full thirty feet across. Now, as he rides with "The Terror" well in hand, Barnahas is aware of a gray head with flaring nostrils, of a neck outstretched, of a powerful shoulder, a heaving flank, and Carnaby goes by. "The Terror" sees this too and, snorting, bores savagely upon the bit—but in front of him gallops Tressider's chestnut, and beside him races the Captain's sorrel. So, foot by foot, and yard by yard, the gray wins by. Over a hedge—across a ditch, they race together till, as they approach the water-jump, behold! once more "The Terror" gallops half a length behind Sir Mortimer's gray.

The Marquis and the Viscount, racing knee and knee, have increased their twelve yards by half, and now, as Barnabas watches, down go their heads, in go their spurs, and away go chestnut and bay, fast and faster, take off almost together, land fairly, and are steadied down again to a rolling gallop.

And now, away races Carnaby, with Barnabas hard upon his left, the pace quickens to a stretching gallop,—the earth flies beneath them. Barnabas marks his take-off and rides for it—touches "The Terror" with his spur and—in that moment, Carnaby's gray swerves. Barnabas sees the danger and, clenching his teeth, swings "The Terror" aside, just in time; who, thus balked, yet makes a brave attempt,—leaps, is short, and goes down with a floundering splash, flinging Barnabas clear.

Half-stunned, half-blinded, plastered with mud and ooze, Barnabas staggers up to his feet, is aware in a dazed manner that horses are galloping down upon him, thundering past and well-nigh over him; is conscious also that "The Terror" is scrambling up and, even as he gets upon his legs, has caught the reins, vaulted into the saddle, and strikes in his spurs,—whereat "The Terror" snorts, rears and sets off after the others. And a mighty joy fills his heart, for now the hand upon his bridle restrains him no longer—nay, rather urges him forward; and far in the distance gallop others of his kind, others whom he scorns, one and all—notably a certain gray. Therefore as he spurns the earth beneath him faster and faster, the heart of "The Terror" is uplifted and full of rejoicing.

But,—bruised, bleeding and torn, all mud from heel to head, and with a numbness in his brain Barnabas rides, stooped low in the saddle, for he is sick and very faint. His hat is gone, and the cool wind in his hair revives him somewhat, but the numbness remains. Yet it is as one in a dream that he finds his stirrups, and is vaguely conscious of voices about him—a thudding of hoofs and the creak of leather. As one in a dream he lifts "The Terror" to a fence that vanishes and gives place to a hedge which in turn is gone, or is magically transfigured into an ugly wall. And, still as one in a dream, he is thereafter aware of cries and shouting, and knows that horses are galloping beside him—riderless. But on and ever on races the great, black horse—head stretched out, ears laid back, iron hoofs pounding—on and on, over hedge and ditch and wall—over fence and brook—past blown and weary stragglers—his long stride unfaltering over ploughland and fallowland, tireless, indomitable—on and ever on until Barnabas can distinguish, at last, the horsemen in front.

Therefore, still as one in a dream, he begins to count them to himself, over and over again. Yet, count how he will, can make them no more than seven all told, and he wonders dully where the rest may be.

Well in advance of the survivors the Viscount is going strong, with Slingsby and the Marquis knee and knee behind; next rides Carnaby with two others, while Tressider, the thinnish, youngish gentleman, brings up the rear. Inch by inch Barnabas gains upon him, draws level and is past, and so "The Terror" once more sees before him Sir Mortimer's galloping gray.

But now—something is wrong in front,—there is a warning yell from the Marquis—up flashes the Captain's long arm, for "Moonraker" has swerved suddenly, unaccountably,—loses his stride, and falls back until he is neck and neck with "The Terror." Thus, still as one in a dream, Barnabas is aware, little by little, that the Viscount's hat and whip are gone, and that he is swaying oddly in the saddle with "Moonraker's" every stride—catches a momentary glimpse of a pale, agonized face, and hears the Viscount speaking:

"No go, Bev!" he pants. "Oh, Bev, I'm done! 'Moonraker's' game, but—I'm—done, Bev—arm, y'know—devilish shame, y'know—"

And Barnabas sees that the Viscount's sleeve is all blood from the elbow down. And in that moment Barnabas casts off the numbness, and his brain clears again.

"Hold on, Dick!" he cries.

"Can't Bev,—I—I'm done. Tried my best—but—I—" Barnabas reaches out suddenly—but is too far off—the Viscount lurches forward, loses his stirrups, sways—and "Moonraker" gallops—riderless. But help is at hand, for Barnabas sees divers rustic onlookers who run forward to lift the Viscount's inanimate form. Therefore he turns him back to the race, and bends all his energies upon this, the last and grimmest part of the struggle; as for "The Terror," he vents a snort of joyful defiance, for now he is galloping again in full view of Sir Mortimer Carnaby's foam-flecked gray.

And now—it's hey! for the rush and tear of wind through the hair! for the muffled thunder of galloping hoofs! for the long, racing stride, the creak of leather! Hey! for the sob and pant and strain of the conflict!

Inch by inch the great, black horse creeps up, but Carnaby sees him coming, and the gray leaps forward under his goading heels,—is up level with Slingsby and the Marquis,—but with "The Terror" always close behind.

Over a hedge,—across a ditch,—and down a slope they race together, —knees in, heads low,—to where, at the bottom, is a wall. An ancient, mossy wall it is, yet hideous for all that, an almost impossible jump, except in one place, a gap so narrow that but one may take it at a time. And who shall be first? The Marquis is losing ground rapidly—a foot—a yard—six! and losing still, races now a yard behind Barnabas. Thus, two by two, they thunder down upon the gap that is but wide enough for one. Slingsby is plying his whip, Carnaby is rowelling savagely, yet, neck and neck, the sorrel and the gray race for the jump, with Barnabas and the Marquis behind.

"Give way, Slingsby!" shouts Sir Mortimer.

"Be damned if I do!" roars the Captain, and in go his spurs.

"Pull over, Slingsby!" shouts Sir Mortimer.

"No, b'gad! Pull over yourself," roars the Captain. "Give way, Carnaby—I have you by a head!"

An exultant yell from Slingsby,—a savage shout from Sir Mortimer—a sudden, crunching thud, and the gallant sorrel is lying a twisted, kicking heap, with Captain Slingsby pinned beneath.

"What, Beverley!" he cries, coming weakly to his elbow, "well ridden, b'gad! After him! The 'Rascal' 's done for, poor devil! So am I, —it's you or Carnaby now—ride, Beverley, ride!" And so, as Barnabas flashes past and over him, Captain Slingsby of the Guards sinks back, and lies very white and still.

A stake-fence, a hedge, a ditch, and beyond that a clear stretch to the winning-post.

At the fence, Carnaby sees "The Terror's" black head some six yards behind; at the hedge, Barnabas has lessened the six to three; and at the ditch once again the great, black horse gallops half a length behind the powerful gray. And now, louder and louder, shouts come down the wind!

"The gray! It's Carnaby's gray! Carnaby's 'Clasher' wins! 'Clasher'! 'Clasher'!"

But, slowly and by degrees, the cries sink to a murmur, to a buzzing drone. For, what great, black horse is this which, despite Carnaby's flailing whip and cruel, rowelling spur, is slowly, surely creeping up with the laboring gray? Who is this, a wild, bare-headed figure, grim and bloody, stained with mud, rent and torn, upon whose miry coat yet hangs a crushed and fading rose?

Down the stretch they race, the black and the gray, panting, sobbing, spattered with foam, nearer and nearer, while the crowd rocks and sways about the great pavilion, and buzzes with surprise and uncertainty.

Then all at once, above this sound, a single voice is heard, a mighty voice, a roaring bellow, such, surely, as only a mariner could possess.

"It's Mr. Beverley, sir!" roars the voice. "Beverley! Beverley—hurrah!"

Little by little the crowd takes up the cry until the air rings with it, for now the great, black horse gallops half a length ahead of the sobbing gray, and increases his lead with every stride, by inches—by feet! On and on until his bridle is caught and held, and he is brought to a stand. Then, looking round, Barnabas sees the Marquis rein up beside him, breathless he is still, and splashed with mud and foam, but smiling and debonair as he reaches out his hand.

"Congratulations, Beverley!" he pants. "Grand race!—I caught Carnaby—at the post. Now, if it hadn't been for—my cravat—" But here the numbness comes upon Barnabas again, and, as one in a dream, he is aware that his horse is being led through the crowd—that he is bowing to some one in the gaudy pavilion, a handsome, tall, and chubby gentleman remarkable for waistcoat and whiskers.

"Well ridden, sir!" says the gentleman. "Couldn't have done it better myself, no, by Gad I couldn't—could I, Sherry?"

"No, George, by George you couldn't!" answered a voice.

"Must take a run down to Brighton, Mr.—Mr.—ah, yes—Beverley. Show you some sport at Brighton, sir. A magnificent race, —congratulate you, sir. Must see more of you!"

Then, still as one in a dream, Barnabas bows again, sees Martin at "The Terror's" bridle, and is led back, through a pushing, jostling throng all eager to behold the winner, and thus, presently finds himself once more in the quiet of the paddock behind the "White Hart" inn.

Stiffly and painfully he descends from the saddle, hears a feeble voice call his name and turning, beholds a hurdle set in the shade of a tree, and upon the hurdle the long, limp form of Captain Slingsby, with three or four strangers kneeling beside him.

"Ah, Beverley!" said he faintly. "Glad you beat Carnaby, he—crowded me a bit—at the wall, y' know. Poor old 'Rascal' 's gone, b'gad—and I'm going, but prefer to—go—out of doors,—seems more room for it somehow—give me the sky to look at. Told you it would be a grand race, and—b'gad, so it was! Best I—ever rode—or ever shall. Eh—what, Beverley? No, no—mustn't take it—so hard, dear fellow. B'gad it—might be worse, y' know. I—might have lost, and—lived—been deeper in Gaunt's clutches than ever,—then. As it is, I'm going beyond—beyond his reach—for good and all. Which is the purest—bit of luck I ever had. Lift me up a little—will you, Beverley? Deuced fine day, b'gad! And how green the grass is—never saw it so green before—probably because—never troubled to look though, was always so—deuced busy, b'gad!—The poor old 'Rascal' broke his back, Beverley—so did I. They—shot 'The Rascal,' but—"

Here the Captain sighed, and closed his eyes wearily, but after a moment opened them again.

"A fine race, gentlemen!" said he, addressing the silent group, "a fine race well ridden—and won by—my friend, Beverley. I'll warrant him a—true-blue, gentlemen. Beverley, I—I congratulate—"

Once more he closed his eyes, sighed deeply and, with the sigh, Captain Slingsby of the Guards had paid his debts—for good and all.

CHAPTER LIV

WHICH CONCERNS ITSELF CHIEFLY WITH A LETTER

And now, the "Galloping Countryman" found himself famous, and, being so, made the further, sudden discovery that all men were his "warmest friends," nay, even among the gentler sex this obtained, for the most dragon-like dowagers, the haughtiest matrons, became infinitely gracious; noble fathers were familiarly jocose; the proudest beauties wore, for him, their most bewitching airs, since as well as being famous, he was known to be one of the wealthiest young men about town; moreover His Royal Highness had deigned to notice him, and Her Grace of Camberhurst was his professed friend. Hence, all this being taken into consideration, it is not surprising that invitations poured in upon him, and that the doors of the most exclusive clubs flew open at his step.

Number Five St. James's Square suddenly became a rendezvous of Sport and Fashion, before its portal were to be seen dashing turn-outs of all descriptions, from phaetons to coaches; liveried menials, bearing cards, embossed, gild-edged, and otherwise, descended upon St. James's Square in multi-colored shoals; in a word, the Polite World forthwith took Barnabas to its bosom, which, though perhaps a somewhat cold and flinty bosom, made up for such minor deficiencies by the ardor of its embrace. By reason of these things, the legs of the Gentleman-in-Powder were exalted,—that is to say, were in a perpetual quiver of superior gratification, and Barnabas himself enjoyed it all vastly—for a week.

At the end of which period behold him at twelve o'clock in the morning, as he sits over his breakfast (with the legs of the Gentleman-in-Powder planted, statuesque, behind his chair), frowning at a stupendous and tumbled pile of Fashionable note-paper, and Polite cards.

"Are these all?" he inquired, waving his hand towards the letters.

"Them, sir, is—hall!" answered the Gentleman-in-Powder.

"Then ask Mr. Peterby to come to me," said Barnabas, his frown growing blacker.

"Cer-tainly, sir!" Here the Gentleman-in-Powder posed his legs, bowed, and took them out of the room. Then Barnabas drew a letter from his pocket and began to read as follows:

The Gables,
Hawkhurst.

> MY DEAR BARNABAS,—As Cleone's letter looks very long (she sits opposite me at this precise moment writing to you, and blushing very prettily over something her pen has just scribbled—I can't quite see what, the table is too wide), mine shall be short, that is, as short as possible. Of course we are all disappointed not to have seen you here since the race—that terrible race (poor, dear

Captain Slingsby,—how dreadful it was!) but of course, it is quite right you should stay near the Viscount during his illness. I rejoice to hear he is so much better. I am having my town house, the one in Berkeley Square, put in order, for Cleone has had quite enough of the country, I think, so have I. Though indeed she seems perfectly content (I mean Cleone) and is very fond of listening to the brook. O Youth! O Romance! Well, I used to listen to brooks once upon a time—before I took to a wig. As for yourself now, Barnabas, the Marquis writes to tell me that your cravats are 'all the thing,' and your waistcoats 'all the go,' and that your new coat with the opened cuff finds very many admirers. This is very well, but since Society has taken you up and made a lion of you, it will necessarily expect you to roar occasionally, just to maintain your position. And there are many ways of roaring, Barnabas. Brummell (whom I ever despised) roared like an insolent cat—he was always very precise and cat-like, and dreadfully insolent, but insolence palls, after a while—even in Society. Indeed I might give you many hints on Roaring, Barnabas, but—considering the length of Cleone's letter, I will spare you more, nor even give you any advice though I yearn to—only this: Be yourself, Barnabas, in Society or out, so shall I always subscribe myself:

Your affectionate friend,
FANNY CAMBERHURST.

3 P.M.—I have opened this letter to tell you that Mr. Chichester and Ronald called here and stayed an hour. Ronald was full of his woes, as usual, so I left him to Cleone, and kept Mr. Chichester dancing attendance on me. And, oh dear me! to see the white rage of the man! It was deliciously thrilling, and I shivered most delightfully.

"You sent for me, sir?" said Peterby, as Barnabas re-folded the letter.

"Yes, John. Are you sure there is no other letter this morning from—from Hawkhurst?"

"Quite, sir."

"Yet the Duchess tells me that the Lady Cleone wrote me also. This letter came by the post this morning?"

"Yes, sir."

"And no other? It's very strange!"

But here, the Gentleman-in-Powder re-appeared to say that the Marquis of Jerningham desired to see Mr. Beverley on a matter of importance, and that nobleman presenting himself, Peterby withdrew.

"Excuse this intrusion, my dear Beverley," said the Marquis as the door closed, "doocid early I know, but the—ah—the matter is pressing. First, though, how's Devenham, you saw him last night as usual, I suppose?"

"Yes," answered Barnabas, shaking hands, "he ought to be up and about again in a day or two."

"Excellent," nodded the Marquis, "I'll run over to Half-moon Street this afternoon. Is Bamborough with him still?"

"No, his Lordship left yesterday."

"Ha!" said the Marquis, and taking out his snuff-box, he looked at it, tapped it, and put it away again. "Poor old Sling," said he gently, "I miss him damnably, y'know, Beverley."

"Marquis," said Barnabas, "what is it?"

"Well, I want you to do me a favor, my dear fellow, and I don't know how to ask you—doocid big favor—ah—I was wondering if you would consent to—act for me?"

"Act for you?" repeated Barnabas, wholly at a loss.

"Yes, in my little affair with Carnaby—poor old Sling, d' you see. What, don't you twig, Beverley, haven't you heard?"

"No!" answered Barnabas, "you don't mean that you and Carnaby are going—to fight?"

"Exactly, my dear fellow, of course! He fouled poor old Sling at the wall, y'know—you saw it, I saw it, so naturally I mean to call him to account for it. And he can't refuse—I spoke doocid plainly, and White's was full. He has the choice of weapons,—pistols I expect. Personally, I should like it over as soon as possible, and anywhere would do, though Eltham for preference, Beverley. So if you will oblige me—"

But here, once again the Gentleman-in-Powder knocked to announce: "Mr. Tressider."

The thinnish, youngish gentleman in sandy whiskers entered with a rush, but, seeing the Marquis, paused.

"What, then—you 're before me, are you, Jerningham?" he exclaimed; then turning, he saluted Barnabas, and burst into a torrent of speech. "Beverley!" he cried, "cursed early to call, but I'm full o' news—bursting with it, damme if I'm not—and tell it I must! First, then, by Gad!—it was at White's you'll understand, and the card-room was full—crammed, sir, curse me if it wasn't, and there's Carnaby and Tufton Green, and myself and three or four others, playing hazard, d'ye see,—when up strolls Jerningham here. 'It's your play, Carnaby,' says I. 'Why then,' says the Marquis,—'why then,' says he, 'look out for fouling!' says he, cool as a cucumber, curse me! 'Eh—what?' cries Tufton, 'why—what d' ye mean?' 'Mean?' says the Marquis, tapping his snuff-box, 'I mean that Sir Mortimer Carnaby is a most accursed rascal' (your very words, Marquis, damme if they weren't). Highly dramatic, Beverley—could have heard a pin drop—curse me if you couldn't! End of it was they arranged a meeting of course, and I was Carnaby's second, but—"

"Was?" repeated the Marquis.

"Yes, was,—for begad! when I called on my man this morning he'd bolted, damme if he hadn't!"

"Gone?" exclaimed the Marquis in blank amazement.

"Clean gone! Bag and baggage! I tell you he's bolted, but—with all due respect to you, Marquis, only from his creditors. He was devilish deep in with Gaunt, I know, beside Beverley here. Oh damme yes, he only did it to bilk his creditors, for Carnaby was always game, curse me if he wasn't!"

Hereupon the Marquis had recourse to his snuff-box again.

"Under the circumstances," said he, sighing and shaking his head, "I think I'll go and talk with our invalid—"

"No good, my boy, if you mean Devenham," said Tressider, shaking his head, "just been there,—Viscount's disappeared too—been away all night!"

"What?" cried Barnabas, springing to his feet, "gone?"

"Damme if he hasn't! Found his fellow in the devil of a way about it, and his little rascal of a groom blubbering on the stairs."

"Then I must dress! You'll excuse me, I know!" said Barnabas, and rang for Peterby. But his hand was even yet upon the bellrope when stumbling feet were heard outside, the door was flung wide, and the Viscount himself stood upon the threshold.

Pale and haggard of eye, dusty and unkempt, he leaned there, then staggering to a chair he sank down and so lay staring at the floor.

"Oh, Bev!" he groaned, "she's gone—Clemency's gone, I—I can't find her, Bev!"

Now hereupon the Marquis very quietly took up his hat and, nodding to Barnabas, linked his arm in Tressider's and went softly from the room, closing the door behind him.

"Dick!" cried Barnabas, bending over him, "my dear fellow!"

"Ever since you spoke, I—I've wanted her, Bev. All through my illness I've hungered for her—the sound of her voice,—the touch of her hand. As soon as I was strong enough—last night, I think it was—I went to find her, to—to kneel at her feet, Bev. I drove down to Frittenden and oh, Bev—she was gone! So I started back—looking for her all night. My arm bothered me—a bit, you know, and I didn't think I could do it. But I kept fancying I saw her before me in the dark. Sometimes I called to her—but she—never answered, she's—gone, Bev, and I—"

"Oh, Dick—she left there weeks ago—"

"What—you knew?"

"Yes, Dick."

"Then oh, Bev,—tell me where!"

"Dick, I—can't!"

"Why—why?"

"I promised her to keep it secret."

"Then—you won't tell me?"

"I can't."

"Won't! won't! Ah, but you shall, yes, by God!"

"Dick, I—"

"By God, but you shall, I say you shall—you must—where is she?" The Viscount's pale cheek grew suddenly suffused, his eyes glared fiercely, and his set teeth gleamed between his pallid lips. "Tell me!" he demanded.

"No," said Barnabas, and shook his head.

Then, in that moment the Viscount sprang up and, pinning him with his left hand, swung Barnabas savagely to the wall.

"She's mine!" he panted, "mine, I tell you—no one shall take her from me, neither you nor the devil himself. She's mine—mine. Tell me where she is,—speak before I choke you—speak!"

But Barnabas stood rigid and utterly still. Thus, in a while, the griping fingers fell away, the Viscount stepped back, and groaning, bowed his head.

"Oh, Bev," said he, "forgive me, I—I'm mad I think. I want her so and I can't find her. And I had a spill last night—dark road you see, and only one hand,—and I'm not quite myself in consequence. I'll go—"

But, as he turned toward the door, Barnabas interposed.

"Dick, I can't let you go like this—what do you intend to do?"

"Will you tell me where she is?"

"No, but—"

"Then, sir, my further movements need not concern you."

"Dick, be reasonable,—listen—"

"Have the goodness to let me pass, sir."

"You are faint, worn out—stay here, Dick, and I—"

"Thanks, Beverley, but I accept favors from my friends only—pray stand aside."

"Dick, if you'll only wait, I'll go to her now—this moment—I'll beg her to see you—"

"Very kind, sir!" sneered the Viscount, "you are—privileged it seems. But, by God, I don't need you, or any one else, to act as go-between or plead my cause. And mark me, sir! I'll find her yet. I swear to you I'll never rest until I find her again. And now, sir, once and for all, I have the honor to wish you a very good day!" saying which the Viscount bowed, and, having re-settled his arm in its sling, walked away down the corridor, very upright as to back, yet a little uncertain in his stride nevertheless, and so was gone.

Then Barnabas, becoming aware of the polite letters, and cards, embossed, gilt-edged and otherwise, swept them incontinent to the floor and, sinking into a chair, set his elbows upon the table, and leaning his head upon his hands fell into a gloomy meditation. It was thus that the Gentleman-in-Powder presently found him, and, advancing into the room with insinuating legs, coughed gently to attract his attention, the which proving ineffectual, he spoke:

"Ex-cuse me, sir, but there is a—person downstairs, sir—at the door, sir!"

"What kind of person?" inquired Barnabas without looking up.

"A most ex-tremely low person, sir—very common indeed, sir. Won't give no name, sir, won't go away, sir. A very 'orrid person—in gaiters, sir."

"What does he want?" said Barnabas, with head still bent.

"Says as 'ow 'e 'as a letter for you, sir, but—"

Barnabas was on his feet so quickly that the Gentleman-in-Powder recoiled in alarm.

"Show him up—at once!"

"Oh!—cer-tainly, sir!" And though the bow of the Gentleman-in-Powder was all that it should be, his legs quivered disapprobation as they took him downstairs.

When next the door opened it was to admit the person in gaiters, a shortish, broad-shouldered, bullet-headed person he was, and his leggings were still rank of the stables; he was indeed a very horsey person who stared and chewed upon a straw. At sight of Barnabas he set a stubby finger to one eyebrow, and chewed faster than ever.

"You have a letter for me, I think?"

"Yessir!"

"Then give it to me."

The horsey person coughed, took out his straw, looked at it, shook his head at it, and put it back again.

"Name o' Beverley, sir?" he inquired, chewing feverishly.

"Yes."

Hereupon the horsey person drew a letter from his pocket, chewed over it a moment, nodded, and finally handed it to Barnabas, who, seeing the superscription, hurriedly broke the seal. Observing which, the horsey person sighed plaintively and shook his head, alternately chewing upon and looking at his straw the while Barnabas read the following:

Oh, Barnabas dear, when shall I see you again? I
am very foolish to-day perhaps, but though the sun shines
gloriously, I am cold, it is my heart that is cold, a
deadly chill—as if an icy hand had touched it. And I
seem to be waiting—waiting for something to happen,
something dreadful that I cannot avert. I fear you will
think me weak and fanciful, but, dear, I cannot help wondering
what it all means. You ask me if I love you.
Can you doubt? How often in my dreams have I seen
you kneeling beside me with your neck all bare and the
dripping kerchief in your hand. Oh, dear Wood of Annersley!
it was there that I first felt your arms about me,
Barnabas, and I dream of that too—sometimes. But
last night I dreamed of that awful race,—I saw you
gallop past the winning post again, your dear face all cut
and bleeding, and as you passed me your eyes looked into
mine—such an awful look, Barnabas. And then it

seemed that you galloped into a great, black shadow that swallowed you up, and so you were lost to me, and I awoke trembling. Oh Barnabas, come to me! I want you here beside me, for although the sky here is blue and cloudless, away to the north where London lies, there is a great, black shadow like the shadow of my dream, and God keep all shadows from you, Barnabas. So come to me—meet me to-morrow—there is a new moon. Come to Oakshott's Barn at 7:30, and we will walk back to the house together.

I am longing to see you, and yet I am a little afraid also, because my love is not a quiet love or gentle, but such a love as frightens me sometimes, because it has grown so deep and strong.

This window, you may remember, faces north, and now as I lift my eyes I can see that the shadow is still dark over London, and very threatening. Come to me soon, and that God may keep all shadows from you is the prayer of

Your
CLEONE.

Now when he had finished reading, Barnabas sighed, and glancing up, found the horsey person still busy with his straw, but now he took it from his mouth, shook his head at it more sternly than ever, dropped it upon the carpet and set his foot upon it; which done, he turned and looked at Barnabas with a pair of very round, bright eyes.

"Now," said he, "I should like to take the liberty o' axing you one or two questions, Mr. Barty, sir,—or as I should say, p'r'aps, Mr. Beverley."

"What," exclaimed Barnabas, starting up, "it's you again, Mr. Shrig?"

"That werry same i-dentical, sir. Disguises again, ye see. Yesterday, a journeyman peg-maker vith a fine lot o' pegs as I didn't vant to sell—to-day a groom looking for a job as I don't need. Been a-keeping my ogles on Number Vun and Number Two, and things is beginning to look werry rosy, sir, yes, things is werry promising indeed."

"How do you mean?"

"Vell, to begin vith," said Mr. Shrig, taking the chair Barnabas proffered, "you didn't 'appen to notice as that theer letter had been broke open and sealed up again, did ye?"

"No," said Barnabas, staring at what was left of the seal.

"No, o' course you didn't—you opened it too quick to notice anything—but I did."

"Oh, surely not—"

"That theer letter," said Mr. Shrig impressively, "vas wrote you by a certain lady, vasn't it?"

"Yes."

"And I brought you that theer letter, didn't I?"

"Yes, but—"

"And 'oo do ye suppose give me that theer letter, to bring to you,—the lady? Oh no! I'll tell you 'oo give it me,—it vas—shall ve say, Number Two, the Accessory afore the fact,—shall ve call 'im C.? Werry good! Now, 'ow did C. or Number Two, 'appen to give me that theer letter? I'll tell you. Ven Number Vun and Number Two, B. and C., vent down to Hawkhurst, I vent down to Hawkhurst. They put up at the 'Qveen's 'ead,' so I 'angs about the 'Qveen's 'ead,'—offers myself as groom—I'm 'andy vith an 'orse—got in the 'abit o' doing odd jobs for Number Vun and Number Two, and, last night, Number Two gives me that theer letter to deliver, and werry pertickler 'e vas as I should give it into your werry own daddle, 'e also gives me a guinea and tells as 'ow 'e don't vant me no more, and them's the circumstances, sir."

"But," said Barnabas in frowning perplexity, "I don't understand. How did he get hold of the letter?"

"Lord, sir, 'ow do I know that? But get it 'e did—'e likewise broke the seal."

"But—why?"

"Vell now, first, it's a love-letter, ain't it?"

"Why—I—"

"Werry good! Now, sir, might that theer letter be making a app'intment—come?"

"Yes, an appointment for to-morrow evening."

"Ah! In a nice, qviet, lonely place—say a vood?"

"Yes, at a very lonely place called Oakshott's Barn."

"Come, that's better and better!" nodded Mr. Shrig brightly, "that's werry pretty, that is—things is rosier than I 'oped, but then, as I said afore, things is allus blackest afore the dawn. Oakshott's Barn, eh? Ecod, now, but it sounds a nice, lonesome place—just the sort o' place for it, a—a—capital place as you might call it." And Mr. Shrig positively chuckled and rubbed his chubby hands together; but all at once, he shook his head gloomily, and glancing at Barnabas, sighed deeply. "But you—von't go, o' course, sir?"

"Go?"

"To Oakshott's Barn, to-morrow evening?"

"Yes, of course," answered Barnabas, "the appointment is for seven-thirty."

"Seven-thirty!" nodded Mr. Shrig, "and a werry nice time for it too! Sunset, it'll be about—a good light and not too long to vait till dark! Yes, seven-thirty's a werry good time for it!"

"For what?"

"V'y," said Mr. Shrig, lowering his voice suddenly, "let's say for 'it'!"

"'It,'" repeated Barnabas, staring.

"Might I jest take a peep at that theer letter, v'ere it says seven-thirty, sir?"

"Yes," said Barnabas, pointing to a certain line of Cleone's letter, "here it is!"

"Ah," exclaimed Mr. Shrig, nodding and rubbing his hands again, "your eyes is good 'uns, ain't they, sir?"

"Yes."

"Then jest take a good look at that theer seven-thirty, vill you, sir—come, vot do you see?"

"That the paper is roughened a little, and the ink has run."

"Yes, and vot else? Look at it a bit closer, sir."

"Why," said Barnabas staring hard at the spot, "it looks as though something had been scratched out!"

"And so it has, sir. If you go there at seven-thirty, it von't be a fair lady as'll be vaiting to meet you. The time's been altered o' course—jest as I 'oped and expected."

"Ah!" said Barnabas, slowly and very softly, and clenched his fist.

"So now, d'ye see, you can't go—can ye?" said Mr. Shrig in a hopeless tone.

"Yes!" said Barnabas.

"Eh? Vot—you vill?"

"Most assuredly!"

"But—but it'll be madness!" stammered Mr. Shrig, his round eyes rounder than ever, "it'll be fair asking to be made a unfort'nate wictim of, if ye go. O' course it 'ud be a good case for me, and good cases is few enough—but you mustn't go now, it 'ud be madness!"

"No," said Barnabas, frowning darkly, "because I shall go—before seven-thirty, you see."

CHAPTER LV

WHICH NARRATES SUNDRY HAPPENINGS AT OAKSHOTT'S BARN

Even on a summer's afternoon Oakshott's Barn is a desolate place, a place of shadows and solitude, whose slumberous silence is broken only by the rustle of leaves, the trill of a skylark high overhead, or the pipe of throstle and blackbird.

It is a place apart, shut out from the world of life and motion, a place suggestive of decay and degeneration, and therefore a depressing place at all times.

Yet, standing here, Barnabas smiled and uncovered his head, for here, once, SHE had stood, she who was for him the only woman in all the world. So having paused awhile to look about him, he presently went on into the gloom of the barn, a gloom damp and musty with years and decay.

Now glancing sharply this way and that, Barnabas espied a ladder or rather the mouldering remains of one, that led up from the darkest corner to a loft; up this ladder, with all due care, he mounted, and thus found himself in what had once served as a hay-loft, for in one corner there yet remained a rotting pile. It was much lighter up here, for in many places the thatch was quite gone, while at one end of the loft was a square opening or window. He was in the act of looking from this window when, all at once he started and crouched down, for, upon the stillness broke a sudden sound,—the rustling of leaves, and a voice speaking in loud, querulous tones. And in a while as he watched, screening himself from all chance of observation, Barnabas saw two figures emerge into the clearing and advance towards the barn.

"I tell you C-Chichester, it will be either him or m-me!"

"If he—condescends to fight you, my dear Ronald."

"C-condescend?" cried Barrymaine, and it needed but a glance at his flushed cheek and swaying figure to see that he had been drinking more heavily than usual. "C-condescend, damn his insolence! Condescend, will he? I'll give him no chance for his c-cursed condescension, I—I tell you, Chichester, I'll—"

"But you can't make a man fight, Ronald."

"Can't I? Why then if he won't fight I'll—"

"Hush! don't speak so loud!"

"Well, I will, Chichester,—s-so help me God, I will!"

"Will—what, Ronald?"

"W-wait and see!"

"You don't mean—murder, Ronald?"

"I didn't s-say so, d-did I?"

"Of course not, my dear Barrymaine, but—shall I take the pistols?" And Mr. Chichester stretched out his hand towards a flat, oblong box that Barrymaine carried clutched beneath his arm. "Better give them to me, Ronald."

"No,—w-why should I?"

"Well,—in your present mood—"

"I—I'm not—d-drunk,—damme, I'm not, I tell you! And I'll give the f-fellow every chance—honorable meeting."

"Then, if he refuses to fight you, as of course he will, you'll let him go to—ah—make love to Cleone?"

"No, by God!" cried Barrymaine in a sudden, wild fury, "I-I'll sh-shoot him first!"

"Kill him?"

"Yes, k-kill him!"

"Oh no you won't, Ronald, for two reasons. First of all, it would be murder—!"

"Murder!" Barrymaine repeated, "so it would—murder! Yes, by God!"

"And secondly, you haven't the nerve. Though he has clandestine meetings with your sister, though he crush you into the mud, trample you under his feet, throw you into a debtor's prison to rot out your days—though he ruin you body and soul, and compromise your sister's honor—still you'd never—murder him, Ronald, you couldn't, you haven't the heart, because it would be—murder!"

Mr. Chichester's voice was low, yet each incisive, quick-spoken word reached Barnabas, while upon Barrymaine their effect was demoniac. Dropping his pistol-case, he threw up wild arms and shook his clenched fists in the air.

"Damn him!" he cried, "damn him! B-bury me in a debtor's prison, will he? Foul my sister's honor w-will he? Never! never! I tell you I'll kill him first!"

"Murder him, Ronald?"

"Murder? I t-tell you it's no murder to kill his sort. G-give me the pistols."

"Hush! Come into the barn."

"No. W-what for?"

"Well, the time is getting on, Ronald,—nearly seven o'clock, and your ardent lovers are usually before their time. Come into the barn."

"N-no,—devilish dark hole!"

"But—he'll see you here!"

"What if he does, can't g-get away from me,—better f-for it out here—lighter."

"What do you mean? Better—for what?"

"The m-meeting."

"What—you mean to try and make him fight, do you?"

"Of course—try that way first. Give him a ch-chance, you know, —c-can't shoot him down on s-sight."

"Ah-h!" said Mr. Chichester, very slowly, "you can't shoot him on sight—of course you can't. I see."

"What? W-what d'ye see? Devilish dark hole in there!"

"All the better, Ronald,—think of his surprise when instead of finding an armful of warm loveliness waiting for him in the shadows, he finds the avenging brother! Come into the shadows, Ronald."

"All right,—yes, the shadow. Instead of the sister, the b-brother—yes, by God!"

Now the flooring of the loft where Barnabas lay was full of wide cracks and fissures, for the boards had warped by reason of many years of rain and sun; thus, lying at full length, Barnabas saw them below, Barrymaine leaning against the crumbling wall, while Mr. Chichester stooped above the open duelling-case.

"What—they're loaded are they?" said he.

"Of c-course!"

"They're handsome tools, Ronald, and with your monogram, I see!"

"Yes. Is your f-flask empty, Chichester?"

"No, I think not," answered Mr. Chichester, still stooping above the pistol in his hand.

"Then give it me, will you—m-my throat's on fire."

"Surely you 've had enough, Ronald? Did you know this flint was loose?"

"I'm n-not drunk, I t-tell you. I know when I've had enough, g-give me some brandy, Chit, I know there's p-precious little left."

"Why then, fix this flint first, Ronald, I see you have all the necessary tools here." So saying, Mr. Chichester rose and began feeling through his pockets, while Barrymaine, grumbling, stooped above the pistol-case. Then, even as he did so, Mr. Chichester drew out a silver flask, unscrewed it, and thereafter made a certain quick, stealthy gesture behind his companion's back, which done, he screwed up the flask again, shook it, and, as Barrymaine rose, held it out to him:

"Yes, I'm afraid there's very little left, Ronald," said he. With a murmur of thanks Barrymaine took the flask and, setting it to his lips, drained it at a gulp, and handed it back.

"Gad, Chichester!" he exclaimed, "it tastes damnably of the f-flask—faugh! What time is it?"

"A quarter to seven!"

"Th-three quarters of an hour to wait!"

"It will soon pass, Ronald, besides, he's sure to be early."

"Hope so! But I—I think I'll s-sit down."

"Well, the floor's dry, though dirty."

"D-dirty? So it is, but beggars can't be c-choosers and—dev'lish drowsy place, this!—I'm a b-beggar—you know t-that, and—pah! I think I'm l-losing my—taste for brandy—"

"Really, Ronald? I've thought you seemed over fond of it—especially lately."

"No—no!" answered Barrymaine, speaking in a thick, indistinct voice and rocking unsteadily upon his heels, "I'm not—n-not drunk, only—dev'lish sleepy!" and swaying to the wall he leaned there with head drooping.

"Then you'd better—lie down, Ronald."

"Yes, I'll—lie down, dev'lish—drowsy p-place—lie down," mumbled Barrymaine, suiting the action to the word; yet after lying down full length, he must needs struggle up to his elbow again to blink at Mr. Chichester, heavy eyed and with one hand to his wrinkling brow. "Wha-what w-was it we—came for? Oh y-yes—I know—Bev'ley, of course! You'll w-wake me—when he c-comes?"

"I'll wake you, Ronald."

"S-such a c-cursed—drowsy—" Barrymaine sank down upon his side, rolled over upon his back, threw wide his arms, and so lay, breathing stertorously.

Then Mr. Chichester smiled, and coming beside him, looked down upon his helpless form and flushed face and, smiling still, spoke in his soft, gentle voice:

"Are you asleep, Ronald?" he inquired, and stirred Barrymaine lightly with his foot, but, feeling him so helpless, the stirring foot grew slowly more vicious. "Oh Ronald," he murmured, "what a fool you are! what a drunken, sottish fool you are. So you'd give him a chance, would you? Ah, but you mustn't, Ronald, you shan't, for your sake and my sake. My hand is steadier than yours, so sleep, my dear Ronald, and wake to find that you have rid us of our good, young Samaritan—once and for all, and then—hey for Cleone, and no more dread of the Future. Sleep on, you swinish sot!"

Mr. Chichester's voice was as soft as ever, but, as he turned away, the sleeping youth started and groaned beneath the sudden movement of that vicious foot.

And now Mr. Chichester stooped, and taking the pistols, one by one, examined flint and priming with attentive eye, which done, he crossed to a darkened window and, bursting open the rotting shutter, knelt and levelled one of the weapons, steadying his wrist upon the sill; then, nodding as though satisfied, he laid the pistols upon the floor within easy reach, and drew out his watch.

Slowly the sun declined, and slowly the shadows lengthened about Oakshott's Barn, as they had done many and many a time before; a rabbit darted across the clearing, a blackbird called to his mate in the thicket, but save for this, nothing stirred; a great quiet was upon the place, a stillness so profound that Barnabas could distinctly hear the scutter of a rat in the shadows behind him, and the slow, heavy breathing of the sleeper down below. And ever that crouching figure knelt beside the broken shutter, very silent, very still, and very patient.

But all at once, as he watched, Barnabas saw the rigid figure grow suddenly alert, saw the right arm raised slowly, stealthily, saw the pistol gleam as it was levelled across the sill; for now, upon the quiet rose a sound faint and far, yet that grew and ever grew, the on-coming rustle of leaves.

Then, even as Barnabas stared down wide-eyed, the rigid figure started, the deadly pistol-hand wavered, was snatched back, and Mr. Chichester leapt to his feet. He stood a moment hesitating as one at a sudden loss, then crossing to the unconscious form of Barrymaine, he set the pistol under his lax hand, turned, and vanished into the shadow.

Thereafter, from the rear of the barn, came the sound of a blow and the creak of a rusty hinge, quickly followed by a rustle of leaves that grew fainter and fainter, and so was presently gone. Then Barnabas rose, and coming to the window, peered cautiously out, and there, standing before the barn surveying its dilapidation with round, approving eyes, his nobbly stick beneath his arm, his high-crowned, broad-brimmed hat upon his head, was Mr. Shrig.

CHAPTER LVI

OF THE GATHERING OF THE SHADOWS

Surprise and something very like disappointment were in Mr. Shrig's look as Barnabas stepped out from the yawning doorway of the barn.

"V'y, sir," said he, consulting a large-faced watch. "V'y, Mr. Beverley, it's eggs-actly twenty minutes arter the time for it!"

"Yes," said Barnabas.

"And you—ain't shot, then?"

"No, thank heaven."

"Nor even—vinged?"

"Nor even winged, Mr. Shrig."

"Fate," said Mr. Shrig, shaking a dejected head at him, "Fate is a werry wexed problem, sir! 'Ere's you now, Number Three, as I might say, the unfort'nate wictim as was to be—'ere you are a-valking up to Fate axing to be made a corp', and vot do you get? not so much as a scrat—not a westige of a scrat, v'ile another unfort'nate wictim vill run avay from Fate, run? ah! 'eaven's 'ard! and werry nat'ral too! and vot does 'e get? 'e gets made a corp' afore 'e knows it. No, sir, Fate's a werry wexed problem, sir, and I don't understand it, no, nor ever shall."

"But this was very simple," said Barnabas, slipping his hand in Mr. Shrig's arm, and leading him away from the barn, "very simple indeed, I got here before they came, and hid in the loft. Then, while they were waiting for me down below, you came and frightened them away."

"Ah! So they meant business, did they?"

"Yes," said Barnabas, nodding grimly, "they certainly meant business, —especially Mr. Chich—"

"Ssh!" said Mr. Shrig, glancing round, "call 'im Number Two. Sir, Number Two is a extra-special, super-fine, over-weight specimen, 'e is. I've knowed a many 'Capitals' in my time, but I never knowed such a Capital o' Capital Coves as 'im. Sir, Vistling Dick vas a innercent, smiling babe, and young B. is a snowy, pet lamb alongside o' Number Two. Capital Coves like 'im only 'appen, and they only 'appen every thousand year or so. Ecod! I 'm proud o' Number Two. And talking of 'im, I 'appened to call on Nick the Cobbler, last night."

"Oh?"

"Ah! and I found 'im vith 'is longest awl close 'andy—all on account o' Number Two."

"How on his account?" demanded Barnabas, frowning suddenly.

"Vell, last evening, Milo o' Crotona, a pal o' Nick's, and a werry promising bye 'e is too, 'appened to drop in sociable-like, and it seems as Number Two followed 'im. And werry much Number Two frightened that 'andsome gal, by all accounts. She wrote you a letter, vich she give me to deliver, and—'ere it is."

So Barnabas took the letter and broke the seal. It was a very short letter, but as he read Barnabas frowned blacker than ever.

"Mr. Shrig," said he very earnestly as he folded and pocketed the letter, "will you do something for me—will you take a note to my servant, John Peterby? You'll find him at the 'Oak and Ivy' in Hawkhurst village."

"Vich, seeing as you're a pal, sir, I vill. But, sir," continued Mr. Shrig, as Barnabas scribbled certain instructions for Peterby on a page of his memorandum, "vot about yourself—you ain't a-going back there, are ye?" and he jerked his thumb over his shoulder towards the barn, now some distance behind them.

"Of course," said Barnabas, "to keep my appointment."

"D'ye think it's safe—now?"

"Quite,—thanks to you," answered Barnabas. "Here is the note, and if you wish, John Peterby will drive you back to London with him."

"V'y, thank'ee sir,—'e shall that,—but you, now?" Mr. Shrig paused, and, somewhat diffidently drew from his side pocket a very business-like, brass-bound pistol, which he proffered to Barnabas, "jest in case they should 'appen to come back, sir," said he.

But Barnabas laughingly declined it, and shook his chubby hand instead.

"Vell," said Mr. Shrig, pocketing note and weapon, "you're true game, sir, yes, game's your breed, and I only 'ope as you don't give me a case—though good murder cases is few and far between, as I've told you afore. Good-by, sir, and good luck."

So saying, Mr. Shrig nodded, touched the broad rim of his castor, and strode away through the gathering shadows.

And when he was gone, and the sound of his going had died away in the distance, Barnabas turned and swiftly retraced his steps; but now he went with fists clenched, and head forward, as one very much on the alert.

Evening was falling and the shadows were deepening apace, and as he went, Barnabas kept ever in the shelter of the trees until he saw before him once more, the desolate and crumbling barn of Oakshott. For a moment he paused, eyeing its scarred and battered walls narrowly, then, stepping quickly forward, entered the gloomy doorway and, turning towards a certain spot, started back before the threatening figure that rose up from the shadows.

"Ah! So you 've c-come at last, sir!" said Barrymaine, steadying himself against the wall with one hand while he held the pistol levelled in the other, "ins-stead of the weak s-sister you find the avenging brother! Been waiting for you hours. C-cursed dreary hole this, and I fell asleep, but—"

"Because you were drugged!" said Barnabas.

"D-drugged, sir! W-what d' you mean?"

"Chichester drugged the brandy—"

"Chichester?"

"He meant to murder me while you slept and fix the crime on you—"

"Liar!" cried Barrymaine, "you came here to meet my s-sister, but instead of a defenceless girl you meet me and I'm g-going to settle with you—once and for all—t-told you I would, last time we met. There's another pistol in the c-case yonder—pick it up and t-take your ground."

"Listen to me," Barnabas began.

"N-not a word—you're going to fight me—"

"Never!"

"Pick up that pistol—or I'll sh-shoot you where you stand!"

"No!"

"I'll c-count three!" said Barrymaine, his pale face livid against the darkness behind, "One! Two!—"

But, on the instant, Barnabas sprang in and closed with him, and, grappled in a fierce embrace, they swayed a moment and staggered out through the gaping doorway.

Barrymaine fought desperately. Barnabas felt his coat rip and tear, but he maintained his grip upon his opponent's pistol hand, yet twice the muzzle of the weapon covered him, and twice he eluded it before Barrymaine could fire. Therefore, seeing Barrymaine's intention, reading his deadly purpose in vicious mouth and dilated nostril, Barnabas loosed one hand, drew back his arm, and smote—swift and hard. Barrymaine uttered a cry that seemed to Barnabas to find an echo far off, flung out his arms and, staggering, fell.

Then Barnabas picked up the pistol and, standing over Barrymaine, spoke.

"I—had to—do it!" he panted. "Did I—hurt you much?"

But Ronald Barrymaine lay very white and still, and, stooping, Barnabas saw that he had struck much harder than he had meant, and that Barrymaine's mouth was cut and bleeding.

Now at this moment, even as he sank on his knees, Barnabas again heard a cry, but nearer now and with the rustle of flying draperies, and, glancing up, saw Cleone running towards them.

"Cleone!" he cried, and sprang to his feet.

"You—struck him!" she panted.

"I—yes, I—had to! But indeed he isn't much hurt—" But Cleone was down upon her knees, had lifted Barrymaine's head to her bosom and was wiping the blood from his pale face with her handkerchief.

"Cleone," said Barnabas, humbly, "I—indeed I—couldn't help it. Oh, Cleone—look up!" Yet, while he spoke, there came a rustling of leaves near by and glancing thither, he saw Mr. Chichester surveying them, smiling and debonair, and, striding forward, Barnabas confronted him with scowling brow and fierce, menacing eyes.

"Rogue!" said he, his lips curling, "Rascal!"

"Ah!" nodded Mr. Chichester gently, "you have a pistol there, I see!"

"Your despicable villainy is known!" said Barnabas. "Ha!—smile if you will, but while you knelt, pistol in hand, in the barn there, had you troubled to look in the loft above your head you might have murdered me, and none the wiser. As it is, I am alive, to strip you of your heritage, and you still owe me twenty thousand guineas. Pah! keep them to help you from the country, for I swear you shall be hounded from every club in London; men shall know you for what you are. Now go, before you tempt me to strangle you for a nauseous beast. Go, I say!"

Smiling still, but with a devil looking from his narrowed eyes, Mr. Chichester slowly viewed Barnabas from head to foot, and, turning, strolled away, swinging his tasselled walking cane as he went, with Barnabas close behind him, pistol in hand, even as they had once walked months before.

Now at this moment it was that Cleone, yet kneeling beside Barrymaine, chanced to espy a crumpled piece of paper that lay within a yard of her, and thus, half unwitingly, she reached out and took it up, glanced at it with vague eyes, then started, and knitting her black brows, read these words:

My Dear Barnabas,—The beast has discovered me.
I thought I only scorned him, but now I know I fear him,
too. So, in my dread, I turn to you. Yes, I will go now—
anywhere you wish. Fear has made me humble, and I
accept your offer. Oh, take me away—hide me, anywhere,
so shall I always be

Your grateful,
CLEMENCY.

Thus, in a while, when Barrymaine opened his eyes it was to see Cleone kneeling beside him with bent head, and with both hands clasped down upon her bosom, fierce hands that clenched a crumpled paper between them. At first he thought she was weeping, but, when she turned towards him, he saw that her eyes were tearless and very bright, and that on either cheek burned a vivid patch of color.

"Oh, Ronald!" she sighed, her lips quivering suddenly, "I—am glad you are better—but—oh, my dear, I wish I—were dead!"

"There, there, Clo!" he muttered, patting her stooping shoulder, "I f-frightened you, I suppose. But I'm all right now, dear. W-where's Chichester?"

"I—don't know, Ronald."

"But you, Cleone? You came here to m-meet this—this Beverley?"

"Yes, Ronald."

"D'you know w-what he is? D'you know he's a publican's son?—a vile, low fellow masquerading as a g-gentleman? Yes, he's a p-publican's son, I tell you!" he repeated, seeing how she shrank at this. "And you s-stoop to such as he—s-stoop to meet him in s-such a place as this! So I came to save you f-from yourself!"

"Did you, Ronald?"

"Yes—but oh, Cleone, you don't love the fellow, do you?"

"I think I—hate him, Ronald."

"Then you won't m-meet him again?"

"No, Ronald."

"And you'll try to be a little kinder—to C-Chichester?" Cleone shivered and rose to her feet.

"Come!" said she, her hands once more clasped upon her bosom, "it grows late, I must go."

"Yes. D-devilish depressing place this! G-give me your arm, Clo." But as they turned to go, the bushes parted, and Barnabas appeared.

"Cleone!" he exclaimed.

"I—I'm going home!" she said, not looking at him.

"Then I will come with you,—if I may?"

"I had rather go—alone—with my brother."

"So pray s-stand aside, sir!" said Barrymaine haughtily through his swollen lips, staggering a little despite Cleone's arm.

"Sir," said Barnabas pleadingly, "I struck you a while ago, but it was the only way to save you from—a greater evil, as you know—"

"He means I threatened to s-shoot him, Clo—so I did, but it was for your sake, to sh-shield you from—persecution as a brother should."

"Cleone," said Barnabas, ignoring Barrymaine altogether, "if there is any one in this world who should know me, and what manner of man I am, surely it is you—"

"Yes, she knows you—b-better than you think, she knows you for a publican's son, first of all—"

"May I come with you, Cleone?"

"No, sir, n-not while I'm here. Cleone, you go with him, or m-me, so—choose!"

"Oh, Ronald, take me home!" she breathed.

So Barrymaine drew her arm through his and, turning his back on Barnabas, led her away. But, when they had gone a little distance, he frowned suddenly and came striding after them.

"Cleone," said he, "why are you so strange to me,—what is it, —speak to me."

But Cleone was dumb, and walked on beside Ronald Barrymaine with head averted, and so with never a backward glance, was presently lost to sight among the leaves.

Long after they had gone, Barnabas stood there, his head bowed, while the shadows deepened about him, dark and darker. Then all at once he sighed again and, lifting his head, glanced about him; and because of the desolation of the place, he shivered; and because of the new, sharp pain that gripped him, he uttered a bitter curse, and so, becoming aware of the pistol he yet grasped, he flung it far from him and strode away through the deepening gloom.

On he went, heeding only the tumult of sorrow and anger that surged within him. And so, betimes, reached the "Oak and Ivy" inn, where, finding Peterby and the phaeton already gone, according to his instructions, he hired post-horses and galloped away for London.

Now, as he went, though the evening was fine, it seemed to him that high overhead was a shadow that followed and kept pace with him, growing dark and ever darker; and thus as he rode he kept his gaze upon this menacing shadow.

As for my lady, she, securely locked within the sanctuary of her chamber, took pen and paper and wrote these words:

"You have destroyed my faith, and with that all else. Farewell."

Which done, she stamped a small, yet vicious foot upon a certain crumpled letter, and thereafter, lying face down upon her bed, wept hot, slow, bitter tears, stifling her sobs with the tumbled glory of her hair, and in her heart was an agony greater than any she had ever known.

CHAPTER LVII

BEING A PARENTHETICAL CHAPTER ON DOUBT, WHICH, THOUGH UNINTERESTING, IS VERY SHORT

It will perhaps be expected that, owing to this unhappy state of affairs, Barnabas should have found sleep a stranger to his pillow; but, on the contrary, reaching London at daybreak, he went to bed, and there, wearied by his long ride, found a blessed oblivion from all his cares and sorrows. Nor did he wake till the day was far spent and evening at hand. But, with returning consciousness came Memory to harrow him afresh, came cold Pride and glowing Anger. And with these also was yet another emotion, and one that he had never known till now, whose name is Doubt; doubt of himself and of his future—that deadly foe to achievement and success—that ghoul-like incubus which, once it fastens on a man, seldom leaves him until courage, and hope, and confidence are dead, and nothing remains but a foreknowledge and expectation of failure.

With this grisly spectre at his elbow Barnabas rose and dressed, and went downstairs to make a pretence of breaking his fast.

"Sir," said Peterby, watching how he sat staring down moodily at the table, "sir, you eat nothing."

"No, John, I'm not hungry," he answered, pushing his plate aside. "By the way, did you find the cottage I mentioned in my note? Though, indeed, you've had very little time."

"Yes, sir, I found one just beyond Lewisham, small, though comfortable. Here is the key, sir."

"Thank you, John," said Barnabas, and thereafter sat staring gloomily at the key until Peterby spoke again:

"Sir, pray forgive me, but I fear you are in some trouble. Is it your misunderstanding with Viscount Devenham? I couldn't help but overhear, and—"

"Ah, yes—even the Viscount has quarrelled with me," sighed Barnabas, "next it will be the Marquis, I suppose, and after him—Gad, John Peterby—I shall have only you left!"

"Indeed, sir, you will always have me—always!"

"Yes, John, I think I shall."

"Sir, when you—gave a miserable wretch another chance to live and be a man, you were young and full of life."

"Yes, I was very, very young!" sighed Barnabas.

"But you were happy—your head was high and your eye bright with confident hope and purpose."

"Yes, I was very confident, John."

"And therefore—greatly successful, sir. Your desire was to cut a figure in the Fashionable World. Well, to-day you have your wish—to-day you are famous, and yet—"

"Well, John?"

"Sir, to-day I fear you are—not happy."

"No, I'm not happy," sighed Barnabas, "for oh! John Peterby, what shall it profit a man though he gain the whole world, and lose his soul!"

"Ah, sir—you mean—?"

"I mean—the Lady Cleone, John. Losing her, I lose all, and success is worse than failure."

"But, sir,—must you lose her?"

"I fear so. Who am I that she should stoop to me among so many? Who am I to expect so great happiness?"

"Sir," said Peterby, shaking his head, "I have never known you doubt yourself or fortune till now!"

"It never occurred to me, John."

"And because of this unshaken confidence in yourself you won the steeplechase, sir—unaided and alone you won for yourself a place in the most exclusive circles in the World of Fashion—without friends or influence you achieved the impossible, because you never doubted."

"Yes, I was very confident, John, but then, you see, I never thought anything impossible—till now."

"And therefore you succeeded, sir. But had you constantly doubted your powers and counted failure even as a possibility, you might still have dreamed of your success—but never achieved it."

"Why then," sighed Barnabas, rising, "it seems that Failure has marked me for her own at last, for never was man fuller of doubt than I."

CHAPTER LVIII

HOW VISCOUNT DEVENHAM FOUND HIM A VISCOUNTESS

Night was falling as, turning out of St. James's Square, Barnabas took his way along Charles Street and so, by way of the Strand, towards Blackfriars. He wore a long, befrogged surtout buttoned up to the chin, though the weather was warm, and his hat was drawn low over his brows; also in place of his tasselled walking-cane he carried a heavy stick.

For the first half mile or so he kept his eyes well about him, but, little by little, became plunged in frowning thought, and so walked on, lost in gloomy abstraction. Thus, as he crossed Blackfriars Bridge he was quite unaware of one who followed him step by step, though upon the other side of the way; a gliding, furtive figure, and one who also went with coat buttoned high and face hidden beneath shadowy hat-brim.

On strode Barnabas, all unconscious, with his mind ever busied with thoughts of Cleone and the sudden, unaccustomed doubt in himself and his future that had come upon him.

Presently he turned off to the right along a dirty street of squalid, tumble-down houses; a narrow, ill-lighted street which, though comparatively quiet by day, now hummed with a dense and seething life.

Yes, a dark street this, with here and there a flickering lamp, that served but to make the darkness visible, and here and there the lighted window of some gin-shop, or drinking-cellar, whence proceeded a mingled clamor of voices roaring the stave of some song, or raised in fierce disputation.

On he went, past shambling figures indistinct in the dusk; past figures that slunk furtively aside, or crouched to watch him from the gloom of some doorway; past ragged creatures that stared, haggard-eyed; past faces sad and faces evil that flitted by him in the dark, or turned to scowl over hunching shoulders. Therefore Barnabas gripped his stick the tighter as he strode along, suddenly conscious of the stir and unseen movement in the fetid air about him, of the murmur of voices, the desolate wailing of children, the noise of drunken altercation, and all the sordid sounds that were part and parcel of the place. Of all this Barnabas was heedful, but he was wholly unaware of the figure that dogged him from behind, following him step by step, patient and persistent. Thus, at last, Barnabas reached a certain narrow alley, beyond which was the River, dark, mysterious, and full of sighs and murmurs. And, being come to the door of Nick the Cobbler, he knocked upon it with his stick.

It was opened, almost immediately, by Clemency herself.

"I saw you coming," she said, giving him her hand, and so led him through the dark little shop, into the inner room.

"I came as soon as I could. Clemency."

"Yes, I knew you would come," she answered, with bowed head.

"I am here to take you away to a cottage I have found for you—a place in the country, where you will be safe until I can find and bring your father to you."

As he ended, she lifted her head and looked at him through gathering tears.

"How good—how kind of you!" she said, very softly, "and oh, I thank you, indeed I do—but—"

"But, Clemency?"

"I must stay—here."

"In this awful place! Why?"

Clemency flushed, and looking down at the table, began to pleat a fold in the cloth with nervous fingers.

"Poor little Nick hasn't been very well lately, and I—can't leave him alone—" she began.

"Then bring him with you."

"And," she continued slowly, "when I wrote you that letter I was—greatly afraid, but I'm—not afraid any longer. And oh, I couldn't leave London yet—I couldn't!"

Now while she spoke, Barnabas saw her clasp and wring her hands together, that eloquent gesture he remembered so well. Therefore he leaned across the table and touched those slender fingers very gently.

"Why not? Tell me your trouble, my sister."

Now Clemency bowed her dark head, and when she spoke her voice was low and troubled: "Because—he is ill—dangerously ill, Milo tells me, and I—I am nearer to him here in London. I can go, sometimes, and look at the house where he lies. So you see, I cannot leave him, yet."

"Then—you love him, Clemency?"

"Yes," she whispered, "yes, oh yes, always—always! That was why I ran away from him. Oh, I love him so much that I grew afraid of my love, and of myself, and of him. Because he is a great gentleman, and I am only—what I am."

"A very good and beautiful woman!" said Barnabas.

"Beauty!" she sighed, "oh, it is only for that he—wanted me, and dear heaven! I love him so much that—if he asked me—I fear—" and she hid her burning face in hands that trembled.

"Clemency!"

The word was hoarse and low, scarcely more than a whisper, but, even so, Clemency started and lifted her head to stare wide-eyed at the figure leaning in the doorway, with one hand outstretched to her appealingly; a tall figure, cloaked from head to foot, with hat drawn low over his brows, his right arm carried in a sling. And as she gazed, Clemency uttered a low, soft cry, and rose to her feet.

"My Lord!" she whispered, "oh, my Lord!"

"Dearest!"

The Viscount stepped into the room and, uncovering his head, sank upon his knees before her.

"Oh, Clemency," said he, "the door was open and I heard it all—every word. But, dearest, you need never fear me any more—never any more, because I love you. Clemency, and here, upon my knees, beg you to honor me by—marrying me, if you will stoop to such a pitiful thing as I am. Clemency dear, I have been ill, and it has taught me many things, and I know now that I—cannot live without you. So, Clemency, if you will take pity on me—oh! Clemency—!"

The Viscount stopped, still kneeling before her with bent head, nor did he look up or attempt to touch her as he waited her answer.

Then, slowly, she reached out and stroked that bowed and humble head, and, setting her hands upon his drooping shoulders, she sank to her knees before him, so that now he could look into the glowing beauty of her face and behold the deep, yearning tenderness of her eyes.

"Dear," said she very gently, "dear, if you—want me so much you have only to—take me!"

"For my Viscountess, Clemency!"

"For your—wife, dear!"

And now, beholding their great happiness, Barnabas stole from the room, closing the door softly behind him.

Then, being only human, he sighed deeply and pitied himself mightily by contrast.

CHAPTER LIX

WHICH RELATES, AMONG OTHER THINGS, HOW BARNABAS LOST HIS HAT

Now as Barnabas stood thus, he heard another sigh, and glancing up beheld Mr. Shrig seated at the little Cobbler's bench, with a guttering candle at his elbow and a hat upon his fist, which he appeared to be examining with lively interest.

"Sir," said he, as Barnabas approached, wondering, "I'm taking the liberty o' looking at your castor."

"Oh!" said Barnabas.

"Sir, it's a werry good 'at as 'ats go, but it's no kind of an 'at for you to-night."

"And why not, Mr. Shrig?"

"Because it ain't much pertection ag'in windictiveness—in the shape of a bludgeon, shall ve say, and as for a brick—v'y, Lord! And theer's an uncommon lot of windictiveness about to-night; it's a-vaiting for you—as you might say—round the corner."

"Really, Mr. Shrig, I'm afraid I don't understand you."

"Sir, d' ye mind a cove o' the name o' 'Vistling Dick,' as got 'isself kicked to death by an 'orse?"

"Yes."

"And d' ye mind another cove commonly known as 'Dancing Jimmy,' and another on 'em as is called 'Bunty Fagan'?"

"Yes, they tried to rob me once."

"Right, sir,—only I scared 'em off, you'll remember. Conseqvently, p'r'aps you ain't forgot certain other coves as you and me had a bit of a turn-up vith v'en I sez to you 'Run,' and you sez to me 'No,' and got a lump on your sconce like an 'ard-biled egg according?"

"Yes, I remember of course, but why—"

"Sir, they 're all on 'em out on the windictive lay again to-night, —only, this time, it's you they 're arter."

"Me—are you sure?"

"And sartin! Corporal Richard Roe, late Grenadiers, give me the office, and Corporal Richard's never wrong, sir. Corporal Dick's my pal as keeps the 'Gun' in Gray's Inn Lane, you may remember, and the 'Gun' 's a famous chaffing-crib for the flash, leary coves. So, v'en the Corp tipped me the vord, sir, I put my castor on my sconce, slipped a barker in my cly, took my stick in my fib—or as you might say 'daddle,' d' ye see, and toddled over to keep a ogle on you. And, sir, if it hadn't been for the young gent as shadowed ye all the way to Giles's Rents, it's my opinion as they'd ha' done you into a corp as you come along."

"But why should they want to do for me?"

"V'y, sir, they'd do for their own mothers, j'yful, if you paid 'em to!"

"But who would employ such a gang?"

"Vell, sir, naming no names, there's a party as I suspect from conclusions as I've drawed, a party as I'm a-going to try to ketch this here werry night, sir—as I mean to ketch in flay-grant de-lick-too, vich is a law term meaning—in the werry act, sir, if you'll help me?"

"Of course I will," said Barnabas, a little eagerly, "but how?"

"By doing eggs-actly as I tell you, sir. Is it a go?"

"It is," nodded Barnabas.

"V'y, then, to begin vith, that theer coat o' yours,—it's too long to run in—off vith it, sir!"

Barnabas smiled, but off came the long, befrogged surtout.

"Now—my castor, sir" and Mr. Shrig handed Barnabas his famous hat. "Put it on, sir, if you please. You'll find it a bit 'eavyish at first, maybe, but it's werry good ag'in windictiveness."

"Thank you," said Barnabas, smiling again, "but it's too small, you see."

"That's a pity!" sighed Mr. Shrig, "still, if it von't go on, it von't. Now, as to a vepping?"

"I have my stick," said Barnabas, holding it up. Mr. Shrig took it, balanced it in his grasp and passed it back with a nod of approval.

"V'y then, sir, I think ve may wenture," said he, and rising, put on his hat, examined the priming of the brass-bound pistol, and taking the nobbly stick under his arm, blew out the candle and crossed to the door; yet, being there, paused. "Sir," said he, a note of anxiety in his voice, "you promise to do eggs-actly vot I say?"

"I promise!"

"Ven I say 'run' you'll run?"

"Yes."

"Then come on, sir, and keep close behind me."

So saying, Mr. Shrig opened the door and stepped noisily out into the narrow court and waited while Barnabas fastened the latch; even then he paused to glance up at the sombre heaven and to point out a solitary star that twinkled through some rift in the blackness above.

"Going to be a fine night for a little walk," said he, "Oliver vill be in town later on."

"Oliver?" inquired Barnabas.

"Ah! that's flash for the moon, sir. Jest a nice light there'll be. This vay, sir." With the words Mr. Shrig turned sharp to his left along the alley towards the River.

"Why this way, Mr. Shrig?"

"First, sir, because they're a-vaiting for you at t'other end o' the alley, and second, because v'en they see us go this vay they'll think they've got us sure and sartin, and follow according, and third, because at a certain place along by the River I've left Corporal Dick and four o' my specials, d'ye see. S-sh! Qviet now! Oblige me with your castor—your 'at, sir."

Wonderingly, Barnabas handed him the article in question, whereupon Mr. Shrig, setting it upon the end of the nobbly stick, began to advance swiftly where the shadow lay blackest, and with an added caution, motioning to Barnabas to do the like.

They were close upon the River now, so close that Barnabas could hear it lapping against the piles, and catch the indefinable reek of it. But on they went, swift and silent, creeping ever in the gloom of the wall beside them, nearer and nearer until presently the River flowed before them, looming darker than the dark, and its sullen murmur was all about them; until Mr. Shrig, stopping all at once, raised the hat upon his stick and thrust it slowly, inch by inch, round the angle of the wall. And lo! even as Barnabas watched with bated breath, suddenly it was gone—struck away into space by an unseen weapon, and all in an instant it seemed, came a vicious oath, a snarl from Mr. Shrig, the thud of a blow, and a dim shape staggered sideways and sinking down at the base of the wall lay very silent and very still.

"Run!" cried Mr. Shrig, and away he went beside the River, holding a tortuous course among the piles of rotting lumber, dexterously avoiding dim-seen obstacles, yet running with a swiftness wonderful to behold. All at once he stopped and glanced about him.

"What now?" inquired Barnabas.

"S-sh! d'ye 'ear anything, sir?"

Sure enough, from the darkness behind, came a sound there was no mistaking, the rush and patter of pursuing feet, and the feet were many.

"Are we to fight here?" demanded Barnabas, buttoning his coat.

"No, not yet, sir. Ah! there's Oliver—told you it vould be a fine night. This vay, sir!" And turning to the left again, Mr. Shrig led the way down a narrow passage. Half-way along this dim alley he paused, and seating himself upon a dim step, fell to mopping his brow.

"A extra-special capital place, this, sir!" said he. "Bankside's good enough for a capital job, but this is better, ah, a sight better! Many a unfort'nate wictim has been made a corp' of, hereabouts, sir!"

"Yes," said Barnabas shivering, for the air struck chill and damp, "but what do we do now?"

"V'y, sir, I'll tell you. Ve sit here, nice and qviet and let 'em run on till they meet my four specials and Corporal Richard Roe, late Grenadiers. My specials has their staves and knows how to use 'em, and the Corp has 's 'ook,—and an 'ook ain't no-vise pleasant as a vepping. So, ven they come running back, d' ye see, theer's you vith your stick, an' me vith my barker, an' so ve 'ave 'em front and rear."

"But can we stop them—all?"

"Ah!" nodded Mr. Shrig, "all as the Corp 'as left of 'em. Ye see they know me, most on 'em, and likevise they knows as v'en I pull a barker from my cly that theer barker don't miss fire. Vot's more, they must come as far as this passage or else drownd theirselves in the River, vich vould save a lot o' trouble and expense, and—s-sh!"

He broke off abruptly and rose to his feet, and Barnahas saw that he held the brass-bound pistol in his hand. Then, as they stood listening, plain and more plain was the pad-pad of running feet that raced up to the mouth of the alley where they stood—past it, and so died down again. Hereupon Mr. Shrig took out his large-faced watch and, holding it close to his eyes, nodded.

"In about vun minute they'll run up ag'in the Corp," said he, "and a precious ugly customer they'll find him, not to mention my specials—ve'll give 'em another two minutes." Saying which, Mr. Shrig reseated himself upon the dim step, watch in hand. "Sir," he continued, "I'm sorry about your 'at—sich a werry good 'at, too! But it 'ad to be yours or mine, and sir,—axing your pardon, but there's a good many 'ats to be 'ad in London jest as good as yourn, for them as can afford 'em, but theer ain't another castor like mine—no, not in the U-nited Kingdom."

"Very true," nodded Barnabas, "and no hat ever could have had a more—useful end, than mine."

"V'y yes, sir—better your castor than your sconce any day," said Mr. Shrig, "and now I think it's about time for us to—wenture forth. But, sir," he added impressively, "if the conclusion as I've drawed is correct, theer's safe to be shooting if you're recognized, so keep in the shadder o' the wall, d' ye see. Now, are ye ready?—keep behind me—so. Here they come, I think."

Somewhere along the dark River hoarse cries arose, and the confused patter of running feet that drew rapidly louder and more distinct. Nearer they came until Barnahas could hear voices that panted out fierce curses; also he heard Mr. Shrig's pistol click as it was cocked.

So, another minute dragged by and then, settling his broad-brimmed hat more firmly, Mr. Shrig sprang nimbly from his lurking-place and fronted the on-comers with levelled weapon:

"Stand!" he cried, "stand—in the King's name!"

By the feeble light of the moon, Barnabas made out divers figures who, checking their career, stood huddled together some yards away, some scowling at the threatening posture of Mr. Shrig, others glancing back over their shoulders towards the dimness behind, whence came a shrill whistle and the noise of pursuit.

"Ah, you may look!" cried Mr. Shrig, "but I've got ye, my lambs—all on ye! You, Bunty Fagan, and Dancing Jimmy, I know you, and you know me, so stand—all on ye. The first man as moves I'll shoot—stone dead, and v'en I says a thing I—"

A sudden, blinding flash, a deafening report, and, dropping his pistol, Mr. Shrig groaned and staggered up against the wall. But Barnabas was ready and, as their assailants rushed, met them with whirling stick.

It was desperate work, but Barnabas was in the mood for it, answering blow with blow, and shout with shout.

"Oh, Jarsper!" roared a distant voice, "we're coming. Hold 'em, Jarsper!"

So Barnabas struck, and parried, and struck, now here, now there, advancing and retreating by turns, until the flailing stick splintered in his grasp, and he was hurled back to the wall and borne to his knees. Twice he struggled up, but was beaten down again, —down and down into a choking blackness that seemed full of griping hands and cruel, trampling feet.

Faint and sick, dazed with his hurts, Barnabas rose to his knees and so, getting upon unsteady feet, sought to close with one who threatened him with upraised bludgeon, grasped at an arm, missed, felt a stunning shock,—staggered back and back with the sounds of the struggle ever fainter to his failing senses, tripped, and falling heavily, rolled over upon his back, and so lay still.

CHAPTER LX

WHICH TELLS OF A RECONCILIATION

"Oh, Lord God of the weary and heavy-hearted, have mercy upon me! Oh, Father of the Sorrowful, suffer now that I find rest!"

Barnabas opened his eyes and stared up at a cloudless heaven where rode the moon, a silver sickle; and gazing thither, he remembered that some one had predicted a fine night later, and vaguely wondered who it might have been.

Not a sound reached him save the slumberous murmur that the River made lapping lazily against the piles, and Barnabas sighed and closed his eyes again.

But all at once, upon this quiet, came words spoken near by, in a voice low and broken, and the words were these:

"Oh, Lord of Pity, let now thy mercy lighten upon me, suffer that I come to Thee this hour, for in Thee is my trust. Take back my life, oh, Father, for, without hope, life is a weary burden, and Death, a boon. But if I needs must live on, give me some sign that I may know. Oh, Lord of Pity, hear me!"

The voice ceased and, once again, upon the hush stole the everlasting whisper of the River. Then, clear and sharp, there broke another sound, the oncoming tread of feet; soft, deliberate feet they were, which yet drew ever nearer and nearer while Barnabas, staring up dreamily at the moon, began to count their steps. Suddenly they stopped altogether, and Barnabas, lying there, waited for them to go on again; but in a while, as the silence remained unbroken, he sighed and turning his throbbing head saw a figure standing within a yard of him.

"Sir," said Mr. Chichester, coming nearer and smiling down at prostrate Barnabas, "this is most thoughtful—most kind of you. I have been hoping to meet you again, more especially since our last interview, and now, to find you awaiting me at such an hour, in such a place,—remote from all chances of disturbance, and—with the River so very convenient too! Indeed, you couldn't have chosen a fitter place, and I am duly grateful."

Saying which, Mr. Chichester seated himself upon the mouldering remains of an ancient wherry, and slipped one hand into the bosom of his coat.

"Sir," said he, leaning towards Barnabas, "you appear to be hurt, but you are not—dying, of course?"

"Dying!" repeated Barnabas, lifting a hand to his aching brow, "dying,—no."

"And yet, I fear you are," sighed Mr. Chichester, "yes, I think you will be most thoroughly dead before morning,—I do indeed." And he drew a pistol from his pocket, very much as though it were a snuff-box.

"But before we write 'Finis' to your very remarkable career," he went on, "I have a few,—a very few words to say. Sir, there have been many women in my life, yes, a great many, but only one I ever loved, and you, it seems must love her too. You have obtruded yourself wantonly in my concerns from the very first moment we met. I have always found you an obstacle, an obstruction. But latterly you have become a menace, threatening my very existence for, should you dispossess me of my heritage I starve, and, sir—I have no mind to starve. Thus, since it is to be your life or mine, I, very naturally, prefer that it shall be yours. Also you threatened to hound me from the clubs—well, sir, had I not had the good fortune to meet you tonight, I had planned to make you the scorn and laughing-stock of Town, and to drive you from London like the impostor you are. It was an excellent plan, and I am sorry to forego it, but necessity knows no law, and so to-night I mean to rid myself of the obstacle, and sweep it away altogether." As he ended, Mr. Chichester smiled, sighed, and cocked his pistol. But, even as it clicked, a figure rose up from behind the rotting wherry and, as Mr. Chichester leaned towards Barnabas, smiling still but with eyes of deadly menace, a hand, pale and claw-like in the half-light, fell and clenched itself upon his shoulder.

At the touch Mr. Chichester started and, uttering an exclamation, turned savagely; then Barnabas struggled to his knees, and pinning his wrist with one hand, twisted the pistol from his grasp with the other and, as Mr. Chichester sprang to his feet, faced him, still upon his knees, but with levelled weapon.

"Don't shoot!" cried a voice.

"Shoot?" repealed Barnabas, and got unsteadily upon his legs. "Shoot—no, my hands are best!" and, flinging the pistol far out into the River, he approached Mr. Chichester, staggering a little, but with fists clenched.

"Sir," cried the voice again, "oh, young sir, what would you do?"

"Kill him!" said Barnabas.

"No, no—leave him to God's justice, God will requite him—let him go."

"No!" said Barnabas, shaking his head. But, as he pressed forward intent on his purpose, restraining hands were upon his arm, and the voice pleaded in his ear:

"God is a just God, young sir—let the man go—leave him to the Almighty,"

And the hands upon his arm shook him with passionate entreaty. Therefore Barnabas paused and, bowing his head, clasped his throbbing temples between his palms and so, stood a while. When he looked up again, Mr. Chichester was gone, and the Apostle of Peace stood before him, his silver hair shining, his pale face uplifted towards heaven.

"I owe you—my life!" said Barnabas.

"You are alive, young sir, which is good, and your hands are not stained with a villain's blood, which is much better. But, as for me—God pity me!—I came here to-night, meaning to be a self-murderer—oh, God forgive me!"

"But you—asked for—a sign, I think," said Barnabas, "and you—live also. And to-night your pilgrimage ends, in Clemency's loving arms."

"Clemency? My daughter? Oh, sir,—young sir, how may that be? They tell me she is dead."

"Lies!" said Barnabas, "lies! I spoke with her tonight." The Apostle of Peace stood a while with bowed head; when at last he looked up, his cheeks were wet with tears.

"Then, sir," said he, "take me to her. Yet, stay! You are hurt, and, if in my dark hour I doubted God's mercy, I would not be selfish in my happiness—"

"Happiness!" said Barnabas, "yes—every one seems happy—but me."

"You are hurt, young sir. Stoop your head and let me see."

"No," sighed Barnabas, "I'm well enough. Come, let me take you to Clemency."

So, without more ado, they left that dreary place, and walked on together side by side and very silent, Barnabas with drooping head, and his companion with eyes uplifted and ever-moving lips.

Thus, in a while, they turned into the narrow court, and reaching the door of Nick the Cobbler, Barnabas knocked and, as they waited, he could see that his companion was trembling violently where he leaned beside him against the wall. Then the door was opened and Clemency appeared, her shapely figure outlined against the light behind her.

"Mr. Beverley," she exclaimed, "dear brother, is it you—"

"Yes, Clemency, and—and I have kept my promise, I have brought you—" But no need for words; Clemency had seen. "Father!" she cried, stretching out her arms, "oh, dear father!"

"Beatrix," said the preacher, his voice very broken, "oh, my child, —forgive me—!" But Clemency had caught him in her arms, had drawn him into the little shop, and, pillowing the silvery head upon her young bosom, folded it there, and so hung above him all sighs, and tears, and tender endearments.

Then Barnabas closed the door upon them and, sighing, went upon his way. He walked with lagging step and with gaze ever upon the ground, heedless alike of the wondering looks of those he passed, or of time, or of place, or of the voices that still wailed, and wrangled, and roared songs; conscious only of the pain in his head, the dull ache at his heart, and the ever-growing doubt and fear within him.

CHAPTER LXI

HOW BARNABAS WENT TO HIS TRIUMPH

The star of Barnabas Beverley, Esquire, was undoubtedly in the ascendant; no such radiant orb had brightened the Fashionable Firmament since that of a certain Mr. Brummell had risen to scintillate a while ere it paled and vanished before the royal frown.

Thus the Fashionable World turned polite eyes to mark the course of this new luminary and, if it vaguely wondered how long that course might be, it (like the perspicacious waiter at the "George") regarded Barnabas Beverley, Esquire, as one to be flattered, smiled upon, and as worthy of all consideration and respect.

For here was one, not only young, fabulously rich and a proved sportsman, but a dandy, besides, with a nice taste and originality in matters sartorial, more especially in waistcoats and cravats, which articles, as the Fashionable World well knows, are the final gauge of a man's depth and possibilities.

Thus, the waistcoats of Barnabas Beverley, Esquire, or their prototypes to a button, were to be met with any day sunning themselves in the Mall, and the styles of cravat affected by Barnabas Beverley, Esquire, were to be observed at the most brilliant functions, bowing in all directions.

Wherefore, all this considered, what more natural than that the Fashionable World should desire to make oblation to this, its newest (and consequently most admired) ornament, and how better than to feed him, since banquets are a holy rite sanctified by custom and tradition?

Hence, the Fashionable World appointed and set apart a day whereon, with all due pomp and solemnity, to eat and drink to the glory and honor of Barnabas Beverley, Esquire.

Nevertheless (perverse fate!) Barnabas Beverley was not happy, for, though his smile was as ready as his tongue, yet, even amid the glittering throng, yea, despite the soft beams of Beauty's eyes, his brow would at times grow dark and sombre, and his white, strong fingers clench themselves upon the dainty handkerchief of lace and cambric fashion required him to carry. Yet even this was accepted in all good faith, and consequently pale checks and a romantic gloom became the mode.

No, indeed, Barnabas was not happy, since needs must he think ever of Cleone. Two letters had he written her, the first a humble supplication, the second an angry demand couched in terms of bitter reproach. Yet Cleone gave no sign; and the days passed. Therefore, being himself young and proud, he wrote no more, and waited for some word of explanation, some sign from her; then, as the days lengthened into weeks, he set himself resolutely to forget her, if such a thing might be.

The better to achieve a thing so impossible, he turned to that most fickle of all goddesses whose name is Chance, and wooed her fiercely by day and by night. He became one of her most devoted slaves; in noble houses, in clubs and hells, he sought her. Calm-eyed, grim-lipped he wooed her, yet with dogged assiduity; he became a familiar figure at those very select gaming-tables where play was highest, and tales of his recklessness and wild prodigality began to circulate; tales of huge sums won and lost with the same calm indifference, that quiet gravity which marked him in all things.

Thus a fortnight has elapsed, and to-night the star of Barnabas Beverley, Esquire, has indeed attained its grand climacteric, for to-night he is to eat and drink with ROYALTY, and the Fashionable World is to do him honor.

And yet, as he stands before his mirror, undergoing the ordeal of dressing, he would appear almost careless of his approaching triumph; his brow is overcast, his cheek a little thinner and paler than of yore, and he regards his resplendent image in the mirror with lack-lustre eyes.

"Your cravat, sir," says Peterby, retreating a few paces and with his head to one side the better to observe its effect, "your cravat is, I fear, a trifle too redundant in its lower folds, and a little severe, perhaps—"

"It is excellent, John! And you say—there is still no letter from—from Hawkhurst?"

"No, sir, none," answered Peterby abstractedly, and leaning forward to administer a gentle pull to the flowered waistcoat. "This coat, sir, is very well, I think, and yet—y-e-es, perhaps it might be a shade higher in the collar, and a thought tighter at the waist. Still, it is very well on the whole, and these flattened revers are an innovation that will be quite the vogue before the week is out. You are satisfied with the coat, I hope, sir?"

"Perfectly, John, and—should a letter come while I am at the banquet you will send it on—at once, John."

"At once, sir!" nodded Peterby, crouching down to view his young master's shapely legs in profile. "Mr. Brummell was highly esteemed for his loop and button at the ankle, sir, but I think our ribbon is better, and less conspicuous, that alone should cause a sensation."

"Unless, John," sighed Barnabas, "unless I receive a word to-night I shall drive down to Hawkhurst as soon as I can get away, so have the curricle and grays ready, will you?"

"Yes, sir. Pardon me one moment, there is a wrinkle in your left stocking, silk stockings are very apt to—"

But here the legs of the Gentleman-in-Powder planted themselves quivering on the threshold to announce:—

"Viscount Devenham!"

He still carried his arm in a sling, but, excepting this, the Viscount was himself again, Bright-eyed, smiling and debonair. But now, as Peterby withdrew, and Barnabas turned to greet him, gravely polite—he hesitated, frowned, and seemed a little at a loss.

"Egad!" said he ruefully, "it seems a deuce of a time since we saw each other, Beverley."

"A fortnight!" said Barnabas.

"And it's been a busy fortnight for both of us, from what I hear."

"Yes, Viscount."

"Especially for—you."

"Yes, Viscount."

"Beverley," said he, staring very hard at the toe of his varnished shoe, "do you remember the white-haired man we met, who called himself an Apostle of Peace?"

"Yes, Viscount."

"Do you remember that he said it was meant we should be—friends?"

"Yes."

"Well I—think he was right,—I'm sure he was right. I—didn't know how few my friends were until I—fell out with you. And so—I'm here to—to ask your pardon, and I—don't know how to do it, only—oh, deuce take it! Will you give me your hand, Bev?"

But before the words had well left his lips, Barnabas had sprang forward, and so they stood, hand clasped in hand, looking into each other's eyes as only true friends may.

"I—we—owe you so much, Bev—Clemency has told me—"

"Indeed, Dick," said Barnabas, a little hastily, "you are a fortunate man to have won the love of so beautiful a woman, and one so noble."

"My dear fellow," said the Viscount, very solemn, "it is so wonderful that, sometimes, I—almost fear that it can't be true."

"The love of a woman is generally a very uncertain thing!" said Barnabas bitterly.

"But Clemency isn't like an ordinary woman," said the Viscount, smiling very tenderly, "in all the world there is only one Clemency and she is all truth, and honor, and purity. Sometimes, Bev, I feel so—so deuced unworthy, that I am almost afraid to touch her."

"Yes, I suppose there are a few such women in the world," said Barnabas, turning away. "But, speaking of the Apostle of Peace, have you met him again—lately?"

"No, not since that morning behind the 'Spotted Cow.' Why?"

"Well, you mentioned him."

"Why yes, but only because I couldn't think of any other way of—er—beginning. You were so devilish high and haughty, Bev."

"And what of Clemency?"

"She has promised to—to marry me, next month,—to marry me—me, Bev. Oh, my dear fellow, I'm the very happiest man alive, and, egad, that reminds me! I'm also the discredited and disinherited son of a flinty-hearted Roman."

"What Dick,—do you mean he has—cut you off?"

"As much as ever he could, my dear fellow, which reduces my income by a half. Deuced serious thing, y' know, Bev. Shall have to get rid of my stable, and the coach; 'Moonraker' must go, too, I'm afraid. Yes, Bev," sighed the Viscount, shaking his head at the reflection of his elegant person in the mirror, "you behold in me a beggar, and the cause—Clemency. But then, I know I am the very happiest beggar in all this wide world, and the cause—Clemency!"

"I feared your father would never favor such a match, Dick, but—"

"Favor it! Oh, bruise and blister me!—"

"Have you told Clemency?"

"Not yet—"

"Has he seen her?"

"No, that's the deuce of it, she's away with her father, y' know. Bit of a mystery about him, I fancy—she made me promise to be patient a while, and ask no questions."

"And where is she?"

"Haven't the least idea. However, I went down to beard my Roman, y' know, alone and single handed. Great mistake! Had Clemency been with me the flintiest of Roman P's would have relented, for who could resist—Clemency? As it was, I did my best, Bev—ran over her points—I mean—tried to describe her, y' know, but it was no go, Bev, no go—things couldn't have gone worse!"

"How?"

"'Sir,' says I—in an easy, off-hand tone, my dear fellow, and it was *after* dinner, you'll understand,—'Sir, I've decided to act upon your very excellent advice, and get married. I intend to settle down, at once!' 'Indeed, Horatio?' says he,—(Roman of eye, Bev) 'who is she, pray?' 'The most glorious woman in the world, sir!' says I. 'Of course,' says he, 'but—which?' This steadied me a little, Bev, so I took a fresh grip and began again: 'Sir,' says I, 'beauty in itself is a poor thing at best—' 'Therefore,' says my Roman (quick as a flash, my dear fellow) 'therefore it is just as well that beauty should not come—entirely empty-handed!' 'Sir,' says I—(calmly, you'll understand, Bev, but with just sufficient firmness to let him see that, after all, he was only a father) 'Sir,' says I, 'beauty is a transient thing at best, unless backed up by virtue, honor, wisdom, courage, truth, purity, nobility of soul—' 'Horatio,' says my father (pulling me up short, Bev) 'you do well to put these virtues first but, in the wife of the future Earl of Bamborough, I hearken for such common, though necessary attributes as birth, breeding, and position, neither of which you have yet mentioned, but I'm impatient, perhaps, and these come at the end of your list,—pray continue.' 'Sir,' says I, 'my future wife is above such petty considerations!' 'Ah!' says my Roman, 'I feared so! She is then, a—nobody, I presume?' 'Sir—most beautiful girl in all England,' says I. 'Ha!' says my Roman, nodding, 'then she *is* a nobody; that settles it.' 'She's all that is pure and good!' says I. 'And a nobody, beyond a doubt!' says he. 'She's everything sweet, noble and brave,' says I. 'But—a nobody!' says he again. Now I'll confess I grew a little heated at this, my dear fellow, though I kept my temper admirably—oh, I made every allowance for him, as a self-respecting son should, but, though filial, I maintained a front of adamant, Bev. But, deuce take it! he kept on at me with his confounded 'nobody' so long that I grew restive at last and jibbed. 'So you are determined to marry a nobody, are you, Horatio?' says he. 'No, my Lord,' says I, rising, (and with an air of crushing finality, Bev) 'I am about to be honored with the hand of one who, by stress of circumstances, was for some time waiting maid at the 'Spotted Cow' inn, at Frittenden.' Well, Bev—that did it, y' know! My Roman couldn't say a word, positively gaped at me and, while he gaped, I bowed, and walked out entirely master of the situation. Result— independence, happiness, and—beggary."

"But, Dick,—how shall you live?"

"Oh, I have an old place at Devenham, in the wilds of Kent,—we shall rusticate there."

"And you will give up Almack's, White's—all the glory of the Fashionable World?"

"Oh, man!" cried the Viscount, radiant of face, "how can all these possibly compare? I shall have Clemency!"

"But surely you will find it very quiet, after London and the clubs?"

"Yes, it will be very quiet at Devenham, Bev," said the Viscount, very gently, "and there are roses there, and she loves roses, I know! We shall be alone in the world together,—alone! Yes, it will be very quiet, Bev—thank heaven!"

"The loneliness will pall, after a time, Dick—say a month. And the roses will fade and wither—as all things must, it seems," said Barnabas bitterly, whereupon the Viscount turned and looked at him and laid a hand upon his shoulder.

"Why, Bev," said he, "my dear old Bev,—what is it? You're greatly changed, I think; it isn't like you to be a cynic. You are my friend, but if you were my bitterest enemy I should forgive you, full and freely, because of your behavior to Clemency. My dear fellow, are you in any trouble—any danger? I have been away only a week, yet I come back to find the town humming with stories of your desperate play. I hear that D'Argenson plucked you for close on a thousand the other day—"

"But I won fifteen hundred the same night, Dick."

"And lost all that, and more, to the Poodle later!"

"Why—one can't always win, Dick."

"Oh, Bev, my dear fellow, do you remember shaking your grave head at me because I once dropped five hundred in one of the hells?"

"I fear I must have been very—young then, Dick!"

"And to-day, Bev, to-day you are a notorious gambler, and you sneer at love! Gad! what a change is here! My dear fellow, what does it all mean?"

Barnabas hesitated, and this history might have been very different in the ending but, even as he met the Viscount's frank and anxious look, the door was flung wide and Tressider, the thinnish, youngish gentleman in sandy whiskers, rushed in, followed by the Marquis and three or four other fine gentlemen, and, beholding the Viscount, burst into a torrent of speech:

"Ha! Devenham! there you are,—back from the wilds, eh? Heard the latest? No, I'll be shot if you have—none of you have, and I'm bursting to tell it—positively exploding, damme if I'm not. It was last night, at Crockford's you'll understand, and every one was there—Skiffy, Apollo, the Poodle, Red Herrings, No-grow, the Galloping Countryman and your obedient humble. One o'clock was striking as the game broke up, and there's Beverley yawning and waiting for his hat, d' ye see, when in comes the Golden Ball. 'Ha, Beverley!' says he, 'you gamble, they tell me?' 'Oh, now and then,' says Beverley. 'Why then,' says Golden Ball, 'you may have heard that I do a little that way, myself?' Now you mention it, I believe I have,' says Beverley. 'Ha!' says Golden Ball, winking at the rest of us, 'suppose we have a match, you and I—call your game.' 'Sir,' says Beverley, yawning again, 'it is past one o'clock, and I make it a rule never to play after one o'clock except for rather high stakes,' (Rather high stakes says he! and to the Golden Ball,—oh curse me!) 'Do you, begad!' says Golden Ball, purple in the face—'ha! you may have heard that I occasionally venture a hundred or so myself—whatever the hour! Waiter—cards!' 'Sir,' says Beverley, I've been playing ever since three o'clock this afternoon and I'm weary of cards.' 'Oh, just as you wish,' says Golden Ball, 'at battledore and shuttlecock I'm your man, or rolling the bones, or—' 'Dice, by all means!' says Beverley, yawning again. 'At how much a throw?' says Golden Ball, sitting down and rattling the box. 'Well,' says Beverley, 'a thousand, I think, should do to begin with!' ('A thou-sand,' says he, damme if he didn't!) Oh Gad, but you should have seen the Golden Ball, what with surprise and his cravat, I thought he'd choke—shoot me if I didn't! 'Done!' says he at last (for we were all round the table thick as flies you'll understand) — and to it they went, and in less than a quarter of an hour, Beverley had bubbled him of close on seven thousand! Quickest thing I ever saw, oh, curse me!"

"Oh, Bev," sighed the Viscount, under cover of the ensuing talk and laughter, "what a perfectly reckless fellow you are!"

"Why, you see, Dick," Barnabas answered, as Peterby re-entered with his hat and cloak, "a man can't always lose!"

"Beverley," said the Marquis, proffering his arm, "I have my chariot below; I thought we might drive round to the club together, you and Devenham and I, if you are ready?"

"Thank you, Marquis, yes, I'm quite ready."

Thus, with a Marquis on his right, and a Viscount on his left, and divers noble gentlemen in his train, Barnabas went forth to his triumph.

CHAPTER LXII

WHICH TELLS HOW BARNABAS TRIUMPHED IN SPITE OF ALL

Never had White's, that historic club, gathered beneath its roof a more distinguished company; dukes, royal and otherwise, elbow each other on the stairs; earls and marquises sit cheek by jowl; viscounts and baronets exchange snuff-boxes in corners, but one and all take due and reverent heed of the flattened revers and the innovation of the riband.

Yes, White's is full to overflowing for, to-night, half the Fashionable World is here, that is to say, the masculine half; beaux and wits; bucks and Corinthians; dandies and macaronis; all are here and, each and every, with the fixed and unshakable purpose of eating and drinking to the glory and honor of Barnabas Beverley, Esquire. Here, also, is a certain "Mr. Norton," whom Barnabas immediately recognizes by reason of his waistcoat and his whiskers. And Mr. Norton is particularly affable and is graciously pleased to commend the aforesaid flattened revers and riband; indeed so taken with them is he, that he keeps their wearer beside him, and even condescends to lean upon his arm as far as the dining-room.

Forthwith the banquet begins and the air hums with talk and laughter punctuated by the popping of corks; waiters hurry to and fro, dishes come and dishes vanish, and ever the laughter grows, and the buzz of talk swells louder.

And Barnabas? Himself "the glass of fashion and the mould of form," in very truth "the observed of all observers," surely to-night he should be happy! For the soaring pinions of youth have borne him up and up at last, into the empyrean, far, far above the commonplace; the "Coursing Hound," with its faded sign and weatherbeaten gables, has been lost to view long and long ago (if it ever really existed), and to-night he stands above the clouds, his foot upon the topmost pinnacle; and surely man can attain no higher, for to-night he feasts with princes.

Thus Barnabas sits among the glare and glitter of it all, smiling at one, bowing to another, speaking with all by turns, and wondering in his heart—if there is yet any letter from Hawkhurst. And now the hurrying tread of waiters ceases, the ring and clatter of glass and silver is hushed, the hum of talk and laughter dies away, and a mottle-faced gentleman rises, and, clutching himself by the shirt-frill with one hand, and elevating a brimming glass in the other, clears his throat, and holds forth in this wise:

"Gentlemen, I'm an Englishman, therefore I'm blunt,—deuced blunt—damned blunt! Gentlemen, I desire to speak a word upon this happy and memorable occasion, and my word is this: Being an Englishman I very naturally admire pluck and daring—Mr. Beverley has pluck and daring—therefore I drink to him. Gentlemen, we need such true-blue Englishmen as Beverley to keep an eye on old Bony; it is such men as Beverley who make the damned foreigners shake in their accursed shoes. So long as we have such men as Beverley amongst us, England will scorn the foreign yoke and stand forth triumphant, first in peace, first in war. Gentlemen, I give you Mr. Beverley, as he is a true Sportsman I honor him, as he is an Englishman he is my friend. Mr. Beverley, gentlemen!"

Hereupon the mottle-faced gentleman lets go of his shirt-frill, bows to Barnabas and, tossing off his wine, sits down amid loud acclamations and a roaring chorus of "Beverley! Beverley!" accompanied by much clinking of glasses.

And now, in their turn, divers other noble gentlemen rise in their places and deliver themselves of speeches, more or less eloquent, flowery, witty and laudatory, but, one and all, full of the name and excellences of Barnabas Beverley, Esquire; who duly learns that he is a Maecenas of Fashion, a sportsman through and through, a shining light, and one of the bulwarks of Old England, b'gad! etc., etc., etc.

To all of which he listens with varying emotions, and with one eye upon the door, fervently hoping for the letter so long expected. But the time is come for him to respond; all eyes are upon him, and all glasses are filled; even the waiters become deferentially interested as, amid welcoming shouts, the guest of the evening rises, a little flushed, a little nervous, yet steady of eye.

And as Barnabas stands there, an elegant figure, tall and graceful, all eyes may behold again the excellent fit of that wonderful coat, its dashing cut and flattened revers, while all ears await his words. But, or ever he can speak, upon this silence is heard the tread of heavy feet beyond the door and Barnabas glances there eagerly, ever mindful of the letter from Hawkhurst; but the feet have stopped and, stifling a sigh, he begins:

"My Lords and gentlemen! So much am I conscious of the profound honor you do me, that I find it difficult to express my—"

But here again a disturbance is heard at the door—a shuffle of feet and the mutter of voices, and he pauses expectant; whereat his auditors cry angrily for "silence!" which being duly accorded, he begins again:

"Indeed, gentlemen, I fear no words of mine, however eloquent, can sufficiently express to you all my—"

"Oh, Barnabas," cries a deep voice; "yes, it *is* Barnabas!" Even as the words are uttered, the group of protesting waiters in the doorway are swept aside by a mighty arm, and a figure strides into the banqueting-room, a handsome figure, despite its country habiliments, a commanding figure by reason of its stature and great spread of shoulder, and John Barty stands there, blinking in the light of the many candles.

Then Barnabas closed his eyes and, reaching out, set his hand upon the back of a chair near by, and so stood, with bent head and a strange roaring in his ears. Little by little this noise grew less until he could hear voices, about him, an angry clamor:

"Put him out!"

"Throw the rascal into the street!"

"Kick him downstairs, somebody!"

And, amid this ever-growing tumult, Barnabas could distinguish his father's voice, and in it was a note he had never heard before, something of pleading, something of fear.

"Barnabas? Barnabas? Oh, this be you, my lad—bean't it, Barnabas?"

Yet still he stood with bent head, his griping fingers clenched hard upon the chair-back, while the clamor about him grew ever louder and more threatening.

"Throw him out!"

"Pitch the fellow downstairs, somebody!"

"Jove!" exclaimed the Marquis, rising and buttoning his coat, "if nobody else will, I'll have a try at him myself. Looks a promising cove, as if he might fib well. Come now, my good fellow, you must either get out of here or—put 'em up, you know,—dooce take me, but you must!"

But as he advanced, Barnabas lifted his head and staying him with a gesture, turned and beheld his father standing alone, the centre of an angry circle. And John Barty's eyes were wide and troubled, and his usually ruddy cheek showed pale, though with something more than fear as, glancing slowly round the ring of threatening figures that hemmed him in, he beheld the white, stricken face of his son. And, seeing it, John Barty groaned, and so took a step towards the door; but no man moved to give him way.

"A—a mistake, gentlemen," he muttered, "I—I'll go!" Then, even as the stammering words were uttered, Barnabas strode forward into the circle and, slipping a hand within his father's nerveless arm, looked round upon the company, pale of cheek, but with head carried high.

"My Lords!" said he, "gentlemen! I have the honor—to introduce to you—John Barty, sometime known as 'Glorious John'—ex-champion of England and—landlord of the 'Coursing Hound' inn—my father!"

A moment of silence! A stillness so profound that it seemed no man drew breath; a long, long moment wherein Barnabas felt himself a target for all eyes—eyes wherein he thought to see amazement that changed into dismay which, in turn, gave place to an ever-growing scorn of him. Therefore he turned his back upon them all and, coming to the great window, stood there staring blindly into the dark street.

"Oh, Barnabas!" he heard his father saying, though as from a long way off, "Barnabas lad, I—I—Oh, Barnabas—they're going! They're leaving you, and—it's all my fault, lad! Oh, Barnabas,—what have I done! It's my fault, lad—all my fault. But I heard you was sick, Barnabas, and like to die,—ill, and calling for me,—for your father, Barnabas. And now—Oh, my lad! my lad!—what have I done?"

"Never blame yourself, father, it—wasn't your fault," said Barnabas with twitching lips, for from the great room behind him came the clatter of chairs, the tread of feet, with voices and stifled laughter that grew fainter and fainter, yet left a sting behind.

"Come away, John," said a voice, "we've done enough to-night—come away!"

"Yes, Natty Bell, yes, I be coming—coming. Oh, Barnabas, my lad, —my lad,—forgive me!"

Now in a while Barnabas turned; and behold! the candles glowed as brightly as ever, silver and glass shone and glittered as bravely as ever, but—the great room was empty, that is to say—very nearly. Of all that brilliant and fashionable company but two remained. Very lonely figures they looked, seated at the deserted table—the Viscount, crumbling up bread and staring at the table-cloth, and the Marquis, fidgeting with his snuff-box, and frowning at the ceiling.

To these solitary figures Barnabas spoke, albeit his voice was hoarse and by no means steady:

"My Lords," said he, "why haven't you—followed the others?"

"Why, you see," began the Marquis, frowning at the ceiling harder than ever, and flicking open his snuff-box, "you see—speaking for myself, of course, I say speaking for myself, I—hum!—the fact is—ha!—that is to say—oh, dooce take it!" And, in his distress, he actually inhaled a pinch of snuff and immediately fell a-sneezing, with a muffled curse after every sneeze.

"Sirs," said Barnabas, "I think you'd better go. You will be less—conspicuous. Indeed, you'd better go."

"Go?" repeated the Viscount, rising suddenly. "Go, is it? No, damme if we do! If you are John Barty's son, you are still my friend, and—there's my hand—Barnabas."

"Mine—too!" sneezed the Marquis, "'s soon as I've got over the—'ffects of this s-snuff—with a curse to it!"

"Oh Dick!" said Barnabas, his head drooping, "Marquis—"

"Name's Bob to—my friends!" gasped the Marquis from behind his handkerchief. "Oh, damn this snuff!"

"Why, Bev," said the Viscount, "don't take it so much to heart, man. Deuced unpleasant, of course, but it'll all blow over, y' know. A week from now and they'll all come crawling back, y' know, if you only have the courage to outface 'em. And we are with him—aren't we, Jerny?"

"Of course!" answered the Marquis, "dooce take me—yes! So would poor old Sling have been."

"Sirs," said Barnabas, reaching out and grasping a hand of each, "with your friendship to hearten me—all things are possible—even this!"

But here a waiter appeared bearing a tray, and on the tray a letter; he was a young waiter, a very knowing waiter, hence his demeanor towards Barnabas had already undergone a subtle change—he stared at Barnabas with inquisitive eyes and even forgot to bow until—observing the Viscount's eye and the Marquis's chin, his back became immediately subservient and he tendered Barnabas the letter with a profound obeisance.

With a murmured apology Barnabas took it and, breaking the seal, read these words in Cleone's writing:

"You have destroyed my faith, and with my faith all else. Farewell."

Then Barnabas laughed, sudden and sharp, and tore the paper across and across, and dropping the pieces to the floor, set his foot upon them.

"Friends," said he, "my future is decided for me. I thank you deeply, deeply for your brave friendship—your noble loyalty, but the fiat has gone forth. To-night I leave the World of Fashion for one better suited to my birth, for it seems I should be only an amateur gentleman, as it were, after all. My Lords, your most obedient, humble servant,—good-by!"

So Barnabas bowed to each in turn and went forth from the scene of his triumph, deliberate of step and with head carried high as became a conqueror.

And thus the star of Barnabas Beverley, Esquire, waxed and waned and vanished utterly from the Fashionable Firmament, and, in time, came to be regarded as only a comet, after all.

CHAPTER LXIII

WHICH TELLS HOW BARNABAS HEARD THE TICKING OF A CLOCK

It was a dark night, the moon obscured as yet by a wrack of flying cloud, for a wind was abroad, a rising wind that blew in fitful gusts; a boisterous, blustering, bullying wind that met the traveller at sudden corners to choke and buffet him and so was gone, roaring away among roofs and chimneys, rattling windows and lattices, extinguishing flickering lamps, and filling the dark with stir and tumult.

But Barnabas strode on heedless and deaf to it all. Headlong he went, his cloak fluttering, his head stooped low, hearing nothing, seeing nothing, taking no thought of time or direction, or of his ruined career, since none of these were in his mind, but only the words of Cleone's letter.

And slowly a great anger came upon him with a cold and bitter scorn of her that cast out sorrow; thus, as he went, he laughed suddenly, —a shrill laugh that rose above the howl of the wind, that grew even wilder and louder until he was forced to stop and lean against an iron railing close by.

"An Amateur Gentleman!" he gasped, "An Amateur Gentleman! Oh, fool! fool!" And once again the fierce laughter shook him in its grip and, passing, left him weak and breathless.

Through some rift in the clouds, the moon cast a fugitive beam and thus he found himself looking down into a deep and narrow area where a flight of damp, stone steps led down to a gloomy door; and beside the door was a window, and the window was open.

Now as he gazed, the area, and the damp steps, and the gloomy door all seemed familiar; therefore he stepped back, and gazing up, saw a high, flat-fronted house, surely that same unlovely house at whose brass-knockered front door Captain Slingsby of the Guards had once stood and rapped with trembling hand.

The place was very silent, and very dark, save for one window where burned a dim light, and, moved by sudden impulse, Barnabas strode forward and, mounting the two steps, seized the knocker; but, even as he did so the door moved. Slowly, slowly it opened, swinging back on noiseless hinges, wider and wider until Barnabas could look into the dimness of the unlighted hall beyond. Then, while he yet stood hesitating, he heard a sound, very faint and sweet, like the chime of fairy bells, and from the dark a face peered forth, a face drawn, and lined, and ghastly pale, whose staring eyes were wide with horror.

"You!" said a voice, speaking in a harsh whisper, "is it you? Alas, Barnaby Bright! what would you—here? Go away! Go away! Here is an evil place, a place of sin, and horror, and blood—go away! go away!"

"But," said Barnabas, "I wish to see—"

"Oh, Barnaby Bright,—hear me! Did I not tell you he was marked for destruction, that evil begetteth evil, and the sword, the sword? I have watched, and watched, and to-night my watch is ended! Go away! Go away!"

"What is it? what do you mean?" demanded Barnabas.

With his eyes still fixed and staring, and without turning his head, Billy Button raised one hand to point with a rigid finger at the wall, just within the doorway.

"Look!" he whispered.

Then, glancing where he pointed, Barnabas saw a mark upon the panelling—a blur like the shadow of a hand; but even as he stared at it, Billy Button, shuddering, passed his sleeve across it and lo! it was gone!

"Oh, Barnaby Bright!" he whispered, "there is a shadow upon this place, as black as death, even as I told you—flee from the shadow, —come away! come away!"

As he breathed the words, the madman sprang past him down the steps, tossed up his long arms towards the moon with a wild, imploring gesture, and turning, scudded away on his naked, silent feet.

Now after a while Barnabas stepped into the gloomy hall and stood listening; the house was very silent, only upon the stillness he could hear the loud, deliberate tick of the wizen-faced clock upon the stairs, and, as he stood there, it seemed to him that to-night it was trying to tell him something. Barnabas shivered suddenly and drew his long cloak about him, then, closing the door, took a step along the dark hall, yet paused to listen again, for now it seemed to him that the tick of the clock was louder than ever.

"Go—back! Go—back!"

Could that be what it meant? Barnabas raised a hand to his brow and, though he still shivered, felt it suddenly moist and clammy. Then, clenching his teeth, he crept forward, guiding himself by the wall; yet as he went, above the shuffle of his feet, above the rustle of his cloak against the panelling, he could hear the tick of the clock—ever louder, ever more insistent:

"Go—back! Go—back!"

He reached the stairs at last and, groping for the banister, began to ascend slowly and cautiously, often pausing to listen, and to stare into the darkness before and behind. On he went and up, past the wizen-faced clock, and so reached the upper hall at the further end of which was the dim light that shone from behind a half-closed door.

Being come to the door, Barnabas lifted his hand to knock, yet stood again hesitating, his chin on his shoulder, his eyes searching the darkness behind him, whence came the slow, solemn ticking of the clock:

"Come—back! Come—back!"

For a long moment he stood thus, then, quick and sudden, he threw wide the door and stepped into the room.

A candle flared and guttered upon the mantel, and by this flickering light he saw an overturned chair, and, beyond that, a litter of scattered papers and documents and, beyond that again, Jasper Gaunt seated at his desk in the corner. He was lolling back in his chair like one asleep, and yet—was this sleep?

Something in his attitude, something in the appalling stillness of that lolling figure, something in the utter quiet of the whole place, filled Barnabas with a nameless, growing horror. He took a step nearer, another, and another—then stopped and, uttering a choking gasp, fell back to the wall and leaned there suddenly faint and sick. For, indeed, this was more than sleep. Jasper Gaunt lolled there, a horrid, bedabbled thing, with his head at a hideous angle and the dagger, which had been wont to glitter so evilly from the wall, smitten sideways through his throat.

Barnabas crouched against the wall, his gaze riveted by the dull gleam of the steel; and upon the silence, now, there crept another sound soft and regular, a small, dull, plashing sound; and, knowing what it was, he closed his eyes and the faintness grew upon him. At length he sighed and, shuddering, lifted his head and moved a backward step toward the door; thus it was he chanced to see Jasper Gaunt's right hand—that white, carefully-tended right hand, whose long, smooth fingers had clenched themselves even tighter in death than they had done in life. And, in their rigid grasp was something that struck Barnabas motionless; that brought him back slowly, slowly across that awful room to sink upon one knee above that pale, clenched hand, while, sweating, shuddering with loathing, he forced open those stiffening fingers and drew from their dead clutch something that he stared at with dilating eyes, and with white lips suddenly compressed, ere he hid it away in his pocket.

Then, shivering, he arose and backed away, feeling behind him for the door, and so passed out into the passage and down the stairs, but always with his pale face turned toward the dim-lit room where Jasper Gaunt lolled in his chair, a bedabbled, wide-eyed thing of horror, staring up at the dingy ceiling.

Thus, moving ever backwards, Barnabas came to the front door, felt for the catch, but, with his hand upon it, paused once more to listen; yet heard only the thick beating of his own heart, and the loud, deliberate ticking of the wizen-faced clock upon the stairs. And now, as he hearkened, it seemed to him that it spoke no more but had taken on a new and more awful sound; for now its slow, rhythmic beat was hatefully like another sound, a soft sound and regular, a small, dull, plashing sound,—the awful tap! tap! tap! of great, slow-falling drops of blood.

CHAPTER LXIV

WHICH SHOWS SOMETHING OF THE HORRORS OF REMORSE

With this dreadful sound in his ears, Barnabas hurried away from that place of horror; but ever the sound pursued him, it echoed in his step, it panted in his quickened breathing, it throbbed in the pulsing of his heart. Wherever he looked, there always was Jasper Gaunt lolling in his chair with his head dangling at its horrible angle,—the very night was full of him.

Hot-foot went Barnabas, by dingy streets and silent houses, and with his chin now on one shoulder, now on the other; and thus, he presently found himself before a certain door and, remembering its faulty catch, tried it but found it fast. Therefore he knocked, softly at first, but louder and louder until at length the door was plucked suddenly open and a woman appeared, a slatternly creature who bore a candle none too steadily.

"Now then, owdacious," she began, somewhat slurring of speech. "What d'ye want—this time o' night—knocking at 'spectable door of a person?"

"Is Mr. Barrymaine in?"

"Mist' Barrymaine?" repeated the woman, scattering grease-spots as she raised the candle in her unsteady hand, "what d'ye wan' this time o'—"

Here, becoming aware of the magnificence of the visitor's attire, she dropped Barnabas a floundering curtsy and showered the step with grease-spots.

"Can I see Mr. Barrymaine?"

"Yes, sir—this way, sir, an' min' the step, sir. See Mist' Barrymaine, yes, sir, firs' floor—an' would you be so good as to ax 'im to keep 'is feet still, or, as you might say, 'is trotters, sir—"

"His feet?"

"Also 'is legs, sir, if you'd be so very obleeging, sir."

"What do you mean?"

"Come an' listen, sir!" So saying, the woman opened a door and stood with a finger pointing unsteadily upwards. "Been a-doing of it ever since 'e came in a hour ago. It ain't loud, p'r'aps, but it's worriting—very worriting. If 'e wants to dance 'e might move about a bit 'stead o' keeping in one place all the time—'ark!" And she pointed with her quavering finger to a certain part of the ceiling whence came the tramp! tramp! of restless feet; and yet the feet never moved away.

"I'll go up!" said Barnabas, and, nodding to the slatternly woman, he hurried along the passage and mounting the dark stair, paused before a dingy door. Now, setting his ear to the panel, he heard a sound—a muffled sound, hoarse but continuous, ever and anon rising to a wail only to sink again, yet never quite ceasing. Then, feeling the door yield to his hand, Barnabas opened it and, stepping softly into the room, closed it behind him.

The place was very dark, except where the moon sent a fugitive beam through the uncurtained window, and face downward across this pale light lay a huddled figure from whose unseen lips the sounds issued—long, awful, gasping sobs; a figure that stirred and writhed like one in torment, whose clenched hands beat themselves upon the frayed carpet, while, between the sobbing and the beat of those clenched hands, came broken prayers intermingled with oaths and moaning protestations.

Barnabas drew a step nearer, and, on the instant, the grovelling figure started up to an elbow; thus, stooping down, Barnabas looked into the haggard face of Ronald Barrymaine.

"Beverley!" he gasped, "w-what d'you want? Go away,—l-leave me!"

"No!" said Barnabas, "it is you who must go away—at once. You must leave London to-night!"

"W-what d' you mean?"

"You must be clear of England by to-morrow night at latest."

Barrymaine stared up at Barnabas wide-eyed and passed his tongue to and fro across his lips before he spoke again:

"Beverley, w-what d' you—mean?"

"I know why you keep your right hand hidden!" said Barnabas.

Barrymaine shivered suddenly, but his fixed stare never wavered, only, as he crouched there, striving to speak yet finding no voice, upon his furrowed brow and pallid cheek ran glittering lines of sweat. At last he contrived to speak again, but in a whisper now:

"W-what do you mean?"

"I mean that tonight I found this scrap of cloth, and I recognized it as part of the cuff of your sleeve, and I found it clenched in Jasper Gaunt's dead hand."

With a hoarse, gasping cry Barrymaine cast himself face down upon the floor again and writhed there like one in agony.

"I d-didn't mean to—oh, God! I never m-meant it!" he groaned and, starting to his knees, he caught at Barnabas with wild, imploring hands: "Oh, Beverley, I s-swear to you I n-never meant to do it. I went there tonight to l-learn the truth, and he th-threatened me—threatened me, I tell you, s-so we fought and he was s-strong and swung me against the w-wall. And then, Beverley—as we s-struggled—somehow I g-got hold of—of the dagger and struck at him—b-blindly. And—oh, my God, Beverley—I shall never forget how he—ch-choked! I can hear it now! But I didn't mean to—do it. Oh, I s-swear I never meant it, Beverley—s-so help me, God!"

"But he is dead," said Barnabas, "and now—"

"Y-you won't give me up, Beverley?" cried Barrymaine, clinging to his knees. "I wronged you, I know—n-now, but don't g-give me up. I'm not afraid to d-die like a g-gentleman should, but—the gallows—oh, my God!"

"No, you must be saved—from that!"

"Ah—w-will you help me?"

"That is why I came."

"W-what must I do?"

"Start for Dover—to-night."

"Yes—yes, Dover. B-but I have no money."

"Here are twenty guineas, they will help you well on your way. When they are gone you shall have more."

"Beverley, I—wronged you, but I know now who my c-creditor really is—I know who has been m-my enemy all along—oh, blind f-fool that I've been,—but I know—now. And I think it's t-turned my brain. Beverley,—my head's all confused—wish D-Dig were here. But I shall be better s-soon. It was D-Dover you said, I think?"

"Yes,—but now, take off that coat."

"B-but it's the only one I've got!"

"You shall have mine," said Barnabas and, throwing aside his cloak, he stripped off that marvellous garment (whose flattened revers were never to become the vogue, after all), and laid it upon the table beside Barrymaine who seemed as he leaned there to be shaken by strange twitchings and tremblings.

"Oh, Beverley," he muttered, "it would have been a good th-thing for me if somebody had s-strangled me at birth. No!—d-don't light the candle!" he cried suddenly, for Barnabas had sought and found the tinder-box, "don't! d-don't!"

But Barnabas struck and the tinder caught, then, as the light came, Barrymaine shrank away and away, and, crouching against the wall, stared down at himself, at his right sleeve ripped and torn, and at certain marks that spattered and stained him, here and there, awful marks much darker than the cloth. Now as he looked, a great horror seemed to come upon him, he trembled violently and, stumbling forward, sank upon his knees beside the table, hiding his sweating face between his arms. And, kneeling thus, he uttered soft, strange, unintelligible noises and the table shook and quivered under him.

"Come, you must take off that coat!"

Very slowly Barrymaine lifted his heavy head and looked at Barnabas with dilating eyes and with his mouth strangely drawn and twisted.

"Oh, Beverley!" he whispered, "I—I think I'm—"

"You must give me that coat!" persisted Barnabas.

Still upon his knees, Barrymaine began to fumble at the buttons of that stained, betraying garment but, all at once, his fingers seemed to grow uncertain, they groped aimlessly, fell away, and he spoke in a hoarse whisper, while upon his lip was something white, like foam.

"I—oh I—Beverley, I—c-can't!"

And now, all at once, as they stared into each other's eyes, Barnabas leaning forward, strong and compelling, Barrymaine upon his knees clinging weakly to the table, sudden and sharp upon the stillness broke a sound—an ominous sound, the stumble of a foot that mounted the stair.

Uttering a broken cry Barrymaine struggled up to his feet, strove desperately to speak, his distorted mouth flecked with foam, and beating the air with frantic hands pitched over and thudded to the floor.

Then the door opened and Mr. Smivvle appeared who, calling upon Barrymaine's name, ran forward and fell upon his knees beside that convulsed and twisted figure.

"My God, Beverley!" he cried, "how comes he like this—what has happened?"

"Are you his friend?"

"Yes, yes, his friend—certainly! Haven't I told you the hand of a Smivvle, sir—"

"Tonight he killed Jasper Gaunt."

"Eh? Killed? Killed him?"

"Murdered him—though I think more by accident than design."

"Killed him! Murdered him!"

"Yes. Pull yourself together and listen. Tomorrow the hue and cry will be all over London, we must get him away—out of the country if possible."

"Yes, yes—of course! But he's ill—a fit, I think."

"Have you ever seen him so before?"

"Never so bad as this. There, Barry, there, my poor fellow! Help me to get him on the couch, will you, Beverley?"

Between them they raised that twitching form; then, as Mr. Smivvle stooped to set a cushion beneath the restless head, he started suddenly back, staring wide-eyed and pointing with a shaking finger.

"My God!" he whispered, "what's that? Look—look at his coat."

"Yes," said Barnabas, "we must have it off."

"No, no—it's too awful!" whimpered Mr. Smivvle, shrinking away, "see—it's—it's all down the front!"

"If this coat is ever found, it will hang him!" said Barnabas. "Come, help me to get it off."

So between them it was done; thereafter, while Mr. Smivvle crouched beside that restless, muttering form, Barnabas put on his cloak and, rolling up the torn coat, hid it beneath its ample folds.

"What, are you going, Beverley?"

"Yes—for one thing to get rid of this coat. On the table are twenty guineas, take them, and just so soon as Barrymaine is fit to travel, get him away, but above all, don't—"

"Who is it?" cried Barrymaine suddenly, starting up and peering wildly over his shoulder, "w-who is it? Oh, I t-tell you there's s-somebody behind me—who is it?"

"Nobody, Barry—not a soul, my poor boy, compose yourself!" But, even as Mr. Smivvle spoke, Barrymaine fell back and lay moaning fitfully and with half-closed eyes. "Indeed I fear he is very ill, Beverley!"

"If he isn't better by morning, get a doctor," said Barnabas, "but, whatever you do—keep Chichester away from him. As regards money I'll see you shan't want for it. And now, for the present, good-by!"

So saying, Barnabas caught up his hat and, with a last glance at the moaning figure on the couch, went from the room and down the stairs, and let himself out into the dingy street.

CHAPTER LXV

WHICH TELLS HOW BARNABAS DISCHARGED HIS VALET

It was long past midnight when Barnabas reached his house in St. James's Square; and gazing up at its goodly exterior he sighed, and thereafter frowned, and so, frowning still, let himself in. Now, late though the hour, Peterby was up, and met him in the hall.

"Sir," said he, anxious of eye as he beheld his young master's disordered dress and the grim pallor of his face, "the Marquis of Jerningham and Viscount Devenham called. They waited for you,—they waited over an hour."

"But they are gone now, of course?" inquired Barnabas, pausing, with his foot on the stair.

"Yes, sir—"

"Good!" nodded Barnabas with a sigh of relief.

"But they left word they would call to-morrow morning, early; indeed they seemed most anxious to see you, sir."

"Ha!" said Barnabas, and, frowning still, went on up the stair.

"Sir," said Peterby, lighting the way into the dressing-room, "you received the—the letter safely?"

"Yes, I received it," said Barnabas, tossing aside his hat and cloak, "and that reminds me,—to-morrow morning you will discharge all the servants."

"Sir?"

"Pay them a month's wages. Also you will get rid of this house and furniture, and all the carriages and horses—except 'The Terror,' —sell them for what they will fetch—no matter how little, only—get rid of them."

"Yes, sir."

"As for yourself, Peterby, I shall require your services no longer. But you needn't lack for a position—every dandy of 'em all will be wild to get you. And, because you are the very best valet in the world, you can demand your own terms."

"Yes, sir."

"And now, I think that is all, I shan't want you again tonight—stay though, before I go to bed bring me the things I wore when I first met you, the garments which as clothes, you told me, didn't exist."

"Sir, may I ask you a question?"

"Oh, yes—if you wish," sighed Barnabas, wearily.

"Are you leaving London, sir?"

"I'm leaving the World of Fashion—yes."

"And you—don't wish me to accompany you, sir."

"No."

"Have I—displeased you in any way?"

"No, it is only that the 'best valet in the world' would be wasted on me any longer, and I shall not need you where I am going."

"Not as a—servant, sir?"

"No."

"Then, sir, may I remind you that I am also a—man? A man who owes all that he is to your generosity and noble trust and faith. And, sir, it seems to me that a man may sometimes venture where a servant may not—if you are indeed done with the Fashionable World, I have done with it also, for I shall never serve any other than you."

Then Barnabas turned away and coming to the mantel leaned there, staring blankly down at the empty hearth; and in a while he spoke, though without looking up:

"The Fashionable World has turned its polite back upon me, Peterby, because I am only the son of a village inn-keeper. But—much more than this—my lady has—has lost her faith in me, my fool's dream is over—nothing matters any more. And so I am going away to a place I have heard described by a pedler of books as 'the worst place in the world'—and indeed I think it is."

"Sir," said Peterby, "when do we start?"

Then, very slowly, Barnabas lifted his heavy head and looked at John Peterby; and, in that dark hour, smiled, and reaching out, caught and grasped his hand; also, when he spoke again, his voice was less hard and not so steady as before:

"Oh, John!" said he, "John Peterby—my faithful John! Come with me if you will, but you come as my—friend."

"And—where are we going, sir?" inquired John, as they stood thus, hand in hand, looking into each other's eyes.

"To Giles's Rents, John,—down by the River."

And thus did Barnabas, in getting rid of the "best valet in the world," find for himself a faithful friend instead.

CHAPTER LXVI

OF CERTAIN CON-CLUSIONS DRAWN BY MR. SHRIG

Number Five St. James's Square was to let; its many windows were blank and shuttered, its portal, which scarcely a week ago had been besieged by Fashion, was barred and bolted, the Gentleman-in-Powder had vanished quite, and with him the glory of Number Five St. James's Square had departed utterly.

Barnabas paused to let his gaze wander over it, from roof to pavement, then, smiling a little bitterly, buried his chin in the folds of his belcher neckerchief and thrusting his hands deep into his pockets, turned and went his way.

And as he went, smiling still, and still a little bitterly, he needs must remember and vaguely wonder what had become of all that Polite notepaper, and all those Fashionable cards, embossed, gilt-edged, and otherwise, that had been wont to pour upon him every morning, and which had so rejoiced the highly susceptible and eloquent legs of the Gentleman-in-Powder.

Evening was falling and the square seemed deserted save for a solitary man in a neckcloth of vivid hue, a dejected-looking man who lounged against the wall under the shade of the trees in the middle of the square, and seemed lost in contemplation of his boots. And yet when Barnabas, having traversed Charles Street and turned into the Haymarket, chanced to look back, he saw that the man was lounging dejectedly after him. Therefore Barnabas quickened his steps, and, reaching the crowded Strand, hurried on through the bustling throng; but just beyond Temple Bar, caught a glimpse of the vivid neckcloth on the opposite side of the road. Up Chancery Lane and across Holborn went Barnabas, yet, as he turned down Leather Lane, there, sure enough, was the man in the neckcloth as dejected as ever, but not twelve yards behind.

Half-way down crowded Leather Lane Barnabas turned off down a less frequented street and halting just beyond the corner, waited for his pursuer to come up. And presently round the corner he came and, in his hurry, very nearly stumbled over Barnabas, who promptly reached out a long arm and pinned him by the vivid neckcloth.

"Why do you follow me?" he demanded.

"Foller you?" repeated the man.

"You have been following me all the way."

"Have I?" said the man.

"You know you have. Come, what do you want?"

"Well, first," said the man, sighing dejectedly, "leggo my neck, will ye be so kind?"

"Not till you tell me why you follow me."

"Why, then," said the man, "listen and I'll tell ye."

"Well?" demanded Barnabas.

But, all at once, and quick as a flash, with a wrench and a cunning twist, the man had broken away and, taking to his heels, darted off down the street and was gone.

For a moment Barnabas stood hesitating, undecided whether to go on to Barrymaine's lodging or no, and finally struck off in the opposite direction, towards Gray's Inn Lane and so by devious ways eventually arrived at the back door of the "Gun," on which he forthwith knocked.

It was opened, almost immediately, by Corporal Richard Roe himself, who stared a moment, smiled, and thereupon extended a huge hand.

"What, is it you, sir?" he exclaimed, "for a moment I didn't know ye. Step in, sir, step in, we're proud to see ye."

So saying, he ushered Barnabas down two steps into the small but very snug chamber that he remembered, with its rows upon rows of shelves whereon a whole regiment of bottles and glasses were drawn up in neat array, "dressed" and marshalled as if on parade; it was indeed a place of superlative tidiness where everything seemed to be in a perpetual state of neatness and order.

In a great elbow chair beside the ingle, with a cushion at his back and another beneath one foot, sat Mr. Shrig puffing at a pipe and with his little reader open on the table at his elbow. He looked a little thinner and paler than usual, and Barnabas noticed that one leg was swathed in bandages, but his smile was as innocent and guileless and his clasp as warm as ever as they greeted each other.

"You must ax-cuse me rising, sir," said he, "the sperrit is villing but natur' forbids, it can't be done on account o' this here leg o' mine,—a slug through the stamper, d' ye see, vich is bad enough, though better than it might ha' been. But it vere a good night on the whole,—thanks to you and the Corp 'ere, I got the whole gang, —though, from conclusions as I'd drawed I'ad 'oped to get—vell, shall ve say Number Two? But Fate was ag'in me. Still, I don't complain, and the vay you fought 'em off till the Corp and my specials come up vas a vonder!"

"Ah! that it were!" nodded the Corporal.

"Though 'ow you wanished yourself avay, and v'ere you wanished to, is more vonderful still."

"Ah, that it is, sir!" nodded the Corporal again.

"Why," explained Barnabas, "I was stunned by a blow on the head, and when I came to, found myself lying out on the wharf behind a broken boat. I should have come round here days ago to inquire how you were, Mr. Shrig, only that my time has been—much occupied—of late."

"Veil, sir," said Mr. Shrig, puffing hard at his pipe, "from all accounts I should reckon as it 'ad. By Goles! but ve vas jest talking about you, sir, the werry i-dentical moment as you knocked at the door. I vas jest running over my little reader and telling the Corp the v'y and the v'erefore as you couldn't ha' done the deed."

"What deed?"

"V'y—*the* deed. The deed as all London is a-talking of,—the murder o' Jasper Gaunt, the money-lender."

"Ah!" said Barnabas thoughtfully. "And so you are quite sure that I—didn't murder Jasper Gaunt, are you. Mr. Shrig?"

"Quite—oh, Lord love you, yes!"

"And why?"

"Because," said Mr. Shrig with his guileless smile, and puffing out a cloud of smoke and watching it vanish ceilingwards, "because I 'appen to know 'oo did."

"Oh!" said Barnabas more thoughtfully than ever. "And who do you think it is?"

"Vell, sir," answered Mr. Shrig ponderously, "from conclusions as I've drawed I don't feel at liberty to name no names nor yet cast no insinivations, but—v'en the other traps (sich werry smart coves too!) 'ave been and gone an' arrested all the innercent parties in London, v'y then I shall put my castor on my napper, and take my tickler in my fib and go and lay my 'ooks on the guilty party."

"And when will that be?"

"Jest so soon as my leg sarves me, sir,—say a veek,—say, two."

"You're in no hurry then?"

"Lord, no, sir, I'm never in an 'urry."

"And you say you think you know who the murderer is?"

"V-y no, sir,—from conclusions as I've drawed I'm sure and sartin 'oo did the deed. But come, sir, vot do you say to a glass o' the Vun and Only, to drink a quick despatch to the guilty party?"

But the clock striking eight, Barnabas shook his head and rose.

"Thank you, but I must be going," said he.

"V'y if you must, you must," sighed Mr. Shrig as they shook hands; "good evening, sir, an' if anything unpleasant should 'appen to you in the next day or two—jest tip me the vord."

"What do you mean by unpleasant, Mr. Shrig?"

"Vell, took up p'r'aps, or shall ve say—arrested,—by some o' the other traps—sich werry smart coves, too!"

"Do you think it likely, Mr. Shrig?"

"Vell, sir," said Mr. Shrig, with his placid smile, "there's some traps as is so uncommon smart that they've got an 'abit of arresting innercent parties verever found, d'ye see. But if they should 'appen to lay their 'ooks on ye, jest tip me the office, sir."

"Thank you," said Barnabas, "I shan't forget," and, with a final nod to Mr. Shrig, turned and followed the Corporal into Gray's Inn Lane.

Now when Barnabas would have gone his way the Corporal stayed him with a very large but very gentle hand, and thereafter stood, rubbing his shaven chin with his shining hook and seeming very much abashed.

"What is it, Corporal?" Barnabas inquired.

"Well, sir," said the soldier diffidently, "it's like this, sir, my pal Jarsper and me, 'aving heard of—of your—altered circumstances, sir, wishes it to be understood as once your pals, ever your pals, come shine, come rain. We likewise wish it to be understood as if at any time a—a guinea would come in 'andy-like, sir—or say two or three, my pal Jarsper and me will be proud to oblige, proud, sir. And lastly, sir, my pal Jarsper and me would 'ave you to know as if at any time you want a friend to your back, there's me and there's 'im—or a roof to your 'ead, why there's ever and always the 'Gun' open to you, sir. We wishes you to understand this and—good evening, sir!"

But, or ever the blushing Corporal could escape, Barnabas caught and wrung his hand:

"And I, Corporal," said he, "I wish you both to know that I am proud to have won two such staunch friends, and that I shall always esteem it an honor to ask your aid or take your hands,—good night, Corporal!"

So saying, Barnabas turned upon his heel, and as he went his step was free and his eye brighter than it had been.

He took an intricate course by winding alleys and narrow side-streets, keeping his glance well about him until at length he came to a certain door in a certain dingy street,—and, finding the faulty latch yield to his hand, entered a narrow, dingy hall and groped his way up the dingiest stairs in the world.

Now all at once he fancied he heard a stealthy footstep that climbed on in the darkness before him, and he paused suddenly, but, hearing nothing, strode on, then stopped again for, plain enough this time, some one stumbled on the stair above him. So he stood there in the gloom, very still and very silent, and thus he presently heard another sound, very soft and faint like the breathing of a sigh. And all at once Barnabas clenched his teeth and spoke.

"Who is it?" he demanded fiercely, "now, by God—if it's you, Chichester—" and with the word, he reached out before him in the dark with merciless, griping hands.

The contact of something warm and soft; a broken, pitiful cry of fear, and he had a woman in his arms. And, even as he clasped that yielding form, Barnabas knew instinctively who it was, and straightway thrilled with a wild joy.

"Madam!" he said hoarsely. "Madam!"

But she never stirred, nay it almost seemed she sank yet closer into his embrace, if that could well be.

"Cleone!" he whispered.

"Barnabas," sighed a voice; and surely no other voice in all the world could have uttered the word so tenderly.

"I—I fear I frightened you?"

"Yes, a little—Barnabas."

"You are—trembling very much."

"Am I—Barnabas?"

"I am sorry that I—frightened you."

"I'm better now."

"Yet you—tremble!"

"But I—think I can walk if—"

"If—?"

"If you will help me, please—Barnabas."

Oh, surely never had those dark and dingy stairs, worn though they were by the tread of countless feet, heard till now a voice so soft, so low and sweet, so altogether irresistible! Such tender, thrilling tones might have tamed Hyrcanean tigers or charmed the ferocity of Cerberus himself. Then how might our

Barnabas hope to resist, the more especially as one arm yet encircled the yielding softness of her slender waist and her fragrant breath was upon his cheek?

Help her? Of course he would.

"It's so very—dark," she sighed.

"Yes, it's very dark," said Barnabas, "but it isn't far to the landing—shall we go up?"

"Yes, but—" my lady hesitated a moment as one who takes breath for some great effort, and, in that moment, he felt her bosom heave beneath his hand. "Oh, Barnabas," she whispered, "won't you—kiss me—first?"

Then Barnabas trembled in his turn, the arm about her grew suddenly rigid and, when he spoke, his voice was harsh and strained.

"Madam," said he, "can the mere kiss of an—inn-keeper's son restore your dead faith?"

Now when he had said this, Cleone shrank in his embrace and uttered a loud cry as if he had offered her some great wrong, and, breaking from him, was gone before him up the stair, running in the dark.

Oh, Youth! Oh, Pride!

So Barnabas hurried after her and thus, as she threw open Barrymaine's door he entered with her and, in his sudden abasement, would have knelt to her, but Ronald Barrymaine had sprung up from the couch and now leaned there, staring with dazed eyes like one new wakened from sleep.

"Ronald," she cried, running to him, "I came as soon as I could, but I didn't understand your letter. You wrote of some great danger. Oh, Ronald dear, what is it—this time?"

"D-danger!" he repeated, and with the word, turned to stare over his shoulder into the dingiest corner: "d-danger, yes, so I am,—but t-tell me who it is—behind me, in the corner?"

"No one, Ronald."

"Yes—yes there is, I tell you," he whispered, "look again—now, d-don't you see him?"

"No, oh no!" answered Cleone, clasping her hands, and shrinking before Barrymaine's wild and haggard look. "Oh, Ronald, there's—no one there!"

"Yes there is, he's always there now—always just behind me. Last night he began to talk to me—ah, no, no—what am I saying? never heed me, Clo. I—I asked you to come because I'm g-going away, soon, very s-soon, Clo, and I know I shall n-never see you again. I suppose you thought it was m-money I wanted, but no—it's not that, I wanted to say good-by because you see I'm g-going away—to-night!"

"Going away, Ronald?" she repeated, sinking to her knees beside the rickety couch, for he had fallen back there as though overcome by sudden weakness. "Dear boy, where are you going—and why?"

"I'm g-going far away—because I must—the s-sooner the better!" he whispered, struggling to his elbow to peer into the corner again. "Yes, the s-sooner the better. But, before I go I want you to promise—to swear, Clo—to s-swear to me—" Barrymaine sat up suddenly and, laying his nervous hands upon her shoulders, leaned down to her in fierce eagerness, "You must s-swear to me n-never to see or have anything to do with that d-devil, Chichester, d' ye hear me, Clo, d' ye hear me?"

"But—oh, Ronald, I don't understand, you always told me he was your friend, I thought—"

"Friend!" cried Barrymaine passionately. "He's a devil, I tell you he's a d-devil, oh—" Barrymaine choked and fell back gasping; but, even as Cleone leaned above him all tender solicitude, he pushed her aside and, springing to his feet, reached out and caught Barnabas by the arm. "Beverley," he cried, "you'll shield her from him—w-when I'm gone, you'll l-look after her, won't you, Beverley? She's the only thing I ever loved—except my accursed self. You will shield her from—that d-devil!"

Then, still clutching Barnabas, he turned and seized Cleone's hands.

"Clo!" he cried, "dearest of sisters, if ever you need a f-friend when I'm gone, he's here. Turn to him, Clo—look up—give him your hand. Y-you loved him once, I think, and you were right—quite r-right. You can t-trust Beverley, Clo—g-give him your hand."

"No, no!" cried Cleone, and, snatching her fingers from Barrymaine's clasp, she turned away.

"What—you w-won't?"

"No—never, never!"

"Why not? Answer me! Speak, I tell you!"

But Cleone knelt there beside the couch, her head proudly averted, uttering no word.

"Why, you don't think, like so many of the fools, that he killed Jasper Gaunt, do you?" cried Barrymaine feverishly. "You don't think he d-did it, do you—do you? Ah, but he didn't—he didn't, I tell you, and I know—because—"

"Stop!" exclaimed Barnabas.

"Stop—no, why should I? She'll learn soon enough now and I'm m-man enough to tell her myself—I'm no c-coward, I tell you—"

Then Cleone raised her head and looked up at her half-brother, and in her eyes were a slow-dawning fear and horror.

"Oh, Ronald!" she whispered, "what do you mean?"

"Mean?" cried Barrymaine, "I mean that I did it—I did it. Yes, I k-killed Jasper Gaunt, but it was no m-murder, Clo—a—a fight, an accident—yes, I s-swear to God I never meant to do it."

"You!" she whispered, "you?"

"Yes, I—I did it, but I swear I never m-meant to—oh, Cleone—" and he reached down to her with hands outstretched appealingly. But Cleone shrank down and down—away from him, until she was crouching on the floor, yet staring up at him with wide and awful eyes.

"You!" she whispered.

"Don't!" he cried. "Ah, don't look at me like that and oh, my God! W-won't you l-let me t-touch you, Clo?"

"I—I'd rather you—wouldn't;" and Barnabas saw that she was shivering violently.

"But it was no m-murder," he pleaded, "and I'm g-going away, Clo—ah! won't you let me k-kiss you good-by—just once, Clo?"

"I'd rather—you wouldn't," she whispered.

"Y-your hand, then—only your hand, Clo."

"I'd rather—you didn't!"

Then Ronald Barrymaine groaned and fell on his knees beside her and sought to kiss her little foot, the hem of her dress, a strand of her long, yellow hair; but seeing how she shuddered away from him, a great sob broke from him and he rose to his feet.

"Beverley," he said, "oh, Beverley, s-she won't let me touch her." And so stood a while with his face hidden in his griping hands. After a moment he looked down at her again, but seeing how she yet gazed at him with that wide, awful, fixed stare, he strove as if to speak; then, finding no words, turned suddenly upon his heel and crossing the room, went into his bed-chamber and locked the door.

Then Barnabas knelt beside that shaken, desolate figure and fain would have comforted her, but now he could hear her speaking in a passionate whisper, and the words she uttered were these:

"Oh, God forgive him! Oh, God help him! Have mercy upon him, oh God of Pity!"

And these words she whispered over and over again until, at length, Barnabas reached out and touched her very gently.

"Cleone!" he said.

At the touch she rose and stood looking round the dingy room like one distraught, and, sighing, crossed unsteadily to the door.

And when they reached the stair, Barnabas would have taken her hand because of the dark, but she shrank away from him and shook her head.

"Sir," said she very softly, "a murderer's sister needs no help, I thank you."

And so they went down the dark stair with never a word between them and, reaching the door with the faulty latch, Barnabas held it open and they passed out into the dingy street, and as they walked side by side towards Hatton Garden, Barnabas saw that her eyes were still fixed and wide and that her lips still moved in silent prayer.

In a while, being come into Hatton Garden, Barnabas saw a hackney coach before them, and beside the coach a burly, blue-clad figure, a conspicuous figure by reason of his wooden leg and shiny, glazed hat.

"W'y, Lord, Mr. Beverley, sir!" exclaimed the Bo'sun, hurrying forward, with his hairy fist outstretched, "this is a surprise, sir, likewise a pleasure, and—" But here, observing my lady's face, he checked himself suddenly, and opening the carriage door aided her in very tenderly, beckoning Barnabas to follow. But Barnabas shook his head.

"Take care of her, Bo'sun," said he, clasping the sailor's hand, "take great care of her." So saying, he closed the door upon them, and stood to watch the rumbling coach down the bustling street until it had rumbled itself quite out of sight.

CHAPTER LXVII

WHICH GIVES SOME ACCOUNT OF THE WORST PLACE IN THE WORLD

A bad place by day, an evil place by night, an unsavory place at all times is Giles's Rents, down by the River.

It is a place of noisome courts and alleys, of narrow, crooked streets, seething with a dense life from fetid cellar to crowded garret, amid whose grime and squalor the wail of the new-born infant is echoed by the groan of decrepit age and ravaging disease; where Vice is rampant and ghoulish Hunger stalks, pale and grim.

Truly an unholy place is Giles's Rents, down by the River.

Here, upon a certain evening, Barnabas, leaning out from his narrow casement, turned wistful-eyed, to stare away over broken roof and chimney, away beyond the maze of squalid courts and alleys that hemmed him in to where, across the River, the sun was setting in a blaze of glory, yet a glory that served only to make more apparent all the filth and decay, all the sordid ugliness of his surroundings.

Below him was a dirty court, where dirty children fought and played together, filling the reeking air with their shrill clamor, while slatternly women stood gossiping in ragged groups with grimy hands on hips, or with arms rolled up in dingy aprons. And Barnabas noticed that the dirty children and gossiping women turned very often to stare and point up at a certain window a little further along the court, and he idly wondered why.

It had been a day of stifling heat, and even now, though evening was at hand, he breathed an air close and heavy and foul with a thousand impurities.

Now as he leaned there, with his earnest gaze bent ever across the River, Barnabas sighed, bethinking him of clean, white, country roads, of murmuring brooks and rills, of the cool green shades of dewy woods full of the fragrance of hidden flower and herb and sweet, moist earth. But most of all he bethought him of a certain wayside inn, an ancient inn of many gables, above whose hospitable door swung a sign whereon a weather-beaten hound, dim-legged and faded of tail, pursued a misty blur that by common report was held to be hare; a comfortable, homely inn of no especial importance perhaps, yet the very best inn to be found in all broad England, none the less. And, as he thought, a sudden, great yearning came upon Barnabas and, leaning his face between his hands, he said within himself:

"'I will arise, and go to my father!'"

But little by little he became aware that the clamor below had ceased and, glancing down into the court, beheld two men in red waistcoats, large men, bewhiskered men and square of elbow. Important men were these, at sight of whom the ragged children stood awed and silent and round of eye, while the gossiping women drew back to give them way. Yes, men of consequence they were, beyond a doubt, and Barnabas noticed that they also stared very often at a certain window a little further up the court and from it to a third man who limped along close behind them by means of a very nobbly stick; a shortish, broadish, mild-looking man whose face was hidden beneath the shadow of the broad-brimmed hat. Nevertheless at sight of this man Barnabas uttered an exclamation, drew in his head very suddenly and thereafter stood, listening and expectant, his gaze on the door like one who waits to meet the inevitable.

And after a while, he saw the latch raised cautiously, and the door begin to open very slowly and noiselessly. It had opened thus perhaps some six inches when he spoke:

"Is that you, Mr. Shrig?"

Immediately the door became stationary and, after some brief pause a voice issued from behind it, a voice somewhat wheezing and hoarse.

"Which your parding I ax, sir," said the voice, "which your parding I 'umbly ax, but it ain't, me being a respectable female, sir, name o' Snummitt, sir—charing, sir, also washing and clear-starching, sir!"

Hereupon, the door having opened to its fullest, Barnabas saw a stout, middle-aged woman whose naturally unlovely look had been further marred by the loss of one eye, while the survivor, as though constantly striving to make amends, was continually rolling itself up and down and to and fro, in a manner quite astonishing to behold.

"Which my name is Snummitt," she repeated, bobbing a curtsy and momentarily eclipsing the rolling eye under the poke of a very large bonnet, "Mrs. Snummitt, sir, which though a widder I'm respectable and of 'igh character and connections. Which me 'aving only one heye ain't by no manner of means to be 'eld ag'in me, seeing as it were took away by a act o' Providence in the shape of another lady's boot-'eel sixteen summers ago come Michaelmas."

"Indeed," said Barnabas, seeing Mrs. Snummitt had paused for breath, "but what—"

"Which I were to give you Mr. Bimby's compliments, sir, and ax if you could oblige him with the loan of a wine-glass?"

"Mr. Bimby?"

"Over-'ead, sir—garret! You may 'ave 'eard 'im, now and then—flute, sir, 'armonious, though doleful."

"And he wants a wine-glass, does he?" said Barnabas, and forthwith produced that article from a rickety corner-cupboard and handed it to Mrs. Snummitt, who took it, glanced inside it, turned it upside-down, and rolled her eye at Barnabas eloquently.

"What more?" he inquired.

"Which I would mention, sir, or shall we say, 'int, as if you could put a little drop o' summat inside of it—brandy, say—'t would be doing a great favor."

"Ah, to be sure!" said Barnabas. And, having poured out a stiff quantum of the spirit, he gave it to Mrs. Snummit, who took it, curtsied, and rolling her solitary orb at the bottle on the table, smiled engagingly.

"Which I would thank you kindly on be'alf o' Mr. Bimby, sir, and, seeing it upon the tip o' your tongue to ax me to partake, I begs to say 'Amen,' with a slice o' lemming cut thin, and thank you from my 'eart."

"I fear I have no lemon," began Barnabas.

"Then we won't say no more about it, sir, not a word. 'Evings forbid as a lemming should come betwixt us seeing as I am that shook on account o' pore, little Miss Pell."

"Who is Miss Pell?"

"She's one as was, sir, but now—ain't," answered Mrs. Snummitt and, nodding gloomily, she took down the brandy in three separate and distinct gulps, closed her eyes, sighed, and nodded her poke bonnet more gloomily than before. "Little Miss Pell, sir, 'ad a attic three doors down, sir, and pore little Miss Pell 'as been and gone and—done it! Which do it I knowed she would."

"Done what?" inquired Barnabas.

"Five long year come shine, come rain, I've knowed pore Miss Pell, and though small, a real lady she were, but lonesome. Last night as ever was, she met me on the stairs, and by the same token I 'ad a scrubbing-brush in one 'and and a bucket in the other, me 'aving been charing for the first floor front, a 'andsome gent with whiskers like a lord, and 'oh, Mrs. Snummitt!' she sez and all of a twitter she was too, 'dear Mrs. Snummitt,' sez she, 'I'm a-going away on a journey,' she sez, 'but before I go,' she sez, 'I should like to kiss you good-by, me being so lonesome,' she sez. Which kiss me she did, sir, and likewise wep' a couple o' big tears over me, pore soul, and then, run away into 'er dark little attic and locked 'erself in, and—done it!"

"What—what did she do?"

"'Ung 'erself in the cupboard, sir. Kissed me only last night she did and wep' over me, and now—cold and stiff, pore soul?"

"But why did she do it?" cried Barnabas, aghast.

"Well, there was the lonesomeness and—well, she 'adn't eat anything for two days it seems, and—"

"You mean that she was hungry—starving?"

"Generally, sir. But things was worse lately on account of 'er heyes getting weak. 'Mrs. Snummitt,' she used to say, 'my heyes is getting worse and worse,' she'd say, 'but I shall work as long as I can see the stitches, and then, Mrs. Snummitt, I must try a change o' scene,' she used to say with a little shiver like. And I used to wonder where she'd go, but—I know now, and—well—the Bow Street Runners 'as just gone up to cut the pore soul down."

"And she killed herself—because she was hungry!" said Barnabas, staring wide-eyed.

"Oh, yes, lots on 'em do, I've knowed three or four as went and done it, and it's generally hunger as is to blame for it. There's Mr. Bimby, now, a nice little gent, but doleful like 'is flute, 'e's always 'ungry 'e is, I'll take my oath—shouldn't wonder if 'e don't come to it one o' these days. And talking of 'im I must be going, sir, and thank you kindly, I'm sure."

"Why, then," said Barnabas as she bobbed him another curtsy, "will you ask Mr. Bimby if he will do me the pleasure to step down and take supper with me?"

"Which, sir, I will, though Mr. Bimby I won't answer for, 'im being busy with the pore young man as 'e brought 'ome last night—it's 'im as the brandy's for. Ye see, sir, though doleful, Mr. Bimby's very kind 'earted, and 'e's always a-nussing somebody or something—last time it were a dog with a broke leg—ah, I've knowed 'im bring 'ome stray cats afore now, many's the time, and once a sparrer. But I'll tell 'im, sir, and thank you kindly."

And in a while, when Mrs. Snummitt had duly curtsied herself out of sight, Barnabas sighed, and turned once more to stare away, over broken roof and crumbling chimney, towards the glory of the sunset. But now, because he remembered poor little Miss Pell who had died because she was so friendless and hungry, and Mr. Bimby who was "always hungry" and played the flute, he stifled his fierce yearning for dewy wood and copse and the sweet, pure breath of the country, and thought no more of his father's inn that was so very far from the sordid grime and suffering of Giles's Rents, down by the River; and setting the kettle on the fire he sank into a chair and stretching out his long legs, fell into a profound meditation.

From this he was roused by the opening of the door, and, glancing up, beheld John Peterby. A very different person he looked from the neat, well-groomed Peterby of a week ago, what with the rough, ill-fitting clothes he wore and the fur cap pulled low over his brows; the gentleman's gentleman had vanished quite, and in his stead was a nondescript character such as might have been met with anywhere along the River, or lounging in shadowy corners. He carried a bundle beneath one arm, and cast a swift look round the room before turning to see the door behind him.

"Ah," said Barnabas nodding, "I'm glad you're back, John, and with plenty of provisions I hope, for I'm amazingly hungry, and besides, I've asked a gentleman to sup with us."

Peterby put down the bundle and, crossing to the hearth, took the kettle, which was boiling furiously, and set it upon the hob, then laying aside the fur cap spoke:

"A gentleman, sir?"

"A neighbor, John."

"Sir," said he, as he began to prepare the tea in that swift, silent manner peculiar to him in all things, "when do you propose we shall leave this place?"

"Why, to tell you the truth, John, I had almost determined to start for the country this very night, but, on second thoughts, I've decided to stay on a while. After all, we have only been here a week as yet."

"Yes, sir, it is just a week sincc—Jasper Gaunt was murdered," said Peterby gently as he stooped to unpack his bundle. Now when he said this, Barnabas turned to look at him again, and thus he noticed that Peterby's brow was anxious and careworn.

"I wish, John," said he, "that you would remember we are no longer master and man."

"Old habits stick, sir."

"And that I brought you to this dismal place as my friend."

"But surely, sir, a man's friend is worthy of his trust and confidence?"

"John Peterby, what do you mean?"

"Sir," said Peterby, setting down the teapot, "as I came along this evening, I met Mr. Shrig; he recognized me in spite of my disguise and he told me to—warn you—"

"Well, John?"

"That you may be arrested—"

"Yes, John?"

"For—the murder of Jasper Gaunt. Oh, sir, why have you aroused suspicion against yourself by disappearing at such a time?"

"Suspicion?" said Barnabas, and with the word he rose and laying his hands upon John Peterby's shoulders, looked into his eyes. Then, seeing the look they held, he smiled and shook his head.

"Oh, friend," said he, "what matters it so long as you know my hands are clean?"

"But, sir, if you are arrested—"

"They must next prove me guilty, John," said Barnabas, sitting down at the table.

"Or an accessory—after the fact!"

"Hum!" said Barnabas thoughtfully, "I never thought of that."

"And, sir," continued Peterby anxiously, "there are two Bow Street Runners lounging outside in the court—"

"But they're not after me yet. So cheer up, John!" Yet in that moment, Peterby sprang to his feet with fists clenched, for some one was knocking softly at the door.

"Quick, sir—the other room—hide!" he whispered. But shaking his head, Barnabas rose and, putting him gently aside, opened the door and beheld a small gentleman who bowed.

A pale, fragile little gentleman this, with eyes and hair of an indeterminate color, while his clothes, scrupulously neat and brushed and precise to a button, showed pitifully shabby and threadbare in contrast with his elaborately frilled and starched cravat and gay, though faded, satin waistcoat; and, as he stood bowing nervously to them, there was an air about him that somehow gave the impression that he was smaller even than Nature had intended.

"Gentlemen," said he, coughing nervously behind his hand, "hem!—I trust I don't intrude. Feel it my obligation to pay my respects, to—hem! to welcome you as a neighbor—as a neighbor. Arthur Bimby, humbly at your service—Arthur Bimby, once a man of parts though now brought low by abstractions, gentlemen, forces not apparent to the human optic, sirs. Still, in my day, I have been known about town as a downy bird, a smooth file, and a knowing card—hem!"

Hereupon he bowed again, looking as unlike a "smooth file" or "knowing card" as any small, inoffensive gentleman possibly could.

"Happy to see you, sir," answered Barnabas, returning his bow with one as deep, "I am Barnabas Barty at your service, and this is my good friend John Peterby. We are about to have supper—nothing very much—tea, sir, eggs, and a cold fowl, but if you would honor us—"

"Sir," cried the little gentleman with a quaver of eagerness in his voice and a gleam in his eye, both quickly suppressed, "hem!—indeed I thank you, but—regret I have already supped—hem—duck and green peas, gentlemen, though I'll admit the duck was tough—deuced tough, hem! Still, if I might be permitted to toy with an egg and discuss a dish of tea, the honor would be mine, sirs—would be mine!"

Then, while Peterby hastened to set the edibles before him, Barnabas drew up a chair and, with many bows and flutterings of the thin, restless hands, the little gentleman sat down.

"Indeed, indeed," he stammered, blinking his pale eyes, "this is most kind, I protest, most kind and neighborly!" Which said, he stooped suddenly above his plate and began to eat, that is to say he swallowed one or two mouthfuls with a nervous haste that was very like voracity, checked himself, and glancing guiltily from unconscious Barnabas to equally unconscious Peterby, sighed and thereafter ate his food as deliberately as might be expected of one who had lately dined upon duck and green peas.

"Ah!" said he, when at length his hunger was somewhat assuaged, "you are noticing the patch in my left elbow, sir?"

"No indeed!" began Barnabas.

"I think you were, sir—every one does, every one—it can't be missed, sir, and I—hem! I'm extreme conscious of it myself, sirs. I really must discard this old coat, but—hem! I'm attached to it—foolish sentiment, sirs. I wear it for associations' sake, it awakens memory, and memory is a blessed thing, sirs, a very blessed thing!"

"Sometimes!" sighed Barnabas.

"In me, sirs, you behold a decayed gentleman, yet one who has lived in his time, but now, sirs, all that remains to me is—this coat. A prince once commended it, the Beau himself condescended to notice it! Yes, sirs, I was rich once and happily married, and my friends were many. But—my best friend deceived and ruined me, my wife fled away and left me, sirs, my friends all forsook me and, to-day, all that I have to remind me of what I was when I was young and lived, is this old coat. To-day I exist as a law-writer, to-day I am old, and with my vanished youth hope has vanished too. And I call myself a decayed gentleman because I'm—fading, sirs. But to fade is genteel; Brummell faded! Yes, one may fade and still be a gentleman, but who ever heard of a fading ploughman?"

"Who, indeed?" said Barnabas.

"But to fade, sir," continued the little gentleman, lifting a thin, bloodless hand, "though genteel, is a slow process and a very weary one. Without the companionship of Hope, life becomes a hard and extreme long road to the ultimate end, and therefore I am sometimes greatly tempted to take the—easier course, the—shorter way."

"What do you mean?"

"Well, sir, there are other names for it, but—hem!—I prefer to call it 'the shorter way.'"

"Do you mean—suicide?"

"Sir," cried Mr. Bimby, shivering and raising protesting hands, "I said 'the shorter way.' Poor little Miss Pell—a lady born, sir—she used to curtsy to me on the stairs, she chose 'the shorter way.' She also was old, you see, and weary. And to-night I met another who sought to take this 'shorter way'—but he was young, and for the young there is always hope. So I brought him home with me and tried to comfort him, but I fear—"

Peterby sprang suddenly to his feet and Mr. Bimby started and turned to glance fearfully towards the door which was quivering beneath the blows of a ponderous fist. Therefore Barnabas rose and crossing the room, drew the latch. Upon the threshold stood Corporal Richard Roe, looming gigantic in the narrow doorway, who, having saluted Barnabas with his shining hook, spoke in his slow, diffident manner.

"Sir," said he, "might I speak a word wi' you?"

"Why, Corporal, I'm glad to see you—come in!"

"Sir," said the big soldier with another motion of his glittering hook, "might I ax you to step outside wi' me jest a moment?"

"Certainly, Corporal," and with a murmured apology to Mr. Bimby, Barnabas followed the Corporal out upon the gloomy landing and closed the door. Now at the further end of the landing was a window, open to admit the air, and, coming to this window, the Corporal glanced down stealthily into the court below, beckoning Barnabas to do the like:

"Sir," said he in a muffled tone, "d' ye see them two coves in the red weskits?" and he pointed to the two Bow Street Runners who lounged in the shadow of an adjacent wall, talking together in rumbling tones and puffing at their pipes.

"Well, Corporal, what of them?"

"Sir, they're a-waiting for you!"

"Are you sure, Corporal? A poor creature committed suicide to-day; I thought they were here on that account."

"No, sir, that was only a blind, they're a-watching and a-waiting to take you for the Gaunt murder. My pal Jarsper knows, and my pal Jarsper sent me here to give you the office to lay low and not to venture out to-night."

"Ah!" said Barnabas, beginning to frown.

"My pal Jarsper bid me say as you was to keep yourself scarce till 'e's got 'is 'ooks on the guilty party, sir."

"Ah!" said Barnabas, again, "and when does he intend to make the arrest?"

"This here very night, sir."

"Hum!" said Barnabas thoughtfully.

"And," continued the Corporal, "I were likewise to remind you, sir, as once your pals, ever and allus your pals. And, sir—good-night, and good-luck to you!" So saying, the Corporal shook hands, flourished his hook and strode away down the narrow stairs, smiling up at Barnabas like a beneficent giant.

And, when he was gone, Barnabas hurried back into the room and, taking pen and paper, wrote this:

You are to be arrested to-night, so I send you my friend, John Peterby. Trust yourself to his guidance.

BEVERLEY.

And having folded and sealed this letter, he beckoned to Peterby.

"John," said he, speaking in his ear, "take this letter to Mr. Barrymaine, give it into his hand, see that he leaves at once. And, John, take a coach and bring him back with you."

So Peterby the silent thrust the note into his bosom, took his fur cap, and sighing, went from the room; and a moment later, glancing cautiously through the window, Barnabas saw him hurry through the court and vanish round the corner.

Then Barnabas turned back to the table, and seeing how wistfully Mr. Bimby eyed the teapot, poured him out another cup; and while they drank together, Mr. Bimby chatted, in his pleasant way, of bitter wrong, of shattered faith and ideals, of the hopeless struggle against circumstance, and of the oncoming terror of old age, bringing with it failing strength and all the horrors of a debtor's prison. And now, mingled with his pity, Barnabas was conscious of a growing respect for this pleasant, small gentleman, and began to understand why a man might seek the "shorter way," yet be no great coward after all.

So Mr. Bimby chattered on and Barnabas listened until the day declined to evening; until Barnabas began to hearken for Peterby's returning footstep on the uncarpeted stair outside. Even in the act of lighting the candles his ears were acutely on the stretch, and thus he gradually became aware of another sound, soft and dull, yet continuous, a sound difficult to locate. But as he stood staring into the flame of the candle he had just lighted, striving meanwhile to account for and place this noise, Mr. Bimby rose and lifted a thin, arresting hand.

"Sir," said he, "do you hear anything?"

"Yes. I was wondering what it could be."

"I think I can tell you, sir," said Mr. Bimby, pointing to a certain part of the cracked and blackened ceiling; "it is up there, in my room—listen!"

And now, all at once Barnabas started and caught his breath, for from the floor above came a soft trampling as of unshod feet, yet the feet never moved from the one spot.

"Indeed," sighed Mr. Bimby, "I greatly fear my poor young friend is ill again. I must go up to him, but first—may I beg—"

"Sir," said Barnabas, his gaze still fixed upon a certain corner of the ceiling, "I should like to go with you, if I may."

"You are very good, sir, very kind, I protest you are," quavered Mr. Bimby, "and hem! if I might suggest—a little brandy—?" But even as Barnabas reached for the bottle, there came a hurry of footsteps on the stair, a hand fumbled at the door and Mr. Smivvle entered with Peterby at his heels.

"Oh, Beverley!" he exclaimed, tugging nervously at his whiskers, "Barry's gone—most distressing—utterly vanished! I just happened to—ah—pop round the corner, my dear fellow, and when I came back he'd disappeared, been looking for him everywhere. Poor Barry—poor fellow, they've got him safe enough by now! Oh Gad, Beverley! what can I do?"

"Sit down," said Barnabas, "I think he's found." So saying he turned and followed Mr. Bimby out of the room.

CHAPTER LXVIII

CONCERNING THE IDENTITY OF MR. BIMBY'S GUEST

It needed but a glance at the huddled figure in the comfortless little attic to assure Barnabas of the identity of Mr. Bimby's "poor young friend"; wherefore, setting down the candle on the broken table, he crossed the room and touched that desolate figure with a gentle hand.

Then Ronald Barrymaine looked up and, seeing Barnabas, struggled to his knees:

"Beverley!" he exclaimed, "oh, thank God! You'll save her from that d-devil—I tried to kill him, b-but he was too quick for me. But you—you'll save her!"

"What do you mean? Is it Cleone? What do you mean—speak!" said Barnabas, beginning to tremble.

"Yes, yes!" muttered Barrymaine, passing a hand across his brow. "Listen then! Chichester knows—he knows, I tell you! He came to me, three days ago I think—while D-Dig was out, and he talked and talked, and questioned me and questioned me, and s-so I—I told him everything—everything! But I had to, Beverley, I had to—*he* made me—yes *he*, Jasper Gaunt. So I told C-Chichester everything and then—he laughed, and I t-tried to k-kill him, but he got away and left me alone with—him. He's always near me now—always c-close behind me where I can't quite s-see him, only sometimes I hear him ch-choke, oh, my God, Beverley!—like he did—that night! I r-ran away to escape him but—oh Beverley!—he's followed me, he was here a moment ago—I heard him, I t-tell you! Oh, Beverley, don't l-look as if you thought me m-mad, I'm not! I'm not! I know it's all an illusion, of c-course, but—"

"Yes," said Barnabas gently, "but what of Cleone?"

"Cleone? Oh, God help me, Beverley, she's going to g-give herself to that devil—to buy his silence!"

"What—what," stammered Barnabas. "What do you mean?"

"I got this to-day—read it and see!" said Barrymaine and drew from his bosom a crumpled letter. Then Barnabas took it, and smoothing it out, read these words:

Ronald dear, I'm sorry I didn't let you kiss me good-by. So sorry that I am going to do all that a woman can to save you. Mr. Chichester has learned your awful secret, and I am the price of his silence. So, because of my promise to our dying mother, and because life can hold nothing for me now, because life and death are alike to me now, I am going to marry him to-night, at his house at Headcorn. Good-by, Ronald dear, and that God may forgive and save you in this life and hereafter, is the undying prayer of

Your Sister, CLEONE.

Barnabas refolded the letter and, giving it back to Barrymaine, took out Natty Bell's great silver watch.

"It is a long way to Headcorn," said he, "I must start at once!"

"Ah! You'll g-go then, Beverley?"

"Go? Of course!"

"Then, oh Beverley, whatever happens—whether you're in time or no, you'll—k-kill him?"

"I think," said Barnabas, putting away his watch, "yes, I think I shall."

"The house is called Ashleydown," continued Barrymaine feverishly, "a b-big house about a m-mile this side the village."

"Ashleydown? I think I've heard mention of it before. But now, you must come with me, Smivvle is downstairs, you shall have my rooms to-night."

"Thanks, Beverley, but do you m-mind—giving me your arm? I get f-faint sometimes—my head, I think, the faintness came on me in the s-street to-night, and I f-fell, I think."

"Indeed, yes, sir," added Mr. Bimby with a little bow, "it was so I found you, sir."

"Ah, yes, you were kind to me, I remember—you have my g-gratitude, sir. Now, Beverley, give me your arm, I—I—oh, God help me!" Barrymaine reached out with clutching fingers, swayed, twisted sideways and would have fallen, had not Barnabas caught him.

"Poor boy!" cried Mr. Bimby, "a fit, I think—so very young, poor boy! You'll need help, sir. Oh, poor boy, poor boy!" So saying, the little gentleman hurried away and presently returned with John and Mr. Smivvle. Thus, between them, they bore Ronald Barrymaine downstairs and, having made him as comfortable as might be in the inner room, left him to the care of the faithful Mr. Smivvle.

Then Barnabas crossed to the narrow window and stood there a while, looking down at the dim figures of the Bow Street Runners who still lounged against the wall in the gathering dusk and talked together in gruff murmurs.

"John," said he at last, "I must trouble you to change coats with me." Peterby slipped off the garment in question, and aided Barnabas to put it on.

"Now, your fur cap, John."

"Sir," said Peterby all anxiety in a moment, "you are never thinking of going out, tonight—it would be madness!"

"Then mad am I. Your cap, John."

"But—if you are arrested—"

"He will be a strong man who stays me tonight, John. Give me your cap."

So Peterby brought the fur cap and, putting it on, Barnabas pulled it low down over his brows and turned to the door. But there Peterby stayed him.

"Sir," he pleaded, "let me go for you."

"No," said Barnabas, shaking his head.

"Then let me go with you,"

"Impossible, John."

"Why?"

"Because," answered Barnabas, grim-lipped, "tonight I go to ride another race, a very long, hard race, and oh, John Peterby—my faithful John, if you never prayed before—pray now, that I may win!"

"Sir," said Peterby, "I will!"

Then Barnabas caught his hand, wrung it, and striding from the room, hurried away down the dark and narrow stair.

CHAPTER LXIX

HOW BARNABAS LED A HUE AND CRY

The shadows were creeping down on Giles's Rents, hiding its grime, its misery and squalor, what time Barnabas stepped out into the court, and, turning his back upon the shadowy River, strode along, watchful-eyed, toward that dark corner where the Bow Street Runners still lounged, smoking their pipes and talking together in their rumbling tones. As he drew nearer he became aware that they had ceased their talk and guessed rather than saw that he was the object of their scrutiny; nor was he mistaken, for as he came abreast of where they stood, one of them lurched towards him.

"Why, hullo, Joe," exclaimed the man, in a tone of rough familiarity, "strike me blue if this ain't fort'nate! 'Ow goes it, Joe?"

"My name isn't Joe," said Barnabas, pausing, for the man had lurched in front of him, barring his way.

"Not Joe, eh?" growled the man, thrusting his head unpleasantly close to Barnabas to peer into his face, "not Joe, eh? Why then p'r'aps it might be—Barnabas, eh? P'r'aps it might be—Beverley, eh? Barnabas Beverley like-wise, eh? All right, Ben!" he called to his mate, "it's our man right enough!"

"What do you mean?" inquired Barnabas, casting a swift glance about him; and thus, he saw a moving shadow some distance down the court, a furtive shape that flitted towards them where the gathering shadows lay thickest. And at the sight, Barnabas clenched his fists and poised himself for swift action.

"What do you want?" he demanded, his gaze still wandering, his ears hearkening desperately for the sound of creeping footsteps behind, "what do you want with me?"

"W'y, we wants you, to be sure," answered Runner No. 1. "We wants you, Barnabas Beverley, Esk-vire, for the murder of Jasper Gaunt. And, wot's more—we've got ye! And, wot's more—you'd better come along nice and quiet in the name o' the—"

But in that moment, even as he reached out to seize the prisoner, Runner No. 1 felt himself caught in a powerful wrestling grip, his legs were swept from under him, and he thudded down upon the cobbles. Then, as Barnahas turned to meet the rush of Runner No. 2, behold a dark figure, that leapt from the dimness behind, and bore No. 2, cursing savagely, staggering back and back to the wall, and pinned him there, while, above the scuffling, the thud of blows and the trample of feet, rose a familiar voice:

"Run, sir—run!" cried John Peterby, "I've got this one—run!"

Incontinent, Barnabas turned, and taking to his heels, set off along the court, but with No. 1 (who had scrambled to his feet again) thundering after him in hot pursuit, roaring for help as he came.

"Stop, thief!" bellowed No. 1, pounding along behind.

"Stop, thief!" roared Barnabas, pounding along in front.

Round the corner into the street of tumble-down houses sped yelling Barnabas, scattering people right and left; round the corner came No. 1 Hard in his rear.

"Stop, thief!" bellowed No. 1, louder than ever.

"Stop, thief!" roared Barnabas, louder still, and running like the wind. Thus, No. 1 continued to bellow along behind, and Barnabas ran on roaring before, by dint of which he had very soon drawn about him divers other eager pursuers who, in their turn, taking up the cry, filled the air with a raving clamor that grew and ever grew. On sped Barnabas, still yelling "thieves," and with a yelling rabblement all about him, on he went by crooked ways, plunging down gloomy courts, doubling sudden corners, leading the pursuit ever deeper into the maze of dark alleys and crooked back streets, until, spying a place suitable to his purpose, he turned aside, and darting down a dark and narrow entry-way, he paused there in the kindly shelter to regain his breath, and heard the hue and cry go raving past until it had roared itself into the distance. Then, very cautiously and with no little difficulty, he retraced his steps, and coming at length to the River, crossed Blackfriars Bridge and hurried west-wards; nor did he stop or slacken his swift pace until he found himself in that quiet, back-street at the end of which his stables were situated. Being come there, he hammered upon the door which was presently opened by old Gabriel Martin himself.

"Martin, I'm in a hurry," said Barnabas, "have 'The Terror' saddled at once, and bring me a pair of spurred boots—quick!"

Without wasting time in needless words, the old groom set the stable-boys running to and fro, and himself brought Barnabas a pair of riding-boots, and aided him to put them on. Which done, Barnabas threw aside the fur cap, stripped off Peterby's rough coat, and looked about for other garments to take their place.

"If it be a coat as you're wanting, sir, there be one as you wore at the race," said Martin, "I keep it upstairs in my room. It be a bit tore, sir, but—"

"It will do," said Barnabas, nodding, "only—hurry, Martin!" By the time the old groom had returned with the scarlet hunting-frock and helped Barnabas into it, "The Terror" was led out from his box, and immediately began to snort and rear and beat a ringing tattoo with his great, round hoofs to a chorus of chirruping and whoa-ing from the stable-boys.

"A bit fresh-ish, p'r'aps, sir!" said Martin, viewing the magnificent animal with glistening eyes, "exercised reg'lar, too! But wot 'e wants is a good, stretching, cross-country gallop."

"Well, he's going to have it, Martin."

"Ah, sir," nodded the old groom, as Barnabas tested girth and stirrup-leathers, "you done mighty well when you bought 'im—theer ain't another 'oss 'is ekal in London—no, nor nowheers else as I knows on. 'E's won one race for you, and done it noble, and wot's more sir—"

"Tonight he must win me another!" said Barnabas, and swung himself into the saddle. "And this will be a much harder and crueller race than he ran before or will ever run again, Martin, I hope. Pray what, time is it?"

"Nigh on to 'alf-past eight, sir."

"So late!" said Barnabas, grim-lipped and frowning as he settled his feet in the stirrups. "Now—give him his head there—stay! Martin, have you a brace of pistols?"

"Pistols! Why yes, sir, but—"

"Lend them to me."

Forthwith the pistols were brought, somewhat clumsy weapons, but serviceable none the less.

"They're loaded, sir!" said Martin as he handed them up.

"Good!" nodded Barnabas, and slipping one into either pocket, gathered up his reins.

"You'll not be back tonight, sir?"

"Not tonight, Martin."

"Good night, sir."

"Good night, Martin."

"Are you ready, sir?"

"Quite ready, Martin."

"Then—stand away there!"

Obediently the stable-boys leapt aside, freeing "The Terror's" proud head, who snorted, reared, and plunged out through the open doorway, swung off sharp to his right and thundered away down the echoing street.

And thus "The Terror" set out on his second race, which was to be a very hard, cruel race, since it was to be run against no four-legged opponent, no thing of flesh and blood and nerves, but against the sure-moving, relentless fingers of Natty Bell's great, silver watch.

CHAPTER LXX

WHICH TELLS HOW BARNABAS RODE ANOTHER RACE

Over Westminster Bridge and down the Borough galloped Barnabas, on through the roaring din of traffic, past rumbling coach and creaking wain, heedless of the shouts of wagoners and teamsters and the indignant cries of startled pedestrians, yet watchful of eye and ready of hand, despite his seeming recklessness.

On sped the great, black horse, his pace increasing as the traffic lessened, on and on along the Old Kent Road, up the hill at New Cross and down again, and so through Lewisham to the open country beyond.

And now the way was comparatively clear save for the swift-moving lights of some chaise or the looming bulk of crawling market-wagons: therefore Barnabas, bethinking him always of the long miles before him, and of the remorseless, creeping fingers of Natty Bell's great watch, slacked his rein, whereat "The Terror," snorting for joy, tossed his mighty crest on high and, bounding forward, fell into his long, racing stride, spurning London further and further into the dimness behind.

Barnabas rode stooped low in the saddle, his watchful eyes scanning the road ahead, a glimmering track bordered by flying hedges, and trees that, looming ghost-like in the dusk, flitted past and, like ghosts, were gone again. Swift, swift sped the great, black horse, the glimmering road below, the luminous heaven above, a glorious canopy whence shone a myriad stars filling the still night with their soft, mysterious glow: a hot, midsummer night full of a great hush, a stillness wherein no wind stirred and upon whose deep silence distant sounds seemed magnified and rose, clear and plain, above the rhythmic drumming of "The Terror's" flying hoofs. Presently, out of the dimness ahead, lights twinkled, growing ever brighter and more numerous and Bromley was before him; came a long, paved street where people turned to stare, and point, and shout at him as he flashed by, and Bromley was behind him, and he was out upon the open road again where hedge, and barn, and tree seemed to leap at him from the dark only to vanish in the dimness behind.

On swept the great, black horse, past fragrant rick and misty pool, past running rills that gurgled in the shadows, by wayside inns whence came the sound of voices and laughter with snatches of song, all quickly lost again in the rolling thunder of those tireless galloping hoofs; past lonely cottages where dim lights burned, over hill, over dale, by rolling meadow and sloping down, past darkling woods whence breathed an air cool and damp and sweet, on up the long ascent of Poll Hill and down into the valley again. Thus, in a while, Barnabas saw more lights before him that, clustering together, seemed to hang suspended in mid-air, and, with his frowning gaze upon these clustering lights, he rode up that long, trying hill that leads into the ancient township of Sevenoaks.

At the further end of the town he turned aside and, riding into the yard of the Castle Inn, called for ale and, while he drank, stood by to watch the hissing ostlers as they rubbed down "The Terror" and gave him sparingly of water. So, into the saddle again and, bearing to the right, off and away for Tonbridge.

But now, remembering the hill country before him, he checked his pace, and thus, as he went, became once more aware of the profound stillness of the night about him, and of a gathering darkness. Therefore lifting his gaze to the heavens, he saw a great, black cloud that grew and spread from east to west, putting out the stars.

Now, with the gathering cloud, came sudden fear to clutch at his heart with icy fingers, a shivering dread lest, after all, he be too late; and, clenching sweating palms, Barnabas groaned, and in that moment "The Terror" leapt snorting beneath the rowelling spur.

Suddenly, as they topped River Hill, out of the murk ahead there met him a puff of wind, a hot wind that came and so was gone again, but far away beyond the distant horizon to his left, the sombre heaven was split and rent asunder by a jagged lightning flash whose quivering light, for one brief instant, showed him a glimpse of the wide valley below, of the winding road, of field and hedgerow and motionless tree and, beyond, the square tower of a church, very small with distance yet, above whose battlements a tiny weather-vane flashed and glittered vividly ere all things vanished, swallowed up in the pitchy dark.

And now came the wind again and in the wind was rain, a few great pattering drops, while the lightning flamed and quivered upon the horizon, and the thunder rolled ever louder and more near.

Came a sudden, blinding flame, that seemed to crackle in the air near by, a stunning thunder-clap shaking the very firmament, and thereafter an aching blackness, upon whose startled silence burst the rain—a sudden, hissing downpour.

Up—up reared "The Terror," whinnying with fear, then strove madly to turn and flee before the fury of wind, and flame, and lashing rain. Three times he swerved wildly, and three times he was checked, as with hand, and voice, and goading spur, Barnabas drove him on again—on down the steep descent, down, down into the yawning blackness of the valley below, on into the raging fury of the storm.

So, buffeted by wind, lashed by stinging rain, blinded by vivid lightning-flash, Barnabas rode on down the hill.

On and ever on, with teeth hard clenched, with eyes fierce and wide, heedless alike of wind and wet and flame, since he could think only of the man he rode to meet. And sometimes he uttered bitter curses, and sometimes he touched and fondled the weapons in his pocket, smiling evilly, for tonight, if he were not blasted by the lightning or crushed beneath his terrified horse, Barnabas meant this man should die.

And now upon the rushing wind were voices, demon voices that shrieked and howled at him, filling the whirling blackness with their vicious clamor.

"Kill him!" they shrieked. "Whether you are in time or no, kill him! kill him!"

And Barnabas, heedless of the death that hissed and crackled in the air about him, fronting each lightning-flash with cruel-smiling mouth, nodded his head to the howling demons and answered:

"Yes, yes, whether in time or no, tonight he dies!"

And now, uplifted with a wild exhilaration, he laughed aloud, exulting in the storm; and now, crushed by fear and dread, and black despair, he raved out bitter curses and spurred on into the storm. Little by little the thought of this man he meant to slay possessed him utterly; it seemed to Barnabas that he could actually hear his soft, mocking laughter; it filled the night, rising high above the hiss of rain and rush of wind—the laugh of a satyr who waits, confident, assured, with arms out-stretched to clasp a shuddering goddess.

On beneath trees, dim-seen, that rocked and swayed bending to the storm, splashing through puddles, floundering through mire, slack of rein and ready of spur, Barnabas galloped hard. And ever the mocking laughter rang in his ears, and ever the demons shrieked to him on the howling wind:

"Kill him! kill him!"

So, at last, amidst rain, and wind, and mud, Barnabas rode into Tonbridge Town, and staying at the nearest inn, dismounted stiffly in the yard and shouted hoarsely for ostlers to bring him to the stables. Being come there, it is Barnabas himself who holds the bucket while the foam-flecked "Terror" drinks, a modicum of water with a dash of brandy. Thereafter Barnabas stands by anxious-eyed what time two ostlers rub down the great, black horse; or, striding swiftly to and fro, the silver watch clutched in impatient hand, he questions the men in rapid tones, as:

"Which is the nearest way to Headcorn?"

"'Eadcorn, sir? Why surely you don't be thinking—"

"Which is the nearest way to Headcorn?" repeats Barnabas, scowling blackly; whereat the fellow answers to the point and Barnabas falls to his feverish striding to and fro until, glancing from the watch in his hand to "The Terror's" lofty crest, observing that his heaving flanks labor no more and that he paws an impatient hoof, Barnabas thrusts watch in fob, tightens girth and surcingle and, having paid his score, swings himself stiffly into the saddle and is off and away, while the gaping ostlers stare after him through the falling rain till he has galloped out of sight.

Away, away, down empty street, over rumbling bridge and so, bearing to the left, on and up the long hill of Pembury.

Gradually the rain ceased, the wind died utterly away, the stars peeped out again. And now, upon the quiet, came the small, soft sound of trickling water, while the air was fragrant with a thousand sweet scents and warm, moist, earthy smells.

But on galloped the great, black horse, by pointed oast-house, by gloomy church, on and ever on, his nostrils flaring, his eye wild, his laboring sides splashed with mire and streaked with foam and blood; on he galloped, faltering a little, stumbling a little, his breath coming in sobbing gasps, but maintaining still his long, racing stride; thundering through sleeping hamlets and waking echoes far and near, failing of strength, scant of breath, but indomitable still.

Oh, mighty "Four-legs"! Oh, "Terror"! whose proud heart scorns defeat! to-night thou dost race as ne'er thou didst before, pitting thy strength and high courage against old Time himself! Therefore on, on, brave horse, enduring thy anguish as best thou may, nor look for mercy from the pitiless human who bestrides thee, who rides grim-lipped, to give death and, if need be, to taste of its bitterness himself, and who, unsparing of himself, shall neither spare thee.

On, on, brave horse, endure as best thou may, since Death rides thee to-night.

Now, in a while, Barnabas saw before him a wide street flanked on either hand by cottages, and with an ancient church beyond. And, as he looked at this church with its great, square tower outlined against the starry heaven, there came, borne to his ears, the fretful wailing of a sleepless child; therefore he checked his going and, glancing about, espied a solitary lighted window. Riding thither, he raised himself in his stirrups and, reaching up, tapped upon the panes; and, in a while, the casement was opened and a man peered forth, a drowsy being, touzled of head and round of eye.

"Pray," said Barnabas, "what village is this?"

"Why, sir," answered the man, "five an' forty year I've lived here, and always heard as it was called Headcorn."

"Headcorn," said Barnabas, nodding, "then Ashleydown should be near here?"

"Why, sir," said the man, nodding in turn, "I do believe you—leastways it were here about yesterday."

"And where is it?"

"Half a mile back down the road, you must ha' passed it, sir. A great house it be though inclined to ruination. And it lays back from the road wi' a pair o' gates—iron gates as is also ruinated, atween two stone pillars wi' a lion a-top of each, leastways if it ain't a lion it's a griffin, which is a fab'lous beast. And talking of beasts, sir, I do believe as that theer dratted child don't never mean to sleep no more. Good night to ye, sir—and may you sleep better a-nights than a married man wi' seven on 'em." Saying which, he nodded, sighed, and vanished.

So back rode Barnabas the way he had come, and presently, sure enough, espied the dim outlines of the two stone columns each with "a lion a-top," and between these columns swung a pair of rusted iron gates; and the gates were open, seeing which Barnabas frowned and set his teeth, and so turned to ride between the gates, but, even as he did so, he caught the sound of wheels far down the road. Glancing thither he made out the twinkling lights of an approaching chaise, and sat awhile to watch its slow progress, then, acting upon sudden impulse, he spurred to meet it. Being come within hail he reined in across the road, and drawing a pistol levelled it at the startled post-boy.

"Stop!" cried Barnabas.

Uttering a frightened oath, the postilion pulled up with a jerk, but as the chaise came to a standstill a window rattled down. Then Barnabas lowered the pistol, and coming up beside the chaise looked down into the troubled face of my Lady Cleone. And her checks were very pale in the light of the lanterns, and upon her dark lashes was the glitter of tears.

CHAPTER LXXI

WHICH TELLS HOW BARNABAS, IN HIS FOLLY, CHOSE THE HARDER COURSE

"You! Is it you—Barnabas?" she whispered and thereafter sighed, a long, quivering sigh. "I—I've been hoping you would come!"

And now, as he looked at her, he saw that her cheeks were suffused, all at once, with a warm and vivid color. "Hoped?" said Barnabas, wondering.

"And—prayed!" she whispered.

"Then, you expected me? You knew I should come?"

"Yes, Barnabas. I—I hoped you would see my—letter to Ronald—that was why I wrote it! And I prayed that you might come—"

"Why?"

"Because I—oh, Barnabas, I'm afraid!"

"You were going to—Chichester?"

"Yes, Barnabas."

"You don't—love him, do you?"

"Love him!" she repeated, "Oh, God!"

And Barnabas saw her shudder violently.

"Yet you were going to him."

"To save my brother. But now—God help me, I can't do it! Oh, it's too hateful and—and I am afraid, Barnabas. I ought to have been at Ashleydown an hour ago, but oh, I—I couldn't, it was too horrible—I couldn't! So I came the longest way; I made the post-boy drive very slowly, I—I was waiting—for you, Barnabas, praying God that you would come to me—"

"Because you—were afraid, my lady."

"Yes, Barnabas."

"And behold, I am here!" said Barnabas. But now, seeing the quiver of her white hands, and the light in her eyes—a sudden glow that was not of the lanterns, he turned his head and looked resolutely away.

"I am here, my lady, to take you back home again," said he.

"Home?" she repeated. "Ah, no, no—I have no home, now! Oh, Barnabas," she whispered, "take me, take me away—to my brother. Let us go away from England to-night—anywhere, take me with you, Barnabas."

Now, as she spoke, her hands came out to him with a swift gesture, full of passionate entreaty. And the lanterns made a shining glory of her hair, and showed him the deep wonder of her eyes, the quick surge of her round, young bosom, the tender quiver of the parted lips as she waited his answer; thus our Barnabas beholding the witchery of her shy-drooping lashes, the scarlet lure of her mouth, the yielding warmth and all the ripe beauty of her, fell suddenly a-trembling and sighed; then, checking the sigh, looked away again across the dim desolation of the country-side, and clenched his hands.

"My lady," said he, his voice hoarse and uncertain, "why do you—tempt me? I am only—an amateur gentleman—why do you tempt me so?" As he spoke he wheeled his horse and motioned to the flinching postboy. "Turn!" he commanded.

"No!" cried Cleone.

"Turn!" said Barnabas, and, as the post-boy hesitated, levelled his pistol.

But now, even as the postilion chirruped to his horses, the chaise door was flung open and Cleone sprang down into the road; but even so, Barnabas barred her way.

"Let me pass!" she cried.

"To Chichester?"

"Yes—God help me. Since you force me to it! Let me go!"

"Get back into the chaise, my lady."

"No, no! Let me pass, I go to save my brother—"

"Not this way!"

"Oh!" she cried passionately, "you force it upon me, yes—you! you! If you won't help me, I must go to him! Dear heaven! there is no other way, let me go—you must—you shall!"

"Go back into the chaise, my lady."

Barnabas spoke very gently but, as she stared up at him, a movement of his horse brought him into the light of the lanterns and, in that moment, her breath caught, for now she beheld him as she had seen him once before, a wild, desperate figure, bare-headed, torn, and splashed with mud; grim of mouth, and in his eyes a look she had once dreamed of and never since forgotten. And, as she gazed, Barnabas spoke again and motioned with his pistol hand.

"Get back into the chaise, my lady."

"No!" she answered, and, though her face was hidden now, he knew that she was weeping. "I'm going on, now—to Ashleydown, to save Ronald, to redeem the promise I gave our mother; I must, I must, and oh—nothing matters to me—any more, so let me go!"

"My lady," said Barnabas, in the same weary tone, "you must get back into the chaise."

"And let Ronald die—and such a death! Never! oh never!"

Barnabas sighed, slipped the pistol into his pocket and dismounted, but, being upon his feet, staggered; then, or ever she knew, he had caught her in his arms, being minded to bear her to the chaise. But in that moment, he looked down and so stood there, bound by the spell of her beauty, forgetful of all else in the world, for the light of the lanterns was all about them, and Cleone's eyes were looking up into his.

"Barnabas," she whispered, "Barnabas, don't let me go!—save me from—that!"

"Ah, Cleone," he murmured, "oh, my lady, do you doubt me still? Can you think that I should fail you?

"Oh, my dear, my dear—I've found a way, and mine is a better way than yours. Be comforted then and trust me, Cleone."

Then, she stirred in his embrace, and, sighing, hid her face close against him and, with her face thus hidden, spoke:

"Yes, yes—I do trust you, Barnabas, utterly, utterly! Take me away with you—tonight, take me to Ronald and let us go away together, no matter where so long as—we go—together, Barnabas." Now when she said this, she could feel how his arms tightened about her, could hear how his breath caught sudden and sharp, and, though she kept her face hid from him, well she knew what look was in his eyes; therefore she lay trembling a little, sighing a little, and with fast-beating heart. And, in a while, Barnabas spoke:

"My lady," said he heavily, "would you trust yourself to—a publican's son?"

"If he would not be—too proud to—take me, Barnabas."

"Oh, my lady—can't you see that if I—if I take you with me tonight, you must be with me—always?"

Cleone sighed.

"And I am a discredited impostor, the—the jest of every club in London!"

Cleone's hand stole up, and she touched his grimly-set chin very gently with one white finger.

"I am become a thing for the Fashionable World to sharpen its wits upon," he continued, keeping his stern gaze perseveringly averted. "And so, my lady—because I cannot any longer cheat folks into accepting me as a—gentleman, I shall in all probability become a farmer, some day."

Cleone sighed.

"But you," Barnabas continued, a little harshly, "you were born for higher and greater fortune than to become the wife of a humble farming fellow, and consequently—"

"But I can make excellent butter, Barnabas," she sighed, stealing a glance up to him, "and I can cook—a little."

Now when she said this, he must needs look down at her again and lo! there, at the corner of her mouth was the ghost of the dimple! And, beholding this, seeing the sudden witchery of her swift-drooping lashes, Barnabas forgot his stern resolutions and stooped his head, that he might kiss the glory of her hair. But, in that moment, she turned, swift and sudden, and yielded him her lips, soft, and warm, and passionate with youth and all the joy of life. And borne away upon that kiss, it seemed to Barnabas, for one brief, mad-sweet instant that all things might be possible; if they started now they might reach London in the dawn and, staying only for Barrymaine, be aboard ship by evening! And it was a wide world, a very fair world, and with this woman beside him—

"It would be so—so very easy!" said he, slowly.

"Yes, it will be very easy!" she whispered.

"Too easy!" said he, beginning to frown, "you are so helpless and lonely, and I want you so bitterly, Cleone! Yes, it would be very easy. But you taught me once, that a man must ever choose the harder way, and this is the harder way, to love you, to long for you, and to bid you—good-by!"

"Oh! Barnabas?"

"Ah, Cleone, you could make the wretchedest hut a paradise for me, but for you, ah, for you it might some day become only a hut, and I, only a discredited Amateur Gentleman, after all."

Then Barnabas sighed and thereafter frowned, and so bore her to the chaise and setting her within, closed the door.

"Turn!" he cried to the postilion.

"Barnabas!"

But the word was lost in the creak of wheels and stamping of hoofs as the chaise swung round; then Barnabas remounted and, frowning still, trotted along beside it. Now in a while, lifting his sombre gaze towards a certain place beside the way, he beheld the dim outline of a finger-post, a very ancient finger-post which (though it was too dark to read its inscription) stood, he knew, with wide-stretched arms pointing the traveller:

TO LONDON. TO HAWKHURST.

And being come opposite the finger-post, he ordered the post-boy to stop, for, small with distance, he caught the twinkling lights of lanterns that swung to and fro, and, a moment later, heard a hail, faint and far, yet a stentorian bellow there was no mistaking. Therefore coming close beside the chaise, he stooped down and looked within, and thus saw that Cleone leaned in the further corner with her face hidden in her hands.

"You are safe, now, my lady," said he, "the Bo'sun is coming, the Captain will be here very soon."

But my lady never stirred.

"You are safe now," he repeated, "as for Ronald, if Chichester's silence can save him, you need grieve no more, and—"

"Ah!" she cried, glancing up suddenly, "what do you mean?"

"That I must go, my lady, and—and—oh, my dear love, this harder way—is very hard to tread. If—we should meet no more after tonight, remember that I loved you—as I always have done and always must, humble fellow though I am. Yes, I think I love you as well as any fine gentleman of them all, and—Cleone—Good-by!"

"Barnabas," she cried, "tell me what you mean to do—oh, Barnabas, where are you going?" And now she reached out her hands as though to stay him. But, even so, he drew away, and, wheeling his horse, pointed towards the twinkling lights.

"Drive on!" he cried to the post-boy.

"Barnabas, wait!"

"Drive on!" he cried, "whip—spur!"

"Barnabas, stay! Oh, Barnabas, listen—"

But as Cleone strove desperately to open the door, the chaise lurched forward, the horses broke into a gallop, and Barnabas, sitting there beneath the ancient finger-post, saw imploring hands stretched out towards him, heard a desolate cry, and—he was alone. So Barnabas sat there amid the gloom, and watched Happiness go from him. Very still he sat until the grind of wheels had died away in the distance; then he sighed, and spurring his jaded horse, rode back towards Headcorn.

And thus did Barnabas, in his folly, forego great joy, and set aside the desire of his heart that he might tread that Harder Way, which yet can be trod only by the foot of—A Man.

CHAPTER LXXII

HOW RONALD BARREYMAINE SQUARED HIS ACCOUNT

A distant clock was striking the hour as Barnabas rode in at the rusted gates of Ashleydown and up beneath an avenue of sombre trees beyond which rose the chimneys of a spacious house, clear and plain against the palpitating splendor of the stars. But the house, like its surroundings, wore a desolate, neglected look, moreover it was dark, not a light was to be seen anywhere from attic to cellar. Yet, as Barnabas followed the sweep of the avenue, he suddenly espied a soft glow that streamed from an uncurtained window giving upon the terrace; therefore he drew rein, and dismounting, led his horse in among the trees and, having tethered him there, advanced towards the gloomy house, his gaze upon the lighted window, and treading with an ever growing caution.

Now, as he went, he took out one of the pistols, cocked it, and with it ready in his hand, came to the window and peered into the room.

It was a long, low chamber with a fireplace at one end, and here, his frowning gaze bent upon the blazing logs, sat Mr. Chichester. Upon the small table at his elbow were decanter and glasses, with a hat and gloves and a long travelling cloak. As Barnabas stood there Mr. Chichester stirred impatiently, cast a frowning glance at the clock in the corner and reaching out to the bell-rope that hung beside the mantel, jerked it viciously, and so fell to scowling at the fire again until the door opened and a bullet-headed, square-shouldered fellow entered, a formidable ruffian with pugilist written in his every feature; to whom Mr. Chichester appeared to give certain commands; and so dismissed him with an impatient gesture of his slim, white hands. As the door closed, Mr. Chichester started up and fell to pacing the floor only to return, and, flinging himself back in his chair, sat scowling at the fire again.

Then Barnabas raised the pistol-butt and, beating in the window, loosed the catch, and, as Mr. Chichester sprang to his feet, opened the casement and stepped into the room.

For a long moment neither spoke, while eyes met and questioned eyes, those of Barnabas wide and bright, Mr. Chichester's narrowed to shining slits. And indeed, as they fronted each other thus, each was the opposite of the other, Barnabas leaning in the window, his pistol hand hidden behind him, a weary, bedraggled figure mired from heel to head; Mr. Chichester standing rigidly erect, immaculate of dress from polished boot to snowy cravat.

"So," said he at last, breaking the ominous silence, "so it's—yes, it is Mr.—Barty, I think, unpleasantly damp and devilish muddy, and, consequently, rather more objectionable than usual."

"I have ridden far, and the roads were bad," said Barnabas.

"Ah! and pray why inflict yourself upon me?"

"For a very good and sufficient reason, sir."

"Ha, a reason?" said Mr. Chichester, lounging against the mantel. "Can it be you have discerned at last that the highly dramatic meeting between father and son at a certain banquet, not so long ago, was entirely contrived by myself—that it was my hand drove you from society and made you the derision of London, Mr. Barty?"

"Why, yes," sighed Barnabas; "I guessed that much, sir."

"Indeed, I admire your perspicacity, Mr. Barty. And now, I presume you have broken into my house with some brutal idea of pummelling me with your fists? But, sir, I am no prizefighter, like you and your estimable father, and I warn you that—"

"Sir," said Barnabas softly, "do not trouble to ring the bell, my mission here is—not to thrash you."

"No? Gad, sir, but you're very forbearing, on my soul you are!" and Mr. Chichester smiled; but his nostrils were twitching as his fingers closed upon the bell-rope. "Now understand me—having shown up your imposture, having driven you from London, I do not propose to trouble myself further with you. True, you have broken into my house, and should very properly be shot like any other rascally thief. I have weapons close by, and servants within call, but you have ceased to interest me—I have other and weightier affairs on hand, so you may go, sir. I give you one minute to take yourself back to your native mud." As he ended, Mr. Chichester motioned airily towards the open window. But Barnabas only sighed again and shook his head.

"Sir," said he, more softly than before, "give me leave to tell you that the Lady Cleone will not keep her appointment here, to-night."

"Ah-h!" said Mr. Chichester slowly, and staring at Barnabas under his drawn brows, "you—mean—?"

"That she was safe home three-quarters of an hour ago."

Mr. Chichester's long, white fingers writhed suddenly upon the bell-rope, released it, and, lifting his hand swiftly, he loosened his high cravat, and so stood, breathing heavily, his eyes once more narrowed to shining slits, and with the scar burning redly upon his cheek.

"So you have dared," he began thickly, "you have dared to interfere again? You have dared to come here, to tell me so?"

"No, sir," answered Barnabas, shaking his head, "I have come here to kill you!"

Barnabas spoke very gently, but as Mr. Chichester beheld his calm eye, the prominence of his chin, and his grimly-smiling mouth, his eyes widened suddenly, his clenched fingers opened, and he reached out again towards the bell-rope. "Stop!" said Barnabas, and speaking, levelled his pistol.

"Ah!" sighed Mr. Chichester, falling back a step, "you mean to murder me, do you?"

"I said 'kill'—though yours is the better word, perhaps. Here are two pistols, you will observe; one is for you and one for me. And we are about to sit down—here, at the table, and do our very utmost to murder each other. But first, I must trouble you to lock the door yonder and bring me the key. Lock it, I say!"

Very slowly, and with his eyes fixed in a wide stare upon the threatening muzzle of the weapon Barnabas held, Mr. Chichester, crossed to the door, hesitated, turned the key, and drawing it from the lock, stood with it balanced in his hand a moment, and then tossed it towards Barnabas.

Now the key lay within a yard of Barnabas who, stepping forward, made as though to reach down for it; but in that instant he glanced up at Mr. Chichester under his brows, and in that instant also, Mr. Chichester took a swift, backward step towards the hearth; wherefore, because of this, and because of the look in Mr. Chichester's eyes, Barnabas smiled, and, so smiling, kicked the key into a far corner.

"Come, sir," said he, drawing another chair up to the table, "be seated!" saying which, Barnabas sat down, and, keeping one pistol levelled, laid the other within Mr. Chichester's reach. "They are both loaded, sir," he continued; "but pray assure yourself."

But Mr. Chichester stood where he was, his eyes roving swiftly from Barnabas to the unlatched window, from that to the door, and so back again to where Barnabas sat, pale, smiling, and with the heavy weapon levelled across the narrow table; and as he stood thus, Mr. Chichester lifted one white hand to his mouth and began to pull at his lips with twitching fingers.

"Come," repeated Barnabas, "be seated, sir."

But Mr. Chichester yet stood utterly still save for the petulant action of those nervous, twitching fingers.

"Sir," Barnabas persisted, "sit down, I beg!"

"I'll fight you—here—and now," said Mr. Chichester, speaking in a strange, muffled tone, "yes—I'll fight you wherever or whenever you wish, but not—not across a table!"

"I think you will," nodded Barnabas grimly. "Pray sit down."

"No!"

"Why, then, we'll stand up for it," sighed Barnabas rising. "Now, sir, take up your pistol."

"No!"

"Then," said Barnabas, his teeth agleam, "as God's above, I'll shoot you where you stand—but first I'll count three!" And once more he levelled the pistol he held.

Mr. Chichester sighed a fluttered sigh, the twitching fingers fell from his mouth and with his burning gaze upon Barnabas, he stepped forward and laid his hand upon the chair-back, but, in the act of sitting down, paused.

"The candles—a little more light—the candles," he muttered, and turning, crossed to the hearth and raised his hand to a branched silver candlestick that stood upon the mantel. But in the moment that his left hand closed upon this, his right had darted upon another object that lay there, and, quick as a flash, he had spun round and fired point-blank.

While the report yet rang on the air, Barnabas staggered, swayed, and, uttering a gasp, sank down weakly into his chair. But, as Mr. Chichester watched him, his eyes wide, his lips parted, and the pistol yet smoking in his hand,

Barnabas leaned forward, and steadying his elbow on the table, slowly, very slowly raised and levelled his weapon.

And now, as he fronted that deadly barrel, Mr. Chichester's face grew suddenly livid, and haggard, and old-looking, while upon his brow the sweat had started and rolled down, glistening upon his cheeks.

The fire crackled upon the hearth, the clock ticked softly in the corner, the table creaked as Barnabas leaned his weight across it, nearer and nearer, but, save for this, the place was very quiet. Then, all at once, upon this silence broke another sound, a distant sound this, but one that grew ever nearer and louder—the grind of wheels and the hoof-strokes of madly galloping horses. Mr. Chichester uttered a gasping cry and pointed towards the window—

"Cleone!" he whispered. "It's Cleone! She's coming, in God's name—wait!"

The galloping hoofs drew rapidly nearer, stopped suddenly, and as Barnabas, hesitating, glanced towards the window, it was flung wide and somebody came leaping through—a wild, terrible figure; and as he turned in the light of the candles, Barnabas looked into the distorted face of Ronald Barrymaine.

For a moment he stood, his arms dangling, his head bent, his glowing eyes staring at Mr. Chichester, and as he stood thus fixing Mr. Chichester with that awful, unwavering stare, a smile twisted his pallid lips, and he spoke very softly:

"It's all r-right, Dig," said he, "the luck's with me at l-last— we're in time—I've g-got him! Come in, D-Dig, and bring the tools—I—I've g-got him!"

Hereupon Mr. Smivvle stepped into the room; haggard of eye he looked, and with cheeks that showed deadly pale by contrast with the blackness of his glossy whiskers, and beneath his arm he carried a familiar oblong box; at sight of Barnabas he started, sighed, and crossing hastily, set the box upon the table and caught him by the arm:

"Stop him, Beverley—stop him!" he whispered hurriedly. "Barry's gone mad, I think, insisted on coming here. Devil of a time getting away, Bow Street Runners—hard behind us now. Means to fight! Stop him, Beverley, for the love of—Ah! by God, what's this? Barry, look—look here!" And he started back from Barnabas, staring at him with horrified eyes. "Barry, Barry—look here!"

But Ronald Barrymaine never so much as turned his head; motionless he stood, his lips still contorted with their drawn smile, his burning gaze still fixed on Mr. Chichester—indeed he seemed oblivious to all else under heaven.

"Come, Dig," said he in the same soft voice, "get out the barkers, and quick about it, d' you hear?"

"But, Barry—oh, my dear fellow, here's poor Beverley, look—look at him!"

"G-give us the barkers, will you—quick! Oh, damnation. Dig, y-you know G-Gaunt and his hangman are hard on my heels! Quick, then, and g-get it over and done with—d'you hear, D-Dig?" So saying, Barrymaine crossed to the hearth and stood there, warming his hands at the blaze, but, even so, he must needs turn his head so that he could keep his gloating eyes always directed to Chichester's pale face.

"I'm w-warming my pistol-hand, Dig," he continued, "mustn't be cold or s-stiff tonight, you see. Oh, I tell you the luck's with me at last! He's b-been so vastly clever, Dig! He's dragged me down to hell, but—tonight I'm g-going to-take him with me."

And ever as he spoke, warming himself at the fire, Ronald Barrymaine kept his burning gaze upon Mr. Chichester's pale face, while Barnabas leaned, twisted in his chair, and Mr. Smivvle busied himself with the oblong box. With shaking hands he took out the duelling-pistols, one by one, and laid them on the table.

"We'll g-give him first choice, eh, Dig?" said Barrymaine. "Ah—he's chosen, I s-see. Now we'll t-take opposite corners of the room and f-fire when you give the word, eh, Dig?"

As he spoke, Barrymaine advanced to the table, his gaze always upon Mr. Chichester, nor did he look away even for an instant, thus, his hand wandered, for a moment, along the table, ere he found and took up the remaining pistol. Then, with it cocked in his hand, he backed away to the corner beside the hearth, and being come there, nodded.

"A good, comfortable distance, D-Dig," said he, "now tell him to take his g-ground."

But even as he spoke, Mr. Chichester strode to the opposite corner of the long room, and turning, stood there with folded arms. Up till now, he had uttered no word, but as Mr. Smivvle leaned back against the wall, midway between them, and glanced from one to the other, Mr. Chichester spoke.

"Sirs," said he, "I shall most certainly kill him, and I call upon you to witness that it was forced upon me."

Now as his voice died away, through the open window came a faint sound that might have been wind in the trees, or the drumming of horse-hoofs, soft and faint with distance.

"Oh, g-give us the word, D-Dig!" said Barrymaine.

"Gentlemen," said Mr. Smivvle, steadying himself against the panelling with shaking hands, "the word will be—Ready? One! Two! Three—Fire! Do you understand?"

An eager "Yes" from Barrymaine, a slight nod from Chichester, yet Mr. Smivvle still leaned there mutely against the wall, as though his tongue failed him, or as if hearkening to that small, soft sound, that might have been wind in the trees.

"The word, Dig—will you give us the word?"

"Yes, yes, Barry, yes, my dear boy—certainly!" But still Mr. Smivvle hesitated, and ever the small sound grew bigger and louder.

"S-speak! Will you s-speak, Dig?"

"Oh, Barry—my dear boy, yes! Ready?"

At the word the two pistols were raised and levelled, almost on the instant, and with his haggard eyes turned towards Barrymaine's corner, Mr. Smivvle spoke again:

"One!—Two!—Three—"

A flash, a single deafening report, and Ronald Barrymaine lurched sideways, caught at the wall, swayed backwards into the corner and leaned there.

"Coward,—you fired too soon!" cried Smivvle, turning upon Mr. Chichester in sudden frenzy, "Villain! Rouge! you fired too soon—!"

"S-stand away, Dig!" said Barrymaine faintly.

"Oh, Barry—you're bleeding! By God, he's hit you!"

"Of c-course, Dig—he never m-misses—neither do I—w-watch now, ah! hold me up, Dig—so! Now, stand away!" But even as Barrymaine, livid of brow and with teeth hard clenched, steadied himself for the shot, loud and clear upon the night came the thudding of swift-galloping horse-hoofs.

And now, for the first time, Barrymaine's gaze left Chichester's face, and fixed itself upon the open casement instead.

"Ha!" he cried, "here comes G-Gaunt at last, D-Dig, and with his hangman at his elbow! But he's t-too late, Dig, he's too l-late—I'm going, but I mean to take our friend—our d-dear friend Chichester w-with me—look now!"

As he spoke he raised his arm, there came the stunning report of the pistol, and a puff of blinding smoke; but when it cleared, Mr. Chichester still stood up rigid in his corner, only, as he stood he lifted his hand suddenly to his mouth, glanced at his fingers, stared at them with wide, horrified eyes. Then his pistol clattered to the floor and he coughed—a hideous, strangling sound, thin and high-pitched. Coughing still, he took a swift pace forward, striving to speak, but choked instead, and so choking, sank to his knees. Even then he strove desperately to utter something, but with it still unspoken, sank down upon his hands, and thence slowly upon his face and lay there very still and quiet.

Then Barrymaine laughed, an awful, gasping laugh, and began to edge himself along the wall and, as he went, he left hideous smears and blotches upon the panelling behind him. Being come to that inanimate figure he stood awhile watching it with gloating eyes. Presently he spoke in a harsh whisper:

"He's dead, D-Dig—quite dead, you see! And he was my f-friend, which was bad! And I trusted him—which was w-worse. A rogue always, Dig, and a l-liar!"

Then Barrymaine groaned, and groaning, spurned that quiet form weakly with his foot and so, pitched down headlong across it.

Now as they lay thus, they together made a great cross upon the floor.

But presently shadows moved beyond the open window, a broad-brimmed, high-crowned hat projected itself into the candle light, and a voice spoke:

"In the King's name! I arrest Ronald Barrymaine for the murder of Jasper Gaunt—in the King's name, genelmen!"

But now, very slowly and painfully, Ronald Barrymaine raised himself upon his hands, lifted his heavy head and spoke in a feeble voice.

"Oh, m-master Hangman," he whispered, "y-you're too l-late—j-just too late!" And so, like a weary child settling itself to rest, he pillowed his head upon his arm, and sighing—fell asleep.

Then Mr. Shrig stepped forward very softly, and beholding that placid young face with its tender, smiling lips, and the lashes that drooped so dark against the dead pallor of the cheek, he took off his broad-brimmed hat and stood there with bent head.

But another figure had followed him, and now sprang toward Barnabas with supporting arms outstretched, and in that moment Barnabas sighed, and falling forward, lay there sprawled across the table.

CHAPTER LXXIII

WHICH RECOUNTS THREE AWAKENINGS

The sunlight was flooding in at the open lattice and, as if borne upon this shaft of glory, came the mingled fragrance of herb and flower and ripening fruit with the blithe carolling of birds, a very paean of thanksgiving; the chirp of sparrows, the soft, rich notes of blackbirds, the warbling trill of thrushes, the far, faint song of larks high in the blue—it was all there, blent into one harmonious chorus of joy, a song that spoke of hope and a fair future to such as were blessed with ears to hear. And by this, our Barnabas, opening drowsy eyes and hearkening with drowsy ears, judged it was yet early morning.

He lay very still and full of a great content because of the glory of the sun and the merry piping of the birds.

But, little by little, as he hearkened, he became conscious of another sound, a very gentle sound, yet insistent because of its regularity, a soft click! click! click! that he could in no wise account for. Therefore he would have turned his head, and straightway wondered to find this so difficult to accomplish; moreover he became aware that he lay in a bed, undressed, and that his arm and shoulder were bandaged. And now, all at once he forgot the bird-song and the sunshine, his brow grew harassed and troubled, and with great caution he lifted his free hand to his neck and began to feel for a certain ribbon that should be there. And presently, having found the ribbon, his questing fingers followed it down into his bosom until they touched a little, clumsily-wrought linen bag, that he had fashioned, once upon a time, with infinite trouble and pains, and in which he had been wont to carry the dried-up wisp of what had once been a fragrant, scarlet rose.

And now, having found this little bag, he lay with brow still troubled as one in some deep perplexity, the while his fingers felt and fumbled with it clumsily. This was the little bag indeed; he knew it by reason of its great, uneven stitches and its many knots and ends of cotton; yes, this was it beyond all doubt, and yet? Truly it was the same, but with a difference.

Now as he lay thus, being full of trouble because of this difference which he could in no wise understand, he drew a deep sigh, which was answered all at once by another; the soft clicking sound abruptly ceased and he knew that some one had risen and now stood looking down at him. Therefore Barnabas presently turned his head and saw a face bent over him, a face with cheeks suspiciously pink, framed in curls suspiciously dark and glossy, but with eyes wonderfully young and bright and handsome; in one small, white hand was a needle and silk, and in the other, a very diminutive piece of embroidery.

"Why, Barnabas!" said the Duchess, very gently, "dear boy—what is it? Ah! you've found it then, already—your sachet? Though indeed it looks more like a pudding-bag—a very small one, of course. Oh, dear me! but you're not a very good needlewoman, are you, Barnabas? Neither am I—I always prick my fingers dreadfully. There—let me open it for you—so! Now, while I hold it, see what is inside."

Then, wondering, Barnabas slipped a clumsy thumb and finger into the little bag and behold the faded wisp had become transfigured and bloomed again in all its virgin freshness. For in his hand there lay a great, scarlet rose, as sweet and fresh and fragrant as though—for all the world as though it had been plucked that very morning.

"Ah, no, no, no," cried the Duchess, reading his look, "it was no hand of mine worked the transformation, dear Barnabas."

"But," murmured drowsy Barnabas, speaking with an effort— "it—was—dead—long ago—?"

"Yet behold it is alive again!" said the Duchess. "And oh, Barnabas dear, if a withered, faded wisp may bloom again—so may a woman's faith and love. There, there, dear boy! Close your eyes and go to sleep again."

So, being very weary, Barnabas closed his eyes and, with the touch of her small, cool fingers in his hair, fell fast asleep.

II

Now as Barnabas lay thus, lost in slumber, he dreamed a dream. He had known full many sleeping visions and fancies of late, but, of them all, surely none had there been quite like this.

For it seemed to him that he was lying out amid the green, dewy freshness of Annersley Wood. And as he lay there, grievously hurt, lo! there came one hasting, light-footed to him through the green like some young nymph of Arcady or Goddess of the Wood, one for whom he seemed to have been waiting long and patiently, one as sweet and fresh and fair as the golden morning and tender as the Spirit of Womanhood.

And, for that he might not speak or move because of his hurt, she leaned above him and her hands touched him, hands very soft, and cool, and gentle, upon his brow, upon his cheek; and every touch was a caress.

Slowly, slowly her arms came about him in a warm, clinging embrace, arms strong and protecting that drew his weary head to the swell of a bosom and pillowed it sweetly there. And clasping him thus, she sighed over him and wept, though very silently, and stooped her lips to him to kiss his brow, his slumberous eyes, and, last of all, his mouth.

So, because of this dream, Barnabas lay in a deep and utter content, for it seemed that Happiness had come to him after all, and of its own accord. But, in a while, he stirred and sighed, and presently opened dreamy eyes, and thus it chanced that he beheld the door of his chamber, and the door was quivering as though it had but just closed. Then, as he lay watching it, sleepy-eyed, it opened again, slowly and noiselessly, and John Peterby entered softly, took a step towards the bed, but, seeing Barnabas was awake, stopped, and so stood there very still.

Suddenly Barnabas smiled, and held out a hand to him.

"Why, John," said he, "my faithful John—is it you?"

"Sir," murmured Peterby, and coming forward, took that extended hand, looking down at Barnabas joyful-eyed, and would have spoken, yet uttered no other word.

"John," said Barnabas, glancing round the faded splendors of the bed-chamber, "where am I, pray?"

"At Ashleydown, sir."

"Ashleydown?" repeated Barnabas, wrinkling his brow.

"Sir, you have been—very ill."

"Ah, yes, I was shot I remember—last night, I think?"

"Sir, it happened over three weeks ago."

"Three weeks!" repeated Barnabas, sitting up with an effort, "three weeks, John?—Oh, impossible!"

"You have been very near death, sir. Indeed I think you would have died but for the tender nursing and unceasing care of—"

"Ah, God bless her! Where is she, John—where is the Duchess?"

"Her Grace went out driving this morning, sir."

"This morning? Why, I was talking with her this morning—only a little while ago."

"That was yesterday morning, sir."

"Oh!" said Barnabas, hand to head, "do you mean that I have slept the clock round?"

"Yes, sir."

"Hum!" said Barnabas. "Consequently I'm hungry, John, deuced sharp set—ravenous, John!"

"That, sir," quoth Peterby, smiling his rare smile, "that is the best news I've heard this three weeks and more, and your chicken broth is ready—"

"Chicken broth!" exclaimed Barnabas, "for shame, John. Bring me a steak, do you hear?"

"But, sir," Peterby remonstrated, shaking his head, yet with his face ever brightening, "indeed I—"

"Or a chop, John, or ham and eggs—I'm hungry; I tell you."

"Excellent!" laughed Peterby, nodding his head, "but the doctor, sir—"

"Doctor!" cried Barnabas, with a snort, "what do I want with doctors? I'm well, John. Bring me my clothes."

"Clothes, sir!" exclaimed Peterby, aghast. "Impossible, sir! No, no!"

"Yes, yes, John—I'm going to get up."

"But, sir—"

"This very moment! My clothes, John, my clothes!"

"Indeed, sir, I—"

"John Peterby," said Barnabas, scowling blackly, "you will oblige me with my garments this instant,—obey me, sir!"

But hereupon, while Barnabas scowled and Peterby hesitated, puckered of brow yet joyful of eye, there came the sound of wheels on the drive below and the slam of a coach door, whereat Peterby crossed to the window and, glancing out, heaved a sigh of relief.

"Who is it?" demanded Barnabas, his scowl blacker than ever.

"Her Grace has returned, sir."

"Very good, John! Present my compliments and sa'y I will wait upon her as soon as I'm dressed."

But hardly had Peterby left the room with this message, than the door opened again and her Grace of Camberhurst appeared, who, catching sight of Barnabas sitting up shock-headed among his pillows, uttered a little, glad cry and hurried to him.

"Why, Barnabas!" she exclaimed, "oh, Barnabas!" and with the words stooped, quick and sudden, yet in the most matter-of-fact manner in the world, and kissed him lightly on the brow.

"Oh, dear me!" she cried, beginning to pat and smooth his tumbled pillows, "how glad I am to see you able to frown again, though indeed you look dreadfully ferocious, Barnabas!"

"I'm—very hungry, Duchess!"

"Of course you are, Barnabas, and God bless you for it!"

"A steak, madam, or a chop, I think—"

"Would be excellent, Barnabas!"

"And I wish to get up, Duchess."

"To be sure you do, Barnabas—there, lie down, so!"

"But, madam, I am firmly resolved—I'm quite determined to get up, at once—"

"Quite so, dear Barnabas—lay your head back on the pillow! Dear me, how comfortable you look! And now, you are hungry you say? Then I'll sit here and gossip to you while you take your chicken broth! You may bring it in, Mr. Peterby."

"Chicken broth!" snarled Barnabas, frowning blacker than ever, "but, madam, I tell you I won't have the stuff; I repeat, madam, that I am quite determined to—"

"There, there—rest your poor tired head—so! And it's all a delicious jelly when it's cold—I mean the chicken broth, of course, not your head. Ah! you may give it to me, Mr. Peterby, and the spoon—thank you! Now, Barnabas!"

And hereupon, observing the firm set of her Grace's mouth, and the authoritative flourish of the spoon she held in her small, though imperious hand, Barnabas submitted and lying back among his pillows in sulky dignity, swallowed the decoction in sulky silence, and thereafter lay hearkening sulkily to her merry chatter until he had sulked himself to sleep again.

III

His third awakening was much like the first in that room, was full of sunshine, and the air vibrant with the song of birds; yet here indeed lay a difference; for now, mingled with the piping chorus, Barnabas was vaguely conscious of another sound, soft and low and oft repeated, a very melodious sound that yet was unlike any note ever uttered by thrush or blackbird, or any of the feathered kind. Therefore, being yet heavy with sleep, Barnabas yawned, and presently turning, propped himself upon his elbow and was just in time to see a shapeless something vanish from the ledge of the open window.

The sun was low as yet, the birds in full song, the air laden with fresh, sweet, dewy scents; and from this, and the profound stillness of the house about him, he judged it to be yet early morning.

Now presently as he lay with his eyes turned ever towards the open casement, the sound that had puzzled him came again, soft and melodious.

Some one was whistling "The British Grenadiers."

And, in this moment a bedraggled object began to make its appearance, slowly and by degrees resolving itself into a battered hat. Inch by inch it rose up over the window-ledge—the dusty crown—the frayed band—the curly brim, and beneath it a face there was no mistaking by reason of its round, black eyes and the untamable ferocity of its whiskers. Hereupon, with its chin resting upon the window-sill, the head gently shook itself to and fro, sighed, and thereafter pronounced these words:

> Devilish pale! Deuced thin! But himself again. Oh, lucky dog! With Fortune eager to dower him with all the treasures of her cornucopia, and Beauty waiting for him with expectant arms, oh, lucky dog! Oh, happy youth! Congratulations, Beverley, glad of it, my dear fellow, you deserve it all and more. Oh, fortunate wight!
>
> But, as for me—you behold the last of lonely Smivvle, sir, of bereaved Digby—of solitary Dig. Poor Barrymaine's star is set and mine is setting—westwards, sir—my bourne is the far Americas, Beverley.

"Ah, Mr. Smivvle!" exclaimed Barnabas, sitting up, "I'm glad to see you—very glad. But what do you mean by America?"

"Sir," answered Mr. Smivvle, shaking his head and sighing again, "on account of the lamentable affair of a month ago, the Bow Street Runners have assiduously chivvied me from pillar to post and from perch to perch, dammem! Had a notion to slip over to France, but the French will insist on talking their accursed French at one, so I've decided for America. But, though hounded by the law, I couldn't go without knowing precisely how you were—without bidding you good-by—without endeavoring to thank you—to thank you for poor Barry's sake and my own, and also to return—"

"Come in," said Barnabas, stretching out his hand, "pray come in—through the window if you can manage it."

In an instant Mr. Smivvle was astride the sill, but paused there to glance about him and twist a whisker in dubious fingers.

"Coast clear?" he inquired. "I've been hanging about the place for a week hoping to see you, but by Gad, Beverley, you're so surrounded by watchful angels—especially one in an Indian shawl, that I didn't dare disturb you, but—"

"Pooh, nonsense—come in, man!" said Barnabas. "Come in, I want your help—"

"My help, Oh Gemini!" and, with the word, Mr. Smivvle was in the room. "My help?" he repeated. "Oh Jupiter—only say the word, my dear fellow."

"Why, then, I want you to aid me to dress."

"Dress? Eh, what, Beverley—get up, is it?"

"Yes. Pray get me my clothes—in the press yonder, I fancy."

"Certainly, my dear fellow, but are you strong enough?" inquired Mr. Smivvle, coming to the press on tip-toe.

"Strong enough!" cried Barnabas in profound scorn, "Of course I am!" and forthwith sprang to the floor and—clutched at the bedpost to save himself from falling.

"Ha—I feared so!" said Mr. Smivvle, hurrying to him with the garments clasped in his arms. "Steady! There, lean on me—I'll have you back into bed in a jiffy."

"Bed!" snorted Barnabas, scowling down at himself. "Bed—never! I shall be as right as a trivet in a minute or so. Oblige me with my shirt."

So, with a little difficulty, despite Mr. Smivvle's ready aid, Barnabas proceeded to invest himself in his clothes; which done, he paced to and fro across the chamber leaning upon Mr. Smivvle's arm, glorying in his returning strength.

"And so you are going to America?" inquired Barnabas, as he sank into a chair, a little wearily.

"I sail for New York in three days' time, sir."

"But what of your place in Worcestershire?"

"Gone, sir," said Mr. Smivvle, beginning to feel for his whisker. "Historic place, though devilish damp and draughty—will echo to the tread of a Smivvle no more—highly affecting thought, sir—oh demmit!"

"As to—funds, now," began Barnabas, a little awkwardly, "are you—have you—"

"Sir, I have enough to begin with—in America. Which reminds me I must be hopping, sir. But I couldn't go without thanking you on behalf of—my friend Barrymaine, seeing he is precluded from—from doing it himself. Sir, it was a great—a great grief to me—to lose him for, as I fancy I told you, the hand of a Smivvle, sir—but he is gone beyond plague or pestilence, or Jews, dammem! And he died, sir, like a gentleman. So, on his behalf I do thank you deeply, and I beg, herewith, to return you the twenty guineas you would have given him. Here they are, sir." So saying, Mr. Smivvle released his whisker and drawing a much worn purse from his pocket, tendered it to Barnabas.

Then, seeing the moisture in Mr. Smivvle's averted eyes, and the drooping dejection of Mr. Smivvle's whiskers, Barnabas took the purse and the hand also, and holding them thus clasped, spoke.

"Mr. Smivvle," said he, "it is a far better thing to take the hand of an honorable man and a loyal gentleman than to kiss the fingers of a prince. This money belonged to your dead friend, let it be an inheritance from him. As to myself, as I claim it an honor to call myself your friend, so let it be my privilege to help you in your new life and—and you will find five thousand guineas to your credit when you reach New York, and—and heaven prosper you."

"Sir—" began Mr. Smivvle, but his voice failing him he turned away and crossing to the window stood there apparently lost in contemplation of the glory of the morning.

"You will let me know how you get on, from time to time?" inquired Barnabas.

"Sir," stammered Mr. Smivvle, "sir—oh, Beverley, I can't thank you—I cannot, but—if I live, you shall find I don't forget and—"

"Hush! I think a door creaked somewhere!" said Barnabas, almost in a tone of relief.

In an instant Mr. Smivvle had possessed himself of his shabby hat and was astride of the window-sill. Yet there he paused to reach out his hand, and now Barnabas might see a great tear that crept upon his cheek—as bright, as glorious as any jewel.

"Good-by, Beverley!" he whispered as their hands met, "good-by, and I shall never forget—never!"

So saying, he nodded, sighed and, swinging himself over the window-ledge, lowered himself from sight.

But, standing there at the casement, Barnabas watched him presently stride away towards a new world, upright of figure and with head carried high like one who is full of confident purpose.

Being come to the end of the drive he turned, flourished his shabby hat and so was gone.

CHAPTER LXXIV

HOW THE DUCHESS MADE UP HER MIND, AND BARNABAS DID THE LIKE

"Gracious heavens—he's actually up—and dressed! Oh Lud, Barnabas, what does this mean?"

Barnabas started and turned to find the Duchess regarding him from the doorway and, though her voice was sharp, her eyes were wonderfully gentle, and she had stretched out her hands to him. Therefore he crossed the room a little unsteadily, and taking those small hands in his, bent his head and kissed them reverently.

"It means that, thanks to you, Duchess, I am well again and—"

"And as pale as a goblin—no, I mean a ghost—trying to catch his death of cold at an open window too—I mean you, not the ghost! And as weak as—as a rabbit, and—oh, dear me, I can't shut it—the casement—drat it! Thank you, Barnabas. Dear heaven, I am so flurried—and even your boots on too! Let me sit down. Lud, Barnabas—how thin you are!"

"But strong enough to go on my way—"

"Way? What way? Which way?"

"Home, Duchess."

"Home, home indeed? You are home—this is your home. Ashleydown is yours now."

"Yes," nodded Barnabas, "I suppose it is, but I shall never live here, I leave today. I am going home, but before I—"

"Home? What home—which home?"

"But before I do, I would thank you if I could, but how may I thank you for all your motherly care of me? Indeed, dear Duchess, I cannot, and yet—if words can—"

"Pho!" exclaimed the Duchess, knitting her brows at him, but with eyes still ineffably soft and tender, "what do you mean by 'home,' pray?"

"I am going back to my father and Natty Bell."

"And to—that inn?"

"Yes, Duchess. You see, there is not, there never was, there never shall be quite such another inn as the old 'Hound.'"

"And you—actually mean to—live there?"

"Yes, for a time, but—"

"Ha—a publican!" exclaimed the Duchess and positively sniffed, though only as a really great lady may.

"—there is a farm near by, I shall probably—"

"Ha—a farmer!" snorted the Duchess.

"—raise horses, madam, and with Natty Bell's assistance I hope—"

"Horses!" cried the Duchess, and sniffed again. "Horses, indeed! Absurd! Preposterous! Quite ridiculous—hush, sir! I have some questions to ask you."

"Well, Duchess?"

"Firstly, sir, what of your dreams? What of London? What of Society?"

"They were—only dreams," answered Barnabas; "in place of them I shall have—my father and Natty Bell."

"Secondly, sir,—what of your fine ambitions?"

"It will be my ambition, henceforth, to breed good horses, madam."

"Thirdly, sir,—what of your money?"

"I shall hope to spend it to much better purpose in the country than in the World of Fashion, Duchess."

"Oh Lud, Barnabas,—what a selfish creature you are!"

"Selfish, madam?"

"A perfect—wretch!"

"Wretch?" said Barnabas, staring.

"Wretch!" nodded the Duchess, frowning, "and pray don't echo my words, sir. I say you are a preposterously selfish wretch, and—so you are!"

"But, madam, why? What do you mean?"

"I mean that you should try to forget yourself occasionally and think of others—me, for instance; look at me—a solitary old woman—in a wig!"

"You, Duchess?"

"Me, Barnabas. And this brings me to fourthly—what of me, sir? —what of me?"

"But, madam, I—"

"And this brings me to fifthly and sixthly and seventhly—my hopes, and dreams, and plans, sir—are they all to be broken, spoiled, ruined by your hatefully selfish whims, sir—hush, not a word!"

"But, Duchess, indeed I don't—"

"Hush, sir, and listen to me. There are days when my wig rebukes me, sir, and my rouge-pot stares me out of countenance; yes, indeed, I sometimes begin to feel almost—middle-aged and, at such times, I grow a little lonely. Heaven, sir, doubtless to some wise end, has always denied me that which is a woman's abiding joy or shame—I mean a child, sir, and as the years creep on, one is apt to be a little solitary, now and then, and at such times I feel the need of a son—so I have determined to adopt you, Barnabas—today! Now! This minute! Not a word, sir, my mind is made up!"

"But," stammered Barnabas, "but, madam, I—I beg you to consider—my father—"

"Is a publican and probably a sinner, Barnabas. I may be a sinner too, perhaps—y-e-s, I fear I am, occasionally. But then I am also a Duchess, and it is far wiser in a man to be the adopted son of a sinful Duchess than the selfish son of a sinful publican, yes indeed."

"But I, madam, what can I say? Dear Duchess, I—the honor you would do me—" floundered poor Barnabas, "believe me if—if—"

"Not another word!" the Duchess interposed, "it is quite settled. As my adopted son Society shall receive you on bended knees, with open arms—I'll see to that! All London shall welcome you, for though I'm old and wear a wig, I'm very much alive, and Society knows it. So no more talk of horses, or farms, or inns, Barnabas; my mind, as I say, is quite made up and—"

"But, madam," said Barnabas gently, "so is mine."

"Ha—indeed, sir—well?"

"Well, madam, today I go to my father."

"Ah!" sighed the Duchess.

"Though indeed I thank you humbly for—your condescension."

"Hum!" said the Duchess.

"And honor you most sincerely for—for—"

"Oh?" said the Duchess, softly.

"And most truly love and reverence you for your womanliness."

"Oh!" said the Duchess again, this time very softly indeed, and with her bright eyes more youthful than ever.

"Nevertheless," pursued Barnabas a little ponderously, "my father is my father, and I count it more honorable to be his son than to live an amateur gentleman and the friend of princes."

"Quite so," nodded the Duchess, "highly filial and very pious, oh, indeed, most righteous and laudable, but—there remains an eighthly, Barnabas."

"And pray, madam, what may that be?"

"What of Cleone?"

Now when the Duchess said this, Barnabas turned away to the window and leaning his head in his hands, was silent awhile.

"Cleone!" he sighed at last, "ah, yes—Cleone!"

"You love her, I suppose?"

"So much—so very much that she shall never marry an innkeeper's son, or a discredited—"

"Bah!" exclaimed the Duchess.

"Madam?"

"Don't be so hatefully proud, Barnabas."

"Proud, madam—I?"

"Cruelly, wickedly, hatefully proud! Oh, dear me! what a superbly virtuous, heroic fool you are, Barnabas. When you met her at the crossroads, for instance—oh, I know all about it—when you had her there—in your arms, why didn't you—run off with her and marry her, as any ordinary human man would have done? Dear heaven, it would have been so deliciously romantic! And—such an easy way out of it!"

"Yes," said Barnabas, beginning to frown, "so easy that it was—wrong!"

"Quite so and fiddlesticks!" sniffed the Duchess.

"Madam?"

"Oh, sir, pray remember that one wrong may sometimes make two right! As it is, you will let your abominable pride—yes, pride! wreck and ruin two lives. Bah!" cried the Duchess very fiercely as she rose and turned to the door, "I've no patience with you!"

"Ah, Duchess," said Barnabas, staying her with pleading hands, "can't you see—don't you understand? Were she, this proud lady, my wife, I must needs be haunted, day and night, by the fear that some day, soon or late, she would find me to be—not of her world—not the man she would have me, but only—the publican's son, after all. Now—don't you see why I dare not?"

"Oh, Pride! Pride!" exclaimed the Duchess. "Do you expect her to come to you, then—would you have her go down on her knees to you, and—beg you to marry her?"

Barnabas turned to the window again and stood there awhile staring blindly out beyond the swaying green of trees; when at last he spoke his voice was hoarse and there was a bitter smile upon his lips.

"Yes, Duchess," said he slowly, "before such great happiness could be mine she must come to me, she must go down upon her knees—proud lady that she is—and beg this innkeeper's son to marry her. So you see, Duchess, I—shall never marry!"

Now when at last Barnabas looked round, the Duchess had her back to him, nor did she turn even when she spoke.

"Then you are going back—to your father?"

"Yes, madam."

"To-day?"

"Yes, madam."

"Then—good-by, Barnabas! And remember that even roses, like all things else, have a habit of fading, sooner or later." And thus, without even glancing at him, the Duchess went out of the room and closed the door softly behind her.

Then Barnabas sank into a chair, like one that is very tired, and sat there lost in frowning thought, and with one hand clasped down upon his breast where hidden away in a clumsily contrived hiding-place a certain rose, even at that moment, was fading away. And in a while being summoned by Peterby, he sighed and, rising, went down to his solitary breakfast.

CHAPTER LXXV

WHICH TELLS WHY BARNABAS FORGOT HIS BREAKFAST

It was a slender little shoe, and solitary, for fellow it had none, and it lay exactly in the middle of the window-seat; moreover, to the casual observer, it was quite an ordinary little shoe, ordinary, be it understood, in all but its size.

Why, then, should Barnabas, chancing to catch sight of so ordinary an object, start up from his breakfast (ham and eggs, and fragrant coffee) and crossing the room with hasty step, pause to look down at this small and lonely object that lay so exactly in the middle of the long, deep window-seat? Why should his hand shake as he stooped and took it up? Why should the color deepen in his pale cheek?

And all this because of a solitary little shoe! A quite ordinary little shoe—to the casual observer! Oh, thou Casual Observer who seeing so much, yet notices and takes heed to so little beyond thy puny self! To whom the fairest prospect is but so much earth and so much timber! To whom music is but an arrangement of harmonious sounds, and man himself but a being erect upon two legs! Oh, thou Casual Observer, what a dull, gross, self-contented clod art thou, who, having eyes and ears, art blind and deaf to aught but things as concrete as—thyself!

But for this shoe, it, being something worn, yet preserved the mould of the little foot that had trodden it, a slender, coquettish little foot, a shapely, active little foot: a foot, perchance, to trip it gay and lightly to a melody, or hurry, swift, untiring, upon some errand of mercy.

All this, and more, Barnabas noted (since he, for one, was no casual observer) as he stood there in the sunlight with the little shoe upon his palm, while the ham and eggs languished forgotten and the coffee grew cold, for how might they hope to vie with this that had lain so lonely, so neglected and—so exactly in the middle of the window-seat?

Now presently, as Barnabas stood thus lost in contemplation of this shoe, he was aware of Peterby entering behind him, and instinctively made as if to hide the shoe in his bosom, but he checked the impulse, turned, and glancing at Peterby, saw that his usually grave lips were quivering oddly at the corners, and that he kept his gaze fixed pertinaciously upon the coffee-pot; whereat the pale cheek of Barnabas grew suffused again, and stepping forward, he laid the little shoe upon the table.

"John," said he, pointing to it, "have you ever seen this before?"

"Why, sir," replied Peterby, regarding the little shoe with brow of frowning portent, "I think I have."

"And pray," continued Barnabas (asking a perfectly unnecessary question), "whose is it, do you suppose?"

"Sir," answered John, still grave of mouth and solemn of eye, "to the best of my belief it belongs to the Lady Cleone Meredith."

"So she—really was here, John?"

"Sir, she came here the same night that you—were shot, and she brought Her Grace of Camberhurst with her."

"Yes, John?"

"And they remained here until today—to nurse you, sir."

"Did they, John?"

"They took turns to be with you—day and night, sir. But it was only my Lady Cleone who could soothe your delirious ravings,—she seemed to have a magic—"

"And why," demanded Barnabas, frowning suddenly, "Why was I never told of her presence?"

"Sir, it was her earnest wish that you were not to know unless—"

"Well, John?"

"Unless you expressly asked for her, by name. And, sir—you never did."

"No," sighed Barnabas, "I never did. But perhaps, after all, it was just as well, John? Under the—circumstances, John?"

But seeing Peterby only shook his head and sighed, Barnabas turned to stare out of the window.

"And she—left this morning—with the Duchess, did she?" he inquired, without looking round.

"Yes, sir."

"Where for?"

"For—London, as I understood, sir."

Hereupon Barnabas was silent for a time, during which Peterby watched him solicitously.

"Is 'The Terror' still here?" Barnabas inquired suddenly.

"Yes, sir, and I took the liberty of sending for Gabriel Martin to look after him."

"Quite right, John. Tell Martin to have him saddled at once."

"You are—going out, sir?"

"Yes, I am going—out."

Peterby bowed and crossed to the door, but paused there, hesitated, and finally spoke:

"Sir, may I ask if you intend to ride—Londonwards?"

"No," answered Barnabas, stifling a sigh, "my way lies in the opposite direction; I am going—back, to the 'Coursing Hound.' And that reminds me—what of you, what are your plans for the future?"

"Sir," stammered Peterby, "I—I had ventured to—to hope that you might—take me with you, unless you wished to—to be rid of me—"

"Rid of you, John!" cried Barnabas, turning at last, "no—never. Why, man, I need you more than ever!"

"Sir," exclaimed Peterby, flushing suddenly, "do you—really mean that?"

"Yes, John—a thousand times, yes! For look you, as I have proved you the best valet in the world—so have I proved you a man, and it is the man I need now, because—I am a failure."

"No, no!"

"Yes, John. In London I attempted the impossible, and today I—return home, a failure. Consequently the future looms rather dark before me, John, and at such times a tried friend is a double blessing. So, come with me, John, and help me to face the future as a man should."

"Ah, sir," answered Peterby, with his sudden radiant smile, "darkness cannot endure, and if the future brings its sorrows, so must it bring its joys. Surely the future stands for hope and—I think—happiness!"

Now as he ended, Peterby raised one hand with forefinger outstretched; and, looking where he pointed, Barnabas beheld—the little shoe. But when he glanced up again, Peterby was gone.

CHAPTER LXXVI

HOW THE VISCOUNT PROPOSED A TOAST

"Oh—hif you please, sir!"

Barnabas started, raised his head, and, glancing over his shoulder, beheld Milo of Crotona. He was standing in the middle of the room looking very cherubic, very natty, and very upright of back; and he stared at Barnabas with his innocent blue eyes very wide, and with every one of the eight winking, twinkling, glittering buttons on his small jacket—indeed, it seemed to Barnabas that to-day his buttons were rather more knowing than usual, if that could well be. Therefore Barnabas dropped his table-napkin, very adroitly, upon a certain object that yet lay upon the table before him, ere he turned about and addressed himself to the Viscount's diminutive "tiger."

"What, my Imp," said he, "where in the world have you sprung from, pray? I didn't see you come in."

"No, sir—'cause you jest 'appened to be lookin' at that there little boot, you did." Thus Master Milo, and his eyes were guileless as an angel's, but—his buttons—!

"Hum!" said Barnabas, rubbing his chin. "But how did you get in, Imp?"

"Froo de winder, sir, I did. An' I 've come to tell you 'is Ludship's compliments, and 'e's a-comin' along wiv 'er, 'e is."

"With—whom?"

"Wiv my lady—'er."

"What lady?"

"Wiv 'is Ludship's lady, 'is Vi-coun-tess,—'er."

"His Viscountess!" repeated Barnabas, staring, "do you mean that the Viscount is—actually married?"

"'T ain't my fault, sir—no fear, it ain't. 'E went and done it be'ind my back—s'morning as ever was, 'e did. I didn't know nothin' about it till it was too late, 'e done it unbeknownst to me, sir, 'e did, an' she done it too a' course, an' the Yurl went an' 'elped 'em to do it, 'e did. So did the Cap'n, and the Doochess an' Lady Cleone—they all 'elped 'em to do it, they did. An' now they're goin' into the country, to Deven'am, an' I'm a-goin' wiv 'em—an' they're a-drivin' over to see you, sir, in 'is Ludship's noo phayton—an' that's all—no, it ain't though."

"What more, Imp?"

"Why, as they all come away from the church—where they'd been a-doin' of it, sir—I met the little, old Doochess in 'er coach, an' she see me, too. 'Why it's the little Giant!' she sez. 'Best respex, mam,' I sez, an' then I see as she'd got Lady Cleone wiv 'er—a fine, 'igh-steppin', 'andsome young filly, I call 'er, an' no error. 'Where are you goin', Giant?' sez the Doochess. 'I'm a-goin' to drop in on Mr. Bev'ley, mam, I am,' I sez. 'Then give 'im my love,' she sez, 'an' tell 'im I shan't never forget 'is pride and 'is selfishness,' she sez,—an' she give me a crown into the bargain, she did. An' then—jest as the coach was a-drivin' off t'other 'un—the young 'un, give me this. 'For Mr. Bev'ley,' she sez in a whisper, and—here it be, sir."

Saying which, Master Milo handed Barnabas a small folded paper whereon, scribbled in Cleone's well-known writing, were these three aphorisms:

1. Pride goeth before destruction, and a haughty spirit before a fall.
2. Selfishness shall find its own reward.
3. Journeys end in lovers' meetings.

Long stood Barnabas devouring these words with his eyes; so puzzled and engrossed was he indeed, that not until Master Milo ventured to touch him on the arm did he look up.

"'Ere's 'is Ludship, sir," explained Milo, jerking his thumb towards the open window, "a-drivin' up the av'noo, sir, in 'is phayton, and wiv 'is noo Vi-coun-tess along of him—and a reg'lar 'igh-stepper she looks, don't she? Arter all, I don't blame 'im for goin' an' doin' of it, I don't. Ye see, I allus 'ad a tender spot for Miss Clemency, mam, I 'ad, and a fine, proper, bang up Vi-coun-tess she do make, an' no error, sir—now don't she?"

"Surely," nodded Barnabas, looking where Milo pointed, "surely she is the handsomest, sweetest young Viscountess in all England, Imp."

So saying, he strode from the room with Master Milo trotting at his heels, and being come out upon the terrace, stood to watch the phaeton's rapid approach.

And, indeed, what words could be found in any language that could possibly do justice to the gentle, glowing beauty of Mistress Clemency Dare, transformed now, for good and all, into Beatrix, Viscountess Devenham? What brush could paint the mantling color of her cheek, the tender light of her deep, soft eyes, the ripe loveliness of her shape, and all the indefinable grace and charm of her? Surely none.

And now, Master Milo has darted forward and sprung to the horses' heads, for the Viscount has leapt to earth and has caught at Barnabas with both hands almost before the phaeton has come to a stand.

"Why, Bev—my dear old fellow, this is a joyful surprise! oh, bruise and blister me!" exclaimed the Viscount, viewing Barnabas up and down with radiant eyes, "to see you yourself again at last—and on this day of all days—this makes everything quite complete, y'know—doesn't it, Clemency? Expected to find you in bed, y'know—didn't we, Clem, dear? And oh—egad, Bev—er—my wife, y'know. You haven't heard, of course, that I—that we—"

"Yes, I've just heard," said Barnabas, smiling, "and God knows, Dick, I rejoice in your joy and wish you every happiness!" And, speaking, he turned and looked into the flushing loveliness of Clemency's face.

"Mr. Beverley—oh, Barnabas—dear brother!" she said softly, "but for you, this day might never have dawned for us—" and she gave both her hands into his. "Oh, believe me, in my joy, as in my sorrow, I shall remember you always."

"And I too, Bev!" added the Viscount.

"And," continued Clemency, her voice a little tearful, "whatever happiness the future may hold will only make that memory all the dearer, Barnabas."

"Gad, yes, that it will, Bev!" added the Viscount. "And, my dear fellow," he pursued, growing somewhat incoherent because of his earnestness, "I want to tell you that—that because I—I'm so deucedly happy myself, y' know, I wish that my luck had been yours—no, I don't mean that exactly, but what I meant to say was that I—that you deserve to—to—oh, blister me! Tell him what I mean, Clemency dear," the Viscount ended, a little hoarsely.

"That you deserve to know a love as great, a joy as deep as ours, dear Barnabas."

"Exactly!" nodded the Viscount, with a fond look at his young wife; "Precisely what I meant, Bev, for I'm the proudest, happiest fellow alive, y' know. And what's more, my dear fellow, in marrying Clemency I marry also an heiress possessed of all the attributes necessary to bowl over a thousand flinty-hearted Roman P's, and my Roman's heart—though tough, was never quite a flint, after all."

"Indeed, sir—he would have welcomed me without a penny!" retorted Clemency, blushing, and consequently looking lovelier than ever.

"Why—to be sure he would!" said Barnabas. "Indeed, who wouldn't?"

"Exactly, Bev!" replied the Viscount, "she cornered him with the first glance, floored him with a second, and had him fairly beaten out of the ring with a third. Gad, if you'd only been there to see!"

"Would I had!" sighed Barnabas.

"Still there's always—the future, y' know!" nodded the Viscount. "Ah, yes, and with an uncommonly big capital F, y' know, Bev. It was decreed that we were to be friends by—well, you remember who, Bev—and friends we always must be, now and hereafter, amen, my dear fellow, and between you and me—and my Viscountess, I think the Future holds more happiness for you than ever the past did. Your turn will come, y' know, Bev—we shall be dancing at your wedding next—shan't we, Clem?"

"No, Dick," answered Barnabas, shaking his head, "I shall never marry."

"Hum!" said the Viscount, fingering his chin and apparently lost in contemplation of a fleecy cloud.

"Of that I am—quite certain."

"Ha!" said the Viscount, staring down at the toe of his glossy boot.

"But," continued Barnabas, "even in my loneliness—"

"His loneliness—hum!" said the Viscount, still contemplating his resplendent boot. "Clemency dear, do you suppose our Barnabas fellow will be groaning over his 'loneliness'—to-morrow, say?" Hereupon, the Viscount laughed suddenly, and for no apparent reason, while even Clemency's red lips curved and parted in a smile.

"But," said Barnabas, looking from one to the other, "I don't understand!"

"Neither do we, Bev. Only, dear fellow, remember this, 'there is a destiny which shapes our ends,' and—occasionally, a Duchess." But here, while Barnabas still glanced at them in perplexity, John Peterby appeared, bearing a tray whereon stood a decanter and glasses.

"Ha!—most excellent Peterby!" cried the Viscount, "you come pat to the occasion, as usual. Fill up for all of us, yes—even my small Imp yonder; I have a toast to give you." And, when the glasses brimmed, the Viscount turned and looked at Barnabas with his boyish smile. "Let us drink," said he, "to the Future, and the Duchess's move!"

So the toast was drunk with all due honors: but when Barnabas sought an explanation, the Viscount laughed and shook his head.

"Pray ask my Viscountess," said he, with a fond look at her, and turned away to rebuckle a trace under the anxious supervision of Master Milo.

"Indeed, no, Barnabas," said Clemency, smiling, "I cannot explain, as Dick well knows. But this I must tell you, while you lay here, very near death, I came to see you often with my dear father."

"Ah!" exclaimed Barnabas, "then you met—her?"

"Yes, I met Cleone, and I—loved her. She was very tired and worn, the first time I saw her; you were delirious, and she had watched over you all night. Of course we talked of you, and she told me how she had found my letter to you, the only one I ever wrote you, and how she had misjudged you. And then she cried, and I took her in my arms and kissed away her tears and comforted her. So we learned to know and love each other, you see."

"I am very glad," said Barnabas, slowly, and with his gaze on the distance, "for her sake and yours."

Now as she looked at him, Clemency sighed all at once, yet thereafter smiled very tenderly, and so smiling, gave him both her hands.

"Oh, Barnabas," said she, "I know Happiness will come to you, sooner or later—when least expected, as it came to me, so—dear Barnabas, smile!"

Then Barnabas, looking from her tearful, pitying eyes to the hand upon whose finger was a certain plain gold ring that shone so very bright and conspicuous because of its newness, raised that slender hand to his lips.

"Thank you, Clemency," he answered, "but why are you—so sure?"

"A woman's intuition, perhaps, Barnabas, or perhaps, because if ever a man deserved to be happy—you do, dear brother."

"Amen to that!" added the Viscount, who had at length adjusted the trace to his own liking and Master Milo's frowning approval. "Good-by, Bev," he continued, gripping the hand Barnabas extended. "We are going down to Devenham for a week or so—Clemency's own wish, and when we come back I have a feeling that the—the shadows, y' know, will have passed quite away, y'know,—for good and all. Good-by, dear fellow, good-by!" So saying, the Viscount turned, rather hastily, sprang into the phaeton and took up the reins.

"Are you right there, Imp?"

"All right, m'lud!" answers that small person with one foot posed negligently on the step, waiting till the last possible moment ere he mounts to his perch behind. So, with a last "good-by" the Viscount touches up his horses, the light vehicle shoots forward with Master Milo swinging suspended in mid-air, who turns to Barnabas, flashes his eight buttons at him, touches his hat to him, folds his arms, and, sitting very stiff in the back, is presently whirled out of sight.

CHAPTER LXXVII

HOW BARNABAS RODE HOMEWARDS, AND TOOK COUNSEL OF A PEDLER OF BOOKS

It was well on in the afternoon when Barnabas, booted and spurred, stepped out into the sunshine where old Gabriel Martin walked "The Terror" to and fro before the door.

"Very glad to see you out and about again, sir," said he, beaming of face and with a finger at his grizzled temple.

"Thank you, Martin."

"And so is the 'oss, sir—look at 'im!" And indeed the great, black horse had tossed up his lofty crest and stood, one slender fore-leg advanced and with sensitive ears pricked forward, snuffing at Barnabas as he came slowly down the steps.

"He doesn't seem to have taken any hurt from the last race we had together," said Barnabas.

"'Arm, sir—lord, no—not a bit, never better! There's a eye for you, there's a coat! I tell you, sir, 'e's in the very pink, that 'e is."

"He does you great credit, Martin."

"Sir," said Martin as Barnabas prepared to mount, "sir, I hear as you ain't thinking of going back to town?"

"To the best of my belief, no, Martin."

"Why, then, sir," said the old groom, his face clouding, "p'r'aps I 'd better be packing up my bits o' traps, sir?"

"Yes, Martin, I think you had," answered Barnabas, and swung himself somewhat awkwardly into the saddle.

"Very good, sir!" sighed old Martin, his gray head drooping. "I done my best for the 'oss and you, sir, but I know I'm a bit too old for the job, p'r'aps, and—"

But at this moment Peterby approached.

"Sir," he inquired, a little anxiously, "do you feel able—well enough to ride—alone?"

"Why, bless you, John, of course I do. I'm nearly well," answered Barnabas, settling his feet in the stirrups, "and that reminds me, you will discharge all the servants—a month's wages, John, and shut up this place as soon as possible. As for Martin here, of course you will bring him with you if he will come. We shall need him hereafter, shan't we, John? And perhaps we'd better offer him another ten shillings a week considering he will have so many more responsibilities on the farm."

So saying, Barnabas waved his hand, wheeled his horse, and rode off down the drive; but, glancing back, when he had gone a little way, he saw that Peterby and the old groom yet stood looking after him, and in the face of each was a brightness that was not of the sun.

On rode Barnabas, filling his lungs with great draughts of the balmy air and looking about him, eager-eyed. And thus, beholding the beauty of wooded hill and dale, already mellowing to Autumn, the heaviness was lifted from his spirit, his drooping back grew straight, and raising his eyes to the blue expanse of heaven, he gloried that he was alive.

But, in a while, remembering Cleone's note, he must needs check his speed, and taking the paper from his bosom, began to con it over:

1. Pride goeth before destruction, and a haughty spirit before a fall.
2. Selfishness shall find its own reward.
3. Journeys end in lovers' meetings.

Now as he rode thus at a hand-pace, puzzling over these cryptic words, he was presently aroused by a voice, somewhat harsh and discordant, singing at no great distance; and the words of the song were these:

"Push about the brisk bowl, 't will enliven the heart
  While thus we sit down on the grass;
The lover who talks of his sufferings and smart
  Deserves to be reckoned an ass, an ass,
  Deserves to be reckoned an ass."

Therefore Barnabas raised his head and, glancing to one side of the way, beheld the singer sitting beneath the hedge. He was a small, merry-eyed man and, while he sang, he was busily setting out certain edibles upon the grass at his feet; now glancing from this very small man to the very large pack that lay beside him, Barnabas reined up and looked down at him with a smile.

"And pray," he inquired, "how do books sell these days?"

"Why, they do and they don't, sir. Sermons are a drug and novels ain't much better, poems is pretty bobbish, but song-books is my meat. And, talking o' songbooks, here's one as is jest the thing for a convivial cock o' the game—a fine, young, slap-up buck like you, my Lord. Here's a book to kill care, drive away sorrer, and give a 'leveller' to black despair. A book as'll make the sad merry, and the merry merrier. Hark to this now!"

So saying, the Pedler drew a book from his pack, and opening it at the title-page, began to read as follows, with much apparent unction and gusto:

THE HEARTY FELLOW:

OR

JOYOUS SOUL'S COMPANION.

BEING A
Chaste, Elegant, and Humourous
COLLECTION OF SONGS,
for the ENTERTAINMENT of:

The TENDER MAID, the PINING LOVER, the CHOICE SPIRIT, the DROLL DOG, the JOVIAL SPORTSMAN, the DARING SOLDIER and the ROUGH, HONEST TAR:
and for all those who would wish to render themselves agreeable, divert the Company, kill Care, and be joyous; where the high-seasoned WIT and HUMOUR will be sufficient Apology for a bad Voice, and by which such as have a tolerable one will be able to Shine without repressing the Laugh of the merrily disposed, or offending the Ear of the chastest Virgin.

To which is added:

A complete Collection of the Various TOASTS, SENTIMENTS, and HOB-NOBS, that have been drank, are now drinking, and some new Ones offered for Adoption.

"There you are, sir—there's a book for you! A book? A whole li-bree—a vaddy-mekkum o' wit, and chock full o' humor! What d' ye say for such a wollum o' sparkling bon mots? Say a guinea, say fifteen bob? say ten? Come—you shall take it for five! Five bob for a book as ain't to be ekalled no-how and no-wheer—"

"Not in Asia, Africa or America?" said Barnabas.

"Eh?" said the Pedler, glancing sharply up at him, "why—what, Lord love me—it's you, is it? aha! So it did the trick for you, did it?"

"What do you mean?"

"Mean, sir? Lord, what should I mean, but that there book on Ettyket, as I sold you—that priceless wollum as I give you—for five bob, months ago, when the larks was a-singing so inspiring."

"Yes, it was a lovely morning, I remember."

"Ah! and you left me that morning, a fine, upstanding young country cove, but to-day—ah, to-day you are a bang up blood—a gent, inside and out, a-riding of a magnificent 'oss—and all on account o' follering the instructions in that 'ere blessed tome as I sold you—for five bob! And dirt-cheap at the money!"

"And I find you exactly as you were," said Barnabas thoughtfully, "yes, even to the bread and cheese."

"There you are wrong, sir—axing your pardon. This time it's 'alf a loaf—medium, a slice o' beef—small, and a cold per-tater—large. But cold per-taters is full o' nourishment, if eat with a contented mind—ah, there's oceans o' nourishment in a cold per-tater—took reg'lar. O' course, for them as is flush o' the rhino, and wants a blow-out, there's nothin' like two o' leg o' beef with a dash o' pea, 'alf a scaffold-pole, a plate o' chats, and a swimmer—it's wholesome and werry filling, and don't cost more than a groat, but give me a cold per-tater to walk on. But you, sir," continued the Pedler, beginning to eat with great appetite, "you, being a reg'lar 'eavy-toddler now, one o' the gilded nobs—and all on account o' that there priceless wollum as I—give away to you—for five bob!

you, being now a blue-blooded aris-to-crat, don't 'ave to walk, so you can go in for plovers or pheasants or partridges, dressed up in hartichokes, p'r'aps, yes—frogs'-legs is your constant fodder now, p'r'aps—not to mention rag-outs and sich. Oh, yes, I reckon you've done a lot, and seen a lot, and—eat a lot since the morning as I give you a priceless wollum worth its weight in solid gold as was wrote by a Person o' Quality—and all for five bob! jest because them larks 'appened to be singing so sentimental—drat 'em! Ah well," sighed the Pedler, bolting the last morsel of beef, "and 'ow did you find London, young sir?"

"Much bigger than I expected."

"Ah, it is a bit biggish till you get used to it. And it's amazing what you can see—if you looks 'ard enough, like the tombs in St. Paul's Churchyard, f'r instance. I knowed of a chap once as spent over a week a-looking for 'em, and never see so much as a single 'eadstone—but then, 'e were born stone-blind, so it were only nat'ral as 'e *should* miss 'em, p'r'aps. But you, young sir, 'ow did you pass your time?"

"Principally in dressing and undressing."

"Ah, jess so, jess so—coats cut 'igh and coats cut low! But what more?"

"And in eating and drinking."

"Ah, French hortolons, p'r'aps, with a occasional tongue of a lark throwed in for a relish, jess so! But what more—did ye marry a duchess, f'r instance?"

"Alas, no!"

"Elope with a earl's daughter, then?"

"No."

"Well—did ye fight any dooels?"

"Not a single one."

"Lord, young sir—you 'ave been a-missing of your opportunities, you 'ave, playing fast and loose wi' Fortun', I calls it—ah, fair flying in the face o' Providence! Now, if instead o' selling books I took to writing of 'em, and tried to write you into a novel, why, Lord, what a poor thing that there novel would be! Who'd want to read it?—why, nobody! Oh, I can see as you've been throwing away your opportunities and wasting your chances shocking, you 'ave."

"Now I wonder," said Barnabas, frowning thoughtfully, "I wonder if I have?"

"Not a doubt of it!" answered the Pedler, swallowing the last of his potato.

"Then the sooner I begin to make up for it, the better."

"Ah!" nodded the Pedler. "I should begin at once, if I was you."

"I will," said Barnabas, gathering up the reins.

"And how, sir?"

"By going my allotted way and—striving to be content."

"Content!" exclaimed the Pedler, "lord, young sir, it's only fools as is ever content! A contented man never done anything much worth 'aving, nor said anything much worth 'caring as ever I 'eard. Never go for to be content, young sir, or you'll never do nothing at all!"

"Why, then," said Barnabas, smiling ruefully, "it is certain that I shall achieve something yet, because—I never shall be content!"

"That's the spirit, young sir—aim 'igh. Jest look at me—born in the gutter, but I wasn't content wi' the gutter so I taught myself to read and write. But I wasn't content to read and write, so I took to the book trade, and 'ere I am to-day travelling the roads and wi' a fairish connection, but I ain't content—Lord, no! I'd like to be a dook a-rolling in a chariot, or a prince o' the blood, or the Prime Minister a-laying down the law. That's the sperrit—shoot 'igh, ah! shoot at the sun and you're bound to 'it summat if it's only a tree or a 'ay-stack. So, if you can't be a dook or a prince, you can allus be—a man—if you try 'ard enough. What—are ye going, young sir?"

"Yes," answered Barnabas, leaning down from the saddle, "good-by, and thank you for your advice," and he stretched out his hand.

Hereupon the pedler of books rose to his feet and rather diffidently clasped the proffered hand. So Barnabas smiled down at him, nodded and rode upon his way, but as for the Pedler, he stood there, staring after him open-mouthed, and with the yellow coins shining upon his palm.

CHAPTER LXXVIII

WHICH TELLS HOW BARNABAS CAME HOME AGAIN, AND HOW HE AWOKE FOR THE FOURTH TIME

Evening was falling as Barnabas came to the top of the hill and, drawing rein, paused there to look down at a certain inn. It was a somewhat small and solitary inn, an ancient inn with many lattices, and with pointed gables whose plaster and cross-beams were just now mellowed by the rosy glow of sunset.

Surely, surely, nowhere in all broad England could there be found just such another inn as this, or one more full of that reposeful dignity which only age can bestow. And in all its length of days never had "The Coursing Hound" looked more restful, more comfortable and home-like than upon this early Autumn evening. And remembering those two gray-headed men, who waited within its hospitable walls, eager to give him welcome, who might, perchance, even now be talking of him one to another, what wonder if, as our Barnabas gazed down at it from worn steps to crooked chimney, from the faded sign before the door of it to the fragrant rick-yard that lay behind it, what wonder (I say) if it grew blurred all at once, and misty, or that Barnabas should sigh so deeply and sit with drooping head, while the old inn blinked its casements innocently in the level rays of the setting sun, like the simple, guileless old inn that it was!

But lo! all at once forth from its weather-beaten porch issued two figures, clean-limbed, athletic figures these—men who strode strong and free, with shoulders squared and upright of back, though the head of each was grizzled with years. On they came, shoulder to shoulder, the one a tall man with a mighty girth of chest, the other slighter, shorter, but quick and active as a cat, and who already had gained a good yard upon his companion; whereupon the big man lengthened his stride; whereupon the slighter man broke into a trot; whereupon the big man fell into a run; whereupon the slighter man followed suit and thus, neck and neck, they raced together up the hill and so, presently reaching the summit, very little breathed considering, pulled up on either side of Barnabas.

"Father!" he cried, "Natty Bell! Oh, it's good to be home again!"

"Man Jack, it's all right!" said Natty Bell, nodding to John, but shaking away at the hand Barnabas had reached down to him, "*our* lad's come back to us, yes, Barnabas has come home, John, and—it *is* our Barnabas—London and Fashion aren't spiled him, John, thank God!"

"No," answered John ponderously, "no, Natty Bell, London aren't spiled him, and—why, Barnabas, I'm glad to see ye, lad—yes, I'm—glad, and—and—why, there y'are, Barnabas."

"Looks a bit palish, though, John!" said Natty Bell, shaking his head, "but that's only nat'ral, arter all, yes—a bit palish, p'r'aps, but, man Jack—what o' that?"

"And a bit thinnish, Natty Bell," replied John, "but Lord! a few days and we'll have him as right as—as ever, yes, quite right, and there y' are, Natty Bell!"

"P'r'aps you might be wishful to tell him, John, as you've had the old 'Hound' brightened up a bit?"

"Why, yes, Barnabas," nodded John, "in honor o' this occasion—though, to be sure, the sign would look better for a touch o' paint here and there—the poor old Hound's only got three legs and a tail left, d' ye see—and the hare, Barnabas, the hare—ain't!"

"P'r'aps we'd better take and let him see for hisself, John?"

"Right, Natty Bell, so he shall."

Thus, presently, Barnabas rode on between them down the hill, looking from one to the other, but saying very little, because his heart was so full.

"And this be the 'oss you wrote us about—hey, Barnabas lad?" inquired Natty Bell, stepping back and viewing 'The Terror' over with an eye that took in all his points. "Ha—a fine action, lad—"

'Pray haven't you heard of a jolly young coal-heaver Who down at Hungerford used for to ply—'

"A leetle—leggy? p'r'aps, Barnabas, and yet—ha!"

'His daddles he used with such skill and dexterity, Winning each mill, sir, and blacking each eye—'

"His cannons'll never trouble him, Barnabas, come rough or smooth, and you didn't say a word too much in your letter. Man Jack—you behold a 'oss as is a 'oss—though, mark you, John, a leetle bit roundish in the barrel and fullish in the shoulder—still, a animal, John, as I'm burning to cock a leg over."

"Why, then, Natty Bell, so you shall," said Barnabas, and forthwith down he swung himself and, being a little careless, wracked his injured shoulder and flinched a little, which the slow-spoken, quick-eyed John was swift to notice and, almost diffidently drew his son's arm through his own. But, Natty Bell, joyful of eye, was already in the saddle; whereat "The Terror," resenting the change, immediately began to dance and to sidle, with, much rearing up in front and lashing out behind, until, finding this all quite unavailing, he set off at a stretching gallop with Natty Bell sitting him like a centaur.

"And now, Barnabas," said John slowly, "'ow might your shoulder be, now?"

"Nearly well, father."

"Good," nodded John, "very good! I thought as you was going to—die, Barnabas, lad. They all did—even the Duchess and Lady—the—the doctors, Barnabas."

"Were you going to say—Lady Cleone, father?"

"Why," answered John, more ponderously than ever, "I won't go for to deny it, Barnabas, never 'aving been a liar—on principle as you know, and—and—there y'are, my lad."

"Have you ever—seen her, then?"

"Seen her," repeated John, beginning to rasp at his great square chin, "seen her, Barnabas, why, as to that—I say, as to that—ah!—here we be, Barnabas," and John Barty exhaled a deep breath, very like a sigh of relief, "you can see from here as the poor old 'Hound' will soon be only tail—not a leg to stand on. I'll have him painted back again next week—and the hare."

So, side by side, they mounted the worn steps of the inn, and side by side they presently entered that long, panelled room where, once on a time, they had fronted each other with clenched fists. Before the hearth stood John Barty's favorite arm-chair and into this, after some little demur, Barnabas sank, and stretched out his booted legs to the fire.

"Why, father," said he, lolling back luxuriously, "I thought you never liked cushions?"

"No more I do, Barnabas. She put them there for you."

"She, father?"

"One o' the maids, lad, one o' the maids and—and there y'are!"

"And now, father, you were telling me of the Lady Cleone—"

"No, I weren't, Barnabas," answered his father hastily and turning to select a pipe from the sheaf on the mantel-shelf, "not me, lad, not me!"

"Why, yes, you spoke of her—in the road."

"In the road? Oh, ah—might ha' spoke of her—in the road, lad."

"Well—do you—know her, father?"

"Know her?" repeated John, as though asking himself the question, and staring very hard at the pipe in his hand, "do I know her—why, yes—oh, yes, I know her, Barnabas. Ye see—when you was so—so near death—" But at this moment the door opened and two neat, mob-capped maids entered and began to spread a cloth upon the table, and scarcely had they departed when in came Natty Bell, his bright eyes brighter than ever.

"Oh, Natty Bell!" exclaimed John, beckoning him near, "come to this lad of ours—do, he's axing me questions, one a-top of t' other till I don't know what! 'Do I know Lady Cleone?' says he; next it'll be 'how' and 'what' and 'where'—tell him all about it. Natty Bell—do."

"Why then—sit down and be sociable, John," answered Natty Bell, drawing another chair to the fire and beginning to fill his pipe.

"Right, Natty Bell," nodded John, seating himself on the other side of Barnabas, "fire away and tell our lad 'ow we came to know her, Natty Bell."

"Why, then, Barnabas," Natty Bell began, as soon as his pipe was in full blast, "when you was so ill, d' ye see, John and me used to drive over frequent to see how you was, d' ye see. But you, being so ill, we weren't allowed to go up and see you, so she used to come down to us and—talk of you. Ah! and very sweet and gentle she was—eh, man Jack?"

"Sweet!" echoed John, shaking his head, "a angel weren't sweeter! Gentle? Ah, Natty Bell, I should say so—and that thoughtful of us—well, there y' are!"

"But one day, Barnabas," Natty Bell continued, "arter we'd called a good many times, she *did* take us up to see you,—didn't she, John?"

"Ah, that she did, Natty Bell, God bless her!"

"And you was a-lying there with shut eyes—very pale and still, Barnabas. But all at once you opened your eyes and—being out o' your mind, and not seeing us—delirious, d' ye see, Barnabas, you began to speak. 'No,' says you very fierce, 'No! I love you so much that I can never ask you to be the wife of Barnabas Barty. Mine must be the harder way, always. The harder way! The harder way!' says you, over and over again. And so we left you, but your voice follered us down the stairs—ah, and out o' the house, 'the harder way!' says you, 'the harder way'—over and over again."

"Ah! that you did, lad!" nodded John solemnly.

"So now, Barnabas, we'd like the liberty to ax you, John and me, what you meant by it?"

"Ah—that's the question, Barnabas!" said John, fixing his gaze on the bell-mouthed blunderbuss that hung over the mantel, "what might it all mean—that's the question, lad."

"It means, father and Natty Bell, that I have been all the way to London to learn what you, being so much wiser than I, tried to teach me—that a sow's ear is not a silk purse, nor ever can be."

"But," said John, beginning to rasp at his chin again, "there's Adam—what of Adam? You'll remember as you said—and very sensible too. Natty Bell—you'll remember as you said—"

"Never mind what I said then, father, I was very young. To-day, since I never can be a gentleman, I have come home so that you may teach me to be a man. And believe me," he continued more lightly as he glanced from the thoughtful brow of Natty Bell to the gloom on his father's handsome face, "oh, believe me—I have no regrets, none—none at all."

"Natty Bell," said John ponderously, and with his gaze still fixed intently upon the blunderbuss, "what do you say to that?"

"Why I say, John, as I believe as our lad aren't speaking the truth for once."

"Indeed, I shall be very happy," said Barnabas, hastily, "for I've done with dreaming, you see. I mean to be very busy, to—to devote my money to making us all happy. I have several ideas already, my head is full of schemes."

"Man Jack," said Natty Bell, puffing thoughtfully at his pipe, "what do *you* say to *that*?"

"Why," answered John, "I say Natty Bell, as it be my belief as our dear lad's nob be full o' only one idee, and that idee is—a woman. Ah, and always will be and—there y'are, Natty Bell."

"For one thing," Barnabas went on more hastily than before, "I'm going to carry out the improvements you suggested years ago for the dear old 'Hound,' father—and you and I, Natty, might buy the farm next door, it's for sale I know, and go in for raising horses. You often talked of it in the old days. Come, what do you say?" he inquired, seeing that neither of his hearers spoke or moved, and wondering a little that his proposals should fall so flat. "What do you think, Natty Bell?"

"Well," answered Natty Bell, "I think, Barnabas, since you ax me so pointed-like, that you'd do much better in taking a wife and raising children."

"Ah—why not, lad?" nodded his father. "It be high time as you was thinking o' settling down, so—why not get married and ha' done with it?"

"Because," answered Barnabas, frowning at the fire, "I can love only one woman in this world, and she is altogether beyond my reach, and—never can be mine—never."

"Ha!" said Natty Bell getting up and staring down into the fire, "Hum!"

'Since boxing is a manly game
And Britain's recreation,
By boxing we will raise our fame
'Bove every other nation.'

"Remember this, Barnabas, when a woman sets her mind on anything, I've noticed as she generally manages to—get it, one way or t' other. So I wouldn't be too sure, if I was you." Saying which, he nodded to John, above his son's drooping head, winked, and went silently out of the room.

Left alone with his son, John Barty sat a while staring up at the bell-mouthed blunderbuss very much as though he expected it to go off at any moment; at last, however, he rose also, hesitated, laid down his pipe upon the mantel-shelf, glanced down at Barnabas, glanced up at the blunderbuss again and finally spoke:

"And remember this, Barnabas, your—your—mother, God bless her sweet soul, was a great lady, but I married her, and I don't think as she ever—regretted it, lad. Ye see, Barnabas, when a good woman really loves a man—that man is the only man in the world for her, and—nothing else matters to her, because her love, being a good love, d' ye see—makes him—almost worthy. The love of a good woman is a sweet thing, lad, a wondrous thing, and may lift a man above all cares and sorrows and may draw him up—ah! as high as heaven at last, and—well—there y' are, Barnabas, dear lad."

Having said this, the longest speech Barnabas ever heard his father utter, John Barty laid his great hand lightly upon his son's bent head and treading very softly, for a man of his inches, followed Natty Bell out of the room.

But now as Barnabas sat there staring into the fire and lost in thought, he became, all at once, a prey to Doubt and Fear once again, doubt of himself, and fear of the future; for, bethinking him of his father's last words, it seemed to him that he had indeed chosen the harder course, since his days, henceforth, must needs stretch away—a dismal prospect wherein no woman's form might go beside him, no soft voice cheer him, no tender hand be stretched out to soothe his griefs; truly he had chosen the harder way, a very desolate way where no light fall of a woman's foot might banish for him its loneliness.

And presently, being full of such despondent thoughts, Barnabas looked up and found himself alone amid the gathering shadows. And straightway he felt aggrieved, and wondered why his father and Natty Bell must needs go off and leave him in this dark hour just when he most needed them.

Therefore he would have risen to seek them out but, in the act of doing so, caught one of his spurs in the rug, and strove vainly to release himself, for try how he would he might not reach down so far because of the pain of his wounded shoulder.

And now, all at once, perhaps because he found himself so helpless, or because of his loneliness and bodily weakness, the sudden tears started to his eyes, hot and scalding, and covering his face, he groaned.

But lo! in that moment of his need there came one, borne on flying feet, to kneel beside him in the fire-glow, and with swift, dexterous fingers to do for him that which he could not do for himself. But when it was done and he was free, she still knelt there with head bent, and her face hidden beneath the frill of her mob-cap.

"Thank you!" he said, very humbly, "I fear I am very awkward, but my shoulder is a little stiff."

But this strange serving-maid never moved, or spoke. And now, looking down at her shapely, drooping figure, Barnabas began to tremble, all at once, and his fingers clenched themselves upon his chair-arms.

"Speak!" he whispered, hoarsely.

Then the great mob-cap was shaken off, yet the face of this maid was still hid from him by reason of her hair that, escaping its fastenings, fell down, over bowed neck and white shoulders, rippling to the floor—a golden glory. And now, beholding the shining splendor of this hair, his breath caught, and as one entranced, he gazed down at her, fearing to move.

"Cleone!" he breathed, at last.

So Cleone raised her head and looked at him, sighing a little, blushing a little, trembling a little, with eyes shy yet unashamed, the eyes of a maid.

"Oh, Barnabas," she murmured, "I am here—on my knees. You wanted me—on my knees, didn't you, Barnabas? So I am here to ask you—" But now her dark lashes fluttered and fell, hiding her eyes from him, "—to beg you to marry me. Because I love you, Barnabas, and because, whatever else you may be, I know you are a man. So—if you really—want me, dear Barnabas, why—take me because I am just—your woman."

"Want you!" he repeated, "want you—oh my Cleone!" and, with a broken, inarticulate cry, he leaned down and would have caught her fiercely against his heart; but she, ever mindful of his wound, stayed him with gentle hand.

"Oh, my dear—your shoulder!" she whispered; and so, clasping tender arms about him, she drew his weary head to her bosom and, holding him thus, covered him with the silken curtain of her hair, and in this sweet shade, stooped and kissed him—his brow, his tearful eyes, and, last of all, his mouth. "Oh, Barnabas," she murmured, "was there ever, I wonder, a man so foolish and so very dear as you, or a woman quite so proud and happy as I?"

"Proud?" he answered, "but you are a great lady, and I am only—"

"My dear, dear—man," sighed Cleone, clasping him a little more closely, "so—when will you marry me? For, oh, my Barnabas, if you must always choose to go the harder way—you must let me tread it with you, to the very end, my dear, brave, honorable man."

And thus did our Barnabas know, at last, that deep and utter content which can come only to those who, forgetful of soul-clogging Self and its petty vanities and shams, may rise above the cynical commonplace and walk with gods.

Now, in a while, as they sat together in the soft glow of the fire, talking very little since Happiness is beyond speech, the door opened and closed and, glancing up, Barnabas was aware of the Duchess standing in the shadows.

"No, no—sit still, dear children," she cried, with a hand out-stretched to each, "I only peeped in to tell you that dinner was almost ready—that is, no, I didn't. I came here to look for Happiness and, thank God, I've found it! You will be married from my house in Berkeley Square, of course. He is a great fool, Cleone, this Barnabas of ours—give him a horse and armor and he would have been a very—knightly fool. And then—he is such a doubting Jonah—no, I mean Thomas, of course,—still he's not quite a fool—I mean Barnabas, not Thomas, who was anything but a fool. Ah! not my hand, dear Barnabas, I still have lips, though I do wear a wig—there, sir. Now you, Cleone. Dear Heaven, how ridiculously bright your eyes are, child. But it's just as well, you must look your best to-night. Besides, the Marquis is coming to dinner, so is the Captain—so awkward with his one arm, dear soul! And the Bo'sun—bless his empty sleeve—no, no—not the Bo'sun's, he has an empty—oh, never mind, and—oh Lud, where am I? Ah, yes—quite a banquet it will be with 'Glorious John' and Mr. Natty. Dear Heaven, how ridiculously happy I am, and I know my wig is all crooked. But—oh, my dears! you have found the most wonderful thing in all this wonderful universe. Riches, rank, fame—they are all good things, but the best, the greatest, the most blessed of all is—Love. For by love the weak are made strong, and the strong gentle—and Age itself—even mine—may be rejuvenated. I'm glad you preferred your own father to an adopted mother, dear Barnabas, even though she is a duchess—for that I must kiss you again—there! And so shall Cleone when I'm gone, so—I'll go. And oh, may God bless you—always, my dears."

So, looking from one to the other, the Duchess turned away and left them together.

And, in a while, looking down at Cleone where she knelt in his embrace, beholding all the charm and witchery of her, the high, proud carriage of her head, the grace and beauty of her shapely body, soft and warm with life and youth, and love, Barnabas sighed for very happiness; whereupon she, glancing up and meeting this look, must needs droop her lashes at him, and blush, and tremble, all in a moment.

"But—you are mine," said Barnabas, answering the blush. "Mine, at last, for ever and always."

"For ever and always, dear Barnabas."

"And yet," said he, his clasp tightening, "I am so unworthy, it almost seems that it cannot possibly be true—almost as if it were a dream."

"Ah no, Barnabas, surely the dream is over and we are awake at last to joy and the fulness of life. And life has given me my heart's desire, and for you, my brave, strong, honorable man—the Future lies all before you."

"Yes," said Barnabas, looking deep into her radiant eyes, "for me there is the Future and—You."

And thus did happiness come to our Barnabas, when least expected, as may it come to each of us when we shall have proved ourselves, in some way, fit and worthy.

CPSIA information can be obtained at www.ICGtesting.com
Printed in the USA
BVOW07s0046060215

386650BV00001B/52/P